hrac

EVERYMAN'S LIBRARY

EVERYMAN,
I WILL GO WITH THEE,
AND BE THY GUIDE,
IN THY MOST NEED
TO GO BY THY SIDE

FRANK O'CONNOR

THE BEST OF FRANK O'CONNOR

SELECTED AND EDITED
BY JULIAN BARNES

EVERYMAN'S LIBRARY
Alfred A. Knopf   New York   London   Toronto

321

CONTENTS

v

CONTENTS

ACKNOWLEDGMENT

———

I am very grateful to Harriet O'Donovan Sheehy, Frank O'Connor's widow, for her forceful encouragement and assistance. She made many useful suggestions, pointed me towards obscure items, and at times stamped a tactful foot. Her selection would inevitably have been different; but she always allowed that the final choice, and responsibility, for this edition was mine.

J.B.

INTRODUCTION

Frank O'Connor was once stopped on the road west of Kinsale by a man who said to him: 'I hear you're a famous writer. I'd like to be a famous writer too, but 'tis bloody hard. The comma and the apostrophe are easy enough, but the semicolon is the very divil.' The man was wrong, of course: the ability to punctuate, and even to spell, correctly are often missing from some of the best writers. What counts is the ability to be on that road, allow yourself to be stopped, listen to what the man says, remember the voice, and know when and how best to use it. O'Connor's art was that of a man who travels his native Ireland at the speed of a bicycle, happy to pause and listen, slow to come to a general conclusion, preferring the particular instance and the gradually revealed truth.

Mrs W. B. Yeats used to address him as 'Michael-Frank', an affectionate combining of his birth-name (Michael O'Donovan) and his pen-name. But that brief hyphen is also an indicator of the proximity between his personal and artistic selves. In some writers, the artistic self is separated off from the daily one: Jekyll closes the study door and turns into Hyde (or, sometimes, vice versa). O'Connor, while containing paradoxes and contradictions as any artist does, was much less of a bifurcated spirit than most. What he was lay very close to what he did; his fiction and non-fiction have similar contours and spirit. And to read the totality of his work is to discover multiple criss-crossings between books, with the same stories alluded to and retold.

But such repetitions, when they occur, don't feel like a writer recycling his material. Instead, the reader is more likely to smile in affectionate recognition as the stories of the Tailor and Anstey, or Mrs Yeats and the next-door dog, or Lord Edward Fitzgerald and the Native American woman, come round again. This is not just because O'Connor is a seductive and trustable narrator to whom we willingly submit, whether he is writing a short story about childhood, describing Celtic architecture, explaining Irish poetry, or fulminating against

ix

the Famine or James Joyce. It is because voice is central to
O'Connor's art. He is that comparatively rare thing in modern
times, an oral prose writer.

When he came to literary awareness, modernism was enjoy-
ing its fullest and most successful expression. In its general
and necessary attack on a dying tradition of panoramic social
realism, it also inflicted major – and to O'Connor's belief,
catastrophic – damage on the notion of the writer's voice.
Modernism fragmented and ironized it, made it unreliable and
shifty, sometimes hidden away altogether. O'Connor wanted
to keep alive in prose, and especially in the short story, what
he believed to be at its heart: the sound of 'an actual man,
talking'.

Talking, but also listening. O'Connor once said that when
he remembered people – even those he was very fond of – he
sometimes couldn't remember their faces, but could always
take off their voices. So, in his art, how a character sounds is
more important than where they live or what they are wearing,
or even what they look like. William Maxwell, O'Connor's
editor for many years at the *New Yorker*, amicably complained
that though he was capable of 'marvellous descriptions', he
didn't go in for them much because they didn't interest him.
They did when he was writing topographically or architectur-
ally – then he looked as closely as anyone – but in the rendering
of human beings into fictional form it all began with voice –
their voice, his voice.

The writer Benedict Kiely once noted that 'O'Connor can
be as outrageously at ease with his own people as a country
priest skelping the courting couples out of the ditches.' His
fellow *New Yorker* writer Maeve Brennan also teased him with
the clerical comparison, imagining St Patrick's Cathedral
with O'Connor 'where he usually is in the afternoons, sitting
in a confession box pretending to be a priest and giving pen-
ance to some old woman'. But the real priest listens, judges,
issues penances, and keeps the sinner's secrets. O'Connor
listened, took notes, did not judge, and turned the confession
into a story. His masters were not the moralists or the modern-
ists, but those like Turgenev ('my hero among writers') who
went with seeming simplicity to the complexity at the heart of

human matters. And the short-story writer he turned to most often was Chekhov. When Maxwell inherited O'Connor's volumes of Chekhov, he described them as 'so lived with – turned down corners, coffee stains, whiskey stains, and perhaps tears'.

In his essay on the Russian in 'The Lonely Art', O'Connor identifies one central, and to him profoundly sympathetic, belief in Chekhov's work: the notion that 'We are not damned for our mortal sins, which so often require courage and dignity, but by our venial sins, which we often commit a hundred times a day until we become as enslaved to them as we could be to alcohol and drugs. Because of them and our toleration of them, we create a false personality for ourselves.' (Again, O'Connor's confessional was an unorthodox one.) In 'The Bishop', written the year before Chekhov died, a bishop, originally from a poor background, is dying a lonely death. He is visited by his old mother who, because of his eminence, at first cannot stop calling him 'Your Grace'. Only towards the end does she break through the 'false personality' society has imposed on her, to the intimate contact mother and son once had: she starts calling him again by the private names she once used when he was a small boy unable to button his trousers. 'It is a final affirmation,' O'Connor writes, 'of Chekhov's faith in life – lonely and sad, immeasurably sad, but beautiful beyond the power of the greatest artist to tell.'

And yet not beyond the power of the artist to try. If Chekhov was O'Connor's prose master, Mozart was his musical master, and there is a conscious iteration in O'Connor's analysis, on the two hundredth anniversary of the composer's death, of what it is that we have come to call 'Mozartean':

It is a way of seeing things which revokes the tragic attitude without turning into comedy, which says, not 'Life is beautiful but so sad' but 'Life is so sad but beautiful', and this way of seeing things, half way between tragedy and comedy, represents a human norm.

That human norm tells us where O'Connor's art came from, and where it is heading.

Julian Barnes

SELECT BIBLIOGRAPHY

SHORT STORIES
Guests of the Nation, London/New York, 1931.
Bones of Contention, New York, 1936; London, 1938.
Crab Apple Jelly, London/New York, 1944.
The Common Chord, London, 1947; New York, 1948.
Traveller's Samples, London/New York, 1951.
Domestic Relations, London/New York, 1957.

The Stories of Frank O'Connor, New York, 1952; London, 1953.
More Stories, New York, 1954.
Collection Two, London, 1964.
Collection Three, London, 1969.
The Cornet Player Who Betrayed Ireland, Dublin, 1981.
Collected Stories, New York, 1982.
My Oedipus Complex and Other Stories, London, 2005.

NOVELS
The Saint and Mary Kate, London/New York, 1936.
Dutch Interior, London/New York, 1940.

AUTOBIOGRAPHY
An Only Child, New York, 1961; London, 1962.
My Father's Son, London, 1968; New York, 1969.

NON-FICTION
The Big Fellow: A Life of Michael Collins, London, 1937.
Irish Miles, London, 1947.
The Road to Stratford, London, 1948 (revised as *Shakespeare's Progress*).
Leinster, Munster and Connaught, London, 1950.
The Mirror in the Roadway: A Study of the Modern Novel, New York, 1956; London, 1957.
The Lonely Voice: A Study of the Short Story, Cleveland, Ohio, 1962; London, 1963.
The Backward Look: A Survey of Irish Literature, London, 1967.

POETRY TRANSLATIONS FROM THE IRISH
Kings, Lords and Commons, New York, 1959; London, 1961.
The Little Monasteries, Dublin, 1963.

OTHER

The Happiness of Getting It Down Right: Letters of Frank O'Connor and William Maxwell, edited by Michael Steinman, New York, 1996.

A Frank O'Connor Reader, edited by Michael Steinman, New York, 1994.

Writers at Work: The Paris Review Interviews, edited by Malcolm Cowley, New York, 1959.

Michael/Frank: Studies on Frank O'Connor, edited by Maurice Sheehy, Dublin/London, 1969.

Frank O'Connor at Work by Michael Steinman, New York, 1990.

Frank O'Connor: New Perspectives, edited by Robert Evans and Richard Harp, West Cornwall, CT, 1998.

Frank O'Connor: Critical Essays, edited by Hilary Lennon, Dublin, 2007. There is also a website sponsored by University College, Cork: www.frankoconnor.ucc.ie

CHRONOLOGY

DATE	AUTHOR'S LIFE	LITERARY CONTEXT
1903	Birth of Michael John O'Donovan in Cork City (17 September) to Mary (Minnie) and Michael O'Donovan over a shop in Douglas Street. His father is an ex-British Army soldier, nicknamed 'Big Mick'. Within a year the family moves to Blarney Street, a slum area. These early years are marked by poverty and illness, made worse by Big Mick's persistent alcoholic binges.	Butler: *The Way of All Flesh.* Mann: *Tonio Kröger.*
1904		Shaw: *John Bull's Other Island.* James: *The Golden Bowl.* Conrad: *Nostromo.* Saki: *Reginald*
1905		Wells: *Kipps.* Forster: *Where Angels Fear to Tread.*
1906		Samuel Beckett born.
1907	Briefly attends Cork's first national school at Strawberry Hill.	Synge: *Playboy of the Western World* (riots at the Abbey Theatre). Adams: *The Education of Henry Adams.*
1908		Bennett: *The Old Wives' Tale.* Forster: *A Room with a View.*
1909		Wells: *Tono Bungay.*
1910	Family moves again, this time to Harrington Square, near O'Donovan relatives. Attends St Patrick's School, but records show that he is often absent due to eye trouble and recurrent illnesses.	Forster: *Howards End.* Wells: *The History of Mr Polly.*
1911		Pound: *Canzoni.* Mansfield: *In a German Pension.* Chesterton: *The Innocence of Father Brown.*

In Ireland, the last of a series of Land Acts makes it easier for tenant farmers to buy their land. Emmeline Pankhurst founds Women's Social and Political Union in Manchester. Wright brothers' first successful powered flight.

Entente Cordiale between Britain and France. Russo-Japanese War (to 1905). Opening of Abbey Theatre (National Theatre of Ireland) in Dublin.

Formation of provisional government (Ulster Unionist Council) in Northern Ireland while in the South Sinn Féin is formed. First Russian Revolution.

Launch of HMS *Dreadnought*, first modern battleship.
Transatlantic wireless telegraphy service between Galway and Canada is opened.

Irish Universities Act leads to foundation of National University of Ireland in Dublin (1909). Asquith Prime Minister in Britain (to 1916).
Irish Transport and General Workers' Union is founded. Lloyd George introduces People's Budget.
Death of Edward VII and accession of George V.

The 84-strong Irish Home Rule Party led by John Redmond supports the Liberals' Parliament Act to reduce the power of the House of Lords in return for another Home Rule Bill. Strikes of dockers, miners, railwaymen and transport workers in Britain.

DATE	AUTHOR'S LIFE	LITERARY CONTEXT
1912	Taught by Daniel Corkery, poet, painter and novelist, who encourages his use of Irish and for a time is almost a surrogate father.	Lady Gregory: *Irish Folk History Plays.* Pound: *Ripostes.* Mann: *Death in Venice.* Alain-Fournier: *Le Grand Meaulnes.*
1913	Transferred to the North Monastery, a school run by the Christian Brothers, renowned for strict discipline. He is unhappy and frequently absent.	Shaw: *Pygmalion.* Lawrence: *Sons and Lovers.* Proust: *A la Recherche du temps perdu* (to 1927).
1914	Father re-enlists in British Army to fight in World War I. Home life becomes peaceful and enjoyable in his father's absence. Begins borrowing books from library and reads omnivorously, which becomes a lifelong habit. Teaches himself rudimentary German and French.	Yeats: *Responsibilities.* Joyce: *Dubliners*; *A Portrait of the Artist as a Young Man* begins serialization in *The Egoist.* Saki: *Beasts and Super-Beasts.*
1915	The monks decide that he is not university material and suggest a transfer to Trade School.	Ford: *The Good Soldier.* Woolf: *The Voyage Out.* Lawrence: *The Rainbow.*
1916	End of formal education. Brief attendance at Trade School.	George Moore: *The Brook Kerith.*
1917	Intensified efforts at self-education. Takes a number of temporary jobs to earn money with which to buy books. Later in the year his first work (never found) is published in a children's newspaper. In the same week he gives a lecture, in Irish, on Goethe.	Yeats: *The Wild Swans at Coole.* Eliot: *Prufrock and other Observations.* Freud: *Introduction to Psychoanalysis.*
1918	Enlists in the First Cork Brigade of the Irish Republican Army and does various odd jobs for it. Gets scholarship to Gaelic League School to learn to teach Irish.	Moore: *A Story-Teller's Holiday.* Strachey: *Eminent Victorians.*
1919	Translates Du Bellay's sonnet, 'Heureux qui, comme Ulysse' into Irish. Published in an English literary journal, it is praised in the (Irish) *Sunday Independent.*	Shaw: *Heartbreak House.* Yeats: *The Player Queen.* Kafka: *In the Penal Colony.*

CHRONOLOGY

HISTORICAL EVENTS

Asquith presents third Home Rule Bill to Parliament. Ulster Covenant pledges opposition to Home Rule. Irish Labour Party founded. Sinking of the *Titanic*.

Home Rule Bill passes the Commons but the Lords are still able to delay it temporarily. Ulster Volunteer Force set up. Irish Volunteer Force (IVF) raised in the South. Strike of Irish Transport and General Workers' Union in Dublin; James Connolly founds Irish Citizens' Army (ICA) to protect strikers. Woodrow Wilson becomes US President.

World War I begins (August). Many thousands of Irishmen of all political persuasions join the British army as volunteers. Home Rule Act placed on statute book but implementation is suspended for the duration of the war.

Battle of Ypres. Einstein's General Theory of Relativity.

Easter Rising of Nationalists in Dublin (24 April) is crushed by the British who execute its leaders, outraging Irish public opinion. Asquith resigns; Lloyd George forms a coalition government (December). Huge death tolls at the battles of Verdun and the Somme. Allies evacuate Gallipoli. Balfour Declaration: Jewish National Home in Palestine.

Release of remaining Easter Rising detainees. Eamon de Valera becomes President of Sinn Féin, taking over from founder Arthur Griffith. Bolshevik Revolution in Russia.

Sinn Féin leads opposition to conscription in Ireland. End of World War I (November). In general election Sinn Féin candidates win, but do not take up 73 of the 105 Irish seats in the House of Commons. Women over 30 gain the vote in Britain. Irish rebel Con Markievicz elected first British female MP.

Sinn Féin MPs declare Irish independence; first meeting of Dáil in Dublin with De Valera as President. IVF and ICA collectively renamed the Irish Republican Army (IRA). Irish War of Independence (to 1921). Versailles Peace Conference. German Republic adopts the Weimar constitution.

DATE	AUTHOR'S LIFE	LITERARY CONTEXT
1920	Invited by Corkery to join his 'literary reading group'; hears classical music for the first time on Corkery's gramophone. Meets Sean O'Faolain who becomes both friend and literary sparring partner.	Wharton: *The Age of Innocence*. Mansfield: *Bliss*. Fitzgerald: *This Side of Paradise*.
1921	Takes the Republican side in the Civil War, following the example of Corkery – as he later admits. (He comes to regret this decision, and writes his book about Michael Collins as 'an act of reparation'.)	O'Neill: *The Emperor Jones*. Lawrence: *Women in Love*. Huxley: *Crome Yellow*. Pirandello: *Six Characters in Search of an Author*. Hašek: *The Good Soldier Svejk* (to 1923).
1922	Actively participates in opposition to the Free State. Three original poems published in *An Long* (Cork Republican newspaper).	Joyce: *Ulysses* published in Paris. Eliot: *The Waste Land*. Woolf: *Jacob's Room*. Galsworthy: *The Forsyte Saga*. Mansfield: *The Garden Party*. Sinclair Lewis: *Babbitt*.
1923	'The Rosary', an original poem, published in the *Catholic Bulletin* (March). Captured by Free State forces in February. Detained at the Women's Prison, Cork, then transferred to Gormanstown Internment Camp (April). Here he teaches Irish to other inmates. Sean T. O'Kelly, later President of Ireland, is a fellow detainee. Released in December.	Yeats awarded Nobel Prize for Literature. First issues of *Dublin Magazine* and *Irish Statesman*. Shaw: *Saint Joan*. O'Casey: *The Shadow of a Gunman*. Svevo: *The Confessions of Zeno*. Rilke: *Duino Elegies*.
1924	Teaches Irish in St Luke's Protestant school in Cork. Begins work as an assistant librarian in Sligo, in the north-west of Ireland. Transferred to Wicklow library after six months.	O'Casey: *Juno and the Paycock*. Mann: *The Magic Mountain*.
1925	'Suibhne Geilt Speaks' (verse translation) published in *Irish Statesman*. First public use of the pseudonym Frank O'Connor (formed from his confirmation	Shaw awarded Nobel Prize. Yeats: *A Vision*. Liam O'Flaherty: *The Informer*. Daniel Corkery: *Hidden Ireland*. Dos Passos: *Manhattan Transfer*.

xviii

CHRONOLOGY

Black and Tans sent to support Irish police force. The first Bloody Sunday in Dublin. A particularly violent year in Cork with the murder by the Black and Tans of Tomas MacCurtain, the first Republican Lord Mayor, and the death on hunger strike of his replacement Terence MacSwiney. Large sections of Cork burned. Government of Ireland Act provides for Home Rule but with separate parliaments for North and South. League of Nations founded. Prohibition in US (to 1933). American women win voting rights. IRA sets fire to Dublin Customs House. First Parliament of Northern Ireland; Ulster Unionist leader Sir James Craig becomes Prime Minister (June). Truce signed between Sinn Féin and the British (July). IRA leader Michael Collins sent to London to negotiate Anglo-Irish Treaty (December). The outcome – Home Rule with dominion status for the South – dismays Republicans. First birth control clinic in Britain.

Irish Free State officially proclaimed and a constitution adopted (January). Resignation of De Valera. Civil war breaks out between pro-and anti-treaty factions of Sinn Féin. Roman Catholic bishops issue a statement excommunicating anyone fighting on the Republican side (October). Assassination of Collins. Sectarian violence escalates in the North. Royal Ulster Constabulary formed. USSR established. Mussolini's Fascist march on Rome. Foundation of BBC. Tomb of Tutankhamun discovered in Luxor. Revival of Ku Klux Khan in USA.

Pro-treaty side victorious in civil war but partition continues to be opposed by the IRA. Prime Minister William Cosgrove of the Cumann na nGaedheal party embarks on programme of national reconstruction. Irish Free State joins the League of Nations. Stalin becomes General Secretary of the Communist Party. Hitler's Munich *putsch* fails. German financial crisis.

Boundary Commission fails to recommend any significant changes to the border with the North, as promised in the Anglo-Irish Treaty. Legislation prohibiting divorce in Free State passed.

DATE	AUTHOR'S LIFE	LITERARY CONTEXT
1925 *cont.*	name, Francis, and his mother's maiden name). Begins to make a name for himself in Dublin literary circles. Meets A.E. (George Russell), publisher of *Irish Statesman* and through him W. B. Yeats and Lady Gregory. Applies for, and obtains the position of Cork's first county librarian.	Fitzgerald: *The Great Gatsby*. Woolf: *Mrs Dalloway*. Kafka: *The Trial*.
1926	Continues writing for *Irish Statesman*, as well as the *Irish Tribune*, contributing poems, essays and book reviews. First short story, 'War', published in *Irish Statesman*.	O'Casey: *The Plough and the Stars*. Hemingway: *The Sun Also Rises*. Kipling: *Debits and Credits*. Kafka: *The Castle*.
1927	Forms the Cork Drama League whose first play is *The Round Table* by Lennox Robinson. Meets Nancy McCarthy, a local chemist and amateur actress and falls in love with her.	Moore: *The Making of an Immortal*. Woolf: *To the Lighthouse*. Cather: *Death Comes for the Archbishop*. Hesse: *Steppenwolf*.
1928	Moves to Dublin to organize the Pembroke District Library, which is officially opened in September 1929. Among many innovations, introduces a music library and story-telling sessions for children. Stories in *Irish Statesman* and *Dublin Magazine*.	Yeats: *The Tower*. Lawrence: *Lady Chatterley's Lover*. Maugham: *Ashenden*. Brecht: *The Threepenny Opera*. Bulgakov begins *The Master and Margarita* (to 1940).
1929	Two different flats in Dublin. Works in Library and writes first novel, *The Saint and Mary Kate*, as well as stories about the Civil War. Essays and poetry published in *Irish Statesman*, two stories in *Dublin Magazine*.	Shaw: *The Apple Cart*. Denis Johnston: *The Old Lady Says 'No!'*. Bowen: *The Last September*. Woolf: *A Room of One's Own*. Faulkner: *The Sound and the Fury*. Hemingway: *A Farewell to Arms*. Hammet: *Red Harvest*.
1930	War stories published in *Irish Statesman* and *Dublin Magazine*, later in his first book of collected stories, *Guests of the Nation*. *Irish Statesman* ceases publication because of a libel action. Seven articles and reviews in last issue as well as poetry and one war story.	Faulkner: *As I Lay Dying*. Hammett: *The Maltese Falcon*. Freud: *Civilization and its Discontents*.

CHRONOLOGY

Radio Eireann set up. Anti-treaty faction of Sinn Féin splits; De Valera forms Fianna Fáil party. Germany admitted to League of Nations. General Strike in Britain. Baird demonstrates television picture.

Assassination of Kevin O'Higgins, Minister for Justice, by militant Republicans. De Valera's Fianna Fáil take up their seats, ending boycott of the Dáil. Lindbergh flies the Atlantic solo. First 'talkie' – *The Jazz Singer.*

First 'Five Year Plan' in USSR. Full suffrage for women in UK. Amelia Earheart becomes the first woman to fly the Atlantic solo. First Mickey Mouse cartoon. Fleming discovers penicillin. Foundation of the Gate Theatre, Dublin.

Passage of the Censorship of Publications Act by the Irish government. Under this law a number of O'Connor's books – and those of many other authors – were banned. Completion of the Shannon Scheme to supply the South with hydro-electric power. Abolition of proportional representation in the North. Wall Street Crash. Period of worldwide Depression begins.

Mahatma Gandhi begins civil disobedience movement in India.

DATE	AUTHOR'S LIFE	LITERARY CONTEXT
1931	Moves to Anglesea Road, near library. Receives $140 from US magazine *Atlantic Monthly* for the story 'Guests of the Nation'. The book *Guests of the Nation* published by Macmillan, London and New York.	Johnston: *The Moon in the Yellow River.* Hammett: *The Glass Key.* Woolf: *The Waves.* Maugham: *Six Stories in the First Person Singular.*
1932	Moves again to Trenton, Ballsbridge. Story in *Yale Review*. *The Wild Bird's Nest* (translations of old Irish poetry) published by Cuala Press, Dublin. *The Saint and Mary Kate* (novel) published by Macmillan, London and New York. Engaged to Nancy McCarthy.	Sean O'Faolain: *Midsummer Night Madness.* Faulkner: *Light in August.* Huxley: *Brave New World.* Musil: *The Man Without Qualities.*
1933	Raglan Road, Ballsbridge. *Guests of the Nation* reprinted. Starts interviewing friends and family of Michael Collins with a view to writing a biography. Amateur group makes film of *Guests of the Nation*.	Yeats: *The Winding Stair; Collected Poems.* Johnston: *A Bride for the Unicorn.* Hemingway: *Winner Take Nothing.* N. West: *Miss Lonelyhearts.* Stein: *The Autobiography of Alice B. Toklas.*
1934	A.E. sells house and moves to London. First autobiographical piece, 'A Boy in Prison', published in *Life and Letters*. Heartbroken when Nancy McCarthy breaks off engagement.	Bowen: *The Cat Jumps.* Beckett: *More Pricks Than Kicks.* Sean O'Faolain: *A Nest of Simple Folk.* Fitzgerald: *Tender is the Night.* H. Miller: *Tropic of Cancer.* Waugh: *A Handful of Dust.*
1935	Appointed to board of directors of the Abbey Theatre. Story 'First Confession' (under the title 'Repentance') published in *Lovat Dickson's Magazine*.	Steinbeck: *Tortilla Flat.* Lewis: *It Can't Happen Here.*
1936	*Three Old Brothers* (original poems) published by Nelson, London. *Bones of Contention* (stories) published by Macmillan, New York. First broadcast on BBC.	Sean O'Faolain: *Bird Alone.* Faulkner: *Absalom, Absalom!* Auden: *Look Stranger!* García Lorca: *The House of Bernardo Alba.*

CHRONOLOGY

Statute of Westminster establishes legal status of dominions of British Commonwealth.

Fianna Fáil wins general election; De Valera forms government. Protectionist economic policies adopted. During the 1930s a number of semi-state companies are set up (e.g. Turf Development Board, Irish Sugar Company, Irish Life). Annuities payable to Irish farmers for land purchase are diverted from British to Irish Exchequer, provoking trade war with Britain. Unemployment in Britain reaches 2,947,000; Hunger Marches. Election of Roosevelt in US. Nazis become largest party in German Reichstag.

De Valera re-elected with increased majority. Abolition of oath of allegiance and reduction of powers of British governor-general. Fine Gael founded. Unemployment Assistance Act. Foundation of Falange (Fascist party) in Spain. Roosevelt announces New Deal. Hitler becomes German Chancellor.

Hitler becomes German *Führer*.

De Valera severs ties with the IRA, imprisoning some of its leaders. Sale and importation of contraceptives made illegal in the Free State. In Germany Nuremberg laws deprive Jews of citizenship.

IRA declared illegal. First Aer Lingus flight. Outbreak of Spanish Civil War (to 1939). Edward VIII abdicates; George VI crowned in UK. Stalin's 'Great Purge' of the Communist Party (to 1938).

DATE	AUTHOR'S LIFE	LITERARY CONTEXT
1937	Appointed managing director of Abbey Theatre. *The Big Fellow: A Life of Michael Collins* published by Nelson, London. *In the Train* and *The Invincibles* (plays), in collaboration with Hugh Hunt, for the Abbey Theatre.	Ó Criomhthain: *The Islandman.* Auden/MacNeice: *Letters from Iceland.* M. J. Farrell: *The Rising Tide.* Steinbeck: *Of Mice and Men.* Hemingway: *To Have and Have Not.* Orwell: *The Road to Wigan Pier.*
1938	*Moses' Rock* (play), in collaboration with Hugh Hunt, for the Abbey Theatre. *Lords and Commons* (translations from Irish) published by Cuala Press, Dublin. Ceases to work as a librarian in order to devote time to writing.	Beckett: *Murphy.* Bowen: *The Death of the Heart.* Brian Coffey: *Third Person.* Dos Passos: *USA.* Greene: *Brighton Rock.* Waugh: *Scoop.* Pritchett: *You Make Your Own Life.* Sartre: *Nausea.*
1939	Marries Evelyn Bowen Speaight, an English actress. They move to a rented house in Woodenbridge, County Wicklow. Steps down from the Abbey Theatre board after the death of Yeats. Birth of first child, Myles. First broadcasts on Radio Eireann.	Yeats: *Last Poems*; *Two Plays.* Joyce: *Finnegans Wake.* O'Brien: *At Swim-Two-Birds.* Death of Yeats. Steinbeck: *The Grapes of Wrath.* H. Miller: *Tropic of Capricorn.* Chandler: *The Big Sleep.* Isherwood: *Goodbye to Berlin.*
1940	Together with Sean O'Faolain, helps establish *The Bell*, a new Irish literary journal. *Dutch Interior* (novel) published by Macmillan, London, and Knopf, New York.	Sean O'Faolain: *Come Back to Erin.* O'Brien: *The Third Policeman* (unpublished until 1967). Hemingway: *For Whom the Bell Tolls.* Chandler: *Farewell, My Lovely.* Greene: *The Power and the Glory.* Dylan Thomas: *Portrait of the Artist as a Young Dog.*
1941	*Dutch Interior* banned by Irish Censorship Board for 'indecency'. Birth of daughter Liadain. Broadcast from London for BBC Home Service.	O'Brien: *An Béal Bocht* (*The Poor Mouth*). Death of Joyce. Fitzgerald: *The Last Tycoon.* Coward: *Blythe Spirit.* Brecht: *Mother Courage.*

CHRONOLOGY

New constitution adopted which ignores the British Crown, claiming sovereignty over 'the whole island of Ireland' but 'pending reintegration' only applying to 26 counties. The nation is to be known as Eire. De Valera becomes Taoiseach (Prime Minister). Bombing of Guernica by German planes. Hitler and Mussolini form Rome–Berlin Axis. Japanese invasion of China.

Douglas Hyde is elected as the first President. Irish government agrees to pay lump sum to Britain to clear annuities debt. British agree to withdraw from naval bases in Eire. End of trade war. Germany annexes Austria. Munich crisis.

Germany occupies Czechoslovakia. Nazi-Soviet Pact; Hitler invades Poland. Ireland declares its neutrality in World War II (though thousands of Irish citizens enlist to fight for Britain). A 'State of Emergency' declared.

IRA leadership attempts to open links with Nazi Germany. Resignation of Neville Chamberlain: Winston Churchill leads coalition ministry in Britain. Fall of France. Battle of Britain. The Blitz.

Heavy German air-raids on Belfast and Derry: fire brigades from Eire are sent to assist victims. Bombs dropped on Dublin in error by German bombers (31 May), killing 334 and injuring 90. Germany invades Russia. Japan attacks Pearl Harbor; US enters war. Hitler invades the Soviet Union.

DATE	AUTHOR'S LIFE	LITERARY CONTEXT
1942	Death of his father in Cork. Works for four weeks at the British Ministry of Information and the BBC in London (January). *The Statue's Daughter* (play) staged at the Gate Theatre, Dublin. *Three Tales* (stories) published by Cuala Press, Dublin. Moves to Sandymount, County Dublin (to 1949). The Irish government, being neutral, worries that the Germans might misinterpret his frequent visits to England, so cancels his passport and bans him from leaving Ireland.	O'Casey: *Red Rose for Me.* Patrick Kavanagh: *The Great Hunger.* Camus: *The Outsider.*
1943	Travel ban rescinded (John Betjeman had successfully approached the Censorship Board for aid). Returns to London in the autumn. Refused work in Radio Eireann. *A Picture Book* with illustrations by Elizabeth Rivers published by Cuala Press, Dublin. Begins publishing controversial articles under the pseudonym Ben Mayo in the *Independent* newspaper.	Bowen: *Seven Winters.*
1944	Spends much time in England working for the BBC. *Crab Apple Jelly* (stories) published by Macmillan, London, and Knopf, New York. Meets and falls in love with Joan Knape, one of a group of English friends who meet after work.	Eliot: *Four Quartets.* Sartre: *Huis clos.*
1945	Birth of Oliver, Michael and Joan's son. Translates *The Midnight Court*, a long poem in Irish by Brian Merriman, published by Fridberg, London/Dublin. First story, 'News for the Church', published in the *New Yorker* magazine. Beginning of long association with the *New Yorker*.	Waugh: *Brideshead Revisited.* Orwell: *Animal Farm.* Betjamin: *New Bats in Old Belfries.*

HISTORICAL EVENTS

North African campaign. Gandhi calls on British to 'Quit India.'

Allied invasion of Italy.

Allied (D-Day) landings in Normandy. Liberation of Paris.

Mussolini shot by partisans. Unconditional surrender of Germany.
De Valera offers condolences to Germany on the death of Hitler. Atomic
bombs dropped on Japan. End of World War II. Nationalists in the North
form Anti-Partition League. Sean O'Kelly becomes Irish President. Period
of rapid inflation in the South. Labour party under Atlee sweeps to victory
in UK. United Nations formed.

DATE	AUTHOR'S LIFE	LITERARY CONTEXT
1946	Birth of Owen, Michael and Evelyn's son. *Selected Stories* published by Fridberg, Dublin. *The Midnight Court* banned in Ireland. 'Judas' (story) translated into French, published in *La France Libre*. Series of literary talks for Leeds BBC.	
1947	*Irish Miles* (travel book) published by Macmillan, London. *The Common Chord* (stories) also published by Macmillan and banned in Ireland. Book reviews in various English journals. Two stories in *New Yorker*, one in *Harper's Bazaar*. Continues to work for BBC. Loans a cottage in Lyme Regis where he instals his mother, wife and children, visiting them at weekends.	Williams: *A Streetcar Named Desire*. Maugham: *Creatures of Circumstance*. Mann: *Doctor Faustus*.
1948	Death of W. B. Yeats. *The Road to Stratford* (Shakespearean criticism) published by Methuen, London. Numerous broadcasts for BBC in London and Belfast. Trip to Denmark to give talk.	Sean O'Faolain: *The Man Who Invented Sin*. Mailer: *The Naked and the Dead*. Greene: *The Heart of the Matter*.
1949	Separates from wife, Evelyn, in August. Lives in Lyme Regis and London with various friends. Spends Christmas in Avignon where he writes *My Oedipus Complex*. Two stories in *New Yorker*, one in *Penguin New Writing No. 37*. Many broadcasts in BBC series *The Critics*. Granted legal separation.	O'Casey: *Cock-a-Doodle Dandy*. Bowen: *The Heat of the Day*. A. Miller: *Death of a Salesman*. Orwell: *Nineteen Eighty-four*.
1950	Lives with Joan and son Oliver in Dublin. *Leinster, Munster and Connaught* (travel book), Robert Hale, London. Three stories in *New Yorker*, one in *Harper's Bazaar*, one in *Today's Woman*, one in *Evening News*. Reads stories on BBC Northern Ireland.	Highsmith: *Strangers on a Train*. Death of Shaw.

CHRONOLOGY

USSR extends influence in Eastern Europe. Beginning of Cold War.

Marshall Plan: US aid for European post-war recovery. India and Pakistan achieve independence as two separate dominions.

De Valera defeated; inter-party government formed in Ireland under John Costello. Soviet blockade of Berlin and Allied airlift. Communist coup in Czechoslovakia. State of Israel established. South African government adopts apartheid as official policy. Assassination of Gandhi.

Republic of Ireland Act passed. Eire withdraws from the Commonwealth and becomes fully independent. Attempts by Eire government to negotiate union with the North firmly resisted by Unionist Prime Minister Basil Brooke. Britain passes Ireland Act, recognizing the Republic but guaranteeing that the North will remain part of the UK unless its parliament decides otherwise. NATO founded (Irish Republic declines to join as Northern Ireland remains part of the UK). Federal Republic of Germany established. Communist Revolution in China.

Economic depression in the Republic throughout the 1950s; emigration increases. Korean War (to 1953).

DATE	AUTHOR'S LIFE	LITERARY CONTEXT
1951	Moves to Lyme Regis with mother, Joan and Oliver. *Traveller's Samples* (stories) published by Macmillan, London, and Knopf, New York. Banned by Censorship Board. Court case to decide custody of chidren. Six broadcasts for BBC. Stories in *Evening News*, *Cornhill Magazine*, *John Bull* and *American Mercury*.	Beckett: *Molloy; Malone Dies.* Salinger: *The Catcher in the Rye.* Styron: *Lie Down in Darkness.* Powell: *A Dance to the Music of Time* (to 1975).
1952	Visits USA to lecture on Anglo-Irish literature and creative writing at Northwestern University, Evanston, Illinois (where he stays with Richard Ellman and family) and later Harvard. *The Stories of Frank O'Connor* published by Knopf, New York. Death of mother (November). Meets Harriet Rich, a mature literature student from Maryland. Controversial article about Ireland in *Holiday Magazine*. Five stories in *New Yorker*.	Hemingway: *The Old Man and the Sea.* Waugh: *Sword of Honour* trilogy (to 1961).
1953	Returns to USA to teach at University of Chicago, Northwestern and Harvard. Divorce made final in April. Buys small Elizabethan house ('Primrose Hill') in Buckinghamshire. Marries Harriet there in December. Gets custody of son Myles who lives there with them. *The Stories of Frank O'Connor*, Hamish Hamilton, London.	Beckett: *Waiting for Godot; Watt; The Unnamable.* Bellow: *The Adventures of Augie March.* Salinger: *Nine Stories.* Borges: *Labyrinths.*
1954	Returns to USA in autumn and lives in apartment in Brooklyn Heights with Harriet and Myles. *More Stories by Frank O'Connor*, Knopf, New York. Stories in *Harper's Magazine*, *Harper's Bazaar*, *Atlantic Monthly* and four in *New Yorker*.	Behan: *The Quare Fellow.* Kingsley Amis: *Lucky Jim.* Dylan Thomas: *Under Milk Wood.* Golding: *Lord of the Flies.*

CHRONOLOGY

DATE	AUTHOR'S LIFE	LITERARY CONTEXT
1955	Brooklyn Heights and Annapolis, Maryland. Reviews and articles in various American papers and journals. Four stories in *New Yorker*.	Nabokov: *Lolita*. Williams: *Cat on a Hot Tin Roof*. Highsmith: *The Talented Mr Ripley*.
1956	*The Mirror in the Roadway: A Study of the Modern Novel*, Knopf, New York. Vintage edition of *Stories*, Knopf. Trips to Ireland and England. Reunion with Nancy McCarthy who becomes a friend of the family. Gives talks at various American universities, including Virginia, Stanford, Berkeley and Michigan. Four Province Films takes option on 'The Majesty of the Law'. Reviews plays for *Holiday Magazine*.	Osborne: *Look Back in Anger*.
1957	*Domestic Relations* (stories) published by Knopf, New York; Hamish Hamilton, London. Makes record about Irish literature for Folkways Records. Film *Rising of the Moon* includes dramatization of 'The Majesty of the Law'. *Mirror in the Roadway* published by Hamish Hamilton, London. Six stories in *New Yorker*. Edits *Modern Irish Short Stories*, Oxford Classics.	Beckett: *Endgame*. Hugh Leonard: *A Leap in the Dark*. Kerouac: *On the Road*.
1958	Brooklyn Heights, Annapolis and Dublin. Birth of daughter Harriet (nicknamed 'Hallie Óg' (young Hallie). First section of autobiography, *An Only Child*, published in *New Yorker*, as well as four stories. TV appearances in New York include *The Last Word* with Bergen Evans, and *Camera Three*, reading a story. In Ireland, reads stories on Radio Eireann.	Behan: *The Hostage*; *Borstal Boy*. Beckett: *Krapp's Last Tape*. Johnston: *The Scythe and the Sunset*. Leonard: *Madigan's Lock*. Capote: *Breakfast at Tiffany's*. Pinter: *The Birthday Party*.
1959	Mespil Flats, Dublin, and Brooklyn Heights. Two more sections of autobiography in *New Yorker* plus one story. *Kings, Lords*	John B. Keane: *Sive*. Burroughs: *Naked Lunch*. Bellow: *Henderson the Rain King*. Grass: *The Tin Drum*.

CHRONOLOGY

Ireland joins the United Nations. Warsaw Pact formed.

IRA reorganizes and begins terrorist campaign in Northern Ireland which peters out by 1962. Suez Crisis. Hungarian uprising. Pakistan becomes the world's first Islamic Republic, but remains within Commonwealth.

De Valera returned to office. Dublin Theatre Festival founded. Treaty of Rome: European Economic Community founded. Harold Macmillan becomes British Prime Minister. Civil Rights Commission established in US to safeguard voting rights. Ghana and Malaya become independent.

T. K. Whitaker's Report on Economic Development.

De Valera stands down to run for President. Seán Lemass, his former deputy, becomes Taoiseach. Government adopts Whitaker's recommendations: protectionist policies abandoned and foreign investment encouraged. Castro comes to power in Cuba.

FRANK O'CONNOR

DATE	AUTHOR'S LIFE	LITERARY CONTEXT
1959 *cont.*	*and Commons* (translations of old Irish poetry) published by Knopf, New York. Banned in Ireland because of inclusion of *The Midnight Court*. Edits *Book of Ireland*. Published in the Collins National Anthologies series, London and Glasgow. Talks at NYU and YMHA Poetry Centre. Reads various stories on Radio Eireann and BBC Northern Ireland.	
1960	Brooklyn Heights. Gives talk at Library of Congress. Goes to Copenhagen for Writers' Conference, where other authors envy his difficult childhood as material for stories. With Liam Clancy produces a reading play about Yeats (called *Yeats and Cuchulain*) at YMHA Poetry Centre. One story in *New Yorker*. First mild symptoms of heart failure.	Updike: *Rabbit, Run.* Pinter: *The Caretaker.* Dahl: *Kiss Kiss.* Spark: *The Ballad of Peckham Rye.*
1961	Palo Alto, California; Mespil Flats and Court Flats, Dublin. Teaches twentieth-century novel and creative writing at Stanford University. Makes *Monitor* (autobiographical film) with Huw Weldon for BBC. *An Only Child*, first volume of autobiography, published by Knopf, New York (sells out in six weeks). *Kings, Lords and Commons* published by Macmillan, London. Suffers slight stroke.	Tom Murphy: *A Whistle in the Dark.* O'Brien: *The Hard Life.* Heller: *Catch-22.* Salinger: *Franny and Zooey.*
1962	Court Flats, Dublin. Awarded honorary doctorate by Trinity College, Dublin. *The Lonely Voice: A Study of the Short Story* published by World Publishing Co. Talks at Yeats Summer School, Sligo. Makes debut on newly established Irish television, in a two-part autobiographical programme called *Self-Portrait*.	Brian Friel: *The Enemy Within.* Nabokov: *Pale Fire.* Albee: *Who's Afraid of Virginia Woolf?* Solzhenitsyn: *One Day in the Life of Ivan Denisovich.*

CHRONOLOGY

Sharpeville massacre in South Africa: ANC outlawed. Cyprus and Nigeria achieve independence. Kennedy elected US President.

The Republic's attempts to join the EEC fail (finally joins in 1972). Radio Telefis Eireann (RTE) begins television broadcasting. Bay of Pigs invasion. Erection of Berlin Wall. Yuri Gagarin becomes first man in space.

IRA calls off its 'Border Campaign', having failed to gain significant support. Cuban missile crisis.

DATE	AUTHOR'S LIFE	LITERARY CONTEXT
1963	Teaching Irish literature at Trinity College, Dublin. Talks about travel, architecture and the theatre as well as reading his own stories on BBC and Radio Eireann. *The Little Monasteries* (translations from Irish), limited edition, Dolmen Press, Dublin. *My Oedipus Complex and Other Stories*, Penguin.	Pynchon: *V.* Salinger: *Raise High the Roof Beam, Carpenters and Seymour: An Introduction.* Plath: *The Bell Jar.* Burgess: *Inside Mr Enderby.*
1964	Two family trips to France. A series of weekly articles in *Sunday Independent* (under own name) about neglect of Irish monuments and architecture as well as reviews of books and plays. Reviews and articles in *Irish Times* and *Spectator.* Broadcasts for BBC Northern Ireland. Ill on and off during year.	Friel: *Philadelphia, Here I Come!* Bellow: *Herzog.*
1965	Operation early in year. Recuperation slow and difficult. Two radio broadcasts, two stories in *Saturday Evening Post. Lonely Voice* published in Macmillan's Papermac. Two sections of second volume of autobiography (*My Father's Son*) printed in *Vogue* and *Kenyon Review.*	Heaney: *Eleven Poems.* John McGahern: *The Dark.* Keane: *The Field.* Mailer: *An American Dream.*
1966	Completes *My Father's Son* (published 1968). New York literary agent sends contract for *The Backward Look: A Survey of Irish Literature*, published by Macmillan, London, Melbourne, Toronto, 1967. Three articles in *Sunday Independent.* Prizewinning BBC adaptation of 'Song Without Words' produced as *Silent Song.* Dies of heart attack at home in Court Flats, 10 March. Buried in Dean's Grange Cemetery, Dublin.	MacNeice: *Collected Poems.* Heaney: *Death of a Naturalist.* Aidan Higgins: *Langrishe, Go Down.* Friel: *The Loves of Cass McGuire.* Leonard: *Mick and Mick.* Pynchon: *The Crying of Lot 49.* Capote: *In Cold Blood.*

C H R O N O L O G Y

Terence O'Neill becomes Prime Minister in Northern Ireland, and seeks greater accommodation with the minority Catholic community. US President John Kennedy visits the Republic. Assassination of Kennedy in Dallas, Texas. Johnson becomes President. Civil war between Greeks and Turks in Cyprus.

First 5-year economic plan exceeds its goals. The 1960s is a period of increased prosperity; rate of emigration declines. The Campaign for Social Justice launched in Northern Ireland. Khrushchev deposed in Russia. US Civil Rights Act prohibits discrimination in US. Nobel Peace Prize awarded to Martin Luther King.

Landmark meetings between O'Neill and Lemass at Stormont and in Dublin. Anglo-Irish trade treaty signed. Lemass introduces free secondary education. War between India and Pakistan. Ian Smith makes Rhodesian Declaration of Independence; Britain declares the regime illegal.

50th anniversary of the Easter Rising celebrated by Catholics throughout Ireland. Lemass stands down and is replaced as Taoiseach by Jack Lynch. Opening of new Abbey Theatre. In the North, Ian Paisley forms the Ulster Constitution Defence Committee (UCDC) to campaign against O'Neill. He also helps to revive the militant loyalist Ulster Volunteer Force, declaring war on the IRA. Mao launches Cultural Revolution in China.

ABOUT THE EDITOR

JULIAN BARNES's novels include *Flaubert's Parrot*, *A History of the World in 10½ Chapters* and *Arthur and George*. He has also published collections of short stories and essays and, most recently, a memoir, *Nothing to be Frightened of*.

1 WAR

WAR WAS the subject which turned Michael O'Donovan into the short story writer Frank O'Connor: war first against the British, then between the Irish in the Civil War. O'Donovan did 'odd jobs', as he put it, for the IRA; later, he chose the Republican side against the Irish Free State, and was interned for a year in 1922–23. The opening ten stories (out of fifteen) in his first collection, *Guests of the Nation* (1931), are all concerned with war.

Thirty-five years later, in *My Father's Son*, his second volume of autobiography, O'Connor looked back dismissingly on *Guests of the Nation* and on his first novel, *The Saint and Mary Kate* (1932):

> I still considered myself a poet, and had little notion of how to write a story and none at all of how to write a novel, so they were produced in hysterical fits of enthusiasm, followed by similar fits of despondency, good passages alternating with bad, till I can no longer read them.

Nor could he bear to reprint them. In later years, he made three separate collections of his stories, totalling 82 of the 150 or so he had published. Yet only two of those first fifteen stories ever made the cut: the title story – which remains one of the most famous fictional accounts of war in the twentieth century – and the final, non-war story, 'The Procession of Life'.

Being an inveterate rewriter, O'Connor unsurprisingly altered these two stories before reprinting them. 'Guests of the Nation' is rewritten at a surface, stylistic level, with minor cuts and additions, the elimination of Kiplingesque renderings of Cockney speech, and such adjustments as 'bugger' for 'blighter'. 'The Procession of Life', about a Cork dockside encounter between an adolescent boy, a nightwatchman, a woman of the streets and a policeman, is much more drastically changed. All the main characters are altered in character and manner, while

Irishisms ('ponny', 'drisheen', '*taoscan*' and even the lovely verb 'connoisseuring') are suppressed. The original story is shorter, stranger, more hallucinatory, and at one point more directly erotic; the later version gives extra background, supplies motive, is more urbane.

But the young O'Connor was not, as the mature O'Connor claimed, unskilled to the point of unreadability. The young O'Connor had the freshness and the fire; the mature O'Connor had the savvy and the caution. For me, the two versions of 'Guests of the Nation' have equal merits; while the earlier version of 'The Procession of Life' is superior. William Maxwell, in the course of an affectionate editorial argument, once told O'Connor, 'Of course you are right about the story, and I am too.' So this collection begins – in similarly admiring disagreement – with seven of the war stories, alongside later non-fictional accounts of those times, from his autobiographies and from *The Big Fellow*, his biography of Michael Collins.

GUESTS OF THE NATION

AT DUSK the big Englishman Belcher would shift his long legs out of the ashes and ask, 'Well, chums, what about it?' and Noble or me would say, 'As you please, chum' (for we had picked up some of their curious expressions), and the little Englishman 'Awkins would light the lamp and produce the cards. Sometimes Jeremiah Donovan would come up of an evening and supervise the play, and grow excited over 'Awkins's cards (which he always played badly), and shout at him as if he was one of our own, 'Ach, you divil you, why didn't you play the tray?' But, ordinarily, Jeremiah was a sober and contented poor devil like the big Englishman Belcher, and was looked up to at all only because he was a fair hand at documents, though slow enough at these, I vow. He wore a small cloth hat and big gaiters over his long pants, and seldom did I perceive his hands outside the pockets of that pants. He reddened when you talked to him, tilting from toe to heel and back and looking down all the while at his big farmer's feet. His uncommon broad accent was a great source of jest to me, I being from the town as you may recognize.

I couldn't at the time see the point of me and Noble being with Belcher and 'Awkins at all, for it was and is my fixed belief you could have planted that pair in any untended spot from this to Claregalway and they'd have stayed put and flourished like a native weed. I never seen in my short experience two men that took to the country as they did.

They were handed on to us by the Second Battalion to keep when the search for them became too hot, and Noble and myself, being young, took charge with a natural feeling of responsibility. But little 'Awkins made us look right fools when he displayed he knew the countryside as well as we did and something more. 'You're the bloke they calls Bonaparte?' he said to me. 'Well, Bonaparte, Mary Brigid Ho'Connell was arskin abaout you and said 'ow you'd a pair of socks belonging to 'er young brother.' For it seemed, as they explained it, that the Second used to have little evenings of their own, and some of the girls of the neighbourhood would turn in, and seeing they were such decent fellows, our lads couldn't well ignore the two Englishmen, but invited them in and were hail-fellow-well-met with them. 'Awkins told me he learned to dance 'The Walls of Limerick' and 'The Siege of Ennis' and 'The Waves of Tory' in a night or two, though naturally he could not return the compliment, because our lads at that time did not dance foreign dances on principle.

So whatever privileges and favours Belcher and 'Awkins had with the Second they duly took with us, and after the first evening we gave up all pretence of keeping a close eye on their behaviour. Not that they could have got far, for they had a notable accent and wore khaki tunics and overcoats with civilian pants and boots. But it's my belief they never had an idea of escaping and were quite contented with their lot.

Now, it was a treat to see how Belcher got off with the old woman of the house we were staying in. She was a great warrant to scold, and crotchety even with us, but before ever she had a chance of giving our guests, as I may call them, a lick of her tongue, Belcher had made her his friend for life. She was breaking sticks at the time, and Belcher, who hadn't been in the house for more than ten minutes, jumped up out of his seat and went across to her.

'Allow me, madam,' he says, smiling his queer little smile; 'please allow me,' and takes the hatchet from her hand. She was struck too parlatic to speak, and ever after Belcher would be at her heels carrying a bucket, or basket, or load of turf, as the case might be. As Noble wittily remarked, he got into looking before she leapt, and hot water or any little thing she wanted Belcher would have it ready for her. For such a huge man (and though I am five foot ten myself I had to look up to him) he had an uncommon shortness – or should I say lack – of speech. It took us some time to get used to him walking in and out like a ghost, without a syllable out of him. Especially because 'Awkins talked enough for a platoon, it was strange to hear big Belcher with his toes in the ashes come out with a solitary 'Excuse me, chum,' or 'That's right, chum.' His one and only abiding passion was cards, and I will say for him he was a good card-player. He could have fleeced me and Noble many a time; only if we lost to him, 'Awkins lost to us, and 'Awkins played with the money Belcher gave him.

'Awkins lost to us because he talked too much, and I think now we lost to Belcher for the same reason. 'Awkins and Noble would spit at one another about religion into the early hours of the morning; the little Englishman as you could see worrying the soul out of young Noble (whose brother was a priest) with a string of questions that would puzzle a cardinal. And to make it worse, even in treating of these holy subjects, 'Awkins had a deplorable tongue; I never in all my career struck across a man who could mix such a variety of cursing and bad language into the simplest topic. Oh, a terrible man was little 'Awkins, and a fright to argue! He never did a stroke of work, and when he had no one else to talk to he fixed his claws into the old woman.

I am glad to say that in her he met his match, for one day when he tried to get her to complain profanely of the drought she gave him a great comedown by blaming the drought upon Jupiter Pluvius (a deity neither 'Awkins nor I had ever even heard of, though Noble said among the pagans he was held to have something to do with rain). And another day the same 'Awkins was swearing at the capitalists for starting the German war, when the old dame laid down her iron, puckered up her little crab's mouth and said, 'Mr 'Awkins, you can say what you please about the war, thinking to deceive me because I'm an ignorant old woman, but I know well what started the war. It was that Italian count that stole the heathen divinity out of the temple in Japan, for believe me, Mr 'Awkins, nothing but sorrow and want follows them that disturbs the hidden powers!' Oh, a queer old dame, as you remark!

So one evening we had our tea together, and 'Awkins lit the lamp and we all sat in to cards. Jeremiah Donovan came in too, and sat down and watched us for a while. Though he was a shy man and didn't speak much, it was easy to see he had no great love for the two Englishmen, and I was surprised it hadn't struck me so clearly before. Well, like that in the story, a terrible dispute blew up late in the evening between 'Awkins and Noble, about capitalists and priests and love for your own country.

'The capitalists,' says 'Awkins, with an angry gulp, 'the

capitalists pays the priests to tell you all abaout the next world, so's you won't notice what they do in this!'

'Nonsense, man,' says Noble, losing his temper, 'before ever a capitalist was thought of people believed in the next world.'

'Awkins stood up as if he was preaching a sermon. 'Oh, they did, did they?' he says with a sneer. 'They believed all the things you believe, that's what you mean? And you believe that God created Hadam and Hadam created Shem and Shem created Jehoshophat? You believe all the silly hold fairy-tale abaout Heve and Heden and the happle? Well, listen to me, chum. If you're entitled to 'old to a silly belief like that, I'm entitled to 'old to my own silly belief – which is, that the fust thing your God created was a bleedin' capitalist with mirality and Rolls Royce complete. Am I right, chum?' he says then to Belcher.

'You're right, chum,' says Belcher, with his queer smile, and gets up from the table to stretch his long legs into the fire and stroke his moustache. So, seeing that Jeremiah Donovan was going, and there was no knowing when the conversation about religion would be over, I took my hat and went out with him. We strolled down towards the village together, and then he suddenly stopped, and blushing and mumbling, and shifting, as his way was, from toe to heel, he said I ought to be behind keeping guard on the prisoners. And I, having it put to me so suddenly, asked him what the hell he wanted a guard on the prisoners at all for, and said that so far as Noble and me were concerned we had talked it over and would rather be out with a column. 'What use is that pair to us?' I asked him.

He looked at me for a spell and said, 'I thought you knew we were keeping them as hostages.' 'Hostages –?' says I, not quite understanding. 'The enemy,' he says in his heavy way, 'have prisoners belong' to us, and now they talk of shooting them. If they shoot our prisoners we'll shoot theirs, and serve them right.' 'Shoot them?' said I, the possibility just beginning to dawn on me. 'Shoot them exactly,' said he. 'Now,' said I, 'wasn't it very unforeseen of you not to tell me and Noble that?' 'How so?' he asks. 'Seeing that we were acting as guards upon them, of course.' 'And hadn't you reason enough to guess that much?' 'We had not, Jeremiah Donovan, we had not. How were we to know when the men were on our hands so long?' 'And what difference does it make? The enemy have our prisoners as long or longer, haven't they?' 'It makes a great difference,' said I. 'How so?' said he sharply; but I couldn't tell him the difference it made, for I was struck too silly to speak. 'And when may we expect to be released from this anyway?' said I. 'You may expect it tonight,' says he. 'Or tomorrow or the next day at latest. So if it's hanging round here that worries you, you'll be free soon enough.'

I cannot explain it even now, how sad I felt, but I went back to the cottage, a miserable man, When I arrived the discussion was still on, 'Awkins holding forth to all and sundry that there was no next world at all and Noble answering in his best canonical style that there was. But I saw 'Awkins was after having the best of it. 'Do you know what, chum?' he was saying, with his saucy smile. 'I think you're jest as big a bleedin' hunbeliever as I am. You say you believe in the next world and you know jest as much abaout the next world as I do, which is sweet damn-all. What's 'Eaven? You dunno. Where's 'Eaven? You dunno. Who's in 'Eaven? You dunno. You know sweet damn-all! I arsk you again, do they wear wings?'

'Very well then,' says Noble, 'they do; is that enough for you? They do wear wings.' 'Where do they get them then? Who makes them? 'Ave they a fact'ry for wings? 'Ave they a sort of store where you 'ands in your chit and tikes your bleedin' wings? Answer me that.'

'Oh, you're an impossible man to argue with,' says Noble. 'Now listen to me −' And off the pair of them went again.

It was long after midnight when we locked up the Englishmen and went to bed ourselves. As I blew out the candle I told Noble what Jeremiah Donovan had told me. Noble took it very quietly. After we had been in bed about an hour he asked me did I think we ought to tell the Englishmen. I having thought of the same thing myself (among many others) said no, because it was more than likely the English wouldn't shoot our men, and anyhow it wasn't to be supposed the Brigade who were always up and down with the Second Battalion and knew the Englishmen well would be likely to want them bumped off. 'I think so,' says Noble. 'It would be sort of cruelty to put the wind up them now.' 'It was very unforeseen of Jeremiah Donovan anyhow,' says I, and by Noble's silence I realized he took my meaning.

So I lay there half the night, and thought and thought, and picturing myself and young Noble trying to prevent the Brigade from shooting 'Awkins and Belcher sent a cold sweat out through me. Because there were men on the Brigade you daren't let nor hinder without a gun in your hand, and at any rate, in those days disunion between brothers seemed to me an awful crime. I knew better after.

It was next morning we found it so hard to face Belcher and 'Awkins with a smile. We went about the house all day scarcely saying a word. Belcher didn't mind us much; he was stretched into the ashes as usual with his usual look of waiting in quietness for something unforeseen to happen, but little 'Awkins gave us a bad time with his audacious gibing and questioning. He was disgusted at Noble's not answering him back. 'Why can't you tike your beating like a man, chum?' he says. 'You with your Hadam and Heve! I'm a Communist – or an Anarchist. An Anarchist, that's what I am.' And for hours after he went round the house, mumbling when the fit took him 'Hadam and Heve! Hadam and Heve!'

I don't know clearly how we got over that day, but get over it we did, and a great relief it was when the tea things were cleared away and Belcher said in his peaceable manner, 'Well, chums, what about it?' So we all sat round the table and 'Awkins produced the cards, and at that moment I heard Jeremiah Donovan's footsteps up the path, and a dark presentiment crossed my mind. I rose quietly from the table and laid my hand on him before he reached the door. 'What do you want?' I asked him. 'I want those two soldier friends of yours,' he says reddening. 'Is that the way it is, Jeremiah Donovan?' I ask. 'That's the way. There were four of our lads went west this morning, one of them a boy of sixteen.' 'That's bad, Jeremiah,' says I.

At that moment Noble came out, and we walked down the path together talking in whispers. Feeney, the local intelligence officer, was standing by the gate. 'What are you going to do about it?' I asked Jeremiah Donovan. 'I want you and Noble to bring them out: you can tell them they're being shifted again; that'll be the quietest way.' 'Leave me out of that,' says Noble suddenly. Jeremiah Donovan looked at him hard for a minute or two. 'All right so,' he said peaceably. 'You and Feeney collect a few tools from the shed and dig a hole by the far end of the bog. Bonaparte and I'll be after you in about twenty minutes. But whatever else you do, don't let anyone see you with the tools. No one must know but the four of ourselves.'

We saw Feeney and Noble go round to the houseen where the tools were kept, and sidled in. Everything if I can so express myself was tottering before my eyes, and I left Jeremiah Donovan to do the explaining as best he could, while I took a seat and said nothing. He told them they were to go back to the Second. 'Awkins let a mouthful of curses out of him at that, and it was plain that Belcher, though he said nothing, was duly perturbed. The old woman was for having them stay in spite of us, and she did not shut her mouth until Jeremiah Donovan lost his temper and said some nasty things to her. Within the house by this time it was pitch dark, but no one thought of lighting the lamp, and in the darkness the two Englishmen fetched their khaki topcoats and said good-bye to the woman of the house. 'Just as a man mikes a 'ome of a bleedin' place,' mumbles 'Awkins, shaking her by the hand, 'some bastard at Headquarters thinks you're too cushy and shunts you off.' Belcher shakes her hand very hearty. 'A thousand thanks, madam,' he says, 'a thousand thanks for everything . . .' as though he'd made it all up.

We go round to the back of the house and down towards the fatal bog. Then Jeremiah Donovan comes out with what is in his mind. 'There were four of our lads shot by your fellows this morning so now you're to be bumped off.' 'Cut that stuff out,' says 'Awkins, flaring up. 'It's bad enough to be mucked about such as we are without you plying at soldiers.' 'It's true,' says Jeremiah Donovan, 'I'm sorry, 'Awkins, but 'tis true,' and comes out with the usual rigmarole about doing our duty and obeying our superiors. 'Cut it out,' says 'Awkins irritably. 'Cut it out!'

Then, when Donovan sees he is not being believed he turns to me. 'Ask Bonaparte here,' he says. 'I don't need to arsk Bonaparte. Me and Bonaparte are chums.' 'Isn't it true, Bonaparte?' says Jeremiah Donovan solemnly to me. 'It is,' I say sadly, 'it is.' 'Awkins stops. 'Now, for Christ's sike. . . .' 'I mean it, chum,' I say. 'You daon't saound as if you mean it. You knaow well you don't mean it.' 'Well, if he don't I do,' says Jeremiah Donovan. 'Why the 'ell sh'd you want to shoot me, Jeremiah Donovan?' 'Why the hell should your people take out four prisoners and shoot them in cold blood upon a barrack square?' I perceive Jeremiah Donovan is trying to encourage himself with hot words.

Anyway, he took little 'Awkins by the arm and dragged him on, but it was impossible to make him understand that we were in earnest. From which you will perceive how difficult it was for me, as I kept feeling my Smith and Wesson and thinking what I would do if they happened to put up a fight or ran for it, and wishing in my heart they would. I knew if only they ran I would never fire on them. 'Was Noble in this?' 'Awkins wanted to know, and we said yes. He laughed. But why should Noble want to shoot him? Why should we want to shoot him? What had he done to us? Weren't we chums (the word lingers painfully in my memory)? Weren't we? Didn't we understand him and didn't he understand us? Did either of us imagine for an instant that he'd shoot us for all the so-and-so brigadiers in the so-and-so British Army? By this time I began to perceive in the dusk the desolate edges of the bog that was to be their last earthly bed, and, so great a sadness overtook my mind, I could not answer him. We walked along the edge of it in the darkness, and every now and then 'Awkins would call a halt and begin again, just as if he was wound up, about us being chums, and I was in despair that nothing but the cold and open grave made ready for his presence would convince him that we meant it all. But all the same, if you can understand, I didn't want him to be bumped off.

At last we saw the unsteady glint of a lantern in the distance and made towards it. Noble was carrying it, and Feeney stood somewhere in the darkness behind, and somehow the picture of the two of them so silent in the boglands was like the pain of death in my heart. Belcher, on recognizing Noble, said ' 'Allo, chum' in his usual peaceable way, but 'Awkins flew at the poor boy immediately, and the dispute began all over again, only that Noble hadn't a word to say for himself, and stood there with the swaying lantern between his gaitered legs.

It was Jeremiah Donovan who did the answering. 'Awkins asked for the twentieth time (for it seemed to haunt his mind) if anybody thought he'd shoot Noble. 'You would,' says Jeremiah Donovan shortly. 'I wouldn't, damn you!' 'You would if you knew you'd be shot for not doing it.' 'I wouldn't, not if I was to be shot twenty times over; he's my chum. And Belcher wouldn't – isn't that right, Belcher?' 'That's right, chum,' says Belcher peaceably. 'Damned if I would. Anyway, who says Noble'd be shot if I wasn't bumped off? What d'you think I'd do if I was in Noble's place and we were out in the middle of a blasted bog?' 'What would you do?' 'I'd go with him wherever he was going. I'd share my last bob with him and stick by 'im through thick and thin.'

'We've had enough of this,' says Jeremiah Donovan, cocking his revolver. 'Is there any message you want to send before I fire?' 'No, there isn't, but ...' 'Do you want to say your prayers?' 'Awkins came out with a cold-blooded remark that shocked even me and turned to Noble again. 'Listen to me, Noble,' he said. 'You and me are chums. You won't come over to my side, so I'll come over to your side. Is that fair? Just you give me a rifle and I'll go with you wherever you want.'

Nobody answered him.

'Do you understand?' he said. 'I'm through with it all. I'm a deserter or anything else you like, but from this on I'm one of you. Does that prove to you that I mean what I say?' Noble raised his head, but as Donovan began to speak he lowered it again without answering. 'For the last time have you any messages to send?' says Donovan in a cold and excited voice.

'Ah, shut up, you, Donovan; you don't understand me, but these fellows do. They're my chums; they stand by me and I stand by them. We're not the capitalist tools you seem to think us.'

I alone of the crowd saw Donovan raise his Webley to the back of 'Awkins's neck, and as he did so I shut my eyes and tried to say a prayer. 'Awkins had begun to say something else when Donovan let fly, and, as I opened my eyes at the bang, I saw him stagger at the knees and lie out flat at Noble's feet, slowly, and as quiet as a child, with the lantern light falling sadly upon his lean legs and bright farmer's boots. We all stood very still for a while watching him settle out in the last agony.

Then Belcher quietly takes out a handkerchief, and begins to tie it about his own eyes (for in our excitement we had forgotten to offer the same to 'Awkins), and, seeing it is not big enough, turns and asks for a loan of mine. I give it to him and as he knots the two together he points with his foot at 'Awkins. ''E's not quite dead,' he says, 'better give 'im another.' Sure enough 'Awkins's left knee as we see it under the lantern is rising again. I bend down and put my gun to his ear; then, recollecting myself and the company of Belcher, I stand up again with a few hasty words. Belcher understands what is in my mind. 'Give 'im 'is first,' he says. 'I don't mind. Poor bastard, we dunno what's 'appening to 'im now.' As by this time I am beyond all feeling I kneel down again and skilfully give 'Awkins the last shot so as to put him forever out of pain.

Belcher who is fumbling a bit awkwardly with the handkerchiefs comes out with a laugh when he hears the shot. It is the first time I have heard him laugh, and it sends a shiver down my spine, coming as it does so inappropriately upon the tragic death of his old friend. 'Poor blighter,' he says quietly, 'and last night he was so curious abaout it all. It's very queer, chums, I always think. Naow; 'e knows as much abaout it as they'll ever let 'im know, and last night 'e was all in the dark.'

Donovan helps him to tie the handkerchiefs about his eyes. 'Thanks, chum,' he says. Donovan asks him if there are any messages he would like to send. 'Naow, chum,' he says, 'none for me. If any of you likes to write to 'Awkins's mother you'll find a letter from 'er in 'is pocket. But my missus left me eight years ago. Went away with another fellow and took the kid with her. I likes the feelin' of a 'ome (as you may 'ave noticed) but I couldn't start again after that.'

We stand around like fools now that he can no longer see us. Donovan looks at Noble and Noble shakes his head. Then Donovan raises his Webley again and just at that moment Belcher laughs his queer nervous laugh again. He must think we are talking of him; anyway, Donovan lowers his gun. ''Scuse me, chums,' says Belcher, 'I feel I'm talking the 'ell of a lot ... and so silly ... abaout me being so 'andy abaout a 'ouse. But this thing come on me so sudden. You'll forgive me, I'm sure.' 'You don't want to say a prayer?' asks Jeremiah Donovan, 'No, chum,' he replies, 'I don't think that'd 'elp. I'm ready if you want to get it over.' 'You understand,' says Jeremiah Donovan, 'it's not so much our doing. It's our duty, so to speak.' Belcher's head is raised like a real blind man's, so that you can only see his nose and chin in the lamplight. 'I never could make out what duty was myself,' he said, 'but I think you're all good lads, if that's what you mean. I'm not complaining.' Noble, with a look of desperation, signals to Donovan, and in a flash Donovan raises his gun and fires. The big man goes over like a sack of meal, and this time there is no need of a second shot.

I don't remember much about the burying, but that it was worse than all the rest, because we had to carry the warm corpses a few yards before we sunk them in the windy bog. It was all mad lonely, with only a bit of lantern between ourselves and the pitch blackness, and birds hooting and screeching all round disturbed by the guns. Noble had to search 'Awkins first to get the letter from his mother. Then having smoothed all signs of the grave away, Noble and I collected our tools, said good-bye to the others, and went back along the desolate edge of the treacherous bog without a word. We put the tools in the houseen and went into the house. The kitchen was pitch black and cold, just as we left it, and the old woman was sitting over the hearth telling her beads. We walked past her into the room, and Noble struck a match to light the lamp. Just then she rose quietly and came to the doorway, being not at all so bold or crabbed as usual.

'What did ye do with them?' she says in a sort of whisper, and Noble took such a mortal start the match quenched in his trembling hand. 'What's that?' he asks without turning round. 'I heard ye,' she said. 'What did you hear?' asks Noble, but sure he wouldn't deceive a child the way he said it. 'I heard ye. Do you think I wasn't listening to ye putting the things back in the houseen?' Noble struck another match and this time the lamp lit for him. 'Was that what ye did with them?' she said, and Noble said nothing – after all what could he say?

So then, by God, she fell on her two knees by the door, and began telling her beads, and after a minute or two Noble went on his knees by the fireplace, so I pushed my way out past her, and stood at the door, watching the stars and listening to the damned shrieking of the birds. It is so strange what you feel at such moments, and not to be written afterwards. Noble says he felt he seen everything ten times as big, perceiving nothing around him but the little patch of black bog with the two Englishmen stiffening into it; but with me it was the other way, as though the patch of bog where the two Englishmen were was a thousand miles away from me, and even Noble mumbling just behind me and the old woman and the birds and the bloody stars were all far away, and I was somehow very small and very lonely. And anything that ever happened me after I never felt the same about again.

ATTACK

LOMASNEY AND I came through the wood after dark, and at the stepping-stones over the little stream we were joined by another man who carried a carbine in the crook of his arm. We went on in silence, Lomasney leading the way across the sodden, slippery ground.

The attack on the barrack was timed to begin at two hours after midnight, and as yet it was only nine o'clock. Beneath us, through the trees, we could see a solitary light burning in one of the barrack bedrooms where some thoughtless policeman had forgotten to close the shutters. Surrounded by barbed wire, its windows shuttered with steel, the old building stood on the outskirts of the village, a formidable nut to crack.

But for a long time now this attack of ours was being promised to the garrison, whose sense of duty had outrun their common sense. Policemen are like that. A soldier never does more than he need do, and so far as possible he keeps on good terms with his enemy: for him the ideal is the least amount of disorder; he only asks not to be taken prisoner or ambushed or blown up too often. But for the policeman there is only one ideal, Order, hushed and entire; to his well-drilled mind a stray shot at a rabbit and a stray shot at a general are one and the same thing, so that in civil commotion he loses all sense of proportion and becomes a helpless, hopeless, gibbering maniac whom in everybody's interests it is better to remove. That at least was how we thought in those days, and the garrison I speak of had been a bad lot, saucy to the villagers and a nuisance to our men for miles around. Oh, it was coming to them – everybody knew that. In the evenings when the policemen were standing outside their door, sunning themselves and enjoying a smoke, some child's voice would be raised from a distance, singing:

> Do you want your old barracks blown down,
>   blown down?
> Do you want your old barracks blown down?

And blown down it would be if Lomasney's new-fangled explosive that was to put TNT in the shade proved a success.

We jumped the fence above the wood and landed in a meadow whose long, wet grass spread a summery fragrance about us. A star or two shone out above the hill, but night was not yet complete. Lomasney let the other man take the lead and waited for me.

'There's something I wanted to say to you, Owen,' he said. 'This house we're going to – there's only an old couple in it. They've had a deal of trouble already, and I'd be sorry to frighten them. So I'll let on we're only sheltering for a few hours, and do you make a joke of it if you can.'

I agreed, and went on with him in silence, waiting for the explanation that I knew was coming. Lomasney was intense and slow, and you could feel a story or a retort springing up in him long before it passed his lips.

'I've known those people since I was a kid,' he went on. 'I used to be friendly with the son of the house one time – he was a deal older than I was, but we hit it off well together. He was a big, handsome, devil-may-care fellow, a great favourite with the girls and a fright to hurl. Everyone was fond of him. He was kept down at home by his father, and so he used to spend his evenings anywhere but at home. He'd walk in on top of you, and sit by the fire as if he was one of the family, and, as soon as not, if you'd a bed to spare he'd spend the night with you.

'Five years ago, he got into trouble. He was keen on a girl in the village. She was married to a waster who used to beat her. One night her husband was knocked out in a row and didn't over it. Paddy hit him, of course, but it was his head cracking off the floor that did for him. Nobody was very sorry for him, but everybody was sorry for Paddy and the girl.

'That night some of Paddy's friends drove him into the city. The people around were very decent; they made up enough money to take him to the States, and he cleared out. It was a stupid thing to do – I know that now – but we were frightened of the law in those days.

'Well, since that night there hasn't been tale nor tiding of him. For a while the old father – he has the devil's own pride – was pretending he got letters through boys that had been with Paddy in New York. Maybe he did, in the beginning, but that was as much as he got. To my own knowledge, Paddy never wrote as much as one line home, and the best we can hope for is that he didn't go the same way as some of the others go. I think he must be dead, and things being as they are, I'd rather he was dead. But you can't convince his father of that. He's as certain as the day that Paddy's alive and flourishing, and it would be as much as your life was worth to contradict him.'

I was strangely moved by this little tale, mostly I think because it came to divert my thoughts from the dark building below to the cottage up the hill.

The man who accompanied us lifted a heavy branch out of a gateway, we pushed it home again, skirted a field of potatoes, and approached the house from the back. Lomasney knocked, and the door was opened by a sharp-eyed, ragged old man whose body was twisted like an apple-tree. He started back when he saw the three of us standing there with our rifles, and let the latch drop with a clatter. Lomasney immediately hailed him in a purposely boisterous tone – too boisterous, I thought, considering our errand – but it had its effect. With a curious gesture he bent forward and drew us in one by one by the hand, giving us as he did so a piercing look that made me wonder if there wasn't a streak of insanity in him. When he took my hand in one of his own old rocky hands and rested the other on my shoulder I felt I understood Lomasney's phrase about contradicting him. There was danger there.

We took our places on a settle beside the fire, opposite an old woman who called out a cracked greeting, but kept her eyes turned away. She wore a black shawl about her shoulders and hair, and her profile was taut in the firelight. The old man lit the lamp. There was a ladder leading to an attic in the centre of the floor, and he took his stand against this, with hands in the pockets of his trousers. He stared at us all in turn, but I came in for the most careful survey. Lomasney made up some legend about me to content the boundless countryman's curiosity in him, and meanwhile, without raising my eyes, I studied him. He was much taller than I had thought him bent beneath the shadow of the doorway, taller and more powerful, with a stubborn and avaricious mouth. His trousers, without as much as a button down the front of it, was in rags, and he hitched it up about his belly with a shrug that displayed the great shoulder-blades and the twisted muscles of his neck. He had a little yellow goat's beard that grew outwards from his chin and made his head appear to be tilted up.

After he had looked his fill at us, he spat out, heaved a chair across to the fire and sat down, spreading his dung-caked legs wide across the hearth.

''Tis late ye're stopping from yeer homes,' he said sourly.

'We've no choice in that,' replied Lomasney.

''Tis late – and foolish.'

'Maybe 'tis.'

''Tis.'

'We've our work to do,' added Lomasney cheerfully.

'Work?' The old man looked at him in pretended wonder. 'Work? Oh, ay.' He slowly quoted two lines of an Irish song. I saw the old woman's shawled head go up with a little jerk. It was her way of smiling at the aptness of it. But Lomasney and the other man looked blank. The old man bent across and laid a stony hand heavily on Lomasney's knee.

Tramping the dews in the morning airley,
And gethering chills for a quarter. . . .

he translated.

'If we are, there's more like us,' said Lomasney, trying to steer the conversation round to politics.

'Wisha, is there?'

'There is, and no one knows that better than yourself, Mike.'

I was amused to see the old man dodging him with a very cleverly assumed ignorance or indifference. After a time I saw that he had long since taken the measure of Lomasney's very earnest and passionate but simple mind, and was getting great enjoyment out of the battle of wits. He dropped his air of boorishness, and a glint of sour amusement flickered in his eyes. A bitter remark or two in Irish flung at his wife showed me the measure of his contempt for the younger man. I let him continue this country sport for a while until I saw Lomasney grow confused. Then I threw in a phrase of my own in Irish to show the old rascal that I understood. At this he looked me up and down wonderingly for a moment, broke into a loud, tempestuous laugh, and shoved back his seat to the table.

'Come, woman!' he shouted. 'Supper! Supper! The young cock is crowing.'

I felt in my heart that he despised me for an interfering young fool.

The old woman filled us out each a jam-crock of milk and cut us a slice of cake. We talked no more during the meal, and when it was over old Kieran produced his beads and knelt beside a chair, touching his forehead with the crucifix. We knelt likewise, all but the old woman, 'whose kneecaps were wake,' she said. Kieran gave out the rosary.

When the prayers proper were finished Lomasney blessed himself hurriedly and half rose, but the old man's voice, angry and strident, broke in to stop him.

'. . . And for my son, Patrick Kieran, who is in the States these five years, Our Father who art in heaven . . .'

And he led us through seven Our Fathers and Hail Marys before he raised the cross on his beads to bless himself.

When he rose his face was flushed, and the same angry, resentful look was on it that it had worn when he opened the door to us.

'I'm sorry,' said Lomasney mildly. 'I forgot about Patrick.'

'Remember him in future,' Kieran said churlishly.

'Have you heard from him lately?' Lomasney asked in the same tone.

'What's that to you, young man?' Kieran shouted with sudden fury, showing his bare yellow gums.

'Oh, nothing, nothing. Don't eat us! I only wondered how he was getting on.'

'He's getting on – he's getting on all right, never fear. He's in Butte, Montana, now in case you want to know.'

'Oh, very well!'

'Why did you ask?'

'Why wouldn't I ask? Wasn't he a friend of mine, man?'

'He have the Son of God to look after him!'

The cry sounded impious, more a challenge than an act of faith.

'Ttttttt!' the old woman sighed moodily into the fire, and Lomasney said no more. Kieran lit a candle and opened the door of a room off the kitchen.

'Stop in there, will ye?'

'We'll be going before morning. We may as well stay in the kitchen.'

'Do what ye're toult, man. There's a fine big bed in there ye can all lie on.'

There was no mistaking the resentment in his tone, and I nudged Lomasney to let him have his way. Having warned him to leave the front door unbolted, we said good night and went into the room. The third man and I removed our boots and lay down, while Lomasney, who had opened the window, sat on a chair beside us and lit a cigarette. The night was calm and clear. Lomasney looked at his watch.

'Midnight,' he said. 'They're cutting the wires now. You fellows may as well try and get an hour's sleep. Will I quench that candle?'

He did so. After a little while he continued softly, to me.

'There! What did I tell you? That old fellow is a devil! . . . You're lying on Patrick's bed now. They keep it made up in case he'd come back without warning – and it's shown to everybody who comes inside the door. . . . A queer old pair! . . . And they say the same blessed prayers still! I'd forgotten they'd be doing that.'

'They are a queer pair,' I said. 'The old woman looks as if she was crushed.'

'So well she might be.'

'And hopeless!'

'Patrick would have been crushed too if he'd stayed at home,' Lomasney added, as if he had thought of it for the first time.

After that it was silence. The lad beside me was asleep, as I soon knew by his regular breathing. Lomasney's cigarette died out, and for close on an hour the two of us remained alone with our thoughts. Once we heard a distant explosion that reminded us sharply of the men who had been out since midnight, felling trees and destroying bridges. I thought of the policemen below listening to that, poor devils! Already they probably knew there was something in the wind, and were padding around half-dressed in their slippers, erecting a barricade behind the doors, and asking one another whether they could hold out till morning.

At last, able to bear it no longer, I rose, and stood beside Lomasney, who was leaning with his two elbows on the window-sill, looking down at the little village in the darkness of its valley.

His watch lay before him on the window-sill, loudly and petu-
lantly ticking the moments away, and his fingers were drumming
a tattoo on the sill. I saw that the barrack was in total darkness.
Lomasney told me in a whisper that there had been four lights
on the top of the building. All had gone out together. Someone
must have heard the explosion and tried to phone.

'For God's sake, let's get outside for a bit,' he said with
ill-suppressed excitement. 'I'm suffocating in here.'

We tiptoed to the door and opened it softly. Suddenly he
caught my arm and drew me back, but not before I had seen
something that startled me far more than his gesture. As I have
said there was a ladder in the centre of the kitchen, and it gave
access to a loft. Now the trap-door that covered the top of the
ladder was open and a light was showing through, but even as
we looked, it was closed with the utmost care, and the kitchen
was in darkness again.

I could feel the excitement of the chase working in Lomasney;
his hand twitched against my arm. Then he made a bound for the
ladder. It shook under his weight with a squeak; the old woman's
voice from another room was suddenly raised in bitter protest,
and – I leaped after him.

I can still see myself with my head through that trap and
Lomasney standing above me with a drawn revolver. We must
have looked a rare pair of grotesques in the light of the candle
that old Kieran was holding – on the defensive too, for if ever
there was murder in a man's eyes there was murder in his. But
what drew our attention was not he, it was the figure that lay on
the straw at his feet. Bearded, emaciated, half-savage; this strange
creature was lying sideways, his body propped on two spindly
arms, staring dully up at us. He wore only a shirt and trousers.

We must have been staring at one another like this for some
time before Lomasney seemed to become conscious of the old
woman's shrill crying below. To add to the confusion our com-
panion was awake and shouting hysterically at me from the foot
of the ladder.

'Go down and stop that woman crying,' said Lomasney
harshly.

Old Kieran looked as though he would resist, but Lomasney
stared coldly past him, pocketed his revolver, and knelt beside
the man on the straw. The old man laid his candle on the dresser.

I made way for him, and he climbed heavily down the ladder, without as much as a backward glance. I heard him talking to the other man, his voice charged with rage, but I did not catch what he was saying. I had eyes and ears only for what was going on in the loft. I noticed even the heap of weekly papers on the floor and the three or four child's games like 'Ludo' and 'Snakes and Ladders' beside them.

'You'd better come down too, Paddy,' said Lomasney gently.

I ran to help him lift young Kieran, but he waved us both aside and feebly rose without our assistance.

'Have you been here always?' asked Lomasney. 'All these long years?' but again the other man just waved his hands, vaguely, as though begging us not to force speech from him.

'Poor devil!' said Lomasney with an anguish of compassion. 'Poor devil! If only I'd known it!'

I took hold of his legs and Lomasney of one arm as we helped him down the ladder to the kitchen. A candle was lighting on the mantelpiece, and the old man, his face and beard thrown into startling relief, was sitting with his back to the ladder, glaring at the ashen heap of burnt turf on the hearth. He said nothing, but the boy's mother, who wore an old coat over her nightdress, held out her bare arms and raised a piercing screech when she saw him. We put him sitting beside her on the settle, and she dropped into a quiet moaning, holding his two hands in hers and caressing them tenderly.

Lomasney jerked the old man's shoulder, and anger and contempt mingled in his voice when he spoke.

'Listen to me now,' he said. 'I'm taking charge here from this on. And I want no more of your cleverness, understand that! You've been too clever too long, confound you, and now you're going to do what I say. . . .

'In two or three days' time you'll go to the city with Patrick. You'll leave him there, and come home without being seen. After that he can come back whenever he pleases – from America that is. We won't say anything about it, and you won't say anything about it, and so far as anybody will know, he will have come from America. Do you understand me?'

'And the policemin?' asked old Kieran sullenly, after a moment's silence. 'How long do you think they'll leave him here? Hey?'

'Tomorrow,' said Lomasney, 'there won't be any policemen there, please God!'

Kieran started. He glanced from Lomasney to me and back again. A look, half cunning, half triumph, stole into his bitter old face.

'So that's what he's here for?' he asked, pointing at me. 'That's what ye're out for? Do you tell me you're out to ind them? Do you?'

'That's what we're out for,' Lomasney answered coldly, fetching his rifle and swinging it across his shoulder.

Kieran chuckled, and the chuckle seemed to shake the whole crazy scaffolding of his bones.

'And I thinking ye were only like children playmaking!' he went on. 'Do it, do it, and remember I'll be on me bended knees praying to Almighty God for ye. Divil a wink I'll sleep this night!'

We left them, old Kieran, who seemed to be possessed of a new lease of life, grown garrulous and maddeningly friendly; the mother sitting very quietly beside her son, who had not as much as opened his mouth but down whose beard the heavy, silent tears were rolling as he gazed vacantly at the candle flame.

Lomasney's voice was exultant as we strode down the fields and picked our way through the wood to join the rest of the attacking party who were assembling in the village street from every house around.

'Lord, O Lord!' he exclaimed gleefully, nipping my arm with his fingers. 'I never went out on a job with a clearer conscience!'

And a few moments later he added:

'But old Mike Kieran isn't quit of me yet, Owen – damn me but he isn't quit of me yet! I'm a bad judge, Owen, if we haven't signed on our best recruit!'

JUMBO'S WIFE

I

WHEN HE had taken his breakfast, silently as his way was after a drunk, he lifted the latch and went out without a word. She heard his feet tramp down the flagged laneway, waking iron echoes, and, outraged, shook her fist after him; then she pulled off the old red flannel petticoat and black shawl she was wearing, and crept back into the hollow of the bed. But not to sleep. She went over in her mind the shame of last night's bout, felt at her lip where he had split it with a blow, and recalled how she had fled into the roadway screaming for help and been brought back by Pa Kenefick, the brother of the murdered boy. Somehow that had sobered Jumbo. Since Michael, the elder of the Kenefick brothers, had been taken out and killed by the police, the people looked up to Pa rather as they looked up to the priest, but more passionately, more devotedly. She remembered how even Jumbo, the great swollen insolent Jumbo had crouched back into the darkness when he saw that slip of a lad walk in before her. 'Stand away from me,' he had said, but not threateningly. 'It was a shame,' Pa had retorted, 'a confounded shame for a drunken elephant of a man to beat his poor decent wife like that,' but Jumbo had said nothing, only 'Let her be, boy, let her be! Go away from me now and I'll quieten down.' 'You'd better quieten down,' Pa had said, 'or you'll answer for it to me, you great bully you,' and he had kicked about the floor the pieces of the delf that Jumbo in his drunken frenzy had shattered one by one against the wall. 'I tell you I won't lay a finger on her,' Jumbo had said, and sure enough, when Pa Kenefick had gone, Jumbo was a quiet man.

But it was the sight of the brother of the boy that had been murdered rather than the beating she had had or the despair at seeing her little share of delf smashed on her, that brought home to Jumbo's wife her own utter humiliation. She had often thought before that she would run away from Jumbo, even, in her wild way, that she would do for him, but never before had she seen so clearly what a wreck he had made of her life. The sight of Pa had reminded her that she was no common trollop but a decent girl; he had said it, 'your decent poor wife,' that was what Pa had said, and it was true; she was a decent poor woman. Didn't the world know how often she had pulled the little home together on her blackguard of a husband, the man who had 'listed in the army under a false name so as to rob her of the separation money, the man who would keep a job only as long as it pleased him, and send her out then to work in the nurseries, picking fruit for a shilling a day?

She was so caught up into her own bitter reflections that when she glanced round suddenly and saw the picture that had been the ostensible cause of Jumbo's fury awry, the glass smashed in it, and the bright colours stained with tea, her lip fell, and she began to moan softly to herself. It was a beautiful piece – that was how she described it – a beautiful, massive piece of big, big castle, all towers, on a rock, and mountains and snow behind. Four shillings and sixpence it had cost her in the Coal Quay market. Jumbo would spend three times that on a drunk; ay, three times and five times that Jumbo would spend, and for all, he had smashed every cup and plate and dish in the house on her poor little picture – because it was extravagance, he said.

She heard the postman's loud double knock, and the child beside her woke and sat up. She heard a letter being slipped under the door. Little Johnny heard it too. He climbed down the side of the bed, pattered across the floor in his nightshirt and brought it to her. A letter with the On-His-Majesty's-Service stamp; it was Jumbo's pension that he drew every quarter. She slipped it under her pillow with a fresh burst of rage. It would keep. She would hold on to it until he gave her his week's wages on Friday. Yes, she would make him hand over every penny of it even if he killed her after. She had done it before, and would do it again.

Little Johnny began to cry that he wanted his breakfast, and she rose, sighing, and dressed. Over the fire as she boiled the kettle she meditated again on her wrongs, and was startled when she found the child actually between her legs holding out the long envelope to the flames, trying to boil the kettle with it. She snatched it wildly from his hand and gave him a vicious slap across the face that set him howling. She stood turning the letter over and over in her hand curiously, and then started as she remembered that it wasn't until another month that Jumbo's pension fell due. She counted the weeks; no, that was right, but what had them sending out Jumbo's pension a month before it was due?

When the kettle boiled she made the tea, poured it out into two tin ponnies, and sat into table with the big letter propped up before her as though she was trying to read its secrets through the manila covering. But she was no closer to solving the mystery when her breakfast of bread and tea was done, and, sudden resolution coming to her, she held the envelope over the spout of the kettle and slowly steamed its fastening away. She drew out the flimsy note inside and opened it upon the table. It was an order, a money order, but not the sort they sent to Jumbo. The writing on it meant little to her, but what did mean a great deal were the careful figures, a two and a five that filled one corner. A two and a five and a sprawling sign before them; this was not for Jumbo – or was it? All sorts of suspicions began to form in her mind, and with them a feeling of pleasurable excitement.

She thought of Pa Kenefick. Pa was a good scholar and the proper man to see about a thing like this. And Pa had been good to her. Pa would feel she was doing the right thing in showing him this mysterious paper, even if it meant nothing but a change in the way they paid Jumbo's pension; it would show how much she looked up to him.

She threw her old black shawl quickly about her shoulders and grabbed at the child's hand. She went down the low arched laneway where they lived – Melancholy Lane, it was called – and up the road to the Kenefick's'. She knocked at their door, and Mrs Kenefick, whose son had been dragged to his death from that door, answered it. She looked surprised when she saw the other woman, and only then Jumbo's wife realized how early it was. She asked excitedly for Pa. He wasn't at home, his mother said, and she didn't know when he would be home, if he came at all. When she saw how crestfallen her visitor looked at this, she asked politely if she couldn't send a message, for women like Jumbo's wife frequently brought information that was of use to the volunteers. No, no, the other woman said earnestly, it was for Pa's ears, for Pa's ears alone, and it couldn't wait. Mrs Kenefick asked her into the parlour, where the picture of the murdered boy, Michael, in his Volunteer uniform hung. It was dangerous for any of the company to stay at home, she said, the police knew the ins and outs of the district too well; there was the death of Michael unaccounted for, and a dozen or more arrests, all within a month or two. But she had never before seen Jumbo's wife in such a state and wondered what was the best thing for her to do. It was her daughter who decided it by telling where Pa was to be found, and immediately the excited woman raced off up the hill towards the open country.

She knocked at the door of a little farmhouse off the main road, and when the door was opened she saw Pa himself, in shirt-sleeves, filling out a basin of hot water to shave. His first words showed that he thought it was Jumbo who had been at her again, but, without answering him, intensely conscious of herself and of the impression she wished to create, she held the envelope out at arm's length. He took it, looked at the address for a moment, and then pulled out the flimsy slip. She saw his brows bent above it, then his lips tightened. He raised his head and called, 'Jim, Liam, come down! Come down a minute!' The tone in which he said it delighted her as much as the rush of footsteps upstairs. Two men descended a ladder to the kitchen, and Pa held out the slip. 'Look at this!' he said. They looked at it, for a long time it seemed to her, turning it round and round and examining the postmark on the envelope. She began to speak rapidly. 'Mr Kenefick will tell you, gentlemen, Mr Kenefick will tell you, the life he leads me. I was never one for regulating me own, gentlemen, but I say before me God this minute, hell will never be full till they have him roasting there. A little pitcher I bought, gentlemen, a massive little piece – Mr Kenefick will tell you – I paid four and sixpence for it – he said I was extravagant. Let me remark he'd spend three times, ay, and six times, as much on filling his own gut as I'd spend upon me home and child. Look at me, gentlemen, look at me lip where he hit me – Mr Kenefick will tell you – I was in gores of blood.' 'Listen now, ma'am,' one of the men interrupted suavely, 'we're very grateful to you for showing us this letter. It's something we wanted to know this long time, ma'am. And now like a good woman will you go back home and not open your mouth to a soul about it, and, if himself ask you anything, say there did ne'er a letter come?' 'Of course,' she said, 'she would do whatever they told her. She was in their hands. Didn't Mr Kenefick come in, like the lovely young man he was, and save her from the hands of that dancing hangman Jumbo? And wasn't she sorry for his mother, poor little 'oman, and her fine son taken away on her? Weren't they all crazy about her?'

The three men had to push her out the door, saying that she had squared her account with Jumbo at last.

II

At noon with the basket of food under her arm, and the child plodding along beside her, she made her way through the northern slums to a factory on the outskirts of the city. There, sitting on the grass beside a little stream – her usual station – she waited for Jumbo. He came just as the siren blew, sat down beside her on the grass, and, without as much as fine day, began to unpack the food in the little basket. Already she was frightened and unhappy; she dreaded what Jumbo would do if ever he found out about the letter, and find out he must. People said he wouldn't last long on her, balloon and all as he was. Some said his heart was weak, and others that he was bloated out with dropsy and would die in great agony at any minute. But those who said that hadn't felt the weight of Jumbo's hand.

She sat in the warm sun, watching the child dabble his fingers in the little stream, and all the bitterness melted away within her. She had had a hard two days of it, and now she felt Almighty God might well have pity on her, and leave her a week or even a fortnight of quiet, until she pulled her little home together again. Jumbo ate placidly and contentedly; she knew by this his drinking bout was almost over. At last he pulled his cap well down over his eyes and lay back with his wide red face to the sun. She watched him, her hands upon her lap. He looked for all the world like a huge, fat, sulky child. He lay like that without stirring for some time; then he stretched out his legs, and rolled over and over and over downhill through the grass. He grunted with pleasure, and sat up blinking drowsily at her from the edge of the cinder path. She put her hand in her pocket. 'Jim, will I give you the price of an ounce of 'baccy?' He stared up at her for a moment. 'There did ne'er a letter come for me?' he asked, and her heart sank. 'No, Jim,' she said feebly, 'what letter was it you were expecting?' 'Never mind, you. Here, give us a couple of lob for a wet!' She counted him out six coppers and he stood up to go.

All the evening she worried herself about Pa Kenefick and his friends – though to be sure they were good-natured, friendly boys. She was glad when Jumbo came in at tea-time; the great bulk of him stretched out in the corner gave her a feeling of security. He was almost in good humour again, and talked a little, telling her to shut up when her tongue wagged too much, or sourly abusing the 'bummers' who had soaked him the evening before. She had cleared away the supper things when a motor-car drove up the road and stopped at the end of Melancholy Lane. Her heart misgave her. She ran to the door and looked out; there were two men coming up the lane, one of them wearing a mask; when they saw her they broke into a trot. 'Merciful Jesus!' she screamed, and rushed in, banging and bolting the door behind her. Jumbo stood up slowly. 'What is it?' he asked. 'That letter.' 'What letter?' 'I showed it to Pa Kenefick, that letter from the barrack.' The blue veins rose on Jumbo's forehead as though they would burst. He could barely speak but rushed to the fire-place and swept the poker above her head. 'If it's the last thing I ever do I'll have your sacred life!' he said in a hoarse whisper. 'Let me alone! Let me alone!' she shrieked. 'They're at the door!' She leaned her back against the door, and felt against her spine the lurch of a man's shoulder. Jumbo heard it; he watched her with narrowed, despairing eyes, and then beckoned her towards the back door. She went on before him on tiptoe and opened the door quietly for him. 'Quick,' he said, 'name of Jasus, lift me up this.' This was the back wall, which was fully twice his own height but had footholes by which he could clamber up. She held his feet in them, and puffing and growling, he scrambled painfully up, inch by inch, until his head was almost level with the top of the wall; then with a gigantic effort he slowly raised his huge body and laid it flat upon the spiny top. 'Keep them back, you!' he said. 'Here,' she called softly up to him, 'take this,' and he bent down and caught the poker.

It was dark in the little kitchen. She crept to the door and listened, holding her breath. There was no sound. She was consumed with anxiety and impatience. Suddenly little Johnny sat up and began to howl. She grasped the key and turned it in the lock once; there was no sound; at last she opened the door slowly.

There was no one to be seen in the lane. Night was setting in – maybe he would dodge them yet. She locked the screaming child in behind her and hurried down to the archway.

The motor-car was standing where it had stopped and a man was leaning over the wheel smoking a cigarette. He looked up and smiled at her. 'Didn't they get him yet?' he asked, 'No,' she said mechanically. 'Ah, cripes!' he swore, 'with the help of God they'll give him an awful end when they ketch him.' She stood there looking up and down the road in the terrible stillness: there were lamps lighting behind every window but not a soul appeared. At last a strange young man in a trench-coat rushed down the lane towards them. 'Watch out there,' he cried. 'He's after giving us the slip. Guard this lane and the one below, don't shoot unless you can get him.' He doubled down the road and up the next laneway.

The young man in the car topped his cigarette carefully, put the butt end in his waistcoat pocket and crossed to the other side of the road. He leaned nonchalantly against the wall and drew a heavy revolver. She crossed too and stood beside him. An old lamplighter came up one of the lanes from the city and went past them to the next gas-lamp, his torch upon his shoulder. 'He's a brute of a man,' the driver said consolingly, 'sure, I couldn't but hit him in the dark itself. But it's a shame now they wouldn't have a gas-lamp at that end of the lane, huh!' The old lamp-lighter disappeared up the road, leaving two or three pale specks of light behind him.

They stood looking at the laneways each end of a little row of cottages, not speaking a word. Suddenly the young man drew himself up stiffly against the wall and raised his left hand towards the fading sky. 'See that?' he said gleefully. Beyond the row of cottages a figure rose slowly against a chimney-pot; they could barely see it in the twilight, but she could not doubt who it was. The man spat upon the barrel of his gun and raised it upon his crooked elbow; then the dark figure leaped out as it were upon the air and disappeared among the shadows of the houses. 'Jasus!' the young man swore softly, 'wasn't that a great pity?' She came to her senses in a flash. 'Jumbo!' she shrieked, 'me poor Jumbo! He's kilt, he's kilt!' and began to weep and clap her hands. The man looked at her in comical bewilderment. 'Well, well!' he said, 'to think of that! And are you his widda, ma'am?' 'God melt and wither you!' she screamed and rushed away towards the spot where Jumbo's figure had disappeared.

At the top of the lane a young man with a revolver drove her back. 'Is he kilt?' she cried. 'Too well you know he's not kilt,' the young man replied savagely. Another wearing a mask came out of a cottage and said 'He's dished us again. Don't stir from this. I'm going round to Samson's Lane.' 'How did he manage it?' the first man asked. 'Over the roofs. This place is a network, and the people won't stir a finger to help us.'

For hours that duel in the darkness went on, silently, without a shot being fired. What mercy the people of the lanes showed to Jumbo was a mercy they had never denied to any hunted thing. His distracted wife went back to the road. Leaving the driver standing alone by his car she tramped up and down staring up every tiny laneway. It did not enter her head to run for assistance. On the opposite side of the road another network of lanes, all steep-sloping, like the others, or stepped in cobbles, went down into the heart of the city. These were Jumbo's only hope of escape, and that was why she watched there, glancing now and then at the maze of lights beneath her.

Ten o'clock rang out from Shandon – shivering, she counted the chimes. Then down one of the lanes from the north she heard a heavy clatter of ironshod feet. Clatter, clatter, clatter; the feet drew nearer, and she heard other, lighter, feet pattering swiftly behind. A dark figure emerged through an archway, running with frantic speed. She rushed out into the middle of the road to meet it, sweeping her shawl out on either side of her head like a dancer's sash. 'Jumbo, me lovely Jumbo!' she screamed. 'Out of me way, y'ould crow!' the wild quarry panted, flying past.

She heard him take the first flight of steps in the southern laneway at a bound. A young man dashed out of the archway a moment after and gave a hasty look around him. Then he ran towards her and she stepped out into the lane to block his passage. Without swerving he rushed into her at full speed, sweeping her off her feet, but she drew the wide black shawl about his head as they fell and rolled together down the narrow sloping passage. They were at the top of the steps and he still struggled frantically to free himself from the filthy enveloping shawl. They rolled from step to step, to the bottom, he throttling her and cursing furiously at her strength; she still holding the shawl tight about his head and shoulders. Then the others came and dragged him off, leaving her choking and writhing upon the ground.

But by this time Jumbo was well beyond their reach.

III

Next morning she walked dazedly about the town, stopping every policeman she met and asking for Jumbo. At the military barrack on the hill they told her she would find him in one of the city police barracks. She explained to the young English officer who spoke to her about Pa Kenefick, and how he could be captured, and for her pains was listened to in wide-eyed disgust. But what she could not understand in the young officer's attitude to her, Jumbo, sitting over the fire in the barrack day-room, had already been made to understand, and she was shocked to see him so pale, so sullen, so broken. And this while she was panting with pride at his escape! He did not even fly at her as she had feared he would, nor indeed abuse her at all. He merely looked up and said with the bitterness of utter resigna-tion, 'There's the one that brought me down!' An old soldier, he was cut to the heart that the military would not take him in, but had handed him over to the police for protection. 'I'm no use to them now,' he said, 'and there's me thanks for all I done. They'd as soon see me out of the way; they'd as soon see the poor old creature that served them out of the way.' 'It was all Pa Kenefick's doings,' his wife put in frantically, 'it was no one else done it. Not that my poor slob of a man ever did him or his any harm. . . .' At this the policemen round her chuckled and Jumbo angrily bade her be silent. 'But I told the officer of the swaddies where he was to be found,' she went on unheeding. 'What was that?' the policemen asked eagerly, and she told them of how she had found Pa Kenefick in the little cottage up the hill.

Every day she went to see Jumbo. When the weather was fine they sat in the little garden behind the barrack, for it was only at dusk that Jumbo could venture out and then only with military or police patrols. There were very few on the road who would speak to her now, for on the night after Jumbo's escape the little cottage where Pa Kenefick had stayed had been raided and smashed up by masked policemen. Of course, Pa and his friends were gone. She hated the neighbours, and dug into her mind with the fear of what might happen to Jumbo was the desire to be quit of Pa Kenefick. Only then, she felt in her blind headlong way, would Jumbo be safe. And what divil's notion took her to show him the letter? She'd swing for Pa, she said, sizing up to the policemen.

And Jumbo grew worse and worse. His face had turned from brick-red to grey. He complained always of pain and spent whole days in bed. She had heard that there was a cure for his illness in red flannel, and had made him a nightshirt of red flannel in which he looked more than ever like a ghost, his hair grey, his face quite colourless, his fat paws growing skinny under the wide crimson sleeves. He applied for admission to the military hospital, which was within the area protected by the troops, and the request was met with a curt refusal. That broke his courage. To the military for whom he had risked his life he was only an informer, a common informer, to be left to the mercy of their enemy when his services were no longer of value. The policemen sympathized with him, for they too were despised by the 'swaddies' as makers of trouble, but they could do nothing for him. And when he went out walking under cover of darkness with two policemen for an escort the people turned and laughed at him. He heard them, and returned to the barrack consumed with a rage that expressed itself in long fits of utter silence or sudden murderous outbursts.

She came in one summer evening when the fit was on him, to find him struggling in the day-room with three of the policemen. They were trying to wrest a loaded carbine from his hands. He wanted blood, he shouted, blood, and by Christ they wouldn't stop him. They wouldn't, they wouldn't, he repeated, sending one of them flying against the hearth. He'd finish a few of the devils that were twitting him before he was plugged himself. He'd shoot everyone, man, woman, and child that came in his way. His frenzy was terrifying and the three policemen were swung this way and that, to right and left, as the struggle swept from wall to door and back. Then suddenly he collapsed and lay unconscious upon the floor. When they brought him round with whiskey he looked from one to the other, and drearily, with terrible anguish, he cursed all the powers about him, God, the King, the republicans, Ireland, and the country he had served.

'Kimberley, Pietermaritzburg, Bethlem, Bloemfontein,' he

moaned. 'Ah, you thing, many's the hard day I put down for you! Devil's cure to me for a crazy man! Devil's cure to me, I say! With me cane and me busby and me scarlet coat — 'twas aisy you beguiled me! . . . The curse of God on you! . . . Tell them to pay me passage, d'you hear me? Tell them to pay me passage and I'll go out to Inja and fight the blacks for you!'

It was easy to see whom he was talking to.

'Go the road resigned, Jim,' his wife counselled timidly from above his head. Seeing him like this she could already believe him dying.

'I will not. . . . I will not go the road resigned.'

'. . . to His blessed and holy Will,' she babbled.

Lifting his two fists from the ground he thumped upon his chest like a drum.

''Tisn't sickness that ails me, but a broken heart,' he cried. 'Tell them to pay me passage! Ah, why didn't I stay with the lovely men we buried there, not to end me days as a public show. . . . They put the croolety of the world from them young, the creatures, they put the croolety of the world from them young!'

The soldiers had again refused to admit him to the military hospital. Now the police had grown tired of him, and on their faces he saw relief, relief that they would soon be shut of him, when he entered some hospital in the city, where everyone would know him, and sooner or later his enemies would reach him. He no longer left the barrack. Disease had changed that face of his already; the only hope left to him now was to change it still further. He grew a beard.

And all this time his wife lay in wait for Pa Kenefick. Long hours on end she watched for him over her half-door. Twice she saw him pass by the laneway, and each time snatched her shawl and rushed down to the barrack, but by the time a car of plain-clothes men drove up to the Keneficks' door Pa was gone. Then he ceased to come home at all, and she watched the movements of his sister and mother. She even trained little Johnny to follow them, but the child was too young and too easily outdistanced. When she came down the road in the direction of the city, all the women standing at their doors would walk in and shut them in her face.

One day the policeman on duty at the barrack door told her

gruffly that Jumbo was gone. He was in hospital somewhere; she would be told where if he was in any danger. And she knew by the tone in which he said it that the soldiers had not taken Jumbo in; that somewhere he was at the mercy of his changed appearance and assumed name, unless, as was likely, he was already too far gone to make it worth the 'rebels'' while to shoot him. Now that she could no longer see him there was a great emptiness in her life, an emptiness that she filled only with brooding and hatred. Everything within her had turned to bitterness against Pa Kenefick, the boy who had been the cause of it all, to whom she had foolishly shown the letter and who had brought the 'dirty Shinners' down on her, who alone had cause to strike at Jumbo now that he was a sick and helpless man.

'God, give me strength!' she prayed. 'I'll sober him, O God, I'll put him in a quiet habitation!'

She worked mechanically about the house. A neighbour's averted face or the closing of a door in her path brought her to such a pitch of fury that she swept out into the road, her shawl stretched out behind her head, and tore up and down, screaming like a madwoman; sometimes leaping into the air with an obscene gesture; sometimes kneeling in the roadway and cursing those that had affronted her; sometimes tapping out a few dance steps, a skip to right and a skip to left, just to rouse herself. 'I'm a bird alone!' she shrieked, 'a bird alone and the hawks about me! Good man, clever man, handsome man, I'm a bird alone!' And 'That they might rot and wither, root and branch, son and daughter, born and unborn; that every plague and pestilence might end them and theirs; that they might be called in their sins' – this was what she prayed in the traditional formula, and the neighbours closed their doors softly and crossed themselves. For a week or more she was like a woman possessed.

IV

Then one day when she was standing by the archway she saw Pa Kenefick and another man come down the road. She stood back without being seen, and waited until they had gone by before she emerged and followed them. It was no easy thing to do upon the long open street that led to the quays, but she pulled her shawl well down over her eyes, and drew up her shoulders so

that at a distance she might look like an old woman. She reached
the foot of the hill without being observed, and after that, to
follow them through the crowded, narrow side-streets of the city
where every second woman wore a shawl was comparatively
easy. But they walked so fast it was hard to keep up with them,
and several times she had to take short-cuts that they did not
know of, thus losing sight of them for the time being. Already
they had crossed the bridge, and she was growing mystified; this
was unfamiliar country and, besides, the pace was beginning to
tell on her. They had been walking now for a good two miles
and she knew that they would soon outdistance her. And all the
time she had seen neither policeman nor soldier.

Gasping she stood and leaned against a wall, drawing the shawl
down about her shoulders for a breath of air. 'Tell me, ma'am,'
she asked of a passer-by, 'where do this road go to?' 'This is the
Mallow Road, ma'am,' the other said, and since Jumbo's wife
made no reply she asked was it any place she wanted. 'No,
indeed,' Jumbo's wife answered without conviction. The other
lowered her voice and asked sympathetically, 'Is it the hospital
you're looking for, poor woman?' Jumbo's wife stood for a
moment until the question sank in. 'The hospital?' she whis-
pered. 'The hospital? Merciful God Almighty!' Then she came
to her senses. 'Stop them!' she screamed, rushing out into the
roadway, 'stop them! Murder! Murder! Stop them!'

The two men who by this time were far ahead heard the shout
and looked back. Then one of them stepped out into the middle
of the road and signalled to a passing car. They leaped in and the
car drove off. A little crowd had gathered upon the path, but
when they understood what the woman's screams signified they
melted silently away. Only the woman to whom she had first
spoken remained. 'Come with me, ma'am,' she said. ''Tis only
as you might say a step from this.'

A tram left them at the hospital gate and Jumbo's wife and the
other woman rushed in. She asked for Jumbo Geany, but the
porter looked at her blankly and asked what ward she was looking
for. 'There were two men here a minute ago,' she said frantically,
'where are they gone to?' 'Ah,' he said, 'now I have you! They're
gone over to St George's Ward. . . .'

In St George's Ward at that moment two or three nuns and a
nurse surrounded the house doctor, a tall young man who was

saying excitedly, 'I couldn't stop them, couldn't stop them! I told them he was at his last gasp, but they wouldn't believe me!' 'He was lying there,' said the nurse pointing to an empty bed, 'when that woman came in with the basket, a sort of dealing woman she was. When she saw him she looked hard at him and then went across and drew back the bedclothes. "Is it yourself is there, Jumbo?" says she, and, poor man, he starts up in bed and says out loud-like "You won't give me away? Promise me you won't give me away." So she laughs and says, "A pity you didn't think of that when you gave Mike Kenefick the gun, Jumbo!" After she went away he wanted to get up and go home. I seen by his looks he was dying and I sent for the priest and Doctor Connolly, and he got wake-like, and that pair came in, asking for a stretcher, and—' The nurse began to bawl.

Just then Jumbo's wife appeared, a distracted, terrified figure, the shawl drawn back from her brows, the hair falling about her face. 'Jumbo Geany?' she asked. 'You're too late,' said the young doctor harshly, 'they've taken him away.' 'No, come back, come back!' he shouted as she rushed towards the window that opened on to the garden at the back of the hospital, 'you can't go out there!' But she wriggled from his grasp, leaving her old black shawl in his hands. Alone she ran across the little garden, to where another building jutted out and obscured the view of the walls. As she did so three shots rang out in rapid succession. She heard a gate slam; it was the little wicket gate on to another road; beside it was a stretcher with a man's body lying on it. She flung herself screaming upon the body, not heeding the little streams of blood that flowed from beneath the armpit and the head. It was Jumbo, clad only in a nightshirt and bearded beyond recognition. His long, skinny legs were naked, and his toes had not ceased to twitch. For each of the three shots there was a tiny wound, two over the heart and one in the temple, and pinned to the cheap flannelette nightshirt was a little typed slip that read

SPY.

They had squared her account with Jumbo at last.

SEPTEMBER DAWN

I

IT WAS LATE September of the finest autumn that had been known for years. For five crowded days the column had held out, flying from one position to another, beaten about by a dozen companies of regular soldiers. At Glenmanus they had taken shelter among the trees, and fought for a few hours with the river protecting them, but, a second column of soldiers having crossed by a temporary bridge a mile or two up the road, they had found themselves completely outflanked. Then they had fought their way across country; seven men holding one ditch while the other seven retreated to the next. Again they had been headed off and again had changed direction. 'It was the sort of game a schoolboy would play with a beetle,' remarked Keown.

This time they had been trapped by a column coming from the direction of Mallow. Finally, in desperation, they had come back by night and along a different route to their old stronghold in Glenmanus, and here they rested while Keown and Hickey, standing apart, held counsel.

Hickey, dressed in a black coat and green riding-breeches, was very tall and slim. He had the reputation of being as conscientious as he was inhuman, and there was a strain of fanaticism in his pale face and in the steely eyes behind their large horn-rimmed spectacles. It was the face of a young scientist or a young priest. He lacked imagination, people said. He also lacked humour. But he was a good soldier and cautious where men's lives were concerned. His companion was stocky and pugnacious, with a fat, good-humoured face and a left eye that squinted atrociously. He was unscrupulous, good-natured, and unreliable, and had a bad reputation for his ways with women. He even boasted of it, and added, with a wink of his sound eye, that there wasn't a parish in Munster where he couldn't find a home and children. He read much more than Hickey, and rarely went anywhere without a book in his pocket. It was most often an indecent French novel, but sometimes he carried about a book of verse which he read aloud to Hickey in his broad, bantering, countryman's voice. He liked to hear himself speak, and, when his column was in billet, practised elocution before a mirror. The two men now stood on the river bank, Hickey idly disturbing the sluggish water with a switch, and Keown, small and ungainly, with a rifle swung across his right shoulder and a sandwich in his hand, eyeing him in silence.

After about ten minutes they returned. Hickey glanced coldly at the twelve volunteers sitting on the grass, chewing sandwiches and drinking spring water out of a rusty water-bottle. Their rifles lay beside them. Most of them had doffed their hats and caps. An autumn sun shone warmly and brightly overhead, and cast spotlights through the yellowing leaves upon their flushed young faces, upturned to his, and their bare brown throats.

'We have decided to disband the column, men,' he said briefly.

'Disband? Do you mean we are to go home?' one of them asked with a quick look of dismay.

'Yes, there's nothing else for it. It's disband or go down together; we can't carry on as we've been doing.'

They stared blankly at him.

'And the rifles, the equipment? What are we to do with them?'

'Dump them.'

'Dump them – after five days?'

'You heard what I said.'

'We're genuinely sorry, boys,' Keown put in kindly. 'Jim and I appreciate more than we can say the way you've stuck by us through it all. Don't think we're ungrateful. We aren't. We've made friends amongst you that we'll always be proud of. But it's better we should lose you this way than another. We want to live for Ireland, not to die for it, and die we will if we stick together any longer. There's no use blinking that. The country here is too damn flat, too damn thickly populated, and there are too many roads.'

There was silence for a moment. The men sat looking desperately at one another and at their leaders. Suddenly one of them, a farm labourer with a thick red moustache, who had been tying up a packet of sandwiches tossed it away; it broke through the leaves, and fell with a little splash in the river. He rose and threw aside his cloth bandolier, and then began to unbuckle his khaki belt. His face was pale, and his hands fumbled nervously at the catch. The others rose too, one after another.

'Faith, it'll be a comfort to sleep at home after a week of this, neighbours.'

The speaker was a handsome youth, scarcely more than a boy.

'Ah, my lad,' said the other man bitterly, 'you'll sleep in a different bed, and a harder bed, before this week is out, and serve you right.'

The speech was greeted with a murmur of approval.

'We must only risk that,' said Keown hastily. 'After all you've only been away from home for a week; they can't have spotted you so easily.'

'Spotted us?' exclaimed the other angrily, squaring up to him. 'Who talks about spotting? Or do you know who you're speaking to? Him and me came up all the way to fight at Passage. We're out of the one house, and we went off together in the dead of night on our bikes to join the brigade. We followed it to Macroom and we were sent back from that. Just as you're sending us back now. We're no seven-day soldiers, but, let me tell you, it's the last time I'll make a fool of myself for ye.'

Keown shrugged his shoulders helplessly without replying.

It was the youngster who showed them where the old dump was. It was dug into the low wall that surrounded the wood, and after some difficulty they succeeded in locating it. He and Keown together took out the heavy stones, one by one, and revealed a deep hollow beneath the wall. There was a long box like a coffin in it, and half a dozen sheets of oilcloth, with some old greasy rags and a tin of oil. The rifles were gathered together – there was no time to oil them – and wrapped in the oilcloth. The same was done with bandoliers, belts, and bayonets. Only the two leaders kept their arms and equipment. Hickey did not even pretend to be interested in the funereal ceremony, but walked moodily about under the shadow of the trees, his spectacles glinting in the stray shafts of sunlight.

When the work was finished, the stones replaced, and all traces of fresh earth cleaned away, the twelve men, looking now merely what in ordinary life they were, farmers' sons or day-labourers, stood awkwardly about, hands behind their backs or buried in their trousers' pockets.

'And now, men, it's time we were going,' said the youngster

in a tone of authority; already he was testing his own leadership of the little group.

Keown grinned and held out his hand to the farm labourer who had spoken so rudely to him. It was taken in silence and held for a moment. The rough unsoldierly faces cleared, and a smile of tenderness, of companionship, crossed them. The youngster strode bravely over to Hickey's side, and held out his hand with all a boy's gaucherie.

'Well, good-bye, Mr Hickey,' he said jauntily. 'See you soon again, I hope.'

'Good-bye, Dermod, boy, and good luck,' said Hickey, smiling faintly, as the others shambled over to say farewell.

Then with a last chorus of 'Good luck' and 'God be with you!' the little group dispersed among the trees, going in different directions to their own homes. Their voices grew faint in the distance, and the two friends were left alone upon the river bank.

II

An hour later as they leaped across the fence above the wood a shot rang out and Keown's hat sailed along beside him to the ground. Hickey flattened himself against the ditch and raised his rifle, but Keown flung himself distractedly on the grass beside his hat, brushed it and contemplated regretfully the little hole on top.

'A man who'd do a thing like that,' he commented with disgust, 'would snatch a slice of bread out of an orphan's mouth!

'But he's a good shot, Jim,' he went on. 'I will say that for him. He's a great shot. One, two, two and a half inches farther down and he'd have got me just where I wouldn't have known when. Ah, well! . . .' He picked himself up gingerly with head well bent. 'A miss is as good as a mile, and talking of miles. . . .'

'I'll stay here until you get across the next field.'

'And where do we go after that, Brother James?'

'It doesn't matter. Anywhere out of this; we can take our bearings later on.'

'At this point in the battle General Hickey gave the order to retreat,' murmured Keown, and scudded across the field, head low, his rifle trailing along the grass. Hickey looked down towards the road.

He could see nobody. The sun was high up in the centre of the heavens, and a great heat had come into the day. Beneath him was the wood, and the broad shallow river shone like steel through the reddening leaves. Beyond it the main road ran white and clear. Beyond the road another hill, more trees, and a house. The house one did not see from the wood, perched as it was like a bonnet on the brow of the hill, but from where he stood he had a clear view of it, outhouses and all. An old mansion of sorts it was, eighteenth century probably, with a wide carriage-way and steps up to the door. As he looked the door opened and a figure appeared, dressed in white; it was a girl whose attention had been attracted by the shot, perhaps also by the knowledge that a column of irregulars was in the vicinity. It amused him to think that he had only to lift his hat or handkerchief on the barrel of his rifle for her to hear more from the same source. Despite his natural caution, the idea became a temptation; he fingered with the safety-catch of his rifle, and began to calculate how many of the enemy there were. Scarcely more than a dozen, he thought, or they would have shown more daring in their approach to the wood. She shaded her eyes with her hand, searching the whole neighbourhood. To wave to her now would be good fun, but dangerous.

He looked round for Keown and saw him hurrying back. Clearly, there was something wrong. But Keown, seeing his attention attracted, came no farther, and made off in another direction, waving his hand in a way that showed the need for haste. Hickey followed, keeping all the time in shelter of the ditch.

When he reached the gap towards which Keown had run, he found him there, sitting on his hunkers, his tongue licking the corners of his mouth, his hands gripping nervously at his rifle.

'James,' he said with affected coolness, 'we must run for it. My tactics are particularly strong upon that point. Leave it to me, James! In the military college I was considered a dab at retreats.'

He pointed to a field that sloped upward from where they crouched to the brow of the hill.

'I'm afraid we'll be exposed crossing the field, but we must only risk it. After that we'll have cover enough. Ready?'

'Are there many of them?' asked Hickey.

'As thick as snakes in the DTs. Are you ready?'

'Ready!' said Hickey.

He closed his eyes and ran. For a full half minute he heard nothing but the beating of his own heart and the soft thud their feet made upon the grass. The sunlight swam in a rosy mist before his darkened eyes, and it seemed as if at any moment the ground might rise out of this nowhere of rosy light and hit him. Suddenly a dozen rifles signalled their appearance with a burst of rapid firing, and immediately on top of this came the unmistakable staccato whirring of a machine-gun. His eyes started open with the shock, and he saw Keown, almost doubled in two, running furiously and well ahead of him. He put on speed. The machine-gun fire grew more intense until it was almost continuous. Then it stopped, and only the rifles kept up their irregular rattle until they too trailed off and were still. It was only then he realized that he was under cover, and that what was driving him forward at such speed was the impetus of his original fear.

Keown waited for him, leaning against an old white-thorn tree, his sides perceptibly widening and narrowing as he breathed. His head seemed to be giddy and shook slightly; his trembling hands mechanically sought in every pocket for cigarettes. A faint smile played about the corners of his mouth, and when he spoke his words came almost in a whisper.

'Rotten shooting, James, but still a narrow squeak.'

'A very narrow squeak,' said Hickey, and said no more, for his own head trembled as if a great hand were holding it in a tight grip and pushing it from side to side at a terrific speed. He stumbled along beside his companion without a word.

About a mile up the glen there was a stream. The two men knelt together beside it and plunged their faces deep into the gleaming, ice-cold water. They rose, half-choking, but dipped into it again, their dripping forelocks blinding their eyes. When the water had cleared a little they sank their hands in, and, still in silence, drank from their cupped palms. Then they dried hands and faces with their handkerchiefs, and each lit a cigarette, taking long pulls of the invigorating smoke.

'It looks to me,' said Keown, with a faint gleam of his old cheerfulness, 'as if this was to be a busy day.'

'It looks to me as if they wanted to locate the column,' Hickey added wearily. 'And now the column is broken up we'd be fools to hang round.'

'You want to get back west?'

'I do.'

'Home to our mountains.'

'Precisely.'

'I don't know how that's to be managed.'

'I do. If once we get outside this accursed ring it will be simple enough. Probably it's closing in already. If we can hold out until nightfall we may be able to slip through; then we have only to cross by Mallow to Donoughmore, and after that everything will be plain sailing.'

'It sounds good. Do you know the way?'

'No, but I think we might get a few miles north of this, don't you?'

'Out of range, Jim, out of range! That's the main thing, the first principle of tactics.'

They shouldered their rifles and went on, keeping to the fields, and taking what cover they could. Hickey's legs were barely able to support him. Keown was in no better condition. Every now and then he sighed, and cast longing glances at the sun which was still upon the peak of heaven and let fall its vertical beams upon the wide expanse of open country, with its green meadow-lands and greying stubble, its golden furze, and squat, pink, all-too-neat farmhouses; or looked disconsolately at the chain of mountains that closed the farthest horizon with a delicate, faint line of blue.

'I know where my mother's son would like to be now,' he said with facetious melancholy.

'So do I,' said Hickey.

'In Kilnamartyr?' asked Keown, thinking still of the mountains. 'God, Kilnamartyr and wan melodious night in Moran's!'

'No. Not in Kilnamartyr. At home – in the city.'

'Your paradise would never do for me, Jim. There are no women in it.'

'Aren't there, now?'

'There are not, you old Mohammedan!'

'How do you know, Antichrist?'

'There aren't, there aren't, there aren't! I'd lay a hundred to one on that.'

'You'd win.'

'Of course I'd win! Don't I know your finicking, Jesuitical

soul? You hate and fear women as you hate and fear the devil – and a bit more. It's a pity, Jim, it's a real pity, because, God increase you, you're a terror to fight; but there's as much poetry in your constitution as there is in a sardine-tin. Will you ever get married, Jim?'

'Not until we've won this war.'

'And if we don't win it?'

'Oh, there's no if; we must win it!'

Keown cast an amused glance at his companion out of the corner of his eye, and they trudged on again in silence.

III

Five times that day they got the alarm and had to take to their heels. Three times it resulted in desultory fighting. One bout lasted a full three-quarters of an hour; it was hard, slogging, ditch-to-ditch fighting, with one holding back the enemy while the other got into position at the farther end of the field. The last alarm came while they were having tea in a farmer's house. There was no suspicion of treachery, and the soldiers, as unprepared as they, had walked up the boreen to the house for tea. The two friends left in haste by the back door, Keown hugging to his breast a floury half-cake snatched from the table in his hurry. The cake had cost him dear, because in securing it he had forgotten his hat (the hat which, as he assured Jim Hickey, he had earmarked as a present for one of his wives). They halved the hot cake and devoured it, regretting the fresh tea upon the table, and the mint of butter now being consumed by the soldiers.

But at last, drawing on to nightfall, they seemed to have left pursuit behind them and took their bearings. Hickey recognized the place. It was close to Mourneabbey and a few miles away lived an old aunt of his. He suggested sleeping there for the night, and Keown jumped at the idea, even consenting to put away his rifle and equipment until morning, lest their appearance should frighten the old woman.

It was darkening when they reached her house, and having stowed their rifles away in a dry wall, they made their way up the long winding boreen to the top of the hill. A sombre maternal peace enveloped the whole countryside; the fields were a rich green that merged into grey and farther off into a deep, shining purple. A stream flashed like a trail of white fire across the land-scape. The beeches along the lane nodded down a withered leaf or two upon their heads, and the glossy trunks glowed a faint silver under the darkness of their boughs. A dog ran to meet them barking noisily.

The house was a long, low, whitewashed building with a four-sided roof, and outhouses on every side. The two men were greeted by Hickey's aunt, an old woman, doubled up with rheumatism, who beamed delightedly upon him through a pair of dark spectacles. They sat down to tea in the kitchen, a long whitewashed room with an open hearth, where the kettle swung from a chain over the fire. Everything in the house was simple and old-fashioned, the open hearth, the bellows one blows by turning a wheel, the churn, the two pictures that hung on opposite walls, one of Robert Emmet and the other of Parnell. Old-fashioned, but comfortable, with a peculiar warmth when she drew the shutters to and lit the lamp. And homely, when she pulled her chair up to the table and questioned Hickey about mother and sisters, tush-tushed playfully his being 'on the run' (he said nothing of the rifles hidden in the wall or their experi-ence during the day) and joked light-heartedly as old people will to whom realities are no longer such, but shadows that drift daily farther and farther away as their hold upon life slackens.

Parnell had been her last great love, and for her the hope of Irish independence had died with him. Hickey was moved by this strange isolation of hers, moved since now more than at any other time what had happened in those far-off days of elections, brass bands and cudgels seemed remote and insubstantial. And so they talked, each failing to understand the other.

Meanwhile, Keown kept one eye upon a young woman who moved silently about the kitchen as he took his meal. She was a country girl who helped the old lady with her housework. Her appearance had a peculiar distinction that was almost beauty. Very straight and slender she was with a broad face that tapered to a point at the chin, a curious unsmiling mouth, large, sensitive nostrils, and wide-set, melancholy eyes. Her hair was dull gold, and was looped up in a great heap at the poll. Her untidy clothes barely concealed a fine figure, and Keown watched with the appreciation of a connoisseur the easy motion of her body, so girlish yet so strong.

His attention was distracted from her by the appearance of a bottle of whiskey, and, ignoring Hickey's warning glance, he filled a stiff glass for himself and sipped it with unction. For a week past he had not been allowed to touch drink; this was one thing Hickey insisted on with fanatical zeal – no bad example must be given to the men.

When the two women had left the room to prepare a bed for their visitors, Keown said, leaning urgently across the table:

'Jim, I give you fair warning that I'm going to fall in love with that girl.'

'You are not.'

'I am, I tell you. And what's more she's going to fall in love with me, you old celibate! So I'm staying on. I've been virtuous too long. A whole week of it! My God, even the Crusaders—'

'You're drinking too much of that whiskey. Put it away!'

'Ah, shut up you, Father James! Aren't we on vacation, anyhow?'

When Hickey's aunt came back she led off the conversation again, but Hickey carefully watched his companion make free with the whiskey and cast bolder and bolder eyes at the girl, and, as he leaned across to fill himself a third glass, snatched the bottle away. That was enough, he said, forcing Keown off with one hand and with the other holding the bottle, and he remained deaf to Keown's assurances that he would take only a glass, a thimbleful, a drop, as he was tired and wanted to go to bed, as well as the old woman's pleading on his behalf that no doubt the young gentleman had had a tiring day and needed a little glass to cheer him up. Hickey could be obstinate when he chose, and he chose then; so Keown went off to bed, sticking out his tongue at him behind the old woman's back, and blinking angrily at the sleep that closed his eyelids in his own despite.

Hickey felt as if he too were more than half asleep, but he remained up until his aunt's husband returned from Mallow. He heard the pony and trap drive into the cobbled yard, and at last the old man entered, his lean brown face flushed with the cold air. The wind was rising, he said cheerfully, and sure enough it seemed to Hickey that he heard a first feeble rustle of branches about the house. 'God sends winds to blow away the falling leaves,' the old man said oracularly. 'Time little Sheela was in bed,' said his wife. The girl called Sheela smiled, and in her queer silent way disappeared into a little room off the kitchen. 'That's another terrible rebel,' the old woman went on, 'though you wouldn't think it of her and the little she have to say. She was never a prouder girl than when she made the bed for the pair of ye tonight. "You never thought," says I to her, "I had such a fine handsome soldier nephew?" . . . Ah, God, ah, God, we weren't so wild in our young days!' 'Happy days!' said her husband nodding and spitting into the ashes. 'But not so wild,' she repeated, 'not so wild!' She brewed fresh tea, and then they sat into the fire and talked family history for what seemed to Hickey an intolerably long time. Once or twice he felt his head sag and realized that he had dropped off momentarily to sleep. It was his aunt who did most of the talking. Occasionally the old man collected his wits for some ponderous sentence, and having made the most of it nodded and smiled quietly with intense satisfaction. He had a brown, bony, innocent face and a short grey beard.

At last he rose and saying solemnly, 'Even the foolish animal must sleep,' went off to bed. Hickey followed him, leaving his aunt to quench the light. Even with Keown in it the house seemed spiritually still, abstracted, and lonely, and thinking of the danger of raids and arrests which their presence brought to it, he half-wished he had not come there. For worlds he would not have disturbed that old couple, spending their last days in childless, childish innocence, without much hope or fear.

He stood at the window of their room before striking a match. The room was a sort of lean-to above the servant's room downstairs, and smelt queerly of apples and decay. The window was low, very low, and he stood back from it. It gave but a faint light and outside he could distinguish nothing but the shadows of some trees grouped about the gable end. The wind, growing louder, pealed through them, and they creaked faintly, while the slightest of slight sounds, as of distant drumming, seemed to emanate from the boards and window-frame of the little bedroom. As he lit the candle and began to undress Keown stirred in the bed, and, raising his fat, pugnacious face and squint eye out of a tumble of white linen and dark hair, said thickly but with sombre indignation, 'In spite of you I'll have that girl. Yes, my f-f-friend, in – spite–of – you—!'

'Ah, go to sleep like a good man!' said Hickey crossly, and clad only in a light summer singlet, slipped into bed beside him.

IV

The wind! That was it, the wind! He could not have slept for long before it woke him. It blew with a sort of clumsy precision, rising slowly in great crescendos that shook the window-panes and seemed to reverberate through the whole ramshackle house. The window was bright so there was no rain. 'God sends winds to blow away the falling leaves,' he thought with a smile.

He lay back and watched the window that seemed to grow brighter as he looked at it, and suddenly it became clear to him that his life was a melancholy, aimless life, and that all this endless struggle and concealment was but so much out of an existence that would mean little anyhow. He had left college two years before when the police first began hunting for him, and he doubted now whether it would ever be in his power to return. He was a different man, and most of the ties he had broken then he would never be able to resume. If they won, of course, the army would be open to him, but the army he knew would not content him long, for soldiering at best was only servitude, and he had lived too desperately to endure the hollow routine of barrack life. Besides, he was a scientist, not a soldier. And if they lost? (He thought bitterly of what Keown had suggested that afternoon and his own reply.) Of course, they mustn't lose, but suppose they did? What was there for him then? America? That was all – America! And his mother, who had worked so hard to educate him and had hoped so much of him, his mother would die, having seen him accomplish nothing, and he would be somewhere very far away. What use would anything be then? And it was quite clear to him that he had realized all this that very morning – or was it the morning before? Above Glenmanus Wood, just at the moment when the door of that old house opened, and a girl dressed in white appeared, a girl to whom it all meant nothing, nothing but that a column of irregulars was somewhere in the neighbourhood and being chased off by soldiers. At that very moment he had felt something explode within him at the inhumanity, the coldness, of it all. He had wanted to wave to her; what was that but the desire for some human contact? And then the presence of immediate danger and the necessity for flight had driven it out of his mind, but now it returned with all the dark power of nocturnal melancholy surging up beneath it; the feeling of his own loneliness, his own unimportance, his own folly.

'What use is it all?' he asked himself aloud, and the wind answered with a low, long-ebbing sound, a murmur, hushed and sustained, that seemed to penetrate the old house and become portion of its secret grief.

He felt his companion stir beside him in the bed. Then Keown sat up. He sat there for a long while silent, and Hickey, fearing the intrusion of his speech lay still and closed his eyes. At last Keown spoke, and his voice startled Hickey by its note of vibrant horror.

'Jim!'

'I mustn't answer,' thought Hickey.

'Jim!' A hand felt about the bed for him and closed on his arm.

'Jim, Jim! Wake up! Listen to me!'

'Well?'

'Do you hear it?'

'What?'

'Listen!'

'Do you mean the wind?'

'Jim!'

'Oh, do for Heaven's sake go to sleep!'

'Listen to that, Jim!'

'I'm listening!'

'Oh, my God! There it is again!'

The wind. It kept up that steady murmur that filled the old house like the bellows filling an organ. Then a clear, startling note rose above the light monotone, and the boards creaked, and the windows strained, and the trees shook with the noise of a breaking wave.

'Jim, I say!'

'Well, what is it?'

'Christ Almighty, man, I can't stand it!'

Keown tossed off the bedclothes, fell back upon the pillows and lay naked with his arms covering his eyes. Hickey started up.

'What's wrong with you?'

'It's them, Jim! It's them!' His voice half-rose into a scream.

'Shut up, do, or you'll wake the whole house! Is that what we came here for? Come on, out with it! What are you snivelling about?'

'I tell you they're outside. Don't you hear them, blast you?'

Hickey's hand closed tightly over his mouth.

'Be quiet! Be quiet! There are old people in this house. I won't have them disturbed I tell you.'

'I won't be quiet. Listen!'

The wind was rising again. Once it dropped at all it took a long time to mobilize its scattered fury. Hickey could feel the other man grow rigid with fear under his hands.

'Listen! Oh, Jim, what am I to do?'

'For the last time I warn you. If you don't keep quiet, so help me, God, I'll smash you up! You've drunk too much, that's what's wrong with you.'

'Oh! oh!'

'Careful now!'

It was coming. The wind rose into a triumphant howl and Keown struggled frantically. He dragged at Hickey's left hand which tried to silence him, and his mouth had formed a shriek when the other's fist descended with a blow that turned it suddenly to a gasp of pain.

'Now, will that keep you quiet?'

Hickey struck again.

'Oh, for Jesus' sake, Jimmie, don't beat me! I'm not telling lies, it's them all right.'

He was sobbing quietly. The first blow must have cut his lip for Hickey felt the blood trickle across his left hand.

'Will you be quiet then?'

'I'll be quiet, Jimmie. Only don't beat me, don't beat me!'

'I won't beat you. Are you cut?'

'Jimmie!'

'Are you cut? I said.'

'Hold my hand, Jimmie!'

Hickey took his hand, and seeing him quieter lay down again beside him. After a few moments Keown's free hand rose and felt his arm and shoulder, even his face, for company. A queer night's rest, thought Hickey ruefully.

For him, at any rate, there was no rest. His companion would lie quiet for a little time, gasping and moaning when the wind blew strongly; but then some more violent blast would come that shook the house, or whirled a loose slate crashing on the cobbles of the yard, and it would begin all over again.

'Jim, they're after me!'

'Be quiet, man! For the good God's sake be quiet!'

'I hear them! I hear them talking in the yard. They're coming for me. Jim, where in Christ's name is my gun? Quick! Quick!'

'There's nobody in the yard, I tell you, and it's nothing but a gale of wind. You and your gun! You're a nice man to trust with a gun! Bawling your heart out because there's a bit of a wind blowing!'

'Ah, Jim, Jim, it's all up with me! All up, all up!'

It was just upon dawn when, from sheer exhaustion, he fell asleep. Hickey rose quietly for fear of disturbing him, pulled on his riding-breeches and coat, and, having lit a cigarette, sat beside the window and smoked. The wind had died down somewhat, and, with the half-light that struggled through the flying clouds above the tree-tops, its rage seemed to count no longer. A grey mist hugged the yard below, and covered all but the tops of the trees. As it cleared, minute by minute, he perceived all about him broken slates, with straw and withered leaves that rustled when the wind blew them about. The mist cleared farther, and he saw the trees looking much barer than they had looked the day before, with broken branches and the new day showing in great, rugged patches between them. The beeches, silver-bright with their sinewy limbs, seemed to him like athletes stripped for a contest. Light, a cold, wintry, forbidding light suffused the chill air. The birds were singing.

At last he heard a door open and shut. Then the bolts on the back door were drawn; he heard a heavy step in the yard, and Sheela passed across it in the direction of one of the outhouses, carrying a large bucket. Her feet, in men's boots twice too big for her, made a metallic clatter upon the cobbles. Her hair hung down her back in one long plait of dull gold, and her body, slender as a hound's, made a deep furrow for it as she walked.

He rose silently, pulled on his stockings, and tiptoed down the creaking stairs to the kitchen. It was almost completely dark, but for the mist of weak light that came through the open door. When he heard her step outside he went to meet her and took a bucket of turf from her hand. They scarcely spoke. She asked if he had been disturbed by the wind and he nodded, smiling. Then she knelt beside the fireplace and turned the little wheel of the bellows. The seed of fire upon the hearth took light and scattered

red sparks about his stockinged feet where he stood, leaning against the mantelpiece. He watched her bent above it, the long golden plait hanging across her left shoulder, the young pointed face taking light from the new-born flame, and as she rose he took her in his arms and kissed her. She leaned against his shoulder in her queer silent way, with no shyness. And for him in that melancholy kiss an ache of longing was kindled, and he buried his face in the warm flesh of her throat as the kitchen filled with the acrid smell of turf; while the blue smoke drifting through the narrow doorway was caught and whirled head-long through grey fields and dark masses of trees upon which an autumn sun was rising.

MACHINE-GUN CORPS IN ACTION

I

WHEN SEAN NELSON and I were looking for a quiet spot in the hills for the brigade printing press we thought of Kilvara, one of the quietest of all the mountain hamlets we knew. And as we drove down the narrow road into it, we heard the most ferocious devil's fusilade of machine-gun fire we had heard since the troubles began.

Nelson slipped the safety-catch of his rifle and I held the car at a crawl. Not that we could see anything or anybody. The firing was as heavy as ever, but no bullet seemed to come near us, and for miles around the vast, bleak, ever-changing screen of hillside with its few specks of cottages was as empty as before.

We seemed to be in the very heart of the invisible battle when suddenly the firing ceased and a little ragged figure – looking, oh, so unspectacular against that background of eternal fortitude – detached itself from behind a hillock, dusted its knees, shouldered a strange-looking machine-gun, and came towards us. It hailed us and signalled us to stop. I pulled up the car, and Nelson lowered his rifle significantly. The little ragged figure looked harmless enough, God knows, and we both had the shyness of unprofessional soldiers.

What we saw was a wild, very under-sized cityman, dressed in an outworn check suit, a pair of musical-comedy tramp's brogues, and a cap which did no more than half conceal his shock of dirty yellow hair. As he came towards us he produced the butt-end of a cigarette, hung it from one corner of his mouth, struck a match upon his boot-sole without pausing in his stride, and carelessly flicked the light across his lips. Then, as he accosted us, he let out a long grey stream of smoke through his nostrils.

'Comrades,' he said companionably. 'Direct me to Jo Kenefick's column, eh? Doing much fighting your end of the line? I'm all the way from Waterford, pure Cork otherwise.'

'Yeh?' we asked in astonishment, though not at the second clause of his statement, of the truth of which his accent left no room for doubt. He knew as much.

'Sure,' he replied, 'sure, sir. You have a look at my boots. All the way without as much as a lift. Couldn't risk that with the baby. Been doing a bit of practice now to keep my hand in.'

'It sounded quite professional to me,' said Nelson mildly.

'Ah!' The little man shook his head. 'Amateur, amateur, but I must keep the old hand in. A beauty though, isn't she? All I've left in the world now.'

He lovingly smoothed off some imaginary rust from his gun, which I took to be of foreign make. I bent out of the car to examine it, but he stepped back.

'No, no. Don't come near her. She's a touchy dame. Guess how much I paid for her? Two pounds. The greatest bargain ever. Two pounds! I heard the Tommy offering it to my wife. By way of a joke, you know. So I said, "You lend me two pounds, old girl, and I'll buy her." Nearly died when she heard I wanted to buy a machine-gun. "Buy a machine-gun – *a machine-gun* – what use would a machine-gun be to her? Wouldn't a mangle be more in her line?" So I said, "Cheerio, old girl, don't get so huffy, a mangle may be a useful article, but it isn't much fun, and anyway, this round is on me." And I rose the money off an old Jew in the Marsh. So help me, God, amen. Wasn't I right?'

'And where are you off to now?' asked Nelson.

'You gentlemen will tell me that, I hope. Jo Kenefick's column, that's where I'm going. Know Tom Casey? No? Well, I served under Tom. He'll tell you all about me, soldier.'

We directed him to Jo's column, which we had left in a village a few miles down the valley.

'You gentlemen wouldn't have an old bob about you, I suppose?' he asked dreamily, and seeing the answer in our eyes hurried on with, 'No, no, of course you wouldn't. Where would you get it? Hard times with us all these days. . . . Or a cigarette? I'm down to my last butt as you may see.'

Out of sheer pity we gave him three of the seven we had between us, and, in acknowledgement of the kindness, he showed us how he could wag both ears in imitation of a dog. It struck me that it was not the first time he had fallen on evil days. Then with a cheerful good-bye he left us, and we sat in the car watching his game, sprightly, dilapidated figure disappear over the mountains on its way to the column. After that we drove into Kilvara.

At the schoolmaster's house we stopped to examine the old school which had been indicated as a likely headquarters for our press. There Nelson set himself to win round the schoolmaster's daughter, a fine, tall, red-haired girl, who looked at us with open hostility. He succeeded so well that she invited us in to tea; but with the tea we had to win over the schoolmaster himself and his second daughter, a much more difficult job. Neither Nelson nor I could fathom what lay beneath their hostility; the family seemed to have no interest in politics outside the court and society column of the daily press; and it was not until the old teacher asked with a snarl whether we had heard firing as we came up that we began to see bottom.

'Ah,' said Nelson laughing, 'you're finished with the tramp.'

'Are we, I wonder?' asked the teacher grimly.

'That man,' said Nelson, 'was the funniest thing I've seen for months.'

'Funny?' exclaimed the younger daughter flaring up. 'I'm glad you think it fun!'

'Well, what did he do to you, anyhow?' asked Nelson irritably. Nelson was touchy about what he called the *bourgeoisie*.

'Do you know,' she asked angrily, 'when my dad said he had no room for him here with two girls in the house, your "funny" friend took his trench mortar, and put it on a sort of camera stand in front of the hall door, and threatened to blow us all into eternity?'

'The little rat!' said Nelson. 'And he actually wanted to stay here?'

'Wanted to stay?' said the daughters together. 'Wanted to stay! Did he stay for a fortnight and the gun mounted all night on the chair beside his bed?'

'Holy Lord God!' said Nelson profanely, 'and we without as much as a good pea-shooter on the armoured car!'

After this the story expanded to an almost incredible extent, for not alone did it concern Kilvara, but other places where the tramp's activities had already become the stuff of legend.

'He'll behave himself when Jo Kenefick gets him,' said Nelson grimly.

'I tell you what, girls,' he went on, 'come back with us in the car and tell Jo Kenefick the story as you told it now.'

At this the girls blushed and giggled, but at last they agreed, and proceeded to ready themselves for the journey, the old schoolmaster meanwhile becoming more and more polite and even going to the trouble of explaining to us the half-dozen different reasons why we could *not* win the war.

I have no intention of describing the journey to Coolenagh and back under an autumn moon – though I can picture it very clearly: mountains and pools and misty, desolate ribbons of mountain road – for that is the story of how we almost retrieved the reputation of the Irish Republican Army in the little hamlet of Kilvara; but what I should like to describe is Jo Kenefick's face when we (that is to say Sean and I, for we judged it unwise to lay Jo open to temptation) told the tale of the tramp's misdeeds.

'Mercy of God!' said Jo. 'Ye nabbed him and let him go again?'

'But didn't he arrive yet?' asked Nelson.

'Arrive?' asked Jo. 'Arrive where, tell me?'

'Here, of course.'

'Here?' asked Jo with a sour scowl. 'And I looking for him this fortnight to massacree him!'

'Damn!' said Nelson, seeing light.

'It was great negligence in ye to let him go,' said Jo severely. 'And I wouldn't mind at all but ye let the gun go too. Do you know I have seventy-five thousand rounds of that stuff in the dump, and he have the only gun in Ireland that will shoot it?'

'He said he bought it for two pounds,' said I.

'He did,' replied Jo. 'He did. And my QM came an hour after and bid fifty. It was an Italian gun not inventoried at all, and it was never looked for in the evacuation. Where did ye find him?'

We told him the exact spot in which we had last seen the gunner.

'Be damn!' said Jo, 'I'll send out a patrol on motor-bikes to catch him. That armoured car isn't much use to me without a gun.'

But when we returned from our joy-ride at two o'clock the following morning – leaving, I hope, two happy maidens in the hills behind – the patrols were back without gunner or gun.

II

Three days later the gunner turned up – between two stalwart country boys with cocked Webleys. He was very downcast, and having explained to Jo Kenefick how he had been sent out of his way by two men answering to our description, he added, a moment after we had made our appearance, that he had been caught in a storm on the hills.

The same night it was decided to make amends for our previous inaction by attacking the nearest town, and that no later than the following morning. The men were hurriedly called together and the plans explained to them. The town was garrisoned by about forty soldiers and the armoured car, driven by me and manned by the tramp, was to prepare the way for the attack.

At dawn I stood in my overalls by the door of the armoured car and lectured the tramp. He was extremely nervous, and tapped the body at every point, looking for what he called leaks. I explained, as clearly as I could to a man who paid no attention to me, that his principal danger would be from inside, and showed him that my revolver was fully loaded to cope with emergencies.

We pulled out of the village and passed little groups of armed men converging on the town. I had to drive slowly, principally because it was impossible to get much speed out of the car, which was far too heavy for its chassis, and needed skilful negotiation, but partly because the lumbering old truck refused to work on reverse and, to avoid occasional detours of a few miles, I had to be careful to get my turns right.

Jo Kenefick, Sean Nelson and some others were waiting for us outside the town and gave us a few necessary directions; then we closed all apertures except that for the machine-gun and the shielded slit through which I watched the road immediately in front of me, and gave the old bus her head downhill. She slowed down of her own accord as we entered a level street the surface of which was far worse than any I had ever seen. As we drew near the spot where I thought the barrack should be I heard the tramp mumble something; I looked back and saw him fiercely sighting his gun; then the most deafening jumble of noise I have ever heard in my life began.

'Slow! Slow!' the tramp shouted, and I held her in as we

lumbered down the main street, letting her rip again as we took a side-street that brought us back to the centre of the town. I knew that the enemy was in occupation of some half-dozen houses. Beyond this I knew nothing of what went on about me. The tramp shouted directions which I followed without question. 'Slow!' he cried when we were passing some occupied post, and two or three times he exclaimed that he had 'got' somebody. This was none of my business. I had enough to do at the wheel.

Besides I was almost deaf from the shooting and the chugging and jumbling of the old bus (all concentrated and magnified within that little steel box until it sounded like the day of judgment and the anger of the Lord) and suffocated by the fumes of petrol and oil that filled it. This went on, as I afterwards calculated, for at least two hours and a half. I could not tell what was happening between our men and the regulars, but I guessed that Kenefick would have bagged some of the supplies we needed under cover of our fire.

Suddenly, in the midst of a terrific burst of firing from the tramp, the engine kicked. My heart stood still. The old bus went on smoothly for a little while, and then, in the middle of the main street, kicked again. I realized that the only hope was to get her out of the town as quickly as possible, and leave the men to escape as best they could. I put her to it, stepping on the gas and praying to her maker. Again she ran smoothly for a few yards and suddenly stopped, not fifty feet from the barrack door as I judged. I let my hands drop from the wheel and sat there in despair. There was no self-starter.

'What's wrong with you, man?' shouted the tramp. 'Start her again, quick.'

'Are any of our men around?' I shouted, indulging a last faint hope.

'How could they be?' yelled the tramp, letting rip an occasional shot. 'Nobody could move in that fire.'

'Then one of us must get out and start her.'

'Get out? Not likely. Stay where you are; you're in no danger.'

'No danger?' I asked bitterly. 'And when they roll a bomb under the car?'

'They'd never think of that!' he said with pathetic consternation.

I pushed open the door that was farthest from the barrack,

pushed it just an inch or so in hope that it would not be detected. It occurred to me that with care, with very great care, one might even creep round under cover as far as the starting-handle. I yelled to the tramp to open heavy fire. He did so with a will, and when I banged the steel door back and knelt on the footboard a perfect tornado of machine-gun bullets was whirling madly in wide circles above my head. Inch by inch I crept along the side of the car, my head just level with the footboard. My progress was maddeningly slow, but I reached the front mudguard in safety, and, still bent double, gave the starting-handle a spin. The car started, jumped, and stood still again with a faint sigh, and at that very moment something happened that I shall never forget the longest day I live.

Silence, an unutterable, appalling silence fell about me. For a full minute I was quite unable to guess what had happened; then it occurred to me – a dreadful revelation – that I had become stone-deaf. I did not dare to move, but crouched there with one hand upon the starter and the other upon the gun in my belt. I looked round me; the street with all its shattered window-panes was quite empty and silent with the silence of midnight. I tried to remember what it was one did when one became suddenly deaf.

Then, the simplest of sounds, my hand jolting the starting-handle, roused me to the knowledge that, whatever else had happened, my hearing must be intact. To make certain I jolted the handle again, and again I distinctly heard the creak. But the silence had now become positively sinister. I gave the handle a ferocious spin, the engine started, and I crept back to the door on hands and knees. Still there was no sound. I raised myself slowly; still nothing. I looked into the car and saw to my horror that it was empty of gunner and gun. Then I glanced along the street and round the farthest corner I saw the last rags of my crew flutter triumphantly before they disappeared for good. The crew had gone over to the enemy, and left me to find my way out of the town as best I could.

I sat in among a heap of spent bullet cases, made the doors tight, and drove lamely out of town. Nobody tried to hinder me nor did I see any sign of our men; it was like a town of the dead, with glass littering the pavements and great gaping holes in every shop window.

I drove for half an hour through a deserted countryside until at last I caught up with a small group of men, two of whom were carrying a stretcher. I drove in amongst them and they surrounded the car, furiously waving rifles and bombs. For safety sake I opened the turret and spoke to them through that.

'Where is he?' they yelled, 'where is he?'

'Where's who?'

'Where's the man with the gun? He hit Mike Cronin one in the leg, and if Mike gets him alive . . .' From the stretcher Mike fully confirmed the intention, adding his vivid impressions of us both.

At that moment Jo Kenefick and Nelson pushed their way through the excited crowd, and probably saved me from a bad mauling. But they were almost as unreasonable and excited as the others; Jo in particular, who promptly threatened to have me court-martialled.

'But how could I know?' I yelled down at him. 'I couldn't see but what was before my eyes. And how does Mike Cronin know it was a bullet from the car he stopped?'

'What else could it be?' asked Jo. 'Where did you let that lunatic go?'

'He went over to the Staters while I was starting the car.'

'Staters!' said Kenefick bitterly. 'He went over to the Staters! Listen to him! And the last man evacuated the town at four o'clock this morning.'

I groaned, the whole appalling truth beginning to dawn upon me.

'And the grub?' I asked.

'Grub? Nobody dared to stir from cover with that fool blazing away. And the people will rend us if ever we show our noses there again.'

That was the truest word Jo Kenefick ever spoke. We did *not* dare to show our noses in the town again, and this time Nelson and I could be of no use as peacemakers.

III

A fortnight later and Jo Kenefick could talk about the affair; if he were pushed to extremity he could even laugh at it, but as his laughter always preceded a bitter little lecture to me about the necessity for foresight and caution, I preferred him in philosophic mood, as when he said:

'Now, you think you have a man when you haven't him at all. There aren't any odds high enough again' a man doing a thing you don't expect him to do. Take that tramp of yours for instance. That man never done a stroke of work in his life. His wife have a little old-clothes shop on the quays. She's a dealing woman – with a tidy stocking, I'd say. She kep' him in 'baccy an' buns an' beer. He never had one solitary thing to worry him. And all of a sudden, lo and behold ye! he wants to be a soldier. Not an ordinary soldier either, mind you, but a free lance; brigadier and bombadier, horse, foot and artillery all at once! What's the odds again' that, I ask you? And which of ye will give me odds on what he's going to do next? Will you?'

'I will not,' said Nelson.

'Nor will I,' said myself.

'There you are,' said Jo. 'My belief is you can't be certain of anything in human nature. As for that skew-eyed machine-gun man of yours, well, there's nothing on heaven or earth I'd put apast him.'

Some hours later Jo's capacity for receiving shocks was put to the test. A mountainy man appeared to complain that the tramp was at his old tricks again. This time it was in connection with a squabble about land; there was a second marriage, a young widow, a large family, and a disputed will in it, but of the rights and wrongs of these affairs no outsider can ever judge. They begin in what is to him a dim and distant past; somebody dies and the survivors dispute over his property; somebody calls somebody else a name; six months later somebody's window is smashed; years after somebody's fences are broken down; the infection spreads to the whole parish; the school is boycotted; there is a riot in the nearest town on fair day; and then, quite casually, some unfortunate wretch who seems to have had nothing to do with the dispute is found in a ditch with portion of his skull blown away.

Not that we gathered anything as lucid or complete from the slob of a mountainy man who talked to us at such length. All he could tell us was that his cousin's house had been machine-gunned, and that, in the opinion of the parish, was carrying the matter too far. Nor did we want to know more. Jo Kenefick was on his feet calling for men when Sean Nelson stopped him.

'Leave it to us, Jo, leave it to us! Remember we've an account to square with him.'

'I'm remembering that,' said Jo slowly. 'And I'm remembering too he got away from ye twice.'

'All the more reason he won't get away a third time.'

'If I leave him to ye,' said Jo, 'will ye swear to me to bring him back here, dead or alive, with his machine-gun?'

'Dead or alive,' nodded Sean.

'And more dead than alive?' said Jo with his heavy humour.

'Oh, more dead than alive!' said Sean.

And so it was that we three, Sean, myself, and the mountainy man set out from the village that evening.

Three-quarters of an hour of jolting and steady climbing and we came to a little valley set between three hills; a stream flowing down the length of it and a few houses set distantly upon the lower slopes. The mountainy man pointed out a comfortable farmhouse backed by a wall of elm-trees as our destination. He refused to come with us, nor indeed did we ask for his company.

The door of the little farmhouse was open, and we walked straight into the kitchen. A young woman was sitting by an open hearth in the twilight, and she rose to greet us.

''Morrow, ma'am,' said Nelson.

'Good morrow and welcome,' she said.

'A man we're looking for, ma'am, a man with a machine-gun, I'm told he's staying here?'

'He is, faith,' she said. 'But he's out at this minute. Won't you sit down and wait for him?'

We sat down. She lifted the kettle on to a hook above the fire and blew on the red turves until they gathered to a flame. It was easy to see that Nelson, the emotional firebrand of the brigade, was impressed. She was a young woman; not an out-and-out beauty, certainly, but good-tempered and kind. Her hair was cut straight across her brow and short at the poll. She was tall, limber and rough, with a lazy, swinging, impudent stride.

'We've been looking for the same man this long time,' said Nelson. 'We've had a good many complaints of him, ma'am, and now he's caused more crossness here, we heard.'

'If that's all you came about,' she said pertly, 'you might have found something better to do.'

'That's for us to say,' said Nelson sharply.

'Clever boy!' she replied with an impudent pretence of surprise, and I saw by the way she set her tongue against her lower lip that Nelson had approached her in the wrong way.

'That man,' I said, 'accidentally shot one of our fellows, and we're afraid something else will happen.'

At this she laughed, a quiet, bubbling, girlish laugh that surprised and delighted me.

'It will,' she said gaily,'something will happen unless you take that gun from him.'

Her attitude had changed completely. Laughing still she told us how the tramp had arrived at her house one night, wet to the skin, and carrying his gun wrapped up in oilcloth. He had heard how her husband's people had been annoying her, had heard something about herself as well and come fired with a sort of quixotic enthusiasm to protect her. On the very night of his arrival he had begun his career as knight-errant by gunning the house of one of the responsible parties, and only her persuasion had discouraged him from doing them further mischief. Three times a day he paraded the boundaries of her farm to make sure that all was well, and at night he would rise and see that the cattle were safely in their stalls and that fences and gates were standing. It was all very idyllic, all very amusing; and as there is little sentiment or chivalry in an Irish countryside there was no doubt that the young widow liked it, and appreciated with a sort of motherly regard the tramp's unnecessary attentions. But Nelson soon made it clear that all this would have to cease. Nelson liked being a little bit officious and did it very well. Her face fell as she listened to him.

'Of course,' he added loftily, 'you won't have any more annoyance. We'll settle that for you, and a great deal better than anyone else could. I'll come back tomorrow and see you straight.'

A few moments later the tramp himself came in; it was amazing how his face changed when he saw us sitting there. Nelson was as solemn as a judge, but for the life of me I could not resist laughing. This encouraged the tramp, who began to laugh, too, as though it were all a very good joke and would go no further. Nelson looked at me severely.

'I see nothing to laugh about,' he said; and to the tramp: 'Be ready to travel back with us inside the next five minutes.'

'Let him have his tea,' said the woman of the house roughly.

'I protest,' said the tramp.

'It's no use protesting,' said Nelson, 'if you don't choose to come you know what the consequences will be.'

'What will they be?' asked the tramp, beginning to grow pale.

'I was ordered to bring you back dead or alive, and dead or alive I'll bring you!'

'There!' said the young woman, putting a teapot on the table. 'Have your tea first, and start shooting after. Will I light the lamp?'

'There's no need,' said Nelson, 'I can shoot quite well in the dark.'

'Aren't you very clever?' she replied.

They glared at one another, and then Nelson pushed over his chair. We took our tea in silence, but after about five minutes the tramp, who had obviously been summoning up his courage, put down his knife with a bang.

'Gentlemen,' he said solemnly. 'I protest. I refuse to return with you. I'm a free citizen of this country and nobody has any rights over me. I warn you I'll resist.'

'Resist away,' growled Nelson into his teacup.

There was silence again. We went on with our tea. Then the latch of the door was lifted and a tall, worn woman dressed in a long black shawl appeared. She stood at the door for a moment, and a very softly-breathed 'So there you are, my man,' warned us whom we were dealing with.

'Maggie! Maggie!' said the tramp. 'Is it you?'

'The same,' she whispered, still in the same hushed, contented voice.

'How did you get here?' he asked.

'I'm searching for you these three days,' she replied soothingly. 'I've a car at the door. Are you ready to come back with me?'

'I – I – I'm sorry, Maggie, but I can't.'

'Och aye, me poor man, and why can't you?' The hush in her voice, even to my ears, was awe-inspiring, but he plunged recklessly into it.

'I'm to go back with these gentlemen, Maggie. By order—'

'Order? Order?' she shrieked, standing to her full height and tossing the shawl back from one shoulder. 'Let me see the order that can take my husband away from me without my will and consent! Let me see the one that's going to do it!'

She threw herself into the middle of the kitchen, the shawl half-flung across one arm, like a toreador going into action. Nelson, without so much as a glance at her, shook his head at the table.

'I'm not taking him against your wishes, ma'am – far be it from me! I'd be the last to try and separate ye. Only I must ask you to take him home with you out of this immediately.'

'Oh! I'll take him home!' she said with a nod of satisfaction. 'Lave that to me.' And with a terrifying shout she turned on the tramp. 'On with your hat, James!'

The poor man stumbled to his feet, looking distractedly at Nelson and me.

'Anything with you?' she rapped out.

'Only me gun.'

'Fetch it along.'

Now Nelson was on his feet protesting.

'No, he can't take that with him.'

'Who's to stop him?'

'I will.'

'Fetch it along, James!'

'And I say he won't fetch it along.' Now it was Nelson who was excited and the woman who was calm.

'There's nobody can interfere with a wife's rights over her husband – and her husband's property.'

'I'll shoot your husband and then I'll show you what I can do with his property,' said Nelson, producing his Webley and laying it beside him on the table.

'What did you give for it?' she asked the tramp.

'Two pounds,' he muttered.

'Give it to you for ten!' she said coolly to Nelson.

'I'll see you damned first,' said Nelson.

'Fetch it along, James,' she said, with an impudent smile.

'There's a car outside waiting to take him somewhere he'll never come back from,' said Nelson. 'I'm warning you not to rouse me.'

'Five so,' she said.

'Go along to hell out of this,' he shouted, 'you and your husband!'

'I'm waiting for me own,' she said.

'You'll get your two pounds,' he said, breathing through his nose.

'Five,' she said, without turning a hair.

'Two!' he bellowed.

'Five!'

'Get along with you now!' he said.

'I rely on your word as an officer and a gentleman,' she shouted suddenly. 'And if you fail me, I'll folly you to the gates of hell. Go on, James,' she said, and without another word the strange pair went out the door.

The young widow rose slowly and watched them through a lifted curtain go down the pathway to the road where a car was waiting for them.

'Well?' she said, turning to me with a sad little smile.

'Well?' said I.

'Well?' said Nelson. 'Somebody's got to stay here and clear up this mess.'

'Somebody had better go and break the news to Jo Kenefick,' said I.

'I can't drive a car,' remarked Nelson significantly.

'It wouldn't be the only thing you can't do,' said the young widow viciously.

Nelson pretended not to hear her.

'You can explain to him how things stand here, and tell him I can't be back until tomorrow.'

'Not before then?' she put in sarcastically.

'I suppose you'll tell me you haven't room for me?' he asked angrily.

'Oh, there's always a spare cowshed if the mountains aren't wide enough,' she retorted.

So I took the hint, and musing upon the contrariness of men and the inhuman persuadableness of motors, I took my machine-gun and drove off through the hills as dark was coming on.

LAUGHTER

WHILE HE was waiting for Eric Nolan to appear he told mother and daughters the story of the last ambush. It was Alec Gorman's story, really, and it needed Alec's secretive excited way of telling it and his hearty peal of laughter as he brought it to a close.

It concerned an impossible young fellow in the neighbourhood who was always begging for admission to the active service unit, always playing about with guns and explosives, and always letting on he was somebody of importance. The soldiers knew of his mania, and did not take the trouble to put him under arrest, much to his own fury and disgust. To anyone who would listen he told the wildest stories about his adventures, and pretended to any and every sort of office; he was quartermaster, company commandant, staff-captain, intelligence officer, and the deuce only knew what besides. And – the crowning touch in the comedy – he had a hare-lip.

Now, one night Alec had a private ambush – quite unauthorized, of course, like everything he did. He launched a bomb at a lorry of soldiers in the street, and then ran away up a dark lane, his cap pulled well down over his eyes, and his hand on the butt of his revolver. By the light of a gas-lamp he saw Hare-lip running breathlessly towards him, in trench coat, riding-breeches and gaiters. When he saw Alec he stopped, and in a tone as authoritative as he could adopt demanded to know what was wrong. At this Alec's delight in devilment made off with his prudence. 'There was an ambush at the cross, mister,' he whined. 'Two fine boys kilt outright – they're picking up the bits of them still, may God punish the blackguards that done it!' Hare-lip stood for a moment as if stupefied. Then he clapped his hands to his eyes in fury and despair (it was a treat to see Alec take off this gesture). His hat fell off and rolled into a puddle. 'Oh, nJesus!' he moaned. 'Oh, nJesus, nand nthey never ntold nme!'

They laughed, mother and daughters. Stephen marvelled at

the courage of the old woman who sat there so coolly while he cleaned his three revolvers. Every other day her house was raided, but crippled as she was with rheumatism, and with two sons in prison it brought no diminution of her high spirits. He liked to see her with a revolver in her hand, turning it over and over, and blinking endlessly at it, a good-humoured wondering smile on her toothless gums. Her younger daughter, plump and debonair, showed the traces more; she had begun to fidget, and her mother covered her with good-humoured abuse.

'I'm sixty-eight years of age, child! I'm forty-six years older than you, and a broomstick wouldn't straighten me back, but I'd make ten of you. Ten of you? I would and twenty! I'd go out in the morning with me little gun in me hand and stand up to a brigade of them. What did I say to their jackeen of a lieutenant the other night? Tell Stephen what I said to him. "Get out o' me way, you rat!" says I, "get out o' me way before I give you me boot where your mother forgot to give you the stick!" I did so, Stephen.'

As for Norah, the elder girl, she was like a mask. That cold and pointed beauty of hers rarely showed feeling.

At last they heard Eric Nolan's knock. He came in, tall, bony, and cynical, a little too carefully dressed for the poor student he was, a little too nonchalant for a revolutionary. He smoked a pipe, carried a silver-mounted walking-stick and wore yellow gloves. There was a calculated but attractive insolence about his way of entering a house and greeting the occupants. He laid his walking-stick on the table, and covered the handle with his hat. Then he made way for Norah who went upstairs to dress, leant against the stair rail and made eyes at Mary whom he disliked and who heartily disliked him. Stephen, adoring even his mannerisms, smiled and tossed the three revolvers on the table.

'There!' he said, 'these are ready anyway. Now what about the bomb, Mrs M'Carthy?'

The old lady fumbled for a moment in her clothes and produced a Mills bomb red with rust. She could not resist the temptation to hold the grisly thing to the light and blink admiringly at it for a moment before she handed it to Stephen.

'Oh, God!' she exclaimed, seeing his hand tremble slightly. 'Look who I'm giving it to. Lord, look, will ye! He's shaking like an aspen leaf.' And she gaily hit him over the knuckles.

'You're no soldier, Stephen. Steady your hand, you cowardly thing!'

At that moment they heard a fierce hammering at the door. Stephen was so startled that he almost dropped the bomb, but the old lady was on her feet in a flash. She snatched the bomb back from him and took up one of the revolvers.

'I'll bring these,' she said tensely. 'Mary, you take the other two. Hurry, you little fool!'

Bent with pain she was already half-way up the stairs. The two young men stood, one at either side of Mary, not daring to speak. She was leaning on the table, looking blankly down on the two oily revolvers which lay beneath her open fingers. She had gone deathly pale. The knocking began again, loud enough to waken the neighbourhood.

Rat-tat-tat!

'Mary, Mary, what are you doing?' the old woman's voice hissed down the stairs.

Rat-tat-tat-tat-tat.

With a slight almost imperceptible shiver, she lifted one of the revolvers and slid it down the bosom of her dress; she did it slowly and deliberately. After a moment the other followed. Eric Nolan went on tiptoe to the outer door, and looked back at Stephen who was standing in the kitchen doorway. 'Ready?' he whispered, and Stephen nodded, too unnerved to speak. He straightened his spectacles with an unsteady hand.

The door opened, there was a rush of heavy feet, and a tall figure dressed in green uniform that was sodden and black with rain stood at the kitchen door. Stephen drew in his breath sharply, and stood back. The uniformed figure lurched helplessly towards him, and without warning Mary staggered and burst into a shriek of excited laughter. Stephen ran to her, and was just in time to put his arm about her and prevent her from falling. He heard Norah taking the stairs three at a time. Her face showed no surprise, but it struck him for the first time that it was a tired, rather dispirited face. With her help he carried Mary to her room.

When he came back to the kitchen the man in uniform was sitting on a chair beside the door; a great flushed face and fuddled, anxious eyes fixed abstractedly upon the opposite wall. Abstractedly too his great hand rose and smoothed down a long dribbling moustache. Eric Nolan stood silently beside him in utter mystification. Then with a supreme effort of will the man came to himself, and glared at Stephen.

'I – I forgot me bracelet,' he said weakly.

'Who in hell are you?' asked Stephen.

'Who am I? Who am I? There's a queshion t'ask! Young man, I'm the Seven Corporal Works of Mercy.... But I forgot me bracelet.'

Nolan chuckled grimly.

'You're probably only one when you're sober,' he said. 'At the moment you're very drunk.'

'Drunk? Of course, I'm drunk. But I'm not *very* drunk. You sh'd see me when I'm took bad!' He clucked his tongue in horror. 'I'm a fright – a fright! Six stitches it took t'mend wan man I hit.'

'What brought you here then?'

'Wha' brought—? I'm a friend of the family, amn't I? Wha' brought *you* here, may I ask?'

Norah came downstairs again, dressed for walking. Stephen looked at her and she nodded.

'Good night, Tom,' she said to the soldier.

'Good night, Norah love! Good night! Good night!'

'Remember me to the other six,' said Nolan amicably, taking up his hat and stick.

The two young men went out with Norah, and stood for a few minutes by the door until her trim little figure, battling with the rain from behind an umbrella, disappeared round the corner of the avenue. Then they followed her nonchalantly, buttoning their heavy coats up at the throat.

When they reached the road she was some distance ahead of them, and this distance they maintained discreetly. They passed a patrol which was walking slowly down the road with rifles at the ready, but they were not halted. That was the effect of Eric's yellow gloves, Stephen thought gleefully.

They reached the top of the dark lane in which Alec had met Hare-lip. Norah, who was standing by the wall in the shadows, handed them the bomb and guns, and with a cold 'Good luck!' went on. Two other men who passed her coming down the lane raised their hats, but she barely glanced at them. Then the little group of four gathered together, and after a

whispered consultation climbed over a wall at the side of the
lane and made their way through tall wet grass to the back of a
row of houses that flanked the main road. At one point a house
had been demolished, and through the gap they had a clear
view of a public-house on the opposite side of the road, its big
front window lit behind red blinds. Somebody was singing
there.

They knelt in the wet grass as they did at the back of the church
on Sundays, putting their overcoats under one knee. Stephen
glanced at his companions. It was as though he still saw them in
the darkness and the falling rain; Eric Nolan, self-conscious and
faintly sarcastic about it all; Stanton, the gloomy little auctioneer,
who as he said in his pompous way did these things 'purely as a
gesture – as a matter of principle'; and Cunningham, the butcher,
who wasn't in the least like a butcher, and bubbled over with an
extraordinary lightness and grace that suggested anything rather
than Ireland. Cunningham was a funk, and admitted to funk with
great elegance and good-humour. The sight of a gun, he said,
was always sufficient to throw him into hysterics, and this was
something more than a good joke, because Stephen had seen him
when his ugly, puckish face suggested that his imagination was
strained almost to breaking point.

Yet, unlike Stanton, he would not have admitted that it was a
matter of principle with him, and perhaps he was speaking the
truth when he said that he did it for the sake of enjoyment.
Otherwise, why should he have come out night after night with
them as he did, good-humouredly letting himself be stuck for
the riskiest jobs, and recounting next day how he had faced them
armed with bromides, aspirin, and whiskey?

For a full half-hour they knelt in the rain, not speaking, almost
afraid to move. The rain penetrated their pants, and the wet cloth
hugged their knees. Stephen smiled as he saw Nolan's yellow
gloves hanging like dead leaves from his left hand. His own cap
sent an icy drizzle down the back of his neck, and the peak
becoming limper sank across his eyes, half-blinding him. He
knew he would be in a foul temper when this was over. The rain
fell with an intolerable persistence. In the public-house over the
way, one song ended and another began.

Suddenly he heard a faint hum and stiffened. He drew his dry
fingers across the lenses of his spectacles which were streaming

with rain, and glanced at the other three. But whether it was his spectacles or his nerves that were at fault, he saw only three shadows that might not have been men at all. He could no longer distinguish them, and as he looked more closely, they seemed to dissolve and disappear into the dark and empty background of the fields.

He felt himself alone there, utterly alone. Once more he dabbed furiously at his glasses, and now two of the figures took shape again and seemed to come to life for a moment. What he saw was the slow raising of one arm, then another; a hand shook and he caught the wet glint of a revolver. He drew his own revolver and looked across the road.

He could see nothing now but the red-lighted window opposite him that seemed all in a moment to have become very small and far away. He levelled his revolver at that; there was nothing else at which to aim. Somebody was singing, but the voice grew fainter as the *rum-brum-brum* of a heavy lorry lurching through the waste mud approached. *Rum-brum* – it came nearer and nearer – *brum* – and suddenly panic seized him. Suppose the lorry were to pass? Suppose that already it had passed unseen? He looked for his companions, but could see nothing except a billowing curtain of darkness on either hand; the red light of the public-house window had blinded him to everything else.

He half-raised himself; the red light went out; the singing continued faintly over the roar of an engine. He sprang to his feet. It took him but the fraction of a second to realize what had happened, and he fired blindly at the spot where the light had been. He fired again, heard a steady sputter of shots beside him, and a dark figure detached itself from the blackness around, and sped away through the thick grass. The song ceased sharply. The light appeared again, but now it was so close he felt he could almost touch it with his hand. He caught his breath sharply and wondered whether the bomb had been a dud or Cunningham had failed to draw the rusty old pin.

On the instant it exploded, but not close to him like the shots; he had forgotten it must burst on the car which had already rounded the corner. The sudden thunder-clap of it left him dazed; he stood for a moment and listened, but heard nothing except the roar of the engine as the lorry made off wildly and unsteadily towards the barrack. His sense of time had vanished.

It had been merely the boom of the gong, the rising of the curtain. He waited.

Already, he could hear in the distance the sound of another lorry tearing up the road. He no longer wished to go, but felt as if he were rooted to the spot. It had happened too quickly to be taken in; he wanted more of it, and still more until the flavour of it was on his tongue. Then a hand caught at his arm, and giving way to the sweet sensation of flight, he ran arm-in-arm with Cunningham. He heard beside him something that was like sobbing, the throaty sobbing of hysteria, and had almost given way to his surprise and consternation before he realized what it was. Not sobbing, but chuckling, a quiet contented chuckling, like a lover's laughter in a dark lane. In spite of himself he found the mirth contagious, and chuckled too. There was something strange in that laugher, something out of another world, in-human and sprightly, as though some gay spirit were breathing through them both.

They cleared the wall, rejoined their companions, and resumed their flight at a jog-trot. Eric Nolan was saying indig-nantly between panting breaths, 'It wouldn't work! The damned thing wouldn't fire! I think it – a shame to – send men out – with guns – like that!' But passing under a street-lamp that was pale in the streaming rain, Stephen saw Cunningham's ugly wet face, flushed with laughter, running beside him and chuckled again. At that moment a dark figure detached itself from the gloom of an archway and came towards them. It was an old woman. She had a tattered coat over her head, and held it tightly beneath her chin; little wisps of grey hair emerged all round it and hung limp with rain. She was very small and very old. Stanton and Nolan went on, but Cunningham and Stephen halted to speak to her. They were above the city now, and it lay far beneath them in the hollow, a little bowl of smudgy, yellow light.

'Tell me, *a ghile*' (that is 'O Brightness'), the old woman cried in a high cracked voice, 'tell me, child! I heard shooting below be the cross. Is it the fighting is on?'

'No, mother,' shouted Cunningham, and it seemed to Stephen that he could no longer control himself. He shook with laughter and looked at the old tramp woman with wild, happy eyes. 'That was no shooting!'

'Wasn't it, son?' she asked doubtfully. 'Lord! oh, Lord!

I thought I heard shooting, and says I to meself, "God direct me," says I like that, "will I risk trapsing down to th' ould doss at all?" And sure then I says, "Wouldn't it be better for you, Moll Clancy, to be shot quick and clane than to die of rheumatics in a mouldy ditch?" And you say they were no shots, child?'

'No, I tell you,' he shouted, catching the old tramp affectionately by the shoulders and shaking her. 'Now listen to me, mother, and I'll tell you how it happened. It was an old woman was the cause of it all. The old woman in the shop below, mother. She's deaf, do you hear me? Stone-deaf, and that's how she spends the winter nights, blowing paper bags!'

She looked at him for a moment and laughed, a high cracked laugh that shook her tiny frame.

'Ah, you devil! You young devil!' she cried gaily.

'Good night, mother!' he shouted and strode on.

'Young devil! Young devil!' she yelled merrily after him, and for a little while she stood watching, until their boyish figures disappeared under the gloom of the trees, and the sound of their running feet died away in the distance. Then, still smiling, she resumed her way into the sleeping city.

SOIRÉE CHEZ UNE BELLE JEUNE FILLE

THIS WAS Helen Joyce's first experience as courier.

On Tuesday morning one of the other girls passed her a note. The class was half asleep, the old professor was half asleep, and as always when he was drowsy his lecture grew more and more unintelligible. She looked at the slip of paper. 'Call at the Western before 5 and say you've come about a room to let. Bring your bicycle. *Destroy this.*' Conspiratorial methods – there was no reason why the message could not have been given verbally. 'And may we not say,' old Turner asked querulously, 'or perhaps it is too serious a thing to say – though Burke – or it may be Newman – I have forgotten which – remarks (though he qualifies the remark – and let me add in passing that whatever we may think – and think we must – though of course within certain limits . . .)'. The day was cloudy and warm; the lecture hall was suffocating, and a girl beside her was lazily sketching Turner who looked for all the world like an old magician or mediaeval alchemist with his long, skinny arms, flowing gown and white beard.

She called at the Western. Its real name was The Western Milk and Butter Emporium, and it was a little dairy in the slums kept by a cripple and his wife. Besides being used as a dairy and a political rendezvous it was also a brothel of sorts, but this she did not learn until long after. Low, dark, cobwebby, with blackened rafters that seemed to absorb whatever light came through the little doorway, it gave her a creepy feeling, 'a hospital feeling,' as she said herself. She looked about her at the case of eggs, the two shining churns of milk, and the half-dozen butter boxes, and wondered who in heaven's name the customers might be.

The cripple led her into a little back room, half kitchen, half bedroom, that was if anything lower and darker and cobwebbier than the shop; it was below the street level and was unfurnished, except for a bed, a kitchen table, and two chairs. Here he produced the dispatch, and gave her directions as to how it was to be delivered. She paid more attention to his appearance than to his instructions. Somehow she had not imagined revolutionaries of his sort. He was low-sized almost to dwarfishness; his voice was a woman's voice, and his eyes, screwed-up close to her own, were distorted by convex spectacles tied with twine. He spoke quickly and clearly but with the accent of a half-educated man; she guessed that he read a great many newspapers, and probably had a brother or cousin in America who sent him supplies. At last he left her, sniggering, 'to dispose of de dispatches as she tought best,' but before she hid the tiny manila envelope in her clothes she took care to bolt the door behind him.

Then she cycled off. The streets were slobbery and greasy. It was one of those uncertain southern days when the sky lifts and lowers, lifts and lowers, endlessly. But if the city streets were greasy the country roads were far worse. Walking, she was ankle-deep in mud, and when she stepped in a pot-hole she had to drag her foot away as though it belonged to someone else. Rain came on in spells and then there was nothing for it but to take shelter under some bush or tree. When it cleared from where she stood she saw it hanging in wait for her on top of the next hill, or above the river, or trailing in a sort of cottony mist along the blue-grey fences. And finally, when a ray of light did break through the dishevelled, dribbling clouds, it was a silvery cold light that made the ploughed lands purple like heather.

For four miles she met nothing upon the road but a wain of hay that swayed clumsily to and fro before her like the sodden hinder-parts of some great unwieldy animal. After that two more miles and not a soul. Civil war was having its effect. Then came a pony and trap driven by an old priest, and again desolation as she cycled into a tantalizingly beautiful sunset that dripped with liquid red and gold. By this time she was so wet that she could enjoy it without thinking of what was to come. She was tired and happy and full of high spirits. At last she was doing the work she had always longed to do, not her own work but Ireland's. The old stuffy, proprietary world she had been reared in was somewhere far away behind her; before her was a world of youth and comradeship and adventure.

She looked with wonder at the flat valley road in front. Along it two parallel lines of pot-holes were overflowing with the momentary glory of the setting sun. It sank, and in the fresh sky above it, grey-green like a pigeon's breast, a wet star flickered out and shone as brightly as a white flower in dew-drenched grass. Then a blob of rain splashed upon her bare hand. Another fell, and still another, and in a moment a brown mist sank like a weighted curtain across the glowing west. The bell on her handle-bars, jogged by the pot-holes, tinkled, and she shivered, clinging to her bicycle.

In a little while she was pushing it up the miry boreen of a farmhouse to which she had been directed. Here her trip should have ended, but, in fact, it did nothing of the sort. There was no one to be seen but an old woman who leaned over her half-door; a very difficult and discreet old woman in a crimson shawl that made a bright patch in the greyness of evening. First, she affected not to hear what Helen said; then she admitted that some men had been there, but where they had gone to or when she had no idea. She doubted if they were any but boys from the next parish. She did not know when they would return, if they returned at all. In fact, she knew nothing of them, had never seen them, and was relying entirely on hearsay.

Helen was almost giving up in despair when the man of the house, a tall, bony, good-natured lad, drove up the boreen in a country cart. 'The boys,' he said, 'were wesht beyant the hill in Crowley's, where all the boys wint, and likely they wouldn't be back before midnight. There was only Mike Redmond and Tom Jordan in it; the resht of the column got shcattered during the day.'

A gaunt figure under the gloom of the trees, he shook rain from the peak of his cap with long sweeps of his arm and smiled. Her heart warmed to him. He offered to lead her to Crowley's, and pushed her bicycle for her as they went down the lane together. 'It was surprising' he said 'that no wan had told her of Crowley's; it was a famous shpot,' and he thought 'everywan knew of it.'

Crowley's was what he called 'a good mile off,' which meant something less than two, and it was still raining. But she found him good company, and inquisitive, as ready to listen as to talk; and soon she was hearing about his brothers in America, and his efforts to learn Irish, and the way he had hidden four rifles when the Black and Tans were coming up the boreen. She said good-bye to him with regret, and went up the avenue to Crowley's alone. It was a comfortable modern house with two broad bay windows that cast an amber glow out into the garden and on to the golden leaves of a laurel that stood before the door.

She knocked and a young woman answered, standing between her and the hall light, while she, half-blinded, asked for Michael Redmond. All at once the young woman pounced upon her and pulled her inside the door.

'Helen!' she gasped. 'Helen Joyce as I'm alive!'

Helen looked at her with astonishment and suddenly remembered the girl with the doll-like features and fair, fluffy hair who held her by the arms. Eric Nolan, the college high-brow, had called her the Darling because she resembled the heroine of some Russian story, and the name had stuck, at least among those who, with Helen and her friends, disliked her. She was not pretty; neither was she intelligent: so the girls said, but the boys replied that she was so feminine! Her eyes were weak and narrowed into slits when she was observing somebody, and when she smiled her lower lip got tucked away behind a pair of high teeth. And as she helped Helen to remove her wet coat and gaiters the latter remembered a habit of hers that had become a college joke, the habit of pulling younger girls aside and asking if there wasn't something wrong with her lip. Not that there ever was, but it provided the Darling with an excuse to pull a long face, and say with a sigh, 'Harry bit me, dear. Whatever am I to do with that boy?' She was so feminine!

She showed Helen into the drawing-room. There were two men inside and they rose to greet her. She handed her dispatch to Michael Redmond, who merely glanced at the contents and put it in his coat pocket. 'There was no answer?' she asked in consternation. 'Not at all,' he replied with a shrug of his shoulders and offered her instead several letters to post. She looked incredulously at him, perilously close to tears.

She was actually sniffing as she followed the Darling upstairs. It was her first experience of headquarters work and already it was too much. She had come all this way and must go back again that night; yet it appeared as if the dispatch she had carried was of no importance to anyone and might as well have been left over until morning, if, indeed, it was worth carrying at all. She did not want to stay for tea and meet Michael Redmond again, but stay she must. Anything was better than facing out immediately, cold and hungry, into the darkness and rain.

She changed her stockings and put on a pair of slippers. When she came downstairs again the room seemed enchantingly cosy. There were thick rugs, a good fire, and a table laid for tea.

She knew Redmond by sight. The other man, Jordan, she had known when she was fifteen or sixteen and went to Gaelic League dances. He used to come in full uniform, fresh from a parade, or after fighting began, in green breeches with leather gaiters, the very cut of a fine soldier. The girls all raved about him.

He looked no older now than he had looked then, and was still essentially the same suave, spectacular young man with the long studious face, the thin-lipped mouth and the dark, smouldering eyes. He was as fiery, as quick in speech, as ever. Eric Nolan had called him The Hero of All Dreams (a nickname which was considered to be in bad taste and had not stuck). In real life the Hero of All Dreams had a little plumbing business in a poor quarter of the city, was married, and had fathered seven children of whom three only were alive.

Michael Redmond, the more urbane and conventional of the two, was genuinely a Don Juan of sorts. He looked rather like an ape with his low, deeply-rounded forehead and retreating chin, his thick lips and short nose. He had small, good-humoured eyes and the most complacent expression Helen had ever seen upon a man. It was a caricature of self-satisfaction. About his forehead and eyes and mouth the skin had contracted into scores of little wrinkles, and each wrinkle seemed to be saying, 'Look! *I* am experience.' His hair was wiry with the alertness of the man's whole nature; it was cut close and going grey in patches. Clearly, he was no longer young. But he exuded enthusiasms, and talked in sharp, quick spurts that were like the crackling of a machine-gun.

Helen found herself rather liking him.

Jordan had been describing their experiences of the day and for Helen's benefit he went back to the beginning. While she was sleeping in her warm bed (he seemed to grudge her the bed) they were being roused out of a cold and comfortless barn in the mountains between Dunmanway and Gugan by word of a column that was conducting a house-to-house search for them. And as they crept out of the barn in the mist of dawn, their feet numbed with cold, they saw troops gathering in the village below with lorries and an armoured car.

Michael Redmond snatched at the tale and swept it forward. As they were making off they had been attacked and forced to take cover behind the heaps of turf that were laid out in rows along the side of the hill. It was only the grouping of the soldiers in the village street that had saved them. (He rubbed his hands gleefully as he said it.) Ten minutes of rapid fire into that tightly-packed mass and it had scattered helter-skelter, leaving three casualties behind. Long before it had time to reform in anything like fighting order they had made their escape. And they had been marching all day.

So being in the neighbourhood, added Jordan slyly, they had called on the Crowleys. Oh, of course, they had called! exclaimed Redmond unaware of any sarcastic intent on his companion's part. May would never have forgiven them if they hadn't. And he smiled at her with a carefully prepared, unctuous smile that showed a pair of gold-stopped teeth and spread slowly to the corners of his mouth while his face contracted into a hundred wrinkles.

'Oh, everyone drops in here,' tinkled the Darling as she flitted about the room. 'Mother calls our house "No Man's Land". Last week we had – let me see – we had seven here, three republicans and four Free Staters.'

'Not all together, I hope?' asked Jordan with a sneer.

'Well, not altogether. But what do you think of this? Vincent Kelly – you know Vincent, Helen, the commanding officer in M— came in one evening about three weeks ago, and who was sitting by the fire but Tom Keogh, all dressed up in riding-breeches and gaiters, on his way to the column!'

'No?'

'Yes, I tell you. The funniest thing you ever saw!'

'And what happened?' asked Helen breathlessly.

'Well, I introduced them. "Commandant Kelly, *Mr Burke*," and Vincent held out his fist like a little gentleman, and said, "How do you do, *Mr Burke*?" And after ten minutes Tommy gave in and said with his best Sunday morning smile, "So sorry I must go, Commandant," and they solemnly shook hands again – just as though they wouldn't have liked to cut one another's throats instead!'

'But do you mean to say—?' Helen was incredulous. 'Do you really mean to say you don't bang the door in these people's faces?'

'Who do you mean?' asked the Darling with equal consterna-
tion. 'Is it Tommy Keogh and Vincent Kelly?'

'No, no. But Free State soldiers?'

'God, no!'

'You don't?'

'Not at all. I've known Vincent Kelly since he was that high.
Why the devil *should* I bang the door in his face? I remember
when he and Tommy were as thick as thieves, when Vincent
wouldn't go to a dance unless Tommy went too. Tomorrow
they'll be as thick again – unless they shoot one another in the
meantime.... And you think I'm going to quarrel with one
about the other?'

'Certainly not,' said Michael Redmond with dignity. 'No one
expects impossibilities.'

'Of course not,' echoed Jordan, his voice tinged with the same
elaborate irony. Obviously he was enjoying Helen's discomfiture.

'But what a ridiculous idea!' gasped the Darling as she poured
out tea.

'Well, I don't understand it,' Helen added weakly.

Whatever explanation she might have received was antici-
pated by a startling incident. They had noticed no previous
sound before the front gate clanged open with a scream of hinges,
and they heard the chug-chug of a car turning in from the road.
The two men started up. Jordan's hand flew to his hip-pocket.

'Don't be silly!' said the Darling. 'As for you,' she added
resentfully to Jordan, 'you seem to have a passion for showing
that you pack a gun.'

His hand fell back to his side.

'Nobody's going to raid us. Besides, if they were, do you really
think they'd drive up to the door like that?'

The car stopped running and she went out into the hall. Her
reasoning seemed sound, and the two men sat down again, Jordan
on the edge of his chair with his hands between his knees. They
looked abashed, but did not take their eyes from the door.

There was a murmur of voices in the hall; the door opened
and again Jordan as if instinctively drew back his arm. In the
doorway stood a tall young man in the uniform of the Regular
Army.

'Don't be afraid, children,' sang the Darling's voice from
behind him. 'You all know one another. You know Doctor

Considine, Helen? – Doctor Considine, Miss Helen Joyce.... Rebels all, Bill! Have a cup of tea.'

The newcomer bowed stiffly, sat down close to the door and accepted in silence the cup of tea which May Crowley handed him. He had a narrow head with blond hair, cropped very close, and an incipient fair moustache. He was restless, almost irritable, and coughed and crossed and recrossed his legs without ceasing, as though he wished himself anywhere but in their company. The other two men showed hardly less constraint, and in the conversation, such as it was, there was a suggestion that everybody had forgotten everybody else's name. The Darling prattled on, but her prattling had no effect and scarcely raised a smile. Even turning on the gramophone did not help to dissipate the general gloom. Considine looked positively penitential.

Suddenly, putting his cup on the table and pushing it decisively away from him, he said without looking round:

'I suppose neither of you fellows would care to come into town with me?'

A mystified silence followed his question.

'I'd be glad of somebody's company,' he added with a sigh.

'But Helen is going back to town, Bill,' said the Darling with astonishment.

'I doubt if she'd care to come back with me,' Considine muttered with rapidly increasing gloom.

'Why shouldn't she? I thought you'd never met before tonight?'

The doctor ignored the insinuation, and turning to Redmond he went on almost appealingly.

'I'd take it as a personal favour.'

'Very sorry,' replied Redmond from behind a suspicious smile. 'I'm afraid it's impossible.'

'What about you?' This to Jordan.

Jordan shook his head.

'Nothing to be afraid of, of course. I'd guarantee to bring you there and back safely.'

Jordan looked at Redmond, who avoided the silent question, and once again, but with less decision, he made a gesture of refusal.

'But what in Heaven's name do you want him for?' asked the Darling. 'It will take you three-quarters of an hour at most to get home. Less if you cross the blown-up bridge. At your age you're not afraid of travelling alone, surely?'

'I'm not alone,' said the doctor.

'Not alone?' three voices asked in unison.

'No. There's a stiff in the car.'

Fully aware of the dramatic quality of his announcement he rose in gloomy meditation, crossed to the window and spun up the blind, as though to assure himself that the 'stiff' was still there. The others looked at one another in stupefaction.

'And how did *you* come by the stiff?' asked the Darling at last.

'A fight outside Dunmanway this morning. He got it through the chest.'

His audience looked at one another again. There was a faint gleam of satisfaction in Michael Redmond's eyes that seemed to say, 'There! What did I tell you?' The doctor sat down and lit a cigarette before he resumed.

'He was all right when we left B——. At least I was certain he'd be all right if only we could operate at once. There was no ambulance – there never is in this bloody army – so I dumped him into the car and drove off for Cork. We had to go slow. The roads were bad, and I was afraid the jolting might be too much for him. I swear to God I couldn't have driven more carefully!'

He took out a handkerchief and wiped the sweat from his face.

'We talked a bit at first. He spoke very intelligently. He was a nice boy, about nineteen. Then I noticed he was sleepy as I thought, nodding and only answering now and again, but I paid no heed to that. It was only to be expected. It was getting dark, too, at the time, and I had to keep my eyes on the road. Then, as I was passing the cross a half-mile back, I got nervous. I can't describe it – it was a sort of eerie feeling. It may have been the trees; trees affect me like that. Or the mist – I don't know. I called back to him and he didn't answer, so I stopped the car and switched on a torch I have (here he fumbled in his pockets, produced the lamp, and switched it on in evidence). Then I saw his tunic was saturated with blood. The poor devil was stone dead.

'So I'm in a bit of a hole,' he added irrelevantly.

They sat still, and for the first time Helen heard the pock-pock of the rain against the window like the faint creak of a loose board.

'I thought there might be someone here who'd come into

town with me. I don't like facing in alone. I'm not ashamed to admit that.'

He was watching Jordan out of the corner of his eye. So were the others, for at the same moment all seemed to become aware of his presence. He seemed to project an aura of emotional disturbance.

'Well,' he began hesitantly, seeing their eyes on him, 'what can I do?' He gave a shrug that said the very opposite of what his face was saying. 'I'll admit I'd like to help you. I don't want to see another man in a hole but – when the thing's impossible?'

'I'd bring you back tomorrow night.'

'Of course. . . .' Jordan hovered upon the brink of an avowal. 'There's another reason. The wife and kiddies. I haven't seen them now for close on three months.'

'You'll be absolutely safe,' said the doctor with growing emphasis. 'Absolutely. I can guarantee that. If necessary I can even speak for the Commanding Officer. Isn't that enough for you?'

Jordan looked at Redmond and Redmond looked back with a shrug that seemed to say, 'Do as you please.' Jordan was alone, and knew it, and his face grew redder and redder as he looked from one to another. A helpless silence fell upon them all, so complete that Helen was positively startled by the doctor's voice saying, almost with satisfaction:

'Plenty of time, you know. It's only seven o'clock.'

She looked at her watch and rose with a little gasp of dismay. At the same moment Jordan too sprang up.

'I may as well chance it,' he said with brazen nonchalance, his hands locked behind his head and a faint smile playing about the corners of his mouth. 'A married man needs a little relaxation now and then.'

'Certainly,' said Michael Redmond.

Though there was no sarcasm in the voice Jordan looked up as though he had been struck.

'You people know nothing about it,' he said sharply, and wounded vanity triumphed over his assumed nonchalance. 'Wait until you're married! Perhaps you'll see things differently then. Wait until you've children of your own.'

He glanced angrily at the girls.

Considine waved a vague, disparaging hand.

'Why, it's the most natural thing in the world,' he said, imparting a sort of general scientific absolution to the sentiment implied. 'The most natural thing in the world.'

The others said nothing. The two girls went upstairs, and while Helen changed back into her shoes and gaiters May Crowley sat on the bed beside her, and a look of utter disgust settled upon her vapid mouth.

'Honest to God,' she said petulantly, 'wouldn't he give you the sick, himself and his wife? Why doesn't he stay at home with her? It's revolting! He should be kept with a column for five years at a time. He's been carrying on for years like that, skipping back like a kid to a jampot, and his poor drag of a wife suffering for him. There she is every twelve months trotting out in that old fur coat of hers – the same old fur coat she got when they were married – and she has to face police and soldiers night after night in that condition! If they raid his house at all they raid it twice a week to keep her company. Because he's such a great soldier! Soldier my eye! If they only knew! But it is revolting, isn't it, Helen?'

'I suppose it is,' replied Helen weakly.

'Of course it is. . . . Michael Redmond is more in my line,' she went on as she stood before the mirror and added a dab of powder to her nose. 'He's a man of the world if you understand me, the sort of man who can talk to a woman. I think I prefer him to any of them, with the exception of Vincent Kelly. . . . Now Vincent is a gentleman if you like. I'm sure you'd love him if only you knew him better. . . . But Jordan! Ugh! Thanks be to God, Bill Considine is taking him out of this. When he looks at you it's as though he was guessing how many children you'd have. He's a breeder, my dear, that's what he is, a breeder!'

Helen did not reply. She was thinking of the dead boy outside in the car.

'Helen, child,' the Darling went on inconsequentially, 'you'd better stop the night.'

'No, really,' said Helen, 'I must get home.'

'I suppose you must.' The Darling looked at her out of indifferent, half-shut eyes. 'Michael is a sweet man! . . . It's the way they hold you, isn't it, dear? I mean, don't you know immediately a man puts his arm round you what his character is like?'

When they came downstairs the others were waiting in a

group under the hall-lamp; Considine in his uniform cap and great coat; Jordan looking more than ever like a hero of romance in trench coat and soft hat, his muddy gaiters showing beneath the ragged edges of his coat.

Michael Redmond opened the door, and they felt the breath of the cold, wet night outside, without a star, and saw the great balloon-like laurel bush in the centre of the avenue, catching the golden beams from doorway and window, and reflecting them from its wet leaves. The car was standing beside it out of range of the light. Helen stood behind for a moment while the others approached it, then fascinated, she followed them. Considine produced his electric torch, and a beam from it shot through the light rain into the darkness of the car. There was nothing to be seen.

Startled, the Darling and Jordan stepped back, and the little group remained for a few seconds looking where the grey light played upon the car's dark hood. Then the doctor laughed, a slight, nervous laugh, and his hand went to the catch of the door. It shot open with a click and something slid out, and hung suspended a few inches above the footboard. It was a man's head, the face upturned, the long, dark hair brushing the footboard of the car, the eyes staring back at them, bright but cold. The face was the face of a boy, but the open mouth, streaked with blood, made it seem like the face of an old man. There was a brown stain across the right cheek, as though the boy had drawn his sleeve across it when the haemorrhage began.

No one said anything; all were too fascinated to speak. Then Michael Redmond's hand went out and, catching the doctor's wrist, forced the light quietly away. It went out, and Redmond lifted the body and thrust it back on the seat.

'Now,' he said, and the pompousness seemed to have gone from his voice. 'You'd better start, doctor.'

'What about you, Miss Joyce?' asked Considine.

'I'm cycling in,' she said.

'We can pace you, of course. The roads are bad, and we shouldn't be able to go fast anyhow.'

'Never mind,' said Redmond roughly. 'It won't take her long to get home.'

Helen liked him more than ever.

He lit her bicycle lamp, and, with a hurried good-bye, she

cycled down the avenue. She had gone the best part of half her way before the car caught up on her. Mentally she thanked Michael Redmond for the delay – 'man of the world, man of the world,' she thought. The car slowed down, and Jordan shouted something which she did not catch and did not reply to. It went on again, and his voice lingered in her ears, faintly repulsive.

The tail-light of the car (the red glass had gone and there was only a white blob leaping along the road) disappeared round a corner, and left her to the wet waste night and the gloom of the trees. Already the rain was beginning to clear; soon there would be a fine spell, with stars perhaps, but the road was full of pot-holes, and she could almost feel the mud that rose in the lamp-light on each side of her front wheel, and spattered her gaiters and coat. And still the voice of Jordan lingered in her ears, and from the depths of her memory rose a bit of a poem that she had heard old Turner quote in college. Had he said that it was one of the finest in the English language? It would be like old Turner to say that. Fat lot he knew about it anyway! But it haunted her mind.

So the two brothers with their murdered man
Rode past fair Florence . . .

IT WAS a period of political unrest, and, in a way, this was a relief, because it acted as a safety valve for my own angry emotions. Indeed, it would be truer to say that the Irish nation and myself were both engaged in an elaborate process of improvisation. I was improvising an education I could not afford, and the country was improvising a revolution it could not afford. In 1916 it had risen to a small, real revolution with uniforms and rifles, but the English had brought up artillery that had blown the centre of Dublin flat, and shot down the men in uniform. It was all very like myself and the Christian Brothers. After that, the country had to content itself with a make-believe revolution, and I had to content myself with a make-believe education, and the curious thing is that it was the make-believe that succeeded.

The elected representatives of the Irish people (those who managed to stay out of gaol) elected what they called a government, with a Ministry of Foreign Affairs that tried in vain to get Woodrow Wilson to see it, a Ministry of Finance that exacted five or ten pounds from small shop-keepers who could ill afford it, a Ministry of Defence that tried to buy old-fashioned weapons at outrageous prices from shady characters, and a Ministry of Home Affairs that established courts of justice with part-time Volunteer policemen and no gaols at all.

It all began innocently enough. People took to attending Gaelic League concerts at which performers sang 'She is Far from the Land', recited 'Let Me Carry Your Cross for Ireland, Lord', or played 'The Fox Chase' on the elbow pipes, and armed police broke them up. I remember one that I attended in the town park. When I arrived, the park was already occupied by police, so after a while the crowd began to drift away towards the open country up the river. A mile or so up it reassembled on the river-bank, but by this time most of the artistes had disappeared. Somebody who knew me asked for a song. At fourteen or fifteen I was delighted by the honour and tried to sing in Irish a seventeenth–century outlaw song about 'Sean O'Dwyer of the Valley'. I broke down after the first verse – I always did break down whenever I had to make any sort of public appearance because the contrast between what was going on in my head and what was going on in the real world was too much for me – but it didn't matter much. [...]

Then the real world began to catch up with the fantasy. Curfew was imposed, first at ten, then at five in the afternoon. The bishop excommunicated everyone who supported the use of physical force, but it went on just the same. One night shots were fired on our road and a lorry halted at the top of the square. An English voice kept on screaming hysterically 'Oh, my back! my back!' but no one could go through the wild shooting of panic-stricken men. Soon afterwards the military came in force, and from our back door we saw a red glare mount over the valley of the city. For hours Father, Mother, and I took turns at standing on a chair in the attic, listening to the shooting and watching the whole heart of the city burn. Father was the most upset of us, for he was full of local pride, and ready to take on any misguided foreigner or Dublin jackeen who was not prepared to admit the superiority of Cork over all other cities. Next morning, when I wandered among the ruins, it was not the business district or the municipal buildings that I mourned for, but the handsome red-brick library that had been so much a part of my life from the time when as a small boy I brought back my first Western adventure story over the railway bridges. Later I stood at the corner by Dillon's Cross where the ambush had been and saw a whole block of little houses demolished by a British tank. One had been the home of an old patriot whom my grandparents called 'Brienie Dill'. A small, silent crowd was held back by soldiers as the tank lumbered across the pavement and thrust at the wall until at last it broke like pie crust and rubble and rafters tumbled. It made a deep impression on me. [...]

All the same I could not keep away from Ireland, and I was involved in most of the activities of that imaginative revolution – at a considerable distance, of course, because I was too young, and anyway, I had Father all the time breathing down my neck. In the absence of proper uniform our Army tended to wear riding-breeches, gaiters, a trench coat, and a soft hat usually pulled low over one eye, and I managed to scrape up most of the essential equipment, even when I had to beg it, as I begged the pair of broken gaiters from Tom MacKernan. I conducted a complicated deal for the Ministry of Defence and bought a French rifle from a man who lived close to Cork Barrack, though, when I had risked a heavy sentence by bringing it home down my trouser leg, all the time pretending I had just met with a serious accident, it turned out that there wasn't a round of ammunition in Ireland to fit it. When the British burned and looted Cork and encouraged the slum-dwellers to join in the looting, I was transferred to the police and put to searching slums in Blarney Lane for jewellery and furs. In a back room in Blarney Lane we located a mink coat which the woman who lived there said had just been sent her by her sister in America. Being a polite and unworldly boy of seventeen, I was quite prepared to take her word for it, but my companion said she hadn't a sister in America, and, shocked by her untruthfulness, I brought the coat back to its rightful owners. That she might have needed it more than they didn't occur to me; I remembered only that I was now a real policeman, and acted as I felt a good policeman should act. [. . .]

My fight for Irish freedom was of the same order as my fight for other sorts of freedom. Still like Dolan's ass, I went a bit of the way with everybody, and in those days everybody was moving in the same direction. Hendrick did not get me to join a debating society, but I got him to join the Volunteers. If it was nothing else, it was a brief escape from tedium and frustration to go out the country roads on summer evenings, slouching along in knee breeches and gaiters, hands in the pockets of one's trench coat and hat pulled over one's right eye. Usually it was only to a parade in some field with high fences off the Rathcooney Road, but sometimes it was a barrack that was being attacked, and we trenched roads and felled trees, and then went home through the wet fields over the hills, listening for distant explosions and scanning the horizon for fires. It was all too much for poor Father, who had already seen me waste my time making toy theatres when I should have been playing football, and drawing naked men when I should have been earning my living. And this time he did at least know what he was talking about. For all he knew I might have the makings of a painter or writer in me, but, as an old soldier himself, he knew that I would never draw even a disability pension. [. . .]

And then, in the depth of winter, came the Treaty with England, which granted us everything we had ever sought except an independent republican government and control of the loyalist province of Ulster. The withholding of these precipitated a Civil War, which, in the light of what we know now, might have been anticipated by anyone with sense, for it was merely an extension into the fourth dimension of the improvisation that had begun after the crushing of the insurrection in 1916. The Nationalist movement had split up into the Free State Party, who accepted the treaty with England, and the Republicans who opposed it by force of arms, as the Irgun was to do much later in Israel. Ireland had improvised a government, and clearly no government that claimed even a fraction less than the imaginary government had claimed could attract the loyalty of young men and women with imagination. They were like a theatre audience that, having learned to dispense with fortuitous properties, lighting, and scenery and begun to appreciate theatre in the raw, were being asked to content themselves with cardboard and canvas. Where there is nothing, there is reality.

But meanwhile the improvisation had cracked: the English could have cracked it much sooner merely by yielding a little to it. When, after election results had shown that a majority of the people wanted the compromise – and when would *they* not have accepted a compromise? – our side continued to maintain that the only real government was the imaginary one, or the few shadowy figures that remained of it, we were acting on the unimpeachable logic of the imagination, that only what exists in the mind is real. What we ignored was that a whole section of the improvisation had cut itself adrift and become a new and more menacing reality. The explosion of the dialectic, the sudden violent emergence of thesis and antithesis from the old synthesis, had occurred under our very noses and we could not see it or control it. Rory O'Connor and Mellowes in seizing the Four Courts were merely echoing Patrick Pearse and the seizure of the Post Office, and Michael Collins, who could so easily have starved them out with a few pickets, imitated the English pattern by blasting the Four Courts with borrowed artillery. And what neither group saw was that every word we said, every act we committed, was a destruction of the improvisation and what we were bringing about was a new Establishment of Church and

State in which imagination would play no part, and young men and women would emigrate to the ends of the earth, not because the country was poor, but because it was mediocre. [. . .]

Imprisonment came as a relief because it took all responsibility out of my hands, and, as active fighting died down and the possibility of being shot in some reprisal execution diminished, it became – what else sums up the period so well? – a real blessing. Not, God knows, that the Women's Gaol in Sunday's Well was anything but a nightmare. The first night I spent there after being taken from the Courthouse I was wakened by the officer of the watch going his round. As he flashed his torch about the cell he told us joyously that there had been a raid on the house of Michael Collins's sister in Blarney Lane and one of the attackers had been captured with a revolver and would be executed. (How was I to know that the irony of circumstances would make me the guest of Michael Collins's sister in that very house before many years had passed?) I fell asleep again, thinking merely that I was very fortunate to be out of the Courthouse where the soldiers would probably have taken it out on me. Towards dawn I was wakened by the tall, bitter-tongued man I knew as 'Mac', and I followed him down the corridor. A Free State officer was standing by the door of one cell, and we went in. Under the window in the gas-light that leaked in from the corridor what seemed to be a bundle of rags was trying to raise itself from the floor. I reached out my hand and shuddered because the hand that took mine was like a lump of dough. When I saw the face of the man, whose hand I had taken, I felt sick, because that was also like a lump of dough. 'So that's how you treat your prisoners?' Mac snarled at the officer. Mac, like my father, was an ex-British soldier, and had the old-fashioned attitude that you did not strike a defenceless man. The officer, who in private life was probably a milkman, began some muttered rigmarole about the prisoner's having tried to burn a widow's home and poured petrol over the sleeping children. 'Look at that!' Mac snarled at me, paying no attention to him. 'Skewered through the ass with bayonets!' I waited and walked with the boy to the head of the iron stairs where the suicide net had been stretched to catch any poor soul who found life too hard, and I watched him stagger painfully down in the gas-light. There were only a half-dozen of us there, and we stood and watched the dawn break over the city

through the high unglazed windows. A few days later the boy
was shot. That scene haunted me for years – partly, I suppose,
because it was still uncertain whether or not I should be next, a
matter that gives one a personal interest in any execution; partly
because of the overdeveloped sense of pity that had made me
always take the part of kids younger or weaker than myself;
mainly because I was beginning to think that this was all our
romanticism came to – a miserable attempt to burn a widow's
house, the rifle butts and bayonets of hysterical soldiers, a poor
woman of the lanes kneeling in some city church and appealing
to a God who could not listen, and then – a barrack wall with
some smug humbug of a priest muttering prayers. (I heard him
the following Sunday give a sermon on the dangers of company-
keeping.) I had been able to think of the Kilmallock skirmish as
though it was something I had read of in a book, but the battered
face of that boy was something that wasn't in any book, and even
ten years later, when I was sitting reading in my flat in Dublin,
the door would suddenly open and he would walk in and the
book would fall from my hands. Certainly, that night changed
something for ever in me. [. . .]

One evening I sat in the hut and listened to a Corkman singing
in a little group about some hero who had died for Ireland and
the brave things he had said and the fine things he had done,
and I listened because I liked these simple little local songs that
continued to be written to the old beautiful ballad airs and that
sometimes had charming verses, like:

I met Pat Hanley's mother and she to me did say,
'God be with my son Pat, he was shot in the runaway;
'If I could kiss his pale cold lips his wounded heart I'd cure
'And I'd bring my darling safely home from the valley of
    Knockanure.'

But half-way through this song I realized that it was about the
boy whose hand I had taken in the Women's Prison in Cork one
morning that spring, and suddenly the whole nightmare came
back. 'It's as well for you fellows that you didn't see that lad's
face when the Free Staters had finished with it,' I said angrily.
I think it must have been that evening that the big row blew up,
and I had half the hut shouting at me. I shouted as well that I was

sick to death of the worship of martyrdom, that the only martyr I had come close to was a poor boy from the lanes like myself, and he hadn't wanted to die any more than I did; that he had merely been trapped by his own ignorance and simplicity into a position from which he couldn't escape, and I thought most martyrs were the same. 'And Pearse?' someone kept on crying. 'What about Pearse? I suppose he didn't want to die either?' 'Of course he didn't want to die,' I said. 'He woke up too late, that was all.' And that did really drive some of the men to fury.

I went to bed myself in a blind rage. Apparently the only proof one had of being alive was one's readiness to die as soon as possible: dead was the great thing to be, and there was nothing to be said in favour of living except the innumerable possibilities it presented of dying in style. I didn't want to die. I wanted to live, to read, to hear music, and to bring my mother to all the places that neither of us had ever seen, and I felt these things were more important than martyrdom.

ALREADY THE Collins of the second phase was beginning to take
shape: the humorous, vital, tense, impatient figure which shoots
through the pages of contemporary history as it shot through the
streets of Dublin with a cry of anguish for 'all the hours we waste
in sleep'. People were already growing accustomed to his ways;
the warning thump of his feet on the stairs as he took them six
at a time, the crash of the door and the searching look, and that
magnetic power of revivifying the stalest air. People still describe
the way in which one became aware of his presence, even when
he was not visible, through that uncomfortable magnetism of the
very air, a tingling of the nerves. First to wake, he sprang out of
bed and stamped about the room as fresh as though he were
leaving a cold bath instead of a warm bed. He was peculiarly
sensitive to touch and drew away when people tried to paw him.
He seemed to be always bundling people out of bed, and not
only the long-suffering O'Hegarty and O'Sullivan, who had the
doubtful pleasure of sharing a room with him, but all the others,
the quiet, simple people who had never thought themselves of
use to humanity. Each of his gestures had a purposeful monu-
mental quality; and his face that strange lighting which evaded
the photographers but which Doyle-Jones has caught in his
bust. One had the impression of a temperament impatient of
all restraint, even that imposed from within, exploding in jerky
gestures, oaths, jests and laughter; so vital that, like his facial
expression, it evades analysis. If I had recorded all the occasions
when he wept I should have given the impression that he was
hysterical. He wasn't; he laughed and wept as a child does (and
indeed, as people in earlier centuries seem to have done) quite
without self-consciousness.

Collins' words and actions, considered separately, are
commonplace enough; one would need a sort of cinema pro-
jector of prose to capture the sense of abounding life they gave
to his contemporaries. People who submitted to their influence

became intoxicated; work seemed easier, danger slighter, the impossible receded. People who did not were exasperated. 'What insolence!' they cried. 'He doesn't even say good morning.' He said neither good morning nor good night; avoided handshakes as he avoided anything in the least savouring of formality; and when ladies accustomed to good society received him he had time only to ask if anyone was inside, and then brushed past them without a glance.

He knew he was a difficult man; he had no home, no constant refuge, passing from house to house and making demands upon its occupants as he did upon the men who worked for him; yet – though a week rarely passed when one of them, host or colleague, hadn't occasion to complain – there were few who did not serve him cheerfully because of the occasions when a fine and sudden delicacy of feeling showed that he appreciated it. Outsiders, seeing how he worked his courier O'Reilly till the beads of sweat stood out on the lad's face, grew indignant, but suddenly the natural good humour and kindness would break through and he would shout 'Give us a couple of eggs for that melt!' Or it would be someone else's turn – his hostess's, perhaps, whom he would bundle off to bed while he sent O'Reilly for champagne, merely because he thought she had a cold. He was a self-willed man – the consideration often came inopportunely and at random, like a misdirected kiss. [. . .]

Collins was naturally a great businessman, and he shouldered his responsibilities in a thoroughly businesslike way. This energetic man, who kept a file for every transaction, who insisted on supervising every detail and went nowhere without his secretary, bore very little resemblance to the Collins of legend and none at all to the revolutionary of fiction. Beside him, Lenin, with his theories, feuds and excommunications, seems a child, and not a particularly intelligent one. He ran the whole Revolution as though it were a great business concern, ignoring all the rules. In his files can be found receipts for the lodging of political refugees side by side with those for sweeping brushes and floor polish. He might be seen a dozen times a day in shops, offices, restaurants, pubs, with solicitors, clergymen, bankers, intellectuals. He permitted no restriction on his freedom and cycled unguarded about the city as though the British Empire had never existed. In the evenings he might be seen at the Abbey Theatre, tossing restlessly in his seat, or in the summer at a race meeting, rubbing shoulders with British officers and Secret-Service men.

The other Collins, the romantic figure, 'which this person was certainly not', as his enemy Brugha said with the clarity of hate, and who has become by far the more widely known, was merely incidental; the real Collins, sitting at his desk, signing corres-pondence, found the necessity for the romantic figure's existence a mere disturbance of routine. Collins, of course, had the roman-tic streak, the power of self-dramatization, which went with his daemonic temperament, but that is a different kettle of fish; his genius was the genius of realism. Answering a business letter in a businesslike way, he would be made aware of the English garrison as a sort of minor interruption and hit out at it as a busy man hits out at a bluebottle.

For the moment the bluebottle took the form of the English police system, which interrupted his work by raiding his offices and imprisoning his staffs: he proceeded grimly to get rid of it. The first victim of the new Intelligence Service was Detective-Sergeant Smith, known as the 'Dog Smith', the Uriah Heep of the force. In July 1919, after several warnings, he was shot down outside his own house in Drumcondra.

It was Collins' first killing. Then, as afterwards, he did every-thing to avoid the necessity for it. With his strange sensitiveness he was haunted for days before by the thought of it. He was morose and silent. When the day of the shooting came, people saw for the first time the curious tension which was repeated over and over again in the years to come. The same scene occurred so often that it became familiar. O'Reilly was usually in waiting somewhere near to bring back a report. As he faltered out the words in answer to the quick glance of his chief, Collins began to stride up and down the room, swinging his arms in wide half circles and grinding his heels into the floor. For ten or fifteen minutes he continued this in silence; then he grabbed a paper and tried to read. But his eyes strayed from the printed columns to the window with an empty, faraway look. Then, raging, he turned upon the unoffending O'Reilly. [. . .]

It was Christmas, which to a man of Collins' temperament was sacred to festivity. His Christmases were always Dickensian, with plenty of drink, good food, relaxed discipline and whole-some good humour. It was a busy time for O'Reilly. There were the seamen, each of whom got a five-pound note and, if they were free, an invitation to meet him in a pub. There were presents to be purchased for the scores of people who had helped him during the year: the women who had sheltered him, the detectives who had given him information – all those not actually part of the movement whose sympathy made so much difference. Each of the presents went out with a little note which the recipient would not dare to treasure. Then, so far as possible, he paid each of his friends a short visit, as though to show what he was like off the job.

After lunch O'Reilly went off on his round of present bearing. Collins had had an early start and a busy day, and was hungry. Rather than give Mrs Devlin the trouble of preparing food, he, O'Connor, O'Sullivan, Tobin and Cullen decided to dine in town. It was four o'clock and only a hundred yards to the Gresham Hotel. The Gresham's private rooms were booked, so they sat in the big dining-room and ordered a meal with wine. They were only halfway through it when a waiter appeared at Collins' elbow.

'You might like to know, sir,' he said in a discreet whisper, 'the Auxiliaries are in the hall.'

They had two minutes in which to prepare before the Auxiliaries burst in upon them, brandishing revolvers and rifles. They rose with their hands in the air. As a preliminary the Auxiliaries searched them.

'Eh, what's this?' asked the man who was searching Collins, and from his hip-pocket produced a bottle of whiskey.

'Stop!' said Collins good-humouredly. 'That's a present for the landlady.'

He gave his name as John Grace. He must be the only revolutionary on record who did not say his name was Smith. The famous notebook was examined but the only word the Auxiliary officer could identify was one which he declared was 'rifles' and which Collins indignantly declared was 'refills'.

When this hitch was got over, he made an excuse and withdrew to the lavatory under escort. O'Connor took up the whiskey he had left behind and invited the Auxiliaries to share it. A corkscrew was produced and another of the guests ordered a second bottle. Noticing his chief so long away, and filled, as they were all filled, with alarm only for his safety, Tobin made a similar excuse. To his consternation he found the officer holding Collins back over a wash basin where the light was most brilliant; teasing his hair about with one hand while in the other he held a photograph of the very man he was examining. The photograph was a bad one, but not so bad that recognition was impossible. To his immense relief the officer released Collins, and the two of them returned to the dining-room. 'Be ready to make a rush for it,' Collins whispered.

But it was unnecessary. The atmosphere in the dining-room had changed from distrust to maudlin pleasantry. The Auxiliaries departed, leaving five men almost crazy with relief. They drank whiskey in neat tumblersful, but it seemed as if nothing could quiet their nerves. They continued to celebrate in Vaughan's Hotel. In a comparatively brief space of time they were drunk and indulging in horseplay, oblivious of their danger. It was the only occasion on which most of those present saw Collins drunk. O'Hegarty, who had missed the dinner party at the Gresham, was begging them to come away before Vaughan's was also raided. They ignored him.

They finally drove to Mrs O'Donovan's in a car and bundled themselves into bed. It was a Christmas none of them was likely to forget.

From MY FATHER'S SON –
A CASE OF HYPNOTISM

WE HAD one extraordinary experience while I was writing the book. The hardest man in Ireland to get at was Joe O'Reilly, Collins' personal servant, his messenger boy, his nurse, and nobody – literally nobody – knew what O'Reilly could tell if he chose, or could even guess why he did not tell it. He was then Aide-de-Camp to the Governor-General; a handsome, brightly spoken, golf-playing man who could have posed anywhere for the picture of the All-American Male.

Hayes' invitation brought him to the house in Guilford Road one evening, and for a couple of hours I had the experience that every biographer knows and dreads. Here was this attractive, friendly, handsome man, completely master of himself, apparently ready to tell everything, but in reality determined on telling nothing.

Hayes was puzzled – after all, he was a historian – and he took over the questioning himself. He was a much more skilful questioner than I, but he too got nowhere.

And then, suddenly, when I was ready to give up and go home, O'Reilly collapsed – if the word even suggests what really happened, which was more like a building caving in. Something had gone wrong with him. Either he had drunk too much, which I thought unlikely because he was perfectly lucid, or, accidentally, either Hayes or I had hypnotized him.

I can remember distinctly the question that precipitated his collapse. I had asked, 'How did Collins behave when he had to have someone shot?' and O'Reilly began his reply carefully, even helpfully, in such a way that it could be of no possible use to me. Then he suddenly jumped up, thrust his hands in his trouser pockets, and began to stamp about the room, digging his heels in with a savagery that almost shook the house. Finally he threw himself on to a sofa, picked up a newspaper, which he pretended to read, tossed it aside after a few moments, and said in a coarse country voice, 'Jesus Christ Almighty, how often have I to tell ye . . . ?' It was no longer Joe O'Reilly who was in the room. It was Michael Collins, and for close on two hours I had an experience that must be every biographer's dream, of watching someone I had never known as though he were still alive. Every gesture, every intonation was imprinted on O'Reilly's brain as if on tape.

I had seen that auto-hypnotism only once before. That was in 1932 when Mother and I were travelling by bus from Bantry. One of the passengers was a violent, cynical, one-legged man who began to beg, and the conductor was too afraid to interfere with him. I took an intense loathing to him and refused to give him money, but he was much less interested in me than in some members of a piper's band who were also travelling. He demanded that they should play for him, and when they merely looked out of the windows he began to imitate the bagpipes himself. After a time I realized that the bagpipes he was imitating were those he had heard during some battle in France fifteen years before. The bagpipes hypnotized him, and now he began imitating the sound of a German scouting plane, the big guns, the whistle of the shells, and as they fell silent he began to mutter in a low frenzied voice to someone who was beside him, 'Hey, Jim! Give us a clip there, Jim! They're coming! Hurry! Jim, Jim!' He reached over to shake someone and then started and sighed. Then he took an ammunition belt that was not there from the shoulders of someone who was long dead and slung it over his own, fitted a clip – that gesture I knew so well – into the heavy stick he carried and began to fire over the back of the seat. Suddenly he sprang into the air and fell in the centre of the bus, unconscious it seemed, and for some reason we were all too embarrassed to do anything. After a few minutes he groaned and reached out to touch his leg – the one that wasn't there. Then he got to his feet and sat back in his seat perfectly silent. I have rarely been so ashamed of myself as I was that day.

But the scene with O'Reilly was almost worse because you could see not only Collins, but also the effect he was having upon a gentle, sensitive boy, and it made you want to intervene between a boy who was no longer there and a ghost. I did it even at the risk of breaking the record. He was sobbing when he described how Collins had crucified him till he decided to leave. 'Here!' was all Collins replied. 'Take this letter on your way.'

'But didn't anybody tell him to lay off you?' I asked angrily.

'Yes, the girl next door,' he said. 'She said, "Collins, do you know what you're doing to that boy?" And Mick said (and suddenly Collins was back in the room again), "I know his value better than you do. He goes to Mass for me every morning. Jesus Christ, do you think I don't know what he's worth to me?"'

When O'Reilly left, the handsome, sprightly young man had disappeared. In his place was an elderly, bewildered man, and you could see what he would be like if Collins had lived. Hayes detained me, and as he refilled my glass he asked, 'Have you ever seen anything so extraordinary?' We both doubted if O'Reillly would turn up next evening.

He did; but this time he looked like the ghost. He gave me a pathetic, accusing look.

'I don't know what you did to me last night,' he muttered. 'I couldn't sleep. I never did anything like that before. I can't stop. It's going on in my head the whole time. I have to talk about it.'

He did so for the rest of the evening, and once again Collins was there. Nowadays a tape recorder in the next room would probably catch most of it, but I had no way of getting it down because I did not dare take out a notebook.

The sequel to that was interesting too, for when the book on Collins was published O'Reilly was reputed to be going through Dublin like a madman, threatening to shoot me. One day, he and I met in the middle of Grafton Street. There was no escaping him and I stopped. 'I've been trying to see you,' he muttered. 'Come in here for a cup of tea.' I went along with him, wondering what I had started, but all he wanted was to tell me the book had already gone out of print and he wanted a half-dozen copies to send to friends. Reality, I suppose, is like that.

2 CHILDHOOD

PREFACE

LIKE MANY fiction-writers, O'Connor was at his most apparently autobiographical when setting his stories in childhood. He was the only child of an overbearing, alcoholic father and a protective mother who encouraged both his bookishness and his 'cissiness'; his mother, brought up by the nuns in an orphanage, had social ambition, while his father was happy to live from day to day and await his British Army pension. The sensitive, artistic boy dreamed of escape from the backstreets of Cork and the embarrassments of family: there was an especially shame-provoking grandmother. Yet the pseudonym 'Frank O'Connor' did not escape far (consisting of his own second name plus his mother's surname); likewise the world experienced by Michael O'Donovan, described in *An Only Child*, frequently overlaps in both tone and incident with the world created by O'Connor. The day he drank his father's beer; how he wanted to murder his grandmother; what happened when he tried to apply the English public school code he had read about in an Irish Trades school. Sometimes a whole section of childhood experience – accompanying his bandsman father on outings – will be transported into fiction ('The Cornet Player Who Betrayed Ireland').

But if you lay the childhood autobiography against the fiction, the result is not reductivism but the opposite. O'Connor can be seen taking what was useful and inventing the rest. He was by nature transformational. William Maxwell said of him that he 'behaved as if he were the oldest of a large family of boys and girls'. So he was – in the sense that he imagined them. He also, when writing about his imaginary siblings and his own distant self, understood and remembered the full peculiarity and relentlessness of children. In *An Only Child* he wrote that 'Children . . . see only one side of any question and because of their powerlessness see this with hysterical clarity.' The child is father to the writer. The adult may learn to view others with increasing generosity, tenderness and forgiveness, but the writer must retain the child's absolutism of eye, and that hysterical clarity, whether writing about childhood or anything else.

MY OEDIPUS COMPLEX

FATHER WAS in the army all through the war – the first war, I mean – so, up to the age of five, I never saw much of him, and what I saw did not worry me. Sometimes I woke and there was a big figure in khaki peering down at me in the candlelight. Sometimes in the early morning I heard the slamming of the front door and the clatter of nailed boots down the cobbles of the lane. These were Father's entrances and exits. Like Santa Claus he came and went mysteriously.

In fact, I rather liked his visits, though it was an uncomfortable squeeze between Mother and him when I got into the big bed in the early morning. He smoked, which gave him a pleasant musty smell, and shaved, an operation of astounding interest. Each time he left a trail of souvenirs – model tanks and Gurkha knives with handles made of bullet cases, and German helmets and cap badges and button-sticks, and all sorts of military equipment – carefully stowed away in a long box on top of the wardrobe, in case they ever came in handy. There was a bit of the magpie about Father; he expected everything to come in handy. When his back was turned, Mother let me get a chair and rummage through his treasures. She didn't seem to think so highly of them as he did.

The war was the most peaceful period of my life. The window of my attic faced south-east. My mother had curtained it, but that had small effect. I always woke with the first light and, with all the responsibilities of the previous day melted, feeling myself rather like the sun, ready to illumine and rejoice. Life never seemed so simple and clear and full of possibilities as then. I put my feet out from under the clothes – I called them Mrs Left and Mrs Right – and invented dramatic situations for them in which they discussed the problems of the day. At least Mrs Right did; she was very demonstrative, but I hadn't the same control of Mrs Left, so she mostly contented herself with nodding agreement.

They discussed what Mother and I should do during the day,

what Santa Claus should give a fellow for Christmas, and what steps should be taken to brighten the home. There was that little matter of the baby, for instance. Mother and I could never agree about that. Ours was the only house in the terrace without a new baby, and Mother said we couldn't afford one till Father came back from the war because they cost seventeen and six. That showed how simple she was. The Geneys up the road had a baby, and everyone knew they couldn't afford seventeen and six. It was probably a cheap baby, and Mother wanted something really good, but I felt she was too exclusive. The Geneys' baby would have done us fine.

Having settled my plans for the day, I got up, put a chair under the attic window, and lifted the frame high enough to stick out my head. The window overlooked the front gardens of the terrace behind ours, and beyond these it looked over a deep valley to the tall, red-brick houses terraced up the opposite hill-side; which were all still in shadow, while those at our side of the valley were all lit up, though with long strange shadows that made them seem unfamiliar; rigid and painted

After that I went into Mother's room and climbed into the big bed. She woke and I began to tell her of my schemes. By this time, thought I never seem to have noticed it, I was petrified in my nightshirt, and I thawed as I talked until, the last frost melted, I fell asleep beside her and woke again only when I heard her below in the kitchen, making the breakfast.

After breakfast we went into town; heard Mass at St Augustine's and said a prayer for Father, and did the shopping. If the afternoon was fine we either went for a walk in the country or a visit to Mother's great friend in the convent, Mother St Dominic. Mother had them all praying for Father, and every night, going to bed, I asked God to send him back safe from the war to us. Little, indeed, did I know what I was praying for!

One morning, I got into the big bed, and there, sure enough, was Father in his usual Santa Claus manner, but later, instead of uniform, he put on his best blue suit, and Mother was as pleased as anything. I saw nothing to be pleased about, because, out of uniform, Father was altogether less interesting, but she only beamed, and explained that our prayers had been answered, and off we went to Mass to thank God for having brought Father safely home.

The irony of it! That very day when he came in to dinner he took off his boots and put on his slippers, donned the dirty old cap he wore about the house to save him from colds, crossed his legs, and began to talk gravely to Mother, who looked anxious. Naturally, I disliked her looking anxious, because it destroyed her good looks, so I interrupted him.

'Just a moment, Larry!' she said gently.

This was only what she said when we had boring visitors, so I attached no importance to it and went on talking.

'Do be quiet, Larry!' she said impatiently. 'Don't you hear me talking to Daddy?'

This was the first time I had heard those ominous words, 'talking to Daddy,' and I couldn't help feeling that if this was how God answered prayers, he couldn't listen to them very attentively.

'Why are you talking to Daddy?' I asked with as great a show of indifference as I could muster.

'Because Daddy and I have business to discuss. Now, don't interrupt again!'

In the afternoon, at Mother's request, Father took me for a walk. This time we went into town instead of out the country, and I thought at first, in my usual optimistic way, that it might be an improvement. It was nothing of the sort. Father and I had quite different notions of a walk in town. He had no proper interest in trams, ships, and horses, and the only thing that seemed to divert him was talking to fellows as old as himself. When I wanted to stop he simply went on, dragging me behind him by the hand; when he wanted to stop I had no alternative but to do the same. I noticed that it seemed to be a sign that he wanted to stop for a long time whenever he leaned against a wall. The second time I saw him do it I got wild. He seemed to be settling himself for ever. I pulled him by the coat and trousers, but, unlike Mother who, if you were too persistent, got into a wax and said: 'Larry, if you don't behave yourself, I'll give you a good slap,' Father had an extraordinary capacity for amiable inattention. I sized him up and wondered would I cry, but he seemed to be too remote to be annoyed even by that. Really, it was like going for a walk with a mountain! He either ignored the wrenching and pummelling entirely, or else glanced down with a grin of amusement from his peak. I had never met anyone so absorbed in himself as he seemed.

At teatime, 'talking to Daddy' began again, complicated this time by the fact that he had an evening paper, and every few minutes he put it down and told Mother something new out of it. I felt this was foul play. Man for man, I was prepared to compete with him any time for Mother's attention, but when he had it all made up for him by other people it left me no chance. Several times I tried to change the subject without success.

'You must be quiet while Daddy is reading, Larry,' Mother said impatiently.

It was clear that she either genuinely liked talking to Father better than talking to me, or else that he had some terrible hold on her which made her afraid to admit the truth.

'Mummy,' I said that night when she was tucking me up, 'do you think if I prayed hard God would send Daddy back to the war?'

She seemed to think about that for a moment.

'No, dear,' she said with a smile. 'I don't think he would.'

'Why wouldn't he, Mummy?'

'Because there isn't a war any longer, dear.'

'But, Mummy, couldn't God make another war, if He liked?'

'He wouldn't like to, dear. It's not God who makes wars, but bad people.'

'Oh!' I said.

I was disappointed about that. I began to think that God wasn't quite what he was cracked up to be.

Next morning I woke at my usual hour, feeling like a bottle of champagne. I put out my feet and invented a long conversation in which Mrs Right talked of the trouble she had with her own father till she put him in the Home. I didn't quite know what the Home was but it sounded the right place for Father. Then I got my chair and stuck my head out of the attic window. Dawn was just breaking, with a guilty air that made me feel I had caught it in the act. My head bursting with stories and schemes, I stumbled in next door, and in the half-darkness scrambled into the big bed. There was no room at Mother's side so I had to get between her and Father. For the time being I had forgotten about him, and for several minutes I sat bolt upright, racking my brains to know what I could do with him. He was taking up more than his fair share of the bed, and I couldn't get comfortable, so I gave him several kicks that made him grunt and stretch. He made room all right, though. Mother waked and felt for me. I settled back comfortably in the warmth of the bed with my thumb in my mouth.

'Mummy!' I hummed, loudly and contentedly.

'Sssh! dear,' she whispered. 'Don't wake Daddy!'

This was a new development, which threatened to be even more serious than 'talking to Daddy.' Life without my early-morning conferences was unthinkable.

'Why?' I asked severely.

'Because poor Daddy is tired.'

This seemed to me a quite inadequate reason, and I was sickened by the sentimentality of her 'poor Daddy.' I never liked that sort of gush; it always struck me as insincere.

'Oh!' I said lightly. Then in my most winning tone: 'Do you know where I want to go with you today, Mummy?'

'No, dear,' she sighed.

'I want to go down the Glen and fish for thornybacks with my new net, and then I want to go out to the Fox and Hounds, and –'

'Don't-wake-Daddy!' she hissed angrily, clapping her hand across my mouth.

But it was too late. He was awake, or nearly so. He grunted and reached for the matches. Then he stared incredulously at his watch.

'Like a cup of tea, dear?' asked Mother in a meek, hushed voice I had never heard her use before. It sounded almost as though she were afraid.

'Tea?' he exclaimed indignantly. 'Do you know what the time is?'

'And after that I want to go up the Rathcooney Road,' I said loudly, afraid I'd forget something in all those interruptions.

'Go to sleep at once, Larry!' she said sharply.

I began to snivel. I couldn't concentrate, the way that pair went on, and smothering my early-morning schemes was like burying a family from the cradle.

Father said nothing, but lit his pipe and sucked it, looking out into the shadows without minding Mother or me. I knew he was mad. Every time I made a remark Mother hushed me irritably. I was mortified. I felt it wasn't fair; there was even something sinister in it. Every time I had pointed out to her the waste of making two beds when we could both sleep in one, she had told me it was healthier like that, and now here was this man, this stranger, sleeping with her without the least regard for her health!

He got up early and made tea, but though he brought Mother a cup he brought none for me.

'Mummy,' I shouted, 'I want a cup of tea, too.'

'Yes, dear,' she said patiently. 'You can drink from Mummy's saucer.'

That settled it. Either Father or I would have to leave the house. I didn't want to drink from Mother's saucer; I wanted to be treated as an equal in my own home, so, just to spite her, I drank it all and left none for her. She took that quietly, too.

But that night when she was putting me to bed she said gently:

'Larry, I want you to promise me something.'

'What is it?' I asked.

'Not to come in and disturb poor Daddy in the morning. Promise?'

'Poor Daddy' again! I was becoming suspicious of everything involving that quite impossible man.

'Why?' I asked.

'Because poor Daddy is worried and tired and he doesn't sleep well.'

'Why doesn't he, Mummy?'

'Well, you know, don't you, that while he was at the war Mummy got the pennies from the Post Office?'

'From Miss MacCarthy?'

'That's right. But now, you see, Miss MacCarthy hasn't any more pennies, so Daddy must go out and find us some. You know what would happen if he couldn't?'

'No,' I said, 'tell us.'

'Well, I think we might have to go out and beg for them like the poor old woman on Fridays. We wouldn't like that, would we?'

'No,' I agreed. 'We wouldn't.'

'So you'll promise not to come in and wake him?'

'Promise.'

Mind you, I meant that. I knew pennies were a serious matter, and I was all against having to go out and beg like the old woman on Fridays. Mother laid out all my toys in a complete ring round the bed so that, whatever way I got out, I was bound to fall over one of them.

When I woke I remembered my promise all right. I got up and sat on the floor and played – for hours, it seemed to me. Then I got my chair and looked out the attic window for more hours. I wished it was time for Father to wake; I wished someone would make me a cup of tea. I didn't feel in the least like the sun; instead, I was bored and so very, very cold! I simply longed for the warmth and depth of the big featherbed.

At last I could stand it no longer. I went into the next room. As there was still no room at Mother's side I climbed over her and she woke with a start.

'Larry,' she whispered, gripping my arm very tightly, 'what did you promise?'

'But I did, Mummy,' I wailed, caught in the very act. 'I was quiet for ever so long.'

'Oh, dear, and you're perished!' she said sadly, feeling me all over. 'Now, if I let you stay will you promise not to talk?'

'But I want to talk, Mummy,' I wailed.

'That has nothing to do with it,' she said with a firmness that was new to me. 'Daddy wants to sleep. Now, do you under-stand that?'

I understood it only too well. I wanted to talk, he wanted to sleep – whose house was it, anyway?

'Mummy,' I said with equal firmness, 'I think it would be healthier for Daddy to sleep in his own bed.'

That seemed to stagger her, because she said nothing for a while.

'Now, once for all,' she went on, 'you're to be perfectly quiet or go back to your own bed. Which is it to be?'

The injustice of it got me down. I had convicted her out of her own mouth of inconsistency and unreasonableness, and she hadn't even attempted to reply. Full of spite, I gave Father a kick, which she didn't notice but which made him grunt and open his eyes in alarm.

'What time is it?' he asked in a panic-stricken voice, not look-ing at Mother but at the door, as if he saw someone there.

'It's early yet,' she replied soothingly. 'It's only the child. Go to sleep again. . . . Now, Larry,' she added, getting out of bed, 'you've wakened Daddy and you must go back.'

This time, for all her quiet air, I knew she meant it, and knew that my principal rights and privileges were as good as lost unless

I asserted them at once. As she lifted me, I gave a screech, enough to wake the dead, not to mind Father. He groaned.

'That damn child! Doesn't he ever sleep?'

'It's only a habit, dear,' she said quietly, though I could see she was vexed.

'Well, it's time he got out of it,' shouted Father, beginning to heave in the bed. He suddenly gathered all the bedclothes about him, turned to the wall, and then looked back over his shoulder with nothing showing only two small, spiteful, dark eyes. The man looked very wicked.

To open the bedroom door, Mother had to let me down, and I broke free and dashed for the farthest corner, screeching. Father sat bolt upright in bed.

'Shut up, you little puppy!' he said in a choking voice.

I was so astonished that I stopped screeching. Never, never had anyone spoken to me in that tone before. I looked at him incredulously and saw his face convulsed with rage. It was only then that I fully realized how God had codded me, listening to my prayers for the safe return of this monster.

'Shut up, you!' I bawled, beside myself.

'What's that you said?' shouted Father, making a wild leap out of the bed.

'Mick, Mick!' cried Mother. 'Don't you see the child isn't used to you?'

'I see he's better fed than taught,' snarled Father, waving his arms wildly. 'He wants his bottom smacked.'

All his previous shouting was as nothing to these obscene words referring to my person. They really made my blood boil.

'Smack your own!' I screamed hysterically. 'Smack your own! Shut up! Shut up!'

At this he lost his patience and let fly at me. He did it with the lack of conviction you'd expect of a man under Mother's horrified eyes, and it ended up as a mere tap, but the sheer indignity of being struck at all by a stranger, a total stranger who had cajoled his way back from the war into our big bed as a result of my innocent intercession, made me completely dotty. I shrieked and shrieked, and danced in my bare feet, and Father, looking awkward and hairy in nothing but a short grey army shirt, glared down at me like a mountain out for murder. I think it must have been then that I realized he was jealous too. And there stood

Mother in her nightdress, looking as if her heart was broken between us. I hoped she felt as she looked. It seemed to me that she deserved it all.

From that morning out my life was a hell. Father and I were enemies, open and avowed. We conducted a series of skirmishes against one another, he trying to steal my time with Mother and I his. When she was sitting on my bed, telling me a story, he took to looking for some pair of old boots which he alleged he had left behind him at the beginning of the war. While he talked to Mother I played loudly with my toys to show my total lack of concern. He created a terrible scene one evening when he came in from work and found me at his box, playing with his regimental badges, Gurkha knives and button-sticks. Mother got up and took the box from me.

'You mustn't play with Daddy's toys unless he lets you, Larry,' she said severely. 'Daddy doesn't play with yours.'

For some reason Father looked at her as if she had struck him and then turned away with a scowl.

'Those are not toys,' he growled, taking down the box again to see had I lifted anything. 'Some of those curios are very rare and valuable.'

But as time went on I saw more and more how he managed to alienate Mother and me. What made it worse was that I couldn't grasp his method or see what attraction he had for Mother. In every possible way he was less winning than I. He had a common accent and made noises at his tea. I thought for a while that it might be the newspapers she was interested in, so I made up bits of news of my own to read to her. Then I thought it might be the smoking, which I personally thought attractive, and took his pipes and went round the house dribbling into them till he caught me. I even made noises at my tea, but Mother only told me I was disgusting. It all seemed to hinge round that unhealthy habit of sleeping together, so I made a point of dropping into their bedroom and nosing round, talking to myself, so that they wouldn't know I was watching them, but they were never up to anything that I could see. In the end it beat me. It seemed to depend on being grown-up and giving people rings, and I realized I'd have to wait.

But at the same time I wanted him to see that I was only waiting, not giving up the fight. One evening when he was being particularly obnoxious, chattering away well above my head, I let him have it.

'Mummy,' I said, 'do you know what I'm going to do when I grow up?'

'No, dear,' she replied. 'What?'

'I'm going to marry you,' I said quietly.

Father gave a great guffaw out of him, but he didn't take me in. I knew it must only be pretence. And Mother, in spite of everything, was pleased. I felt she was probably relieved to know that one day Father's hold on her would be broken.

'Won't that be nice?' she said with a smile.

'It'll be very nice,' I said confidently. 'Because we're going to have lots and lots of babies.'

'That's right, dear,' she said placidly. 'I think we'll have one soon, and then you'll have plenty of company.'

I was no end pleased about that because it showed that in spite of the way she gave in to Father she still considered my wishes. Besides, it would put the Geneys in their place.

It didn't turn out like that, though. To begin with, she was very preoccupied – I supposed about where she would get the seventeen and six – and though Father took to staying out late in the evenings it did me no particular good. She stopped taking me for walks, became as touchy as blazes, and smacked me for nothing at all. Sometimes I wished I'd never mentioned the confounded baby – I seemed to have a genius for bringing calamity on myself.

And calamity it was! Sonny arrived in the most appalling hullabaloo – even that much he couldn't do without a fuss – and from the first moment I disliked him. He was a difficult child – so far as I was concerned he was always difficult – and demanded far too much attention. Mother was simply silly about him, and couldn't see when he was only showing off. As company he was worse than useless. He slept all day, and I had to go round the house on tiptoe to avoid waking him. It wasn't any longer a question of not waking Father. The slogan now was 'Don't-wake-Sonny!' I couldn't understand why the child wouldn't sleep at the proper time, so whenever Mother's back was turned I woke him. Sometimes to keep him awake I pinched him as well. Mother caught me at it one day and gave me a most unmerciful flaking.

One evening, when Father was coming in from work, I was playing trains in the front garden. I let on not to notice him; instead, I pretended to be talking to myself, and said in a loud voice: 'If another bloody baby comes into this house, I'm going out.'

Father stopped dead and looked at me over his shoulder.

'What's that you said?' he asked sternly.

'I was only talking to myself,' I replied, trying to conceal my panic. 'It's private.'

He turned and went in without a word. Mind you, I intended it as a solemn warning, but its effect was quite different. Father started being quite nice to me. I could understand that, of course. Mother was quite sickening about Sonny. Even at mealtimes she'd get up and gawk at him in the cradle with an idiotic smile, and tell Father to do the same. He was always polite about it, but he looked so puzzled you could see he didn't know what she was talking about. He complained of the way Sonny cried at night, but she only got cross and said that Sonny never cried except when there was something up with him – which was a flaming lie, because Sonny never had anything up with him, and only cried for attention. It was really painful to see how simple-minded she was. Father wasn't attractive, but he had a fine intelligence. He saw through Sonny, and now he knew that I saw through him as well.

One night I woke with a start. There was someone beside me in the bed. For one wild moment I felt sure it must be Mother, having come to her senses and left Father for good, but then I heard Sonny in convulsions in the next room, and Mother saying: 'There! There! There!' and I knew it wasn't she. It was Father. He was lying beside me, wide awake, breathing hard and apparently as mad as hell.

After a while it came to me what he was mad about. It was his turn now. After turning me out of the big bed, he had been turned out himself. Mother had no consideration now for any-one but that poisonous pup, Sonny. I couldn't help feeling sorry for Father. I had been through it all myself, and even at that age I was magnanimous. I began to stroke him down and say: 'There! There!' He wasn't exactly responsive.

'Aren't you asleep either?' he snarled.

'Ah, come on and put your arm around us, can't you?' I said, and he did, in a sort of way. Gingerly, I suppose, is how you'd describe it. He was very bony but better than nothing.

At Christmas he went out of his way to buy me a really nice model railway.

From AN ONLY CHILD – MOTHER

WHENEVER I read about juvenile delinquents, I find myself thinking of Mother, because she was whatever the opposite of a juvenile delinquent is, and this was not due to her upbringing in a Catholic orphanage, since whatever it was in her that was the opposite of a juvenile delinquent was too strong to have been due to the effect of any environment, and, indeed, resisted a number of environments to which no reasonable person would subject a child; the gutter where life had thrown her was deep and dirty. One way of describing this quality is to call it gaiety; another is to say that she was a woman who passionately believed in the world of appearances. If something appeared to be so, or if she had been told it was so, then she believed it to be so. This, as every psychologist knows, leads to disillusionments, and when a juvenile delinquent is disillusioned we describe it as a traumatic experience. So far as I could see, up to her death practically all Mother's experiences were traumatic, including, I am afraid, her experience with me. And some small portion of her simple-mindedess she did pass on to me.

She was small and dainty, with long dark hair that she was very proud of. She had only two faults that I ever knew of – she was vain and she was obstinate – and the fact that these qualities were masked by humility and gentleness prevented my recognizing them till I was a grown man. Father, who was as grey as a badger at thirty-five, and in danger of growing bald, in spite of his clippers, was very jealous of her beautiful dark hair, and when-ever he wanted to make her mad he would affect to discover white strands in it. Being an orphan, she had no notion of her own age, and had never known a birthday, but Father had discussed it with my Uncle Tim and satisfied himself that she was several years older than himself. When he believed she was seventy, he got really angry because he was sure she was going to let her vanity deprive her of a perfectly good pension. Mother shrugged this off as another example of his jealousy. To tell the truth, that was what I thought myself. She looked, at the time, like a well-preserved fifty-five. However, to put his mind at rest, I had the date of her birth looked up in the Customs House in Dublin, and discovered that she was only a few months short of seventy. Father was triumphant, but I felt guilty because I feared that the knowledge of her real age would make her become old. I needn't have worried. I think she probably decided finally that though the Registrar of Births and Deaths was a well-intentioned man, he was not particularly bright.

She had a lordly way with any sort of record she could get her hands on that conflicted with her own view of herself – she merely tore it up. Once, the poet George Russell did a charming pencil drawing of her, which I had framed. The next time I came home on holiday, I found the frame filled with snapshots of me, and my heart sank, because I knew what must have happened. 'What did you do with that drawing?' I asked, hoping she might at least have preserved it, and she replied firmly: 'Now, I'm just as fond of A.E. as you are, but I could not have that picture round the house. He made me look like a poisoner.' When she was eighty-five, and we were leaving to live in England, I discovered that she had done the same thing with the photograph in her passport. She was entirely unaffected by my anger. 'The sergeant of the police at Saint Luke's said it,' she proclaimed firmly. 'The man who took that picture should be tried for his life.' I think she was glad to have official authority for her personal view that I had been very remiss in not bringing proceedings against the photographer. When my wife and I separated, the only indication I had of Mother's feelings was when I looked at my photograph album one day and saw that every single photograph of my wife had been destroyed. Where she had been photographed with me or the children her picture had been cut away. It was not all malice, any more than the destruction of her own pictures was all vanity. I am certain it went back to some childish technique of endurance by obliterating impressions she had found too terrible to entertain, as though, believing as she did in the world of appearances, she found it necessary to alter the world of appearances to make it seem right, but in time it came to affect almost everything she did. It even worked in reverse, for one Christmas an old friend, Stan Stewart, sent her a book, but because it came straight from his bookseller, it did not contain an inscription, as books that were sent to me did. After her death, I found the book with a charming inscription from Stan, written in by herself. Her affection for him made her give herself away, for she wrote 'From dear Stan'.

THE GENIUS

I

SOME KIDS are sissies by nature but I was a sissy by conviction. Mother had told me about geniuses; I wanted to be one, and I could see for myself that fighting, as well as being sinful, was dangerous. The kids round the Barrack where I lived were always fighting. Mother said they were savages, that I needed proper friends, and that once I was old enough to go to school I would meet them.

My way, when someone wanted to fight and I could not get away, was to climb on the nearest wall and argue like hell in a shrill voice about Our Blessed Lord and good manners. This was a way of attracting attention, and it usually worked because the enemy, having stared incredulously at me for several minutes, wondering if he would have time to hammer my head on the pavement before someone came out to him, yelled something like 'blooming sissy' and went away in disgust. I didn't like being called a sissy but I preferred it to fighting. I felt very like one of those poor mongrels who slunk through our neighbourhood and took to their heels when anyone came near them, and I always tried to make friends with them.

I toyed with games, and enjoyed kicking a ball gently before me along the pavement till I discovered that any boy who joined me grew violent and started to shoulder me out of the way. I preferred little girls because they didn't fight so much, but otherwise I found them insipid and lacking in any solid basis of information. The only women I cared for were grown-ups, and my most intimate friend was an old washerwoman called Miss Cooney who had been in the lunatic asylum and was very religious. It was she who had told me all about dogs. She would run a mile after anyone she saw hurting an animal and even went to the police about them, but the police knew she was mad and paid no attention.

She was a sad-looking woman with grey hair, high cheekbones, and toothless gums. While she ironed, I would sit for hours in the steaming, damp kitchen, turning over the pages of her religious books. She was fond of me, too, and told me she was sure I would be a priest. I agreed that I might be a Bishop, but she didn't seem to think so highly of Bishops. I told her there were so many other things I might be that I couldn't make up my mind but she only smiled at this. Miss Cooney thought there was only one thing a genius could be and that was a priest.

On the whole, I thought an explorer was what I would be. Our house was in a square between two roads, one terraced above the other, and I could leave home, follow the upper road for a mile past the Barrack, turn left on any of the intervening roads and lanes, and return almost without leaving the pavement. It was astonishing what valuable information you could pick up on a trip like that. When I came home I wrote down my adventures in a book called *The Voyages of Johnson Martin*, with Many Maps and Illustrations, Irishtown University Press, 3s.6d. nett. I was also compiling *The Irishtown University Song Book for Use in Schools and Institutions*, by Johnson Martin, which had the words and music of my favourite songs. I could not read music yet but I copied it from anything that came handy, preferring staff to solfa because it looked better on the page. But I still wasn't sure what I would be. All I knew was that I intended to be famous and have a statue put up to me near that of Father Matthew in Patrick Street. Father Matthew was called the Apostle of Temperance, but I didn't think much of temperance. So far our town hadn't a proper genius and I intended to supply the deficiency.

But my work continued to bring home to me the great gaps in my knowledge. Mother understood my difficulty and worried herself endlessly finding answers to my questions, but neither she nor Miss Cooney had a great store of the sort of information I needed, and Father was more a hindrance than a help. He was talkative enough about subjects that interested himself but they did not greatly interest me. 'Ballybeg,' he would say brightly. 'Market Town. Population 648. Nearest station, Rathkeale.' He was also forthcoming enough about other things, but later Mother would take me aside and explain that he was only joking again. This made me mad because I never knew when he was joking and when he wasn't.

I can see now, of course, that he didn't really like me. It was not the poor man's fault. He had never expected to be the father of a genius and it filled him with forebodings. He looked round him at all his contemporaries who had normal, bloodthirsty, illiterate children, and shuddered at the thought that I would never be good for anything but being a genius. To give him his due, it wasn't himself he worried about, but there had never been anything like it in the family before and he dreaded the shame of it. He would come in from the front door with his cap over his eyes and his hands in his trousers pockets and stare moodily at me while I sat at the kitchen table, surrounded by papers, producing fresh maps and illustrations for my book of voyages or copying the music of 'The Minstrel Boy'.

'Why can't you go out and play with the Horgans?' he would ask wheedlingly, trying to make it sound attractive.

'I don't like the Horgans, Daddy,' I would reply politely.

'But what's wrong with them?' he would ask testily. 'They're fine, manly young fellows.'

'They're always fighting, Daddy.'

'And what harm is fighting? Can't you fight them back?'

'I don't like fighting, Daddy, thank you,' I would say, still with perfect politeness.

'The dear knows, the child is right,' Mother would say, coming to my defence. 'I don't know what sort those children are.'

'Ah, you have him as bad as yourself,' Father would snort and stalk to the front door again, to scald his heart with thoughts of the nice natural son he might have had if only he hadn't married the wrong woman. Granny had always said Mother was the wrong woman for him and now she was being proved right.

She was being proved so right that the poor man couldn't keep his eyes off me, waiting for the insanity to break out. One of the things he didn't like was my Opera House. The Opera House was a cardboard box I had mounted on two chairs in the dark hallway. It had a proscenium cut in it, and I had painted some backdrops of mountain and sea with wings that represented trees and rocks. The characters were pictures cut out, mounted and coloured and moved on bits of stick. It was lit with candles for which I had made coloured screens, greased so that they were transparent, and I made up operas from story-books and bits of songs. I was singing a passionate duet for two of the characters while twiddling the screens to produce the effect of moonlight when one of the screens caught fire and everything went up in a mass of flames. I screamed and Father came to stamp out the blaze, and he cursed me till even Mother lost her temper with him and told him he was worse than six children, after which he wouldn't speak to her for a week.

Another time I was so impressed with a lame teacher I knew that I decided to have a lame leg myself, and there was hell in the home for days because Mother had no difficulty at all in seeing that my foot was already out of shape while Father only looked at it and sniffed contemptuously. I was furious with him, and Mother decided he wasn't much better than a monster. They quarrelled for days over that until it became quite an embarrassment to me because, though I was bored stiff with limping, I felt I should be letting her down by getting better. When I went down the Square, lurching from side to side, Father stood at the gate, looking after me with a malicious knowing smile, and when I had discarded my limp, the way he mocked Mother was positively disgusting.

II

As I say, they squabbled endlessly about what I should be told. Father was for telling me nothing.

'But, Mick,' Mother would say earnestly, 'the child must learn.'

'He'll learn soon enough when he goes to school,' he snarled. 'Why do you be always at him, putting ideas into his head? Isn't he bad enough? I'd sooner the boy would grow up a bit natural.'

But either Mother didn't like children to be natural or she thought I was natural enough as I was. Women, of course, don't object to geniuses half as much as men do. I suppose they find them a relief.

Now, one of the things I wanted badly to know was where babies came from but this was something that no one seemed to be able to explain to me. When I asked Mother she got upset and talked about birds and flowers, and I decided that if she had ever known she must have forgotten it and was ashamed to say so. Miss Cooney when I asked her only smiled wistfully and said: 'You'll know all about it soon enough, child.'

'But, Miss Cooney,' I said with great dignity, 'I have to know now. It's for my work, you see.'

'Keep your innocence while you can, child,' she said in the same tone. 'Soon enough the world will rob you of it, and once 'tis gone 'tis gone forever.'

But whatever the world wanted to rob me of, it was welcome to it from my point of view, if only I could get a few facts to work on. I appealed to Father and he told me that babies were dropped out of aeroplanes and if you caught one you could keep it. 'By parachute?' I asked, but he only looked pained and said: 'Oh, no, you don't want to begin by spoiling them.' Afterwards, Mother took me aside again and explained that he was only joking. I went quite dotty with rage and told her that one of these days he would go too far with his jokes.

All the same, it was a great worry to Mother. It wasn't every mother who had a genius for a son, and she dreaded that she might be wronging me. She suggested timidly to Father that he should tell me something about it, and he danced with rage. I heard them because I was supposed to be playing with the Opera House upstairs at the time. He said she was going out of her mind, and that she was driving me out of my mind as well. She was very upset because she had considerable respect for his judgement.

At the same time when it was a matter of duty she could be very, very obstinate. It was a heavy responsibility, and she disliked it intensely – a deeply pious woman who never mentioned the subject at all to anybody if she could avoid it – but it had to be done. She took an awful long time over it – it was a summer day, and we were sitting on the bank of a stream in the Glen – but at last I managed to detach the fact that mummies had an engine in their tummies and daddies had a starting-handle that made it work, and once it started it went on until it made a baby. That certainly explained an awful lot I had not understood up to this – for instance, why fathers were necessary and why Mother had buffers on her chest while Father had none. It made her almost as interesting as a locomotive, and for days I went round deploring my own rotten luck that I wasn't a girl and couldn't have an engine and buffers instead of a measly old starting-handle like Father.

Soon afterwards I went to school and disliked it intensely. I was too small to be moved up to the big boys, and the other 'infants' were still at the stage of spelling 'cat' and 'dog'. I tried to tell the old teacher about my work, but she only smiled and said: 'Hush, Larry!' I hated being told to hush. Father was always saying it to me.

One day I was standing at the playground gate, feeling very lonely and dissatisfied, when a tall girl from the Senior Girls' School spoke to me. She had a plump, dark face and black pigtails.

'What's your name, little boy?' she asked.

I told her.

'Is this your first time at school?' she asked.

'Yes.'

'And do you like it?'

'No, I hate it,' I replied gravely. 'The children can't spell and the old woman talks too much.'

Then I talked myself, for a change, and she listened attentively while I told her about myself, my voyages, my books, and the time of the trains from all the city stations. As she seemed so interested I told her I would meet her after school and tell her some more.

I was as good as my word. When I had eaten my lunch, instead of going on further voyages I went back to the Girls' School and waited for her to come out. She seemed pleased to see me because she took my hand and brought me home with her. She lived up Gardiner's Hill, a steep, demure suburban road with trees that overhung the walls at either side. She lived in a small house on top of the hill and was one of a family of three girls. Her little brother, John Joe, had been killed the previous year by a car. 'Look at what I brought home with me!' she said when we went into the kitchen, and her mother, a tall, thin woman, made a great fuss of me and wanted me to have my dinner with Una. That was the girl's name. I didn't take anything but while she ate I sat by the range and told her mother about myself. She seemed to like it as much as Una, and when dinner was over Una took me out in the fields behind the house for a walk.

When I went home at teatime, Mother was delighted.

'Ah,' she said, 'I knew you wouldn't be long making nice friends at school. It's about time for you, the dear knows.'

I felt much the same about it, and every fine day at three I waited for Una outside the school. When it rained and Mother would not let me out I was miserable.

One day while I was waiting for her there were two senior girls outside the gate.

'Your girl isn't out yet, Larry,' said one with a giggle.

'And do you mean to tell me Larry has a girl?' the other asked with a shocked air.

'Oh, yes,' said the first. 'Una Dwyer is Larry's girl. He goes with Una, don't you, Larry?'

I replied politely that I did, but in fact I was seriously alarmed. I had not realized that Una would be considered my girl. It had never happened to me before, and I had not understood that my waiting for her would be regarded in such a grave light. Now, I think the girls were probably right anyhow, for that is always the way it has been with me. A woman has only to shut up and let me talk long enough for me to fall head and ears in love with her. But then I did not recognize the symptoms. All I knew was that going with somebody meant you intended to marry them. I had always planned on marrying Mother; now it seemed as if I was expected to marry someone else, and I wasn't sure if I should like it or if, like football, it would prove to be one of those games that two people could not play without pushing.

A couple of weeks later I went to a party at Una's house. By this time it was almost as much mine as theirs. All the girls liked me and Mrs Dwyer talked to me by the hour. I saw nothing unusual about this except a proper appreciation of geniuses. Una had warned me that I should be expected to sing, so I was ready for the occasion. I sang the Gregorian *Credo*, and some of the little girls laughed but Mrs Dwyer only looked at me fondly.

'I suppose you'll be a priest when you grow up, Larry?' she asked.

'No, Mrs Dwyer,' I replied firmly. 'As a matter of fact, I intend to be a composer. Priests can't marry, you see, and I want to get married.'

That seemed to surprise her quite a bit. I was quite prepared to continue discussing my plans for the future, but all the children talked together. I was used to planning discussions so that they went on for a long time, but I found that whenever I began one in the Dwyers', it was immediately interrupted so that I found it hard to concentrate. Besides, all the children shouted, and Mrs Dwyer, for all her gentleness, shouted with them and at them. At first, I was somewhat alarmed, but I soon saw that they meant no particular harm, and when the party ended I was jumping up and down on the sofa, shrieking louder than anyone, while Una, in hysterics of giggling, encouraged me. She seemed to think I was the funniest thing ever.

It was a moonlit November night, and lights were burning in the little cottages along the road when Una brought me home. On the road outside she stopped uncertainly and said: 'This is where little John Joe was killed.'

There was nothing remarkable about the spot, and I saw no chance of acquiring any useful information.

'Was it a Ford or a Morris?' I asked, more out of politeness than anything else.

'I don't know,' she replied with smouldering anger. 'It was Donegan's old car. They can never look where they're going, the old shows!'

'Our Lord probably wanted him,' I said perfunctorily.

'I dare say He did,' Una replied, though she showed no particular conviction. 'That old fool Donegan – I could kill him whenever I think of it.'

'You should get your mother to make you another,' I suggested helpfully.

'Make me a what?' Una exclaimed in consternation.

'Make you another brother,' I repeated earnestly. 'It's quite easy, really. She has an engine in her tummy, and all your daddy has to do is to start it with his starting-handle.'

'Cripes!' Una said and clapped her hand over her mouth in an explosion of giggles. 'Imagine me telling her that!'

'But it's true, Una,' I said obstinately. 'It only takes nine months. She could make you another little brother by next summer.'

'Oh, Jay!' exclaimed Una in another fit of giggles. 'Who told you all that?'

'Mummy did. Didn't your mother tell you?'

'Oh, she says you buy them from Nurse Daly,' said Una and began to giggle again.

'I wouldn't really believe that,' I said with as much dignity as I could muster.

But the truth was I felt I had made a fool of myself again. I realized now that I had never been convinced by Mother's explanation. It was too simple. If there was anything that woman could get wrong she did so without fail. And it upset me, because for the first time I found myself wanting to make a really good impression. The Dwyers had managed to convince me that, whatever else I wanted to be, I did not want to be a priest. I didn't even want to be an explorer, a career which would take me away for long periods from my wife and family. I was prepared to be a composer and nothing but a composer.

That night in bed I sounded Mother on the subject of marriage. I tried to be tactful because it had always been agreed between us that I should marry her and I did not wish her to see that my feelings had changed.

'Mummy,' I asked, 'if a gentleman asks a lady to marry him, what does he say?'

'Oh,' she replied shortly, 'some of them say a lot. They say more than they mean.'

She was so irritable that I guessed she had divined my secret and I felt really sorry for her.

'If a gentleman said "Excuse me, will you marry me?" would that be all right?' I persisted.

'Ah, well, he'd have to tell her first that he was fond of her,' said Mother, who, no matter what she felt, could never bring herself to deceive me on any major issue.

But about the other matter I saw that it was hopeless to ask her any more. For days I made the most pertinacious inquiries at school and received some startling information. One boy had actually come floating down on a snowflake, wearing a bright blue dress, but, to his chagrin and mine, the dress had been given away to a poor child in the North Main Street. I grieved long and deeply over this wanton destruction of evidence. The balance of opinion favoured Mrs Dwyer's solution, but of the theory of engines and starting-handles no one in the school had ever heard. That theory might have been all right when Mother was a girl but it was now definitely out of fashion.

And because of it I had been exposed to ridicule before the family whose good opinion I valued most! It was hard enough to keep up my dignity with a girl who was doing algebra while I hadn't got beyond long division without falling into childish errors that made her laugh. That is another thing I still cannot stand, being made fun of by women. Once they begin they never stop. Once when we were going up Gardiner's Hill together after school she stopped to look at a baby in a pram. The baby grinned at her and she gave him her finger to suck. He waved his fists and sucked like mad and she went off into giggles again.

'I suppose that was another engine?' she said.

Four times at least she mentioned my silliness, twice in front of other girls, and each time, though I pretended to ignore it, I was pierced to the heart. It made me determined not to be exposed again. Once Mother asked Una and her younger sister, Joan, to tea and all the time I was in an agony of self-consciousness, dreading what she would say next. I felt that a woman who had said such things about babies was capable of anything. Then the talk turned on the death of little John Joe, and it all flowed back into my mind on a wave of mortification. I made two efforts to change the conversation, but Mother returned to it. She was full of pity for the Dwyers, full of sympathy for the little boy, and had almost reduced herself to tears. Finally, I got up and ordered Una and Joan to play with me. Then Mother got angry.

'For goodness' sake, Larry, let the children finish their tea!' she snapped.

'It's all right, Mrs Delaney,' Una said good-naturedly. 'I'll go with him.'

'Nonsense, Una!' Mother said sharply. 'Finish your tea and go on with what you were saying. It's a wonder to me your poor mother didn't go out of her mind. How can they let people like that drive cars?'

At this I set up a loud wail. At any moment now, I felt, she was going to get on to babies and advise Una about what her mother ought to do.

'Will you behave yourself, Larry!' Mother said in a quivering voice. 'Or what's come over you in the past few weeks? You used to have such nice manners, and now look at you! A little corner boy! I'm ashamed of you!'

How could she know what had come over me? How could she realize that I was imagining the family circle in the Dwyers' house and Una, between fits of laughter, describing my old-fashioned mother who still talked about babies coming out of people's stomachs? It must have been real love, for I have never known true love in which I wasn't ashamed of Mother.

And she knew it and was hurt. I still enjoyed going home with Una in the afternoons and, while she ate her dinner, I sat at the piano and pretended to play my own compositions, but whenever she called at our house for me I grabbed her by the hand and tried to drag her away so that she and Mother shouldn't start talking.

'Ah, I'm disgusted with you,' Mother said one day. 'One would think you were ashamed of me in front of that little girl. I'll engage she doesn't treat her mother like that.'

Then one day I was waiting for Una at the school gate as usual. Another boy was waiting there as well – one of the seniors. When he heard the screams of the school breaking up he strolled away and stationed himself at the foot of the hill by the crossroads. Then Una herself came rushing out in her wide-brimmed felt hat, swinging her satchel, and approached me with a conspiratorial air.

'Oh, Larry, guess what's happened!' she whispered. 'I can't bring you home with me today. I'll come down and see you during the week, though. Will that do?' '

'Yes, thank you,' I said in a dead cold voice. Even at the most tragic moment of my life I could be nothing but polite. I watched her scamper down the hill to where the big boy was waiting. He looked over his shoulder with a grin, and then the two of them went off together.

Instead of following them, I went back up the hill alone and stood leaning over the quarry wall, looking at the roadway and the valley of the city beneath me. I knew this was the end. I was too young to marry Una. I didn't know where babies came from and I didn't understand algebra. The fellow she had gone home with probably knew everything about both. I was full of gloom and revengeful thoughts. I, who had considered it sinful and dangerous to fight, was now regretting that I hadn't gone after him to batter his teeth in and jump on his face. It wouldn't even have mattered to me that I was too young and weak and that he would have done all the battering. I saw that love was a game that two people couldn't play at without pushing, just like football.

I went home and without saying a word took out the work I had been neglecting so long. That, too, seemed to have lost its appeal. Moodily, I ruled five lines and began to trace the difficult sign of the treble clef.

'Didn't you see Una, Larry?' Mother asked in surprise, looking up from her sewing.

'No, Mummy,' I said, too full for speech.

'Wisha, 'twasn't a falling-out ye had?' she asked in dismay, coming towards me. I put my head on my hands and sobbed. 'Wisha, never mind, childeen!' she murmured, running her hand through my hair. 'She was a bit old for you. You reminded her of her little brother that was killed, of course – that was why. You'll soon make new friends, take my word for it.'

But I did not believe her. That evening there was no comfort for me. My great work meant nothing to me and I knew it was all I would ever have. For all the difference it made, I might as well become a priest. I felt it was a poor, sad, lonesome thing being nothing but a genius.

FIRST CONFESSION

ALL THE trouble began when my grandfather died and my grandmother – my father's mother – came to live with us. Relations in the one house are a strain at the best of times, but, to make matters worse, my grandmother was a real old country woman and quite unsuited to the life in town. She had a fat, wrinkled old face, and, to Mother's great indignation, went round the house in bare feet – the boots had her crippled, she said. For dinner she had a jug of porter and a pot of potatoes with – sometimes – a bit of salt fish, and she poured out the potatoes on the table and ate them slowly, with great relish, using her fingers by way of a fork.

Now, girls are supposed to be fastidious, but I was the one who suffered most from this. Nora, my sister, just sucked up to the old woman for the penny she got every Friday out of the old-age pension, a thing I could not do. I was too honest, that was my trouble; and when I was playing with Bill Connell, the sergeant-major's son, and saw my grandmother steering up the path with the jug of porter sticking out from beneath her shawl I was mortified. I made excuses not to let him come into the house, because I could never be sure what she would be up to when we went in.

When Mother was at work and my grandmother made the dinner I wouldn't touch it. Nora once tried to make me, but I hid under the table from her and took the bread-knife with me for protection. Nora let on to be very indignant (she wasn't, of course, but she knew Mother saw through her, so she sided with Gran) and came after me. I lashed out at her with the bread-knife, and after that she left me alone. I stayed there till Mother came in from work and made my dinner, but when Father came in later Nora said in a shocked voice: 'Oh, Dadda, do you know what Jackie did at dinnertime?' Then, of course, it all came out; Father gave me a flaking; Mother interfered, and for days after that he didn't speak to me and Mother barely spoke to Nora.

And all because of that old woman! God knows, I was heart-scalded.

Then, to crown my misfortunes, I had to make my first Con-fession and Communion. It was an old woman called Ryan who prepared us for these. She was about the one age with Gran; she was well-to-do, lived in a big house on Montenotte, wore a black cloak and bonnet, and came every day to school at three o'clock when we should have been going home, and talked to us of Hell. She may have mentioned the other place as well, but that could only have been by accident, for Hell had the first place in her heart.

She lit a candle, took out a new half-crown, and offered it to the first boy who would hold one finger – only one finger! – in the flame for five minutes by the school clock. Being always very ambitious I was tempted to volunteer, but I thought it might look greedy. Then she asked were we afraid of holding one finger – only one finger! – in a little candle flame for five minutes and not afraid of burning all over in roasting hot furnaces for all eternity. 'All eternity! Just think of that! A whole lifetime goes by and it's nothing, not even a drop in the ocean of your suffer-ings.' The woman was really interesting about Hell, but my attention was all fixed on the half-crown. At the end of the lesson she put it back in her purse. It was a great disappointment; a religious woman like that, you wouldn't think she'd bother about a thing like a half-crown.

Another day she said she knew a priest who woke one night to find a fellow he didn't recognize leaning over the end of his bed. The priest was a bit frightened – naturally enough – but he asked the fellow what he wanted, and the fellow said in a deep, husky voice that he wanted to go to Confession. The priest said it was an awkward time and wouldn't it do in the morning, but the fellow said that last time he went to Confession, there was one sin he kept back, being ashamed to mention it, and now it was always on his mind. Then the priest knew it was a bad case, because the fellow was after making a bad confession and committing a mortal sin. He got up to dress, and just then the cock crew in the yard outside, and – lo and behold! – when the priest looked round there was no sign of the fellow, only a smell of burning timber, and when the priest looked at his bed didn't he see the print of two hands burned in it? That was because the fellow had made a bad confession. This story made a shocking impression on me.

But the worst of all was when she showed us how to examine our conscience. Did we take the name of the Lord, our God, in vain? Did we honour our father and our mother? (I asked her did this include grandmothers and she said it did.) Did we love our neighbour as ourselves? Did we covet our neighbour's goods? (I thought of the way I felt about the penny that Nora got every Friday.) I decided that, between one thing and another, I must have broken the whole ten commandments, all on account of that old woman, and so far as I could see, so long as she remained in the house I had no hope of ever doing anything else.

I was scared to death of Confession. The day the whole class went I let on to have a toothache, hoping my absence wouldn't be noticed; but at three o'clock, just as I was feeling safe, along comes a chap with a message from Mrs Ryan that I was to go to Confession myself on Saturday and be at the chapel for Communion with the rest. To make it worse, Mother couldn't come with me and sent Nora instead.

Now, that girl had ways of tormenting me that Mother never knew of. She held my hand as we went down the hill, smiling sadly and saying how sorry she was for me, as if she were bringing me to the hospital for an operation.

'Oh, God help us!' she moaned. 'Isn't it a terrible pity you weren't a good boy? Oh, Jackie, my heart bleeds for you! How will you ever think of all your sins? Don't forget you have to tell him about the time you kicked Gran on the shin.'

'Lemme go!' I said, trying to drag myself free of her. 'I don't want to go to Confession at all.'

'But sure, you'll have to go to Confession, Jackie,' she replied in the same regretful tone. 'Sure, if you didn't, the parish priest would be up to the house, looking for you. 'Tisn't, God knows, that I'm not sorry for you. Do you remember the time you tried to kill me with the bread-knife under the table? And the language you used to me? I don't know what he'll do with you at all, Jackie. He might have to send you up to the Bishop.'

I remember thinking bitterly that she didn't know the half of what I had to tell – if I told it. I knew I couldn't tell it, and understood perfectly why the fellow in Mrs Ryan's story made a bad confession; it seemed to me a great shame that people wouldn't stop criticizing him. I remember that steep hill down to the church, and the sunlit hillsides beyond the valley of the river, which I saw in the gaps between the houses like Adam's last glimpse of Paradise.

Then, when she had manoeuvred me down the long flight of steps to the chapel yard, Nora suddenly changed her tone. She became the raging malicious devil she really was.

'There you are!' she said with a yelp of triumph, hurling me through the church door. 'And I hope he'll give you the penitential psalms, you dirty little caffler.'

I knew then I was lost, given up to eternal justice. The door with the coloured-glass panels swung shut behind me, the sunlight went out and gave place to deep shadow, and the wind whistled outside so that the silence within seemed to crackle like ice under my feet. Nora sat in front of me by the confession box. There were a couple of old women ahead of her, and then a miserable-looking poor devil came and wedged me in at the other side, so that I couldn't escape even if I had the courage. He joined his hands and rolled his eyes in the direction of the roof, muttering aspirations in an anguished tone, and I wondered had he a grandmother too. Only a grandmother could account for a fellow behaving in that heartbroken way, but he was better off than I, for he at least could go and confess his sins; while I would make a bad confession and then die in the night and be continually coming back and burning people's furniture.

Nora's turn came, and I heard the sound of something slamming, and then her voice as if butter wouldn't melt in her mouth, and then another slam, and out she came. God, the hypocrisy of women! Her eyes were lowered, her head was bowed, and her hands were joined very low down on her stomach, and she walked up the aisle to the side altar looking like a saint. You never saw such an exhibition of devotion; and I remembered the devilish malice with which she had tormented me all the way from our door, and wondered were all religious people like that, really. It was my turn now. With the fear of damnation in my soul I went in, and the confessional door closed of itself behind me.

It was pitch-dark and I couldn't see priest or anything else. Then I really began to be frightened. In the darkness it was a matter between God and me, and He had all the odds. He knew what my intentions were before I even started; I had no chance.

All I had ever been told about Confession got mixed up in my mind, and I knelt to one wall and said: 'Bless me, father, for I have sinned; this is my first confession.' I waited for a few minutes, but nothing happened, so I tried it on the other wall. Nothing happened there either. He had me spotted all right.

It must have been then that I noticed the shelf at about one height with my head. It was really a place for grown-up people to rest their elbows, but in my distracted state I thought it was probably the place you were supposed to kneel. Of course, it was on the high side and not very deep, but I was always good at climbing and managed to get up all right. Staying up was the trouble. There was room only for my knees, and nothing you could get a grip on but a sort of wooden moulding a bit above it. I held on to the moulding and repeated the words a little louder, and this time something happened all right. A slide was slammed back; a little light entered the box, and a man's voice said: 'Who's there?'

''Tis me, father,' I said for fear he mightn't see me and go away again. I couldn't see him at all. The place the voice came from was under the moulding, about level with my knees, so I took a good grip of the moulding and swung myself down till I saw the astonished face of a young priest looking up at me. He had to put his head on one side to see me, and I had to put mine on one side to see him, so we were more or less talking to one another upside-down. It struck me as a queer way of hearing confessions, but I didn't feel it my place to criticize.

'Bless me, father, for I have sinned; this is my first confession,' I rattled off all in one breath, and swung myself down the least shade more to make it easier for him.

'What are you doing up there?' he shouted in an angry voice, and the strain the politeness was putting on my hold of the moulding, and the shock of being addressed in such an uncivil tone, were too much for me. I lost my grip, tumbled, and hit the door an unmerciful wallop before I found myself flat on my back in the middle of the aisle. The people who had been waiting stood up with their mouths open. The priest opened the door of the middle box and came out, pushing his biretta back from his forehead; he looked something terrible. Then Nora came scampering down the aisle.

'Oh, you dirty little caffler!' she said. 'I might have known

you'd do it. I might have known you'd disgrace me. I can't leave
you out of my sight for one minute.'

Before I could even get to my feet to defend myself she bent
down and gave me a clip across the ear. This reminded me that
I was so stunned I had even forgotten to cry, so that people might
think I wasn't hurt at all, when in fact I was probably maimed
for life. I gave a roar out of me.

'What's all this about?' the priest hissed, getting angrier than
ever and pushing Nora off me. 'How dare you hit the child like
that, you little vixen?'

'But I can't do my penance with him, father,' Nora cried,
cocking an outraged eye up at him.

'Well, go and do it, or I'll give you some more to do,' he said,
giving me a hand up. 'Was it coming to Confession you were,
my poor man?' he asked me.

''Twas, father,' said I with a sob.

'Oh,' he said respectfully, 'a big hefty fellow like you must
have terrible sins. Is this your first?'

''Tis, father,' said I.

'Worse and worse,' he said gloomily. 'The crimes of a lifetime.
I don't know will I get rid of you at all today. You'd better wait
now till I'm finished with these old ones. You can see by the
looks of them they haven't much to tell.'

'I will, father,' I said with something approaching joy.

The relief of it was really enormous. Nora stuck out her
tongue at me from behind his back, but I couldn't even be both-
ered retorting. I knew from the very moment that man opened
his mouth that he was intelligent above the ordinary. When I had
time to think, I saw how right I was. It only stood to reason that
a fellow confessing after seven years would have more to tell than
people that went every week. The crimes of a lifetime, exactly
as he said. It was only what he expected, and the rest was the
cackle of old women and girls with their talk of Hell, the Bishop,
and the penitential psalms. That was all they knew. I started to
make my examination of conscience, and barring the one bad
business of my grandmother it didn't seem so bad.

The next time, the priest steered me into the confession box
himself and left the shutter back the way I could see him get in
and sit down at the further side of the grille from me.

'Well, now,' he said, 'what do they call you?'

'Jackie, father,' said I.

'And what's a-trouble to you, Jackie?'

'Father,' I said, feeling I might as well get it over while I had him in good humour, 'I had it all arranged to kill my grandmother.'

He seemed a bit shaken by that, all right, because he said nothing for quite a while.

'My goodness,' he said at last, 'that'd be a shocking thing to do. What put that into your head?'

'Father,' I said, feeling very sorry for myself, 'she's an awful woman.'

'Is she?' he asked. 'What way is she awful?'

'She takes porter, father,' I said, knowing well from the way Mother talked of it that this was a mortal sin, and hoping it would make the priest take a more favourable view of my case.

'Oh, my!' he said, and I could see he was impressed.

'And snuff, father,' said I.

'That's a bad case, sure enough, Jackie,' he said.

'And she goes round in her bare feet, father,' I went on in a rush of self-pity, 'and she knows I don't like her, and she gives pennies to Nora and none to me, and my da sides with her and flakes me, and one night I was so heart-scalded I made up my mind I'd have to kill her.'

'And what would you do with the body?' he asked with great interest.

'I was thinking I could chop that up and carry it away in a barrow I have,' I said.

'Begor, Jackie,' he said, 'do you know you're a terrible child?'

'I know, father,' I said, for I was just thinking the same thing myself. 'I tried to kill Nora too with a bread-knife under the table, only I missed her.'

'Is that the little girl that was beating you just now?' he asked.

' 'Tis, father.'

'Someone will go for her with a bread-knife one day, and he won't miss her,' he said rather cryptically. 'You must have great courage. Between ourselves, there's a lot of people I'd like to do the same to but I'd never have the nerve. Hanging is an awful death.'

'Is it, father?' I asked with the deepest interest – I was always very keen on hanging. 'Did you ever see a fellow hanged?'

'Dozens of them,' he said solemnly. 'And they all died roaring.'

'Jay!' I said.

'Oh, a horrible death!' he said with great satisfaction. 'Lots of the fellows I saw killed their grandmothers too, but they all said 'twas never worth it.'

He had me there for a full ten minutes talking, and then walked out the chapel yard with me. I was genuinely sorry to part with him, because he was the most entertaining character I'd ever met in the religious line. Outside, after the shadow of the church, the sunlight was like the roaring of waves on a beach; it dazzled me; and when the frozen silence melted and I heard the screech of trams on the road my heart soared. I knew now I wouldn't die in the night and come back, leaving marks on my mother's furniture. It would be a great worry to her, and the poor soul had enough.

Nora was sitting on the railing, waiting for me, and she put on a very sour puss when she saw the priest with me. She was mad jealous because a priest had never come out of the church with her.

'Well,' she asked coldly, after he left me, 'what did he give you?'

'Three Hail Marys,' I said.

'Three Hail Marys,' she repeated incredulously. 'You mustn't have told him anything.'

'I told him everything,' I said confidently.

'About Gran and all?'

'About Gran and all.'

(All she wanted was to be able to go home and say I'd made a bad confession.)

'Did you tell him you went for me with the bread-knife?' she asked with a frown.

'I did to be sure.'

'And he only gave you three Hail Marys?'

'That's all.'

She slowly got down from the railing with a baffled air. Clearly, this was beyond her. As we mounted the steps back to the main road she looked at me suspiciously.

'What are you sucking?' she asked.

'Bullseyes.'

'Was it the priest gave them to you?'

' 'Twas.'

'Lord God,' she wailed bitterly, 'some people have all the luck! 'Tis no advantage to anybody trying to be good. I might just as well be a sinner like you.'

From WRITING A STORY – ONE MAN'S WAY

THOSE OF you who know something about my work will realize that even then, when you have taken every precaution against wasting your time, when everything is organized, and, according to the rules, there is nothing left for you but produce a perfect story, you often produce nothing of the kind. My own evidence for that comes from a story I once wrote called 'First Confession'. It is a story about a little boy who goes to confession for the first time and confesses that he had planned to kill his grandmother. I wrote the story twenty-five years ago, and it was published and I was paid for it. I should have been happy, but I was not. No sooner did I begin to re-read the story than I knew I had missed the point. It was too spread out in time.

Many years later a selection of my stories was being published, and I re-wrote the story, concentrating it into an hour. This again was published, and became so popular that I made more money out of it than I'd ever made out of a story before. You'd think that at least would have satisfied me. It didn't.

Years later, I took that story and re-wrote it in the first person because I realized it was one of those stories where it was more important to say 'I planned to kill my grandmother' than to say 'Jackie planned to kill his grandmother'. And since then, you will be glad to know, whenever I wake up at four in the morning and think of my sins, I do not any longer think of the crime I committed against Jackie in describing his first confession. The story is as finished as it is ever going to be, and, to end on a note of confidence, I would wish you to believe that if you work hard at a story over a period of twenty-five or thirty years, there is a reasonable chance that at last you will get it right.

(1959 radio broadcast)

THE STUDY OF HISTORY

THE DISCOVERY of where babies came from filled my life with excitement and interest. Not in the way it's generally supposed to, of course. Oh, no! I never seem to have done anything like a natural child in a standard textbook. I merely discovered the fascination of history. Up to this, I had lived in a country of my own that had no history, and accepted my parents' marriage as an event ordained from the creation; now, when I considered it in this new, scientific way, I began to see it merely as one of the turning-points of history, one of those apparently trivial events that are little more than accidents but have the effect of changing the destiny of humanity. I had not heard of Pascal, but I would have approved his remark about what would have happened if Cleopatra's nose had been a bit longer.

It immediately changed my view of my parents. Up to this, they had been principles, not characters, like a chain of mountains guarding a green horizon. Suddenly a little shaft of light, emerging from behind a cloud, struck them, and the whole mass broke up into peaks, valleys, and foothills; you could even see whitewashed farmhouses and fields where people worked in the evening light, a whole world of interior perspective. Mother's past was the richer subject for study. It was extraordinary the variety of people and settings that woman had had in her background. She had been an orphan, a parlourmaid, a companion, a traveller; and had been proposed to by a plasterer's apprentice, a French chef who had taught her to make superb coffee, and a rich and elderly shopkeeper in Sunday's Well. Because I liked to feel myself different, I thought a great deal about the chef and the advantages of being a Frenchman, but the shopkeeper was an even more vivid figure in my imagination because he had married someone else and died soon after – of disappointment, I had no doubt – leaving a large fortune. The fortune was to me what Cleopatra's nose was to Pascal: the ultimate proof that things might have been different.

'How much was Mr Riordan's fortune, Mummy?' I asked thoughtfully.

'Ah, they said he left eleven thousand,' Mother replied doubtfully, 'but you couldn't believe everything people say.'

That was exactly what I could do. I was not prepared to minimize a fortune that I might so easily have inherited.

'And weren't you ever sorry for poor Mr Riordan?' I asked severely.

'Ah, why would I be sorry, child?' she asked with a shrug. 'Sure, what use would money be where there was no liking?'

That, of course, was not what I meant at all. My heart was full of pity for poor Mr Riordan who had tried to be my father; but, even on the low level at which Mother discussed it, money would have been of great use to me. I was not so fond of Father as to think he was worth eleven thousand pounds, a hard sum to visualize but more than twenty-seven times greater than the largest salary I had ever heard of – that of a Member of Parliament. One of the discoveries I was making at the time was that Mother was not only rather hard-hearted but very impractical as well.

But Father was the real surprise. He was a brooding, worried man who seemed to have no proper appreciation of me, and was always wanting me to go out and play or go upstairs and read, but the historical approach changed him like a character in a fairy-tale. 'Now let's talk about the ladies Daddy nearly married,' I would say; and he would stop whatever he was doing and give a great guffaw. 'Oh, ho, ho!' he would say, slapping his knee and looking slyly at Mother. 'You could write a book about them.' Even his face changed at such moments. He would look young and extraordinarily mischievous. Mother, on the other hand, would grow black.

'You could,' she would say, looking into the fire. 'Daisies!'

' "The handsomest man that walks Cork!" ' Father would quote with a wink at me. 'That's what one of them called me.'

'Yes,' Mother would say, scowling. 'May Cadogan!'

'The very girl!' Father would cry in astonishment. 'How did I forget her name? A beautiful girl! 'Pon my word, a most remarkable girl! And still is, I hear.'

'She should be,' Mother would say in disgust. 'With six of them!'

'Oh, now, she'd be the one that could look after them! A fine head that girl had.'

'She had. I suppose she ties them to a lamp-post while she goes in to drink and gossip.'

That was one of the peculiar things about history. Father and Mother both loved to talk about it but in different ways. She would only talk about it when we were together somewhere, in the Park or down the Glen, and even then it was very hard to make her stick to the facts, because her whole face would light up and she would begin to talk about donkey-carriages or concerts in the kitchen, or oil-lamps, and though nowadays I would probably value it for atmosphere, in those days it sometimes drove me mad with impatience. Father, on the other hand, never minded talking about it in front of her, and it made her angry – particularly when he mentioned May Cadogan. He knew this perfectly well and he would wink at me and make me laugh outright, though I had no idea of why I laughed, and, anyway, my sympathy was all with her.

'But, Daddy,' I would say, presuming on his high spirits, 'if you liked Miss Cadogan so much why didn't you marry her?'

At this, to my great delight, he would let on to be filled with doubt and distress. He would put his hands in his trouser pockets and stride to the door leading into the hallway.

'That was a delicate matter,' he would say, without looking at me. 'You see, I had your poor mother to think of.'

'I was a great trouble to you,' Mother would say, in a blaze.

'Poor May said it to me herself,' he would go on as though he had not heard her, 'and the tears pouring down her cheeks. "Mick," she said, "that girl with the brown hair will bring me to an untimely grave."'

'She could talk of hair!' Mother would hiss. 'With her carroty mop!'

'Never did I suffer the way I suffered then, between the two of them,' Father would say with deep emotion as he returned to his chair by the window.

'Oh, 'tis a pity about ye!' Mother would cry in an exasperated tone and suddenly get up and go into the front room with her book to escape his teasing. Every word that man said she took literally. Father would give a great guffaw of delight, his hands on his knees and his eyes on the ceiling, and wink at me again.

I would laugh with him, of course, and then grow wretched because I hated Mother's sitting alone in the front room. I would go in and find her in her wicker chair by the window in the dusk, the book open on her knee, looking out at the Square. She would always have regained her composure when she spoke to me, but I would have an uncanny feeling of unrest in her and stroke her and talk to her soothingly as if we had changed places and I were the adult and she the child.

But if I was excited by what history meant to them, I was even more excited by what it meant to me. My potentialities were double theirs. Through Mother I might have been a French boy called Laurence Armady or a rich boy from Sunday's Well called Laurence Riordan. Through Father I might, while still remaining a Delaney, have been one of the six children of the mysterious and beautiful Miss Cadogan. I was fascinated by the problem of who I would have been if I hadn't been me, and, even more, by the problem of whether or not I would have known that there was anything wrong with the arrangement. Naturally, I tended to regard Laurence Delaney as the person I was intended to be, and so I could not help wondering whether as Laurence Riordan I would not have been aware of Laurence Delaney as a real gap in my make-up.

I remember that one afternoon after school I walked by myself all the way up to Sunday's Well, which I now regarded as something like a second house. I stood for a while at the garden gate of the house where Mother had been working when she was proposed to by Mr Riordan, and then went and studied the shop itself. It had clearly seen better days, and the cartons and advertisements in the window were dusty and sagging. It wasn't like one of the big stores in Patrick Street, but at the same time, in size and fittings, it was well above the level of a village shop. I regretted that Mr Riordan was dead because I would have liked to see him for myself instead of relying on Mother's impressions, which seemed to me to be biased. Since he had, more or less, died of grief on Mother's account, I conceived of him as a really nice man; lent him the countenance and manner of an old gentleman who always spoke to me when he met me on the road; and felt I could have become really attached to him as a father. I could imagine it all: Mother reading in the parlour while she waited for me to come home up Sunday's Well in a school cap and blazer, like the boys from the Grammar School, and with an expensive leather satchel instead of the old cloth schoolbag I carried over my shoulder. I could see myself walking slowly and with a certain distinction, lingering at gateways and looking down at the river; and later I would go out to tea in one of the big houses with long gardens sloping to the water, and maybe row a boat on the river along with a girl in a pink frock. I wondered only whether I would have any awareness of the National School boy with the cloth schoolbag who jammed his head between the bars of a gate and thought of me. It was a queer, lonesome feeling that all but reduced me to tears.

But the place that had the greatest attraction of all for me was the Douglas Road, where Father's friend Miss Cadogan lived, only now she wasn't Miss Cadogan but Mrs O'Brien. Naturally, nobody called Mrs O'Brien could be as attractive to the imagination as a French chef or an elderly shopkeeper with eleven thousand pounds, but she had a physical reality that the other pair lacked. As I went regularly to the library at Parnell Bridge, I frequently found myself wandering up the road in the direction of Douglas and always stopped in front of the long row of houses where she lived. There were high steps up to them, and in the evening the sunlight fell brightly on the house-fronts till they looked like a screen. One evening as I watched a gang of boys playing ball in the street outside, curiosity overcame me. I spoke to one of them. Having been always a child of solemn and unnatural politeness, I probably scared the wits out of him.

'I wonder if you could tell me which house Mrs O'Brien lives in, please?' I asked.

'Hi, Gussie!' he yelled to another boy. 'This fellow wants to know where your old one lives.'

This was more than I had bargained for. Then a thin, good-looking boy of about my own age detached himself from the group and came up to me with his fists clenched. I was feeling distinctly panicky, but all the same I studied him closely. After all, he was the boy I might have been.

'What do you want to know for?' he asked suspiciously.

Again, this was something I had not anticipated.

'My father was a great friend of your mother,' I explained carefully, but, so far as he was concerned, I might as well have been talking a foreign language. It was clear that Gussie O'Brien had no sense of history.

'What's that?' he asked incredulously.

At this point we were interrupted by a woman I had noticed earlier, talking to another over the railing between the two steep gardens. She was small and untidy-looking and occasionally rocked the pram in an absent-minded way as though she only remembered it at intervals.

'What is it, Gussie?' she cried, raising herself on tiptoe to see us better.

'I don't really want to disturb your mother, thank you,' I said, in something like hysterics, but Gussie anticipated me, actually pointing me out to her in a manner I had been brought up to regard as rude.

'This fellow wants you,' he bawled.

'I don't really,' I murmured, feeling that now I was in for it. She skipped down the high flight of steps to the gate with a laughing, puzzled air, her eyes in slits and her right hand arranging her hair at the back. It was not carroty as Mother described it, though it had red lights when the sun caught it.

'What is it, little boy?' she asked coaxingly, bending forward.

'I didn't really want anything, thank you,' I said in terror. 'It was just that my daddy said you lived up here, and, as I was changing my book at the library, I thought I'd come up and inquire. You can see,' I added, showing her the book as proof, 'that I've only just been to the library.'

'But who is your daddy, little boy?' she asked, her grey eyes still in long, laughing slits. 'What's your name?'

'My name is Delaney,' I said. 'Larry Delaney.'

'Not *Mike* Delaney's boy?' she exclaimed wonderingly. 'Well, for God's sake! Sure, I should have known it from that big head of yours.' She passed her hand down the back of my head and laughed. 'If you'd only get your hair cut I wouldn't be long recognizing you. You wouldn't think I'd know the feel of your old fellow's head, would you?' she added roguishly.

'No, Mrs O'Brien,' I replied meekly.

'Why, then indeed I do, and more along with it,' she added in the same saucy tone, though the meaning of what she said was not clear to me. 'Ah, come in and give us a good look at you! That's my eldest, Gussie, you were talking to,' she added, taking my hand. Gussie trailed behind us for a purpose I only recognized later.

'Ma-a-a-a, who's dat fella with you?' yelled a fat little girl who had been playing hopscotch on the pavement.

'That's Larry Delaney,' her mother sang over her shoulder. I don't know what it was about that woman but there was something about her high spirits that made her more like a regiment than a woman. You felt that everyone should fall into step behind her. 'Mick Delaney's son from Barrackton. I nearly married his old fellow once. Did he ever tell you that, Larry?' she added slyly. She made sudden swift transitions from brilliance to intimacy that I found attractive.

'Yes, Mrs O'Brien, he did,' I replied, trying to sound as roguish as she, and she went off into a delighted laugh, tossing her red head.

'Ah, look at that now! How well the old divil didn't forget me! You can tell him I didn't forget him either. And if I married him, I'd be your mother now. Wouldn't that be a queer old three and fourpence? How would you like me for a mother, Larry?'

'Very much, thank you,' I said complacently.

'Ah, go on with you, you would not,' she exclaimed, but she was pleased all the same. She struck me as the sort of woman it would be easy enough to please. 'Your old fellow always said it: your mother was a *most* superior woman, and you're a *most* superior child. Ah, and I'm not too bad myself either,' she added with a laugh and a shrug, wrinkling up her merry little face.

In the kitchen she cut me a slice of bread, smothered it with jam, and gave me a big mug of milk. 'Will you have some, Gussie?' she asked in a sharp voice as if she knew only too well what the answer would be. 'Aideen,' she said to the horrible little girl who had followed us in, 'aren't you fat and ugly enough without making a pig of yourself? Murder the Loaf we call her,' she added smilingly to me. 'You're a polite little boy, Larry, but damn the politeness you'd have if you had to deal with them. Is the book for your mother?'

'Oh, no, Mrs O'Brien,' I replied. 'It's my own.'

'You mean you can read a big book like that?' she asked incredulously, taking it from my hands and measuring the length of it with a puzzled air.

'Oh, yes, I can.'

'I don't believe you,' she said mockingly. 'Go on and prove it!'

There was nothing I asked better than to prove it. I felt that as a performer I had never got my due, so I stood in the middle of the kitchen, cleared my throat, and began with great feeling to enunciate one of those horribly involved opening paragraphs you found in children's books of the time. 'On a fine evening in Spring, as the setting sun was beginning to gild the blue peaks with its lambent rays, a rider, recognizable as a student by certain niceties of attire, was slowly, and perhaps regretfully making his way . . .' It was the sort of opening sentence I loved.

'I declare to God!' Mrs O'Brien interrupted in astonishment. 'And that fellow there is one age with you, and he can't spell house. How well you wouldn't be down at the library, you caubogue, you! . . . That's enough now, Larry,' she added hastily as I made ready to entertain them further.

'Who wants to read that blooming old stuff?' Gussie said contemptuously.

Later, he took me upstairs to show me his air rifle and model aeroplanes. Every detail of the room is still clear to me: the view into the back garden with its jungle of wild plants where Gussie had pitched his tent (a bad site for a tent as I patiently explained to him, owing to the danger from wild beasts); the three cots still unmade; the scribbles on the walls; and Mrs O'Brien's voice from the kitchen telling Aideen to see what was wrong with the baby, who was screaming his head off from the pram outside the front door. Gussie, in particular, fascinated me. He was spoiled, clever, casual; good-looking, with his mother's small clean features; gay and calculating. I saw that when I left and his mother gave me a sixpence. Naturally I refused it politely, but she thrust it into my trouser pocket, and Gussie dragged at her skirt, noisily demanding something for himself.

'If you give him a tanner you ought to give me a tanner,' he yelled.

'I'll tan you,' she said laughingly.

'Well, give up a lop anyway,' he begged, and she did give him a penny to take his face off her, as she said herself, and after that he followed me down the street and suggested we should go to the shop and buy sweets. I was simple-minded, but I wasn't an out-and-out fool, and I knew that if I went to a sweet-shop with Gussie I should end up with no sixpence and very few sweets. So I told him I could not buy sweets without Mother's permission, at which he gave me up altogether as a sissy or worse.

It had been an exhausting afternoon but a very instructive one. In the twilight I went back slowly over the bridges, a little regretful for that fast-moving, colourful household, but with a new appreciation for my own home. When I went in the lamp was lit over the fireplace and Father was at his tea.

'What kept you, child?' Mother asked with an anxious air, and suddenly I felt slightly guilty, and I played it as I usually did whenever I was at fault – in a loud, demonstrative, grown-up way. I stood in the middle of the kitchen with my cap in my hand and pointed it first at one, then at the other.

'You wouldn't believe who I met!' I said dramatically.

'Wisha, who, child?' Mother asked.

'Miss Cadogan,' I said, placing my cap squarely on a chair, and turning on them both again. 'Miss May Cadogan. Mrs O'Brien as she is now.'

'Mrs O'Brien?' Father exclaimed, putting down his cup. 'But where did you meet Mrs O'Brien?'

'I said you wouldn't believe it. It was near the library. I was talking to some fellows, and what do you think but one of them was Gussie O'Brien, Mrs O'Brien's son. And he took me home with him, and his mother gave me bread and jam, and she gave me *this*.' I produced the sixpence with a real flourish.

'Well, I'm blowed!' Father gasped, and first he looked at me, and then he looked at Mother and burst into a loud guffaw.

'And she said to tell you she remembers you too, and that she sent her love.'

'Oh, by the jumping bell of Athlone!' Father crowed and clapped his hands on his knees. I could see he believed the story I had told and was delighted with it, and I could see, too, that Mother did not believe it and that she was not in the least delighted. That, of course, was the trouble with Mother. Though she would do anything to help me with an intellectual problem, she never seemed to understand the need for experiment. She never opened her mouth while Father cross-questioned me, shaking his head in wonder and storing it up to tell the men in the factory. What pleased him most was Mrs O'Brien's remembering the shape of his head, and later, while Mother was

out of the kitchen, I caught him looking in the mirror and strok-
ing the back of his head.

But I knew too that for the first time I had managed to produce
in Mother the unrest that Father could produce, and I felt
wretched and guilty and didn't know why. This was an aspect of
history I only studied later.

That night I was really able to indulge my passion. At last
I had the material to work with. I was myself as Gussie O'Brien,
standing in the bedroom, looking down at my tent in the garden,
and Aideen as my sister, and Mrs O'Brien as my mother, and,
like Pascal, I re-created history. I remembered Mrs O'Brien's
laughter, her scolding, and the way she stroked my head. I knew
she was kind – casually kind – and hot-tempered, and recognized
that in dealing with her I must somehow be a different sort of
person. Being good at reading would never satisfy her. She
would almost compel you to be as Gussie was: flattering, imper-
tinent, and exacting. Though I couldn't have expressed it in
those terms, she was the sort of woman who would compel you
to flirt with her.

Then, when I had had enough, I deliberately soothed myself
as I did whenever I had scared myself by pretending that there
was a burglar in the house or a wild animal trying to get in the
attic window. I just crossed my hands on my chest, looked up at
the window, and said to myself: 'It is not like that. I am not
Gussie O'Brien. I am Larry Delaney, and my mother is Mary
Delaney, and we live in Number Eight, Wellington Square.
Tomorrow I'll go to school at the Cross, and first there will be
prayers, and then arithmetic, and after that composition.'

For the first time the charm did not work. I had ceased to be
Gussie, all right, but somehow I had not become myself again,
not any self that I knew. It was as though my own identity was a
sort of sack I had to live in, and I had deliberately worked my
way out of it, and now I couldn't get back again because I had
grown too big for it. I practised every trick I knew to reassure
myself. I tried to play a counting game; then I prayed, but even
the prayer seemed different, as though it didn't belong to me
at all. I was away in the middle of empty space, divorced from
mother and home and everything permanent and familiar.
Suddenly I found myself sobbing. The door opened and Mother
came in in her nightdress, shivering, her hair over her face.

'You're not sleeping, child,' she said in a wan and complaining voice.

I snivelled, and she put her hand on my forehead.

'You're hot,' she said. 'What ails you?'

I could not tell her of the nightmare in which I was lost. Instead, I took her hand, and gradually the terror retreated, and I became myself again, shrank into my little skin of identity, and left infinity and all its anguish behind.

'Mummy,' I said, 'I promise I never wanted anyone but you.'

I WAS always very fond of heights, and afterwards it struck me that reading was only another form of height, and a more perilous one. It was a way of looking beyond your own back yard into the neighbours'. Our back yard had a high wall, and by early afternoon it made the whole kitchen dark, and when the evening was fine, I climbed the door of the outhouse and up the roof to the top of the wall. It was on a level with the respectable terrace behind ours, which had front gardens and a fine view, and I often sat there for hours on terms of relative equality with the policeman in the first house who dug close beside me and gave me ugly looks but could not think up a law to keep me from sitting on my own back wall. From this I could see Gardiner's Hill falling headlong to the valley of the city, with its terraces of tall houses and its crest of dark trees. It was all lit up when our little house was already in darkness. In the mornings, the first thing I did when I got up was to mount a chair under the attic window and push up the window-frame to see the same hillside when it was still in shadow and its colours had the stiffness of early-morning light. I have a distinct recollection of climbing out the attic window and, after negotiating the peril of the raised window-frame, crawling up the roof to the ridge to enlarge my field of view, but Mother must have caught me at this, because I do not remember having done it often.

Then there was the quarry that fell sheer from the neighbourhood of the barrack to the Ballyhooley Road. It was a noisome place where people dumped their rubbish and gangs of wild kids had stoning matches after school and poor people from the lanes poked among the rubbish for spoil, but I ignored them and picked my way through the discarded bully-beef tins and climbed to some ledge of rock or hollow in the quarry face, and sat there happily, surveying the whole neighbourhood from Mayfield Chapel, which crowned the hillside on the edge of the open country, to the spire of Saint Luke's Church below me, and

below that again, in the distance was the River Lee with its
funnels and masts, and the blue hills over it. Immediately beneath
me was the Ballyhooley Road, winding up the hill from Saint
Luke's Cross, with its little houses and their tiny front gardens,
and (on the side nearest me) the back yards where the women
came to peg up their washing; and all the time the shadow moved
with a chill you could feel, and the isolated spots of sunlight
contracted and their colour deepened. I felt like some sort of
wild bird, secure from everything and observing everything –
the horse and cart coming up the road, the little girl with her
skipping rope on the pavement, or the old man staggering by on
his stick – all of them unconscious of the eagle eye that watched
them.

THE MAN OF THE WORLD

WHEN I was a kid there were no such things as holidays for me and my likes, and I have no feeling of grievance about it because, in the way of kids, I simply invented them, which was much more satisfactory. One year, my summer holiday was a couple of nights I spent at the house of a friend called Jimmy Leary, who lived at the other side of the road from us. His parents sometimes went away for a couple of days to visit a sick relative in Bantry, and he was given permission to have a friend in to keep him company. I took my holiday with the greatest seriousness, insisted on the loan of Father's old travelling bag and dragged it myself down our lane past the neighbours standing at their doors.

'Are you off somewhere, Larry?' asked one.

'Yes, Mrs Rooney,' I said with great pride. 'Off for my holidays to the Learys'.'

'Wisha, aren't you very lucky?' she said with amusement.

'Lucky' seemed an absurd description of my good fortune. The Learys' house was a big one with a high flight of steps up to the front door, which was always kept shut. They had a piano in the front room, a pair of binoculars on a table near the window, and a toilet on the stairs that seemed to me to be the last word in elegance and immodesty. We brought the binoculars up to the bedroom with us. From the window you could see the whole road up and down, from the quarry at its foot with the tiny houses perched on top of it to the open fields at the other end, where the last gas lamp rose against the sky. Each morning I was up with the first light, leaning out the window in my nightshirt and watching through the glasses all the mysterious figures you never saw from our lane: policemen, railwaymen, and farmers on their way to market.

I admired Jimmy almost as much as I admired his house, and for much the same reasons. He was a year older than I, was well-mannered and well-dressed, and would not associate with most of the kids on the road at all. He had a way when any of them joined us of resting against a wall with his hands in his trousers pockets and listening to them with a sort of well-bred smile, a knowing smile, that seemed to me the height of elegance. And it was not that he was a softy, because he was an excellent boxer and wrestler and could easily have held his own with them any time, but he did not wish to. He was superior to them. He was – there is only one word that still describes it for me – sophisticated.

I attributed his sophistication to the piano, the binoculars, and the indoor john, and felt that if only I had the same advantages I could have been sophisticated, too. I knew I wasn't, because I was always being deceived by the world of appearances. I would take a sudden violent liking to some boy, and when I went to his house my admiration would spread to his parents and sisters, and I would think how wonderful it must be to have such a home; but when I told Jimmy he would smile in that knowing way of his and say quietly: 'I believe they had the bailiffs in a few weeks ago,' and, even though I didn't know what bailiffs were, bang would go the whole world of appearances, and I would realize that once again I had been deceived.

It was the same with fellows and girls. Seeing some bigger chap we knew walking out with a girl for the first time, Jimmy would say casually: 'He'd better mind himself: that one is dynamite.' And, even though I knew as little of girls who were dynamite as I did of bailiffs, his tone would be sufficient to indicate that I had been taken in by sweet voices and broad-brimmed hats, gaslight and evening smells from gardens.

Forty years later I can still measure the extent of my obsession, for, though my own handwriting is almost illegible, I sometimes find myself scribbling idly on a pad in a small, stiff, perfectly legible hand that I recognize with amusement as a reasonably good forgery of Jimmy's. My admiration still lies there somewhere, a fossil in my memory, but Jimmy's knowing smile is something I have never managed to acquire.

And it all goes back to my curiosity about fellows and girls. As I say, I only imagined things about them, but Jimmy knew. I was excluded from knowledge by the world of appearances that blinded and deafened me with emotion. The least thing could excite or depress me: the trees in the morning when I went to early Mass, the stained-glass windows in the church, the blue hilly streets at evening with the green flare of the gas lamps, the smells of cooking and perfume – even the smell of a cigarette packet that I had picked up from the gutter and crushed to my nose – all kept me at this side of the world of appearances, while Jimmy, by right of birth or breeding, was always at the other. I wanted him to tell me what it was like, but he didn't seem to be able.

Then one evening he was listening to me talk while he leant against the pillar of his gate, his pale neat hair framing his pale, good-humoured face. My excitability seemed to rouse in him a mixture of amusement and pity.

'Why don't you come over some night the family is away and I'll show you a few things?' he asked lightly.

'What'll you show me, Jimmy?' I asked eagerly.

'Noticed the new couple that's come to live next door?' he asked with a nod in the direction of the house above his own.

'No,' I admitted in disappointment. It wasn't only that I never knew anything but I never noticed anything either. And when he described the new family that was lodging there, I realized with chagrin that I didn't even know Mrs MacCarthy, who owned the house.

'Oh, they're just a newly married couple,' he said. 'They don't know that they can be seen from our house.'

'But how, Jimmy?'

'Don't look up now,' he said with a dreamy smile while his eyes strayed over my shoulder in the direction of the lane. 'Wait till you're going away. Their end wall is only a couple of feet from ours. You can see right into the bedroom from our attic.'

'And what do they do, Jimmy?'

'Oh,' he said with a pleasant laugh, 'everything. You really should come.'

'You bet I'll come,' I said, trying to sound tougher than I felt. It wasn't that I saw anything wrong in it. It was rather that, for all my desire to become like Jimmy, I was afraid of what it might do to me.

But it wasn't enough for me to get behind the world of appearances. I had to study the appearances themselves, and for three evenings I stood under the gas lamp at the foot of our lane, across the road from the MacCarthys', till I had identified the new lodgers. The husband was the first I spotted, because he came from his work at a regular hour. He was tall, with stiff jet-black hair and a big black guardsman's moustache that somehow failed to conceal the youthfulness and ingenuousness of his face, which was long and lean. Usually, he came accompanied by an older man, and stood chatting for a few minutes outside his door – a black-coated, bowler-hatted figure who made large, sweeping gestures with his evening paper and sometimes doubled up in an explosion of loud laughter.

On the third evening I saw his wife – for she had obviously been waiting for him, looking from behind the parlour curtains, and when she saw him she scurried down the steps to join in the conversation. She had thrown an old jacket about her shoulders and stood there, her arms folded as though to protect herself further from the cold wind that blew down the hill from the open country, while her husband rested one hand fondly on her shoulder.

For the first time, I began to feel qualms about what I proposed to do. It was one thing to do it to people you didn't know or care about, but, for me, even to recognize people was to adopt an emotional attitude towards them, and my attitude to this pair was already one of approval. They looked like people who might approve of me, too. That night I remained awake, thinking out the terms of an anonymous letter that would put them on their guard, till I had worked myself up into a fever of eloquence and indignation.

But I knew only too well that they would recognize the villain of the letter and that the villain would recognize me, so I did not write it. Instead, I gave way to fits of anger and moodiness against my parents. Yet even these were unreal, because on Saturday night when Mother made a parcel of my nightshirt – I had now become sufficiently self-conscious not to take a bag – I nearly broke down. There was something about my own house that night that upset me all over again. Father, with his cap over his eyes, was sitting under the wall-lamp, reading the paper, and Mother, a shawl about her shoulders, was crouched over the fire from her little wickerwork chair, listening; and I realized that they, too, were part of the world of appearances I was planning to destroy, and as I said good-night I almost felt that I was saying good-bye to them as well.

But once inside Jimmy's house I did not care so much. It always had that effect on me, of blowing me up to twice the size, as though I were expanding to greet the piano, the binoculars, and the indoor toilet. I tried to pick out a tune on the piano with one hand, and Jimmy, having listened with amusement for some time, sat down and played it himself as I felt it should be played, and this, too, seemed to be part of his superiority.

'I suppose we'd better put in an appearance of going to bed,' he said disdainfully. 'Someone across the road might notice and tell. *They're* in town, so I don't suppose they'll be back till late.'

We had a glass of milk in the kitchen, went upstairs, undressed, and lay down, though we put our overcoats beside the bed. Jimmy had a packet of sweets but insisted on keeping them till later. 'We may need these before we're done,' he said with his knowing smile, and again I admired his orderliness and restraint. We talked in bed for a quarter of an hour; then put out the light, got up again, donned our overcoats and socks, and tiptoed upstairs to the attic. Jimmy led the way with an electric torch. He was a fellow who thought of everything. The attic had been arranged for our vigil. Two trunks had been drawn up to the little window to act as seats, and there were even cushions on them. Looking out, you could at first see nothing but an expanse of blank wall topped with chimney stacks, but gradually you could make out the outline of a single window, eight or ten feet below. Jimmy sat beside me and opened his packet of sweets, which he laid between us.

'Of course, we could have stayed in bed till we heard them come in,' he whispered. 'Usually you can hear them at the front door, but they might have come in quietly or we might have fallen asleep. It's always best to make sure.'

'But why don't they draw the blind?' I asked as my heart began to beat uncomfortably.

'Because there isn't a blind,' he said with a quiet chuckle. 'Old Mrs MacCarthy never had one, and she's not going to put one in for lodgers who may be gone tomorrow. People like that never rest till they get a house of their own.'

I envied him his nonchalance as he sat back with his legs crossed, sucking a sweet just as though he were waiting in the cinema for the show to begin. I was scared by the darkness and the mystery, and by the sounds that came to us from the road with such extraordinary clarity. Besides, of course, it wasn't my house and I didn't feel at home there. At any moment I expected the front door to open and his parents to come in and catch us.

We must have been waiting for half an hour before we heard voices in the roadway, the sound of a key in the latch and, then, of a door opening and closing softly. Jimmy reached out and touched my arm lightly. 'This is probably our pair,' he whispered. 'We'd better not speak any more in case they might hear us.' I nodded, wishing I had never come. At that moment a faint light became visible in the great expanse of black wall, a faint, yellow stairlight that was just sufficient to silhouette the window frame beneath us. Suddenly the whole room lit up. The man I had seen in the street stood by the doorway, his hand still on the switch. I could see it all plainly now, an ordinary small, suburban bedroom with flowery wallpaper, a coloured picture of the Sacred Heart over the double bed with the big brass knobs, a wardrobe, and a dressing-table.

The man stood there till the woman came in, removing her hat in a single wide gesture and tossing it from her into a corner of the room. He still stood by the door, taking off his tie. Then he struggled with the collar, his head raised and his face set in an agonized expression. His wife kicked off her shoes, sat on a chair by the bed, and began to take off her stockings. All the time she seemed to be talking because her head was raised, looking at him, though you couldn't hear a word she said. I glanced at Jimmy. The light from the window below softly illumined his face as he sucked with tranquil enjoyment.

The woman rose as her husband sat on the bed with his back to us and began to take off his shoes and socks in the same slow, agonized way. At one point he held up his left foot and looked at it with what might have been concern. His wife looked at it, too, for a moment and then swung half-way round as she unbuttoned her skirt. She undressed in swift, jerky movements, twisting and turning and apparently talking all the time. At one moment she looked into the mirror on the dressing-table and touched her cheek lightly. She crouched as she took off her slip, and then pulled her nightdress over her head and finished her undressing beneath it. As removed her underclothes she seemed to throw them anywhere at all, and I had a strong impression that there was something haphazard and disorderly about her. Her husband was different. Everything he removed seemed to be removed in order and then put carefully where he could find it most readily in the morning. I watched him take out his watch, look at it carefully, wind it, and then hang it neatly over the bed.

Then, to my surprise, she knelt by the bed, facing towards the window, glanced up at the picture of the Sacred Heart, made a large hasty Sign of the Cross, and, covering her face with her hands, buried her head in the bedclothes. I looked at Jimmy in dismay, but he did not seem to be embarrassed by the sight. The husband, his folded trousers in his hand, moved about the room slowly and carefully, as though he did not wish to disturb his wife's devotions, and when he pulled on the trousers of his pyjamas he turned away. After that he put on his pyjama jacket, buttoned it carefully, and knelt beside her. He, too, glanced respectfully at the picture and crossed himself slowly and reverently, but he did not bury his face and head as she had done. He knelt upright with nothing of the abandonment suggested by her pose, and with an expression that combined reverence and self-respect. It was the expression of an employee who, while admitting that he might have a few little weaknesses like the rest of the staff, prided himself on having deserved well of the management. Women, his slightly complacent air seemed to indicate, had to adopt these emotional attitudes, but he spoke to God as one man to another. He finished his prayers before his wife; again he crossed himself slowly, rose, and climbed into bed, glancing again at his watch as he did so.

Several minutes passed before she put her hands out before her on the bed, blessed herself in her wide, sweeping way, and rose. She crossed the room in a swift movement that almost escaped me, and next moment the light went out – it was as if the window through which we had watched the scene had disappeared with it by magic, till nothing was left but a blank black wall mounting to the chimney pots.

Jimmy rose slowly and pointed the way out to me with his flashlight. When we got downstairs we put on the bedroom light, and I saw on his face the virtuous and sophisticated air of a collector who has shown you all his treasures in the best possible light. Faced with that look, I could not bring myself to mention the woman at prayer, though I felt her image would be impressed on my memory till the day I died. I could not have explained to him how at that moment everything had changed for me, how, beyond us watching the young married couple from ambush, I had felt someone else watching us, so that at once we ceased to be the observers and became the observed. And the observed in such a humiliating position that nothing I could imagine our victims doing would have been so degrading.

I wanted to pray myself but found I couldn't. Instead, I lay in bed in the darkness, covering my eyes with my hand, and I think that even then I knew that I should never be sophisticated like Jimmy, never be able to put on a knowing smile, because always beyond the world of appearances I would see only eternity watching.

'Sometimes, of course, it's better than that,' Jimmy's drowsy voice said from the darkness. 'You shouldn't judge it by tonight.'

FATHER PLAYED the big drum in the Blackpool Brass and Reed Band, and as I was the only child, I had often to accompany him, much against my will, on his Sunday trips to the band room or on band promenades at holiday resorts. The Cork bands were divided into supporters of William O'Brien and supporters of John Redmond, two rival Irish politicians with little to distinguish them except their personalities – flamboyant in O'Brien and frigid in Redmond. The Blackpool Band was an O'Brienite group, and our policy was 'Conciliation and Consent', whatever that meant. The Redmond supporters we called Molly Maguires, and I have forgotten what their policy was – if they had one. Our national anthem was 'God Save Ireland' and theirs 'A Nation Once Again'. I was often filled with pity for the poor degraded children of the Molly Maguires, who paraded the streets with tin cans, singing (to the tune of 'John Brown's Body': 'We'll Hang William O'Brien on a Sour Apple Tree'. Sometimes passion overcame me till I got a tin can of my own and paraded up and down, singing: 'We'll Hang Johnny Redmond on a Sour Apple Tree'.

The bandsmen shared our attitudes. There were frequent riots, and during election times Father came home with a drumstick up his sleeve – a useful weapon if he was attacked by Molly Maguires. There were even more serious incidents. Bandsmen raided a rival band room and smashed up the instruments, and one of Father's most gloomy songs listed some of the men who had done this:

> Creedy, Reidy, Dessy, and Snell,
> Not judging their souls, they're already in Hell.
> The night of the battle we'll show them some fun;
> We'll hang up the ruffian that stole our big drum.

Almost all the bandsmen were ex-bandsmen of the British Army, as Father was; and I think it may have been something of a tragedy to them that when once they returned to Cork, music became less important than the political faction for whom they made it. Father was devoted to the policy and personality of William O'Brien, who had married the daughter of one of the great Franco-Jewish bankers. It was Sophie Raffalovitch's mother who had started the romance by sending to O'Brien when he was in gaol a verse of Racine with an eagle's feather enclosed, but I am glad that when Sophie O'Brien was old and poor in France during the German occupation, the Irish Government protected her and paid her an allowance. Once, when there were threats of a Molly Maguire attack, Father, an enormously powerful man, acted as bodyguard for William O', and William O' thanked him personally and handed him a pound note. All the same, for several years Father had been big drummer of a Molly Maguire band. It was a superb band, and Father liked music so well that he preferred it to politics. For the sake of the music he even endured the indignity of playing for Johnny Redmond. Naturally, whenever he attended a demonstration at which William O' was criticized, he withdrew, like a good Catholic from a heretical service. What made him leave the Molly band and join the Blackpool Band I never knew. It was a period that for some reason he never liked to talk about, and I suspect that someone in the band must have impugned him by calling him a turncoat. That is the sort of thing that would have broken his spirit, for he was a proud man and a high-principled one, though what his principles were based on was more than I ever discovered. He was the one who insisted on the 'O'Donovan' form of the name, and it must have been his absence at the Boer War that explains my being described as 'Donovan' on my birth certificate. He would not permit a slighting reference to William O'Brien, and reading the *Echo*, the only evening paper in Cork, and a Molly one, was as much a torment as a pleasure to him. 'There were about 130 people present, most of them women, with a sprinkling of children' was how the *Echo* would describe any meeting of O'Brien's, and Father would raise his eyes to Heaven, calling on God to witness that anything the *Echo* said was untrue. 'Oh, listen to George Crosbie, the dirty little caffler!' he would cry with mortification. In days when no one else that I knew seemed to worry about it, he was a passionate believer in buying Irish manufactures, and often sent me back to the shop with a box of English matches that had been passed off on me. He was a strong supporter of Jim Larkin, the Irish Labour leader; for months when he was out on strike we practically didn't eat, but we always bought *The Irish Worker*, Larkin's paper, and I was permitted to read it aloud because my dramatic style of reading suited Larkin's dramatic style of journalism. According to Mother, there was a period in my infancy when Father didn't drink for two years. He had drunk himself penniless, as he frequently did, and some old friend had refused him a loan. The slight had cut him so deep that he stopped drinking at once. The friend was wrong if he assumed that Father would not have repaid that or any other loan, but, still, it was a great pity that he hadn't a few more friends of the sort.

It was no joke to go with Father on one of his Sunday outings with the band, and I often kicked up hell about it, but Mother liked me to go, because she had some strange notion that I could restrain him from drinking too much. Not that I didn't love music, nor that I wasn't proud of Father as, with the drum slung high about his neck, he glanced left and right of it, waiting to give the three taps that brought the bandsmen in. He was a drummer of the classical type: he hated to see a man carry his drum on his belly instead of his chest, and he had nothing but scorn for the showy drummers who swung or crossed their sticks. He was almost disappointingly unpretentious.

But when he was on the drink, I was so uncertain that I always had the feeling that one day he would lose me and forget I had been with him at all. Usually, the band would end its piece in front of a pub at the corner of Coburg Street. The pubs were always shut on Sunday until after last Mass, and when they opened, it was only for an hour or two. The last notes of 'Brian Boru's March' would hardly have been played before Father unslung the drum, thrust it on the young fellows whose job it was to carry it, and dashed across the road to the pub, accompanied by John P., his great buddy. John P. – I never knew what his surname was – was a long string of misery, with an air of unutterable gravity, emphasized by the way he sucked in his cheeks. He was one of the people vaguely known as 'followers of the band' – a group of lonely souls who gave some significance to their simple lives by attaching themselves to the band. They discussed its policies and personalities, looked after the instruments, and knew every pub in Cork that would risk receiving its members after hours. John P., with a look of intense concentration, would give a secret knock on the side door of the pub and utter what seemed to be whispered endearments through the keyhole, and more and more bandsmen would join the group peppering outside, while messengers rushed up to them shouting: 'Come on, can't ye, come on! The bloomin' train will be gone!'

That would be the first of the boring and humiliating waits outside public houses that went on all day and were broken only when I made a scene and Father gave me a penny to keep me quiet. Afterwards it would be the seaside at Aghada – which wasn't so bad because my maternal grandmother's people, the Kellys, still lived there and they would give me a cup of tea – or Crosshaven, or the grounds of Blarney Castle, and in the intervals of playing, the band would sit in various public houses with the doors barred, and if I was inside I couldn't get out, and – what was worse for a shy small boy – if I was out I couldn't get in. It was all very boring and alarming, and I remember once at Blarney, in my discouragement, staking my last penny on a dice game called the Harp, Crown, and Feather in the hope of retrieving a wasted day. Being a patriotic child, with something of Father's high principle, I put my money on the national emblem and lost. This was prophetic, because since then I have lost a great many pennies on the national emblem, but at least it cured me of the more obvious forms of gambling for the rest of my days. [...]

So far keeping him off the drink, I never did it but once, when I drank his pint, became very drunk, smashed my head against a wall, and had to be steered home by himself and John P., both of them mad with frustration and panic, and be put to bed.

THE CORNET PLAYER WHO
BETRAYED IRELAND

AT THIS hour of my life I don't profess to remember what we inhabitants of Blarney Lane were patriotic about: all I remember is that we were very patriotic, that our main principles were something called 'Conciliation and Consent', and that our great national leader, William O'Brien, once referred to us as 'The Old Guard'. Myself and other kids of the Old Guard used to parade the street with tin cans and toy trumpets, singing 'We'll hang Johnnie Redmond on a sour apple tree'. (John Redmond, I need hardly say, was the leader of the other side.)

Unfortunately, our neighbourhood was bounded to the south by a long ugly street leading uphill to the cathedral, and the lanes off it were infested with the most wretched specimens of human-ity who took the Redmondite side for whatever could be got from it in the way of drink. My personal view at the time was that the Redmondite faction was maintained by a conspiracy of publicans and brewers. It always saddened me, coming through this street on my way from school, and seeing the poor misguided children, barefoot and in rags, parading with tin cans and toy trumpets and singing 'We'll hang William O'Brien on a sour apple tree'. It left me with very little hope for Ireland.

Of course, my father was a strong supporter of 'Conciliation and Consent'. The parish priest who had come to solicit his vote for Redmond had told him he would go straight to Hell, but my father had replied quite respectfully that if Mr O'Brien was an agent of the devil, as Father Murphy said, he would go gladly.

I admired my father as a rock of principle. As well as being a house-painter (a regrettable trade which left him for six months 'under the ivy', as we called it), he was a musician. He had been a bandsman in the British Army, played the cornet extremely well, and had been a member of the Irishtown Brass and Reed Band from its foundation. At home we had two big pictures of the band after each of its most famous contests, in Belfast and Dublin. It was after the Dublin contest when Irishtown emerged as the premier brass band that there occurred an unrecorded episode in operatic history. In those days the best band in the city was always invited to perform in the Soldiers' Chorus scene in Gounod's *Faust*. Of course, they were encored to the echo, and then, ignoring conductor and everything else, they burst into a selection from Moore's Irish Melodies. I am glad my father didn't live to see the day of pipers' bands. Even fife and drum bands he looked on as primitive.

As he had great hopes of turning me into a musician too he frequently brought me with him to practices and promenades. Irishtown was a very poor quarter of the city, a channel of mean houses between breweries and builders' yards with the terraced hillsides high above it on either side, and nothing but the white Restoration spire of Shandon breaking the skyline. You came to a little footbridge over the narrow stream; on one side of it was a red-brick chapel, and when we arrived there were usually some of the bandsmen sitting on the bridge, spitting back over their shoulders into the stream. The bandroom was over an undertaker's shop at the other side of the street. It was a long, dark, barn-like erection overlooking the bridge and decorated with group photos of the band. At this hour of a Sunday morning it was always full of groans, squeaks and bumps.

Then at last came the moment I loved so much. Out in the sunlight, with the bridge filled with staring pedestrians, the band formed up. Dickie Ryan, the bandmaster's son, and myself took our places at either side of the big drummer, Joe Shinkwin. Joe peered over his big drum to right and left to see if all were in place and ready; he raised his right arm and gave the drum three solemn flakes: then, after the third thump the whole narrow channel of the street filled with a roaring torrent of drums and brass, the mere physical impact of which hit me in the belly. Screaming girls in shawls tore along the pavements calling out to the bandsmen, but nothing shook the soldierly solemnity of the men with their eyes almost crossed on the music before them. I've heard Toscanini conduct Beethoven, but compared with Irishtown playing 'Marching Through Georgia' on a Sunday morning it was only like Mozart in a girls' school. The mean little houses, quivering with the shock, gave it back to us: the terraced hillsides that shut out the sky gave it back to us: the interested faces of passers-by in their Sunday clothes from the pavements were like mirrors reflecting the glory of the music. When the band stopped and again you could hear the gapped sound of feet, and people running and chattering, it was like a parachute jump into commonplace.

Sometimes we boarded the paddle-steamer and set up our music stands in some little field by the sea, which all day echoed of Moore's Melodies, Rossini, and Gilbert and Sullivan: sometimes we took a train into the country to play at some sports meeting. Whatever it was, I loved it, though I never got a dinner: I was fed on lemonade, biscuits and sweets, and, as my father spent most of the intervals in the pub, I was sometimes half mad with boredom.

One summer day we were playing at a fête in the grounds of Blarney Castle, and, as usual, the band departed to the pub and Dickie Ryan and myself were left behind, ostensibly to take care of the instruments. A certain hanger-on of the band, one John P., who to my knowledge was never called anything else, was lying on the grass, chewing a straw and shading his eyes from the light with the back of his hand. Dickie and I took a side drum each and began to march about with them. All at once Dickie began to sing to his own accompaniment, 'We'll hang William O'Brien on a sour apple tree'. I was so astonished that I stopped drumming and listened to him. For a moment or two I thought he must be mocking the poor uneducated children of the lanes round Shandon Street. Then I suddenly realized that he meant it. Without hesitation I began to rattle my side drum even louder and shouted 'We'll hang Johnnie Redmond on a sour apple tree'. John P. at once started up and gave me an angry glare. 'Stop that now, little boy!' he said threateningly. It was quite plain that he meant me, not Dickie Ryan.

I was completely flabbergasted. It was bad enough hearing the bandmaster's son singing a traitorous song, but then to be told to shut up by a fellow who wasn't even a bandsman; merely a hanger-on who looked after the music stands and carried the big drum in return for free drinks! I realized that I was among enemies. I quietly put aside the drum and went to find my father. I knew that he could have no idea what was going on behind his back in the band.

I found him at the back of the pub, sitting on a barrel and holding forth to a couple of young bandsmen.

'Now, "Brian Boru's March",' he was saying with one finger raised, 'that's a beautiful march. I heard the Irish Guards do that on Salisbury Plain, and they had the English fellows' eyes popping out. "Paddy," one of them says to me (they all call you Paddy), "wot's the name of the shouting march?" But somehow we don't get the same fire into it at all. Now, listen, and I'll show you how that should go!'

'Dadda,' I said in a whisper, pulling him by the sleeve, 'do you know what Dickie Ryan was singing?'

'Hold on a minute now,' he said, beaming at me affectionately. 'I just want to illustrate a little point.'

'But, Dadda,' I went on determinedly, 'he was singing "We'll hang William O'Brien from a sour apple tree".'

'Hah, hah, hah,' laughed my father, and it struck me that he hadn't fully appreciated the implications of what I had said.

'Frank,' he added, 'get a bottle of lemonade for the little fellow.'

'But, Dadda,' I said despairingly, 'when I sang "We'll hang Johnnie Redmond", John P. told me to shut up.'

'Now, now,' said my father with sudden testiness, 'that's not a nice song to be singing.'

This was a stunning blow. The anthem of 'Conciliation and Consent' – not a nice song to be singing!

'But, Dadda,' I wailed, 'aren't we *for* William O'Brien?'

'Yes, yes, yes,' he replied, as if I were goading him, 'but everyone to his own opinion. Now drink your lemonade and run out and play like a good boy.'

I drank my lemonade all right, but I went out not to play but to brood. There was but one fit place for that. I went to the shell of the castle; climbed the stair to the tower and leaning over the battlements watching the landscape like bunting all round me I thought of the heroes who had stood here, defying the might of England. Everyone to his own opinion! What would they have thought of a statement like that? It was the first time that I realized the awful strain of weakness and the lack of strong principle in my father, and understood that the old bandroom by the bridge was in the heart of enemy country and that all round me were enemies of Ireland like Dickie Ryan and John P.

It wasn't until months after that I realized how many there

were. It was Sunday morning, but when we reached the band-room there was no one on the bridge. Upstairs the room was almost full. A big man wearing a bowler hat and a flower in his buttonhole was standing before the fireplace. He had a red face with weak, red-rimmed eyes and a dark moustache. My father, who seemed as surprised as I was, slipped quietly into a seat behind the door and lifted me on to his knee.

'Well, boys,' the big man said in a deep husky voice, 'I suppose ye have a good notion what I'm here for. Ye know that next Saturday night Mr Redmond is arriving in the city, and I have the honour of being Chairman of the Reception Committee.'

'Well, Alderman Doyle,' said the bandmaster doubtfully, 'you know the way we feel about Mr Redmond, most of us anyway.'

'I do, Tim, I do,' said the alderman evenly as it gradually dawned on me that the man I was listening to was the Arch-Traitor, locally known as Scabby Doyle, the builder whose vile orations my father always read aloud to my mother with chagrined comments on Doyle's past history. 'But feeling isn't enough, Tim. Fair Lane Band will be there of course. Watergrasshill will be there. The Butler Exchange will be there. What will the backers of this band, the gentlemen who helped it through so many difficult days, say if we don't put in an appearance?'

'Well, ye see, Alderman,' said Ryan nervously, 'we have our own little difficulties.'

'I know that, Tim,' said Doyle. 'We all have our difficulties in troubled times like these, but we have to face them like men in the interests of the country. What difficulties have you?'

'Well, that's hard to describe, Alderman,' said the bandmaster.

'No, Tim,' said my father quietly, raising and putting me down from his knee, ''tis easy enough to describe. I'm the difficulty, and I know it.'

'Now, Mick,' protested the bandmaster, 'there's nothing personal about it. We're all old friends in this band.'

'We are, Tim,' agreed my father. 'And before ever it was heard of, you and me gave this bandroom its first coat of paint. But every man is entitled to his principles, and I don't want to stand in your light.'

'You see how it is, Mr Doyle,' said the bandmaster appealingly. 'We had others in the band that were of Mick Twomey's persuasion, but they left us to join O'Brienite bands. Mick didn't, nor we didn't want him to leave us.'

'Nor don't,' said a mournful voice, and I turned and saw a tall, gaunt, spectacled young man sitting on the window sill.

'I had three men,' said my father earnestly, holding up three fingers in illustration of the fact, 'three men up at the hours on different occasions to get me to join other bands. I'm not boasting. Tim Ryan knows who they were.'

'I do, I do,' said the bandmaster.

'And I wouldn't,' said my father passionately. 'I'm not boasting, but you can't deny it: there isn't another band in Ireland to touch ours.'

'Nor a cornet player in Ireland to touch Mick Twomey,' chimed in the gaunt young man, rising to his feet. 'And I'm not saying that to coddle or cock him up.'

'You're not, you're not,' said the bandmaster. 'No one can deny he's a musician.'

'And listen here to me, boys,' said the gaunt young man, with a wild wave of his arm, 'don't leave us be led astray by anyone. What were we before we had the old band? Nobody. We were no better than the poor devils that sit on that bridge outside all day, spitting into the river. Whatever we do, leave us be all agreed. What backers had we when we started, only what we could collect ourselves outside the chapel gates on Sunday, and hard enough to get permission for that itself? I'm as good a party man as anyone here, but what I say is, music is above politice. . . . Alderman Doyle,' he begged, 'tell Mr Redmond whatever he'll do not to break up our little band on us.'

'Jim Ralegh,' said the alderman, with his red-rimmed eyes growing moist, 'I'd sooner put my hand in the fire than injure this band. I know what ye are, a band of brothers. . . . Mick,' he boomed at my father, 'will you desert it in its hour of trial?'

'Ah,' said my father testily, 'is it the way you want me to play against William O'Brien?'

'Play against William O'Brien,' echoed the alderman. 'No one is asking you to play *against* anyone. As Jim Ralegh here says, music is above politice. What we're asking you to do is to play for something for the band, for the sake of unity. You know what'll happen if the backers withdraw? Can't you pocket your pride and make this sacrifice in the interest of the band?'

My father stood for a few moments, hesitating. I prayed for once he might see the true light; that he might show this group of misguided men the faith that was in him. Instead he nodded curtly, said 'Very well, I'll play,' and sat down again. The rascally alderman said a few humbugging words in his praise which didn't take me in. I don't think they even took my father in, for all the way home he never addressed a word to me. I saw then that his conscience was at him. He knew that by supporting the band in the unprincipled step it was taking he was showing himself a traitor to Ireland and our great leader, William O'Brien.

Afterwards, whenever Irishtown played at Redmondite demonstrations, my father accompanied them, but the moment the speeches began he retreated to the edge of the crowd, rather like a pious Catholic compelled to attend a heretical religious service, and stood against the wall with his hands in his pockets, passing slighting and witty comments on the speakers to any O'Brienites he might meet. But he had lost all dignity in my eyes. Even his gibes at Scabby Doyle seemed to me false, and I longed to say to him, 'If that's what you believe, why don't you show it?' Even the seaside lost its attraction when at any moment the beautiful daughter of a decent O'Brienite family might point to me and say: 'There is the son of the cornet player who betrayed Ireland.'

Then one Sunday we went to play at some idolatrous function in a seaside town called Bantry. While the meeting was on my father and the rest of the band retired to the pub and I with them. Even by my presence in the Square I wasn't prepared to countenance the proceedings. I was looking idly out of the window when I suddenly heard a roar of cheering and people began to scatter in all directions. I was mystified until someone outside started to shout, 'Come on, boys! The O'Brienites are trying to break up the meeting.' The bandsmen rushed for the door. I would have done the same but my father looked hastily over his shoulder and warned me to stay where I was. He was talking to a young clarinet player of serious appearance.

'Now,' he went on, raising his voice to drown the uproar outside. 'Teddy the Lamb was the finest clarinet player in the whole British Army.'

There was a fresh storm of cheering, and wild with excitement I saw the patriots begin to drive a deep wedge of whirling sticks through the heart of the enemy, cutting them into two fighting camps.

'Excuse me, Mick,' said the clarinet player, going white, 'I'll go and see what's up.'

'Now, whatever is up,' my father said appealingly, 'you can't do anything about it.'

'I'm not going to have it said I stopped behind while my friends were fighting for their lives,' said the young fellow hotly.

'There's no one fighting for their lives at all,' said my father irascibly, grabbing him by the arm. 'You have something else to think about. Man alive, you're a musician, not a bloody infantryman.'

'I'd sooner be that than a bloody turncoat, anyway,' said the young fellow, dragging himself off and making for the door.

'Thanks, Phil,' my father called after him in a voice of a man who had to speak before he has collected his wits. 'I well deserved that from you. I well deserved that from all of ye.' He took out his pipe and put it back into his pocket again. Then he joined me at the window and for a few moments he looked unseeingly at the milling crowd outside. 'Come on,' he said shortly.

Though the couples were wrestling in the very gutters no one accosted us on our way up the street; otherwise I feel murder might have been committed. We went to the house of some cousins and had tea, and when we reached the railway station my father led me to a compartment near the engine; not the carriage reserved for the band. Though we had ten minutes to wait it wasn't until just before the whistle went that Tim Ryan, the bandmaster, spotted us through the window.

'Mick!' he shouted in astonishment. 'Where the hell were you? I had men out all over the town looking for you! Is it anything wrong?'

'Nothing, Tim,' replied my father, leaning out of the window to him. 'I wanted to be alone, that's all.'

'But we'll see you at the other end?' bawled Tim as the train began to move.

'I don't know will you,' replied my father grimly. 'I think ye saw too much of me.'

When the band formed up outside the station we stood on the pavement and watched them. He had a tight hold of my hand. First Tim Ryan and then Jim Ralegh came rushing over to him.

With an intensity of hatred I watched those enemies of Ireland again bait their traps for my father, but now I knew they would bait them in vain.

'No, no, Tim,' said my father, shaking his head, 'I went too far before for the sake of the band, and I paid dear for it. None of my family was ever called a turncoat before today, Tim.'

'Ah, it is a young fool like that?' bawled Jim Ralegh with tears in his wild eyes. 'What need a man like you care about him?'

'A man have his pride, Jim,' said my father gloomily.

'He have,' cried Ralegh despairingly, 'and a fat lot any of us has to be proud of. The band was all we ever had, and if that goes the whole thing goes. For the love of the Almighty God, Mick Twomey, come back with us to the bandroom anyway.'

'No, no, no,' shouted my father angrily. 'I tell you after today I'm finished with music.'

'Music is finished with us you mean,' bawled Jim. 'The curse of God on the day we ever heard of Redmond or O'Brien! We were happy men before it. . . . All right, lads,' he cried, turning away with a wild and whirling motion of his arm. 'Mick Twomey is done with us. Ye can go on without him.'

And again I heard the three solemn thumps on the big drum, and again the street was flooded with a roaring torrent of music, and though it no longer played for me, my heart rose to it and the tears came from my eyes. Still holding my hand, my father followed on the pavement. They were playing 'Brian Boru's March', his old favourite. We followed them through the ill-lit town and as they turned down the side-street to the bridge, my father stood on the kerb and looked after them as though he wished to impress every detail on his memory. It was only when the music stopped and the silence returned to the narrow channel of the street that we resumed our lonely way homeward.

3 WRITERS

PREFACE

FOR ANY Irish prose writer of O'Connor's generation, there was a preliminary and pressing question: James Joyce. Exemplar, liberator, great yet ignorable one-off, crushing presence, artistic warning? O'Connor wrote several times about Joyce, veering from the highest admiration to the sternest disregard; in doing so, he was also elaborating his own aesthetic. Joyce as the delineator of daily life, of the ordinary Ireland O'Connor also took as his subject – the Joyce of the first three hundred pages of *Ulysses* – this he revered along with everyone else. The Joyce which ended in the grotesque unreadability of *Finnegans Wake*, and which got there via increased aestheticism, over-formal planning, obsession with the word rather than life itself, the Joyce whose Ireland remained frozen as a young man's view: all this O'Connor disapproved of. 'I think I like the instinctual as against the intellectual,' he wrote to the American critic Harvey Breit. 'As a writer I like the feeling I get when some story which I've been trying to bring up in the right way gets on its own feet and tells me to go to hell. You don't imagine any story in *Dubliners* told Joyce to go to hell, do you? It wouldn't have the nerve. I'm for the democratic way of life, in literature as in politics. Writers are leaders, not dictators.'

The other writer O'Connor kept coming back to, though for personal as much as artistic reasons, was Yeats. The poet was like a second, literary father to him: though no easier to have around in Dublin than the old soldier Michael O'Donovan had been in Cork. Yeats was O'Connor's literary patron, encouraging and bullying, inspiring and exasperating; he published (and interferingly rewrote) O'Connor's translations from the Irish, and was a toweringly manipulative presence when O'Connor was director of the Abbey Theatre. As with O'Connor's blood father, they were still quarrelling until the day Yeats died.

O'Connor knew all the Irish writers of his day, and had firm views on most of them; few provoked as much affection as 'A.E.'

(George Russell). But literature did not just take place for him in the quarrelsome sophistications of Dublin, or in Parisian exile; it lay also in the oral, the folk, the Gaelic traditions of the country-side. He retold the story of 'The Tailor and Anstey' many times in his work, and – apart from its intrinsic interest – there are perhaps two reasons why O'Connor couldn't keep away from it. First, it is about the collision between a joyless, disapproving modern state and a free yet harmless individual of no means or influence; it is clear where O'Connor's sympathy would lie. Secondly, it is a story of censorship; and O'Connor was himself often banned under the cultural policy of the Irish government. The twenty-first-century reader might well be honestly baffled at the notion that O'Connor's stories ran foul of any censorship board. If so, this would be to grossly underestimate the oppressive puritanism and grey mediocrity of church and state at that time. 'A country ruled by fools and blackguards', he once called it, where life was 'emptiness and horror'. This was also, of course, his subject-matter.

A PORTRAIT of the Artist as a Young Man should be compulsory reading for every young man and woman. I doubt if I was seventeen when I read it first, in a copy removed from the Students' Library at University College, Cork, because of its indecency. Though I had had a more sheltered childhood than most boys, I wasn't in the least shocked or disturbed by it. I felt too strongly that Joyce had understood as no one else seemed to do the problems of the serious adolescent growing up in squalid circumstances. Young people are like that. What they get out of a book is more often what they need for their own adjustment to life than what the author intends. What I got out of Dostoevsky at the same time was not the sadism – I never noticed it – but a realization that the lies I told almost automatically were more comic than serious, and this gradually made me stop telling lies at all.

After this, Joyce was the Irish writer who influenced me most. I came on *Ulysses* also in an erratic way and was moved and excited by everything in it that dealt with Stephen Dedalus, not so much by the chapters that dealt with Bloom. From what I knew of Russian fiction I got the impression that Bloom was a flat figure. I still find him rather flat. When 'Work in Progress' – later titled *Finnegans Wake* – began to appear in print, I learned parts of it by heart and wrote in praise of it in *The Irish Statesman*, though the editor, George Russell, tried in private to restrain my enthusiasm. 'You shouldn't say Joyce is a genius, you know,' he said reprovingly. 'An enormous talent, of course; a colossal talent, but not a genius. Now, James Stephens is a genius.' In those days I looked down on Stephens and repeated Russell's verdict with derision; which shows not only that you can't put an old head on young shoulders but that you shouldn't try.

I even made a youthful pilgrimage to see Joyce and liked him a lot, though I was disturbed by the remark he made when I was leaving. The story of the cork frame has been argued and argued by Joyceans since Desmond MacCarthy first printed it, and the reader must argue it for himself. I had admired an old print of the city of Cork in a peculiar frame and, touching the frame, asked 'What's that?' 'Cork,' said Joyce. 'I know that,' I said, 'but what's the frame?' 'Cork,' replied Joyce. 'I had great difficulty in getting a French frame maker to make it.'

The main significance of that silly little anecdote relates to myself, for after that I began to see cork frames all over Joyce's work, and they always gave me the same slight shock I got when he said 'cork' for the second time. *Finnegans Wake* was the first book of his I lost interest in, because, though I knew it much better than those who criticized it, I always had a lingering doubt whether what I was defending was really supreme artistry or plain associative mania. Later, I stopped rereading great chunks of *Ulysses* which had always bored me – the parodies, the chapter of errors, the scientific catechism – till I was left with only 25 per cent of the book and had to admit that Joyce not only had no sense of organic design but – what was much worse – no vision of human life that had developed beyond the age of twenty-one.

On the other hand, I began to see that he was the greatest master of rhetoric who had ever lived. By rhetoric I mean the technique of literary composition, the relationship of the written word to the object. This, I think, is the aspect of *A Portrait of the Artist* that should appeal most to middle-aged people. His brother, Stanislaus, was shocked when Joyce told him that he was interested in nothing but style, because Stanislaus was a moralist, and his principal interest was in the material and the viewpoint. But Joyce was telling the literal truth; by that time he had ceased to care for anything but the art of writing.

It had not always been so, and this was the tragedy of the relationship between those two brilliant brothers, as it so often is between two strong characters who grow up side by side, mutually dependent. There had been another James Joyce, much closer to Stanislaus, and whom only Stanislaus remembered – poor, angry and idealistic – and to him the material had mattered intensely. One can find this earlier Joyce in *Stephen Hero*, a fragment of the rejected early draft of *A Portrait of the Artist*. Before its publication, I had been hearing of it for years from acquaintances. One of them had told me it was written in the manner of Meredith, and, indeed, it contains a number of awkward ironic references to the hero, like 'this fantastic idealist' and 'this heaven-ascending essayist', which recall Meredith at his archest. But it is not the style of *Stephen Hero* that matters, for it has none; it is the rage, the anguish, the pity, the awkwardness in it. I remember thinking when I read it first, 'This is the worst book ever written, but after it I shall never be able to read *A Portrait of the Artist* again.'

This, of course, was an exaggerated reaction; in fact, I find it hard to reread *Stephen Hero*, while I can always read *A Portrait of the Artist* again, though never in the same way. Less and less do I hear the echoes of my own tormented youth in Cork, and more and more do I find myself admiring the devices of the great master of rhetoric. This is not so much a description of a tormented childhood and youth as a reconstitution of it in another form that excites all the detective instinct in me. I do not know what the total pattern is, but I recognize sections of a total pattern here and there as, when I am out archaeologizing, I can identify portions of some great building from humps and hollows in the ground. First, there is the over-all rhetorical pattern by which the book is divided into three sections – lyric, epic and dramatic. While the character of Stephen is still fluid, his experiences are expressed in lyric form, each ending in a cry; when he finally takes shape as an individual, he speaks in his own particular voice, through his diary.

Under that is the basic psychological development that accompanies and sustains the artistic one, and this has to be understood in terms of Aristotle's *De Anima*. It is not for nothing that young Stephen Dedalus notices the two faucets in the men's room in the Wicklow Hotel which are hot and cold, or the school badges which are red and white – hot and cold – or the illness which makes him sweat and shiver; for these are the extremes between which the individual lives who is neither hot nor cold. 'The mean,' says Aristotle, 'is capable of judgement, for it becomes in reference to each of the extremes another extreme. And as that which is to perceive white or black must not itself be actually white or black, but both of these potentially ... so also in the case of touch, it must not be either hot or cold in itself.' So, too, when Dante says, 'A priest would not be a priest if he did not tell his flock what is right and what is wrong,' and Stephen thinks, 'It was wrong; it was unfair and cruel,' we are present at the birth of a mind which alone decides what is right and wrong and differentiates us from the world of sensation. Aristotle adds: 'Neither is thought, in which right and wrong are determined – i.e. right in the sense of practical judgement, scientific knowledge and true opinion, and wrong in the sense of the opposite of these – thought in this signification is not identical with sensation.'

I have no illusion that I have said the last word on the matter, nor do I think that Joyce stuck to Aristotle any more closely than he stuck to Homer or Vico – in fact, I should be very much surprised if he had. I should suggest that the reader might follow a pattern leading from 'heart' through 'mind', 'soul', 'spirit' and 'imagination' to 'freedom', and see how it works out for him. One of the best student papers I ever read in America was by a young poet who analysed the book in terms of the rubrics.

'Analysed' – the very word is like a knell. Why should a work of art have to be subjected to analysis? And where is the Joyce whom Stanislaus knew and who cared deeply about the things Stanislaus and myself and so many others have cared about and who never grew up? My friend V. S. Pritchett has called Joyce 'a mad grammarian', and I have said myself that his work is 'a rhetorician's dream', saying little more than Joyce himself said to his brother when he told him he was interested only in style. Joyce believed, as Yeats did not, that 'words alone are certain good' and that all that happens to human beings can be expressed fully in language. This, as we say in Ireland, is where the ferryboat left him, because it can't. Experience, as older people know, is always drifting into a world where language cannot follow, where, as Turgenev says, 'perhaps only music can follow'. Robert Browning wrote:

A fancy from a flower-bell, someone's death,
A chorus-ending from Euripides, –
And that's enough for fifty hopes and fears
As old and new at once as nature's self,
To rap and knock and enter in our soul,
Take hands and dance there, a fantastic thing,
Round the ancient idol, on his base again, –
The grand Perhaps!

Younger readers will read, careless of Aristotle and Thomas Aquinas, the pattern of human life and how rhetoric may follow it, and not notice how every word has been brooded upon until nothing can be neglected; and older readers will read, pursuing every hint, in the hope that they may understand their children's revolt. But this great book is one about which they can both hope to be right, because, as an elderly man, I can still think back on the boy who read it first in a provincial town forty-odd years ago and was comforted by it, and almost wish I were sixteen again.

I THINK I almost said 'Thank God' when Joyce died. There must have been young men who said 'Thank God' when Byron died, and I can think of no other writer, unless perhaps Rousseau, who wielded such an influence; who was so much the pool of Narcissus to his generation, as Cyril Connolly put it. [...]

Joyce's writing has all the virtues of a disciple of Flaubert; it is exact, appropriate and detached. 'The streets, shuttered for the repose of Sunday, swarmed with a gaily coloured crowd. Like illumined pearls the lamps shone from the summits of their tall poles upon the living texture below which, changing shape and hue unceasingly, sent up into the warm grey evening air an unchanging, unceasing murmur.' That is Flaubert, though the echo of the word 'unceasingly' is a trick of style which Joyce never tired of and had picked up probably from Pater.

But if the stories in *Dubliners* have Flaubert's virtues, they have also Flaubert's weaknesses. To be absolutely faithful to what one sees and hears and not to speculate on what may lie behind it, for fear of indulging in one's own emotionalism, is a creed that produces obvious limitations. Two boys on the lang from school meet a man who talks to them for a few minutes; goes away and returns. What he is – a sexual maniac – what he has done in the meantime, are only suggested by the tone of his speech and the way it alters after his return. Subject value, emotional or intellectual values, do not exist; there is a certain experience to be conveyed; this is where it begins, this is where it ends – now watch me do it! This is a sort of asceticism which the average reader is incapable of, and it produces in his mind a certain feeling of stiffness, of gaucherie as though he were watching someone behave rather too correctly to be quite well-bred. After the murder of John the Baptist in Flaubert's *Herodias* his disciples carry away the head. The story ends with the line 'As it was very heavy they carried it turn and turn about.' Flaubert intends to show his detachment; his command of himself: this is the point where a lesser writer would have burst out into an emotional passage; but to me the line suggests not self-control but a vague reminiscence of Eliza Doolittle's drawing room manner; it is a literary crick in the neck. After Mr Hynes in Joyce's 'Ivy Day in The Committee Room' recites his moving little ballad on Parnell's death, one of the election canvasser turns to a Unionist and asks if it wasn't fine. ' Mr Crofton,' the story ends, 'said that it was a very fine piece of writing.'

There is something of the same weakness in all Joyce's conversation at least to my ear.

'Pope Leo XIII,' said Mr Cunningham, 'was one of the lights of the age. His great idea, you know, was the union of the Latin and Greek Churches. That was the aim of his life.'

'I often heard he was one of the most intellectual men in Europe,' said Mr Power. 'I mean, apart from his being Pope.'

'So he was,' said Mr Cunningham, 'if not the most so. His motto, you know, as Pope, was *Lux upon Lux* – *Light upon Light*.'

'No, no,' said Mr Fogarty eagerly, 'I think you're wrong there. It was *Lux in Tenebris*, I think – *Light in Darkness*.'

'Oh, yes,' said Mr MacCoy. '*Tenebrae.*'

'Allow me,' said Mr Cunningham positively, 'it was *Lux upon Lux*. And Pius IX his predecessor's motto was *Crux upon Crux* – that is, *Cross upon Cross* – to show the difference between their two pontificates.'

That is good, but it is a little too good; it is observed so carefully – notice the murderous 'if not the most so' – that it ceases to give the impression of conversation at all; there is a queer stifling atmosphere about it; it is conversation without spontaneity, without lyric or dramatic impulse; in a word I feel it is not dialogue but mimicry. And it seems to me that Joyce had so trained himself to remain withdrawn from his work, that very often what he gives us for style is a clever imitation of another man's work, and what passes for conversation is little better than parody. [. . .]

Almost every serious critic of Joyce has felt and said the same things about *Ulysses*: that it is the greatest book of our time, and at the same time that it isn't a great book at all; that it is on the scale of the *Divine Comedy* but that personally one prefers a few pages of George Moore. It is hard to define that sense of discomfort. For myself – and I am a hero-worshipper – the discomfort comes from a strong sense of artistic failure. For close on the first three hundred pages *Ulysses* is absolutely beyond comparison in modern literature. It is, what Joyce intended it to be, the whole of life; the complete man in the complete world: in fact it goes as close as makes no difference to being a scientific description of modern life. I cannot imagine whatever its fate as a work of art that it will ever lose its importance as a document.

In those three hundred pages there are few dull spots and the divagations caused by the arbitrary method of construction are few. It is true the *Sirens* episode, written in musical form and parodying the rhythms of various types of music, as in 'Pat is a waiter who waits while you wait. Hee hee hee hee. He waits while you wait. He he. A waiter is he. Hee hee hee hee' does introduce an element of virtuosity which seems to run counter to the main stream of the book, but the interruption isn't serious, and it gives the texture, already enormously enriched by Dujardin's invention of the interior monologue, a new lift. But in the *Cyclops* episode the attempt to follow the Greek original is, I feel, a serious handicap. Joyce chooses a Gaelic League nationalist of the worst type for his Cyclops, but everything that is said in Cyclops' cave has to be interpreted again in a Cyclopean style, and so the narrative, which anyhow is little better than an amusing parody, has to be halted to allow of new parodies in a fantastic gigantesque style which is anything but amusing. 'The catastrophe was terrific and instantaneous in its effect. The observatory of Dunsink registered in all eleven shocks, all of the fifth grade of Mercalli's scale, and there is no record extant of a similar seismic disturbance in our island since the earthquake of 1534, the year of the rebellion of Silken Thomas.' That might amuse us for a few moments if we read it in the comic column of the morning newspaper, but it is pretty trashy stuff to find in a book. The *Nausikaa* episode which follows, in spite of some splendid visual writing (the presiding organ is the eye!) contains a great deal written in the style of the Heartsease novelettes which is equally trashy. 'A sterling good daughter was Gerty just like a second mother in the house, a ministering angel too with a little heart worth its weight in gold.' And so on. In the next episode the crucial meeting between Bloom and Dedalus takes place at a gathering of medicals in Holles Street Hospital. The presiding organ is naturally the womb. How is the style to symbolize this? Obviously, by suggesting, in a series of parodies of the whole development of English prose, the embryo becoming man. It is at this point, it seems to me, that Joyce's crazy and haphazard organization of his material has tied him up in knots. It is as though the self-conscious literary artist were being doubled by a drunken Dublin medico whose superstition makes him avoid the mortar lines on the pavement and whose intellectual level is Gilbert and Sullivan. Joyce's virtuosity seems to me to belong to a second-rate brain. 'Beneficent Disseminator of blessings to all Thy creatures,' says one of the students, 'how great and universal must be that sweetest of Thy tyrannies which can hold in thrall the free and the bond, the simple swain and the polished cox-comb, the lover in the heyday of reckless passion and the husband of maturer years.' Even as a parody of Sterne it is bad, but com-pared with the naturalistic conversation of the early portions it is intolerable.

Yet it is this chapter which prepares for the crisis of the book, the great scene in the brothel when Bloom sees at last in Stephen the little boy he had lost in death. I feel that the nearer Joyce drew to his climax the more he shirked it, the more he inclined to rely upon virtuosity to see him through. And it is in this chapter, intended by Joyce to be the keystone of the book, that the book falls to pieces; first, because he is following an arbitrary method of construction instead of allowing the material to take organic shape, and second, because that itself is only a symptom: Joyce's self-consciousness makes him as clumsy as an adolescent before the emotions of the situation. If it had been treated in any of the manners of the first half it would have been tremendous; even in the moments of lucidity there are passages of fine intensity, as when Bloom, half-canned, enters the brothel and imagines for a moment that he is entering his own home where his wife has been entertaining her lover. 'On the antlered rack of the hall hang a man's hat and waterproof. Bloom uncovers himself, but seeing them frowns, then smiles, preoccupied.' But Circe in the Greek story turned men into swine, and Joyce must find his correspondences. Dedalus and Bloom are swamped in a series of hallucinations. Bloom tries and sentences himself for an imagi-nary crime; becomes emperor of Ireland, changes his sex, and everything he thinks of takes on visible form. It is hard to see what Joyce intended by the hallucinations. Though they have the form of common daydreams they are distorted in the manner of nightmares, and, even then, contain considerable tracts of parody. The only thing one feels is that they couldn't possibly have taken place in Bloom's mind. When Stephen's mother appears, she appears as one of the many nightmare forms; there is nothing to show that this is the climax of the book, and the essential scene in which Bloom calls on the drunken Stephen first as 'Mr Dedalus', and then as 'Stephen' is crowded into the last two pages and lost. And to make Stephen, tortured by the apparition of his mother, smash the shade of the gas mantel with a cry of 'Nothung' (a reference to Siegfried's splitting of the anvil in the *Valkyrie*) is simply puerility. The book never recovers from the incompetence of the central episode; the two which follow, the one written in journalese and the other in scientific question and answer, are arid beyond belief; and it is saved from mediocrity only by the magnificent last episode which brings us back with a jolt to the mood of the first chapters, saturated in the poetry of everyday life.

Finnegans Wake is an extension of Joyce's problem and his solutions of it. It is haunted by a fundamental Caesarism which will admit no bounds to the human will. *Ulysses* was intended to be life; this is the universe; universal history, universal language. The conception, which in Joyce is always adventurous, is touched with megalomania. His hero is a Chapelizod publican with a wife, twin sons and a daughter, and he falls asleep and dreams of himself as Dublin, of his sons as North Side and South Side, of his daughter as a cloud and of his wife as the Liffey. He has been flirting with a nursemaid and imagines himself being tried by a court consisting of the Four Evangelists and the Twelve Apostles. There are no characters, merely principles; the men are earth and the women water; they change their shapes and reappear in all the great stories of history and mythology, and the language changes with them. *Requiem eternam dona ei Domine*, becomes, for the giant, Rockquiem eternuel give Donal aye in dolmeny.

There are lovely things in the book, and magic in every page of the Anna Livia episode, but the whole thing, now I have had time to study it, seems to me a colossal failure. It gives the impression of being a continuation of the parodistic and hallucinatory portions of *Ulysses*, and I cannot get over the feeling that the second-rate brain with its utter intellectual poverty, its superstitions and puns and jingle, has got complete control. I feel that more particularly from the style of the rewriting, always a clue to a writer's mind. It seems to me that every rewriting has added to the pedantry. Even Mr Edmund Wilson, a fine critic and devotee of *Finnegans Wake*, finds on examining the four printed versions of Anna Livia that Joyce should have stopped after the third – the little Faber edition. I don't know the first draft which appeared in *Le Navire d'Argent* but of the three I do know I prefer the first. The early 'Well, that's the limmat! As El Negro said when he looked in La Plate' becomes in the Faber edition 'As El Negro winced when he wonced in La Plate.' 'Tell me every tiny bit. I want to know every single thing' becomes 'Tell me every tiny teign. I want to know every single ingul.' 'It's a long long way, walking weary!' is turned into 'Tez thelon langlo, walking weary,' and where the improvement is I cannot for the life of me see, but I do see a mind turning in on itself and not caring any longer for the business of communication. I feel it as a sort of disintegration of the material, as though the mind behind had softened from abstraction through pedantry into mere whimsy. [. . .]

And yet even as I wrote the last words an idea came knocking at my head. The framework of life, the tensions of thought, morality and emotion that hold civilization together, because they are unseen, rot many times as fast as the fabric. The slum landlords of the intellect, the people with a vested interest in antiquated ideas, who make their profit out of old tenements scream at the first cry of danger. They talk of 'the decline of reticence' and shut their ears. They are the politicians, the professors and the popular novelists. And yet if civilization is to exist we must destroy everything in literature that seems to be false, that does not apply to the world about us and the men and women we meet. Those who destroy the false standards are the saints and heroes of our time. It is they who within the changing world keep changing those invisible tensions without which life would be impossible.

I seemed to hear the doorbell ring and the maid's step on the stairs.

'Mr James Joyce to see you, sir.'

GEORGE RUSSELL, the Editor of the *Irish Statesman*, did his edit-
ing from an attic room in a Georgian house in Merrion Square,
which he had papered in brown wrapping-paper and decorated
with gods and goddesses in dark browns and gold. He sat behind
a large desk to the side of the fireplace – a big, burly north of
Ireland Presbyterian with wild hair and beard and a pipe hanging
from his discoloured teeth. He usually sat well back in his chair,
beaming benevolently through his spectacles, his legs crossed,
and his socks hanging down over his ankles. Sometimes in an
earnest mood he leaned forward with his two fat hands on his
knees, his head lowered as he looked at you over the specs, giving
his appearance almost an elfin quality. He was an extraordinarily
restless, fidgety man, forever jumping up to find some poem he
was about to print (usually lost in the heap of papers, prints, and
manuscripts in his desk) or some book he was reviewing. With
him was his secretary, Susan Mitchell, a deaf woman with a sweet,
faded face, who was supposed to have loved him platonically for
the best part of her life.

Phibbs, like many of the younger writers, despised Russell,
whom he regarded as an old windbag. I was prepared to do the
same, but, while we were still arguing, Phibbs said, 'The differ-
ence between your generation and ours is that we have had no
youth.' 'Oh, really!' Russell replied with an air of great concern,
and I disgraced myself by a roar of laughter in which Russell
joined. One of his favourite quotations was a phrase from *The
Three Musketeers* – 'I perceive if we do not kill one another we
shall be good friends'; and I think at that moment Russell and
I decided we should be friends, for as we were leaving he put his
arm round my shoulder and said, 'Send me something for the
paper.'

I did, and he printed it, and another source of income became
open to me. Admittedly it was small, but when one has never

had anything the occasional guinea or two guineas seems like wealth. I could now spend a night in a hotel – though six and sixpence for bed and breakfast struck me as wicked – so I went to Dublin, mastered even my timidity, and visited him in his house in Rathgar on Sunday evening. I went through the performance I went through so often in later years, climbed the steps, pulled the bell, heard the smelly old dog begin to yelp; and then Russell, shouting and kicking excitedly at the dog, pulled me in by the hand. He had the usual Dublin combination of living- and dining-room, filled with paintings, mostly by himself, and all in glaring colours that matched the glaring overhead light. Corkery, who had once visited him, had told me that the pictures were 'like Hampstead Heath on Sunday night'.

For the first hour he sat uneasily in his big chair in the middle of the room, intent on the doorbell, which was always anticipated by the infernal dog. It was like sitting in the middle of Grand Central Station. Visitors to Dublin – Americans, Japanese, and Chinese – were always dropping in, as well as a gang of adoring old ladies whom I called 'The Holy Women'. He lectured to them all, telling American agriculturists how to organize co-operatives and Indians how to understand Gandhi, and suggesting new themes to poets and story-tellers. He talked in set patterns and phrases which had endured for years, some indeed of which could be traced back to his boyhood.

'You know, A.E.,' I said to him years later, 'back in 1904 Joyce has you saying: "The only question about a work of art is, out of how deep a life does it spring." '

'Well, that's clever of him,' Russell replied. 'That's true, you know. I may have said that.'

He said it at least once a day. What was more he did not realize that I was joking him.

He was a creature of habit, and his conversation, like his life, like his pictures, ran in patterns; well-formed phrases, ideas, quotations, and anecdotes that he repeated year after year without altering an inflection. He was unskilful in the way he introduced them, and they were usually so general in their application that they had a tendency to obliterate the point in discussion. 'Leonardo advised young painters to study the stains in old marble to discover compositions for their own paintings' was a standard phrase that was exceedingly difficult to relate to any subject one was considering. After a time you got to see Leonardo hovering in the air a mile off and found yourself trying to ward him off as if he were a wasp. [. . .]

I don't think I ever left that house or the office without an armful of books, good, bad, and indifferent, and later, when I was in hospital, Russell continued to send me regular parcels of them – 'to raise your soul above the troubles of the flesh' as he would explain.

He was that sort of man. Within half an hour he enveloped you in universal curiosity and affection in which shyness was forgotten. It was like an old fur coat, a little bit smelly and definitely designed for someone of nobler stature, but, though it might threaten you with suffocation, it never left you feeling cold. He would find you a new doctor, a new wife, a new lodging, or a new job, and if you were ill would cheerfully come and nurse you. [. . .]

As all Russell's discoveries had to be pronounced on by Yeats, Russell ordered me to visit him on one of his Monday evenings. In those days Sunday was Russell's night, Monday Yeats's, Tuesday afternoon Sarah Purser's, Sunday afternoon Seamus O'Sullivan's. Yeats's Mondays were peculiar because they were all male; on Monday nights he discussed sex, except when Lady Gregory was staying, and, of course, it would be my rotten luck to be ordered to the presence when she was staying and no one else came, so that I had to face Yeats and herself alone. At that time I did not know Mrs Yeats, who could manage to make even me feel at home. To complete my confusion, Lady Gregory wore a mantilla as though for an audience with the Pope.

It was all too much for a raw youth who was terrified of social occasions anyhow. Yeats's study was kept deliberately dark, and everything in it was expensive and beautiful; the masks from his dance plays, the tall bookcases with the complete sets of the classics, and the long, orderly table with the tall silver candlesticks. Even Corkery could not have said that the pictures were 'like Hampstead Heath on Sunday evening'. And nothing less like Russell could be imagined than the tall man in the well-cut blue suit with the silk shirt and bow-tie who came shuffling in, holding his hand out high as though he expected you to kiss his ring – a beautiful ring, as it happened. Never could you imagine an Irish country-man giving Yeats an approving look and shouting, 'Bring in the whiskey now, Mary, and be *continually* bringing in the hot water,' which was how Russell was received in one Irish town. Later, the very sight of Yeats at the door would send Mother scuttling to her bedroom. There was something ecclesiastical about the blind man's stare, the ceremonial washing of the hands and the languid unction of the voice. That night I noticed that he said 'weld' and 'midder' for 'world' and 'murder'.

There was a touch of the bird about him as well; the eyes, like those of a bird, seemed to be at the sides rather than the front of the face, and his laugh tended to be harsh, abrupt, and remote – a caw, as Moore called it. When he was happy and forgot himself, animation seemed to flow over him. He sat forward, arms on his knees, washing his hands over and over, the pose sometimes broken by a loud, harsh, throaty laugh and the tossing back of the big bird's head while he sat bolt upright in his chair gripping his lapels and raising his brows with a triumphant stare; sometimes he broke it by tweaking his nose; most characteristically perhaps by raising his index finger for attention. But when he was really excited his whole face lit up as from a light inside. It was astonishing, because even in old age when he was looking most wretched and discontented that blaze of excitement would sweep over his face like a glory, like a blast of sunlight over a moor, and from behind the mask a boy's tense eager face looked out at you. [. . .]

Russell was extraordinarily inquisitive about women, and with an ingenuousness that even I found upsetting. Though he never talked to me of his wife, and rarely of the one son he mentioned at all, I had the feeling that he was unhappy in his marriage and inclined to think that women were a plague.

'Do you have flirtations with pretty girls?' he asked me one night.

'Sometimes,' I admitted – I should have hated to confess how rarely.

'And do they get you to write poems for them?'

'Yes.'

'That's fine,' he said happily. 'Write them all the poems they want, but take care they don't marry you. That's the devil of it.'

When he came back from his first American tour he was in a

wild state of excitement about American girls. He had spent a birthday in Vassar or some other women's college and the girls had made him a birthday cake with a great mass of candles. Afterwards, one of them had come up and kissed him, and when he started, said, 'Oh, boy, do be your age!'

'They must be the most beautiful girls the world has ever seen,' he said to me. 'If only you could get them to sit in a corner and keep quiet, you could admire them for hours. But they *will* talk!'

At the same time he tried to arrange a marriage between Simone Tery, a beautiful French journalist, and me. He showed his love for Simone as I never knew him to show love for anyone, but knowing his passion for generalization I assumed – quite correctly, I think – that I was not the only young Irish writer he had chosen as a husband for her. He merely adored her, and wanted somebody in Dublin to marry her so that he could be sure of entertainment one evening a week. He got off on the wrong foot with Simone and myself, because when we met for dinner he looked at me and said, 'Isn't she nice?' and then at Simone and said, 'Isn't he nice?' and for the rest of the evening we sat and glowered at one another. He made it worse by congratulating her on not using 'any of those horrible cosmetics that American girls ruin their beauty with', and she, made up as skilfully as only a Frenchwoman can be, modestly lowered her eyes and said, 'I only use them on particular occasions, A.E.'

He was very impressed one night when I repeated a bawdy story a girl had told me and said with great solemnity: 'That is a wonderful example of the economy of Nature which I am always impressing on you. Nature intended me to be a lyric poet, so I *never* met a girl who told stories like that. She intended you to be a realistic novelist, so she just throws girls of that sort in your way.' [...]

Yeats was a natural organizer, never happy unless he was organizing something or somebody – a great bully, as I discovered later, and an outrageous flatterer. When he began to bully me I always gave him lip, almost on principle. After my father, I never quarrelled so much with anyone, and even if one allows that I am a bit in the same line myself, it takes two to make a disagreement last as long as ours. One might say that I was discovering my real father at last, and that all the old attitudes induced by my human father came on top. Yet I can truthfully say that when, towards the end of his life, I became his devoted slave, it was entirely due to his generosity, because with no one else was I so crude and uppish.

His principal weakness was that he was easily bored, and L. A. G. Strong was not the only one who bored him. George Russell bored him too, and many others, and he made no effort to conceal it. This, I think, cost him the affection of a number of people who would have been better friends than some of those he made.

Apart from these things, I think of him as a shy and rather lonely man who desperately wanted to be friends, and was utterly loyal to the friends he made. It took a long time to appreciate that shyness in him because it tended to make him portentous and overwhelming in society and even in the home. Once, when Michael Yeats was pulling his sister's hair and Mrs Yeats failed to separate them, Daddy was summoned. He stalked slowly and solemnly to an armchair, sat down, and recited, 'Let dogs delight to bark and bite', and then stalked out again, apparently feeling he had done all that was expected of a father. The children never became intimate with him: even the marvellous 'Prayer for My Daughter' was written while Anne was safely in another building. Michael once got his own back by asking in a piercing voice as his father went by, 'Mummy, who is that man?' and Yeats was deeply hurt. [. . .]

He knew, too, though I never told him so, that I did not share his interest in spiritualism. One night I asked him bluntly if he ever had had an experience that could not be explained in strictly rational terms. He thought for a while and grew embarrassed.

'Yes, once. I think I can tell you. You are, after all, a man of the world. I was having a love affair with a certain woman and she said she was pregnant. I was very worried because I felt that if she was, I must marry her. I came home to Ireland and confessed to an old aunt. "Don't believe her," she said. "She's having you on." So I went to a certain famous medium and asked for her help without telling her what my trouble was. She went into a trance and produced some writing that neither of us could read. Finally I took it to the British Museum and they told me to come back in a week. When I went back the head of one of the departments said, "Mr Yeats, this is a most remarkable document. It is written in the form of Hebrew taught in the German universities in the seventeenth century." '

Then Yeats looked at me triumphantly, his head tossed back, the big, blind eyes behind the spectacles challenging me to explain that one if I could.

'Never mind what sort of Hebrew it was written in,' I said. 'Did it tell you whether you were the father of the child or not?'

The practical Corkman! He sat back wearily – rationalists are so hard to argue with.

'Oh, no, no,' he said vaguely. 'It just said things like "O great poet of our race!" ' Clearly he thought this important, but I didn't. As a story-teller I felt that the point had got lost. [. . .]

But no reasonable human being could fight for long with Yeats. As well as a successor for Hunt I had to find a successor for Tanya Moiseiwitsch, who insisted on leaving with him, and I arranged to send Yeats's daughter, Anne, who had been assisting Tanya, to study stage design with Baty and Jouvet in Paris. I had warned Anne Yeats that Baty was a magnificent director with no notion of acting, and Jouvet a magnificent director of players with no notion of stage design. God alone knows what complicated intrigue Yeats saw in this, for it would simply never have occurred to him that I had been watching his daughter's work with interest, but as no one was allowed to excel Yeats in courtesy he arranged to publish a superb edition of my translation of 'The Lament for Art O'Leary', with coloured drawings by his brother, Jack.

A short time later I invited myself out to Rathfarnham to present a friend of mine to Mrs Yeats. At once Yeats started explaining to me that as a father he could not possibly allow his daughter to go to Paris unprotected, and that she must go to the Old Vic instead, where she could be looked after by some aunt, cousin, or friend. I replied that nothing I had seen in the Old Vic had given me the idea that we had anything to learn from it and that I wouldn't consent to spend a penny of the theatre's money on sending Anne there. Yeats grew sulkier and sulkier, but George, seeing us to the door later in the evening, lifted my spirits by doing a dance step in the hall. 'That old bully!' she said. 'It's about time someone stood up to him. He's always trying to push people around.'

It was not the first time she had saved an evening for me. I knew the apparent childish selfishness of Yeats, because once when I was seeing him home, he went to his club, and told me that George was ill with some infectious disease and that he couldn't go home. I, thinking of George by herself in the house, said 'Oh, that's awful!' and Yeats replied mournfully, 'Yes. You see, I can't even get at my books.' But I also saw the other side, which apparently Higgins didn't see. Once, when we went in a taxi to some Board meeting, I paid the taxi driver and Yeats grabbed the money frantically from his hand and created a scene while he tried to find money of his own – always a difficult task for him as he never could make out where his pockets were. I said, 'Oh, stop it, W.B.,' and he turned on me. 'You don't understand, O'Connor,' he gasped. 'I wouldn't mind, but my wife would never forgive me.' Maybe only a story-teller can understand that, but I knew that a man who worried about what he was going to tell his wife about who paid the taxi fare was a man in love, whatever anybody else might think. [. . .]

A great man is one who acts and speaks from a vision of himself. It is not that he is always right and everyone else wrong – often it is the other way round – but that even when he is wrong he is speaking from 'the foul rag-and-bone shop of the heart', the central volcano from which all creation comes. In so far as he interprets his country, as Yeats interpreted Ireland, he has no other source of authority. Once when we were arguing about politics, Yeats quoted a remark of de Valera's of which his enemies were making great capital – 'When I want to know what Ireland thinks, I look into my own heart.' 'Where else could he look?' growled Yeats.

But it takes a large heart to hold even a small country, and since Yeats' death there has been no other that could hold us, with all our follies and heroism.

SLIGO IS Yeats, and will be now for ever. A great poet impresses himself on a landscape like a phase of history, and for me East Dorset will always be as much Hardy as Celt or Saxon. One can scarcely look at the toppled-down crown of Knocknarea to the south without remembering 'The host is riding from Knocknarea', or at the long, shiplike beak of Ben Bulben to the north without remembering 'When first I saw her on Ben Bulben's side'. People have swum Lough Gill to reach Innisfree without knowing that the island Yeats really wrote of goes by the unpoetic name of Cat Island. One north of Ireland man with the strong utilitarian northern streak in him was heard to murmur as he looked over Sligo bridge at the foaming weir: 'I would that we were, my beloved, white swans on the foam of the sea. Man dear, there's enough water there to wash all the water-closets in Sligo.'

Now, nine years after his death, Yeats' remains have been returned to Sligo. It was his own wish, the completion of a work long planned, the crowning of a life which was like some great work of art nobly conceived, nobly executed and here brought to a triumphant conclusion.

> Under bare Ben Bulben's head
> In Drumcliffe churchyard Yeats is laid. . . .
> On limestone quarried near the spot
> By his command these words are cut:
> > Cast a cold eye
> > On life, on death.
> > Horseman, pass by!

As an epitaph it is all right, but as an epitaph on Yeats it is hard to think of anything more inappropriate. The lines of his by which I shall always remember him are those that haunted me all day after I had heard of his death:

Strong sinew and soft flesh
Are foliage round the shaft
Before the arrowsmith
Has stripped it; and I pray
That I, all foliage gone,
May shoot into my joy.

The truth is that of all the men I have known there was none
who cast a more eager eye on both life and death. He was a blazing
enthusiast who, into his seventies, retained all the spontaneity and
astonishment of a boy of seventeen. [...]

When we weren't quarrelling, which was often enough, we
usually got on well, because his adolescent eagerness, his passion
for abstract conversation, was the sort of thing I had been used
to when Sean O'Faolain and I were boys in Cork and made our-
selves intellectually drunk over 'objectivity' and 'subjectivity',
Keats and Shelley. We had long, excited and very muddled argu-
ments about Hegelianism, Fascism, Communism, pacifism; and
sometimes the clash of ideas would release the lightning of phrase
or anecdote, always perfectly apt. Once when I quoted the
remark of an Irish politician that 'the great difference between
England and Ireland is that in England you can say what you like
so long as you do the right thing, in Ireland you can do what you
like so long as you say the right thing,' he capped it with 'My
father used to say that the great difference between England and
Ireland is that every Englishman has rich relations and every
Irishman poor ones.'

His first enthusiasm after I got to know him was the establish-
ment of an Academy of Letters, and he had a lovely time chasing
about in taxis, giving lunch-parties, sending wires and pulling
wires. He was an outrageous old flatterer. At that time I hadn't
even published a book and was being accepted into the Academy
on trust, but when I asked whether Mr Somebody or Other was
important enough to be a member Yeats replied: 'Why worry
about literary eminence? You and I will provide that.'

Then he became a Fascist and started parading Dublin in a
bright blue shirt. In his early revolutionary days he wanted
the secret society he belonged to to steal the Coronation Stone
from Westminster Abbey. In his Fascist phase he wanted the
Blueshirts to rebuild Tara and transfer the capital there. He had

neighbours who, he decided, were Blueshirts too, and these had a dog. Mrs Yeats, who was democratic in sympathies, kept hens, and the Blueshirt dog worried the democratic hens. Naturally, Yeats supported the dog. One day Mrs Yeats' favourite hen disappeared, and she wrote to the neighbours to complain of the dog. By return the neighbours replied that the dog had been destroyed. Mrs Yeats, who was very fond of animals, was conscience-stricken, but Yeats was delighted at what he regarded as a true Blueshirt respect for law and order. One evening he called at my flat in a state of high glee. The democratic hen had returned safe and sound and Mrs Yeats was overwhelmed with remorse. Another victory over the democracies!

Then I became a director of the Abbey Theatre, and our rows went on almost uninterruptedly until his death. He wanted *Coriolanus* produced in coloured shirts, in hopes of starting anti-Fascist riots as in Paris, but I dug in my heels about that. In time I almost became one of his enthusiasms myself, which was flattering but rather embarrassing, as he had fathered more bad art and literature than any great writer of his time. 'Within five years,' he told me once, 'So-and-So will be a European figure.' 'Russell,' he said to A.E., who was refusing to enthuse over another of his protégés, 'I wish you and I had the same chance of immortality as that young man.' But one liked the boyish eagerness which prompted it, the questioning way he read you some God-awful poem and tried to persuade you it was 'profound,' 'Shakespearean,' 'the greatest thing produced in our time.'

In his later years he got into a perfect fever over eugenics. It began by his asking me one night if I thought genius could be passed on from one generation to the next. I said I thought not; talent, perhaps, but not genius, and he got very cross, and only then did I realize that he was thinking of his son Michael. Then his face lit up, and he said: 'I had an old aunt who used to say you could pass on anything you liked, provided you took care not to marry the girl next door.'

After that the enthusiasm really got under way. Somebody or other, who was the greatest something or other of our time, had invented a method of testing intelligence that dispensed altogether with acquired knowledge and only tested natural aptitude. This had revealed the alarming fact that if you took children out of a slum and put them in decent surroundings their natural aptitude did not improve, so that the standard of human intelligence was steadily declining. One of the tests turned out to be a labyrinth problem, the second a picture of a heap of clothes on a strand, with a blank space in the middle of the clothes, which the unfortunate children were supposed to fill in with the name of the object that should have been represented. Being myself from a slum, I didn't like to admit that I didn't know from Adam what the appropriate object was, but curiosity compelled me to ask.

'Oh,' said Yeats, 'a dog. To guard the clothes.'

Intelligent or not, it struck me that the capacity of human beings for deluding themselves was practically infinite.

'By the way,' I asked, 'do you think you'd ever have passed an intelligence test?'

He thought about that for a while.

'No,' he admitted regretfully, 'I suppose I wouldn't.'

In the last letter I received from him, written on his deathbed, he suggested that if I wanted his help I should wire and he would return and reorganize the entire Board of the theatre! I used to feel years younger after a visit to him. Disillusionment and cynicism simply dropped away from me when he was round.

CENTENARY ADDRESS AT THE GRAVESIDE OF W. B. YEATS

CEUD BLIAN o shoin do rugadh William Butler Yeats. 'Ach da nesclaiti an doras anois,' dubhairt Richard Best liom la amhain, 'is da dtagadh Oscar Wilde no John Synge isteach, ta fhios agam nach naithneochfainn iad mar bheidis nios sine is nios laige na mar ataim-se fein anois. Ach ni mar sin a chim iad.' Thuigeas cionnas mar a chonnaic se iad:

> I see them walking in an air of glory
>> Whose light doth trample on my days . . .

Is mar sin a chim Yeats. Is beodha anois e na le linn a bheatha fein, agus nil le deunamh agam ach an rud is doigh liom ba mhaith leis adearfainn do radh. Ba mhaith leis go labrochfainn an Ghaoluinn, mar biodh nach raibh aon teanga aige fein ach an Beurla (agus gur chuireas i niul do oiche amhain nach ro-mhaith a mheasas a bhi an Beurla fein aige) ba mhian leis nach bhfoghluimeochfadh a mhac ach an Ghreigis agus an Ghaoluinn – niorbh fiu puinn leis an Laidin mar, dar leis, nar scriobhadh aon rud foghanta riamh innti – ach ba theanga na sibhialtachta an Chreigis, agus bhi gach aon rud eile le foghluim as an nGaoluinn. Nilim deimhnitheach go raibh iomlan an chirt aige.

This is the hundredth birthday of William Butler Yeats. His personality and work have never seemed more alive than they do now, which makes this a day of rejoicing rather than of regret. My own task is an easy one because I have merely to say a few of the things I think he would have wished me to say. I know he would have wished me to speak Irish, because though he was no linguist he was fascinated by the Irish language and literature. One night he told me that all he wished his son to learn at school was Greek and Irish. Latin, according to him, had never produced a real writer, but Greek was the language of civilization, and everything else a man needed to know could be learned from Irish.

Another thing he would have wished me to do – and which I must do since none of the eminent people who have written of him in his centenary year has done so – is to say how much he owed to the young Englishwoman he married, and who made possible the enormous development of his genius from 1916 onward. This should be said by someone who was closer to them both than I was, but it was obvious even to a casual acquaintance. It is not too much to say that if Yeats had not married, or indeed, if he had married someone else, that the story of his later work would probably have been very different. In many ways he was a most fortunate man; fortunate in his parentage, because it is not every poet who has a genius for a father, and most fortunate in his marriage.

He would have wished me too to commemorate along with him his great friends and collaborators, Lady Gregory and John Synge. He was a man with a genius for friendship; with a great memory for small kindnesses done him and a great generosity in forgetting injuries. No one without that sweetness of character could have detached Lady Gregory from her career as a London literary hostess and left her collecting folk stories in Gort, or John Synge from his Paris attic to live a lonely life on Aran. No one without it could have been so cruelly hurt at the bitterness shown to Synge in his last years. For a long time before Yeats' marriage he withdrew gradually from Ireland and the Irish theatre to their great loss, but even that hurt he learned to ignore if not to forget. In this again, I think, we in Ireland may owe a debt to Mrs Yeats.

I have introduced the issues of love and friendship deliberately because in the summing-up of any man's achievement there are always two things to be taken into account – the man's character and the character of the circumstances he had to deal with.

The character of the circumstances is admirably expressed in his choice of a burial place, which my friends in Radio Eireann describe as 'a quiet churchyard'. To the eye of the amateur historian like myself Drumcliffe is no Stoke Poges, but an important Columban monastery whose history reaches back to the sixth or seventh century. Indeed, Colam Cille may well have stood where we are standing now. If ever we in Ireland were to become conscious of our heritage, we should probably find at the other side of the road from the round tower the foundations of a beautiful twelfth-century church, and under the road itself, where trucks and cars pass by, we should find paved roadways, high crosses and numerous tombstones of abbots and kings. Yeats was not the first great man to be buried here; but this is the sort of Ireland he inherited, and that we still inherit – a ruined, fragmented country, divorced from its past. His father before him had inherited it, and on it he blamed what he thought were our faults as a people. 'The faults of the Irishman,' he wrote, 'his foolish swagger and wild exaggeration of himself and everything, is because, notwithstanding his love for his native land, he is not allowed to have pride in it. The individual personality is enormously strengthened by the national personality – the Frenchman is more himself because of Paris.'

In Yeats' youth he had been divorced from the religion of his ancestors by his father's good-natured atheism, qualified by palmistry; and from the time he was a boy he set out to fashion a religion for himself from fragments of Greek and Indian mythology and the poetry of Shelley and Blake. In the same way by a system of education that is still with us he had been divorced from his country's past, though its monuments were all about him, on Knocknarea, in Carrowmore, in Sligo and Dromahair; and in the same patient, stubborn way he set himself to re-create an Early Ireland of his own from a handful of translations of old sagas and poems. Even when he was an old man, you could still make him happy with some fragment of Irish literature he did not know, and this was not easy because he knew almost everything that had been written by an Irishman.

This is where the character of the man and the character of the circumstances met, for a fragmented country offers little to a young writer with a vigorous mind. If Paris strengthens the Frenchman's character, Dublin enfeebles the Irishman's. We must, I think, be the only civilized country whose universities have no chair of the national literature. Ireland would have killed Joyce if he had not left it; he felt sure it had killed Yeats, and told him so, a little too soon perhaps.

But in fact the same background that would have killed Joyce gave Yeats his opportunity. He had the sort of eclectic, synthetic mind that can always discover 'the right twigs for an eagle's nest'; the sort of mind that can build happily among ruins. He compared himself with the bee – 'O honey bees, come build in the empty house of the stare.' It needed a mind like his, strong, but full of sweetness to build in this empty house of ours, and to see beyond the quarrelling sects and factions an older Ireland where men could still afford to be brave and generous and gay.

> And I choose the laughing lip
> That shall not turn from laughing, whatever rise or fall;
> The heart that grows no bitterer, although betrayed by all;
> The hand that loves to scatter; the life like a gambler's throw.

That is the real voice of Yeats; faithful to his own party, but never embittered, never unjust. Once, during his supposed Fascist period a certain famous Englishman approached him at a party in London and said, 'Of course, you support Mr Cosgrave's party, Yeats,' and Yeats replied, 'Oh, I support the gunmen – on both sides!' ('And the damn fool turned his back on me,' he added when he told me the story.) Even his worst enemy he would remember for some kind or chivalrous gesture. Once when a journalist who had attacked himself and Maud Gonne died he said to me, 'And yet all the time, that man knew one secret about Maud Gonne that could have destroyed her influence forever. I went to see him in his office and said, "You must never say that!" and he went on attacking us as bitterly as ever, but he never said it.'

He dreamed of an Ireland where people would disagree without recrimination and excommunication. When he opposed the Divorce Bill in the Senate it was because it made a further cleavage between Catholic and Protestant, and his speech begins in a characteristic way, 'It is perhaps the deepest political passion with this nation that North and South should be united.' One night he said to me, 'You may live to see what I shall never see – the day when Irishmen can disagree without each demanding that the other shall worship at his own narrow conventicle.' He was criticizing the greatest single weakness in our people, our tendency to turn everything we love from our language to our religion into a test of orthodoxy.

It is part of the fragmentation of our national life, and the part that is most injurious to our culture, for culture is an interpenetration and mingling of all the creative forces within a country. Because we leave our literary history to be written by Americans and Englishmen, we fail to see how in Yeats' prime the language movement and the literary movement fed one another, and were themselves fed by other creative activities like co-operative creameries and the beautiful stained glass of Loughrea Cathedral and Cong parish church.

A poet's work endures, but if it has been fruitful, it changes its meaning from generation to generation. This is Yeats' hundredth birthday, and his first birthday into immortality. Today we establish a tradition, and I can only hope it will be a worthy one. I should like to think that as a hundredth birthday present we might do something that would ensure that no young Irishman would ever again grow up so ignorant of his own past; that we might establish a chair of Irish literature in one of our universities, or restore Sligo Abbey, which is as beautiful as any Oxford college, as a repository of the great collection of Yeats relics that Miss Niland has already acquired.

Through centuries after this, if our civilization lasts, others will speak where I am speaking now and other audiences will listen. I hope that what they will praise in Yeats will not be the things that we praise, for that would merely mean that we had left our work undone, and that the tradition we establish today may be the basis of another different Ireland:

That we in coming days may be
Still the indomitable Irishry.

Drumcliffe, June 13th, 1965.

THE TAILOR, when I knew him first, was over eighty, a crippled little Kerryman with soft, round, rosy cheeks exactly like a baby's and two brilliant, mischievous baby eyes. His eyes were the first thing that attracted you. He had no teeth, and he spoke very fast from far back in his throat, and talk and laughter mixed and bubbled like water and wind in a pipe. Most fine days he sat on the road outside his house, maybe minding the cow, but never doing anything much else in the nature of work; the most approachable man in the world, for he had no slyness and distrusted no human being, wherever he might come from. If a Chinese had happened to pass the way, the Tailor would have saluted him politely and asked him how the divil things were by them in China, and, if the man was an intelligent, conversible sort of man who could pass a shrewd comment or crack a joke, the Tailor would have brought him home to Anstey, his wife, and accepted him as a friend along with Kirsten, the Danish girl, Ripley, the American, Seumas, the sculptor, and the English colonel – his 'scholars', as he called them.

Not only did he not distrust people, but, what is much rarer in Ireland, country or town, he did not distrust ideas or conventions. I could not say if this was charity, natural good breeding or simple intellectual independence, but, if someone had dropped in an auto-giro and offered the Tailor a lift, the old man would have gone without giving it a thought, in spite of the shrieks and curses of Anstey. 'Take the world easy and the world will take you easy,' the Tailor told her, but he never managed to get her to appreciate it, because she was a woman of the ancient world, and love and hatred stuck like hooks in her heart.

There are only two dialects of Irish, plain Irish and toothless Irish, and, lacking a proper acquaintance with the latter, I think I missed the cream of the old man's talk, though his English was very colourful and characteristic. But I noticed how almost every phrase he spoke was rounded off by an apt allusion. When Anstey hurried, the Tailor, enthroned on his butter-box by the fire, reproved her and instantly followed up with the story of the Gárlach Coileánach's mother. 'A year is past since my mother was lost; she'd be round the lake since then.' Or when someone spoke of a girl having a baby he came back with: 'She's having last year's laugh's cry.' In Irish, poems, rhymes and proverbs tumbled from him literally in hundreds.

He had all the traditional stuff – the pishogues about the fairies and the pookas, and the witch-doctors born on Good Friday and christened on Easter Sunday, whose power was entirely in their thumbs. He remembered when a cock who grew old was not killed, but plucked and put out on the mountain to die – some savage offering. All that was part of his environment, and it was probably only his fluency and sheer delight in story-telling that made him so much more impressive than other old shanachies I have met. But it was his character which kept him from succumbing to the charms of the invisible world and maintained his lively curiosity about the real one. He was excellent on the history of the parish, on the old days and the faction fights between Cork and Kerrymen which took place in these mountains. He described the Horgan family of Kenmare, whose landlord was attempting to suppress the faction fights and warned them that if they attended another they would be evicted, and how they all preferred to face the workhouse or the emigrant ship rather than let down their kinsmen. He described Sean Mor Lucy, the most powerful man ever was in these parts, with his cry of 'Two o'clock and not a blow shtruck yet,' coming late to the faction fight because he had met a bull and never passed a bull without fighting it. It was the same Sean Mor who was nearly beaten by a black wrestler at the fair of Macroom and was saved only by a neighbour shouting: 'What do you stand on, Sean?' 'Because,' the Tailor added to my astonishment, 'the black man's weakness is in his shin and his elbow.' How, I still wonder, did folk-lore, which can never get anything right, pass on such an extraordinary bit of information as the anatomical formation of a negro's foot?

But the Tailor was at his best as a yarn-spinner, and I never heard a better. Unlike the usual traditional story-tellers, whose stories have been transmitted to them from previous generations and whose own creative powers seem to be non-existent, the Tailor could take a simple little incident of life in the valley, embroider it here and there with a traditional touch, and it became a masterpiece. So, for instance, with the story of the inquest in Mr Cross's book on him, and with the story of his friend Jerry Coakley, 'The Captain'. The Captain had a cat called Moonlighter, who, according to the Tailor, was so bleddy human that he always joined in the Captain's favourite patriotic song, 'We'll plant a tree in Ould Ireland'. One night the Captain, who slept stark naked, found himself with a terrible toothache. In anguish he left his little hut and ran down the road towards the river, followed by Moonlighter. He buried his face in the icy water till the shock killed the toothache, and then, seeing that it was a fine moonlight night, he thought he might as well put in a little poaching. He caught a salmon and tossed it on the bank, but Moonlighter dug his teeth in the salmon, who gave a mighty leap which carried himself and Moonlighter back into the river, where the Captain had the divil's own job to rescue the cat.

The pleasantest Christmas of my life was spent in the inn in Gougane Barra, though most of the day I was with the Tailor and Anstey. On Christmas Eve the valley was like something out of a fairy-tale, with the still mountain lake mirroring the little white cottages and the little grey fields by day, and at night a hundred candles from a score of cottages. There was only one other visitor at the inn, a middle-aged woman who said she had come there for a quiet holiday. Anstey made great play of that; herself and myself to be all alone in the hotel and no wan at all to oblige the poor woman; what would she think the men of the county were like? The cottage was nearly full after supper, a row of old men sitting on the settle with their hats down over their eyes and their sticks between their knees, while the Tailor sat by the fire in front of them on his butter-box. I brought the whiskey and the Tailor supplied the beer. I have never seen the Tailor in better form. He knew I wanted the words and music of a beautiful song which had never been recorded, and he had brought down the only old man in the locality who knew it. The talk began with stories of ghosts and pookas, and then the Tailor sang his favourite song, a version of the Somerset song, 'The Herring'.

And phwat do you think I made of his belly?
A lovely girril, her name it was Nelly,
   Sing falderol, falal, falal.
And what do you think I made of his back?
A lovely boy, his name it was Jack. . . .

Then it was the turn of the other old man, and he hummed and hawed about it.

   ''Tis a bit barbarous.'

'Even so, even so,' said the Tailor, who had his own way with censorships, ''twasn't you made or composed it.'

When the evening was fair and the sunlight was yellow

'That's a powerful line,' interjected the singer after the Gaelic words *buidheachtan na gréine*. 'There's a cartload of meaning in that line.'

When the evening was fair and the sunlight was yellow
   I halted beholding a maiden bright,
Coming to me by the edge of the mountain;
   Her cheeks had a berry-bright, rosy light;
      The honey-gold hair down her shoulders was twining,
      Swinging and billowing, surging and shining,
      Sweeping the grass as she passed by me smiling,
   Driving her geese at the fall of night.

The tune was exquisite and there was nothing in the song you could call barbarous except the young woman's warmly expressed objection to sleeping alone instead of having a companion to 'drive the geese' with her. But with the whiskey it loosened the tongues of the old men, and they quoted with gusto the supposed dying words of Owen Roe O'Sullivan and told scandalous stories about the neighbours, and then the Tailor sang his party piece about the blacksmith:

John Riordan was well-known in Muskerry
   For soldering old iron and the fastening of shoes,
And all the old ladies in the range of the valley
   Knew the click of his hammer on their ticky-tack-toos.

Late that night as we stumbled out along the little causeway from the cabin to the road one of the old men slapped me vigorously on the shoulder and roared: 'Well, thanks be to the Almighty God, Frinshias, we had wan grand dirty night.' I admit that at the time I was a little surprised, but, remembering it afterwards, I felt that to thank God for a good uproariously bawdy party was the very hallmark of a deeply religious mind. I don't know, but I commend the idea to moralists.

But then a young man from London came to live in the neighbourhood, to whom the Tailor became deeply attached, and Mr Eric Cross began to write down his stories and sayings in a little book which appeared as 'The Tailor and Anstey'. For those of us who knew the old couple it is beyond criticism, for it preserves them for us in all their warmth and humanity. That the Tailor saw nothing wrong in the idea of a book goes without saying; he no more minded it than he would have minded an airman or a Chinese. But I still blame myself for not realizing that to all good Irishmen a book is anathema. Mr de Valera's Department of Justice banned the book as being 'in its general tendency indecent'. Then three priests came to the cabin one day, and that dying old man was forced to go on his knees and burn his own copy of the book at his own hearth – 'eight and sixpence worth,' Anstey continued to echo mournfully. To her eight and sixpence was a week's income. This was followed by a boycott; the cottage where night after night you had seen a half-dozen men sitting on the settle with their hats over their eyes was shunned as if it had the plague.

Yet in Ireland there were professors, priests, folk-lorists by the hundred who had accepted the hospitality of that kind old couple, and been glad to listen, as I had, to the 'indecent' talk round the fire at night, and none of them had the courage to protest but one pious Catholic reviewer in the *Sunday Independent*, who had enthused over the book on its appearance and had the courage to repeat his statements word for word when the campaign against it began.

But the one man who really took up the case was no advocate of Gaelic Ireland, but a Southern Unionist, Sir John Keane. He raised it in the Senate, and Mr de Valera's stalwarts, no longer content with attacking the book, attacked the old couple about whom it was written – 'a dirty old man' and 'a moron'. Nobody who does not know the Irish countryside can realize the extent of the tragedy which descended on that old couple at the end of their days. 'When people are as old as we are there is little more the world can do to them,' the Tailor said, masking his grief with philosophy. But Anstey had never learned philosophy. You could see the old woman was eating her heart out.

Then the Tailor died, the happy, holy, peaceful death which anyone who knew him would have expected for him; Anstey went to the District Hospital, and there she too died. And then when Mr de Valera's buffoons had made laughing-stocks of themselves by banning several works of Catholic piety, and even to conciliate their own supporters had to invent some machinery for ridding themselves of the odium they had brought on their country, they established a Censorship Appeal Board.

And, lo and behold! it was instantly discovered that 'The Tailor and Anstey' was not, after all, an indecent book and might safely be put into the hands of anybody. Strangely, up to that moment not one member of that Appeal Board had felt it necessary to express any view about the book when it might have meant so much to a poor old man and woman. When they did nerve themselves to speak it was too late. No friend or neighbour could come rushing up the Gougane Barra road to tell the Tailor that he was not after all 'a dirty old man' and Anstey that she was not 'a moron'.

But one lesson it did teach me, and others too, I think: that it would be far better that the language and traditions of Ireland should go into the grave with that great-hearted couple than that we should surrender our children to the professors and priests and folk-lorists.

4 LONELY VOICES

PREFACE

THOUGH O'CONNOR published two early novels, his principal output over the thirty-five years of his writing life was the short story. He disliked the way the novel was developing in the first part of the twentieth century: he thought it was becoming over-technical, and he especially disapproved of the 'twenty-four-hour novel' introduced by Joyce and Virginia Woolf. 'Everyone was publishing twenty-four-hour novels at the time, and the unities had at last been brought back into literature. As if the uni-ties mattered a damn, as though what you wanted in the novel wasn't the organic feeling of life.' For O'Connor, a novel was a piece of fiction in which characters were tested through time; therefore *Ulysses* and its like were novels which instead of being 'a development, an extension into time' were merely 'an exten-sion sideways'. Elephantinely misconceived short stories, in other words.

In his approach to writing, O'Connor was firm-minded, even dogmatic, but never theoretical. His favourite line from Goethe was, 'Grey, my dear friend, is all your theory, and green the golden tree of Life.' Nevertheless, all writers develop over time a collage of certainties, and a tendency to generalize outwards from their own work; while those who work in academe, as O'Connor did, are perhaps more likely to be tempted by the notion of a unifying theory. In O'Connor's case, this was first pronounced in a lecture series at Stanford in 1961, and published in 1963 as *The Lonely Voice*. The novelist Russell Banks described the effect on him of what has become a classic textbook in American writing schools: 'When at last I read *The Lonely Voice* ... the effect on me at 37 was like the effect on me at 27 of Forster's *Aspects of the Novel* and at 17 of Pound's *ABC of Reading*: gratitude for having received sound instruction and profound annoyance with myself for not having got it sooner.'

O'Connor's central thesis is that 'There is in the short story at its most characteristic something we do not often find in the novel – an intense awareness of human loneliness.' The story is especially good at dealing with 'submerged population groups', which helps explain its strength in America, where such groups abound. Thus the form's characteristic personnel consists of 'outlawed figures wandering at the fringes of society'. Though by O'Connor's own definition, almost every single story he wrote might qualify for this section, the ones that follow are those which deal most directly with the lonely, and the voices the writer gives to them.

THE PROCESSION OF LIFE

AT LAST his father had fulfilled his threat. He was locked out. Since his mother died, a year ago, it had been a cause of dire penalties and direr threats, this question of hours. 'Early to bed,' his father quoted, insisting that he should be home by ten o'clock. He, a grown boy of sixteen to be home at ten o'clock like any kid of twelve! He had risked being late a dozen times before, but tonight had cooked it properly. There was the door locked against him, not a light in the house, and a stony ear to all his knockings and whisperings.

By turns he felt miserable and elated. He had tried sleeping in a garden, but that wasn't a success. Then he had wandered aimlessly into the city and been picked up by a policeman. He looked so young and helpless that the policeman wanted to take him to the barracks, but this was not included in his plans for the night. So he promised the policeman that he would go home directly, and no sooner was he out of the policeman's sight, than he doubled down the quay at the opposite side of the bridge. He walked on for at least a mile until he judged himself safe. The quays were lonely and full of shadows, and he sighed with relief when he saw a watchman's fire glowing redly on the waterfront. He went up to it, and said good-night to the watchman, who was an oldish, bearded man with a sour and repulsive face.

He sat in his little sentry-box, smoking his pipe, and looked, thought Larry, for all the world like a priest in the confessional. But he was swathed in coats and scarves, and a second glance made Larry think not of a priest but of some heathen idol; his face was so bronzed above the grey beard and glowed so majestically in the flickering light of the brazier.

Larry didn't like his situation at all, but he felt his only hope was to stick near the watchman. The city smouldering redly between its hills was in some way unfamiliar and frightening. So were the quays all round him. There were shadowy heaps of timber lying outside the range of the watchman's fire, and behind these he imagined all sorts of strange and frightening things. The river made a clucking, lonely sound against the quay wall, and three or four ships, almost entirely in darkness, swayed about close to the farther bank. He heard the noisy return of a party of sailors from across the water, and once two Lascars went past him in the direction of the bridge.

But the watchman did not seem to welcome Larry's company as much as Larry welcomed his. He was openly incredulous when Larry said he had been locked out.

'Locked out?' he asked suspiciously. 'Then why didn't you kick up hell, huh?'

'What's that, sir?' asked Larry, startled.

'Why didn't you bate the door and kick up hell's delights?'

'God, sir, I'd be afraid to do that!'

At this the watchman started blindly from his box, rubbing the sleep from his eyes and swaying about in the heavy fumes of the brazier.

'Afraid?' he exclaimed scornfully. 'A boy of your age to be afraid of his own father? When I was your age I wouldn't let meself be treated like that. I had a girl of me own, and the first time me ould fella' – God rest him! – tried to stop me going with her I up with the poker, and hit him such a clout over the poll they had to put six stitches in him in the Infirmary after.'

Larry shuddered.

'And what did he do then, sir?' he asked innocently.

'What did he do then?' growled the watchman. 'Ech, he was a quiet man after that I tell you! He couldn't look at me after in the light of day but he'd get a reeling in his head.'

'Lord, sir,' said Larry, 'you must have hit him a terrible stroke!'

'Oh, I quietened him,' said the watchman complacently. 'I quietened him sure enough. . . . And there's a big fella' like you now, and you'd let your father bate you, and never rise a hand in your own self-defence?'

'I would, God help me!' said Larry.

'I suppose you never touched a drop of drink in your life?'

'I did not.'

'And you never took a girl out for a walk?'

'I didn't.'

'Had you ever as much as a pipe in your mouth, tell me?'

'I took a couple of pulls out of me father's pipe once,' said Larry brokenly. 'And I was retching until morning.'

'No wonder you're locked out!' said the watchman contemptuously. 'No wonder at all! I think if I'd a son like you 'twould give me all I could do to keep me hands off him. Get out of me sight!'

Terrified at this extraordinary conclusion, Larry retreated to the edge of the circle of light. He dared not go farther.

'Get out of me sight!' said the watchman again.

'You won't send me away now, sir?' asked Larry in despair.

'Won't I?' asked the watchman ironically. 'Won't I just? There's people comes here at every hour of the night, and am I going to have it said I gethered all the young blackguards of the city about me?'

'I'd go mad with lonesomeness,' Larry cried, his voice rising on a note of fear.

'You'll find company enough in the tramp's shelter on the Marina.'

'I won't go, I won't go! I'll dodge behind the timbers if a stranger comes.'

'You'll do nothing of the kind,' the watchman shouted, losing his temper. 'Clear out now and don't let me see your ugly mug again.'

'I won't go!' Larry repeated hysterically, evading him by running round the brazier. 'I'm frightened, I tell you.'

He had plainly heard the sound of quick footsteps coming in his direction, and he was determined that he would stay. The watchman, too, had heard them, and was equally determined that he would go.

'Bad luck to you!' he whispered despairingly, 'what misfortune brought you this way tonight. If you don't go away I'll strangle you and drop your naked body in the river for the fish to ate. Be off with you, you devil's brat!'

He succeeded in chasing Larry for a few yards when the footsteps suddenly stopped and a woman's voice called out:

'Anybody there?'

'I am,' said the watchman, surlily abandoning the chase.

'I thought you were lost,' the woman said, and her voice sounded in Larry's ears like a peal of bells. He came nearer to the brazier on tiptoe so that the watchman would not perceive him.

'Do you want tea?' the watchman asked sourly.

'Well, you are a perfect gentleman,' the woman's voice went on with a laugh. 'Nice way to speak to a lady!'

'Oh, I know the sort of a lady you are!' the watchman grumbled.

'Squinty!' and now her voice sounded caressing. 'Are you really sore because I left you down the other night? I was sorry, Squinty, honest to God I was, but he was a real nice fella' with tons of dough, and he wanted me so bad!'

Larry, fascinated by the mysterious woman, drew nearer and nearer to the circle of light.

'It isn't only the other night,' the watchman snarled. 'It's every night. You can't see a man but you want to go off with him. I warn you, my girl—'

But his girl was no longer listening to him.

'Who's that?' she whispered sharply, peering into the shadows where Larry's boyish face was half-hidden.

'Blast you!' shouted the watchman furiously. 'Aren't you gone yet?'

The woman strode across to where Larry stood and caught him by the arm. He tried to draw back, but she pulled him into the light of the brazier.

'I say, kid,' she said, 'aren't you bashful? Let's have a look at you! ... Why, he's a real beauty, that's what he is.'

'I'll splinter his beauty for him in wan minit if he don't get out of this!' the watchman cried. 'I'll settle him. He have the heart played out of me this night already.'

'Ah, be quiet, Squinty!' said the woman appeasingly.

'I'll be the death of him!'

'No, you won't. ... Don't you be afraid of him, kid. He's not as bad as he sounds. ... Make a drop of tea for him, Squinty, the poor kid's hands are freezing.'

'I won't make tea for him. I have no liquors to spare for young ragamuffins and sleepouts.'

'Aah, do as you're told!' the woman said disgustedly.

'You know there's only two ponnies,' said the watchman, subsiding.

'Well, him and me'll drink out of the one. Won't we kid?'

And with amazing coolness she put him sitting on an impro-vised bench before the fire, sat close beside him, and drew his hand comfortingly about her slender waist. Larry held it shyly; for the moment he wasn't even certain that he might lawfully hold it at all. He looked at this magical creature in the same shy way. She had a diminutive face, coloured a ghostly white, and crimson lips that looked fine in the firelight. She was perfumed, too, with a scent that he found overpowering and sweet. There was something magical and compelling about her. And stranger than all, the watchman had fallen under her spell. He brewed the tea and poured it out into two ponnies, grumbling to himself the while.

'You *know* he have no right to set down there,' he was saying. 'Nice trouble I'd be getting into if someone came along and seen a . . . seen a woman of the streets and a young reformatory school brat settin' be the fire. . . . Eh, me lady? . . . Oh, very well, very well. . . . This'll be put a stop to, this can't go on forever. . . . And you think I don't know what you're up to, huh? Hm? No, no, my dear, you can't fool an old soldier like me that way. This'll be put a stop to.'

'What are you saying, Squinty?' the woman asked.

'Oh, don't mind me! Don't mind me!' The watchman laughed bitterly. 'I don't count, but all the same this'll be put a stop to . . . there's your tea!'

He handed her one of the ponnies, then retreated into his watch box with the second. Inside he fumbled in his pockets, removed a little parcel of bread and butter, and tossed her half, which she deftly caught and shared with Larry. Larry had begun to feel that miracles were a very ordinary thing after all.

'Get outside that, kid,' she said kindly to Larry, handing him the ponny of boiling tea. ''Twill warm up your insides. What happened you to be out so late? Kissed the girl and lost the tram?'

'Me ould fella'—' said Larry, sipping and chewing, 'me ould fella' – locked me out! Bad luck to him!' he added with a startling new courage.

'Oh, ay, oh, ay!' commented the watchman bitterly from his box. 'That's the way they speaks of their fathers nowadays! No respect for age or anything else. Better fed than taught.'

'Never mind him, darling,' said the woman consolingly. 'He's old-fashioned, that's what he is!'

Then as Larry made a frightened sign to her, she laughed.

'Are you afraid he'll hear me? Oh, Squinty doesn't mind a bit.

We're old friends. He know quite well what I think of him –
don't you, Squinty?' Her voice dropped to a thrilling whisper,
and her hand fondled Larry's knee in a way that sent a shiver of
pleasure through him. 'Will you come home with me, darling?'
she asked, without listening to the watchman's reply.

'Oh, I know, I know,' the latter answered. 'Nice name this
place'll be getting with you and all the immoral men and boys
of the city making your rondeyvoos here. Sailors . . . tramps . . .
reformatory school brats . . . all sorts and conditions. This'll be
put a stop to, my lady. Mark my words, this'll be put a stop to.
I know what you're saying, I know what you're whispering. It's
no use, my dear. You can't deceive me.'

'I was only asking him if he'd e'er a place to stop.'

'And what is it to you if he haven't, my lady?'

'God help us, you wouldn't like your own son to be out here
all night, catching his death of cold or maybe dropping asleep
and falling stupid in the fire.'

'I wouldn't like me own son to be connaisseuring with the
likes of you either.'

'He might meet with worse,' said the woman, bridling up.

'And where would you bring him?'

'Never mind where I'd bring him! I'd bring him a place he'd
be welcome in anyway, not like here.'

The watchman suddenly changed his tone, becoming violent,
and at the same time conciliatory.

'You wouldn't leave me here lonesome by meself after all you
promised me?' he cried.

'I won't remain here to be insulted either.'

'He can stay, he can stay,' said the watchman submissively.
'I won't say a cross word to him.'

'He'd rather go home with me,' said the woman. 'Wouldn't
you, darling?'

'I would,' said Larry decisively.

'Don't you go! Don't you go, young fellow!' shouted the
watchman. 'She's an immoral woman. . . . Oh, you low creature,'
he continued, 'aren't you ashamed of yourself? Leaving me lone-
some night after night, and chasing off with any stranger that
comes the way. Last time it was the dandy fellow off the Swedish
boat, and now it's a common brat that his own father won't
leave in.'

'Now, now, don't be snotty!' said the young woman reprovingly. 'It's not becoming to your years. And if you're good maybe I'll come round and see you tomorrow night.'

'You'll say that and not mean a word of it!' exclaimed the watchman. 'Oh, you low creature. You haven't a spark of honour or decency.'

'Come on home, darling, before he loses his temper,' said the woman good-humouredly. She rose and took Larry's hand, and with a loud 'Good-bye' to the watchman, guided him on to the roadway. As she did so there came the sound of heavy footsteps thudding along the wooden jetty. The woman started nervously and pushed Larry before her towards the shadow of the timber.

'Here, kid,' she whispered, 'we'll go round by the timbers and up the Park. Hurry! Hurry! I hear someone coming.'

The steps drew nearer, and suddenly she dropped Larry's hand and crouched back into the shadows. He heard a quick, stifled cry that terrified him.

'Oh, Sacred Heart, he seen me!' she said, and then in a tense, vicious whisper she cried to the unseen, 'May the divil in hell melt and blind you, you clumsy Tipperary lout!'

'Is that you I seen, Molly?' a jovial voice called from the darkness, and a moment later Larry saw the glint of the fire on an array of silver buttons.

'Yes, constable, it's me,' the woman answered, and Larry could scarcely recognize her voice for the moment, it was so unctuous, so caressing. But again came the fierce mutter beside him, 'Bad luck and end to you, y'ould ram, what divil's notion took you to come this way tonight?'

'Are you alone?' the policeman asked, emerging from the shadows.

'No, constable,' she sniggered.

'Is there someone with you?'

'Yes, constable . . . a friend.'

'Oh, a friend, is there? And what's your friend doing out at this hour of the night?' He strode across to Larry and shook his arm. 'So you're the friend, me young hopeful? And what have you here at this hour of the night, huh?'

'He was seeing me home, constable, and I took a bit of a weakness so we sat here a while with Squinty.'

'Answer me!' thundered the policeman to Larry. 'And don't try to tell any lies. What have you out at this hour?'

'Me father' – gasped Larry, 'me father – locked me out – sir.'

'Mmmm. Your father locked you out, did he? Well, I'm thinking it wouldn't do you any harm to lock you in, d'you hear? How would you like that, eh?'

'Bah!' grunted the watchman.

'What did you say, Squinty?'

'I said right, constable. Right every time! If I'd me way with that sort of young fellow I'd make drisheens of his hide.'

'And what about you, Molly?'

'He's a friend of mine, constable,' the woman said ingratiatingly. 'Let him go now and he won't do it again. I'm finding him a place to sleep – the poor child is perished with the cold. Leave him to me, constable. I'll look after him for the night.'

'Aisy now, aisy!' the policeman interrupted heavily. 'We're all friends, aren't we?'

'Yes, constable.'

'And we want to do the best we can by one another, don't we?'

'Yes, constable.'

'I've a word to say to you, so I think I'll take your advice and let the boy go. Squinty will keep an eye on him, won't you, Squinty?'

'You may swear I'll keep an eye on him,' the watchman said viciously.

'That's all right then. Are you satisfied now, Molly?'

'Yes, constable,' she said between her teeth.

'The same place?'

'Yes, constable.'

She turned on her heel and went off slowly along the quay. The darkness was thinning. A faint brightness came from above the hill at the other side of the river. The policeman glanced at it and sighed.

'Well, it's a fine day, thanks be to God,' he said. 'I had a quiet night of it, and after this I'll have a grand sleep for myself. Will you try a drop, Squinty?'

'I will then,' said the watchman greedily.

The policeman took a flask from his pocket and drank from it. He handed it to the watchman, who took another swig and gave it back to him. The policeman held it up to the fire. He closed his left eye and whistled brightly for a few moments.

'There's a *taoscán* in it still,' he commented. 'I suppose you don't drink, young fellow?'

'I don't,' said Larry sourly, 'but I'd drink it now if you'd give it to me.'

'I will, I will,' said the policeman laughing. 'And I after taking your girl from you and all. 'Tis the least I might do. But never mind, young fellow. There's plenty more where she came from.'

Larry choked over a mouthful of the neat whiskey and handed back the empty flask. The policeman drew out a packet of cheap cigarettes and held it towards him.

'Wish me luck!' he said.

'Good luck!' said Larry, taking a cigarette.

'Fathers are a curse anyway,' said the other confidentially. 'But I mustn't be keeping me little pusher waiting. So long, men.'

'So long,' said Larry and the watchman together.

The policeman disappeared between the high walls of timber, and Larry sat by the brazier and recklessly lit his cigarette. The watchman, too, lit his pipe, and smoked silently and contentedly, spitting now and again out of sheer satisfaction. The faint brightness over the hill showed clearer and clearer, until at last the boy could distinguish the dim outlines of riverside and ships and masts. He shivered. The air seemed to have become colder. The watchman began to mumble complacently to himself within his box.

'Ah, dear me,' he said, launching a spit in the direction of the brazier, 'dear me, honesty is the best policy. . . . Yes, my lady, honesty is the best policy after all, that's what I say. . . . I told you I'd (spit) put a stop to your goings-on, my lady; your (spit) Swedish skippers and your dandy boys, and now you're quiet enough, my lady. . . . Now you're quiet enough.'

Larry rose.

'Where are you going now?' asked the watchman sourly.

'I'm going home,' said Larry.

'Stop where you are now! Didn't you hear what the policeman said?'

'I don't care what the policeman said. I'm going home.'

'Home? Aren't you afraid?'

'What would I be afraid of?' asked Larry contemptuously.

'Ah, my boy,' said the watchman with fierce satisfaction, 'your old fella' will hammer hell out of you when he gets you inside the door!'

'Will he?' asked Larry. 'Will he now? I'd bloody well like to see him try it.'

And whistling jauntily, he went off in the direction of the city.

OLD DAN BRIDE was breaking brosna for the fire when he heard a step on the path. He paused, a bundle of saplings on his knee.

Dan had looked after his mother while the life was in her, and after her death no other woman had crossed his threshold. Signs on it, his house had that look. Almost everything in it he had made with his own hands in his own way. The seats of the chairs were only slices of log, rough and round and thick as the saw had left them, and with the rings still plainly visible through the grime and polish that coarse trouser-bottoms had in the course of long years imparted. Into these Dan had rammed stout knotted ash-boughs that served alike for legs and back. The deal table, bought in a shop, was an inheritance from his mother and a great pride and joy to him though it rocked whenever he touched it. On the wall, unglazed and fly-spotted, hung in mysterious isolation a Marcus Stone print, and beside the door was a calendar with a picture of a racehorse. Over the door hung a gun, old but good, and in excellent condition, and before the fire was stretched an old setter who raised his head expectantly whenever Dan rose or even stirred.

He raised it now as the steps came nearer and when Dan, laying down the bundle of saplings, cleaned his hands thoughtfully on the seat of his trousers, he gave a loud bark, but this expressed no more than a desire to show off his own watchfulness. He was half human and knew people thought he was old and past his prime.

A man's shadow fell across the oblong of dusty light thrown over the half-door before Dan looked round.

'Are you alone, Dan?' asked an apologetic voice.

'Oh, come in, come in, sergeant, come in and welcome,' exclaimed the old man, hurrying on rather uncertain feet to the door which the tall policeman opened and pushed in. He stood there, half in sunlight, half in shadow, and seeing him so, you would have realized how dark the interior of the house really was. One side of his red face was turned so as to catch the light, and behind it an ash tree raised its boughs of airy green against the sky. Green fields, broken here and there by clumps of red-brown rock, flowed downhill, and beyond them, stretched all across the horizon, was the sea, flooded and almost transparent with light. The sergeant's face was fat and fresh, the old man's face, emerging from the twilight of the kitchen, had the colour of wind and sun, while the features had been so shaped by the struggle with time and the elements that they might as easily have been found impressed upon the surface of a rock.

'Begor, Dan,' said the sergeant, ''tis younger you're getting.'

'Middling I am, sergeant, middling,' agreed the old man in a voice which seemed to accept the remark as a compliment of which politeness would not allow him to take too much advantage. 'No complaints.'

'Begor, 'tis as well because no one would believe them. And the old dog doesn't look a day older.'

The dog gave a low growl as though to show the sergeant that he would remember this unmannerly reference to his age, but indeed he growled every time he was mentioned, under the impression that people had nothing but ill to say of him.

'And how's yourself, sergeant?'

'Well, now, like the most of us, Dan, neither too good nor too bad. We have our own little worries, but, thanks be to God, we have our compensations.'

'And the wife and family?'

'Good, praise be to God, good. They were away from me for a month, the lot of them, at the mother-in-law's place in Clare.'

'In Clare, do you tell me?'

'In Clare. I had a fine quiet time.'

The old man looked about him and then retired to the bed-room, from which he returned a moment later with an old shirt. With this he solemnly wiped the seat and back of the log-chair nearest the fire.

'Sit down now, sergeant. You must be tired after the journey. 'Tis a long old road. How did you come?'

'Teigue Leary gave me the lift. Wisha now, Dan, don't be putting yourself out. I won't be stopping. I promised them I'd be back inside an hour.'

'What hurry is on you?' asked Dan. 'Look, your foot was only on the path when I made up the fire.'

'Arrah, Dan, you're not making tea for me?'

'I am not making it for you, indeed; I'm making it for myself, and I'll take it very bad of you if you won't have a cup.'

'Dan, Dan, that I mightn't stir, but 'tisn't an hour since I had it at the barracks!'

'Ah, whisht, now, whisht! Whisht, will you! I have something here to give you an appetite.'

The old man swung the heavy kettle on to the chain over the open fire, and the dog sat up, shaking his ears with an expression of the deepest interest. The policeman unbuttoned his tunic, opened his belt, took a pipe and a plug of tobacco from his breast pocket, and crossing his legs in an easy posture, began to cut the tobacco slowly and carefully with his pocket knife. The old man went to the dresser and took down two handsomely decorated cups, the only cups he had, which, though chipped and handle-less, were used at all only on very rare occasions; for himself he preferred his tea from a basin. Happening to glance into them, he noticed that they bore signs of disuse and had collected a lot of the fine white turf-dust that always circulated in the little smoky cottage. Again he thought of the shirt, and, rolling up his sleeves with a stately gesture, he wiped them inside and out till they shone. Then he bent and opened the cupboard. Inside was a quart bottle of pale liquid, obviously untouched. He removed the cork and smelt the contents, pausing for a moment in the act as though to recollect where exactly he had noticed that particular smoky smell before. Then, reassured, he stood up and poured out with a liberal hand.

'Try that now, sergeant,' he said with quiet pride.

The sergeant, concealing whatever qualms he might have felt at the idea of drinking illegal whiskey, looked carefully into the cup, sniffed, and glanced up at old Dan.

'It looks good,' he commented.

'It should be good,' replied Dan with no mock modesty.

'It tastes good too,' said the sergeant.

'Ah, sha,' said Dan, not wishing to praise his own hospitality in his own house, ''tis of no great excellence.'

'You'd be a good judge, I'd say,' said the sergeant without irony.

'Ever since things became what they are,' said Dan, carefully guarding himself against a too-direct reference to the peculiarities of the law administered by his guest, 'liquor isn't what it used to be.'

'I've heard that remark made before now, Dan,' said the sergeant thoughtfully. 'I've heard it said by men of wide experience that it used to be better in the old days.'

'Liquor,' said the old man, 'is a thing that takes time. There was never a good job done in a hurry.'

' 'Tis an art in itself.'

'Just so.'

'And an art takes time.'

'And knowledge,' added Dan with emphasis. 'Every art has its secrets, and the secrets of distilling are being lost the way the old songs were lost. When I was a boy there wasn't a man in the barony but had a hundred songs in his head, but with people running here, there and everywhere, the songs were lost. . . . Ever since things became what they are,' he repeated on the same guarded note, 'there's so much running about the secrets are lost.'

'There must have been a power of them.'

'There was. Ask any man today that makes whiskey do he know how to make it out of heather.'

'And was it made of heather?' asked the policeman.

'It was.'

'You never drank it yourself?'

'I didn't, but I knew old men that did, and they told me that no whiskey that's made nowadays could compare with it.'

'Musha, Dan, I think sometimes 'twas a great mistake of the law to set its hand against it.'

Dan shook his head. His eyes answered for him, but it was not in nature for a man to criticize the occupation of a guest in his own home.

'Maybe so, maybe not,' he said noncommittally.

'But sure, what else have the poor people?'

'Them that makes the laws have their own good reasons.'

'All the same, Dan, all the same, 'tis a hard law.'

The sergeant would not be outdone in generosity. Politeness required him not to yield to the old man's defence of his superiors and their mysterious ways.

'It is the secrets I'd be sorry for,' said Dan, summing up. 'Men die and men are born, and where one man drained another will plough, but a secret lost is lost forever.'

'True,' said the sergeant mournfully. 'Lost forever.'

Dan took his cup, rinsed it in a bucket of clear water by the door and cleaned it again with the shirt. Then he placed it carefully at the sergeant's elbow. From the dresser he took a jug of milk and a blue bag containing sugar; this he followed up with a slab of country butter and – a sure sign that he had been expecting a visitor – a round cake of homemade bread, fresh and uncut. The kettle sang and spat and the dog, shaking his ears, barked at it angrily.

'Go away, you brute!' growled Dan, kicking him out of his way.

He made the tea and filled the two cups. The sergeant cut himself a large slice of bread and buttered it thickly.

'It is just like medicines,' said the old man, resuming his theme with the imperturbability of age. 'Every secret there was is lost. And leave no one tell me that a doctor is as good a man as one that had the secrets of old times.'

'How could he be?' asked the sergeant with his mouth full.

'The proof of that was seen when there were doctors and wise people there together.'

'It wasn't to the doctors the people went, I'll engage?'

'It was not. And why?' With a sweeping gesture the old man took in the whole world outside his cabin. 'Out there on the hillsides is the sure cure for every disease. Because it is written' – he tapped the table with his thumb – 'it is written by the poets "wherever you find the disease you will find the cure." But people walk up the hills and down the hills and all they see is flowers. Flowers! As if God Almighty – honour and praise to Him! – had nothing better to do with His time than be making old flowers!'

'Things no doctor could cure the wise people cured,' agreed the sergeant.

'Ah, musha, 'tis I know it,' said Dan bitterly. 'I know it, not in my mind but in my own four bones.'

'Have you the rheumatics at you still?' the sergeant asked in a shocked tone.

'I have. Ah, if you were alive, Kitty O'Hara, or you, Nora Malley of the Glen, 'tisn't I'd be dreading the mountain wind or the sea wind; 'tisn't I'd be creeping down with my misfortunate red ticket for the blue and pink and yellow dribble-drabble of their ignorant dispensary.'

'Why then indeed,' said the sergeant, 'I'll get you a bottle for that.'

'Ah, there's no bottle ever made will cure it.'

'That's where you're wrong, Dan. Don't talk now till you try it. It cured my own uncle when he was that bad he was shouting for the carpenter to cut the two legs off him with a handsaw.'

'I'd give fifty pounds to get rid of it,' said Dan magniloquently. 'I would and five hundred.'

The sergeant finished his tea in a gulp, blessed himself and struck a match which he then allowed to go out as he answered some question of the old man. He did the same with a second and third, as though titillating his appetite with delay. Finally he succeeded in getting his pipe alight and the two men pulled round their chairs, placed their toes side by side in the ashes, and in deep puffs, lively bursts of conversation, and long, long silences, enjoyed their smoke.

'I hope I'm not keeping you?' said the sergeant, as though struck by the length of his visit.

'Ah, what would you keep me from?'

'Tell me if I am. The last thing I'd like to do is waste another man's time.'

'Begor, you wouldn't waste my time if you stopped all night.'

'I like a little chat myself,' confessed the policeman.

And again they became lost in conversation. The light grew thick and coloured and, wheeling about the kitchen before it disappeared, became tinged with gold; the kitchen itself sank into cool greyness with cold light on the cups and basins and plates of the dresser. From the ash tree a thrush began to sing. The open hearth gathered brightness till its light was a warm, even splash of crimson in the twilight.

Twilight was also descending outside when the sergeant rose to go. He fastened his belt and tunic and carefully brushed his clothes. Then he put on his cap, tilted a little to side and back.

'Well, that was a great talk,' he said.

''Tis a pleasure,' said Dan, 'a real pleasure.'

'And I won't forget the bottle for you.'

'Heavy handling from God to you!'

'Good-bye now, Dan.'

'Good-bye, sergeant, and good luck.'

Dan didn't offer to accompany the sergeant beyond the door. He sat in his old place by the fire, took out his pipe once more, blew through it thoughtfully, and just as he leaned forward for a twig to kindle it, heard the steps returning. It was the sergeant. He put his head a little way over the half-door.

'Oh, Dan!' he called softly.

'Ay, sergeant?' replied Dan, looking round, but with one hand still reaching for the twig. He couldn't see the sergeant's face, only hear his voice.

'I suppose you're not thinking of paying that little fine, Dan?'

There was a brief silence. Dan pulled out the lighted twig, rose slowly and shambled towards the door, stuffing it down in the almost empty bowl of the pipe. He leaned over the half-door while the sergeant with hands in the pockets of his trousers gazed rather in the direction of the laneway, yet taking in a considerable portion of the sea line.

'The way it is with me, sergeant,' replied Dan unemotionally, 'I am not.'

'I was thinking that, Dan; I was thinking you wouldn't.'

There was a long silence during which the voice of the thrush grew shriller and merrier. The sunken sun lit up rafts of purple cloud moored high above the wind.

'In a way,' said the sergeant, 'that was what brought me.'

'I was just thinking so, sergeant, it only struck me and you going out the door.'

'If 'twas only the money, Dan, I'm sure there's many would be glad to oblige you.'

'I know that, sergeant. No, 'tisn't the money so much as giving that fellow the satisfaction of paying. Because he angered me, sergeant.'

The sergeant made no comment on this and another long silence ensued.

'They gave me the warrant,' the sergeant said at last, in a tone which dissociated him from all connection with such an un-neighbourly document.

'Did they so?' exclaimed Dan, as if he was shocked by the thoughtlessness of the authorities.

'So whenever 'twould be convenient for you —'

'Well, now you mention it,' said Dan, by way of throwing out a suggestion for debate, 'I could go with you now.'

'Ah, sha, what do you want going at this hour for?' protested the sergeant with a wave of his hand, dismissing the notion as the tone required.

'Or I could go tomorrow,' added Dan, warming to the issue.

'Would it be suitable for you now?' asked the sergeant, scaling up his voice accordingly.

'But, as a matter of fact,' said the old man emphatically, 'the day that would be most convenient to me would be Friday after dinner, because I have some messages to do in town, and I wouldn't have the journey for nothing.'

'Friday will do grand,' said the sergeant with relief that this delicate matter was now practically disposed of. 'If it doesn't they can damn well wait. You could walk in there yourself when it suits you and tell them I sent you.'

'I'd rather have yourself there, sergeant, if it would be no inconvenience. As it is, I'd feel a bit shy.'

'Why then, you needn't feel shy at all. There's a man from my own parish there, a warder; one Whelan. Ask for him; I'll tell him you're coming, and I'll guarantee when he knows you're a friend of mine he'll make you as comfortable as if you were at home.'

'I'd like that fine,' Dan said with profound satisfaction. 'I'd like to be with friends, sergeant.'

'You will be, never fear. Good-bye again now, Dan. I'll have to hurry.'

'Wait now, wait till I see you to the road.'

Together the two men strolled down the laneway while Dan explained how it was that he, a respectable old man, had had the grave misfortune to open the head of another old man in such a way as to require his removal to hospital, and why it was that he couldn't give the old man in question the satisfaction of paying in cash for an injury brought about through the victim's own unmannerly method of argument.

'You see, sergeant,' Dan said, looking at another little cottage up the hill, 'the way it is, he's there now, and he's looking at us as sure as there's a glimmer of sight in his weak, wandering, watery eyes, and nothing would give him more gratification than for me to pay. But I'll punish him. I'll lie on bare boards for him. I'll suffer for him, sergeant, so that neither he nor any of his children after him will be able to raise their heads for the shame of it.'

On the following Friday he made ready his donkey and butt and set out. On his way he collected a number of neighbours who wished to bid him farewell. At the top of the hill he stopped to send them back. An old man, sitting in the sunlight, hastily made his way indoors, and a moment later the door of his cottage was quietly closed.

Having shaken all his friends by the hand, Dan lashed the old donkey, shouted: 'Hup there!' and set out alone along the road to prison.

AFTER FOURTEEN YEARS

NICHOLAS COLEMAN arrived in B— on a fair day. The narrow streets were crowded with cattle that lurched and lounged dangerously as the drovers goaded them out of the way of passing cars. The air was charged with smells and dust and noise. Jobbers swung their sticks and shouted at one another across the street; shopkeepers displayed their wares and haggled with customers on the high pavements; shrill-voiced women sold apples, cigarettes and lemonade about the statue of the Maid of Erin in the market-place, and jovial burly farmers with shrewd ascetic faces under their Spanish hats jostled him as they passed.

He was glad when he succeeded in getting his business done and could leave the town for a while. It unnerved him. Above the roofs one could see always the clear grey-green of a hill that rose sharply above them and seemed as if at any moment it might fall and crush them. The sea road was better. There were carts on that too, and creels passed full of squealing animals; but at least one had the great bay with its many islands and its zone of violet hills through which sunlight and shadow circulated ceaselessly, without effort, like the flowing of water. The surface of the bay was very calm, and it seemed as if a rain of sunlight were pelting upon a bright flagstone and being tossed back again in a faint glittering spray, so that when one looked at it for long it dazzled the eye. Three or four fishing smacks and a little railway steamer with a bright red funnel were all that the bay held.

He had his dinner over an old shop in the market-place, but he was so nervous that he ate little. The farmers and jobbers tried to press him into conversation, but he had nothing to say; they talked of prices and crops, the Government and the County Council, about all of which he knew next to nothing. Eventually they let him be, much to his relief.

After dinner he climbed the hill that led out of town. The traffic had grown less: he climbed, and as the town sank back against the growing circle of the bay it seemed a quiet place enough, too quiet perhaps. He felt something like awe as he went up the trim gravel path to the convent. 'At seven,' he thought, 'the train will take me back to the city. At ten I shall be walking through Patrick Street on my way home. Tomorrow I shall be back at my old stool in the office. I shall never see this place again, never!'

But in spite of this, and partly because of it, his heart beat faster when the lay sister showed him into the bare parlour, with its crucifix, its polished floor, its wide-open windows that let in a current of cool air.

And at last *she* came; a slim figure in black with starched white facings. He scarcely looked at her, but took her hand, smiling, embarrassed and silent. She too was ill at ease.

They sat together on a garden seat from which he saw again the town and the bay, even more quiet now. He heard nothing of its noise but the desolate screech of a train as it entered the station. Her eyes took it all in dispassionately, and now and again he glanced shyly up at her fine profile. That had not changed, and he wondered whether he had altered as little as she. Perhaps he hadn't, perhaps for her at least he was still the same as he had always been. Yet – there was a change in her! Her face had lost something; perhaps it was intensity; it no longer suggested the wildness and tenderness that he knew was in her. She looked happier and stronger.

'And Kate?' she asked after they had talked for a little while. 'How is she?'

'Oh, Kate is very well. They have a nice house in Passage – you know Tom has a school there. It's just over the river – the house, I mean; sometimes I go down to them on a Sunday evening for tea. . . . They have five children now; the eldest is sixteen.'

'Yes, of course – Marie. Why, she was called after me! She's my godchild.'

'Yes, yes, fancy I'd forgotten! You were always with Kate in those days.'

'I'd love to see Marie. She has written to me for my feastday ever since she was nine.'

'Has she? I didn't know. They don't talk to me about it.'

A faint flush mounted her cheek; for a moment she was silent, and if he had looked at her he would have seen a sudden look of doubt and pain in her eyes. But he did not look up, and she continued.

'Kate writes to me off and on too – but you know Kate! It was from her I heard of your mother's death. That must have been a terrible blow to you.'

'Yes, it was very sudden. I was the only one with her when it came.'

'We had Mass for her here. How did she die? Was she —?'

'She died hard. She didn't want to leave me.'

'Oh!'

Her lips moved silently for a little.

'I've never forgotten her. She was so gentle, so – so unobtrusive, and Fair Hill used to be such a happy place then, before Kate married, when there were only the three of ourselves. . . . Do you remember, I used to go without my dinner to come up after school? . . . And so the house is gone?'

'Yes, the house is gone.'

'And Jennifer? The parrot?'

'Jennifer died long ago. She choked herself with an apple.'

'And Jasper?'

'Jasper too. An Alsatian killed him. I have another now, a sheep-dog, a great lazy fellow. He's made friends with the Kerry Blue next door and the Kerry Blue comes with us and catches rabbits for him. He's fond of rabbits, but he's so big, so big and lazy!'

'You're in lodgings. Why didn't you go to live with Kate and Tom? You know they'd have been glad to have you.'

'Why should I? They were married; they had children at the time; they needed the house for themselves. . . . Besides, you know what I am. I'm a simple fellow, I'm not a bit clever, I don't read books or papers. At dinner the cattle-jobbers were trying to get me talking politics, and honest, I didn't know what they were at! What would Tom and his friends from the University have thought of a stupid creature like me?'

'No, you spent all your time in the country. I remember you getting up at five and going out with the dogs, around White's Cross and back through Ballyvolane. Do you still do that?'

'Yes, every fine morning and most Sundays. But I had to give up the birds when mother died.'

'Ah, the birds! What a pity! I remember them too, and how beautifully they sang.' She laughed happily, without constraint. 'The other girls envied me so much because you were always giving me birds' eggs, and I swapped them for other things, and

I came back to you crying, pretending I'd lost them. . . . I don't think you ever guessed what a cheat I was. . . . Ah, well! And you're still in the factory.'

'Still in the factory! . . . You were right, you see. Do you remember you said I'd stick there until I grew grey hairs. You used to be angry with me then, and that worried me, and I'd give a spurt or two – No, no, I never had any ambition – not much anyhow – and as well be there as any place else. . . . And now I'm so used to it that I couldn't leave even if I wanted to. I live so quietly that even coming here has been too much of an adventure for me. All the time I've been saying "Tomorrow I shall be back at work, tomorrow I shall be back at work." I'll be glad to get home.'

'Yes, I can understand that.'

'Can you? You used to be different.'

'Yes, but things *are* different here. One works. One doesn't think. One doesn't want to think. I used to lie abed until ten at one time, now I'm up at half-past five every morning and I'm not a bit more tired. I'm kept busy all day. I sleep sound. I don't dream. And I hate anything that comes to disturb the routine.'

'Like me?'

'No, not like you. I hate being ill, lying in bed listening to the others and not working myself.'

'And you don't get into panics any longer?'

'No, no more panics.'

'You don't weep? You're not ambitious any longer? – that's so strange! . . . Yes, it *is* good to have one's life settled, to fear nothing and hope for nothing.'

She cast a quick, puzzled look at him.

'Do you still go to early Mass?' she asked.

'Yes, just as before.'

They fell into silence again. A little mist was rising from the town; one side of the bay was flanked with a wall of gold; a cool wind from the sea blew up to them, stirring the thick foliage and tossing her light, black veil. A bell rang out suddenly and she rose.

'What are your lodgings like?' she asked, her cheeks reddening. 'I hope you look after yourself and that they feed you properly. You used to be so careless.'

'Oh, yes, yes. They're very decent. And you – how do you find the place agreeing with you? Better than the city?'

'Oh, of course,' she said wearily, 'it is milder here.'

They went silently up the path towards the convent and parted as they had met, awkwardly, almost without looking at one another.

'No,' he thought, as he passed through the convent gate, 'that's over!' But he knew that for days, perhaps for months, birds and dogs, flowers, his early-morning walks through the country, the trees in summer, all those things that had given him pleasure would give him nothing but pain. The farmers coming from the fair, shouting to one another forward and back from their lumbering carts brought to mind his dreams of yesterday, and he grieved that God had created men without the innocence of natural things, had created them subtle and capricious, with memories in which the past existed like a statue, perfect and unapproachable.

And as the train carried him back to the city the clangour of its wheels that said 'ruthutta ruthutta ruthutta' dissolved into a bright mist of conversation through which he distinctly heard a woman's voice, but the voice said nothing; it was like memory, perfect and unapproachable; and his mind was weighed down by an infinite melancholy that merged with the melancholy of the dark countryside through which he passed – a countryside of lonely, steel-bright pools that were islanded among the silhouettes of hills and trees. Ironically he heard himself say again, 'Yes, it *is* good to have one's life settled, to fear nothing and hope for nothing.'

And the train took him ever farther and farther away and replied with its petulant metallic voice –

'Ruthutta ruthutta ruthutta!'

MAY NIGHT

IT WAS a night in May, warm and dim and full of the syrupy smell of whitethorn. In a black sky a single star, blue and misty, was burning. Two tramps sat by the roadside. One was tall and thin, and in the ash-coloured twilight one might have seen that he had a long face with a drooping moustache. The other was a small man who looked fat; but that was only because he was swathed in coats, one more ragged than the next. He must have been wearing four or five in all. He had a ragged black beard that jutted out all over his face. His black hat was pasted perfectly flat over his scattered black locks that streamed about his shoulders, inside and outside the coats. Even in daylight all you could see of his person would be two beady black eyes, very bright, a stub of a nose no bigger than the butt of a cigar, and, when he moved his hands, the tips of his dirty fingers which were otherwise lost to view.

'Man,' he was saying in a high sing-song voice, 'is an animal. An animal must live. Therefore man must live. That's a syllogism; if you don't agree with it you must contradict the major or the minor or say the conclusion doesn't follow. But a man is made in the image of God and he must try and live decent. Only you, Horgan, you son of a bitch, you're worse than an animal. An animal bites because 'tis his nature to, but you bite because you likes it. Horgan,' he said, spitting, 'you're neither a man nor an animal. Why do you hang around me?'

'I don't hang around you.'

'You do. You do hang around me. No one else would leave you do it. But I'm a weak man and I leaves you. You're a constant source of timptation to me. When I gets angry I hits you and then I do be sorry.'

'Where would you be only for me? Who carries you away when you're drunk? Only for me the guards would have you now.'

'I admit I gets drunk,' replied the fat man sternly. 'Not like you. Nothing makes you drunk, which is another reason I say you're not a man at all. And you leads me into timptation. When you're with me I wants to hit you. I wants to hit you now.'

'You try it and see what you'll get.'

'If I lose me temper I'll hit you,' said the fat man, spitting on his stick. 'I'll hit you such a crack you won't get over it. . . .' After a moment he sighed. 'O Lord, behold the timptation I'm put in with this fellow. Some day I'll do for him. . . . What did you hang that dog for?' he cried fiercely. 'What harm was he doing you? One of God's creatures! You savage!'

'Don't you call me a savage!'

'Savage, savage, dirty savage!' said the fat man thickly.

'By Chrisht, I'll shtrangle you!'

'Come on! Come on! Do it!' cried the fat man, springing to his feet with extraordinary agility and brandishing his stick. As the other began clumsily to rise there was a sound of footsteps on the road. The fat man lowered his stick with an oath and resumed his seat, back to back with his companion. The tall man lit his pipe. There they sat, looking in opposite directions and muttering the most fiendish maledictions at one another under their breath; the fat man in particular showed a decided ability to manufacture curses. Some minutes later the footsteps drew level with them, and the figure of a man emerged from the darkness. The flame in the bowl of the tall man's pipe attracted his attention. He stopped.

'Good-night, men,' he said with a soft, country accent. 'Would ye have a light?'

'Certainly,' said the tall man in a whining and obsequious tone. 'You're welcome to a light from the pipe, the little that's in it, God help us.'

The stranger bent over him. In the light which the tramp sucked from his pipe he saw with his small, shrewd eyes the pale face of a young man. What he saw there caused him suddenly to drop his obsequiousness, and when he spoke again it was in a blustering tone.

'Where are you going to?' he asked.

'The city,' replied the young man after a barely perceptible pause.

'Looking for work?'

'Ay.' Again there was the same slight pause.

'And you'll get it I suppose.'

'What's that?'

'You'll get it, you'll get it,' repeated the tall tramp, and into his voice had crept a perceptible snarl. 'The foxy country boy. Ye'd live where honest men would starve.'

'I dunno would we.'

'Oh, don't you? Well, I know. I know men that can't get a living in their own city on account of the country johnnies.'

'Never mind him,' broke in the fat man. 'He's not from the city at all. No one knows where he comes from.'

'Don't they? Don't they now? If they don't they know damn well where you come from. With your bag under your arm!'

'Be quiet, you, Horgan! Be quiet now!'

'I will not be quiet,' hissed Horgan. 'Look at him now, young fellow! Look at him now! The man that was to be a priest. And when they were turning him out they cursed him to have the bag on his back the longest day he'd live, and he thinks when he's carrying it under his oxter that he's cheating them!'

'Ay,' said the fat man slowly in a deep voice, 'I was, I was to be a priest. And I know curses, curses that'll bring the big, blind boils out on you so that you'll stink for ever – and you going the roads.'

'Don't you curse me!' exclaimed Horgan, not quite sure of himself.

'Ah,' said the fat man with satisfaction, shaking his head so that his long locks wagged about him, 'I'll give you a hot little *maledico vobis* that'll make you wish you never seen the light, Horgan. You mind what I say.'

'How far more have I to go?' asked the stranger.

'Fourteen mile,' replied the fat tramp.

''Tis a long road.'

''Tis so. Set down, can't you?'

'I will for a minute.'

'There's a lot looking for work.'

'There is.'

''Tis to England you should go,' said the fat man decisively. 'They give them money for nothing there. If I could put by a few ha'pence I'd go to England. I'd rent a little house of my own and drop the drink and go to Mass regular.'

'England!' said the young man bitterly. 'I tramped every mile of it.'

'And no work?'

'No work.'

He turned and lay on his stomach, biting a blade of grass.

'And didn't they give you the money?'

'God's curse on the ha'penny.'

'Lord, O Lord! The liars there are!' The tramp fumbled in his bag. 'A biteen of bread?. . . The liars!' he added indignantly under his breath.

The young man took the crust and began to gnaw it moodily. A car whizzed by, its lights picking them out like pieces of scenery against the theatrical green of the hedges and the dead white of the hawthorn. Screwing up their eyes, the two tramps looked at their companion.

'You could have asked for a lift,' said the man with the beard.

'I'm in no hurry.'

''Tis hard enough to get work in the city, I hear tell.'

'I'm not going there to get work.'

'Take my advice,' said the fat man with animation, 'don't go on the roads! Don't go on the roads, young man! 'Tis a cur-dog's life.'

'I'm not going on the roads.'

'And what are you going to do?' It was the truculent voice of Horgan, breaking a sudden silence.

'What do you think?'

'Are you going to try for the army?'

'No.'

'For the guards?'

'They wouldn't take me.'

'Then what is it? Jasus, you're making a great secret of it.'

''Tis no secret. I'm going to say good-bye to misfortune.'

There was another silence, deeper, longer. The fat tramp caught his breath and grabbed the young man's arm.

'Don't do it!' he cried. 'No, don't do it!'

'And why not?' The young man sat bolt upright and the tramp felt a pair of wild eyes piercing him in the darkness. 'Why not, I say?'

'Because 'tis a sin, a terrible sin. Life comes from God. God is good. So life is a good thing – that's a syllogism. And if you kill yourself you'll be damned.'

'I'm damned as it is.'

'No, no, no! You don't know what it is. I know, I know, but I can't tell you. There's no one can tell you, no one! But you feel it in here' – he beat his breast frantically – 'the fire, the blackness, the loneliness, the fear. Don't do it young man, don't do it!' His voice rose to an angry impotent cry.

'Don't be a fool, Kenfick,' said Horgan; and there was the same rancour and jealousy and malice in his voice. 'He's telling lies. What's he going there for? Why can't he do it anywhere else? He's telling lies.'

'Jasus!' The stranger suddenly bent across the fat man and gripped Horgan by the throat. 'Are 'oo contradicting me, are 'oo?'

'Never mind him!' said Kenfick.

'Are 'oo contradicting me?'

'I'm not, I'm not,' screamed Horgan, frightened out of his wits and brazening it out with spleen, 'I'm asking a civil question.'

The young man's grip relaxed. He resumed his former position, lying on his stomach.

'Tell us,' said the fat man, stretching out a conciliatory hand. 'Never mind that black devil. Young man, I like you. Tell us what happened.'

'You know it all now,' replied the young man after a moment's hesitation. 'I was in England looking for work. I tramped every bit of it. I came home at the latter end. My mother said: "Go out and look for work. I can't keep you here." So I went out and I looked. I tramped Munster looking for it, begging my way. Then I came back to her. "Did you get work?" says she. "No," says I, "I didn't." "Then you must go away again," says she, "I can't keep you." I took up a bit of rope that was lying in the back room and I went out to the shed. I tied it to a rafter. Then I put a box underneath it and I tied the rope around my neck. The door opened and in she walked. "Is it hanging your-self you are?" says she. "It is," says I. "You can't do it here," says she. "Is it to be putting me to the expense of burying you?" "What'll I do then?" says I. "My feet are bleeding, and I can't tramp no more." "You can go down to the city," says she, "where the tide will wash your body away and there'll be no call for me to bury you."'

As the stranger concluded his story the fat tramp sighed angrily. He pulled his old hat farther over his eyes.

'She's no mother,' he muttered thickly. 'She's a wolf. Never mind her. Spit on her! Faugh! . . . Oh!' he cried, his voice rising to a wail, 'my mother; why didn't I mind her when I had her? And all the times she cried over me, and all the prayers she said for me, and all in the hope that one day she'd kneel for my blessing! Oh, God, what blinds us, what blinds us, O God, that we don't see our own destruction?' Bawling his lament with hoarse sobs, he began hitting the grass about him with great sweeps of his stick. 'Listen, boy,' he continued eagerly. 'Come with me. I makes it out well; all the priests knows me; they're good to me. Sometimes I makes one and six a day.'

'Are you going to drop me then?' asked Horgan angrily.

'I am. I'm sick of you.'

'I'll lay you out,' cried Horgan, drawing back his fist.

'Will you? Will you? Will you?' Kenfick lifted his stick. 'Leave me see you now. Bah! You haven't it in you, Horgan. You're a coward, Horgan!'

'Don't you call me a coward!'

'You are a coward!'

'I won't come between ye,' said the stranger, rising. 'I'll go me road. I'll be no man's dog any more, waiting for the bite to fill me. There's no use your telling me about hell no more, mister,' he added in a husky voice. 'I was afraid of it once, but I'm afraid of it no longer.'

'Young man, young man,' cried Kenfick, 'beware! You don't know what you're saying. 'Tis blasphemy, young man. Almighty God, have mercy on us all this night. Almighty God, forgive him and save him!'

'Save!' snarled Horgan. 'Look at who talks of saving. He saved you nicely, didn't He?'

'Yes, He did, He did. I sees what none of ye sees; I sees the world and the people of the world, and I sees the black angels and the white angels fighting always around them. Don't do it, young man. Stop with me.'

'A grand life you have to offer him,' sneered Horgan.

''Tisn't a grand life, but 'tisn't a bad life either.'

''Twould be better for him be dead than tied to the likes of you.'

'Shut up, you!'

'I will not shut up. What'll he say when he have a month of

you, dragging you along the road and you stinking with drink, pulling you out the convent gate and you shouting back dirty words at the nuns?'

'If I do inself, isn't it their own fault?' hissed the fat man. 'Why don't they give me the few coppers I ask for without whinging and whining? What is it to them what I does with them? What do they think I'm going to buy with them? A house and shop? But women are all alike. A man have sense. A man don't ask are you going to buy drink with it. Look at the priests! They gives me whiskey because they have sense.'

'Because they're afraid of your dirty tongue.'

'Because they have sense, they likes whiskey themselves. And they knows I'm not a bad man. They knows I'm only weak. And some day when I've a bit of money put by I'll go and live in a town and have a little house of my own, and every day of my life I'll answer the Holy Mass. And Almighty God knows it, and He's not angry with me, and some day He'll lift me up out of the gutter. I know He will, I know it well. And I know what He'll do to you, Horgan. Will I tell you?'

'Don't you say anything bad about me.'

'Ah, you're afraid! You know damn well what's coming to you and you're afraid.'

'I am not afraid.'

'Young man, young man, look at him now!' Kenfick had Horgan by the neck of the coat, shaking him back and forward. 'Look at him!' he shouted triumphantly. 'The man that was talking about death.'

And at that instant the tramps saw that the stranger was gone, vanished into the darkness of the spring night, his footsteps unheard on the thick wet grass. Horgan laughed bitterly. The fat man sat back and began to tie up his old bag. Suddenly he broke into a whine.

'O Lord!' he said, 'I should have told him. At the hour of death . . . an aspiration . . . My Jesus, mercy. . . . Almighty God, forgive and save him, forgive and save us all.'

For some time after he could be heard muttering ejaculations and prayers. Then Horgan lit a cigarette and he grew rigid.

'Horgan,' he said sternly, 'where did you get that fag?'

'Where do you think?' asked the other with a snarl.

'Did you steal them from that boy?'

'What do you think I was doing while the pair of ye were gassing?'

The fat man sighed bitterly. After about three minutes of silence there was the heavy thud of a stick, a scream of pain, and in an instant the two were struggling like madmen in the grass.

THERE IS A LONE HOUSE

THE WOMAN stood at the foot of the lane, her right hand resting on the gate, her left fumbling at the neck of her blouse. Her face was lined, particularly about mouth and forehead; it was a face that rarely smiled, but was soft for all that, and plump and warm. She was quite grey. From a distance, this made her seem old; close at hand it had precisely the opposite effect, and tended to emphasize sharply what youthfulness still lingered in her, so that one thought of her as having suffered terribly at some time in the past.

The man came down the road, whistling a reel, the crisp, sprinkled notes of which were like the dripping of water in a cistern. She could hear his footsteps from a long way off, keeping irregular time to the elfin music, and drew aside a whitehorn bush by the gateway to watch him from cover. Apparently satisfied by her inspection, she kicked away the stone that held the gate in place, and, as he drew level with her, stepped out into the roadway. When he saw her he stopped, bringing down his ash plant with a twirl, but she did not look up.

'Morrow, ma'am,' he cried jovially.

Then she did look up, and a helpless blush that completely and utterly belied the apparent calculation of her previous behaviour flowed over her features, giving them a sudden, startling freshness. 'Good morrow and good luck,' she answered in a low voice.

'Is it far to Ballysheery, ma'am?'

''Tis seven miles.'

'Seven Irish, ma'am?'

'Seven English.'

'That's better.'

She drew her tongue across her lips to moisten them. The man was young. He was decently dressed, but flaunted a rough, devil-may-care expression. He wore no hat, and his dark hair was all a tangle. You were struck by the length of his face, darkened by hot June suns; the high-boned nose jutting out rather too far, the irregular, discoloured teeth, the thick cracked lips, the blue eyes so far apart under his narrow, bony forehead that they seemed to sink back into the temples. A craggy face with high cheekbones, all hills and hollows, it was rendered extraordinarily mobile by the unexpected shadows that caught it here and there as the pale eyes drew it restlessly about. She judged him to be about twenty-six or -seven.

'You seemed to be belting it out fine enough.'

'How's that, ma'am?'

'I heard you whistling.'

'That's to encourage the feet, ma'am. . . . You'll pardon my asking, is there any place around a man would get a cup of tea, ma'am?'

'There's no one would grudge you that, surely.'

Another would have detected the almost girlish timidity of the answer, but not he. He appeared both puzzled and disappointed.

'I'll go a bit farther so,' he said stiffly.

'What hurry is on you?'

' 'Tis my feet gets cramped.'

'If you come with me you can rest them a while.'

'God increase you, ma'am,' he replied.

They went up the boreen together. The house was on top of a hill, and behind it rose the mountainside, studded with rocks. There were trees about it, and in front a long garden with a hedge of fuchsia, at one side of which ran a stream. There were four or five apple trees, and beside the kitchen garden were a few flower-beds with a profusion of tall snap-dragon, yellow, red and white.

She put on the kettle and turned the wheel of the bellows. The kitchen filled with blue turf smoke, and the man sat beside the door, almost invisible behind a brilliant column of dust motes, whirling spirally in the evening sunlight. But his hands lay on his knees in a pool of light, great brown hands with knuckles like polished stones. Fascinated, she watched them, and as she laid the table she almost touched them for sheer pleasure. His wild eyes, blue as the turf smoke, took in everything about the kitchen with its deal table, chairs and dresser, all scrubbed white; its delft arranged with a sort of pedantic neatness that suggests the old maid.

'This is a fine, fancy place, ma'am,' he said.

''Tis a quiet place.'

''Tis so. The men are all away?'

'There are no men.'

'Oh!'

'Only a boy that does turns for me.'

'Oh!'

That was all he said before he turned to his meal. He was half-starved, she decided, as she watched him wolf the warm, crumbling bread. He saw her grey eyes fixed on him and laughed brightly.

'I has a great stroke, ma'am.'

'You have, God bless you. I might have boiled you another egg.'

When tea was over he sighed, stretching himself in his chair, and lit his pipe.

'Would you mind if I took off my boots, ma'am?' he asked shyly.

'Why would I? Take them off and welcome.'

'My feet is crucified.'

She bent and took up the boot he removed.

'No wonder. Your boots are in need of mending.'

He laughed at her expressive politeness.

'Mending, ma'am? Did you say mending? They're long past praying for.'

'They are, that's true. I wonder. . . . There's an old pair inside these years and years. They'd be better than the ones you have if they'd fit you.'

She brought them in, good substantial boots but stiff, and a trifle large for him. Not that he was in a state to mind.

'God, but they're grand, ma'am, they're grand! One little patch now, and they'd be as good as new. Better than new, for they're a better boot than I could ever buy in a shop. Wait now! Wait!' With boyish excitement he foraged in his pockets, and from the lining of his coat produced a piece of leather. He held it up with the air of a professional conjurer. 'Watch me now. Are you watching?' The leather fitted over the slight hole and he gave a whoop of joy. She found him last and hammer; he provided tacks from a paper bag in a vest pocket, and set to mending the damage with something like a tradesman's neatness.

'Is that your trade?' she asked curiously.

'One of my trades, ma'am. Cobbler, carpenter, plumber, gardener, thatcher, painter, poet; everything under the sun and moon, and nothing for long. But a cobbler is what I do be most times.'

He walked the kitchen in his new boots with all a child's inconsequent pleasure. There was something childlike about him, she decided, and she liked it. He peered at the battered alarm clock on the smoky heights of the mantelpiece and sighed.

'I'd like to stop here always,' he said wistfully, 'but I suppose I'd better be going.'

'What hurry is on you?'

'Seven miles, ma'am. Two hours. Maybe more. And I have to be in the old doss early if I want to get a place to sleep.'

But he sat down once more and put a match to his pipe.

'Not, mind you, ma'am, that there's many could put me out of a warm corner if I'd a mind to stay in it. No indeed, but unless I had a drop in me I'd never fight for a place. Never. I'm apt to be cross when I'm drunk, but I never hit a man sober yet only once. That was a foxy tinker out of the Ranties, and the Ranties are notorious cross men, ma'am. You see, there was a little blind man, ma'am, trying to sleep, and this Ranty I'm talking about, whenever he saw the blind man dozing, he'd give his beard a tug. So I got that mad I rose up, and without saying as much as by your leave, I hit him such a terrible blow under the chin the blood hopped out on me in the dark. Yes, ma'am, hopped clean out on me. That was a frightful hard blow.' He looked at her for approval and awe, and saw her, womanlike, draw up her shoulders and shiver. His dramatic sense was satisfied.

It was quite dark when he rose to go. The moon was rising over the hills to the left, far away, and the little stream beside the house sounded very loud in the stillness.

'If there was e'er an old barn or an outhouse,' he said as if to himself.

'There's a bed inside,' she answered. He looked round at her in surprise.

'Ah, I wouldn't ask to stop within,' he exclaimed.

Suddenly her whole manner changed. All the brightness, if brightness it could be called, seemed to drop away from her, leaving her listless, cold and melancholy.

'Oh, please yourself,' she said shortly, as if banishing him from her thoughts. But still he did not go. Instead, he sat down again, and they faced one another across the fireplace, not speaking, for he too had lost his chatter. The kitchen was in darkness except for the dwindling glow of the turf inside its cocoon of grey dust, and the wan nightlight above the half-door. Then he laughed, rubbing his palms between his knees.

'And still you know, I'd ask nothing better,' he added shyly.

'What's that?'

'I'd ask nothing better than to stop.'

'Go or stop as you like.'

'You see,' he went on, ignoring her gathering surprise, 'I'm an honest fellow. I am, on my oath, though maybe you wouldn't think it, with the rough talk I have, and the life I lead. You could leave me alone with a bag of sovereigns, not counting them, and I'd keep them safe for you. And I'm just the same other ways. I'm not a bit forward. They say a dumb priest loses his benefit, and I'm just like that. I'm apt to lose me benefit for want of a bit of daring.'

Then (and this time it was he who was surprised) she laughed, more with relief, he thought, than at anything he had said. She rose and closed the door, lit the lamp and hung up the heavy kettle. He leaned back in his chair with a fresh sigh of pleasure, stretching out his feet to the fire, and in that gesture she caught something of his nostalgia. He settled down gratefully to one of those unexpected benefits which are the bait with which life leads us onward.

When she rose next morning, she was surprised to find him about before her, the fire lit, and the kettle boiling. She saw how much he needed a shave, and filled out a pan of water for him. Then when he began to scrub his face with the soap, she produced a razor, strop and brush. He was enchanted with these, and praised the razor with true lyric fire.

'You can have it,' she said. 'Have them all if they're any use to you.'

'By God, aren't they though,' he exclaimed reverently.

After breakfast he lit his pipe and sat back, enjoying to the full the last moments which politeness would impose upon hospitality.

'I suppose you're anxious to be on your road?' she asked awkwardly. Immediately he reddened.

'I suppose I'm better to,' he replied. He rose and looked out. It was a grey morning and still. The green stretched no farther than the hedge; beyond that lay a silver mist, flushed here and there with rose. 'Though 'tis no anxiety is on me – no anxiety at all,' he added with a touch of bitterness.

'Don't take me up wrong,' she said hastily. 'I'm not trying to hunt you. Stop and have your dinner. You'll be welcome.'

'I chopped a bit of kindling for you,' he replied, looking shyly at her from under lowered lids. 'If there was something else I could be doing, I'd be glad enough to stop, mind you.'

There was. Plenty else to be doing. For instance, there was an outhouse that needed whitewashing, and blithely enough he set about his task, whistling. She came and watched him; went, and came again, standing silently beside him, a strange stiff figure in the bright sunlight, but he had no feeling of supervision. Because he had not finished when dinner was ready he stayed to tea, and even then displayed no hurry to be gone. He sang her some of his poems. There was one about Mallow Races, another about a girl he had been in love with as a boy, 'the most beautiful girl that was ever seen in Kerry since the first day,' so he naively told her. It began:

> I praise no princesses or queens or great ladies
>> Or figures historical noted for style,
> Or beauties of Asia or Mesopotamia,
>> But sweet Annie Bradie, the rose of Dunmoyle.

A sort of confidence had established itself between them. The evening passed quickly in talk and singing – in whistling too, for he was a good whistler, and sometimes performed for dancing: to judge by his own statements he was a great favourite at wakes and weddings and she could understand that.

It was quite dark when they stopped the conversation. Again he made as if to go, and again in her shy, cold way she offered him the chance of staying. He stayed.

For days afterward there seemed to be some spell upon them both. A week passed in excuses and delays, each morning finding him about long before she appeared with some new suggestion, the garden to be weeded, potatoes to be dug, the kitchen to be whitewashed. Neither suggested anything but as it were from hour to hour, yet it did not occur to the man that for her as for him their companionship might be an unexpected benefit.

He did her messages to the village whenever Dan, the 'boy', a sullen, rather stupid, one-eyed old man, was absent, and though she gave no sign that she did not like this, he was always surprised afresh by the faint excitement with which she greeted his return; had it been anyone else one might have called her excitement gaiety, but gay was hardly a word one could apply to her, and the emotion quickly died and gave place to a sullen apathy.

She knew the end must come soon, and it did. One evening he returned from an errand, and told her someone had died in the village. He was slightly shocked by her indifference. She would not go with him to the wake, but she bade himself go if he pleased. He did please. She could see there was an itch for company on him; he was made that way. As he polished his boots he confessed to her that among his other vocations he had tried being a Trappist monk, but stuck it only for a few months. It wasn't bad in summer, but it was the divil and all in winter, and the monks told him there were certain souls like himself the Lord called only for six months of the year (the irony of this completely escaped him).

He promised to be back before midnight, and went off very gay. By this time he had formed his own opinion of the woman. It was not for nothing she lived there alone, not for nothing a visitor never crossed the threshold. He knew she did not go to Mass, yet on Sunday when he came back unexpectedly for his stick, he had seen her, in the bedroom, saying her Rosary. Something was wrong, but he could not guess what.

Her mood was anything but gay and the evening seemed to respond to it. It was very silent after the long drought; she could hear the thrush's beak go tip-tap among the stones like a fairy's hammer. It was making for rain. To the north-west the wind had piled up massive archways of purple cloud like a ruined cloister, and through them one's eyes passed on to vistas of feathery cloudlets, violet and gold, packed thick upon one another. A cold wind had sprung up: the trees creaked, and the birds flew by, their wings blown up in a gesture of horror. She stood for a long while looking at the sky, until it faded, chilled by the cold wind. There was something mournful and sinister about it all.

It was quite dark when she went in. She sat over the fire and waited. At half past eleven she put down the kettle and brewed herself tea. She told herself she was not expecting him, but still she waited. At half past twelve she stood at the door and listened for footsteps. The wind had risen, and her mind filled slowly with its childish sobbing and with the harsh gushing of the stream beside the house. Then it began to rain. To herself she gave him until one. At one she relented and gave him another half-hour, and it was two before she quenched the light and went to bed. She had lost him, she decided.

She started when an hour or more later she heard his footsteps up the path. She needed no one to tell her he was alone and drunk: often before she had waited for the footsteps of a drunken old man. But instead of rushing to the door as she would have done long ago, she waited.

He began to moan drowsily to himself. She heard a thud followed by gusty sighing; she knew he had fallen. Everything was quiet for a while. Then there came a bang at the door which echoed through the house like a revolver shot, and something fell on the flagstones outside. Another bang and again silence. She felt no fear, only a coldness in her bowels.

Then the gravel scraped as he staggered to his feet. She glanced at the window. She could see his head outlined against it, his hands against its frame. Suddenly the voice rose in a wail that chilled her blood.

'What will the soul do at the judgment? Ah, what will the soul do? I will say to ye, "Depart from me into everlasting fire that was prepared for the divil and his angels. Depart from me, depart!"'

It was like a scream of pain, but immediately upon it came a low chuckle of malice. The woman's fists clenched beneath the clothes. 'Never again,' she said to herself aloud, 'never again!'

'Do you see me, do you?' he shouted. 'Do you see me?'

'I see you,' she whispered to herself.

'For ye, for ye, I reddened the fire,' went on the man, dropping back into his whine, 'for ye, for ye, I dug the pit. The black bitch on the hill, let ye torment her for me, ye divils. Forever, forever! Gather round, ye divils, gather round, and let me see ye roast the black bitch that killed a man. . . . Do you hear me, do you?'

'I hear you,' she whispered.

'Listen to me!

"When the old man was sleeping
   She rose up from her bed,
And crept into his lone bedroom
   And cruelly struck him dead;
'Twas with a hammer she done the deed,
   May God it her repay,
And then she . . . then she . . ."

'How does it go? I have it.

"And then she lifted up the body
   And hid it in the hay."

Suddenly a stone came crashing through the window and a cold blast followed it. 'Never again,' she cried, hammering the bedframe with her fists, 'dear God, never again.' She heard the footsteps stumbling away. She knew he was running. It was like a child's malice and terror.

She rose and stuffed the window with a rag. Day was breaking. When she went back to bed she was chilled and shaken. Despairing of rest, she rose again, lit a candle and blew up the fire.

But even then some unfamiliar feeling was stirring at her heart. She felt she was losing control of herself and was being moved about like a chessman. Sighing, she slipped her feet into heavy shoes, threw an old coat about her shoulders, and went to the door. As she crossed the threshold she stumbled over something. It was a boot; another was lying some little distance away. Something seemed to harden within her. She placed the boots inside the door and closed it. But again came the faint thrill at her heart, so light it might have been a fluttering of untried wings and yet so powerful it shook her from head to foot, so that almost before she had closed the door she opened it again and went out, puzzled and trembling, into a cold noiseless rain. She called the man in an extraordinarily gentle voice as though she were afraid of being heard; then she made the circle of the farmhouse, a candle sheltered in the palm of her hand.

He was lying in the outhouse he had been whitewashing. She stood and looked down at him for a moment, her face set in a grim mask of disgust. Then she laid down the candle and lifted him, and at that moment an onlooker would have been conscious of her great physical strength. Half lifting, half guiding, her steered the man to the door. On the doorstep he stood and said something to her, and immediately, with all her strength, she struck him across the mouth. He staggered and swore at her, but she caught him again and pushed him across the threshold. Then she went back for the candle, undressed him and put him to bed.

It was bright morning when she had done.

That day he lay on in bed, and came into the kitchen about two o'clock looking sheepish and sullen. He was wearing his own ragged boots.

'I'm going now,' he said stiffly.

'Please yourself,' she answered coolly. 'Maybe you'd be better.'

He seemed to expect something more, and because she said nothing he felt himself being put subtly in the wrong. This was not so surprising, because even she was impressed by her own nonchalance that seemed to have come suddenly to her from nowhere.

'Well?' he asked, and his look seemed to say, 'Women are the divil and all!' One could read him like a book.

'Well?'

'Have you nothing to say for yourself?'

'Have you nothing to say for yourself?' she retorted. 'I had enough of your blackguarding last night. You won't stop another hour in this house unless you behave yourself, mark me well, you won't.'

He grew very red.

'That's strange,' he answered sulkily.

'What's strange?'

'The likes of you saying that to me.'

'Take it or leave it. And if you don't like it, there's the door.'

Still he lingered. She knew now she had him at her mercy, and the nonchalance dropped from her.

'Aren't you a queer woman?' he commented, lighting his pipe. 'One'd think you wouldn't have the face to talk like that to an honest man. Have you no shame?'

'Listen to who's talking of shame,' she answered bitterly. 'A pity you didn't see yourself last night, lying in your dirt like an old cow. And you call yourself a man. How ready you were with your stones!'

'It was the shock,' he said sullenly.

'It was no shock. It was drink.'

'It was the shock I tell you. I was left an orphan with no one to tell me the badness of the world.'

'I was left an orphan too. And I don't go round crying about the badness of the world.'

'Oh, Christ, don't remind me what you were. 'Tis only myself, the poor fool, wouldn't know, and all the old chat I had about the man I drew blood from, as if I was a terrible fellow entirely. I might have known to see a handsome woman living lonely that she wouldn't be that way only no man in Ireland would look at the side of the road she walked on.'

He did not see how the simple flattery of his last words went through her, quickening her with pleasure; he noticed only the savage retort she gave him, for the sense of his own guilt was growing stronger in him at every moment. Her silence was in part the cause of that; her explanation would have been his triumph. That at least was how he had imagined it. He had not been prepared for this silence which drew him like a magnet. He could not decide to go, yet his fear of her would not allow him to remain. The day passed like that. When twilight came she looked across at him and asked:

'Are you going or stopping?'

'I'm stopping, if you please,' he answered meekly.

'Well, I'm going to bed. One sleepless night is enough for me.'

And she went, leaving him alone in the kitchen. Had she delayed until darkness fell, he would have found it impossible to remain, but there was no suspicion of this in her mind. She understood only that people might hate her; that they might fear her never entered her thoughts.

An hour or so later she looked for the candle and remembered that she had left it in his room. She rose and knocked at his door. There was no answer. She knocked again. Then she pushed in the door and called him. She was alarmed. The bed was empty. She laid her hand to the candle (it was lying still where she had left it, on the dresser beside the door) but as she did so she heard his voice, husky and terrified.

'Keep away from me! Keep away from me, I tell you!'

She could discern his figure now. He was standing in a corner, his little white shirt half-way up his thighs, his hand grasping something, she did not see what. It was some little while before the explanation dawned on her, and with it came a sudden feeling of desolation within her.

'What ails you?' she asked gently. 'I was only looking for the candle.'

'Don't come near me!' he cried.

She lit the candle, and as he saw her there, her face as he had never seen it before, stricken with pain, his fear died away. A moment later she was gone, and the back door slammed behind her. It was only then he realized what his insane fear had brought him to, and the obsession of his own guilt returned with a terrible clarity. He walked up and down the little room in desperation.

Half an hour later he went to her room. The candle was burning on a chair beside the bed. She lifted herself on the pillow and looked at him with strangely clear eyes.

'What is it?' she asked.

'I'm sorry,' he answered. 'I shouldn't be here at all. I'm sorry. I'm queer. I'll go in the morning and I won't trouble you any more.'

'Never mind,' she said, and held out her hand to him. He came closer and took it timidly. 'You wouldn't know.'

'God pity me,' he said. 'I was distracted. You know I was distracted. You were so good to me, and that's the way I paid you out. But I was going out of my mind. I couldn't sleep.'

'Sure you couldn't.' She drew him down to her until his head was resting on the pillow, and made him lie beside her.

'I couldn't, I couldn't,' he said into her ear. 'I wint raving mad. And I thought whin you came into the room –'

'I know, I know.'

'I did, whatever came over me.'

'I know.' He realized that she was shivering all over.

She drew back the clothes from him. He was eager to explain, to tell her about himself, his youth, the death of his father and mother, his poverty, his religious difficulties, his poetry. What was wrong with him was, he was wild; could stick to no trade, could never keep away from drink.

'You were wild yourself,' he said.

'Fifteen years ago. I'm tame now in earnest.'

'Tell me about it,' he said eagerly, 'talk to me, can't you? Tell me he was bad. Tell me he was a cruel old uncle to you. Tell me he beat you. He used to lock you up for days, usedn't he, to keep you away from boys? He must have been bad or you'd never had done what you did, and you only a girl.'

But still she said nothing. Bright day was in the room when he fell asleep, and for a long while she lay, her elbow on the pillow, her hand covering her left breast, while she looked at him. His mouth was wide open, his irregular teeth showed in a faint smile. Their shyness had created a sort of enchantment about them, and she watched over his sleep with something like ecstasy, ecstasy which disappeared when he woke, to find her the same hard quiet woman he knew.

After that she ceased making his bed in the small room, and he slept with her. Not that it made any difference to their relations. Between them after those few hours of understanding persisted a fierce, unbroken shyness, the shyness of lonely souls. If it rasped the nerves of either, there was no open sign of it, unless a curiously irritable tenderness revealed anything of their thoughts. She was forever finding things done for her; there was no longer any question of his going, and he worked from morning until late night with an energy and intelligence that surprised her. But she knew he felt the lack of company, and one evening she went out to him as he worked in the garden.

'Why don't you go down to the village now?' she asked.

'Ah, what would I be doing there?' But it was clear that it had been on his mind at that very moment.

'You might drop in for a drink and a chat.'

'I might do that,' he agreed.

'And why don't you?'

'Me? I'd be ashamed.'

'Ashamed? Ashamed of what? There's no one will say anything to you. And if they do, what are you, after all, but a working man?'

It was clear that this excuse had not occurred to him, but it would also have been clear to anyone else that she would have thought poorly of such as gave it credit. So he got his coat and went.

It was late when he came in, and she saw he had drunk more than his share. His face was flushed and he laughed too easily. For two days past a bottle of whiskey had been standing on the dresser (what a change for her!) but if he had noticed it he had made no sign. Now he went directly to it and poured himself out a glass.

'You found it,' she said with a hint of bitterness.

'What's that?'

'You found it, I say.'

'Of course I did. Have a drop yourself.'

'No.'

'Do. Just a drop.'

'I don't want it.'

He crossed to her, stood behind her chair for a moment; then he bent over and kissed her. She had been expecting it, but on the instant she revolted.

'Don't do that again,' she said appealingly, wiping her mouth.

'You don't mind me, do you?' he sniggered, still standing behind her.

'I do. I mind it when you're drunk.'

'Well, here's health.'

'Don't drink any more of that.'

'Here's health.'

'Good health.'

'Take a drop yourself, do.'

'No, I tell you,' she answered angrily.

'By God, you must.'

He threw one arm about her neck and deliberately spilt the whiskey between her breasts. She sprang up and threw him away from her. Whatever had been in her mind was now forgotten in her loathing.

'Bad luck to you!' she cried savagely.

'I'm sorry,' he said quickly. 'I didn't mean it.' Already he was growing afraid.

'You didn't mean it,' she retorted mockingly. 'Who thought you to do it then? Was it Jimmie Dick? What sort of woman do you think I am, you fool? You sit all night in a public-house talking of me, and when you come back you try to make me out as loose and dirty as your talk.'

'Who said I was talking of you?'

'I say it.'

'Then you're wrong.'

'I'm not wrong. Don't I know you, you poor sheep? You sat there, letting them make you out a great fellow, because they thought you were like themselves and thought I was a bitch, and you never as much as opened your mouth to give them the lie. You sat there and gaped and bragged. That's what you are.'

'That's not true.'

'And then you come strutting back, stuffed with drink, and think I'll let you make love to me, so that you can have something to talk about in the public-house.'

Her eyes were bright with tears of rage. She had forgotten that something like this was what she knew would happen when she made him go to the village, so little of our imagination can we bear to see made real. He sank into a chair, and put his head between his hands in sulky dignity. She lit the candle and went off to bed.

She fell asleep and woke to hear him stirring in the kitchen. She rose and flung open the door. He was still sitting where she had seen him last.

'Aren't you going to bed at all tonight?' she asked.

'I'm sorry if I disturbed you,' he replied. The drunkenness had gone, and he did look both sorry and miserable. 'I'll go now.'

'You'd better. Do you see the time?'

'Are you still cross? I'm sorry, God knows I am.'

'Never mind.'

''Twas all true.'

'What was true?' She had already forgotten.

'What you said. They were talking about you, and I listened.'

'Oh, that.'

'Only you were too hard on me.'

'Maybe I was.'

She took a step forward. He wondered if she had understood what he was saying at all.

'I was fond of you all right.'

'Yes,' she said.

'You know I was.'

'Yes.'

She was like a woman in a dream. She had the same empty feeling within her, the same sense of being pushed about like a chessman, as on the first night when she carried him in. He put his arm about her and kissed her. She shivered and clung to him, life suddenly beginning to stir within her.

*

One day, some weeks later, he told her he was going back home on a visit; there were cousins he wished to see; something or other; she was not surprised. She had seen the restlessness on him for some time past and had no particular belief in the cousins. She set about preparing a parcel of food for him, and in this little attention there was something womanly that touched him.

'I'll be back soon,' he said, and meant it. He could be moved easily enough in this fashion, and she saw through him. It was dull being the lover of a woman like herself; he would be best married to a lively girl of eighteen or so, a girl he could go visiting with and take pride in.

'You're always welcome,' she said. 'The house is your own.'

As he went down the boreen he was saying to himself 'She'll be lost! She'll be lost!' but he would have spared his pity if he had seen how she took it.

Her mood shifted from busy to idle. At one hour she was work-ing in the garden, singing, at another she sat in the sun, motionless and silent for a long, long time. As weeks went by and the year drifted into a rainy autumn, an astonishing change took place in her, slowly, almost imperceptibly. It seemed a physical rather than a spiritual change. Line by line her features divested themselves of strain, and her body seemed to fall into easier, more graceful curves. It would not be untrue to say she scarcely thought of the man, unless it was with some slight relief to find herself alone again. Her thoughts were all contracted within herself.

One autumn evening he came back. For days she had been expecting him; quite suddenly she had realized that he would return, that everything was not over between them, and very placidly accepted the fact.

He seemed to have grown older and maturer in his short absence; one felt it less in his words than in his manner. There was decision in it. She saw that he was rapidly growing into a deferred manhood, and was secretly proud of the change. He had a great fund of stories about his wanderings (never a word of the mythical cousins); and while she prepared his supper, she listened to him, smiling faintly, almost as if she were not listening at all. He was as hungry now as the first evening she met him, but everything was easier between them; he was glad to be there and she to have him.

'Are you pleased I came?' he asked.

'You know I'm pleased.'

'Were you thinking I wouldn't come?'

'At first I thought you wouldn't. You hadn't it in your mind to come back. But afterward I knew you would.'

'A man would want to mind what he thinks about a woman like you,' he grumbled good-humouredly. 'Are you a witch?'

'How would I be a witch?' Her smile was attractive.

'Are you?' He gripped her playfully by the arm.

'I am not and well you know it.'

'I have me strong doubts of you. Maybe you'll say now you know what happened? Will you? Did you ever hear of a man dreaming three times of a crock of gold? Well, that's what happened me. I dreamt three times of you. What sign is that?'

'A sign you were drinking too much.'

''Tis not. I know what sign it is.'

He drew his chair up beside her own, and put his arm about her. Then he drew her face round to his and kissed her. At that moment she could feel very clearly the change in him. His hand crept about her neck and down her breast, releasing the warm smell of her body.

'That's enough love-making,' she said. She rose quickly and shook off his arm. A strange happy smile like a newly open flower lingered where he had kissed her. 'I'm tired. Your bed is made in there.'

'My bed?'

She nodded.

'You're only joking me. You are, you divil, you're only joking.'

His arms out, he followed her, laughing like a lad of sixteen. He caught at her, but she forced him off again. His face altered suddenly, became sullen and spiteful.

'What is it?'

'Nothing.'

''Tis a change for you.'

''Tis.'

'And for why?'

'For no why. Isn't it enough for you to know it?'

'Is it because I wint away?'

'Maybe.'

'Is it?'

'I don't know whether 'tis or no.'

'And didn't I come back as I said I would?'

'You did. When it suited you.'

'The divil is in ye all,' he said crossly.

Later he returned to the attack; he was quieter and more persuasive; there was more of the man in him, but she seemed armed at every point. He experienced an acute sense of frustration. He had felt growing in him this new, lusty manhood, and returned with the intention of dominating her, only to find she too had grown, and still outstripped him. He lay awake for a long time, thinking it out, but when he rose next morning the barrier between them seemed to have disappeared. As ever she was dutiful, unobtrusive; by day at any rate she was all he would have her to be. Even when he kissed her she responded; of his hold on her he had no doubt, but he seemed incapable of taking advantage of it.

That night when he went to bed he began to think again of it, and rage grew in him until it banished all hope of sleep. He rose and went into her room.

'How long is this going to last?' he asked thickly.

'What?'

'This. How long more are you going to keep me out?'

'Maybe always,' she said softly, as if conjuring up the prospect.

'Always?'

'Maybe.'

'Always? And what in hell do you mean by it? You lure me into it, and then throw me away like an old boot.'

'Did I lure you into it?'

'You did. Oh, you fooled me right enough at the time, but I've been thinking about it since. 'Twas no chance brought you on the road the first day I passed.'

'Maybe I did,' she admitted. She was stirred again by the quickness of his growth. 'If I did you had nothing to complain of.'

'Haven't I now?'

'Now is different.'

'Why? Because I wint away?'

'Because you didn't think me good enough for you.'

'That's a lie. You said that before, and you know 'tis a lie.'

'Then show it.'

He sat on the bed and put his face close to hers.

'You mean, to marry you?'

'Yes.'

'You know I can't.'

'What hinders you?'

'For a start, I have no money. Neither have you.'

'There's money enough.'

'Where would it come from?'

'Never you mind where 'twould come from. 'Tis there.'

He looked at her hard.

'You planned it well,' he said at last. 'They said he was a miser. . . . Oh, Christ, I can't marry you!'

'The divil send you better meat than mutton,' she retorted coarsely.

He sat on the edge of the bed, his big hand caressing her cheek and bare shoulder.

'Why don't you tell the truth?' she asked. 'You have no respect for me.'

'Why do you keep on saying that?'

'Because 'tis true.' In a different voice she added: 'Nor I hadn't for myself till you went away. Take me now or leave me. . . . Stop that, you fool!'

'Listen to me –'

'Stop that then! I'm tame now, but I'm not tame enough for that.'

Even in the darkness she could feel that she had awakened his old dread of her; she put her arms about his head, drew him down to her, and whispered in his ear.

'Now do you understand?' she said.

A few days later he got out the cart and harnessed the pony. They drove into the town three miles away. As they passed through the village people came to their doors to look after them. They left the cart a little outside the town, and, following country practice, separated to meet again on the priest's doorstep. The priest was at home, and he listened incredulously to the man's story.

'You know I'll have to write to your parish priest first,' he said severely.

'I know,' said the man. 'You'll find and see he have nothing against me.'

The priest was shaken.

'And this woman has told you everything?'

'She told me nothing. But I know.'

'About her uncle?'

'About her uncle,' repeated the man.

'And you're satisfied to marry her, knowing that?'

'I'm satisfied.'

'It's all very strange,' said the priest wearily. 'You know,' he added to the woman, 'Almighty God has been very merciful to you. I hope you are conscious of all He in His infinite mercy has done for you, who deserve it so little.'

'I am. From this out I'll go to Mass regularly.'

'I hope,' he repeated emphatically, 'you are fully conscious of it. If I thought there was any lightness in you, if I thought for an instant that you wouldn't make a good wife to this man, my conscience wouldn't allow me to marry you. Do you understand that?'

'Never fear,' she said, without lifting her eyes. 'I'll make him a good wife. And he knows it.'

The man nodded. 'I know it,' he said.

The priest was impressed by the solemn way in which she spoke. She was aware that the strength which had upheld her till now was passing from her to the young man at her side; the future would be his.

From the priest's they went to the doctor's. He saw her slip on a ring before they entered. He sat in the room while the doctor examined her. When she had dressed again her eyes were shining. The strength was passing from her, and she was not sorry to see it pass. She laid a sovereign on the table.

'Oho,' exclaimed the doctor, 'how did you come by this?' The man started and the woman smiled.

'I earned it hard,' she answered.

The doctor took the coin to the window and examined it.

'By Jove,' he said, 'it's not often I see one of these.'

'Maybe you'll see more of them,' she said with a gay laugh. He looked at her from under his eyes and laughed too; her brightness had a strange other-world attraction.

'Maybe I will,' he replied. 'In a few months' time, eh? Sorry I can't give you change in your own coin. Ah, well! Good luck, anyway. And call me in as often as you please.'

SPRING HAD only come and already he was tired to death; tired of the city, tired of his job. He had come up from the country intending to do wonders, but he was as far as ever from that. He would be lucky if he could carry on, be at school each morning at half past nine and satisfy his half-witted principal.

He lodged in a small red-brick house in Rathmines that was kept by a middle-aged brother and sister who had been left a bit of money and thought they would end their days enjoyably in a city. They did not enjoy themselves, regretted their little farm in Kerry, and were glad of Ned Keating because he could talk to them about all the things they remembered and loved.

Keating was a slow, cumbrous young man with dark eyes and a dark cow's-lick that kept tumbling into them. He had a slight stammer and ran his hand through his long limp hair from pure nervousness. He had always been dreamy and serious. Sometimes on market days you saw him standing for an hour in Nolan's shop, turning the pages of a schoolbook. When he could not afford it he put it back with a sigh and went off to find his father in a pub, just raising his eyes to smile at Jack Nolan. After his elder brother Tom had gone for the church he and his father had constant rows. Nothing would do Ned now but to be a teacher. Hadn't he all he wanted now? his father asked. Hadn't he the place to himself? What did he want going teaching? But Ned was stubborn. With an obstinate, almost despairing determination he had fought his way through the training college into a city job. The city was what he had always wanted. And now the city had failed him. In the evenings you could still see him poking round the second-hand bookshops on the quays, but his eyes were already beginning to lose their eagerness.

It had all seemed so clear. But then he had not counted on his own temper. He was popular because of his gentleness, but how many concessions that involved! He was hesitating, good-natured, slow to see guile, slow to contradict. He felt he was constantly underestimating his own powers. He even felt he lacked spontaneity. He did not drink, smoked little, and saw dangers and losses everywhere. He blamed himself for avarice and cowardice. The story he liked best was about the country boy and the letter box. 'Indeed, what a fool you think I am! Put me letther in a pump!'

He was in no danger of putting his letter in a pump or anywhere else for the matter of that. He had only one friend, a nurse in Vincent's Hospital, a wild, lighthearted, lightheaded girl. He was very fond of her and supposed that some day when he had money enough he would ask her to marry him; but not yet: and at the same time something that was both shyness and caution kept him from committing himself too far. Sometimes he planned excursions besides the usual weekly walk or visit to the pictures but somehow they seldom came to anything.

He no longer knew why he had come to the city, but it was not for the sake of the bed-sitting room in Rathmines, the oblong of dusty garden outside the window, the trams clanging up and down, the shelf full of second-hand books, or the occasional visit to the pictures. Half humorously, half despairingly, he would sometimes clutch his head in his hands and admit to himself that he had no notion of what he wanted. He would have liked to leave it all and go to Glasgow or New York as a labourer, not because he was romantic, but because he felt that only when he had to work with his hands for a living and was no longer sure of his bed would he find out what all his ideals and emotions meant and where he could fit them into the scheme of his life.

But no sooner did he set out for school next morning, striding slowly along the edge of the canal, watching the trees become green again and the tall claret-coloured houses painted on the quiet surface of the water, than all his fancies took flight. Put his letter in a pump indeed! He would continue to be submissive and draw his salary and wonder how much he could save and when he would be able to buy a little house to bring his girl into; a nice thing to think of on a spring morning: a house of his own and a wife in the bed beside him. And his nature would continue to contract about him, every ideal, every generous impulse another mesh to draw his head down tighter to his knees till in ten years' time it would tie him hand and foot.

*

Tom, who was a curate in Wicklow, wrote and suggested that they might go home together for the long weekend, and on Saturday morning they set out in Tom's old Ford. It was Easter weather, pearly and cold. They stopped at several pubs on the way and Tom ordered whiskeys. Ned was feeling expansive and joined him. He had never quite grown used to his brother, partly because of old days when he felt that Tom was getting the education he should have got, partly because his ordination seemed to have shut him off from the rest of the family, and now it was as though he were trying to surmount it by his boisterous manner and affected bonhomie. He was like a man shouting to his comrades across a great distance. He was different from Ned; lighter in colour of hair and skin; fat-headed, fresh-complexioned, deep-voiced, and autocratic; an irascible, humorous, friendly man who was well-liked by those he worked for. Ned, who was shy and all tied up within himself, envied him his way with men in garages and barmaids in hotels.

It was nightfall when they reached home. Their father was in his shirtsleeves at the gate waiting to greet them, and immediately their mother rushed out as well. The lamp was standing in the window and threw its light as far as the whitewashed gateposts. Little Brigid, the girl from up the hill who helped their mother now she was growing old, stood in the doorway in half-silhouette. When her eyes caught theirs she bent her head in confusion.

Nothing was changed in the tall, bare, whitewashed kitchen. The harness hung in the same place on the wall, the rosary on the same nail in the fireplace, by the stool where their mother usually sat; table under the window, churn against the back door, stair without banisters mounting straight to the attic door that yawned in the wall – all seemed as unchanging as the sea outside. Their mother sat on the stool, her hands on her knees, a coloured shawl tied tightly about her head, like a gipsy woman with her battered yellow face and loud voice. Their father, fresh-complexioned like Tom, stocky and broken-bottomed, gazed out the front door, leaning with one hand on the dresser in the pose of an orator while Brigid wet the tea.

'I said ye'd be late,' their father proclaimed triumphantly, twisting his moustache. 'Didn't I, woman? Didn't I say they'd be late?'

'He did, he did,' their mother assured them. ''Tis true for him.'

'Ah, I knew ye'd be making halts. But damn it, if I wasn't put astray by Thade Lahy's car going east!'

'And was that Thade Lahy's car?' their mother asked in a shocked tone.

'I told ye 'twas Thade Lahy's,' piped Brigid, plopping about in her long frieze gown and bare feet.

'Sure I should know it, woman,' old Tomas said with chagrin. 'He must have gone into town without us noticing him.'

'Oye, and how did he do that?' asked their mother.

'Leave me alone now,' Tomas said despairingly. 'I couldn't tell you, I could not tell you.'

'My goodness, I was sure that was the Master's car,' their mother said wonderingly, pulling distractedly at the tassels of her shawl.

'I'd know the rattle of Thade Lahy's car anywhere,' little Brigid said very proudly and quite unregarded.

It seemed to Ned that he was interrupting a conversation that had been going on since his last visit, and that the road outside and the sea beyond it, and every living thing that passed before them, formed a pantomime that was watched endlessly and passionately from the darkness of the little cottage.

'Wisha, I never asked if ye'd like a drop of something,' their father said with sudden vexation.

'Is it whiskey?' boomed Tom.

'Why? Would you sooner whiskey?'

'Can't you pour it out first and ask us after?' growled Tom.

'The whiskey, is it?'

''Tis not. I didn't come all the ways to this place for what I can get better at home. You'd better have a bottle ready for me to take back.'

'Coleen will have it. Damn it, wasn't it only last night I said to Coleen that you'd likely want a bottle? Some way it struck me you would. Oh, he'll have it, he'll have it.'

'Didn't they catch that string of misery yet?' asked Tom with the cup to his lips.

'Ah, man alive, you'd want to be a greyhound to catch him. God Almighty, hadn't they fifty police after him last November, scouring the mountains from one end to the other and all they caught was a glimpse of the white of his ass. Ah, but the priest preached a terrible sermon against him – by name, Tom, by name!'

'Is old Murphy blowing about it still?' growled Tom.

'Oh, let me alone now!' Tomas threw his hands to heaven and strode to and fro in his excitement, his bucket-bottom wagging. Ned knew to his sorrow that his father could be prudent, silent, and calculating; he knew only too well the cock of the head, the narrowing of the eyes, but, like a child, the old man loved innocent excitement and revelled in scenes of the wildest passion, all about nothing. Like an old actor he turned everything to drama. 'The like of it for abuse was never heard, never heard, never heard! How Coleen could ever raise his head again after it! And where the man got the words from! Tom, my treasure, my son, you'll never have the like.'

'I'd spare my breath to cool my porridge,' Tom replied scornfully. 'I dare say you gave up your own still so?'

'I didn't, Tom, I didn't. The drop I make, 'twould harm no one. Only a drop for Christmas and Easter.'

The lamp was in its own place on the rear wall, and made a circle of brightness on the fresh lime wash. Their mother was leaning over the fire with joined hands, lost in thought. The front door was open and night thickening outside, the coloured night of the west; and as they ate, their father walked to and fro in long ungainly strides, pausing each time at the door to give a glance up and down the road and at the fire to hoist his broken bottom to warm. Ned heard steps come up the road from the west. His father heard them too. He returned to the door and glued his hand to the jamb. Ned covered his eyes with his hands and felt that everything was as it had always been. He could hear the noise of the strand as a background to the voices.

'God be with you, Tomas,' the voice said.

'God and Mary be with you, Teig.' (In Irish they were speaking.) 'What way are you?'

'Well, honour and praise be to God. 'Tis a fine night.'

''Tis, 'tis, 'tis so indeed. A grand night, praise be to God.'

'Musha, who is it?' their mother asked, looking round.

''Tis young Teig,' their father replied, looking after him.

'Shemus's young Teig?'

''Tis, 'tis, 'tis.'

'But where would Shemus's young Teig be going at this hour of night? 'Tisn't to the shop?'

'No, woman, no, no, no. Up to the uncle's I suppose.'

'Is it Ned Willie's?'

'He's sleeping at Ned Willie's,' Brigid chimed in in her high-pitched voice, timid but triumphant. ''Tis since the young teacher came to them.'

There was no more to be said. Everything was explained and Ned smiled. The only unfamiliar voice, little Brigid's, seemed the most familiar of all.

Tom said first Mass next morning and the household, all but Brigid, went. They drove, and Tomas in high glee sat in front with Tom, waving his hand and shouting greetings at all they met. He was like a boy, so intense was his pleasure. The chapel was perched high above the road. Outside the morning was grey and beyond the windy edge of the cliff was the sea. The wind blew straight in, setting cloaks and petticoats flying.

After dinner as the two boys were returning from a series of visits to the neighbours' houses their father rushed down the road to meet them, shaking them passionately by the hand and asking were they well. When they were seated in the kitchen he opened up the subject of his excitement.

'Well,' he said, 'I arranged a grand little outing for ye tomorrow, thanks be to God,' and to identify further the source of his inspiration he searched at the back of his neck for the peak of his cap and raised it solemnly.

'Musha, what outing are you talking about?' their mother asked angrily.

'I arranged for us to go over the bay to your brother's.'

'And can't you leave the poor boys alone?' she bawled. 'Haven't they only the one day? Isn't it for the rest they came?'

'Even so, even so, even so,' Tomas said with mounting passion. 'Aren't their own cousins to lay eyes on them?'

'I was in Carriganassa for a week last summer,' said Tom.

'Yes, but I wasn't, and Ned wasn't. 'Tis only decent.'

''Tisn't decency is worrying you at all but drink,' growled Tom.

'Oh!' gasped his father, fishing for the peak of his cap to swear with, 'that I might be struck dead!'

'Be quiet, you old heathen!' crowed his wife. 'That's the truth, Tom my pulse. Plenty of drink is what he wants where he won't be under my eye. Leave ye stop at home.'

'I can't stop at home, woman,' shouted Tomas. 'Why do you be always picking at me? I must go whether they come or not. I must go, I must go, and that's all there is about it.'

'Why must you?' asked his wife.

'Because I warned Red Pat and Dempsey,' he stormed. 'And the woman from the island is coming as well to see a daughter of hers that's married there. And what's more, I borrowed Cassidy's boat and he lent it at great inconvenience, and 'twould be very bad manners for me to throw his kindness back in his face. I must go.'

'Oh, we may as well all go,' said Tom.

It blew hard all night and Tomas, all anxiety, was out at break of day to watch the whitecaps on the water. While the boys were at breakfast he came in and, leaning his arms on the table with hands joined as though in prayer, he announced in a caressing voice that it was a beautiful day, thank God, a pet day with a moist gentle little bit of a breezheen that would only blow them over. His voice would have put a child to sleep, but his wife continued to nag and scold, and he stumped out again in a fury and sat on the wall with his back to the house and his legs crossed, chewing his pipe. He was dressed in his best clothes, a respectable blue tailcoat and pale frieze trousers with only one patch on the seat. He had turned his cap almost right way round so that the peak covered his right ear.

He was all over the boat like a boy. Dempsey, a haggard, pock-marked, melancholy man with a soprano voice of astounding penetration, took the tiller and Red Patrick the sail. Tomas clambered into the bows and stood there with one knee up, leaning forward like a figurehead. He knew the bay like a book. The island woman was perched on the ballast with her rosary in her hands and her shawl over her eyes to shut out the sight of the waves. The cumbrous old boat took the sail lightly enough and Ned leaned back on his elbows against the side, rejoicing in it all.

'She's laughing,' his father said delightedly when her bows ran white.

'Whose boat is that, Dempsey?' he asked, screwing up his eyes as another brown sail tilted ahead of them.

' 'Tis the island boat,' shrieked Dempsey.

' 'Tis not, Dempsey. 'Tis not indeed, my love. That's not the island boat.'

'Whose boat is it then?'

'It must be some boat from Carriganassa, Dempsey.'

' 'Tis the island boat I tell you.'

'Ah, why will you be contradicting me, Dempsey, my treasure? 'Tis not the island boat. The island boat has a dark brown sail; 'tis only a month since 'twas tarred, and that's an old tarred sail, and what proves it out and out, Dempsey, the island-boat sail has a patch in the corner.'

He was leaning well over the bows, watching the rocks that fled beneath them, a dark purple. He rested his elbow on his raised knee and looked back at them, his brown face sprinkled with spray and lit from below by the accumulated flickerings of the water. His flesh seemed to dissolve, to become transparent, while his blue eyes shone with extraordinary brilliance. Ned half-closed his eyes and watched sea and sky slowly mount and sink behind the red-brown, sun-filled sail and the poised and eager figure.

'Tom!' shouted his father, and the battered old face peered at them from under the arch of the sail, with which it was almost one in tone, the silvery light filling it with warmth.

'Well?' Tom's voice was an inexpressive boom.

'You were right last night, Tom, my boy. My treasure, my son, you were right. 'Twas for the drink I came.'

'Ah, do you tell me so?' Tom asked ironically.

' 'Twas, 'twas, 'twas,' the old man said regretfully. ' 'Twas for the drink. 'Twas so, my darling. They were always decent people, your mother's people, and 'tis her knowing how decent they are makes her so suspicious. She's a good woman, a fine woman, your poor mother, may the Almighty God bless her and keep her and watch over her.'

'Aaa-men,' Tom chanted irreverently as his father shook his old cap piously towards the sky.

'But Tom! Are you listening, Tom?'

'Well, what is it now?'

'I had another reason.'

'Had you indeed?' Tom's tone was not encouraging.

'I had, I had, God's truth, I had. God blast the lie I'm telling you, Tom, I had.'

''Twas boasting out of the pair of ye,' shrieked Dempsey from the stern, the wind whipping the shrill notes from his lips and scattering them wildly like scraps of paper.

''Twas so, Dempsey, 'twas so. You're right, Dempsey. You're always right. The blessing of God on you, Dempsey, for you always had the true word.' Tomas's laughing leprechaun countenance gleamed under the bellying, tilting, chocolate-coloured sail and his powerful voice beat Dempsey's down. 'And would you blame me?'

'The O'Donnells hadn't the beating of them in their own hand,' screamed Dempsey.

'Thanks be to God for all His goodness and mercy,' shouted Tomas, again waving his cap in a gesture of recognition towards the spot where he felt the Almighty might be listening, 'they have not. They have not so, Dempsey. And they have a good hand. The O'Donnells are a good family and an old family and a kind family, but they never had the like of my two sons.'

'And they were stiff enough with you when you came for the daughter,' shrieked Dempsey.

'They were, Dempsey, they were. They were stiff. They were so. You wouldn't blame them, Dempsey. They were an old family and I was nothing only a landless man.' With a fierce gesture the old man pulled his cap still further over his ear, spat, gave his moustache a tug and leaned at a still more precarious angle over the bow, his blue eyes dancing with triumph. 'But I had the gumption, Dempsey. I had the gumption, my love.'

The islands slipped past; the gulf of water narrowed and grew calmer, and white cottages could be seen scattered under the tall ungainly church. It was a wild and rugged coast, the tide was full, and they had to pull in as best they could among the rocks. Red Patrick leaped lightly ashore to draw in the boat. The others stepped after him into several inches of water and Red Patrick, himself precariously poised, held them from slipping. Rather shamefastly, Ned and Tom took off their shoes.

'Don't do that!' shrieked their father. 'We'll carry ye up. Mother of God, yeer poor feet!'

'Will you shut your old gob?' Tom said angrily.

They halted for a moment at the stile outside Caheragh's. Old Caheragh had a red beard and a broad, smiling face. Then they went on to O'Donnell's who had two houses, modern and old, separated by a yard. In one lived Uncle Maurice and his family and in the other Maurice's married son, Sean. Ned and Tom remained with Sean and his wife. Tom and he were old friends. When he spoke he rarely looked at Tom, merely giving him a sidelong glance that just reached to his chin and then dropped his eyes with a peculiar timid smile. ''Twas,' Ned heard him say, and then: 'He did,' and after that: 'Hardly.' Shuvaun was tall, nervous, and matronly. She clung to their hands with an excess of eagerness as though she couldn't bear to let them go, uttering ejaculations of tenderness, delight, astonishment, pity, and admiration. Her speech was full of diminutives: 'childeen', 'handeen', 'boateen'. Three young children scrambled about the floor with a preoccupation scarcely broken by the strangers. Shuvaun picked her way through them, filling the kettle and cutting the bread, and then, as though afraid of neglecting Tom, she clutched his hand again. Her feverish concentration gave an impression that its very intensity bewildered her and made it impossible for her to understand one word they said. In three days' time it would all begin to drop into place in her mind and then she would begin quoting them.

Young Niall O'Donnell came in with his girl; one of the Deignans from up the hill. She was plump and pert; she had been in service in town. Niall was a well-built boy with a soft, wild-eyed, sensuous face and a deep mellow voice of great power. While they were having a cup of tea in the parlour where the three or four family photos were skyed, Ned saw the two of them again through the back window. They were standing on the high ground behind the house with the spring sky behind them and the light in their faces. Niall was asking her something but she, more interested in the sitting-room window, only shook her head.

'Ye only just missed yeer father,' said their Uncle Maurice when they went across to the other house for dinner. Maurice was a tight-lipped little man with a high bald forehead and a snappy voice. 'He went off to Owney Pat's only this minute.'

'The devil!' said Tom. 'I knew he was out to dodge me. Did you give him whiskey?'

'What the hell else could I give him?' snapped Maurice. 'Do you think 'twas tea the old coot was looking for?'

Tom took the place of honour at the table. He was the favourite. Through the doorway into the bedroom could be seen a big canopy bed and on the whiteness of a raised pillow a skeleton face in a halo of smoke-blue hair surmounted with what looked suspiciously like a mauve tea-cosy. Sometimes the white head would begin to stir and everyone fell silent while Niall, the old man's pet, translated the scarcely audible whisper. Sometimes Niall would go in with his stiff ungainly swagger and repeat one of Tom's jokes in his drawling, powerful bass. The hens stepped daintily about their feet, poking officious heads between them, and rushing out the door with a wild flutter and shriek when one of the girls hooshed them. Something timeless, patriarchal, and restful about it made Ned notice everything. It was as though he had never seen his mother's house before.

'Tell me,' Tom boomed with mock concern, leaning over confidentially to his uncle and looking under his brows at young Niall, 'speaking as a clergyman and for the good of the family and so on, is that son of yours coorting Delia Deignan?'

'Why? Was the young blackguard along with her again?' snapped Maurice in amusement.

'Of course I might be mistaken,' Tom said doubtfully.

'You wouldn't know a Deignan, to be sure,' Sean said dryly.

'Isn't any of them married yet?' asked Tom.

'No, by damn, no,' said Maurice. 'Isn't it a wonder?'

'Because,' Tom went on in the same solemn voice, 'I want someone to look after this young brother of mine. Dublin is a wild sort of place and full of temptations. Ye wouldn't know a decent little girl I could ask?'

'Cait! Cait!' they all shouted, Niall's deep voice loudest of all.

'Now all the same, Delia looks a smart little piece,' said Tom.

'No, Cait! Cait! Delia isn't the same since she went to town. She has notions of herself. Leave him marry Cait!'

Niall rose gleefully and shambled in to the old man. With a gamesome eye on the company Tom whispered:

'Is she a quiet sort of girl? I wouldn't like Ned to get anyone rough.'

'She is, she is,' they said, 'a grand girl!'

Sean rose quietly and went to the door with his head bowed.

'God knows, if anyone knows he should know and all the times he manhandled her.'

Tom sat bolt upright with mock indignation while the table rocked. Niall shouted the joke into his grandfather's ear. The mauve tea-cosy shook; it was the only indication of the old man's amusement.

The Deignans' house was on top of a hill high over the road and commanded a view of the countryside for miles. The two brothers with Sean and the O'Donnell girls reached it by a long winding boreen that threaded its way uncertainly through little grey rocky fields and walls of unmortared stone which rose against the sky along the edges of the hill like lacework. On their way they met another procession coming down the hill. It was headed by their father and the island woman, arm in arm, and behind came two locals with Dempsey and Red Patrick. All the party except the island woman were well advanced in liquor. That was plain when their father rushed forward to shake them all by the hand and ask them how they were. He said that divil such honourable and kindly people as the people of Carriganassa were to be found in the whole world, and of these there was no one a patch on the O'Donnells; kings and sons of kings as you could see from one look at them. He had only one more call to pay and promised to be at Caheragh's within a quarter of an hour.

They looked over the Deignans' half-door. The kitchen was empty. The girls began to titter. They knew the Deignans must have watched them coming from Maurice's door. The kitchen was a beautiful room; woodwork and furniture, homemade and shapely, were painted a bright red-brown and the painted dresser shone with pretty ware. They entered and looked about them. Nothing was to be heard but the tick of the cheap alarm clock on the dresser. One of the girls began to giggle hysterically. Sean raised his voice.

'Are ye in or are ye out, bad cess to ye!'

For a moment there was no reply. Then a quick step sounded in the attic and a girl descended the stairs at a run, drawing a black knitted shawl tighter about her shoulders. She was perhaps twenty-eight or thirty, with a narrow face, sharp like a ferret's, and blue nervous eyes. She entered the kitchen awkwardly sideways, giving the customary greetings but without looking at anyone.

'A hundred welcomes. . . . How are ye? . . . 'Tis a fine day.'

The O'Donnell girls giggled again. Nora Deignan looked at

them in astonishment, biting nervously at the tassel of her shawl. She had tiny sharp white teeth.

'What is it, aru?' she asked.

'Musha, will you stop your old cimeens,' boomed Tom, 'and tell us where's Cait from you? You don't think 'twas to see your ugly puss that we came up here?'

'Cait!' Nora called in a low voice.

'What is it?' another voice replied from upstairs.

'Damn well you know what it is,' bellowed Tom, 'and you cross-eyed expecting us since morning. Will you come down out of that or will I go up and fetch you?'

There was the same hasty step and a second girl descended the stairs. It was only later that Ned was able to realize how beautiful she was. She had the same narrow pointed face as her sister, the same slight features sharpened by a sort of animal instinct, the same blue eyes with their startled brightness; but all seemed to have been differently composed, and her complexion had a transparency as though her whole nature were shining through it. 'Child of Light, thy limbs are burning through the veil which seems to hide them,' Ned found himself murmuring. She came on them in the same hostile way, blushing furiously. Tom's eyes rested on her; soft, bleary, emotional eyes incredibly unlike her own.

'Have you nothing to say to me, Cait?' he boomed, and Ned thought his very voice was soft and clouded.

'Oh, a hundred welcomes.' Her blue eyes rested for a moment on him with what seemed a fierce candour and penetration and went past him to the open door. Outside a soft rain was beginning to fall; heavy clouds crushed down the grey landscape, which grew clearer as it merged into one common plane; the little grey bumpy fields with the walls of grey unmortared stone that drifted hither and over across them like blown sand, the whitewashed farmhouses lost to the sun sinking back into the brown-grey hillsides.

'Nothing else, my child?' he growled, pursing his lips.

'How are you?'

'The politeness is suffocating you. Where's Delia?'

'Here I am,' said Delia from the doorway immediately behind him. In her furtive way she had slunk round the house. Her bland impertinence raised a laugh.

'The reason we called,' said Tom, clearing his throat, 'is this young brother of mine that's looking for a wife.'

Everyone laughed again. Ned knew the oftener a joke was repeated the better they liked it, but for him this particular joke was beginning to wear thin.

'Leave him take me,' said Delia with an arch look at Ned who smiled and gazed at the floor.

'Be quiet, you slut!' said Tom. 'There are your two sisters before you.'

'Even so, I want to go to Dublin. . . . Would you treat me to lemonade, mister?' she asked Ned with her impudent smile. 'This is a rotten hole. I'd go to America if they left me.'

'America won't be complete without you,' said Tom. 'Now, don't let me hurry ye, ladies, but my old fellow will be waiting for us in Johnny Kit's.'

'We'll go along with you,' said Nora, and the three girls took down three black shawls from inside the door. Some tension seemed to have gone out of the air. They laughed and joked between themselves.

'Ye'll get wet,' said Sean to the two brothers.

'Cait will make room for me under her shawl,' said Tom.

'Indeed I will not,' she cried, starting back with a laugh.

'Very shy you're getting,' said Sean with a good-natured grin.

' 'Tisn't that at all but she'd sooner the young man,' said Delia.

'What's strange is wonderful,' said Nora.

Biting her lip with her tiny front teeth, Cait looked angrily at her sisters and Sean, and then began to laugh. She glanced at Ned and smilingly held out her shawl in invitation, though at the same moment angry blushes chased one another across her forehead like squalls across the surface of a lake. The rain was a mild, persistent drizzle and a strong wind was blowing. Everything had darkened and grown lonely, and, with his head in the blinding folds of the shawl, which reeked of turf-smoke, Ned felt as if he had dropped out of Time's pocket.

They waited in Caheragh's kitchen. The bearded old man sat in one chimney corner and a little barelegged boy in the other. The dim blue light poured down the wide chimney on their heads in a shower with the delicacy of light on old china, picking out surfaces one rarely saw; and between them the fire burned a bright orange in the great whitewashed hearth with the black, swinging bars and pothook. Outside the rain fell softly, almost soundlessly, beyond the half-door. Delia, her black shawl trailing from her shoulders, leaned over it, acting the part of watcher as in a Greek play. Their father's fifteen minutes had strung themselves out to an hour and two little barefooted boys had already been sent to hunt him down.

'Where are they now, Delia?' one of the O'Donnells would ask.

'Crossing the fields from Patsy Kit's.'

'He wasn't there so.'

'He wouldn't be,' the old man said. 'They'll likely go on to Ned Kit's now.'

'That's where they're making for,' said Delia. 'Up the hill at the far side of the fort.'

'They'll find him there,' the old man said confidently.

Ned felt as though he were still blanketed by the folds of the turf-reeking shawl. Something seemed to have descended on him that filled him with passion and loneliness. He could scarcely take his eyes off Cait. She and Nora sat on the form against the back wall, a composition in black and white, the black shawl drawn tight under the chin, the cowl of it breaking the curve of her dark hair, her shadow on the gleaming wall behind. She did not speak except to answer some question of Tom's about her brother, but sometimes Ned caught her looking at him with naked eyes. Then she smiled swiftly and secretly and turned her eyes again to the door, sinking back into pensiveness. Pensiveness or vacancy? he wondered. While he gazed at her face with the animal instinctiveness of its over-delicate features it seemed like a mirror in which he saw again the falling rain, the rocks and hills and angry sea.

The first announced by Delia was Red Patrick. After him came the island woman. Each had last seen his father in a different place. Ned chuckled at a sudden vision of his father, eager and impassioned and aflame with drink, stumping with his broken bottom across endless fields through pouring rain with a growing procession behind him. Dempsey was the last to come. He doubted if Tomas would be in a condition to take the boat at all.

'What matter, aru?' said Delia across her shoulder. 'We can find room for the young man.'

'And where would we put him?' gaped Nora.

'He can have Cait's bed,' Delia said innocently.

'Oye, and where would Cait sleep?' Nora asked and then skitted and covered her face with her shawl. Delia scoffed. The men laughed and Cait, biting her lip furiously, looked at the floor. Again Ned caught her eyes on him and again she laughed and turned away.

Tomas burst in unexpected on them all like a sea wind that scattered them before him. He wrung Tom's hand and asked him how he was. He did the same to Ned. Ned replied gravely that he was very well.

'In God's holy name,' cried his father, waving his arms like a windmill, 'what are ye all waiting for?'

The tide had fallen. Tomas grabbed an oar and pushed the boat on to a rock. Then he raised the sail and collapsed under it and had to be extricated from its drenching folds, glauming and swearing at Cassidy's old boat. A little group stood on a naked rock against a grey background of drifting rain. For a long time Ned continued to wave back to the black shawl that was lifted to him. An extraordinary feeling of exultation and loss enveloped him. Huddled up in his overcoat he sat with Dempsey in the stern, not speaking.

'It was a grand day,' his father declared, swinging himself to and fro, tugging at his Viking moustache, dragging the peak of his cap farther over his ear. His gestures betrayed a certain lack of rhythmical cohesion; they began and ended abruptly. 'Dempsey, my darling, wasn't it a grand day?'

' 'Twas a grand day for you,' shrieked Dempsey, as if his throat would burst.

' 'Twas, my treasure, 'twas a beautiful day. I got an honourable reception and my sons got an honourable reception.'

By this time he was flat on his belly, one leg completely over the edge of the boat. He reached back a clammy hand to his sons.

' 'Twas the best day I ever had,' he said. 'I got porter and I got whiskey and I got poteen. I did so, Tom, my calf. Ned, my brightness, I went to seven houses and in every house I got seven drinks and with every drink I got seven welcomes. And your mother's people are a hand of trumps. It was no slight they put on me at all even if I was nothing but a landless man. No slight, Tom. No slight at all.'

Darkness had fallen, the rain had cleared, the stars came out of a pitch-black sky under which the little tossing, nosing boat seemed lost beyond measure. In all the waste of water nothing could be heard but the splash of the boat's sides and their father's voice raised in tipsy song.

> 'The evening was fair and the sunlight was yellow,
>   I halted, beholding a maiden bright
> Coming to me by the edge of the mountain,
>   Her cheeks had a berry-bright rosy light.'

Ned was the first to wake. He struck a match and lit the candle. It was time for them to be stirring. It was just after dawn, and at half past nine he must be in his old place in the schoolroom before the rows of pinched little city faces. He lit a cigarette and closed his eyes. The lurch of the boat was still in his blood, the face of Cait Deignan in his mind, and as if from far away he heard a line of the wild love-song his father had been singing: 'And we'll drive the geese at the fall of night.'

He heard his brother mumble something and nudged him. Tom looked big and fat and vulnerable with his fair head rolled sideways and his heavy mouth dribbling on to the sleeve of his pyjamas. Ned slipped quietly out of bed, put on his trousers, and went to the window. He drew the curtains and let in the thin cold daylight. The bay was just visible and perfectly still. Tom began to mumble again in a frightened voice and Ned shook him. He started out of his sleep with a cry of fear, grabbing at the bedclothes. He looked first at Ned, then at the candle and drowsily rubbed his eyes.

'Did you hear it too?' he asked.

'Did I hear what?' asked Ned with a smile.

'In the room,' said Tom.

'There was nothing in the room,' replied Ned. 'You were ramaishing so I woke you up.'

'Was I? What was I saying?'

'You were telling no secrets,' said Ned with a quiet laugh.

'Hell!' Tom said in disgust and stretched out his arm for a cigarette. He lit it at the candle flame, his drowsy red face puckered and distraught. 'I slept rotten.'

'Oye!' Ned said quietly, raising his eyebrows. It wasn't often

Tom spoke in that tone. He sat on the edge of the bed, joined his hands and leaned forward, looking at Tom with wide gentle eyes.

'Is there anything wrong?' he asked.

'Plenty.'

'You're not in trouble?' Ned asked without raising his voice.

'Not that sort of trouble. The trouble is in myself.'

Ned gave him a look of intense sympathy and understanding. The soft emotional brown eyes were searching him for a judgment. Ned had never felt less like judging him.

'Ay,' he said gently and vaguely, his eyes wandering to the other side of the room while his voice took on its accustomed stammer, 'the trouble is always in ourselves. If we were contented in ourselves the other things wouldn't matter. I suppose we must only leave it to time. Time settles everything.'

'Time will settle nothing for me,' Tom said despairingly. 'You have something to look forward to. I have nothing. It's the loneliness of my job that kills you. Even to talk about it would be a relief but there's no one you can talk to. People come to you with their troubles but there's no one you can go to with your own.'

Again the challenging glare in the brown eyes and Ned realized with infinite compassion that for years Tom had been living in the same state of suspicion and fear, a man being hunted down by his own nature; and that for years to come he would continue to live in this way, and perhaps never be caught again as he was now.

'A pity you came down here,' stammered Ned flatly. 'A pity we went to Carriganassa. 'Twould be better for both of us if we went somewhere else.'

'Why don't you marry her, Ned?' Tom asked earnestly.

'Who?' asked Ned.

'Cait.'

'Yesterday,' said Ned with the shy smile he wore when he confessed something, 'I nearly wished I could.'

'But you can, man,' Tom said eagerly, sitting upon his elbow. Like all men with frustration in their hearts he was full of schemes for others. 'You could marry her and get a school down here. That's what I'd do if I was in your place.'

'No,' Ned said gravely. 'We made our choice a long time ago. We can't go back on it now.'

Then with his hands in his trouser pockets and his head bowed he went out to the kitchen. His mother, the coloured shawl about her head, was blowing the fire. The bedroom door was open and he could see his father in shirtsleeves kneeling beside the bed, his face raised reverently towards a holy picture, his braces hanging down behind. He unbolted the half-door, went through the garden and out on to the road. There was a magical light on everything. A boy on a horse rose suddenly against the sky, a startling picture. Through the apple-green light over Carriganassa ran long streaks of crimson, so still they might have been enamelled. Magic, magic, magic! He saw it as in a children's picture-book with all its colours intolerably bright; something he had outgrown and could never return to, while the world he aspired to was as remote and intangible as it had seemed even in the despair of youth.

It seemed as if only now for the first time was he leaving home; for the first time and forever saying good-bye to it all.

THE BRIDAL NIGHT

IT WAS sunset, and the two great humps of rock made a twilight in the cove where the boats were lying high up the strand. There was one light only in a little whitewashed cottage. Around the headland came a boat and the heavy dipping of its oars was like a heron's flight. The old woman was sitting on the low stone wall outside her cottage.

''Tis a lonesome place,' said I.

''Tis so,' she agreed, 'a lonesome place, but any place is lonesome without one you'd care for.'

'Your own flock are gone from you, I suppose?' I asked.

'I never had but the one,' she replied, 'the one son only,' and I knew because she did not add a prayer for his soul that he was still alive.

'Is it in America he is?' I asked. (It is to America all the boys of the locality go when they leave home.)

'No, then,' she replied simply. 'It is in the asylum in Cork he is on me these twelve years.'

I had no fear of trespassing on her emotions. These lonesome people in the wild places, it is their nature to speak; they must cry out their sorrows like the wild birds.

'God help us!' I said. 'Far enough!'

'Far enough,' she sighed. 'Too far for an old woman. There was a nice priest here one time brought me up in his car to see him. All the ways to this wild place he brought it, and he drove me into the city. It is a place I was never used to, but it eased my mind to see poor Denis well-cared-for and well-liked. It was a trouble to me before that, not knowing would they see what a good boy he was before his madness came on him. He knew me; he saluted me, but he said nothing until the superintendent came to tell me the tea was ready for me. Then poor Denis raised his head and says: "Leave ye not forget the toast. She was ever a great one for her bit of toast." It seemed to give him ease and he cried after. A good boy he was and is. It was like him after seven long years to think of his old mother and her little bit of toast.'

'God help us,' I said for her voice was like the birds', hurrying high, immensely high, in the coloured light, out to sea to the last islands where their nests were.

'Blessed be His holy will,' the old woman added, 'there is no turning aside what is in store. It was a teacher that was here at the time. Miss Regan her name was. She was a fine big jolly girl from the town. Her father had a shop there. They said she had three hundred pounds to her own cheek the day she set foot in the school, and – 'tis hard to believe but 'tis what they all said: I will not belie her – 'twasn't banished she was at all, but she came here of her own choice, for the great liking she had for the sea and the mountains. Now, that is the story, and with my own eyes I saw her, day in day out, coming down the little pathway you came yourself from the road and sitting beyond there in a hollow you can hardly see, out of the wind. The neighbours could make nothing of it, and she being a stranger, and with only the book Irish, they left her alone. It never seemed to take a peg out of her, only sitting in that hole in the rocks, as happy as the day is long, reading her little book or writing her letters. Of an odd time she might bring one of the little scholars along with her to be picking posies.

'That was where my Denis saw her. He'd go up to her of an evening and sit on the grass beside her, and off and on he might take her out in the boat with him. And she'd say with that big laugh of hers: "Denis is my beau." Those now were her words and she meant no more harm by it than the child unborn, and I knew it and Denis knew it, and it was a little joke we had, the three of us. It was the same way she used to joke about her little hollow. "Mrs Sullivan," she'd say, "leave no one near it. It is my nest and my cell and my little prayer-house, and maybe I would be like the birds and catch the smell of the stranger and then fly away from ye all." It did me good to hear her laugh, and whenever I saw Denis moping or idle I would say it to him myself: "Denis, why wouldn't you go out and pay your attentions to Miss Regan and all saying you are her intended?" It was only a joke. I would say the same thing to her face, for Denis was such a quiet boy, no way rough or accustomed to the girls at all – and how would he in this lonesome place?

'I will not belie her, it was she saw first that poor Denis was after more than company, and it was not to this cove she came at all then but to the little cove beyond the headland, and 'tis hardly she would go there itself without a little scholar along with her. "Ah," I says, for I missed her company, "isn't it the great stranger Miss Regan is becoming?" and Denis would put on his coat and go hunting in the dusk till he came to whatever spot she was. Little ease that was to him, poor boy, for he lost his tongue entirely, and lying on his belly before her, chewing an old bit of grass, is all he would do till she got up and left him. He could not help himself, poor boy. The madness was on him, even then, and it was only when I saw the plunder done that I knew there was no cure for him only to put her out of his mind entirely. For 'twas madness in him and he knew it, and that was what made him lose his tongue – he that was maybe without the price of an ounce of 'baccy – I will not deny it: often enough he had to do without it when the hens would not be laying, and often enough stirabout and praties was all we had for days. And there was she with money to her name in the bank! And that wasn't all, for he was a good boy; a quiet, good-natured boy, and another would take pity on him, knowing he would make her a fine steady husband, but she was not the sort, and well I knew it from the first day I laid eyes on her, that her hand would never rock the cradle. There was the madness out and out.

'So here was I, pulling and hauling, coaxing him to stop at home, and hiding whatever little thing was to be done till evening the way his hands would not be idle. But he had no heart in the work, only listening, always listening, or climbing the cnuceen to see would he catch a glimpse of her coming or going. And, oh, Mary, the heavy sigh he'd give when his bit of supper was over and I bolting the house for the night, and he with the long hours of darkness forninst him – my heart was broken thinking of it. It was the madness, you see. It was on him. He could hardly sleep or eat, and at night I would hear him, turning and groaning as loud as the sea on the rocks.

'It was then when the sleep was a fever to him that he took to walking in the night. I remember well the first night I heard him lift the latch. I put on my few things and went out after him. It was standing here I heard his feet on the stile. I went back and latched the door and hurried after him. What else could I do, and this place terrible after the fall of night with rocks and hills and water and streams, and he, poor soul, blinded with the dint of sleep. He travelled the road a piece, and then took to the hills, and I followed him with my legs all torn with briars and furze. It was over beyond by the new house that he gave up. He turned to me then the way a little child that is running away turns and clings to your knees; he turned to me and said: "Mother, we'll go home now. It was the bad day for you ever you brought me into the world." And as the day was breaking I got him back to bed and covered him up to sleep.

'I was hoping that in time he'd wear himself out, but it was worse he was getting. I was a strong woman then, a mayen-strong woman. I could cart a load of seaweed or dig a field with any man, but the night-walking broke me. I knelt one night before the Blessed Virgin and prayed whatever was to happen, it would happen while the light of life was in me, the way I would not be leaving him lonesome like that in a wild place.

'And it happened the way I prayed. Blessed be God, he woke that night or the next night on me and he roaring. I went in to him but I couldn't hold him. He had the strength of five men. So I went out and locked the door behind me. It was down the hill I faced in the starlight to the little house above the cove. The Donoghues came with me: I will not belie them; they were fine powerful men and good neighbours. The father and the two sons came with me and brought the rope from the boats. It was a hard struggle they had of it and a long time before they got him on the floor, and a longer time before they got the ropes on him. And when they had him tied they put him back into bed for me, and I covered him up, nice and decent, and put a hot stone to his feet to take the chill of the cold floor off him.

'Sean Donoghue spent the night sitting beside the fire with me, and in the morning he sent one of the boys off for the doctor. Then Denis called me in his own voice and I went into him. "Mother," says Denis, "will you leave me this way against the time they come for me?" I hadn't the heart. God knows I hadn't. "Don't do it, Peg," says Sean. "If 'twas a hard job trussing him before, it will be harder the next time, and I won't answer for it."

' "You're a kind neighbour, Sean," says I, "and I would never make little of you, but he is the only son I ever reared and I'd sooner he'd kill me now than shame him at the last."

'So I loosened the ropes on him and he lay there very quiet all day without breaking his fast. Coming on to evening he asked me for the sup of tea and he drank it, and soon after the doctor and another man came in the car. They said a few words to Denis but he made them no answer and the doctor gave me the bit of writing. "It will be tomorrow before they come for him," says he, "and 'tisn't right for you to be alone in the house with the man." But I said I would stop with him and Sean Donoghue said the same.

'When darkness came on there was a little bit of a wind blew up from the sea and Denis began to rave to himself, and it was her name he was calling all the time. "Winnie," that was her name, and it was the first time I heard it spoken. "Who is that he is calling?" says Sean. "It is the schoolmistress," says I, "for though I do not recognize the name, I know 'tis no one else he'd be asking for." "That is a bad sign," says Sean. "He'll get worse as the night goes on and the wind rises. 'Twould be better for me go down and get the boys to put the ropes on him again while he's quiet." And it was then something struck me, and I said: "Maybe if she came to him herself for a minute he would be quiet after." "We can try it anyway," says Sean, "and if the girl has a kind heart she will come."

'It was Sean that went up for her. I would not have the courage to ask her. Her little house is there on the edge of the hill; you can see it as you go back the road with the bit of garden before it the new teacher left grow wild. And it was a true word Sean said for 'twas worse Denis was getting, shouting out against the wind for us to get Winnie for him. Sean was a long time away or maybe I felt it long, and I thought it might be the way she was afeared to come. There are many like that, small blame to them. Then I heard her step that I knew so well on the boreen beside the house and I ran to the door, meaning to say I was sorry for the trouble we were giving her, but when I opened the door Denis called out her name in a loud voice, and the crying fit came on me, thinking how lighthearted we used to be together.

'I couldn't help it, and she pushed in apast me into the bedroom with her face as white as that wall. The candle was lighting on the dresser. He turned to her roaring with the mad look in his eyes, and then went quiet all of a sudden, seeing her like that overright him with her hair all tumbled in the wind. I was coming behind her. I heard it. He put up his two poor hands and the red mark of the ropes on his wrists and whispered to her: "Winnie, asthore, isn't it the long time you were away from me?"

' "It is, Denis, it is indeed," says she, "but you know I couldn't help it."

' "Don't leave me any more now, Winnie," says he, and then he said no more, only the two eyes lighting out on her as she sat by the bed. And Sean Donoghue brought in the little stooleen for me, and there we were, the three of us, talking, and Den is paying us no attention only staring at her.

' "Winnie," says he, "lie down here beside me."

' "Oye," says Sean, humouring him, "don't you know the poor girl is played out after her day's work? She must go home to bed."

' "No, no, no," says Denis and the terrible mad light in his eyes. "There is a high wind blowing and 'tis no night for one like her to be out. Leave her sleep here beside me. Leave her creep in under the clothes to me the way I'll keep her warm."

' "Oh, oh, oh, oh," says I, "indeed and indeed, Miss Regan, 'tis I'm sorry for bringing you here. 'Tisn't my son is talking at all but the madness in him. I'll go now," says I, "and bring Sean's boys to put the ropes on him again."

' "No, Mrs Sullivan," says she in a quiet voice. "Don't do that at all. I'll stop here with him and he'll go fast asleep. Won't you, Denis?"

' "I will, I will," says he, "but come under the clothes to me. There does a terrible draught blow under that door."

' "I will indeed, Denis," says she, "if you'll promise me to go to sleep."

' "Oye whisht, girl," says I. " 'Tis you that's mad. While you're here you're in my charge, and how would I answer to your father if you stopped in here by yourself?"

' "Never mind about me, Mrs Sullivan," she said. "I'm not a bit in dread of Denis. I promise you there will no harm come to me. You and Mr Donoghue can sit outside in the kitchen and I'll be all right here."

'She had a worried look but there was something about her there was no mistaking. I wouldn't take it on myself to cross the girl. We went out to the kitchen, Sean and myself, and we heard every whisper that passed between them. She got into the bed beside him: I heard her. He was whispering into her ear the sort of foolish things boys do be saying at that age, and then we heard no more only the pair of them breathing. I went to the room door and looked in. He was lying with his arm about her and his head on her bosom, sleeping like a child, sleeping like he slept in his good days with no worry at all on his poor face. She did not look at me and I did not speak to her. My heart was too full. God help us, it was an old song of my father's that was going through my head: "Lonely Rock is the one wife my children will know".

'Later on, the candle went out and I did not light another. I wasn't a bit afraid for her then. The storm blew up and he slept through it all, breathing nice and even. When it was light I made a cup of tea for her and beckoned her from the room door. She loosened his hold and slipped out of bed. Then he stirred and opened his eyes.

' "Winnie," says he, "where are you going?"

' "I'm going to work, Denis," says she. "Don't you know I must be at school early?"

' "But you'll come back to me tonight, Winnie?" says he.

' "I will, Denis," says she. "I'll come back, never fear."

'And he turned on his side and went fast asleep again.

'When she walked into the kitchen I went on my two knees before her and kissed her hands. I did so. There would no words come to me, and we sat there, the three of us, over our tea, and I declare for the time being I felt 'twas worth it all, all the troubles of his birth and rearing and all the lonesome years ahead.

'It was a great ease to us. Poor Denis never stirred, and when the police came he went along with them without commotion or handcuffs or anything that would shame him, and all the words he said to me was: "Mother, tell Winnie I'll be expecting her."

'And isn't it a strange and wonderful thing? From that day to the day she left us there did no one speak a bad word about what she did, and the people couldn't do enough for her. Isn't it a strange thing and the world as wicked as it is, that no one would say the bad word about her?'

Darkness had fallen over the Atlantic, blank grey to its farthest reaches.

A BACHELOR'S STORY

EVERY OLD bachelor has a love story in him if only you can get at it. This is usually not very easy because a bachelor is a man who does not lightly trust his neighbour, and by the time you can identify him as what he is, the cause of it all has been elevated into a morality, almost a divinity, something the old bachelor himself is afraid to look at for fear it might turn out to be stuffed. And woe betide you if he does confide in you, and you, by word or look, suggest that you do think it is stuffed, for that is how my own friendship with Archie Boland ended.

Archie was a senior Civil Servant, a big man with a broad red face and hot blue eyes and a crust of worldliness and bad temper overlaying a nature that had a lot of sweetness and fun in it. He was a man who affected to believe the worst of everyone, but he saw that I appreciated his true character, and suppressed his bad temper most of the time, except when I trespassed on his taboos, religious and political. For years the two of us walked home together. We both loved walking, and we both liked to drop in at a certain pub by the canal bridge where they kept good draught stout. Whenever we encountered some woman we knew, Archie was very polite and even effusive in an old-fashioned way, raising his hat with a great sweeping gesture and bowing low over the hand he held as if he were about to kiss it, which I swear he would have done on the least encouragement. But afterwards he would look at me under his eyebrows with a knowing smile and tell me things about their home life which the ladies would have been very distressed to hear, and this, in turn, would give place to a sly look that implied that I was drawing my own conclusions from what he said, which I wasn't, not usually.

'I know what you think, Delaney,' he said one evening, carefully putting down the two pints and lowering himself heavily into his seat. 'You think I'm a bad case of sour grapes.'

'I wasn't thinking anything at all,' I said.

'Well, maybe you mightn't be too far wrong at that,' he conceded, more to his own view of me than to anything else. 'But it's not only that, Delaney. There are other things involved. You see, when I was your age I had an experience that upset me a lot. It upset me so much that I felt I could never go through the same sort of thing again. Maybe I was too idealistic.'

I never heard a bachelor yet who didn't take a modest pride in his own idealism. And there in the far corner of that pub by the canal bank on a rainy autumn evening, Archie took the plunge and told me the story of the experience that had turned him against women, and I put my foot in it and turned him against me as well. Ah, well, I was younger then!

You see, in his earlier days Archie had been a great cyclist. Twice he had cycled round Ireland, and had made any amount of long trips to see various historic spots, battlefields, castles and cathedrals. He was no scholar, but he liked to know what he was talking about and had no objection to showing other people that they didn't. 'I suppose you know that place you were talking about, James?' he would purr when someone in the office stuck his neck out. 'Because if you don't, I do.' No wonder he wasn't too popular with the staff.

One evening Archie arrived in a remote Connemara village where four women teachers were staying, studying Irish, and after supper he got to chatting with them, and they all went for a walk along the strand. One was a young woman called Madge Hale, a slight girl with blue-grey eyes, a long clear-skinned face, and a rather breathless manner, and Archie did not take long to see that she was altogether more intelligent than the others, and that whenever he said something interesting her whole face lit up like a child's.

The teachers were going on a trip to the Aran Islands next day, and Archie offered to join them. They visited the tiny oratories, and, as none of the teachers knew anything about these, Archie in his well-informed way described the origin of the island mon-asteries and the life of the hermit monks in the early mediaeval period. Madge was fascinated and kept asking questions about what the churches had looked like, and Archie, flattered into doing the dog, suggested that she should accompany him on a bicycle trip the following day, and see some of the later monas-teries. She agreed at once enthusiastically. The other women laughed, and Madge laughed, too, though it was clear that she didn't really know what they were laughing about.

Now, this was one sure way to Archie's heart. He disliked women because they were always going to parties or the pictures, painting their faces, and taking aspirin in cartloads. There was altogether too much nonsense about them for a man of his grave taste, but at last he had met a girl who seemed absolutely devoid of nonsense and was serious through and through.

Their trip next day was a great success, and he was able to point out to her the development of the monastery church through the mediaeval abbey to the preaching church. That evening when they returned, he suggested, half in jest, that she should borrow the bicycle and come back to Dublin with him. This time she hesitated, but it was only for a few moments as she considered the practical end of it, and then her face lit up in the same eager way, and she said in her piping voice: 'If you think I won't be in your way, Archie.'

Now, she was in Archie's way, and very much in his way, for he was a man of old-fashioned ideas, who had never in his life allowed a woman he was accompanying to pay for as much as a cup of tea for herself, who felt that to have to excuse himself on the road was little short of obscene, and who endured the agonies of the damned when he had to go to a country hotel with a pretty girl at the end of the day. When he went to the reception desk he felt sure that everyone believed unmentionable things about him and he had an overwhelming compulsion to lecture them on the subject of their evil imaginations. But for this, too, he admired her – by this time any other girl would have been wondering what her parents and friends would say if they knew she was spending the night in a country hotel with a man, but the very idea of scandal never seemed to enter Madge's head. And it was not, as he shrewdly divined, that she was either fast or flighty. It was merely that it had never occurred to her that anything she and Archie might do could involve any culpability.

That settled Archie's business. He knew she was the only woman in the world for him, though to tell her this when she was more or less at the mercy of his solicitations was something that did not even cross his mind. He had a sort of old-fashioned chivalry that set him above the commoner temptations. They cycled south through Clare to Limerick, and stood on the cliffs overlooking the Atlantic; the weather held fine, and they drifted through the flat apple country to Cashel and drank beer and

lemonade in country pubs, and finally pushed over the hills to
Kilkenny, where they spent their last evening wandering in the
dusk under the ruins of mediaeval abbeys and inns, studying
effigies and blazons; and never once did Archie as much as hold
her hand or speak to her of love. He scowled as he told me this,
as though I might mock him from the depths of my own small
experience, but I had no inclination to do so, for I knew the
enchantment of the senses that people of chaste and lonely char-
acter feel in one another's company and that haunts the memory
more than all the passionate embraces of lovers.

When they separated outside Madge's lodgings in Rathmines
late one summer evening, Archie felt that he was at last free to
speak. He held her hand as he said good-bye.

'I think we had quite good fun, don't you?' he asked.

'Oh, yes, Archie,' she cried, laughing in her delight. 'It was
wonderful. It was the happiest holiday I ever spent.'

He was so encouraged by this that he deliberately retained
hold of her hand.

'That's the way I feel,' he said, beginning to blush. 'I didn't
want to say it before because I thought it might embarrass you.
I never met a woman like you before, and if you ever felt you
wanted to marry me I'd be honoured.'

For a moment, while her face darkened as though all the
delight had drained from it, he thought that he had embarrassed
her even now.

'Are you sure, Archie?' she asked nervously. 'Because you
don't know me very long, remember. A few days like that is not
enough to know a person.'

'That's a thing that soon rights itself,' Archie said oracularly.

'And, besides, we'd have to wait a long while,' she added. 'My
people aren't very well off; I have two brothers younger than
me, and I have to help them.'

'And I have a long way to go before I get anywhere in the
Civil Service,' he replied good-humouredly, 'so it may be quite
a while before I can do what I like, as well. But those are things
that also right themselves, and they right themselves all the
sooner if you do them with an object in mind. I know my own
character pretty well,' he added thoughtfully, 'and I know it
would be a help to me. And I'm not a man to change his mind.'

She still seemed to hesitate; for a second or two he had a strong impression that she was about to refuse him, but then she thought better of it. Her face cleared in the old way, and she gave her nervous laugh.

'Very well, Archie,' she said. 'If you really want me, you'll find me willing.'

'I want you, Madge,' he replied gravely, and then he raised his hat and pushed his bicycle away while she stood outside her gate in the shadow of the trees and waved. I admired that gesture even as he described it. It was so like Archie, and I could see that such a plighting of his word would haunt him as no passionate love-making would ever do. It was magnificent, but it was not love. People should be jolted out of themselves at times like those, and when they are not so jolted it frequently means, as it did with Archie, that the experience is only deferred till a less propitious time.

However, he was too innocent to know anything of that. To him the whole fantastic business of walking out with a girl was miracle enough in itself, like being dumped down in the middle of some ancient complex civilization whose language and customs he was unfamiliar with. He might have introduced her to history, but she introduced him to operas and concerts, and in no time he was developing prejudices about music as though it was something that had fired him from boyhood, for Archie was by nature a gospel-maker. Even when I knew him, he shook his head over my weakness for Wagner. Bach was the man, and somehow Bach at once ceased to be a pleasure and became a responsibility. It was part of the process of what he called 'knowing his own mind'.

On fine Sundays in autumn they took their lunch and walked over the mountains to Enniskerry, or cycled down the Boyne Valley to Drogheda. Madge was a girl of very sweet disposition, so that they rarely had a falling-out, and even at the best of times this must have been an event in Archie's life, for he had an irascible, quarrelsome, gospel-making streak. It was true that there were certain evenings and weekends that she kept to herself to visit her old friends and an ailing aunt in Miltown, but these did not worry Archie, who believed that this was how a conscientious girl should be. As a man who knew his own mind, he liked to feel that the girl he was going to marry was the same.

Oh, of course it was too perfect! Of course, an older hand

would have waited to see what price he was expected to pay for all those perfections, but Archie was an idealist, which meant that he thought Nature was in the job solely for his benefit. Then one day Nature gave him a rap on the knuckles just to show him that the boot was on the other foot.

In town he happened to run into one of the group of teachers he had met in Connemara during the holidays and invited her politely to join him in a cup of tea. Archie favoured one of those long mahogany teahouses in Grafton Street where daylight never enters; he was a creature of habit, and this was where he had eaten his first lunch in Dublin, and there he would continue to go till some minor cataclysm like marriage changed the current of his life.

'I hear you're seeing a lot of Madge,' said the teacher gaily as if this were a guilty secret between herself and Archie.

'Oh, yes,' said Archie as if it weren't. 'And with God's help I expect to be doing the same for the rest of my life.'

'So I heard,' she said joyously. 'I'm delighted for Madge, of course. But I wonder whatever happened that other fellow she was engaged to?'

'Why?' asked Archie, who knew well that she was only pecking at him and refused to let her see how sick he felt. 'Was she engaged to another fellow?'

'Ah, surely she must have told you that!' the teacher cried with mock consternation. 'I hope I'm not saying anything wrong,' she added piously. 'Maybe she wasn't engaged to him after all. He was a teacher, too, I believe – somewhere on the South Side. What was his name?'

'I'll ask her and let you know,' replied Archie blandly. He was giving nothing away till he had had more time to think of it.

All the same he was in a very ugly temper. Archie was one of those people who believe in being candid with everybody, even at the risk of unpleasantness, which might be another reason that he had so few friends when I knew him. He might, for instance, hear from somebody called Mahony that another man called Devins had said he was inclined to be offensive in argument, which was a reasonable enough point of view, but Archie would feel it his duty to go straight to Devins and ask him to repeat the remark, which, of course, would leave Devins wondering who it was that had been trying to make mischief for him, so he would

ask a third man whether Mahony was the tell-tale, and a fourth
would repeat the question to Mahony, till eventually, I declare
to God, Archie's inquisition would have the whole office by
the ears.

Archie, of course, had felt compelled to confess to Madge
every sin of his past life, which, from the point of view of
this narrative, was quite without importance, and he naturally
assumed when Madge did not do the same that it could only be
because she had nothing to confess. He realized now that this
was a grave mistake since everyone has something to confess,
particularly women.

He could have done with her what he would have done with
someone in the office and asked her what she meant, but this did
not seem sufficient punishment to him. Though he didn't recog-
nize it, Archie's pride was deeply hurt. He regarded Madge's
silence as equivalent to an insult, and in the matter of insults he
felt it was his duty to give as good as he got. So, instead of having
it out with her as another man might have done, he proceeded
to make her life a misery. He continued to walk out with her as
though nothing had happened, and then brought the conversa-
tion gently round to various domestic disasters which had or had
not occurred in his own experience and all of which had been
caused solely by someone's deceit. This was intended to scare the
wits out of Madge, as no doubt it did. Then he called up a friend
of his in the Department of Education and asked him out for
a drink.

'The Hale girl?' his friend said thoughtfully. 'Isn't she engaged
to that assistant in St Joseph's? Wheeler, a chap with a lame leg?
I think I heard that. Why? You're not keen on her yourself by
any chance?'

'Ah, you know me,' Archie replied with a fat smile.

'Why then, indeed, I do not,' said his friend. 'But if you mean
business you'd want to hurry up. Now you mention it, they were
only supposed to be waiting till he got a headship somewhere.
He's a nice fellow, I believe.'

'So I'm told,' said Archie, and went away with a smile on his
lips and murder in his heart. Those forthright men of the world
are the very devil once they get a bee in their bonnets. Othello
had nothing on a Civil Servant of twelve years' standing and a
blameless reputation. So he still continued to see Madge, though

now his method of tormenting her was to press her about those
odd evenings she was supposed to spend with her aunt or those
old friends she spoke of. He realized that some of those evenings
were probably really spent as innocently as she described them,
since she showed neither embarrassment nor distress at his prob-
ing and gibing. It was the others that caused her to wince, and
those were the ones he concentrated on.

'I could meet you when you came out, you know,' he said in
a benign tone that almost glowed.

'But I don't know when I'll be out, Archie,' she replied,
blushing and stammering.

'Ah, well, even if you didn't get out until half past ten – and
that would be late for a lady her age – it would still give us time
for a little walk. That's if the night was fine, of course. It's all
very well, doing your duty by old friends, but you don't want to
deny yourself every little pleasure.'

'I couldn't promise anything, Archie, really I couldn't,' she
said almost angrily, and Archie smiled to himself, the smug smile
of the old inquisitor whose helpless victim has begun to give
himself away.

The road where Madge lived was one of those broad Victorian
roads you find scattered all over the hills at the south side of
Dublin, with trees along the pavement and deep gardens leading
to pairs of merchants' houses, semi-detached and solidly built,
with tall basements and high flights of steps. Next night, Archie
was waiting at the corner of a side-street in the shadow, feeling
like a detective as he watched her house. He had been there only
about ten minutes when she came out and tripped down the
steps. When she emerged from the garden, she turned right up
the hill, and Archie followed, guided more by the distinctive
clack of her heels than by the glimpses he caught of her passing
swiftly under a street lamp.

She reached the bus stop at the top of the road, and a man
came up and spoke to her. He was a youngish man in a bright
tweed coat, hatless and thin, dragging a lame leg. He took her
arm, and they went off together in the direction of the Dodder
bank. As they did, Archie heard her happy, eager, foolish laugh,
and it sounded exactly as though she were laughing at him.

He was beside himself with misery. He had got what he had
been seeking, which was full confirmation of the woman's guilt,

and now he had no idea what to do with it. To follow them and have it out on the river bank in the darkness was one possibility, but he realized that Wheeler – if this was Wheeler – probably knew as little of him as he had known of Wheeler, and that it would result only in general confusion. No, it was that abominable woman he would have to have it out with. He returned slowly to his post, turned into a public-house just round the corner, and sat swallowing whiskey in silence until another customer unwittingly touched on one of his pet political taboos. Then he sprang to his feet, and, though no one had invited his opinion, he thundered for several minutes against people with slave minds, and stalked out with a virtuous feeling that his wrath had been entirely disinterested.

This time he had to wait for over half an hour in the damp and cold, and this did not improve his temper. Then he heard her footsteps, and guessed that the young man had left her at the same spot where they had met. It could, of course, have been the most innocent thing in the world, intended merely to deceive inquisitive people in her lodging house, but to Archie it seemed all guile and treachery. He crossed the road and stood under a tree beside the gate, so well concealed that she failed altogether to see him till he stepped out to meet her. Then she started back.

'Who's that?' she asked in a startled whisper, and then, after a look, added with what sounded like joy and was probably merely relief: 'Oh, Archie, it's you!' Then, as he stood there glowering at her, her tone changed again and he could detect the consternation as she asked:

'What are you doing here, Archie?'

'Waiting,' Archie replied in a voice as hollow as his heart felt.

'Waiting? But for what, Archie?'

'An explanation.'

'Oh, Archie!' she exclaimed with childish petulance. 'Don't talk to me that way!'

'And what way would you like me to talk to you?' he retorted, letting fly with his anger. 'I suppose you're going to tell me now you were at your aunt's?'

'No, Archie,' she replied meekly. 'I wasn't. I was out with a friend.'

'A friend?' repeated Archie.

'Not a friend exactly either, Archie,' she added in distress.

'Not exactly,' Archie repeated with grim satisfaction. 'With your fiancé, in fact?'

'That's true, Archie,' she admitted. 'I don't deny that. You must let me explain.'

'The time for explanations is past,' Archie thundered magnificently, though the moment before he had been demanding one. 'The time for explanations was three months ago. For three months and more, your whole life has been a living lie.'

This was a phrase Archie had thought up, entirely without assistance, drinking whiskey in the pub. He may have failed to notice that it was not entirely original. It was intended to draw blood, and it did.

'I wish you wouldn't say things like that, Archie,' Madge said in an unsteady voice. 'I know I didn't tell you the whole truth, but I wasn't trying to deceive you.'

'No, of course you weren't trying,' said Archie. 'You don't need to try. What you ought to try some time is to tell the truth.'

'But I am telling the truth,' she said indignantly. 'I'm not a liar, Archie, and I won't have you saying it. I couldn't help getting engaged to Pat. He asked me, and I couldn't refuse him.'

'You couldn't refuse him?'

'No. I told you you should let me explain. It happened before, and I won't have it happen again.'

'What happened?'

'Oh, it's a long story, Archie. I once refused a boy at home in our own place and – he died.'

'He died?' Archie said incredulously.

'Well, he committed suicide. It was an awful thing to happen, but it wasn't my fault. I was young and silly, and I didn't know how dangerous it was. I thought it was just all a game, and I led him on and made fun of him. How could I know the way a boy would feel about things like that?'

'Hah!' Archie grunted uncertainly, feeling that as usual she had thought too quickly for him, and that all his beautiful anger accumulated over weeks would be wasted on some pointless argument. 'And I suppose you felt you couldn't refuse me either?'

'Well, as a matter of fact, Archie,' she said apologetically, 'that was the way I felt.'

'Good God!' exploded Archie.

'It's true, Archie,' she said in a rush. 'It wasn't until weeks after that I got to like you really, the way I do now. I was hoping all that time we were together that you didn't like me that way at all, and it came as a terrible blow to me, Archie. Because, as you see, I was sort of engaged already, and it's not a situation you'd like to be in yourself, being engaged to two girls at the one time.'

'And I suppose you thought *I*'d commit suicide?' Archie asked incredulously.

'But I didn't know, Archie. It wasn't until afterwards that I really got to know you.'

'You didn't know!' he said, choking with anger at the suggestion that he was a man of such weak and commonplace stuff. 'You didn't *know*! Good God, the vanity and madness of it! And all this time you couldn't tell me about the fellow you say committed suicide on account of you.'

'But how could I, Archie?' she asked despairingly. 'It's not the sort a thing a girl likes to think of, much less to talk about.'

'No,' he said, breathing deeply, 'and so you'll go through life, tricking and deceiving every honourable man that comes your way – all out of pure kindness of heart. That be damned for a yarn!'

'It's not a yarn, Archie,' she cried hotly. 'It's true, and it never happened with anyone, only Pat and you, and one young fellow at home, but the last I heard of him he was walking out with another girl, and I dare say he's over it by now. And Pat would have got over it the same if only you'd had patience.'

The picture of yet a third man engaged to his own fiancée was really too much for Archie, and he knew that he could never stand up to this little liar in argument.

'Madge,' he said broodingly, 'I do not like to insult any woman to her face, least of all a woman I once respected, but I do not believe you. I can't believe anything you say. You have behaved to me in a deceitful and dishonourable manner, and I can't trust you any longer.'

Then he turned on his heel and walked heavily away, remembering how on this very spot, a few months before, he had turned away with his heart full of hope, and he realized that everything people said about women was true down to the last bitter gibe, and that never again would he trust one of them.

'That was the end of my attempts at getting married,' he

finished grimly. 'Of course, she wrote and gave me the names of two witnesses I could refer to if I didn't believe her, but I couldn't even be bothered replying.'

'Archie,' I asked in consternation, 'you don't mean that you really dropped her?'

'Dropped her?' he repeated, beginning to scowl. 'I never spoke to the woman again, only to raise my hat to her whenever I met her on the street. I don't even know what happened to her after, whether she married or not. I have some pride.'

'But, Archie,' I said despairingly, 'suppose she was simply telling the truth?'

'And suppose she was?' he asked in a murderous tone.

Then I began to laugh. I couldn't help it, though I saw it was making him mad. It was raining outside on the canal bank, and I wasn't laughing at Archie so much as at myself. Because, for the first time, I found myself falling in love with a woman from the mere description of her, as they do in the old romances, and it was an extraordinary feeling, as though there existed somewhere some pure essence of womanhood that one could savour outside the body.

'But damn it, Archie,' I cried, 'you said yourself she was a serious girl. All you're telling me now is that she was a sweet one as well. It must have been hell for her, being engaged to two men in the same town and trying to keep both of them happy till the other fellow got tired of her and left her free to marry you.'

'Or free for a third man to come along and put her in the same position again,' said Archie with a sneer.

I must say I had not expected that one, and for a moment it stopped me dead. But there is no stopping a man who is in love with a shadow as I was then, and I was determined on finding justification for myself.

'But after all, Archie,' I said, 'isn't that precisely why you marry a woman like that? Can you imagine marrying one of them if the danger wasn't there? Come, Archie, don't you see that the whole business of the suicide is irrelevant? Every nice girl behaves exactly as though she had a real suicide in her past. That's what makes her a nice girl. It's not easy to defend it rationally, but that's the way it is. Archie, I think you made a fool of yourself.'

'It's not possible to defend it rationally or any other way,'

Archie said with finality. 'A woman like that is a woman without character. You might as well stick your head in a gas-oven and be done with it as marry a girl like that.'

And from that evening on, Archie dropped me. He even told his friends that I had no moral sense and would be bound to end up bad. Perhaps he was right, perhaps I shall end up as badly as he believed; but, on the other hand, perhaps I was only saying to him all the things he had been saying to himself for years in the bad hours coming on to morning, and he only wanted reassurance from me, not his own sentence on himself pronounced by another man's lips. But, as I say, I was very young and didn't understand. Nowadays I should sympathize and congratulate him on his narrow escape, and leave it to him to proclaim what an imbecile he was.

LONELY ROCK

I

IN ENGLAND during the war I had a great friend called Jack Courtenay who was assistant manager in one of the local factories. His job was sufficiently important to secure his exemption from military service. His family was originally from Cork, but he had come to work in England when he was about eighteen and married an English girl called Sylvia, a school-teacher. Sylvia was tall, thin, fair and vivacious, and they got on very well together. They had two small boys, of seven and nine. Jack was big-built, handsome, and solemn-looking, with a gravity which in public enabled him to escape from the usual English suspicion of Irish temperament and in private to get away with a schoolboy mania for practical joking. I have known him invite someone he liked to his office to discuss an entirely imaginary report from the police, accusing the unfortunate man of bigamy and deserting a large family. He could carry on a joke like that for a long time without a shadow of a smile, and end up by promising his victim to try and persuade the police that it was all a case of mistaken identity.

He was an athlete, with an athlete's good nature when he was well and an athlete's hysteria when he wasn't. A toothache or a cold in the head could drive him stark, staring mad. Then he retired to bed (except when he could create more inconvenience by not doing so) and conducted guerrilla warfare against the whole houeshold, particularly the children, who were diverting the attention which should have come to himself. His face, normally expressionless, could convey indescribable agonies on such occasions, and even I felt that Sylvia went too far with her air of indifference and boredom. 'Do stop that shouting!' or 'Why don't you see the dentist?' were remarks that caused me almost as much pain as they caused her husband.

Fortunately, his ailments were neither serious nor protracted, and Sylvia didn't seem to mind so much about his other weakness, which was girls. He had a really good eye for a girl and a corresponding vanity about the ravages he could create in them, so he was forever involved with some absolutely stunning blonde. At Christmas I was either dispatching or receiving presents that Sylvia wasn't supposed to know about. These flirtations (they were nothing more serious) never went too far. The man was a born philanderer. Because I was fresh from Ireland and disliked his schoolboy jokes, he regarded me as a puritan and gave me friendly lectures with a view to broadening my mind and helping me to enjoy life. Sylvia's mind he had apparently broadened already.

'Did you know that Jack's got a new girl, Phil?' she asked, while he beamed proudly on both of us. 'Such a relief after the last! Didn't he show you the last one's photo? Oh, my dear, the commonest-looking piece.'

'Now, now, who's jealous?' Jack would say severely, wagging his finger at her.

'Really, Jack,' she would reply with bland insolence, 'I'd have to have a very poor opinion of myself to be jealous of that. Didn't you say she was something in Woolworth's?'

To complete the picture of an entirely emancipated household, I was supposed to be in love with her and to indulge in all sorts of escapades behind his back. We did our best to keep up the game, but I am afraid she found me rather heavy going.

There was a third adult in the house; this was Jack's mother, whom Sylvia, with characteristic generosity, had invited to live with them. At the same time I don't think she had had any idea what she was letting herself in for. It was rather like inviting a phase of history. Mrs Courtenay was a big, bossy, cheerful woman and an excellent housekeeper, so Jack and Sylvia had at least the advantage of being able to get away together whenever they liked. The children were fond of her and she spoiled them, but at the same time her heart was not in them. They had grown up outside her scope and atmosphere. Her heart was all the time in the little house in Douglas Street in Cork, with the long garden and the apple trees, the old cronies who dropped in for a cup of tea and a game of cards, and the convent where she went to Mass and to visit the lifelong friend whom Sylvia persisted in calling Sister Mary Misery. Sister Mary Misery was always in some trouble and always inviting the prayers of her friends. Mrs Courtenay's nostalgia was almost entirely analogical, and the precise degree of pleasure she received from anything was conditioned by its resemblance to something or somebody in Cork. Her field of analogy was exceedingly wide, as when she admired a photograph of St Paul's because it reminded her of the Dominican Church in Cork.

Jack stood in great awe of his mother, and this was something Sylvia found it difficult to understand. He did not, for instance, like drinking spirits before her, and if he had to entertain while she was there, he drank sherry. When at ten o'clock sharp the old woman rose and said: 'Wisha, do you know, I think I'll go to my old doss; good night to ye,' he relaxed and started on the whiskey.

There was hardly a day, wet or fine, well or ill, but Mrs Courtenay was up for morning Mass. This was practically her whole social existence, as her only company, apart from me, was Father Whelan, the parish priest; a nice, simple poor man, but from Waterford – 'not at all the same thing,' as Sylvia observed. For a Waterford man he did his best. He lent her the papers from home; sometimes newspapers, but mostly religious papers: 'simple papers for simple people,' he explained to Sylvia, just to show that he wasn't taken in.

But if he implied that Mrs Courtenay was simple, he was wrong.

'Wisha, hasn't Father Tom a beautiful face, Phil?' she would exclaim with childish pleasure as she held out the photograph of some mountainous sky-pilot. 'You'd never again want to hear another Passion sermon after Father Tom. Poor Father Whelan does his best, but of course he hasn't the intellect.'

'How could he?' Sylvia would say gravely. 'We must remember he's from Waterford.'

Mrs Courtenay never knew when Sylvia was pulling her leg.

'Why then, indeed, Sylvia,' she said, giving a reproving look over her spectacles, 'some very nice people came from Waterford.'

Though Mrs Courtenay couldn't discuss it with Sylvia, who might have thought her prejudiced, she let me know how shocked she was by the character of the English, who seemed from the age of fifteen on to do nothing but fall in and out of love. Mrs Courtenay had heard of love; she was still very much in love with her own husband, who had been dead for years, but this was a serious matter and had nothing whatever in common with those addle-pated affairs you read of in the newspapers. Fortunately, she never knew the worst, owing to her lack of familiarity with the details. Once an old schoolmistress friend of Sylvia's with a son the one age with Jack tried to start a little chat with her about the dangers young men had to endure, but broke down under the concentrated fire of Mrs Courtenay's innocence.

'Willie's going to London worries me a lot,' she said darkly.

'Why, then, indeed, ma'am, I wouldn't blame you,' said Mrs Courtenay. 'The one time I was there, the traffic nearly took the sight out of my eyes.'

'And it's not the traffic only, is it, Mrs Courtenay?' asked the schoolmistress, a bit taken aback. 'I mean, we send them out into the world healthy, and we want them to come back to us healthy.'

'Ah, indeed,' said Mrs Courtenay triumphantly, 'wasn't it only the other day I was saying the same thing to you, Sylvia? Whatever he gets to eat in London, Jack's digestion is never the same.'

Not to wrong her, I must admit that she wasn't entirely ignorant of the subject, for she mentioned it herself to me (very confidentially while Sylvia was out of the room) in connection with a really nice sodality man from the Watercourse Road who got it through leaning against the side of a ship.

Sylvia simply did not know what to make of her mother-in-law's ingenuousness, which occasionally bordered on imbecility, but she was a sufficiently good housekeeper herself to realize that the old woman had plenty of intelligence, and she respected the will-power that kept her going, cheerful and uncomplaining, through the trials of loneliness and old age.

'We're very busy these days,' she would sigh after Mrs Courtenay had gone to bed, and she was enjoying what her husband called 'the first pussful.' 'We're doing another novena for Sister Mary Misery's sciatica. The last one misfired, but we'll wear Him down yet! Really, she talks as if God were a Corkman!'

'Well,' said Jack, 'some very nice people came from Cork.'

'But it's fantastic, Jack! It's simply fantastic!' Sylvia cried, slamming her palm on the arm-rest of her chair. 'She's upstairs now, talking to God as she talked to us. She feels she will wear Him down, exactly as she says.'

'She probably will,' said I.

'I shouldn't be in the least surprised,' Sylvia added viciously. 'She's worn me down.'

II

Naturally, Jack and Sylvia both told me of the absolutely stunning brunette he had met in Manchester, driving a Ministry car. Then, for some reason, the flow of confidences dried up. I guessed that something had gone wrong with the romance, but knew better than to ask questions. I knew that Jack would tell me in his own good time. He did too, one grey winter evening when we had walked for miles up the hills and taken refuge from the wind in a little bar-parlour where a big fire was roaring. When he brought in the pints, he told me in a slightly superior way with a smile that didn't seem quite genuine that he was having trouble about Margaret.

'Serious?' I asked.

'Well, she's had a baby,' he said with a shrug.

He expected me to be shocked, and I was, but not for his reasons. It was clear that he was badly shaken, did not know how his philandering could have gone so far or had such consequences, and was blaming the drink or something equally irrelevant.

'That's rotten luck,' I said.

'That's the worst of it,' he said. 'It's not luck.'

'Oh!' I said. I was beginning to realize vaguely the mess in which he had landed himself. 'You mean she—?'

'Yes,' he cut in. 'She wanted it. Now she wants to keep it, and her family won't let her, so she's left home.'

'Oh,' I said again. 'That is rotten.'

'It's not very pleasant,' he said, unconsciously trying to reassert himself in his old part as a man of the world by lowering the key of the conversation.

'Does Sylvia know?'

'Good Lord, no,' he exclaimed with a frown, and this time it was he who was shocked. 'There's no point in upsetting her.'

'She'll be a damn sight more upset if she hears of it from someone else,' I said.

'Yes,' he replied after a moment. 'I see your point.'

I don't know whether he did or not. He had the sort of

sensitiveness which leads men into the most preposterous situa-
tions in the desire not to give pain to people they love. It never
minimizes the pain in the long run, of course, or so it seemed to
me. I had no experience of that sort of situation and was all for
giving the pain at once and getting it over. I should even have
been prepared to break the news to Sylvia myself, just to be sure
she had someone substantial to bawl on. Nowadays I wouldn't
rush into it so eagerly.

Instead, Sylvia talked to me about it, in her official tone. It was
a couple of months later. She had managed to get rid of her
mother-in-law for half an hour, and we were drinking cocktails.

'Did you know Jack's got himself into a scrape with the
brunette, Phil?' she said lightly, crossing her legs and smoothing
her skirt. 'Has he told you?'

I could have shaken her. There was no need to do the stiff
upper lip on me, and at any rate I couldn't reply to it. I like a bit
more intimacy myself.

'He has,' I said uncomfortably. 'How are things going?'

'Baby's ill, and she's had to chuck her job. Jack is really quite
worried.'

'I don't wonder,' I said. 'What's he going to do?'

'What can he do?' she exclaimed with a shrug and a mow. 'He
should look after the girl. I've told him I'll divorce him.'

I hardly knew what to say to this. Sweet reasonableness may be
all very well, but usually it bears no relation to the human facts.

'Is that what you want to do?'

'Well, my feelings don't count for much in this.'

'That's scarcely how Jack looks at it,' I said.

'So he says,' she muttered with a shrug.

'Oh, don't be silly, Sylvia!' I said.

She looked at me for a moment as though she might throw
something at me, and I almost wished she would.

'Oh, well,' she said at last, 'if that's how he feels he should
bring her here. You can't even imagine what girls in her position
have to go through. It'll simply drive her to suicide, and then he
will have something to worry about. I do wish you'd speak to
him, Phil.'

'What's his objection?'

'Mother doesn't know we drink,' she said maliciously. 'Any-
how, as if it would ever cross her mind that he was responsible!

She probably thinks it's something you catch from leaning against a tree.'

'I'll talk to him,' I said. I had a feeling that between them they would be bound to make a mess of it.

'Tell him Granny need never know,' she said. 'He doesn't even have to pretend he knows the girl. She can be a friend of mine. And at a time like this, who's going to inquire about her husband? We can kill him off in the most horrible manner. She just loves tragedies.'

This was more difficult than it sounded. Jack didn't want to talk at all, and when he talked he was in a bad humour. I had had to take him out to the local pub, and we talked in low voices between the family parties and the dart-players. Jack's masculine complacency revolted as much at taking advice from me as at taking help from Sylvia. He listened in a peculiar way he had, frowning with one side of his face, as if with half his mind he was considering your motion while with the other he ruled it out of order.

'I'm afraid it's impossible,' he said stiffly.

'Well, what are you going to do?'

'Sylvia said she'd divorce me,' he replied in a sulky voice that showed it would be a long time before he forgave Sylvia for her high-minded offer.

'Is that what you want?'

'But, my dear fellow, it's not a matter of what I want,' he said scoffingly.

'You mean you won't accept Sylvia's kindness, is that it?'

'I won't go on my knees to anybody, for anything.'

'Do you want her to go on her knees to you?'

'Oh,' he replied ungraciously, 'if that's how she feels –'

'You wouldn't like me to get a note from her?' I asked. (I knew it was mean, but I couldn't resist it.)

III

That was how Margaret came to be invited to the Courtenays'. I promised to look in, the evening she came. It was wet, and the narrow sloping High Street with its rattling inn-signs looked the last word in misery. As I turned up the avenue to the Courtenays', the wind was rising. In the distance it had blown a great gap through the cloud, and the brilliant sky had every tint of metal from blue steel at the top to bronze below. Mrs Courtenay opened the door to me.

'They're not back from the station yet,' she said cheerfully. 'Would you have a cup of tea?'

'No,' I said. 'All I want is to get warm.'

'I suppose they'll be having it when they come in,' she said. 'The train must be late.'

Just then the taxi drove up, and Sylvia came in with Margaret, a short, slight girl with a rather long, fine-featured face; the sort of face that seems to have been slightly shrunken to give its features a certain precision and delicacy. Jack came in, carrying the baby's basket, and set it on a chair in the hall. His mother went straight to it, as though she could see nothing else.

'Isn't he lovely, God bless him?' she said, showing her gums while her whole face lit up.

'I'd better get him settled down,' Margaret said nervously with a quick, bright smile.

'Yes,' Sylvia said. 'Margaret and I will take him up. Will you pour her a drink first, Jack?'

'Certainly,' said Jack, beginning to beam. 'Nothing I like so much. Whiskey, Mrs Harding?'

'Oh, whiskey – Mr Courtenay,' she replied with her sudden, brilliant laugh.

'Won't you call me Jack,' he asked with a mock-languishing air. I think he was almost enjoying the mystification, which had something in common with his own practical jokes.

While the girls went upstairs with the baby, Mrs Courtenay sat before the fire, her hands joined in her lap. Her eyes had a faraway look.

'God help us!' she sighed. 'Isn't she young to be a widow?'

At ten Mrs Courtenay drew the shawl about her shoulders, said as usual 'I'll go to my old doss,' and went upstairs. Some time later we were interrupted by a sickly little whine. Margaret jumped up with an apologetic smile.

'That's Teddy,' she said. 'I shan't be a minute.'

'I shouldn't trouble, dear,' Sylvia said in her bland, insolent way, and we heard a door open softly. 'I rather thought Granny would come to the rescue,' she explained.

'He'll be afraid of a stranger,' Margaret said tensely, and we all listened again. We heard the old woman's voice, soft and almost continuous, and the crying ceased abruptly. Apparently Teddy didn't consider Mrs Courtenay a stranger. I noticed as if for the first time the billows of wind break over the house.

Next morning, when Teddy had been settled in the garden in his pram, Mrs Courtenay said: 'I think I'll take him for a little walk. They get very tired of the one place.' She apparently knew things about babies that weren't in any textbook, and uttered them in a tone of quiet authority which made textbooks an impertinence. She didn't appear again until lunch-time, having taken him to the park – 'they're very fond of trees.' His father's death in an air-crash in the Middle East had proved a safe introduction to the other women, and Mrs Courtenay, who usually complained of the standoffishness of the English, returned in high good humour, full of gossip – the untold numbers blinded, drowned, and burned to death, and the wrecked lives of young women who became too intimate with foreigners. The Poles, in particular, were a great disappointment to her – such a grand Catholic nation, but so unreliable.

That evening, when we heard the shriek from the bedroom, there was no question about who was to deal with it. 'Don't upset yourselves,' Mrs Courtenay said modestly, pulled the shawl firmly about her, and went upstairs. Margaret, a very modern young woman, had Teddy's day worked out to a time-table, stipulating when he should be fed, lifted, and loved, but it had taken that baby no time to discover that Mrs Courtenay read nothing but holy books and believed that babies should be fed, lifted, and loved when it suited themselves. Margaret frowned and shook herself in her frock.

'I'm sure it's bad for him, Sylvia,' she said.

'Oh, dreadful,' Sylvia sighed with her heartless air as she threw one long leg over the arm of the chair. 'But Granny is thriving on it. Haven't you noticed?'

A curious situation was developing in the house, which I watched with fascination. Sylvia, who had very little use for sentiment, was quite attracted by Margaret. 'She really is charming, Phil,' she told me in her bland way. 'Really, Jack has remarkably good taste.' Margaret, a much more dependent type, after hesitating for a week, developed quite a crush on Sylvia. It was Jack who was odd man out. Their friendship was a puzzle to him, and what they said and thought about him when they were together was more than he could imagine, but judging by the frown that frequently drew down one side of his face, he felt it couldn't be very nice.

Sylvia was older, shrewder, more practical, and Margaret's guilelessness took her breath away. Margaret's experience of love had been very limited; she had fluttered round with some highly inappropriate characters, and from them drew vast generalizations, mostly derogatory, which included all races and men. Jack had been the first real man in her life, and she had grabbed at the chance of having his child. Now she envisaged nothing but a future dedicated to the memory of a couple of weekends with him and to the upbringing of his child. Sylvia in her cool way tried to make her see things more realistically.

'Really, Phil,' she told me, 'she is the sweetest girl, but, oh, dear, she's such an impossible romantic. What she really needs is a husband to knock some of the romance out of her.'

I had a shrewd idea that she regarded me as a likely candidate for the honours of knocking the romance out of Margaret, but I felt the situation was already complicated enough. At the same time, it struck me as ironic that the world should be full of men who would be glad of a decent wife, while a girl like Margaret, whom any man could be proud of, made a fool of herself over a married man.

IV

One Saturday afternoon I went up early, just after lunch, for my walk with Jack. He wasn't ready, so I sat in the front room with Sylvia, Margaret, and Mrs Courtenay. I had the impression that there were feelings, at least on the old lady's part, and I was right. It had taken Teddy a week to discover that she had a bedroom of her own, and when he did, he took full advantage of it. She had now become his devoted slave, and when we met, I had to be careful that she didn't suspect me of treating him with insufficient respect. Two old women on the road had made a mortal enemy of her because of that. And it wasn't only strangers. Margaret too came in for criticism.

The criticism this afternoon had been provoked first by

Margaret's inhuman refusal to feed him half an hour before his feeding time, and secondly by the pointed way the two younger women went on with their talk instead of joining her in keeping him company. In Margaret this was only assumed. She was inclined to resent the total occupation of her baby by Mrs Courtenay, but this was qualified by Teddy's antics and quite suddenly she would smile and then a quick frown would follow the smile. Sylvia was quite genuinely uninterested. She had the capacity for surrounding herself in her own good manners.

The old woman could, of course, have monopolized me, but it gave her more satisfaction to throw me to the girls and make their monstrous inhumanity obvious even to themselves.

'Wisha, go on, Phil,' she said with her sweet, distraught smile. 'You'll want to be talking. He'll be getting his dinner soon anyway. The poor child is famished.'

Most of this went over my head, and I joined the girls gladly enough, while Mrs Courtenay, playing quietly with Teddy, suffered in silence. Just then the door opened quietly behind her and Jack came in. She started and looked up.

'Ah, here's Daddy now!' she said triumphantly. 'Daddy will play with us.'

'Daddy will do nothing of the sort,' retorted Jack with remarkable presence of mind. 'Daddy wants somebody to play with him. Ready, Phil?'

But even this didn't relax the tension in the room. Margaret looked dumbfounded. She looked at Jack and grinned; then frowned and looked at me. Sylvia raised her shoulders. Meanwhile her mother-in-law, apparently quite unaware of the effect she had created, was making Teddy sit up and show off his tricks. Sylvia followed us to the door.

'Does she suspect anything?' she asked anxiously with one hand on the jamb.

'Oh, not at all,' Jack said with a shocked expression that almost caused one side of his face to fold up. 'That's only her way of speaking.'

'Hm,' grunted Sylvia. 'Curious way of speaking.'

'Not really, Sylvia,' I said. 'If she suspected anything, that's the last thing in the world she'd have said.'

'Like leaning against a ship?' Sylvia said. 'I dare say you're right.'

But she wasn't sure. Jack walked down the avenue without speaking, and I knew he was shaken too.

'Awkward situation,' he said between his teeth.

Since Margaret's arrival he had become what for him was almost forthcoming. It was mainly the need for someone to confide in. He couldn't any longer confide in Margaret or Sylvia because of their friendship.

'I don't think it meant what Sylvia imagined,' I said as we set off briskly up the hill. We both liked the hilly country behind the town, the strong thrust of the landscape that made walking like a bird's flight on a stormy day.

'I dare say not, but still, it's awkward – two women in a house!'

'I suppose so.'

'You know what I mean?'

I thought I did, and I liked his delicacy. Being a chap who never cared to hurt people's feelings, he probably left both girls very much alone. Having had so much to do with them both, and being the sort who is accustomed to having a lot to do with women, he probably found this a strain. They must have found it so likewise, because their behaviour had grown decidedly obstreperous. One evening I had watched them, with their arms about one another's waists, guying him, and realized that behind it there was an element of hysteria. The situation was becoming impossible.

We had come out on the common, with the little red houses to one side, and the uplands sweeping away from them.

'Last night Sylvia woke me when the alert went, to keep Margaret company,' he went on in a tone in which pain, bewilderment, and amusement were about equally blended. It was as though he were fastidiously holding up something small, frail, and not quite clean for your inspection. 'She said she'd go if I didn't. I'd have preferred her to go, but then she got quite cross. She said: "Margaret won't like it, and you've shown her little enough consideration since she came."'

'Rather tactless of Sylvia,' I said.

'I know,' he added with a bewildered air. 'And it's so unlike her. She said I didn't understand women.'

'And did you go?'

'I had to.'

I could fill in the gaps in his narrative and appreciate his embarrassment. Obviously, before he went to Margaret's room, he had to go to his mother's to explain Sylvia's anxiety for her old school friend, and having done everything a man could do to spare the feelings of three women, had probably returned to bed with the feeling that they were all laughing at him. And though he told it lightly, I had the feeling that it was loneliness which made him tell it at all, and that he would never again be quite comfortable with either Sylvia or Margaret. 'Now your days of philandering are over,' was running through my head. I wasn't sure that he would be quite such a pleasant friend.

Margaret remained for some months until the baby was quite well and she had both got a job and found a home where Teddy would be looked after. She was full of gaiety and courage, but I had the feeling that her way was not an easy one either. Even without the aid of a husband, the romance had been knocked out of her. It was marked by the transference of her allegiance from Jack to Sylvia. And Sylvia was lonesome too. She kept pressing me to come to the house when Jack was away. She corresponded with Margaret and went to stay with her when she was in town. They were linked by something which excluded Jack. To each of them her moment of sacrifice had come, and each had risen to it, but nobody can live on that plane forever, and now there stretched before them the commonplace of life with no prospect that ever again would it call on them in the same way. Never again would Sylvia and Jack be able to joke about his philandering, and the house seemed the gloomier for it, as though it had lost a safety valve.

Mrs Courtenay too was lonely after Teddy, though with her usual stoicism she made light of it. 'Wisha, you get very used to them, Phil,' she said to me as she pulled her shawl about her. Now she felt that she had no proper introduction when she went to the park, was jealous of the mothers and grandmothers who met there, and decided that the English were as queer and standoffish as she had always supposed them to be. For weeks she slept badly and talked with resignation of 'being in the way' and 'going to her long home'. She never asked about Teddy, always about his mother, and when Margaret, who seemed suddenly to have got over her dislike of the old woman, sent her a photo of the child, she put it away in a drawer and did not refer to it again.

One evening, while Sylvia was in the kitchen, she startled me by a sudden question.

'You never hear about Mrs Harding?' she asked.

'I believe she's all right,' I said. 'Sylvia could tell you. She hears from her regularly.'

'They don't tell me,' she said resignedly, folding her arms and looking broodingly into the fire – it was one of her fictions that no one ever told her anything. 'Wisha, Phil,' she added with a smile, 'you don't think she noticed me calling Jack his daddy?'

She turned a searching look on me. It was one of those occasions when whatever you say is bound to be wrong.

'Who's that, Mrs Courtenay?'

'Sylvia. She didn't notice?'

'I wouldn't say so. Why?'

'It worries me,' she replied, looking into the fire again. 'It could make mischief.'

'I doubt it,' I said. 'I don't think Sylvia noticed anything.'

'I hope not. I made a novena that she wouldn't. She's a nice, simple poor girl.'

'She's one in a thousand,' I said.

'Why then, indeed, Phil, there aren't many like her,' she agreed humbly. 'I could have bitten my tongue out when I said it. But, of course, I knew from the first minute I saw him in the hall. Didn't you?'

'Know what?' I stammered, wondering if I looked as red as I felt.

'That Jack was his daddy,' she said in a low voice. 'Sure you must.'

'Oh, yes,' I said. 'He mentioned it.'

'He didn't say anything to me,' she said, but without reproach. You could see she knew that Jack would have good reason for not telling her. 'I suppose he thought I'd tell Sylvia, but of course I wouldn't dream of making mischief. And the two of them such great friends too – wisha, isn't life queer, Phil?'

In the kitchen Sylvia suddenly began to sing 'Lili Marlene'. It was then the real poignancy of the situation struck me. I had seen it only as the tragedy of Jack and Sylvia and Margaret, but what was their loneliness to that of the old woman, to whom tragedy presented itself as in a foreign tongue? Now I realized why she did not care to look at the photograph of Margaret's son.

'It might be God's will her poor husband was killed,' Mrs Courtenay said. 'God help us, I can never get the poor boy out of my head. I pray for him night and morning. 'Twould be such a shock to him if he ever found out. And the baby so lovely and all – oh, the dead image of Jack at his age!'

Sylvia accompanied me to the door as usual. Now when we kissed good-night it wasn't such an act on her part; not because she cared any more for me but because she was already seeking for support in the world outside. The bubble in which she lived was broken. I was tempted to tell her about her mother-in-law, but something held me back. Women like their own mystifications, which give them a feeling of power; they dislike other people's, which they always describe as slyness. Besides, it would have seemed like a betrayal. I had shifted my allegiance.

5 IRELAND

PREFACE

IN 1958 O'CONNOR was interviewed by the *Paris Review* in his Brooklyn apartment, which had a view across the river to lower Manhattan and the New York Harbor. On the writer's table, the interviewer noted 'a typewriter, a small litter of papers, and a pair of binoculars'. O'Connor explained that the binoculars were for watching liners 'on the way to Ireland'. He added that he returned there once a year, and that if he didn't, he would die.

O'Connor was profoundly attached to the land of his birth: to its traditions and history, its landscape, archaeology and culture, its lunacies, its smells and sounds, and above all, to its people. He loathed sentimental Irishry, and as his second wife Harriet Sheehy recalled, 'He nearly threw up when an American hotel operator said, "Top of the morning to you, Mr O'Connor".' But he was fascinated by, and cared deeply about, the rural and small-town folk he turned into characters in such stories as 'The Majesty of the Law', 'Uprooted', or 'In the Train'. Many of his stories were first published in the *New Yorker*, then perhaps the world's most sophisticated magazine; but he was writing them 'for the man and woman down the country who reads them and says, "Yes. That is how it is. That is life as I know it." '

O'Connor had many harsh things to say about Ireland, about the moral stagnation and intellectual repression of both Church and State. He wrote a weekly newspaper column in which he frequently attacked the government for neglecting the high crosses and the ruins of romanesque churches, for allowing Georgian houses to be knocked down, and for its censorship policy. He suffered from this himself: much of his work was banned for its 'general indecent tendency'. In theory, Ireland was the perfect place for a writer to work; and yet – even leaving aside the matter of censorship – the country's bureaucracy made it near-impossible. 'A writer must fight and think and waste his time in useless efforts to create an atmosphere in which he can exist and work.'

But such professional exasperation only emphasized the attachment O'Connor felt to all that was non-official Ireland. He wrote three topographical books about the country – though category is a fairly fluid concept with O'Connor; there are times, reading his *Leinster, Munster and Connaught*, when you feel you might have wandered into the beginning of a short story (and sometimes, of course, you have). He tried to make sense of Ireland's fractured history, and the literature it produced, in *The Backward Look*; and he sought to preserve and convey the literary past in his translations of Irish poetry, of which he published five volumes. The collection *Kings, Lords & Commons*, includes two of the great long Irish poems, 'The Midnight Court' and 'The Lament for Art O'Leary'; also verse high and low from 600 AD to the nineteenth century. The notes at the head of the poems that follow are the translator's own. 'Kilcash' was read by Brendan Kennelly at O'Connor's burial on 12th March 1966 at Dean's Grange cemetery, Co. Dublin.

A LEARNED MISTRESS

It is part of the legend of Irish history that the Renaissance missed Ireland completely, but Ireland was a part, however minute, of Europe, and in their dank and smoky castles, the Irish and Anglo-Irish aristocracy lived a life that fundamentally differed little from the life that went on in the castles of the Loire. Isobel Campbell, the great Countess of Argyle, wrote a poem to her chaplain's — but really, I can't say what — and the joke was taken up by her Campbell kinsmen, who still wrote classical Irish. She might have written this little poem, and who will dare to say that it does not breathe the whole spirit of the Renaissance?

Tell him it's all a lie;
   I love him as much as my life;
He needn't be jealous of me —
   I love him and loathe his wife.

If he kill me through jealousy now
   His wife will perish of spite,
He'll die of grief for his wife —
   Three of us dead in a night.

All blessings from heaven to earth
   On the head of the woman I hate,
And the man I love as my life,
   Sudden death be his fate.

ADVICE TO LOVERS

The way to get on with a girl
    Is to drift like a man in a mist,
Happy enough to be caught,
    Happy to be dismissed.

Glad to be out of her way,
    Glad to rejoin her in bed,
Equally grieved or gay
    To learn that she's living or dead.

I AM STRETCHED ON YOUR GRAVE

I am stretched on your grave
   And would lie there forever;
If your hands were in mine
   I'd be sure we'd not sever.
My apple tree, my brightness,
   'Tis time we were together
For I smell of the earth
   And am stained by the weather.

When my family thinks
   That I'm safe in my bed
From night until morning
   I am stretched at your head,
Calling out to the air
   With tears hot and wild
My grief for the girl
   That I loved as a child.

Do you remember
   The night we were lost
In the shade of the blackthorn
   And the chill of the frost?
Thanks be to Jesus
   We did what was right,
And your maidenhead still
   Is your pillar of light.

The priests and the friars
   Approach me in dread
Because I still love you
   My love and you dead,
And would still be your shelter
   From rain and from storm,
And with you in the cold grave
   I cannot sleep warm.

A WORD OF WARNING

To go to Rome
   Is little profit, endless pain;
The Master that you seek in Rome,
   You find at home, or seek in vain.

A GREY EYE WEEPING

*With the breaking of the Treaty of Limerick by the English in 1691
the Irish Catholics descended into a slavery worse than anything
experienced by Negroes in the Southern States. (When the Irish came
to America, the Negroes called them 'White Niggers'.) This period
is best represented in the few authentic poems of Egan O'Rahilly,
a Kerry poet who lived between 1670 and 1726. In this fine poem he
approaches, not one of the masters he would have approached fifty
years before – the MacCarthys – but Lord Kenmare, one of the new
Anglo-Irish gentry. Hence the bitter repetition of the fellow's name.
O'Rahilly himself would have considered 'Valentine' a ridiculous
name for anyone calling himself a gentleman, and as for 'Brown',
he would as soon have addressed a 'Jones' or a 'Robinson'.
O'Rahilly is a snob, but one of the great snobs of literature.*

That my old bitter heart was pierced in this black doom,
That foreign devils have made our land a tomb,
That the sun that was Munster's glory has gone down
Has made me a beggar before you, Valentine Brown.

That royal Cashel is bare of house and guest,
That Brian's turreted home is the otter's nest,
That the kings of the land have neither land nor crown
Has made me a beggar before you, Valentine Brown.

Garnish away in the west with its master banned,
Hamburg the refuge of him who has lost his land,
An old grey eye, weeping for lost renown,
Have made me a beggar before you, Valentine Brown.

EGAN O'RAHILLY

YEATS . . . published two books of my translations from the Irish and rewrote them in the process. Gogarty once invited me to come to Yeats's flat with him – 'He's writing a few little lyrics for me, and I'd like to see how he's getting on.' It was rather like that. I went one night to Yeats' for dinner and we fought for God knows how long over a single line of an O'Rahilly translation I had done – 'Has made me travel to seek you, Valentine Brown.' At first I was fascinated by the way he kept trying it out, changing pitch and intonation. 'Has made me – no! Has made me travel to seek you – No, that's wrong, HAS MADE ME TRAVEL TO SEEK YOU, VALENTINE BROWN – no!'

Long before that evening I had tired of the line, and hearing it repeated endlessly in Yeats' monotone I felt it sounded worse.

'It's tautological,' I complained. 'It should be something like "Has made me a beggar before you, Valentine Brown," ' and he glared at me as if he had never seen me before.

'No beggars! No beggars!' he roared, and I realized that, like other theatre men I have known, he thought the writer's place was at home.

All the same, it was as interesting to work over poetry with him as it was later to work over plays. He was an absolute master of both, and his principal virtue was his principal defect. He had absolutely no ear for music that I could discern, though this, of course, never shook his faith in his own musical genius. He told a story of how he had gone to Dr Sigerson's one day when Sigerson had an old countrywoman in a hypnotic trance and made her feel Yeats' face. 'Poet,' she had said, then 'great poet,' then 'musician'. 'And then I knew she was a genuine medium,' Yeats declared.

KILCASH

Kilcash was the home of one branch of the Butler family. Although I don't think Yeats, who had Butler blood in him, knew this, it was one of his favourite poems, and there is a good deal of his work in it.

What shall we do for timber?
    The last of the woods is down.
Kilcash and the house of its glory
    And the bell of the house are gone,
The spot where that lady waited
    Who shamed all women for grace
When earls came sailing to greet her
    And Mass was said in the place.

My grief and my affliction
    Your gates are taken away,
Your avenue needs attention,
    Goats in the garden stray.
The courtyard's filled with water
    And the great earls where are they?
The earls, the lady, the people
    Beaten into the clay.

No sound of duck or geese there,
    Hawk's cry or eagle's call,
No humming of the bees there
    That brought honey and wax for all,
Nor even the song of the birds there
    When the sun goes down in the west,
No cuckoo on top of the boughs there,
    Singing the world to rest.

There's mist there tumbling from branches,
    Unstirred by night and by day,
And darkness falling from heaven,
    For our fortune has ebbed away,
There's no holly nor hazel nor ash there,
    The pasture's rock and stone,
The crown of the forest has withered,
    And the last of its game is gone.

I beseech of Mary and Jesus
    That the great come home again
With long dances danced in the garden,
    Fiddle music and mirth among men,
That Kilcash the home of our fathers
    Be lifted on high again,
And from that to the deluge of waters
    In bounty and peace remain.

HOPE

*If seven hundred years of history can be summed up in four lines,
they are all here.*

Life has conquered, the wind has blown away
Alexander, Caesar and all their power and sway;
Tara and Troy have made no longer stay –
Maybe the English too will have their day.

WE WERE sitting in the hotel having coffee when the door opened and two men shuffled in. At first I took them to be a farmer and a drover, but then I realized that they were really father and son. It was market day in town and they were the only country people who came in, so I marked them down as individualists. The old man came in without raising his eyes or his knees, as if he were pushing some weight before him with his belly, like an engine. They sat down at a glass-topped table, the old man taking off his hat and laying it on a chair beside him. He had a glib of white hair which reached to the bridge of his nose, and a Punchinello chin. His son had the same sort of glib, but it was brown. He too took off his cap and put it on the remaining chair, but he was less a man of the world than his father, and as if he thought it might be considered presumptuous, or perhaps unsafe, or even that he might be charged extra for occupying the chair, he took it back and stowed it away on the ground beneath him.

I watched the pair of them in fascination. There they sat, slumped in their chairs with their arms hanging by their sides, staring intently at the glass top of the table, like two mountains overlooking a lake. One or other of them must have ordered something, though it seemed to me that they didn't, and that the order was understood. The waitress first brought a loaf and the younger man steadily cut slice after slice until it was all cut up. She brought a bowl of soup for the older man who slowly broke several slices of bread into it. She brought a cup of tea for the other, and he buttered one slice of bread, only to find himself with a bit of butter left on his knife which he didn't know what to do with. He looked at it steadily for a while, and then, having a brain-wave, he buttered himself a second slice. After that he took good care not to experiment any further with the butter but saucered his tea. They never spoke during the whole meal, but when they had finished, and there wasn't crust or crumb of the loaf remaining, the old man took a dirty cloth purse from his trousers pocket and handed the young man a coin. The young man looked at it in astonishment. 'Is it a bob a head?' he muttered. 'Don't know what it is,' replied the other.

Those now, so far as I could gather, were the only words uttered by either of them, so I feel that they are important enough to be placed on record. The young man retrieved his cap, put it on and went into the kitchen. He returned a few minutes later with what appeared to be a sixpenny bit and a few coppers and stood by his own chair turning them over and over as he looked at them. Maybe he was trying to do the sum, or maybe he was wondering whether he oughtn't to ask his father for the change. I do not know what wild schemes may have been passing through his mind at that moment. He may even have been thinking of buying a packet of cigarettes – he was only about thirty-five and capable of any flightiness. His father ignored him, and went on looking at the table, still masticating in the manner of the late Mr Gladstone. He wasn't in the least uneasy. Probably he had had other sons. He knew all young men were wild like that at least once in their lives. They all settled down in time.

At last the young man gave it up; cast a longing look at the money and returned it. Without looking up the old man took it, put his hand in his trousers pocket, took out the big cloth purse and quietly put back the change. They went out exactly as they had come in, the old man still masticating, and I followed them with my eyes till they disappeared up the street. I felt exactly as if someone had punctured me and left me slowly dissolving through the legs of my trousers.

CORK AND MENTAL AGE OF CITIES

WATERFORD IS one thing, Cork another. I once travelled in the train from Kilkenny with an amiable lunatic. 'Could you tell me the name of that castle?' I asked, and he put on a grave face, scratched his head and replied slowly: 'That comes under the heading of fortification.' 'But the bridge!' I urged. 'What do you call the bridge beside it?' A look of real anguish came over the lunatic's face as he scratched his head again. 'That,' he replied, 'comes under the heading of navigation.'

Something of the same pain affects me when I turn to try and write of my native city. 'That comes under the heading of auto-biography.' Just in flashes and for a day or two only I can see it under the heading of topography: a charming old town with the spire of Shandon, two sides of it limestone and two sandstone, rising above the river, as beautiful as any of the Wren spires in the city of London, and the bow fronts which undulate along Patrick Street and the Grand Parade, with their front doors high up as in round towers, and flights of steps so high that they go up parallel to the pavement, because the river flows beneath, and areas had to be built upon street-level. I can admire as if I were a stranger the up and down of it on the hills as though it had been built in a Cork accent. But it doesn't last. Objectively I am observing, subjectively I am observed, and in a way I know all too well.

That isn't, I think, because I am naturally melancholy or introspective, or because my memories of childhood are mainly unhappy ones. For a great part of my childhood I was very happy, but I cannot help thinking that towns need to be classified according to their maximum mental age, which should appear in every directory beside their population. It would be difficult for the average person over eighteen to be happy in Cork. Of course, there are worse towns, towns where the mental age is nearer twelve, and Dublin's own mental age is not so high –

twenty-three or -four at best. In the history of the world only a
few towns have existed where a man could grow old in the fullest
development of his mental faculties, and one of these murdered
Socrates.

CORK

Apart from the usual miseries of adolescence and (with me) of
poverty, our youth was happy enough. We knew that Cork was
the most musical city in the United Kingdom – the visiting tenors
told us that. It was also the most appreciative of great literature –
visiting Shakespearean actors confirmed it. At some street corner
Thackeray had heard two newsboys discuss I forget what classical
text. We listened, but we must have got hold of the wrong news-
boys, or perhaps it was the wrong text. We admired the university
buildings, which he had said were worthy of Oxford High Street.
Before we knew what the High was like that sounded like a
compliment. We liked the Italianate names which some old fogy
had foisted on the suburbs at either side of the river – Monte-
notte, Tivoli and the Marina – and walking along the river banks
we remembered Rudin, and the German girls murmuring *Guten
Abend* in the dusk, and I quoted Mignon's Song:

> You know the land that is the citron's home,
> Where golden fruit shines in the leafy gloom;
> From the blue sky a breath of rapture blows;
> High grows the laurel, still the myrtle grows:
>> You know it well, it haunts me so,
>> There, there, with you, my sweetheart, let me go.

The town was full of marvellous characters – Chekhov charac-
ters, Dostoevsky characters; as in the usual English conception
of the Irish, you had only to record what they said and produce
a masterpiece.

We recorded what they said all right, but it never mounted up
to what you could call a masterpiece. We developed the defensive
attitude of the provincial to the outsider, and yet were miserable
if we hadn't an outsider to practise it on. O'Faolain ran a paper;
I ran a dramatic society which produced *The Cherry Orchard*. We
had to drop the line 'At your age you should have a mistress', but

we were one better than the company playing *Juno and the Pay-cock*, in which the heroine had to have tuberculosis instead of a baby. Denouncing my misguided efforts to make a theatre, a priest wrote in the local paper that 'Mike the Moke' (meaning me) 'will go down to posterity at the head of the Pagan Dublin Muses'. Though not on so high a literary plane, he was of one mind with another local priest who in his sermons deplored 'the madness and melancholy of the moderns meandering in the marshes of mediocrity without God!' Oh, we had characters all right, but they did not respond to the sort of romantic treatment we tried to give them.

SLIGO

Something of Sligo's uniqueness comes of the fact that it is largely Protestant and has the explosive feeling of a border county, where, if people are not occupied in murdering one another, they may well settle down to write poetry and produce plays. It has nothing of the snug, smug majority orthodoxy of Protestant towns like Portadown or Catholic towns like Clona-kilty. Dundalk, on the other side of the country, though less spectacular, has something of the same explosiveness. 'I per-ceive,' as one of the Three Musketeers says, 'that if we do not kill one another we shall become very good friends.'

I saw this incipient explosiveness at work for the first time when I went to Sligo as a young fellow on my first job. I lodged in the house of a Corkwoman, who, within a few days, told me in confidence that Sligo people were *awful*. I am always fascinated by the views of people on inhabitants of another locality; they are so like the views of English people on French or of Mr Hilaire Belloc on the Anglo-Saxons. 'Thank God to be back to civiliza-tion!' as the woman in Dover said to me after she had left the Channel packet. 'Thank God to be back to non-robbery!' as her husband added. When I asked the Corkwoman how awful the Sligo people were, she said they had no nature. She had been in one house where a pot of boiling water had toppled over on the daughter of the house, and, after one glance at her, her mother had said calmly: 'No loss on her.' My landlady's husband was an ex-soldier. Occasionally of an evening after the mechanical chimes in the Catholic cathedral had played 'The Men of the West' with a missing note which always sent shudders down my spine, a window at the opposite side of the street would open and a neighbour's gramophone would play 'God Save the King'. Almost at the first insulting bars my landlord, ordinarily the placidest of men, would burst into my bedroom with a portable gramophone, throw open my window, thrust out the gramophone and put on a record of 'A Soldier's Song'. It was merely a matter of gramophones instead of machine-guns.

When I went back there many years later as adjudicator in a local festival, I found not one festival, but two. The country companies performed before me, and then, with make-up still on, dashed off to the other side of the town to perform before the rival adjudicator, and at the end of the week the differing marks were compared and criticized with such passion that the adjudicators themselves might have become involved, only that by that time they had pocketed their cheques and returned to their wives and families.

I advise anyone who is looking for a really funny film-script to turn his attention to an Irish festival. It is one of those occasions when anything in the world may happen. Once I remember in Dunmanway judging a schoolchildren's play about the Babes in the Wood, in which the Babes, instead of being covered up with leaves by the birds, as I was always told, were covered by the Blessed Virgin, who appeared, followed by a small boy with an electric torch, which he focused more or less on the back of her neck to represent a halo. A friend in Wexford judged a performance of 'Everyman', in which the seven deadly sins were represented in tableaux; Lust was portrayed as a lot of small boys sitting at café tables, with small girls on their knees, all singing: 'Daisy, Daisy, give me your answer, do'.

I saw nothing so good in Sligo, though some companies ran it close. In one production the scenery was a poster pinned up in the middle of the stage. For the prison scenes the poster had bars painted on it. That was all, and, so perverse and extraordinary an art is the theatre, it was entirely and absolutely satisfying and left me feeling that I never wanted to see a painted flat again.

From THE BACKWARD LOOK

IN 1801 THE Act of Union put an end to the independent parliament of Ireland and made the country part of the United Kingdom. Up to 1801, in spite of the country's having been ravaged by two middle- and lower-class invasions from England, the people were still largely feudal in attitude. What happened to them happened mainly from above. The Irish parliamentary tree under which they sat was not a satisfactory one and conducted more lightning than it produced fruits, but, for good or ill, things dropped unexpectedly from it. It might be a minor concession to Catholics or a new reign of terror, but they could observe it and speculate on it. At any time it might drop something really worth while, such as Catholic Emancipation or some qualified recognition of the Irish language.

Now the tree had been cut down, and what dropped under the greater tree in London, hundreds of miles away, they could not observe; nor could they anticipate much of it. In other words, the people were left to their own devices, and their devices were unbelievably inadequate. Since the vast majority of them could not really possess either homes or land, they had lost all their traditional skills. Outside of Ulster they had lost even the two skills without which civilization cannot exist – carpentry and cookery. When they went abroad they could neither build nor cook, so they made bad settlers. They were merely a few million unskilled rustics, speaking a half-dead language they could neither read nor write, thrown in with well-educated populations who were highly skilled in industrial techniques. Neither abroad nor at home could they compete; their only hope was to survive, and even this they were in no position to do well. The culminating point of the period is the Famine. 'Famine' is a useful word when you do not wish to use words like 'genocide' or 'extermination'. [...]

There were three distinct waves of Irish emigration to the United States. The first, up to 1801, was satisfactory enough from the American point of view; and this was not, as historians would have us believe, because the emigrants were all clean-living, hard-working Scottish Presbyterians, temporarily domiciled in Ulster. The second wave, up to 1845, was quite different. The best observer of pre-Famine Ireland, the evangelist Asenath Nicholson, asked what she was doing in Ireland, replied: 'To learn the true condition of the poor Irish at home, and ascertain why so many moneyless, half-clad, illiterate emigrants are daily landed on our shores.' The third wave of emigrants, after the Famine, was practically hopeless – illiterate, drunken, and despairing. [. . .]

Nicholson's *Ireland's Welcome to the Stranger* is almost entirely unknown, though in its own right it is one of the really remarkable travel books, like Huc's *Travels in Tartary and Thibet*. Like Huc's book, which describes the experiences of two Catholic missionaries on their way to Lhasa, it has also a certain comic charm, because it is the story of an American Protestant missionary who trudged through Ireland distributing tracts, slept in country cabins, and lived, like the natives, on a few potatoes. What makes the situation funnier is that this stout Protestant seems to have fallen madly in love with the Capuchin priest and temperance advocate Father Matthew. We may even suspect that he fell a little in love with her, because she admits rather coyly that he gave her a gold brooch. Her book is a love song; a Protestant love song to a Catholic people, and it is significant that the preface to the only edition is dated from Dublin on 10 June, 1847. Mrs Nicholson had come back to run a soup kitchen and rescue what poor human fragments she could from the ruin that she had foreseen.

What gives the book its historical importance is that she was a genuine missionary. Unlike the great George Petrie, who was tramping the country at the same time, recording music, poetry and old buildings, she was not in the least interested in culture, and what she reveals of it she reveals unconsciously and without prejudice. The Nicholson family had had nine servant girls all from the one village of Johnstown, County Kilkenny, and she went there to see their relatives and reassure them. There was nothing these poor people could do for her but invite her to join their Sunday dance. This, as a good missionary, she had to refuse, so she went to church instead. But on her return, she tells us, 'a crowd of all ages walked in, decently attired for the day, and without the usual welcomes or any apology, the hero who first introduced me seated himself by my side, took out his flute, wet his fingers, saying, "This is for you, Mrs N. and what will you have?" '

Then she goes on:

> The cabin was too small to contain the three score and ten who had assembled, and with one simultaneous movement, without speaking, all rushed out, bearing me along, and placed me upon a cart before the door, the player at my right hand. And then a dance began, which, to say nothing of the day, was to me of no ordinary kind. Not a laugh – not a loud word was heard; no affected airs, which the young are prone to assume; but as soberly as though they were in a funeral procession, they danced for an hour, wholly for my amusement, and for my welcome. Then each approached, gave me the hand, bade me God speed, leaped over the stile, and in stillness walked away. It was a true and hearty Irish welcome in which the aged as well as the young partici-pated. A matron of sixty, of the Protestant faith, was holding by the hand a grandchild of seven years, and standing by the cart where I stood; and she asked when they had retired, if I did not enjoy it? 'What are these wonderful people?' was my reply. I had never seen the like.

This is something you do not get at all from English descrip-tions of Irish life at the time and even have to deduce from the work of a native cultural enthusiast like Petrie. The moment the paragraph begins we are right into the score of *Don Giovanni*: this is a dance of the peasants to welcome the lady of the castle; and we realize that debased, hungry and ragged as they were, the Irish were still a race of artists, 'But thrown upon this filthy modern tide and by its formless spawning fury wrecked.'

What keeps Mrs Nicholson's book from depressing us with its suffering and polemic is that, quite unintentionally, it is filled with music and dancing.

> I sat down to enjoy [the morning] upon a moss-hillock, and commenced singing, for the Kerry mountains are the best conductors of sound of any I have ever met . . . I had sung

but a passage, when, from over a widestretched valley, a mountain boy, with a herd of cattle, struck up a lively piper's song, so clear and shrill that I gladly exchanged my psalmody for morning notes like these. . . . I listened till a pause ensued, and again commenced; instantly he responded, and though the distance was a mile at least, yet alternately we kept up the song till his was lost in the distance.

It was not that the people were too simple to realize the Dachau-like nightmare of their circumstances, or that Mrs Nicholson, the Puritan Yankee, did not understand the reasons for them, but as she says herself, 'So fond are the Irish of music, that in some form or other, they must and will have it.' After the description of her curmudgeonly reception by the O'Connells of Derrynane, she gives us a characteristic picture of the country folk gathering seaweed on the strand below. 'And all you have for your labour is the potato?' she says bitterly to one middle-aged woman.

'That's all, ma'am, that's all; and it's many of us that can't get the sup of milk with 'em, no, nor the salt; but we can't help it, we must be content with what the good God sends us.'
    She hitched her basket over her shoulder, and in company with one older than herself, skipped upon the sand made wet with rain, and turning suddenly about, gave me a pretty specimen of Kerry dancing, as practised by the peasantry. 'The sand is too wet, ma'am, to dance right well on,' and again, shouldering her basket, with a 'God speed ye on ye'r journey,' leaped away.

Here, as in so many other passages, the evangelist and reformer almost drops away in sheer delight.

    I looked after them among the rocks, more with admiration for the moment, than with pity; for what hearts, amid splendour and ease, lighter than these? And what heads and stomachs, faring sumptuously every day, freer from aches than theirs, with the potato and the sup of milk? This woman, who danced before me, was more than fifty, and I do not believe that the daughter of Herodias herself, was more graceful in her movements, more beautiful in complexion or symmetry, than was this 'dark-haired' matron of the mountains of Kerry.

I have, perhaps, stressed such passages unduly, but I feel that if we are to understand the real awfulness of post-Famine Ireland, we need a clearer idea of what the people were like before it. When George Petrie in a passage that should be famous tries to tell us what the effect of the Famine really was, he does not speak of the shrunken population, the hundreds of gutted villages, the Famine pits or the emigration boats. In the Introduction to his collection of Irish music he says:

> The green pastoral plains, the fruitful valleys, as well as the wild hillsides and the dreary bogs had equally ceased to be animate with human life. 'The land of song' was no longer tuneful; or, if a human sound met the traveller's ear, it was only that of the feeble and despairing wail for the dead. This awful, unwonted silence, which, during the famine and subsequent years, almost everywhere prevailed, struck more fearfully upon their imaginations, as many Irish gentlemen informed me, and gave them a deeper feeling of the desolation with which the country had been visited, than any other circumstance which had forced itself upon their attention . . .

[. . .] Protestant schools were of little interest or use to Catholics, because, as Asenath Nicholson was told when she inspected Lady Wicklow's school: 'They are educated according to their rank; they belong to the lower order, and reading, writing, arithmetic and a little knowledge of the maps is all the education they will ever need.'

It was the same all over Ireland, and by the time she reached Kerry Mrs Nicholson was getting very impatient with it.

> 'But have they not talents to be cultivated and is this not a professedly Christian school, instituted by missionaries?' 'It is,' she answered; 'but I must do as I am bidden. They are poor, and must be educated according to their station.' Again I enforced the obligation imposed on us by Christ to 'occupy till he come'. She did not understand me; and

though she belonged to the Protestant Church, I could not see that her dark understanding had ever been enlightened by the Spirit of God, or that she was any more capable of teaching spiritual things than the Catholics about her whom she viewed as being so dark.

Because they did not wish to be educated according to what Protestants thought their station in life, the people had to turn for education to the hedge-schools – those nurseries of the secret societies – and the very few Church schools, in both of which Latin was taught. [...]

Having reviewed Miss Woodham-Smith's *The Great Hunger* I realize that it is a subject one cannot discuss without bringing down an old house on one's head. The word 'famine' itself is question-begging for it means 'an extreme and general scarcity of food', and to use it of a country with a vast surplus of food – cows, sheep, pigs, poultry, eggs and corn – is simply to debase language. Irish historians, who are firmly convinced that the Famine was all a mistake in the office, explain it in terms of an economic theory called *laissez-faire*. This is another cock that won't fight, for the *Shorter Oxford Dictionary* defines it as 'a phrase expressive of the principle of the non-interference of government with the action of individuals, especially in trade and in industrial affairs'. Anyone who can believe that the British maintained a garrison of 100,000 men in Ireland for the purpose of *not* interfering in trade and industrial affairs attaches some meaning to the word 'history' that escapes me. The *Oxford History of England* sums up the Famine adequately in a single sentence: 'It was the misfortune of Ireland that the fate of Governments was decided at Westminster.'

But behind Irish history for the last fifty years of the nineteenth century looms the shadow of the Famine – not the Famine as historians see it but as ordinary people saw it. In a passage from the autobiography of Father Peter O'Leary he describes a single small family he and his parents were friendly with – Paddy Buckley, his wife, Kate, and their two young children, Sheela and Little Diarmuid.

Then came the Famine, and Sheela, her father, mother and Little Diarmuid had to go down to Macroom and enter the Workhouse. As soon as they were inside they were separated. The father was put among the men, the mother among the women. Sheela was put with the little girls and Little Diarmuid with the infants. The whole workhouse and all the poor people in it were swamped with every sort of serious illness: the people almost as fast as they came in, falling with hunger – God between us and all harm! – dying as soon as the disease struck them. There was no room for half of them. Those who could not get in merely lay out on the river bank below the bridge. You saw them there every morning after the night out, stretched in rows, some moving and some very still, with no stir from them. Later people came and lifted those who no longer moved, and heaved them into carts and carried them up to a place near Carrigastyra, where a big, wide, deep pit was open for them, and thrust them all together into the pit. The same was done with those who were dead in the Workhouse after the night.

The father and mother questioned as much as they could about Sheela and Little Diarmuid ... When they found that the two children were already dead, they became so miserable and lonely that they would not stay in the place. They were separated, but they managed to communicate with one another. They agreed on escaping. Patrick slipped out of the house first. He stood waiting at the top of Bothar na Sop for Kate. After a time he saw her coming, but she walked very slowly. She had the disease. They continued up towards Carrigastyra and came to the place where the big pit was. They knew their two children were below in the pit with the hundreds of other bodies. They stayed by the pit and wept for a long time. Above in Derrylea, west of Cahireen, was the little hut where they had lived before they went into the poorhouse. They left the big pit and went north-westwards to Derrylea where the hut was. It was six miles away and night was coming but they kept on. They were hungry and Kate was ill. They had to walk very slowly. When they had gone a couple of miles Kate had to stop. She could go no further. They met neighbours. They were given a drink and a little food, but no one would let them in because they had come direct from the poorhouse, and the wife was ill. Paddy took his wife up on his back and continued towards the hut. . . .

Next day a neighbour came to the hut. He saw the two of them dead and his wife's feet clasped in Paddy's bosom as though he were trying to warm them. It would seem that he felt the death agony come on Kate and her legs grow cold, so he put them inside his own shirt to take the chill from them.

From that passage more than from anything in the history books we can learn what Petrie meant in the passage I have quoted. For the first time in its recorded history a people who loved music had ceased to sing. It is scarcely to be wondered at.

IF . . . YOU ask me, 'Is it a good country to live in?' I can only reply, 'How could it be?' and then, after a moment's reflection, 'Anyway, what matter?' It is a mess, and one which will take more than my lifetime to clear up, but it can be cleared up and is a job worth the doing.

At any rate I am not tempted to live anywhere else. Dublin, where I spend my days, is a beautiful city with the mountains behind it and the sea in front, and what more can a man ask? It has no industries to speak of, except beer and biscuits. It has the worst slums in Europe, which is what happens when you build a great aristocratic capital of four-storey Georgian mansions without the industry to support it. (Families of six and seven people live in one room, with spindly-legged children dragging water up the great ruined staircases from the yard.)

Dublin is a pleasant town in the sense that whether you have money or not, or whether you are famous or not, you can know everybody worth knowing, and everybody worth knowing will know you. If an attaché in one of the embassies wants me to meet some visitor and I am not at home, he can ring up my favourite teashop, and if the waitresses don't know where I am, the old man who sells papers at the corner of Grafton Street certainly will.

And except for the waitresses and busmen, they all call me by my Christian name! That is one of the few rigid conventions of a highly unconventional society. Dublin has never forgiven Yeats for not having allowed it to call him 'Willie'. I have long given up struggling against it, and even defend hotly a member of the new government who insists on his senior officials calling him 'Seán'. This is a convention that interpenetrates the whole of Irish life. Once in England a priest friend told me of another priest, an old man, who came to him in tears because their English bishop didn't like him and was about to get rid of him. 'But why do you say that, Dan?' 'Oh,' groaned the old man, 'he wrote me a terrible letter! A terrible letter!' 'But what did he say?'

'Oh, it isn't what he said so much as the way he said it – he began *Dear Murphy*.'

I knew exactly what the old priest felt, because in Ireland it is always the personal element that counts, the fact that there are people whom you call by their Christian names who will be prepared to help you in any difficulty. To live comfortably in Dublin you need to know a doctor who knows a specialist or two; a solicitor who knows a counsel; a Catholic priest; a man in each goverment department and a few men in the principal businesses, and you need to know them all by their Christian names.

As the American scholar Conrad Arensberg points out in the best book ever written on Ireland, *The Irish Countryman*, the whole of Irish lift centres about this personal element. You don't buy in the best or cheapest shop. You buy from a shopkeeper with whom your family stands in that particular relationship; he marries a country girl and attracts other customers who stand in the same relationship with his wife's family, and when the relationship is exhausted, the business changes hands. The visible sign of the relationship is your debit balance. You pay money 'off' the account, but you never pay off the account itself except as a declaration of war.

In the abstract, of course, it is a terrible system. All abstract considerations like justice, truth and personal integrity melt before it. Year after year the bishops denounce the sin of perjury, but it simply has no effect; the overriding element is always the personal relationship, and people simply do not regard perjury committed on that score as a sin at all. Lawyers tell me that the only place in Ireland where you can expect testimony that is not perjured is Wexford, which has a strong English racial backbone, but my own experience of Wexford was rather different. I was misguided enough to ask an old man the way (a thing you must never do unless you already know the way and are merely in search of copy).

'Are you married?' asked the old man in the way old men in Ireland have of plunging off at a tangent.

'I am not,' I said with resignation.

'Don't ever marry a girl without feeling her first,' said the old man firmly. 'The parish priest will tell you differently, but priests have no experience. There was a man in a house near me that married a girl like that, and the first night they were together, whatever occasion he had of grabbing hold of her, he felt the child jump inside her. I would never marry a girl without feeling her first, and I would never give information about a neighbour.'

'You're a man of high principles,' said I.

'I am,' said he. 'There was another man living near me that got into trouble about a man that was shot. The police came and asked me questions about him but I put them astray. I never give information about a neighbour.'

As I said, in the abstract it is a terrible system, but in practice it has enormous advantages, for real loneliness is very, very rare, and suicide so exceptional that it is always like a slap in the face for the whole community. An Irishman's friends have been very remiss if he ever achieves suicide.

The farther west you go, the stronger this personal element becomes, the weaker the abstraction of law. Sometimes, sitting in a country cottage, listening to the conversation, noting the stresses and the elaboration of personal implications, I have the feeling of listening to people speaking a foreign language. I know one Englishman who thinks the world begins and ends in a certain parish in Donegal, where, on Christmas Eve, the police politely sent up word to the pub where he was staying that they would have to raid it at eleven, and would the customers mind going across the fields to another pub which they wouldn't be raiding until half past eleven. So at eleven all the customers trooped over the fields in the darkness, and at half past eleven back they came after collecting the customers from the other pub, and at midnight the police solemnly retired to their barracks with the whiskey thoughtfully supplied by the two publicans.

I notice it most of all in Donegal. Once, a friend and I walked too far and called at a village post office to inquire if there was a bus back. There was no bus – as you will have gathered, there rarely is – but the postmistress sent out a little girl to inquire if any car was leaving the village that evening. None was, so, in spite of our protests, she rang up the next village; no car was leaving that either. At this she proceeded to give the other postmistress a bit of her mind, and in what must have been an apologetic tone, the other suggested a third village from which MacGinley's car usually set out about that hour. But when, on ringing up, our postmistress discovered that MacGinley's car was broken, there was hell to pay. She immediately rang the police in the nearest town, and ordered them to stop the first car coming in our direction and tell the driver to pick us up. He did, too, and there was no damn nonsense about obliging anyone.

Let me recount one further incident which haunts my memory, perhaps because I have never solved the mystery behind it. Once some friends and I saw from the road a handsome Georgian house among the trees. A certain lack of symmetry suggested to me that it was only a screen, and that behind it was an older manor house, so we went up the drive to see. Through the open window of a ground-floor room a Tibetan mastiff howled for somebody's blood – preferably ours.

We knocked and the door was opened by a pleasant elderly woman who invited us in. The hall was magnificent. After a while a timid elderly man appeared and agreed to let us look over the house, but first he had to put the mastiff away – 'we keep him for protection'. We enthusiastically agreed that the mastiff should be put away. There were obviously no servants. The two old people, brother and sister, were alone in this house and as frightened of us as we of the dog.

It was only after they had shown us the splendid panelled interior that it began to dawn on them that we had no intentions on their lives. Really, people were very nice! They had recently had a fire and the neighbours had come and helped to put it out! We introduced ourselves and they did the same. They bore a famous Norman name – let us call it De Courcy.

'You're here a long time then?'

'Oh, yes, since the Twelfth Century. The chapel is Twelfth Century. Perhaps you'd like to see it?'

They led the way across the avenue, and there, under the trees, was a ruined chapel. It made me more certain than ever that the place was a converted manor house. They kept the chapel beautifully; the floor cemented, a modern religious statue inside the door, a beautiful mediaeval Virgin and Child on the altar.

'You see,' said the old man. 'Twelfth Century.'

'Fifteenth, surely,' I said, looking at the details of the windows.

'Oh, I think not,' he said, getting very rattled. 'Father—said it was Twelfth Century. We found some tiles when we were cementing the floor. Perhaps you could tell from those.'

He produced the tiles and they put my nose badly out of joint, because they were undoubtedly Twelfth Century. It emerged in conversation that the old couple owned no land but the little field behind the house. By this time they had begun to perceive that instead of plotting to murder them we were rapidly falling head and ears in love with them, and, growing more and more reckless, they insisted on our remaining for drinks. They began to think up other things to detain us. The dove house? Were we interested in dove houses?

'Or perhaps you'd like to see our courtyard?'

I nearly replied, 'Would we hell!' A man who has made a fool of himself about a little thing like dating a chapel needs something to restore his confidence, and the courtyard proved conclusively that the house was an old manor house.

I could scarcely wait to get home to look it up. There it was in the reference books, all right; old manor house, reconstructed in the early Eighteenth Century by some Cromwellian whose name you could chain a Bible to. But of the De Courcys not a word!

To this day I don't know what the story is; brother and sister with a Norman name, without land or servants, in a recon-structed manor house going back long before Cromwell. Are they the last of the original Norman owners? How on earth did the house come into the possession of these people and why did they want to own it?

I don't know, but I feel that if I did, it would make all this history unnecessary, because all Ireland would be in it. Its romance would be the romance of Irish history. No one who does not love the sense of the past should ever come near us; nobody who does, whatever our faults may be, should give us the hard word.

6 BETTER QUARRELLING

PREFACE

o'connor was that demographically unlikely thing in the Ireland of his time, an only child. And he was a writer who believed that the short story found its best focus as an expression of 'the lonely voice'. But he was also an observer of what the rest of Ireland believed itself to be, so he both understood and portrayed the dynamics of large wrangling families, of parochial village life, of the hugger-mugger city. 'It is better to be quarrelling than lonely,' as the saying has it. In 1949, he wrote in *Holiday* magazine that 'real loneliness [in Ireland] is very, very rare, and suicide so exceptional that it is always like a slap in the face for the whole community'.

One lonely voice is a monologue; two lonely voices are a quarrel; a dozen enough for a novel. O'Connor wrote wonderfully well about sibling rivalries, fluctuations of friendship, the emotional pragmatism that lack of choice entails, and the quarrels that echo through villages and down generations. That he did so in the short story rather than the novel is less to do with the nature of Irish society than with the nature of his own particular genius.

FOR THE first two or three years in Dublin, I organized my library and wrote two books: *Guests of the Nation*, the book of Civil War stories from lodgings in Ranelagh; the novel, *The Saint and Mary Kate*, from my first flat in Anglesea Road, which was neither cheerful nor comfortable, but where at last I had my own books, records, pictures and furniture about me. I still considered myself a poet, and had little notion of how to write a story and none at all of how to write a novel, so they were produced in hysterical fits of enthusiasm, followed by similar fits of despondency, good passages alternating with bad, till I can no longer read them.

All the same, for all its intolerable faults, I knew that *The Saint and Mary Kate* was a work of art, something I had never succeeded in producing before, and as I wrote it, I read it aloud to Mother, who either went into fits of laughter or looked puzzled and said restlessly, 'Well, aren't you a terrible boy!' It became the principal argument of the pious Catholics against me, and at one library conference in Cork I had to sit and listen to a denunciation of it as a scandalous and heretical work by the editor of the 'Three Thousand Best Books', who was so drunk that he could not stand straight on the platform.

George Russell enthused about it, not with the enthusiasm of a schoolteacher whose favourite pupil has passed an examination with honours, but with that of an inhibited man who rejoices in any sort of emotional outpouring – the excitement he displayed over Hugo and Dumas. He was passionately inquisitive about the character of the heroine, and a dozen times at least brought the conversation round to what she would be like to live with. This was something I didn't know myself, because I wasn't really writing about any woman in particular – I didn't know enough of them for that – but about that side of women that appealed to me – the one that has no patience with abstractions. I, of course, was full of abstractions.

From THE SAINT AND MARY KATE

PHIL HAD to admit that as Mary Kate grew older she displayed a distressing lukewarmness about the fierce modesty with which he surrounded himself. She even enjoyed the letter which he brought her from Gregory. Which led them into a peculiar discussion, during which Mary Kate made the most dramatic advance of her life, by announcing that she thought a lot of talk was made about nothing, and, personally, if Phil, for instance, wanted to kiss her she wouldn't mind.

Then she looked away and tried to pretend that she did not know how furiously she was blushing, and Phil's eyes sank to the floor and he blushed too. There was a dreadful moment of suspense.

'No,' he said at last; 'if I kissed you it would mean I was going to marry you.'

'No, it wouldn't,' she retorted promptly. 'You could kiss a girl without marrying her.'

'*I* couldn't,' he said between his teeth. 'I'd never kiss a woman I hadn't made up my mind to marry.'

'Why?' she asked.

'Because it wouldn't be fair to marry some one else after.'

She determined not to let him see how this thrust had gone home.

'But suppose the girl wouldn't mind?'

'I'm not thinking about her. I'm thinking of the woman I'd marry.'

'But she might have been kissed before that.'

'Not if she was my wife,' said Phil flatly without looking up, his face grown redder than ever. 'I'll never marry a woman that isn't like my own mother, and I'd expect it of her that she'd be as I'd be.'

'Oh, but that's silly,' said Mary Kate, a little wave of perturbation and jealousy mixed rising within her. 'You wouldn't expect any girl to be like your mother.'

'*I* would,' he maintained obstinately.

'But if she was like your mother no one would want to marry her,' she exclaimed with exasperation.

'Why not?'

'Because no one marries mothers,' she replied hotly. 'You marry girls, not mothers.'

'Well, they become mothers, don't they?' he demanded.

'They do,' she admitted reluctantly, 'they do.' Adding as an afterthought, 'Not to their husbands, though.' Which, even if accidental, was a considerable piece of psychology.

But this conversation left them both disturbed. Phil was disturbed because her words when he repeated them later to himself made him hot all over and made his skin so sensitive that the pillow against his cheek was momentarily transformed into the cool fresh cheek of Mary Kate, and when he laid one hand lightly on another and stroked it, it was as if he were stroking some one else's hand, and the fingers that were his own seemed cool and twig-like, reminding him of Mary Kate's long translucent fingers resting on the edge of his table. He shivered with longing, and twice that night he had to get up and kneel in prayer to bring his vagrom imaginations under control.

For Mary Kate it was even worse. She had already gone through most of what Phil was going through only without his sense of guilt. And now she had to go to bed, her ears still hot with his cruel snub, and with the knowledge that unless she stayed unkissed for as long as Phil's fidgets continued (an utter impossibility, she recognized) she would forfeit her chance of being his wife; and even if she were to practise her will power to that extent (it seemed still more impossible when you thought it out in terms of will power) there was always the still greater chance of the respectable woman of forty-five or so who would somehow remind him of his mother. Like Dona Nobis, for instance! Mary Kate had no grudge against Dona Nobis, but the respectable woman of forty-five she pictured as a pious woman with one tooth.

It was a great curse, she thought, tossing restlessly in her bed, to fall in love for the first time with a boy whose tastes in women ran to motherhood, and who attached to kissing an importance out of all proportion to the event. Well, it was his own fault, she decided bitterly, finding the bed too hot for her; he couldn't say but that she had given him his chance, and when he had married his old woman and grown tired of her she would tell him so.

She pictured herself stepping into a motor-car beside a handsome young man in grey tweeds, when Phil walked up worn and old, a long streak of grey through his hair. And she would say (very sprightly of course and with no sign of grief), 'Well, Phil, I suppose you sometimes think of the night I offered to let you kiss me?' And since she suddenly found herself sobbing as she said this, and tears were a great relief, she allowed her imagination to build whole castles of such lachrymose stuff. She would be found dead, and Phil would lament over her and remember that he had not taken the chance to kiss her in life, and kiss her now that she was dead.

She sobbed at great length, and found herself considerably more cheerful.

She got up, and as she walked across the squeaking floor, her little feet shining ghostlily at her from under the sweep of her nightdress, the toes caught up, and warming one another in an instinctive embrace, she decided that Phil might go to blue blazes, and for her part she was not going to worry her head about him any more. The point was that she was getting too old to be going on like this (the night was cold) and she wanted a boy. If she couldn't have Phil, well, she couldn't, and any other boy would do just as well (it was queer how you could make up your mind like this at night) – and every one admitted she was a beauty, and boys already looked back at her when they met her in the street (Phil was a little fool).

So she returned to bed, and surrendered herself to imaginary arms and lips that with disappointing celerity launched her into oblivion.

THE LUCEYS

IT'S EXTRAORDINARY, the bitterness there can be in a town like ours between two people of the same family. More particularly between two people of the same family. I suppose living more or less in public as we do we are either killed or cured by it, and the same communal sense that will make a man be battered into a reconciliation he doesn't feel gives added importance to whatever quarrel he thinks must not be composed. God knows, most of the time you'd be more sorry for a man like that than anything else.

The Luceys were like that. There were two brothers, Tom and Ben, and there must have been a time when the likeness between them was greater than the difference, but that was long before most of us knew them. Tom was the elder; he came in for the drapery shop. Ben had to have a job made for him on the County Council. This was the first difference and it grew and grew. Both were men of intelligence and education but Tom took it more seriously. As Ben said with a grin, he could damn well afford to with the business behind him.

It was an old-fashioned shop which prided itself on only stocking the best, and though the prices were high and Tom in his irascible opinionated way refused to abate them – he said haggling was degrading! – a lot of farmers' wives would still go nowhere else. Ben listened to his brother's high notions with his eyes twinkling, rather as he read the books which came his way, with profound respect and the feeling that this would all be grand for some other place, but was entirely inapplicable to the affairs of the County Council. God alone would ever be able to disentangle these, and meanwhile the only course open to a prudent man was to keep his mind to himself. If Tom didn't like the way the County Council was run, neither did Ben, but that was the way things were, and it rather amused him to rub it in to his virtuous brother.

Tom and Ben were both married. Tom's boy, Peter, was the great friend of his cousin, Charlie – called 'Charliss' by his Uncle

Tom. They were nice boys; Peter a fat, heavy, handsome lad who blushed whenever a stranger spoke to him, and Charlie with a broad face that never blushed at anything. The two families were always friendly; the mothers liked to get together over a glass of port wine and discuss the fundamental things that made the Lucey brothers not two inexplicable characters but two aspects of one inexplicable family character; the brothers enjoyed their regular chats about the way the world was going, for intelligent men are rare and each appreciated the other's shrewdness.

Only young Charlie was occasionally mystified by his Uncle Tom; he hated calling for Peter unless he was sure his uncle was out, for otherwise he might be sent into the front room to talk to him. The front room alone was enough to upset any high-spirited lad, with its thick carpet, mahogany sideboard, orna-mental clock, and gilt mirror with cupids. The red curtains alone would depress you, and as well as these there was a glass-fronted mahogany bookcase the length of one wall, with books in sets, too big for anyone only a priest to read: *The History of Ireland*, *The History of the Popes*, *The Roman Empire*, *The Life of Johnson* and *The Cabinet of Literature*. It gave Charlie the same sort of shivers as the priest's front room. His uncle suited it, a small, frail man, dressed in clerical black with a long pinched yellow face, tight lips, a narrow skull going bald up the brow, and a pair of tin specs.

All conversations with his uncle tended to stick in Charlie's mind for the simple but alarming reason that he never under-stood what the hell they were about, but one conversation in particular haunted him for years as showing the dangerous state of lunacy to which a man could be reduced by reading old books. Charlie was no fool, far from it; but low cunning and the most genuine benevolence were mixed in him in almost equal parts, producing a blend that was not without charm but gave no room for subtlety or irony.

'Good afternoon, Charliss,' said his uncle after Charlie had tied what he called 'the ould pup' to the leg of the hallstand. 'How are you?'

'All right,' Charlie said guardedly. (He hated being called Charliss, it made him sound such a sissy.)

'Take a seat, Charliss,' said his uncle benevolently. 'Peter will be down in a minute.'

'I won't,' said Charlie. 'I'd be afraid of the ould pup.'

'The expression, Charliss,' said his uncle in that rasping little voice of his, 'sounds like a contradiction in terms, but, not being familiar with dogs, I presume 'tis correct.'

'Ah, 'tis,' said Charlie, just to put the old man's mind at rest.

'And how is your father, Charliss?'

'His ould belly is bad again,' said Charlie. 'He'd be all right only the ould belly plays hell with him.'

'I'm sorry to hear it,' his uncle said gravely. 'And tell me, Charliss,' he added, cocking his head on one side like a bird, 'what is he saying about me now?'

This was one of the dirtiest of his Uncle Tom's tricks, assuming that Charlie's father was saying things about him, which to give Ben his due, he usually was. But on the other hand, he was admitted to be one of the smartest men in town, so he was entitled to do so, while everyone without exception appeared to agree that his uncle had a slate loose. Charlie looked at him cautiously, low cunning struggling with benevolence in him, for his uncle though queer was open-handed, and you wouldn't want to offend him. Benevolence won.

'He's saying if you don't mind yourself you'll end up in the poorhouse,' he said with some notion that if only his uncle knew the things people said about him he might mend his ways.

'Your father is right as always, Charliss,' said his uncle, rising and standing on the hearth with his hands behind his back and his little legs well apart. 'Your father is perfectly right. There are two main classes of people, Charliss – those who gravitate towards the poorhouse and those who gravitate towards the 'jail. . . . Do you know what "gravitate" means, Charliss?'

'I do not,' said Charlie without undue depression. It struck him as being an unlikely sort of word.

' "Gravitate", Charliss, means "tend" or "incline". Don't tell me you don't know what they mean!'

'I don't,' said Charlie.

'Well, do you know what this is?' his uncle asked smilingly as he held up a coin.

'I do,' said Charlie, humouring him as he saw that the conversation was at last getting somewhere. 'A tanner.'

'I am not familiar with the expression, Charliss,' his uncle said tartly and Charlie knew, whatever he'd said out of the way, his uncle was so irritated that he was liable to put the tanner back. 'We'll call it sixpence. Your eyes, I notice, gravitate towards the sixpence' (Charlie was so shocked that his eyes instantly gravitated towards his uncle), 'and in the same way, people gravitate, or turn naturally, towards the jail or poorhouse. Only a small number of either group reach their destination, though – which might be just as well for myself and your father,' he added in a low impressive voice, swaying forward and tightening his lips. 'Do you understand a word I'm saying, Charliss?' he added with a charming smile.

'I do not,' said Charlie.

'Good man! Good man!' his uncle said approvingly. 'I admire an honest and manly spirit in anybody. Don't forget your sixpence, Charliss.'

And as he went off with Peter, Charlie scowled and muttered savagely under his breath: 'Mod! Mod! Mod! The bleddy mon is mod!'

When the boys grew up Peter trained for a solicitor while Charlie, one of a large family, followed his father into the County Council. He grew up a very handsome fellow with a square, solemn, dark-skinned face, a thick red lower lip, and a mass of curly black hair. He was reputed to be a great man with greyhounds and girls and about as dependable with one as with the other. His enemies called him 'a crooked bloody bastard' and his father, a shrewd man, noted with alarm that Charlie thought him simple-minded.

The two boys continued the best of friends, though Peter, with an office in Asragh, moved in circles where Charlie felt himself lost; professional men whose status was calculated on their furniture and food and wine. Charlie thought that sort of entertainment a great pity. A man could have all the fun he wanted out of life without wasting his time on expensive and unsatisfactory meals and carrying on polite conversation while you dodged between bloody little tables that were always falling over, but Charlie, who was a modest lad, admired the way Peter never knocked anything over and never said: 'Chrisht!' Wine, coffee cups, and talk about old books came as easy to him as talk about a dog or a horse.

Charlie was thunderstruck when the news came to him that

Peter was in trouble. He heard it first from Mackesy the detective, whom he hailed outside the courthouse. (Charlie was like his father in that; he couldn't let a man go by without a greeting.)

'Hullo, Matt,' he shouted gaily from the courthouse step. 'Is it myself or my father you're after?'

'I'll let ye off for today,' said Mackesy, making a garden seat of the crossbar of his bicycle. Then he lowered his voice so that it didn't travel further than Charlie. 'I wouldn't mind having a word with a relative of yours, though.'

'A what, Matt?' Charlie asked, skipping down the steps on the scent of news. (He was like his father in that, too.) 'You don't mean one of the Luceys is after forgetting himself?'

'Then you didn't hear about Peter?'

'Peter! Peter in trouble! You're not serious, Matt?'

'There's a lot of his clients would be glad if I wasn't, Cha,' Mackesy said grimly. 'I thought you'd know about it as ye were such pals.'

'But we are, man, we are,' Charlie insisted. 'Sure, wasn't I at the dogs with him – when was it? – last Thursday? I never noticed a bloody thing, though, now you mention it, he was lashing pound notes on that Cloonbullogue dog. I told him the Dalys could never train a dog.'

Charlie left Mackesy, his mind in a whirl! He tore through the cashier's office. His father was sitting at his desk, signing paying-orders. He was wearing a grey tweed cap, a grey tweed suit, and a brown cardigan. He was a stocky, powerfully built man, with a great expanse of chest, a plump, dark, hairy face, long quizzical eyes that tended to close in slits; hair in his nose, hair in his ears; hair on his high cheekbones that made them like small cabbage-patches.

He made no comment on Charlie's news, but stroked his chin and looked worried. Then Charlie shot out to see his uncle. Quill, the assistant, was serving in the shop and Charlie stumped in behind the counter to the fitting room. His uncle had been looking out the back, all crumpled up. When Charlie came in he pulled himself erect with fictitious jauntiness. With his old black coat and wrinkled yellow face he had begun to look like an old rabbi.

'What's this I hear about Peter?' began Charlie, who was never one to be ceremonious.

'Bad news travels fast, Charlie,' said his uncle in his dry little voice, clamping his lips so tightly that the wrinkles ran up his cheeks from the corners of his mouth. He was so upset that he forgot even to say 'Charliss'.

'Have you any notion how much it is?' asked Charlie.

'I have not, Charlie,' Tom said bitterly. 'I need hardly say my son did not take me into his confidence about the extent of his robberies.'

'And what are you going to do?'

'What can I do?' The lines of pain belied the harsh little staccato that broke up every sentence into disjointed phrases as if it were a political speech. 'You saw yourself, Charliss, the way I reared that boy. You saw the education I gave him. I gave him the thing I was denied myself, Charliss. I gave him an honourable profession. And now for the first time in my life I am ashamed to show my face in my own shop. What can I do?'

'Ah, now, ah, now, Uncle Tom, we know all that,' Charlie said truculently, 'but that's not going to get us anywhere. What can we do now?'

'Is it true that Peter took money that was entrusted to him?' Tom asked oratorically.

'To be sure he did,' replied Charlie without the thrill of horror which his uncle seemed to expect. 'I do it myself every month, only I put it back.'

'And is it true he ran away from his punishment instead of standing his ground like a man?' asked Tom, paying no attention to him.

'What the hell else would he do?' asked Charlie, who entirely failed to appreciate the spiritual beauty of atonement. 'Begod, if I had two years' hard labour facing me you wouldn't see my heels for dust.'

'I dare say you think I'm old-fashioned, Charliss,' said his uncle, 'but that's not the way I was reared, nor the way my son was reared.'

'And that's where the ferryboat left ye,' snorted Charlie. 'Now that sort of thing may be all very well, Uncle Tom, but 'tis no use taking it to the fair. Peter made some mistake, the way we all make mistakes, but instead of coming to me or some other friend, he lost his nerve and started gambling, Chrisht, didn't I see it happen to better men? You don't know how much it is?'

'No, Charliss, I don't.'

'Do you know where he is, even?'

'His mother knows.'

'I'll talk to my old fellow. We might be able to do something. If the bloody fool might have told me on Thursday instead of backing that Cloonbullogue dog!'

Charlie returned to the office to find his father sitting at his desk with his hands joined and his pipe in his mouth, staring nervously at the door.

'Well?'

'We'll go over to Asragh and talk to Toolan of the Guards ourselves,' said Charlie. 'I want to find out how much he let himself in for. We might even get a look at the books.'

'Can't his father do it?' Ben asked gloomily.

'Do you think he'd understand them?'

'Well, he was always fond of literature,' Ben said shortly.

'God help him,' said Charlie. 'He has enough of it now.'

''Tis all his own conceit,' Ben said angrily, striding up and down the office with his hands in his trouser pockets. 'He was always good at criticizing other people. Even when you got in here it was all influence. Of course, he'd never use influence. Now he wants us to use it.'

'That's all very well,' Charlie said reasonably, 'but this is no time for raking up old scores.'

'Who's raking up old scores?' his father shouted angrily.

'That's right,' Charlie said approvingly. 'Would you like me to open the door so that you can be heard all over the office?'

'No one is going to hear me at all,' his father said in a more reasonable tone – Charlie had a way of puncturing him. 'And I'm not raking up any old scores. I'm only saying now what I always said. The boy was ruined.'

'He'll be ruined with a vengeance unless we do something quick,' said Charlie. 'Are you coming to Asragh with me?'

'I am not.'

'Why?'

'Because I don't want to be mixed up in it at all. That's why. I never liked anything to do with money. I saw too much of it. I'm only speaking for your good. A man done out of his money is a mad dog. You won't get any thanks for it, and anything that goes wrong, you'll get the blame.'

Nothing Charlie could say would move his father, and Charlie was shrewd enough to know that everything his father said was right. Tom wasn't to be trusted in the delicate negotiations that would be needed to get Peter out of the hole, the word here, the threat there; all the complicated machinery of family pressure. And alone he knew he was powerless. Despondently he went and told his uncle and Tom received the news with resignation, almost without understanding.

But a week later Ben came back to the office deeply disturbed. He closed the door carefully behind him and leaned across the desk to Charlie, his face drawn. For a moment he couldn't speak.

'What ails you?' Charlie asked with no great warmth.

'Your uncle passed me just now in the Main Street,' whispered his father.

Charlie wasn't greatly put out. All of his life he had been made a party to the little jabs and asides of father and uncle, and he did not realize what it meant to a man like his father, friendly and popular, this public rebuke.

'That so?' he asked without surprise. 'What did you do to him?'

'I thought you might know that,' his father said, looking at him with a troubled air from under the peak of his cap.

'Unless 'twas something you said about Peter?' suggested Charlie.

'It might, it might,' his father agreed doubtfully. 'You didn't – ah – repeat anything I said to you?'

'What a bloody fool you think I am!' Charlie said indignantly. 'And indeed I thought you had more sense. What did you say?'

'Oh, nothing. Nothing only what I said to you,' replied his father and went to the window to look out. He leaned on the sill and then tapped nervously on the frame. He was haunted by all the casual remarks he had made or might have made over a drink with an acquaintance – remarks that were no different from those he and Tom had been passing about one another all their lives. 'I shouldn't have said anything at all, of course, but I had no notion 'twould go back.'

'I'm surprised at my uncle,' said Charlie. 'Usually he cares little enough what anyone says of him.'

But even Charlie, who had moments when he almost under-stood his peppery little uncle, had no notion of the hopes he had raised and which his more calculating father had dashed. Tom Lucey's mind was in a rut, a rut of complacency, for the idealist too has his complacency and can be aware of it. There are moments when he would be glad to walk through any mud, but he no longer knows the way; he needs to be led; he cannot degrade himself even when he is most ready to do so. Tom was ready to beg favours from a thief. Peter had joined the Air Force under an assumed name, and this was the bitterest blow of all to him, the extinction of the name. He was something of an amateur genealogist, and had managed to convince himself, God knows how, that his family was somehow related to the Gloucestershire Lucys. This was already a sort of death.

The other death didn't take long in coming. Charlie, in the way he had, got wind of it first, and, having sent his father to break the news to Min, he went off himself to tell his uncle. It was a fine spring morning. The shop was empty but for his uncle, standing with his back to the counter studying the shelves.

'Good morning, Charliss,' he crackled over his shoulder. 'What's the best news?'

'Bad, I'm afraid, Uncle Tom,' Charlie replied, leaning across the counter to him.

'Something about Peter, I dare say?' his uncle asked casually, but Charlie noticed how, caught unawares, he had failed to say 'my son', as he had taken to doing.

'Just so.'

'Dead, I suppose?'

'Dead, Uncle Tom.'

'I was expecting something of the sort,' said his uncle. 'May the Almighty God have mercy on his soul! . . . Con!' he called at the back of the shop while he changed his coat. 'You'd better close up the shop. You'll find the crepe on the top shelf and the mourning-cards in my desk.'

'Who is it, Mr Lucey?' asked Con Quill. ''Tisn't Peter?'

''Tis, Con, 'tis, I'm sorry to say,' and Tom came out briskly with his umbrella over his arm. As they went down the street two people stopped them: the news was already round.

Charlie, who had to see about the arrangements for the funeral, left his uncle outside the house and so had no chance of averting the scene that took place inside. Not that he would have had much chance of doing so. His father had found Min in a state of collapse. Ben was the last man in the world to look after a woman, but he did manage to get her a pillow, put her legs on a chair and cover her with a rug, which was more than Charlie would have given him credit for. Min smelt of brandy. Then Ben strode up and down the darkened room with his hands in his pockets and his cap over his eyes, talking about the horrors of aeroplane travel. He knew he was no fit company for a woman of sensibility like Min, and he almost welcomed Tom's arrival.

'That's terrible news, Tom,' he said.

'Oh, God help us!' cried Min. 'They said he disgraced us but he didn't disgrace us long.'

'I'd sooner 'twas one of my own, Tom,' Ben said excitedly. 'As God is listening to me I would. I'd still have a couple left, but he was all ye had.'

He held out his hand to Tom. Tom looked at it, then at him, and then deliberately put his own hands behind his back.

'Aren't you going to shake hands with me, Tom?' Ben asked appealingly.

'No, Ben,' Tom said grimly. 'I am not.'

'Oh, Tom Lucey!' moaned Min with her crucified smile. 'Over your son's dead body!'

Ben looked at his brother in chagrin and dropped his hand. For a moment it looked as though he might strike him. He was a volatile, hot-tempered man.

'That wasn't what I expected from you, Tom,' he said, making a mighty effort to control himself.

'Ben,' said his brother, squaring his frail little shoulders, 'you disrespected my son while he was alive. Now that he's dead I'd thank you to leave him alone.'

'I disrespected him?' Ben exclaimed indignantly. 'I did nothing of the sort. I said things I shouldn't have said. I was upset. You know the sort I am. You were upset yourself and I dare say you said things you regret.'

''Tisn't alike, Ben,' Tom said in a rasping, opinionated tone. 'I said them because I loved the boy. You said them because you hated him.'

'I hated him?' Ben repeated incredulously. 'Peter? Are you out of your mind?'

'You said he changed his name because it wasn't grand enough for him,' Tom said, clutching the lapels of his coat and stepping from one foot to another. 'Why did you say such a mean, mock-ing, cowardly thing about the boy when he was in trouble?'

'All right, all right,' snapped Ben. 'I admit I was wrong to say it. There were a lot of things you said about my family, but I'm not throwing them back at you.'

'You said you wouldn't cross the road to help him,' said Tom. Again he primmed up the corners of his mouth and lowered his head. 'And why, Ben? I'll tell you why. Because you were jealous of him.'

'I was jealous of him?' Ben repeated. It seemed to him that he was talking to a different man, discussing a different life, as though the whole of his nature was being turned inside out.

'You were jealous of him, Ben. You were jealous because he had the upbringing and education your own sons lacked. And I'm not saying that to disparage your sons. Far from it. But you begrudged my son his advantages.'

'Never!' shouted Ben in a fury.

'And I was harsh with him,' Tom said, taking another nervous step forward while his neat waspish little voice grew harder. 'I was harsh with him and you were jealous of him, and when his hour of trouble came he had no one to turn to. Now, Ben, the least you can do is to spare us your commiserations.'

'Oh, wisha, don't mind him, Ben,' moaned Min. 'Sure, every-one knows you never begrudged my poor child anything. The man isn't in his right mind.'

'I know that, Min,' Ben said, trying hard to keep his temper. 'I know he's upset. Only for that he'd never say what he did say – or believe it.'

'We'll see, Ben, we'll see,' said Tom grimly.

That was how the row between the Luceys began, and it con-tinued like that for years. Charlie married and had children of his own. He always remained friendly with his uncle and visited him regularly; sat in the stuffy front room with him and listened with frowning gravity to Tom's views, and no more than in his childhood understood what the old man was talking about. All he gathered was that none of the political parties had any prin-ciple and the country was in a bad way due to the inroads of the uneducated and ill-bred. Tom looked more and more like a rabbi. As is the way of men of character in provincial towns, he tended more and more to become a collection of mannerisms, a caricature of himself. His academic jokes on his simple customers became more elaborate; so elaborate, in fact, that in time he gave up trying to explain them and was content to be set down as merely queer. In a way it made things easier for Ben; he was able to treat the breach with Tom as another example of his brother's cantankerousness, and spoke of it with amusement and good nature.

Then he fell ill. Charlie's cares were redoubled. Ben was the world's worst patient. He was dying and didn't know it, wouldn't go to hospital, and broke the heart of his wife and daughter. He was awake at six, knocking peremptorily for his cup of tea; then waited impatiently for the paper and the post. 'What the hell is keeping Mick Duggan? That fellow spends half his time gossiping along the road. Half past nine and no post!' After that the day was a blank to him until evening when a couple of County Council chaps dropped in to keep him company and tell him what was afoot in the courthouse. There was nothing in the long low room, plastered with blue and green flowered wallpaper, but a bedside table, a press, and three or four holy pictures, and Ben's mind was not on these but on the world outside – feet passing and repassing on errands which he would never be told about. It broke his heart. He couldn't believe he was as bad as people tried to make out; sometimes it was the doctor he blamed, sometimes the chemist who wasn't careful enough of the bottles and pills he made up – Ben could remember some shocking cases. He lay in bed doing involved calculations about his pension.

Charlie came every evening to sit with him. Though his father didn't say much about Tom, Charlie knew the row was always there in the back of his mind. It left Ben bewildered, a man without bitterness. And Charlie knew he came in for some of the blame. It was the illness all over again: someone must be slipping up somewhere; the right word hadn't been dropped in the right quarter or a wrong one had been dropped instead. Charlie, being so thick with Tom, must somehow be to blame. Ben did not understand the inevitable. One night it came out.

'You weren't at your uncle's?' Ben asked.

'I was,' Charlie said with a nod. 'I dropped in on the way up.'

'He wasn't asking about me?' Ben asked, looking at him out of the corner of his eye.

'Oh, he was,' Charlie said with a shocked air. 'Give the man his due, he always does that. That's one reason I try to drop in every day. He likes to know.'

But he knew this was not the question his father wanted answered. That question was: 'Did you say the right words? Did you make me out the feeble figure you should have made me out, or did you say the wrong thing, letting him know I was better?' These things had to be managed. In Charlie's place Ben would have managed it splendidly.

'He didn't say anything about dropping up?' Ben asked with affected lightness.

'No,' Charlie said with assumed thoughtfulness. 'I don't remember.'

'There's blackness for you!' his father said with sudden bitterness. It came as a shock to Charlie; it was the first time he had heard his father speak like that, from the heart, and he knew the end must be near.

'God knows,' Charlie said, tapping one heel nervously, 'he's a queer man. A queer bloody man!'

'Tell me, Charlie,' his father insisted, 'wouldn't you say it to him? 'Tisn't right and you know 'tisn't right.'

''Tisn't,' said Charlie, tearing at his hair, 'but to tell you the God's truth I'd sooner not talk to him.'

'Yes,' his father added in disappointment. 'I see it mightn't do for you.'

Charlie realized that his father was thinking of the shop, which would now come to him. He got up and stood against the fireplace, a fat, handsome, moody man.

'That has nothing to do with it,' he said. 'If he gave me cause I'd throw his bloody old shop in his face in the morning. I don't want anything from him. 'Tis just that I don't seem to be able to talk to him. I'll send Paddy down tonight and let him ask him.'

'Do, do,' his father said with a knowing nod. 'That's the very thing you'll do. And tell Julie to bring me up a drop of whiskey and a couple of glasses. You'll have a drop yourself?'

'I won't.'

'You will, you will. Julie will bring it up.'

Charlie went to his brother's house and asked him to call on Tom and tell him how near the end was. Paddy was a gentle, good-natured boy with something of Charlie's benevolence and none of his guile.

'I will to be sure,' he said. 'But why don't you tell him? Sure, he thinks the world of you.'

'I'll tell you why, Paddy,' Charlie whispered with his hand on his brother's sleeve. 'Because if he refused me I might do him some injury.'

'But you don't think he will?' Paddy asked in bewilderment.

'I don't think at all, Paddy,' Charlie said broodingly. 'I know.'

He knew all right. When he called on his way home the next afternoon his mother and sister were waiting for him, hysterical with excitement. Paddy had met with a cold refusal. Their hysteria was infectious. He understood now why he had caught people glancing at him curiously in the street. It was being argued out in every pub, what Charlie Lucey ought to do. People couldn't mind their own bloody business. He rapped out an oath at the two women and took the stairs three at a time. His father was lying with his back to the window. The whiskey was still there as Charlie had seen it the previous evening. It tore at his heart more than the sight of his father's despair.

'You're not feeling too good?' he said gruffly.

'I'm not, I'm not,' Ben said, lifting the sheet from his face. 'Paddy didn't bring a reply to that message?' he added questioningly.

'Do you tell me so?' Charlie replied, trying to sound shocked.

'Paddy was always a bad man to send on a message,' his father said despondently, turning himself painfully in the bed, but still not looking at Charlie. 'Of course, he hasn't the sense. Tell me, Charlie,' he added in a feeble voice, 'weren't you there when I was talking about Peter?'

'About Peter?' Charlie exclaimed in surprise.

'You were, you were,' his father insisted, looking at the window. 'Sure, 'twas from you I heard it. You wanted to go to Asragh to look at the books, and I told you if anything went wrong you'd get the blame. Isn't that all I said?'

Charlie had to readjust his mind before he realized that his father had been going over it all again in the long hours of loneliness and pain, trying to see where he had gone wrong. It seemed to make him even more remote. Charlie didn't remember what his father had said; he doubted if his uncle remembered.

'I might have passed some joke about it,' his father said., 'but sure I was always joking him and he was always joking me. What the hell more was there in it?'

'Oh, a chance remark!' agreed Charlie.

'Now, the way I look at that,' his father said, seeking his eyes for the first time, 'someone was out to make mischief. This town is full of people like that. If you went and told him he'd believe you.'

I will, I will,' Charlie said, sick with disgust. 'I'll see him myself today.'   .

He left the house, cursing his uncle for a brutal egotist. He felt the growing hysteria of the town concentrating on himself and knew that at last it had got inside him. His sisters and brothers, the people in the little shops along the street, expected him to bring his uncle to book, and failing that, to have done with him. This was the moment when people had to take their side once and for all. And he knew he was only too capable of taking sides.

Min opened the door to him, her red-rimmed eyes dirty with tears and the smell of brandy on her breath. She was near hysterics, too.

'What way is he, Charlie?' she wailed.

'Bad enough, Aunt Min,' he said as he wiped his boots and went past her. 'He won't last the night.'

At the sound of his voice his uncle had opened the sitting-room door and now he came out and drew Charlie in by the hand. Min followed. His uncle didn't release his hand, and betrayed his nervousness only by the way his frail fingers played over Charlie's hand, like a woman's.

'I'm sorry to hear it, Charliss,' he said.

'Sure, of course you are, Uncle Tom,' said Charlie, and at the first words the feeling of hysteria within him dissolved and left only a feeling of immense understanding and pity. 'You know what brought me?'

His uncle dropped his hand.

'I do, Charliss,' he said and drew himself erect. They were neither of them men to beat about the bush.

'You'll come and see the last of him,' Charlie said, not even marking the question.

'Charliss,' Tom said with that queer tightening at the corners of his mouth, 'I was never one to hedge or procrastinate. I will not come.'

He almost hissed the final words. Min broke into a loud wail.

'Talk to him, Charlie, do! I'm sick and tired of it. We can never show our faces in the town again.'

'And I need hardly say, Charliss,' his uncle continued with an air of triumph that was almost evil, 'that that doesn't trouble me.'

'I know,' Charlie said earnestly, still keeping his eyes on the withered old face with the narrow-winged, almost transparent nose. 'And you know that I never interfered between ye. Whatever disagreements ye had, I never took my father's side against you. And 'twasn't for what I might get out of you.'

In his excitement his uncle grinned, a grin that wasn't natural, and that combined in a strange way affection and arrogance, the arrogance of the idealist who doesn't realize how easily he can be fooled.

'I never thought it, boy,' he said, raising his voice. 'Not for an instant. Nor 'twasn't in you.'

'And you know too you did this once before and you regretted it.'

'Bitterly! Bitterly!'

'And you're going to make the same mistake with your brother that you made with your son?'

'I'm not forgetting that either, Charliss,' said Tom. 'It wasn't today nor yesterday I thought of it.'

'And it isn't as if you didn't care for him,' Charlie went on remorselessly. 'It isn't as if you had no heart for him. You know he's lying up there waiting for you. He sent for you last night and you never came. He had the bottle of whiskey and the two glasses by the bed. All he wants is for you to say you forgive him. . . . Jesus Christ, man,' he shouted with all the violence in him roused, 'never mind what you're doing to him. Do you know what you're doing to yourself?'

'I know, Charliss,' his uncle said in a cold, excited voice. 'I know that too. And 'tisn't as you say that I have no heart for him. God knows it isn't that I don't forgive him. I forgave him long years ago for what he said about – one that was very dear to me. But I swore that day, Charliss, that never the longest day I lived would I take your father's hand in friendship, and if God was to strike me dead at this very moment for my presumption I'd say the same. You know me, Charliss,' he added, gripping the lapels of his coat. 'I never broke my word yet to God or man. I won't do it now.'

'Oh, how can you say it?' cried Min. 'Even the wild beasts have more nature.'

'Some other time I'll ask you to forgive me,' added Tom, ignoring her.

'You need never do that, Uncle Tom,' Charlie said with great simplicity and humbleness. ''Tis yourself you'll have to forgive.'

At the door he stopped. He had a feeling that if he turned he would see Peter standing behind him. He knew his uncle's barren pride was all he could now offer to the shadow of his son, and that it was his dead cousin who stood between them. For a moment he felt like turning and appealing to Peter. But he was never much given to the supernatural. The real world was trouble enough for him, and he went slowly homeward, praying that he might see the blinds drawn before him.

PEASANTS

WHEN Michael John Cronin stole the funds of the Carrick-nabreena Hurling, Football and Temperance Association, commonly called the Club, everyone said: 'Devil's cure to him!' ''Tis the price of him!' 'Kind father for him!' 'What did I tell you?' and the rest of the things people say when an acquaintance has got what is coming to him.

And not only Michael John but the whole Cronin family, seed, breed, and generation, came in for it; there wasn't one of them for twenty miles round or a hundred years back but his deeds and sayings were remembered and examined by the light of this fresh scandal. Michael John's father (the heavens be his bed!) was a drunkard who beat his wife, and his father before him a land-grabber. Then there was an uncle or grand-uncle who had been a policeman and taken a hand in the bloody work at Mitchelstown long ago, and an unmarried sister of the same whose good name it would by all accounts have needed a regiment of husbands to restore. It was a grand shaking-up the Cronins got altogether, and anyone who had a grudge in for them, even if it was no more than a thirty-third cousin, had rare sport, dropping a friendly word about it and saying how sorry he was for the poor mother till he had the blood lighting in the Cronin eyes.

There was only one thing for them to do with Michael John; that was to send him to America and let the thing blow over, and that, no doubt, is what they would have done but for a certain unpleasant and extraordinary incident.

Father Crowley, the parish priest, was chairman of the committee. He was a remarkable man, even in appearance; tall, powerfully built, but very stooped, with shrewd, loveless eyes that rarely softened to anyone except two or three old people. He was a strange man, well on in years, noted for his strong political views, which never happened to coincide with those of any party, and as obstinate as the devil himself. Now what should

Father Crowley do but try to force the committee to prosecute Michael John?

The committee were all religious men who up to this had never as much as dared to question the judgments of a man of God: yes, faith, and if the priest had been a bully, which to give him his due he wasn't, he might have danced a jig on their backs and they wouldn't have complained. But a man has principles, and the like of this had never been heard of in the parish before. What? Put the police on a boy and he in trouble?

One by one the committee spoke up and said so. 'But he did wrong,' said Father Crowley, thumping the table. 'He did wrong and he should be punished.'

'Maybe so, father,' said Con Norton, the vice-chairman, who acted as spokesman. 'Maybe you're right, but you wouldn't say his poor mother should be punished too and she a widow-woman?'

'True for you!' chorused the others.

'Serves his mother right!' said the priest shortly. 'There's none of you but knows better than I do the way that young man was brought up. He's a rogue and his mother is a fool. Why didn't she beat Christian principles into him when she had him on her knee?'

'That might be, too,' Norton agreed mildly. 'I wouldn't say but you're right, but is that any reason his Uncle Peter should be punished?'

'Or his Uncle Dan?' asked another.

'Or his Uncle James?' asked a third.

'Or his cousins, the Dwyers, that keep the little shop in Lissna-carriga, as decent a living family as there is in County Cork?' asked a fourth.

'No, father,' said Norton, 'the argument is against you.'

'Is it indeed?' exclaimed the priest, growing cross. 'Is it so? What the devil has it to do with his Uncle Dan or his Uncle James? What are ye talking about? What punishment is it to them, will ye tell me that? Ye'll be telling me next 'tis a punishment to me and I a child of Adam like himself.'

'Wisha now, father,' asked Norton incredulously, 'do you mean 'tis no punishment to them having one of their own blood made a public show? Is it mad you think we are? Maybe 'tis a thing you'd like done to yourself?'

'There was none of my family ever a thief,' replied Father Crowley shortly.

'Begor, we don't know whether there was or not,' snapped a little man called Daly, a hot-tempered character from the hills.

'Easy, now! Easy, Phil!' said Norton warningly.

'What do you mean by that?' asked Father Crowley, rising and grabbing his hat and stick.

'What I mean,' said Daly, blazing up, 'is that I won't sit here and listen to insinuations about my native place from any foreigner. There are as many rogues and thieves and vagabonds and liars in Cullough as ever there were in Carricknabreena – ay, begod, and more, and bigger! That's what I mean.'

'No, no, no, no,' Norton said soothingly. 'That's not what he means at all, father. We don't want any bad blood between Cullough and Carricknabreena. What he means is that the Crowleys may be a fine substantial family in their own country, but that's fifteen long miles away, and this isn't their country, and the Cronins are neighbours of ours since the dawn of history and time, and 'twould be a very queer thing if at this hour we handed one of them over to the police. . . . And now, listen to me, father,' he went on, forgetting his role of pacificator and hitting the table as hard as the rest, 'if a cow of mine got sick in the morning, 'tisn't a Cremin or a Crowley I'd be asking for help, and damn the bit of use 'twould be to me if I did. And everyone knows I'm no enemy of the Church but a respectable farmer that pays his dues and goes to his duties regularly.'

'True for you! True for you!' agreed the committee.

'I don't give a snap of my finger what you are,' retorted the priest. 'And now listen to me, Con Norton. I bear young Cronin no grudge, which is more than some of you can say, but I know my duty and I'll do it in spite of the lot of you.'

He stood at the door and looked back. They were gazing blankly at one another, not knowing what to say to such an impossible man. He shook his fist at them.

'Ye all know me,' he said. 'Ye know that all my life I'm fighting the long-tailed families. Now, with the help of God, I'll shorten the tail of one of them.'

Father Crowley's threat frightened them. They knew he was an obstinate man and had spent his time attacking what he called the 'corruption' of councils and committees, which was all very well as long as it happened outside your own parish. They dared not oppose him openly because he knew too much about all of them and, in public at least, had a lacerating tongue. The solution they favoured was a tactful one. They formed themselves into a Michael John Cronin Fund Committee and canvassed the parishioners for subscriptions to pay off what Michael John had stolen. Regretfully they decided that Father Crowley would hardly countenance a football match for the purpose.

Then with the defaulting treasurer, who wore a suitably contrite air, they marched up to the presbytery. Father Crowley was at his dinner but he told the houskeeper to show them in. He looked up in astonishment as his dining-room filled with the seven committeemen, pushing before them the cowed Michael John.

'Who the blazes are ye?' he asked, glaring at them over the lamp.

'We're the Club Committee, father,' replied Norton.

'Oh, are ye?'

'And this is the treasurer – the ex-treasurer, I should say.'

'I won't pretend I'm glad to see him,' said Father Crowley grimly.

'He came to say he's sorry, father,' went on Norton. 'He is sorry, and that's as true as God, and I'll tell you no lie. . . .' Norton made two steps forward and in a dramatic silence laid a heap of notes and silver on the table.

'What's that?' asked Father Crowley.

'The money, father. 'Tis all paid back now and there's nothing more between us. Any little crossness there was, we'll say no more about it, in the name of God.'

The priest looked at the money and then at Norton.

'Con,' he said, 'you'd better keep the soft word for the judge. Maybe he'll think more of it than I do.'

'The judge, father?'

'Ay, Con, the judge.'

There was a long silence. The committee stood with open mouths, unable to believe it.

'And is that what you're doing to us, father?' asked Norton in a trembling voice. 'After all the years, and all we done for you, is

it you're going to show us up before the whole country as a lot
of robbers?'

'Ay, ye idiots, I'm not showing ye up.'

'You are then, father, and you're showing up every man,
woman, and child in the parish,' said Norton. 'And mark my
words, 'twon't be forgotten for you.'

The following Sunday Father Crowley spoke of the matter
from the altar. He spoke for a full half-hour without a trace of
emotion on his grim old face, but his sermon was one long, ven-
omous denunciation of the 'long-tailed families' who, according
to him, were the ruination of the country and made a mockery
of truth, justice and charity. He was, as his congregation agreed,
a shockingly obstinate old man who never knew when he was
in the wrong.

After Mass he was visited in his sacristy by the committee.
He gave Norton a terrible look from under his shaggy eyebrows,
which made that respectable farmer flinch.

'Father,' Norton said appealingly, 'we only want one word
with you. One word and then we'll go. You're a hard character,
and you said some bitter things to us this morning; things we
never deserved from you. But we're quiet, peaceable poor men
and we don't want to cross you.'

Father Crowley made a sound like a snort.

'We came to make a bargain with you, father,' said Norton,
beginning to smile.

'A bargain?'

'We'll say no more about the whole business if you'll do one
little thing – just one little thing – to oblige us.'

'The bargain!' the priest said impatiently. 'What's the bargain?'

'We'll leave the matter drop for good and all if you'll give the
boy a character.'

'Yes, father,' cried the committee in chorus. 'Give him a
character! Give him a character!'

'Give him a what?' cried the priest.

'Give him a character, father, for the love of God,' said Norton
emotionally. 'If you speak up for him, the judge will leave him
off and there'll be no stain on the parish.'

'Is it out of your minds you are, you half-witted angashores?'
asked Father Crowley, his face suffused with blood, his head
trembling. 'Here am I all these years preaching to ye about

decency and justice and truth and ye no more understand me than that wall there. Is it the way ye want me to perjure myself? Is it the way ye want me to tell a damned lie with the name of Almighty God on my lips? Answer me, is it?'

'Ah, what perjure!' Norton replied wearily. 'Sure, can't you say a few words for the boy? No one is asking you to say much. What harm will it do you to tell the judge he's an honest, good-living, upright lad, and that he took the money without meaning any harm?'

'My God!' muttered the priest, running his hands distractedly through his grey hair. 'There's no talking to ye, no talking to ye, ye lot of sheep.'

When he was gone the committeemen turned and looked at one another in bewilderment.

'That man is a terrible trial,' said one.

'He's a tyrant,' said Daly vindictively.

'He is, indeed,' sighed Norton, scratching his head. 'But in God's holy name, boys, before we do anything, we'll give him one more chance.'

That evening when he was at his tea the committeemen called again. This time they looked very spruce, businesslike, and independent. Father Crowley glared at them.

'Are ye back?' he asked bitterly. 'I was thinking ye would be. I declare to my goodness, I'm sick of ye and yeer old committee.'

'Oh, we're not the committee, father,' said Norton stiffly.

'Ye're not?'

'We're not.'

'All I can say is, ye look mighty like it. And, if I'm not being impertinent, who the deuce are ye?'

'We're a deputation, father.'

'Oh, a deputation! Fancy that, now. And a deputation from what?'

'A deputation from the parish, father. Now, maybe you'll listen to us.'

'Oh, go on! I'm listening, I'm listening.'

'Well, now, 'tis like this, father,' said Norton, dropping his airs and graces and leaning against the table. ''Tis about that little business this morning. Now, father, maybe you don't understand us and we don't understand you. There's a lot of misunderstanding in the world today, father. But we're quiet simple poor men that want to do the best we can for everybody, and a few words or a few pounds wouldn't stand in our way. Now, do you follow me?'

'I declare,' said Father Crowley, resting his elbows on the table, 'I don't know whether I do or not.'

'Well, 'tis like this, father. We don't want any blame on the parish or on the Cronins, and you're the one man that can save us. Now all we ask of you is to give the boy a character –'

'Yes, father,' interrupted the chorus, 'give him a character! Give him a character!'

'Give him a character, father, and you won't be troubled by him again. Don't say no to me now till you hear what I have to say. We won't ask you to go next, nigh or near the court. You have pen and ink beside you and one couple of lines is all you need write. When 'tis over you can hand Michael John his ticket to America and tell him not to show his face in Carricknabreena again. There's the price of his ticket, father,' he added, clapping a bundle of notes on the table. 'The Cronins themselves made it up, and we have his mother's word and his own word that he'll clear out the minute 'tis all over.'

'He can go to pot!' retorted the priest. 'What is it to me where he goes?'

'Now, father, can't you be patient?' Norton asked reproachfully. 'Can't you let me finish what I'm saying? We know 'tis no advantage to you, and that's the very thing we came to talk about. Now, supposing – just supposing for the sake of argument – that you do what we say, there's a few of us here, and between us, we'd raise whatever little contribution to the parish fund you'd think would be reasonable to cover the expense and trouble to yourself. Now do you follow me?'

'Con Norton,' said Father Crowley, rising and holding the edge of the table, 'I follow you. This morning it was perjury, and now 'tis bribery, and the Lord knows what 'twill be next. I see I've been wasting my breath. . . . And I see too,' he added savagely, leaning across the table towards them, 'a pedigree bull would be more use to ye than a priest.'

'What do you mean by that, father?' asked Norton in a low voice.

'What I say.'

'And that's a saying that will be remembered for you the longest day you live,' hissed Norton, leaning towards him till they were glaring at one another over the table.

'A bull,' gasped Father Crowley. 'Not a priest.'

''Twill be remembered.'

'Will it? Then remember this too. I'm an old man now. I'm forty years a priest, and I'm not a priest for the money or power or glory of it, like others I know. I gave the best that was in me – maybe 'twasn't much but 'twas more than many a better man would give, and at the end of my days . . .' lowering his voice to a whisper he searched them with his terrible eyes, '. . . at the end of my days, if I did a wrong thing, or a bad thing, or an unjust thing, there isn't man or woman in this parish that would brave me to my face and call me a villain. And isn't that a poor story for an old man that tried to be a good priest?' His voice changed again and he raised his head defiantly. 'Now get out before I kick you out!'

And true to his word and character not one word did he say in Michael John's favour the day of the trial, no more than if he was black. Three months Michael John got and by all accounts he got off light.

He was a changed man when he came out of jail, downcast and dark in himself. Everyone was sorry for him, and people who had never spoken to him before spoke to him then. To all of them he said modestly: 'I'm very grateful to you, friend, for overlooking my misfortune.' As he wouldn't go to America, the committee made another whip-round and between what they had collected before and what the Cronins had made up to send him to America, he found himself with enough to open a small shop. Then he got a job in the County Council, and an agency for some shipping company, till at last he was able to buy a public-house.

As for Father Crowley, till he was shifted twelve months later, he never did a day's good in the parish. The dues went down and the presents went down, and people with money to spend on Masses took it fifty miles away sooner than leave it to him. They said it broke his heart.

He has left unpleasant memories behind him. Only for him, people say, Michael John would be in America now. Only for him he would never have married a girl with money, or had it to lend to poor people in the hard times, or ever sucked the blood of Christians. For, as an old man said to me of him: 'A robber he is and was, and a grabber like his grandfather before him, and an enemy of the people like his uncle, the policeman; and though some say he'll dip his hand where he dipped it before, for myself I have no hope unless the mercy of God would send us another Moses or Brian Boru to cast him down and hammer him in the dust.'

FISH FOR FRIDAY

NED MACCARTHY, the teacher in a village called Abbeyduff, was wakened one morning by his sister-in-law. She was standing over him with a cynical smile and saying in a harsh voice:

'Wake up! 'Tis started.'

'What's started, Sue?' Ned asked wildly, jumping up in bed with an anguished air.

'Why?' she asked dryly. 'Are you after forgetting already? You'd better dress and go for the doctor.'

'Oh, the doctor!' sighed Ned, remembering all at once why he was sleeping alone in the little back room and why that unpleasant female who so obviously disapproved of him was in the house.

He dressed in a hurry, said a few words of encouragement to his wife, talked to the children while swallowing a cup of tea, and got out the old car. He was a sturdy man in his early forties with fair hair and pale grey eyes, nervous and excitable. He had plenty to be excitable about – the house, for instance. It was a fine house, an old shooting lodge, set back at a distance of two fields from the road, with a lawn in front leading to the river and steep gardens climbing the wooded hills behind. It was, in fact, an ideal house, the sort he had always dreamed of, where Kitty could keep a few hens and he could dig the garden and get in a bit of shooting. But scarcely had he settled in when he realized it had all been a mistake. A couple of rooms in town would have been better. The loneliness of the long evenings when dusk had settled on the valley was something he had never even imagined.

He had lamented it to Kitty, who had suggested the old car, but even this had its drawbacks because the car demanded as much attention as a baby. When Ned was alone in it he chatted to it encouragingly; when it stopped because he had forgotten to fill the tank he kicked it viciously, as if it were a wicked dog, and the villagers swore that he had actually been seen stoning it. This, coupled with the fact that he sometimes talked to himself when he hadn't the car to talk to, had given rise to the legend that he had a slate loose.

He drove down the lane and across the little footbridge to the main road, and then stopped before the public-house at the corner, which his friend Tom Hurley owned.

'Anything you want in town, Tom?' he shouted from the car.

'What's that, Ned?' replied a voice from within, and Tom himself, a small, round, russet-faced man, came out with his wrinkled grin.

'I have to go into town. I wondered, was there anything you wanted?'

'No, no, Ned, thanks, I don't think so,' replied Tom in his nervous way, all the words trying to come out together. 'All we wanted was fish for the dinner, and the Jordans are bringing that.'

'That stuff!' exclaimed Ned, making a face. 'I'd sooner 'twas them than me.'

'Och, isn't it the devil, Ned?' Tom spluttered with a similar expression of disgust. 'The damn smell hangs round the shop all day. But what the hell else can you do on a Friday? You going for a spin?'

'No,' replied Ned with a sigh. 'It's Kitty. I have to call the doctor.'

'Oh, I see,' said Tom, beginning to beam. His expression exaggerated almost to caricature whatever emotion his interlocutor might be expected to feel. 'Ah, please God, it'll go off all right. Come in and have a drink.'

'No, thanks, Tom,' Ned said with resignation. 'I'd better not.'

'Ah, hell to your soul, you will,' fussed Tom. 'It won't take you two minutes. Hard enough it was for me to keep you off it the time the first fellow arrived.'

'That's right, Tom,' Ned said in surprise as he left the car and followed Tom into the pub. 'I'd forgotten about that. Who was it was here?'

'Ah, God!' moaned Tom, 'you had half the countryside in here. Jack Martin and Owen Hennessey, and that publican friend of yours from town – Cronin, ay, Cronin. There was a dozen of ye here. The milkman found ye next morning, littering the floor, and ye never even locked the doors after ye! Ye could have had my licence endorsed on me.'

'Do you know, Tom,' Ned said with a complacent smile, 'I'd forgotten about that completely. My memory isn't what it was. I suppose we're getting old.'

'Ah, well,' Tom said philosophically, pouring out a large drink for Ned and a small one for himself, ''tis never the same after the first. Isn't it astonishing, Ned, the first,' he added in his eager way, bending over the counter, 'what it does to you? God, you feel as if you were beginning life again. And by the time the second comes, you're beginning to wonder will the damn thing ever stop. . . . God forgive me for talking,' he whispered, beckoning over his shoulder with a boyish smile. 'Herself wouldn't like to hear me.'

''Tis true just the same, Tom,' Ned said broodingly, relieved at understanding a certain gloom he had felt during the preceding weeks. 'It's not the same. And that itself is only an illusion. Like when you fall in love, and think you're getting the one woman in the world, while all the time it's just one of Nature's little tricks for making you believe you're enjoying yourself when you're only putting yourself wherever she wants you.'

'Ah, well,' said Tom with his infectious laugh, 'they say it all comes back when you're a grandfather.'

'Who the hell wants to be a grandfather?' asked Ned with a sniff, already feeling sorry for himself with his home upset, that unpleasant female in the house, and more money to be found.

He drove off, but his mood had darkened. It was a beautiful bit of road between his house and the town, with the river below him on the left, and the hills at either side with the first wash of green on them like an unfinished sketch, and, walking or driving, it was usually a delight to him because of the thought of civilization at the other end. It was only a little seaside town, but it had shops and pubs and villas with electric light, and a water supply that did not fold up in May, and there were all sorts of interesting people to be met there, from summer visitors to Government inspectors with the latest news from Dublin. But now his heart didn't rise. He realized that the rapture of being a father does not repeat itself, and it gave him no pleasure to think of being a grandfather. He was decrepit enough as he was.

At the same time he was haunted by some memory of days when he was not decrepit, but careless and gay. He had been a Volunteer and roamed the hills for months with a column, wondering where he would spend the night. Then it had all seemed uncomfortable and dangerous enough, and, maybe like the illusion of regeneration at finding himself a father, it had been merely an illusion of freedom, but, even so, he felt he had known it and now knew it no more. It was linked in his mind with high hills and wide vistas, but now his life seemed to have descended into a valley like that he was driving along, with the river growing deeper and the hills higher as they neared the sea. He had descended into it by the quiet path of duty: a steady man, a sucker for responsibilities – treasurer of the Hurling Club, treasurer of the Republican Party, secretary for three other organizations. Bad! Bad! He shook his head reprovingly as he looked at the trees, the river, and the birds who darted from the hedges as he approached, and communed with the car.

'You've nothing to complain of, old girl,' he said encouragingly. 'It's all Nature. It gives you an illusion of freedom, but all the time it's bending you to its own purposes as if you were only cows or trees.'

Being nervous, he didn't like to drive through a town. He did it when he had to, but it made him flustered and fidgety so that he missed seeing whoever was on the streets, and the principal thing about a town was meeting people. He usually parked his car outside Cronin's pub on the way in, and then walked the rest of the way. Larry Cronin was an old comrade of revolutionary days who had married into the pub.

He parked the car and went to tell Larry. This was quite unnecessary as Larry knew every car for miles around and was well aware of Ned's little weakness, but it was a habit, and Ned was a man of more habits than he realized himself.

'I'm just leaving the old bus for half an hour, Larry,' he called through the door in a plaintive tone that conveyed regret for the inconvenience he was causing Larry and grief for the burden being put on himself.

'Come in, man, come in!' cried Larry, a tall, engaging man with a handsome face and a wide smile that was quite sincere if Larry liked you and damnably hypocritical if he didn't. His mouth was like a show-case with the array of false teeth in it. 'What the hell has you out at this hour of morning?'

'Oh, Nature, Nature,' said Ned with a laugh, digging his hands in his trouser pockets.

'How do you mean, Nature?' asked Larry, who did not understand the allusive ways of intellectuals but appreciated them none the less.

'Kitty, I mean,' Ned said. 'I'm going to get the doctor. I told you she was expecting again.'

'Ah, the blessings of God on you!' Larry cried jovially. 'Is this the third or the fourth? Christ, you lose count, don't you? You might as well have a drop as you're here. For the nerves, I mean. 'Tis hard on the nerves. That was a hell of a night we had the time the boy, was born.'

'Wasn't it?' said Ned, beaming at being reminded of something that seemed to have become a legend. 'I was just talking to Tom Hurley about it.'

'Ah, what the hell does Hurley know about it?' asked Larry, filling him out a drink in his lordly way. 'The bloody man went to bed at two. That fellow is too cautious to be good. But Martin gave a great account of himself. Do you remember? The whole first act of *Tosca*, orchestra and all. Tell me, you didn't see Jack since he was home?'

'Jack?' Ned exclaimed in surprise, looking up from his drink. (He felt easier in his mind now, being on the doctor's doorstep.) 'Was Jack away?'

'Arrah, Christ, he was,' said Larry, throwing his whole weight on the counter. 'In Paris, would you believe it? He's on the batter again, of course. Wait till you hear him on Paris! 'Tis only the mercy of God if the parish priest doesn't get to hear of it. Martin would want to mind himself.'

'That's where you're wrong, Larry,' Ned said with sudden bitterness, not so much against Jack Martin as against Life itself. 'Martin doesn't have to mind himself. The parish priest will mind him. If an inspector comes snooping round while Martin is on it, Father Clery will be taking him out to look at antiquities.'

'Ah, 'tis the God's truth for you,' Larry said in mournful disapproval. 'But you or I couldn't do it. Christ, man, we'd get slaughtered alive. 'Tisn't worried you are about Kitty?' he asked in a gentler tone.

'Ah, no, Larry,' said Ned. 'It's not that. It's just that at times like this a man feels himself of no importance. You know what I mean? A messenger boy would do as well. We're all dragged down to the same level.'

'And damn queer we'd be if we weren't,' said Larry with his good-natured smile. 'Unless, that is, you'd want to have the bloody baby yourself.'

'Ah, it's not only that, Larry,' Ned said irritably. 'It's not that at all. But a man can't help thinking.'

'Why, then indeed, that's true for you,' said Larry, who, as a result of his own experience in the pub, had developed a gloomy and philosophic view of human existence. After all, a man can't be looking at schizophrenia for ten hours a day without feeling that Life isn't simple. 'And 'tis at times like this you notice it – men coming and going, like the leaves on the trees. Isn't it true for me?'

But that wasn't what Ned was thinking about at all. He was thinking of his lost youth and what had happened in it to turn him from a firebrand into a father.

'No, Larry, that's not what I mean,' he said, drawing figures on the counter with the bottom of his glass. 'It's just that you can't help wondering what's after happening you. There were so many things you wanted to do that you didn't do, and you wonder if you'd done them would it be different. And here you are, forty-odd, and your life is over and nothing to show for it! It's as if when you married some good went out of you.'

'Small loss, as the fool said when he lost Mass,' retorted Larry, who had found himself a comfortable berth in the pub and lost his thirst for adventure.

'That's the bait, of course,' Ned said with a grim smile. 'That's where Nature gets us every time.'

'Arrah, what the hell is wrong with Nature?' asked Larry. 'When your first was born you were walking mad around the town, looking for people to celebrate it with. Now you sound as though you were looking for condolences. Christ, man, isn't it a great thing to have someone to share your troubles and give a slap in the ass to, even if she does let the crockery fly once in a while? What the hell about an old bit of china?'

'That's all very well, Larry,' Ned said, scowling, 'if – *if*, mind – that's all it costs.'

'And what the hell else does it cost?' asked Larry. 'Twenty-one meals a week and a couple of pounds of tea on the side. Sure, 'tis for nothing!'

'But *is* that all?' Ned asked fiercely. 'What about the days on the column?'

'Ah, that was different, Ned,' Larry said with a sigh while his eyes took on a faraway look. 'But, sure, everything was different then. I don't know what the hell is after coming over the country at all.'

'The same thing that's come over you and me,' said Ned. 'Middle age. But we had our good times, even apart from that.'

'Oh, begod, we had, we had,' Larry admitted wistfully.

'We could hop in a car and not come home for a fortnight if the fancy took us.'

'We could, man, we could,' said Larry, showing a great mouthful of teeth. 'Like the time we went to the Junction Races and came back by Donegal. Ah, Christ, Ned, youth is a great thing. Isn't it true for me?'

'But it wasn't only youth,' cried Ned. 'We had freedom, man. Now our lives are run for us by women the way they were when we were kids. This is Friday, and what do I find? Hurley waiting for someone to bring home the fish. You're waiting for the fish. I'll go home to a nice plate of fish. One few words in front of an altar, and it's fish for Friday the rest of our lives.'

'Still, Ned, there's nothing nicer than a good bit of fish,' Larry said dreamily. 'If 'tis well done, mind you. *If* 'tis well done. And 'tisn't often you get it well done. I grant you that. God, I had some fried plaice in Kilkenny last week that had me turned inside out. I declare to God, if I stopped that car once I stopped it six times, and by the time I got home I was shaking like an aspen.'

'And yet I can remember you in Tramore, letting on to be a Protestant just to get bacon and eggs,' Ned said accusingly.

'Oh, that's the God's truth,' Larry said with a wondering grin. 'I was a devil for meat, God forgive me. It used to make me mad, seeing the Protestants lowering it. And the waitress, Ned – do you remember the waitress that wouldn't believe I was a Protestant till I said the Our Father the wrong way for her? She said I had too open a face for a Protestant. How well she'd know a thing like that about the Our Father, Ned?'

'A woman would know anything she had to know to make a man eat fish,' Ned said, rising with gloomy dignity. 'And you may be reconciled to it, Larry, but I'm not. I'll eat it because I'm damned with a sense of duty, and I don't want to get Kitty into trouble with the neighbours, but with God's help I'll see one more revolution before I die if I have to swing for it.'

'Ah, well,' sighed Larry, 'youth is a great thing, sure enough. . . . Coming, Hanna, coming!' he replied as a woman's voice yelled from the bedroom above them. He gave Ned a smug wink to suggest that he enjoyed it, but Ned knew that that scared little rabbit of a wife of his would be wanting to know what all the talk was about his being a Protestant, and would then go to Confession and tell the priest that her husband had said heretical prayers and ask him was it a reserved sin and should Larry go to the Bishop. It was no life, no life, Ned thought as he sauntered down the hill past the church. And it was a great mistake taking a drink whenever he felt badly about the country, because it always made the country seem worse.

Suddenly someone clapped him on the shoulder. It was Jack Martin, the vocational-school teacher, a small, plump, nervous man, with a baby complexion, a neat greying moustache, and big blue innocent eyes. Ned's grim face lit up. Of all his friends, Martin was the one he warmed to most. He was a talented man and a good baritone. His wife had died a few years before and left him with two children, but he had never married again and had been a devoted, if over-anxious, father. Yet always two or three times a year, particularly approaching his wife's anniversary, he went on a tearing drunk that left some legend behind. There was the time he had tried to teach Italian music to the tramp who played the penny whistle in the street, and the time his house-keeper had hidden his trousers and he had shinned down the drainpipe and appeared in the middle of town in pyjamas, bowing in the politest way possible to the ladies who passed.

'MacCarthy, you scoundrel!' he said delightedly in his shrill nasal voice, 'you were hoping to give me the slip. Come in here one minute till I tell you something. God, you'll die!'

'If you'll just wait there ten minutes, Jack, I'll be along to you,' Ned said eagerly. 'There's just one job, one little job I have to do, and then I'll be able to give you my full attention.'

'Yes, but you'll have one drink before you go,' Martin said cantankerously. 'You're not a messenger boy yet. One drink and I'll release you on your own recognizances to appear when required. You'll never guess where I was, Ned. I woke up there – as true as God!'

Ned, deciding good-humouredly that five minutes' explana-tion in the bar was easier than ten minutes' argument in the street, allowed himself to be steered to a table by the door. It was quite clear that Martin was 'on it'. He was full of clockwork vitality, rushing to the counter for fresh drinks, fumbling for money, trying to carry glasses without spilling, and talking, talking, all the time. Ned beamed at him. Drunk or sober, he liked the man.

'Ned,' Martin burst out ecstatically, 'I'll give you three guesses where I was.'

'Let me see,' said Ned in mock meditation. 'I suppose 'twould never be Paris?' and then laughed outright at Martin's injured air.

'You can't do anything in this town,' Martin said bitterly. 'I suppose next you'll be telling me about the women I met there.'

'No,' said Ned gravely, 'it's Father Clery who'll be telling you about them – from the pulpit.'

'To hell with Clery!' snapped Martin. 'No, Ned, this is se-e-e-rious. It only came to me in the past week. You and I are wasting our bloody time in this bloody country.'

'Yes, Jack,' said Ned, settling himself in his seat with sudden gravity, 'but what else can you do with Time?'

'Ah, this isn't philosophy, man,' Martin said testily. 'This is – is se-e-e-rious, I tell you.'

'I know how serious it is, all right,' Ned said complacently, 'because I was only saying it to Larry Cronin ten minutes ago. Where the hell is our youth gone?'

'But that's only a waste of time, too, man,' Martin said impatiently. 'You couldn't call that youth. Drinking bad porter in pubs after closing time and listening to somebody singing "The Rose of Tralee". That's not life, man.'

'No,' said Ned, nodding, 'but what is life?'

'How the hell would I know?' asked Martin. 'I suppose you have to go out and look for it the way I did. You're not going to find the bloody thing here. You have to go south, where they have sunlight and wine and good cookery and women with a bit of go in them.'

'And don't you think it would be the same thing there?' Ned asked relentlessly while Martin raised his eyes to the ceiling and moaned.

'Oh, God, dust and ashes! Dust and ashes! Don't we get enough of that every Sunday from Clery? And Clery knows no more about it than we do.'

Now, Ned was very fond of Martin, and admired the vitality

with which in his forties he still pursued a fancy, but all the same he could not let him get away with the simpleminded notion that life was merely a matter of topography.

'That is a way life has,' he pronounced oracularly. 'You think you're seeing it, and it turns out it was somewhere else at the time. It's like women – the girl you lose is the one that could have made you happy. I suppose there are people in the south wishing they could be in some wild place like this – I admit it's not likely, but I suppose it could happen. No, Jack, we might as well resign ourselves to the fact that, wherever the hell life was, it wasn't where we were looking for it.'

'For God's sake, man!' Martin exclaimed irritably. 'You talk like a man of ninety-five.'

'I'm forty-two,' Ned said with quiet emphasis, 'and I have no illusions left. You still have a few. Mind,' he went on with genuine warmth, 'I admire you for it. You were never a fighting man like Cronin or myself, but you put up a better fight than either of us. But Nature has her claws in you as well. You're light and airy now, but what way will you be this time next week? And even now,' he added threateningly, 'even at this minute, you're only that way because you've escaped from the guilt for a little while. You've got down the drainpipe and you're walking the town in your night clothes, but sooner or later they'll bring you back and make you put your trousers on.'

'But it isn't guilt, Ned,' Martin interrupted. 'It's my stomach. I can't keep it up.'

'It isn't only your stomach, Jack,' Ned said triumphantly, having at last steered himself into the open sea of argument. 'It's not your stomach that makes you avoid me in the Main Street.'

'Avoid you?' Martin echoed, growing red. 'When did I avoid you?'

'You did avoid me, Jack,' said Ned with a radiant smile of forgiveness. 'I saw you, and, what's more, you said it to Cronin. Mind,' he added generously, 'I'm not blaming you. It's not your fault. It's the guilt. You're pursued by guilt the way I'm pursued by a sense of duty, and they'll bring the pair of us to our graves. I can even tell you the way you'll die. You'll be up and down to the chapel ten times a day for fear once wasn't enough, with your head bowed for fear you'd catch a friend's eye and be led astray, beating your breast, lighting candles, and counting indulgences, and every time you see a priest your face will light up as if he was a pretty girl, and you'll raise your hat and say "Yes, father," and "No, father," and "Father, whatever you please." And it won't be your fault. That's the real tragedy of life, Jack – we reap what we sow.'

'I don't know what the hell is after coming over you,' Martin said in bewilderment. 'You – you're being positively personal, MacCarthy. I never tried to avoid anybody. I resent that statement. And the priests know well enough the sort I am. I never tried to conceal it.'

'I know, Jack, I know,' Ned said gently, swept away by the flood of his own melancholy rhetoric, 'and I never accused you of it. I'm not being personal, because it's not a personal matter. It's Nature working through you. It works through me as well, only it gets me in a different way. I turn every damn thing into a duty, and in the end I'm fit for nothing. And I know the way I'll die too. I'll disintegrate into a husband, a father, a schoolmaster, a local librarian, and fifteen different sort of committee officials, and none of them with justification enough to remain alive – unless I die on a barricade.'

'What barricade?' asked Martin, who found all this hard to follow.

'Any barricade,' said Ned wildly. 'I don't care what 'tis for so long as 'tis a fight. I don't want to be a messenger boy. I'm not even a good one. Here I am, arguing with you in a pub instead of doing what I was sent to do. Whatever the hell that was,' he added with a hearty laugh as he realized that for the moment – only for the moment, of course – he had forgotten what it was. 'Well, that beats everything,' he said with a grin. 'But you see what I mean. What duty does for you. I'm after forgetting what I came for.'

'Ah, that's only because it wasn't important,' said Martin, who was anxious to talk of Paris.

'That's where you're wrong again, Jack,' said Ned, really beginning to enjoy the situation. 'Maybe, 'twas of no importance to us but it was probably of great importance to Nature. It's we that aren't important. What was the damn thing? My memory has gone to hell. One moment. I have to close my eyes and empty my mind. That's the only way I have of beating it.'

He closed his eyes and lay back limply in his seat, though even through his self-induced trance he smiled lightly at the absurdity of it all.

'No good,' he said, starting out of it briskly. 'It's an extraordinary thing, the way it disappears as if the ground opened and swallowed it. And there's nothing you can do. 'Twill come back of its own accord, and there won't be rhyme nor reason to that either. I was reading an article about a German doctor who says you forget because it's too unpleasant to think about.'

'It's not a haircut?' Martin asked helpfully, but Ned, a tidy man, just shook his head.

'Or clothes?' Martin went on. 'Clothes are another great thing with them.'

'No,' Ned said frowning. 'I'm sure 'twas nothing for myself.'

'Or for the kids? Shoes or the like?'

'Something flashed across my mind just then,' murmured Ned.

'If it's not that it must be groceries.'

'I don't see how it could,' Ned said argumentatively. 'Williams delivers them every week, and they're always the same.'

'In that case,' Martin said flatly, 'it's bound to be something to eat. They're always forgetting things – bread or butter or milk.'

'I suppose so,' Ned said in bewilderment, 'but I'm damned if I know what. Jim!' he called to the barman. 'If you were sent on a message today, what would you say 'twould be?'

'Fish, Mr Mac,' the barman replied promptly. 'Every Friday.'

'Fish!' repeated Martin exultantly. 'The very thing!'

'Fish?' repeated Ned, feeling that some familiar chord had been struck. 'I suppose it could be. I know I offered to bring it to Tom Hurley, and I was having a bit of an argument with Larry Cronin about it. I remember he said he rather liked it.'

'Like it?' cried Martin. 'I can't stand the damn stuff, but the housekeeper has to have it for the kids.'

'Ah, 'tis fish, all right, Mr Mac,' the barman said knowingly. 'In an hour's time you wouldn't be able to forget it with the smell around the town.'

'Well, obviously,' Ned said, resigning himself to it, 'it has something to do with fish. It may not be exactly fish, but it's something like it.'

'Whether it is or not, she'll take it as kindly meant,' said Martin comfortingly. 'Like flowers. Women in this country seem to think they're alike.'

'It's extraordinary,' said Ned as they went out. 'We have minds we have less control of than we have of our cars. Wouldn't you think with all their modern science they'd find some way of curing a memory like that?'

Two hours later the two friends, more loquacious than ever, drove up to Ned's house for lunch. 'Mustn't forget the fish,' Ned said as he reached back in the car for it. At that moment he heard the wail of a newborn infant and went very white.

'What the hell is that, Ned?' Martin asked in alarm.

'That, Martin,' said Ned, 'is the fish, I'm afraid.'

'I won't disturb you, now, Ned,' Martin said hastily, getting out of the car. 'I'll get a snack from Tom Hurley.'

'Courage, man!' said Ned frowningly. 'Here you are and here you'll stop. But why fish, Martin? That's what I can't understand. Why did I think it was fish?'

OLD-AGE PENSIONERS

ON FRIDAY evening as I went up the sea road for my evening walk I heard the row blowing up at the other side of the big ash-tree, near the jetty. I was sorry for the sergeant, a decent poor man. When a foreign government imposed a cruel law, providing for the upkeep of all old people over seventy, it never gave a thought to the policeman who would have to deal with the consequences. You see, our post office was the only one within miles. That meant that each week we had to endure a procession of old-age pensioners from Caheragh, the lonely, rocky promontory to the west of us, inhabited – so I am told – by a strange race of people, alleged to be descendants of a Portuguese crew who were driven ashore there in days gone by. That I couldn't swear to; in fact, I never could see trace or tidings of any foreign blood in Caheragh, but I was never one for contradicting the wisdom of my ancestors. But government departments have no wisdom, ancestral or any other kind, so the Caheraghs drew their pensions with us, and the contact with what we considered civilization being an event in their lonesome lives, they usually brought their families to help in drinking them. That was what upset us. To see a foreigner drunk in our village on what we rightly considered our money was more than some of us could stand.

So Friday, as I say, was the sergeant's busy day. He had a young guard called Coleman to assist him, but Coleman had troubles of his own. He was a poet, poor fellow, and desperately in love with a publican's daughter in Coole. The girl was incapable of making up her mind about him, though her father wanted her to settle down; he told her all young men had a tendency to write poetry up to a certain age, and that even himself had done it a few times until her mother knocked it out of him. But her view was that poetry, like drink, was a thing you couldn't have knocked out of you, and that the holy all of it would be that

Coleman would ruin the business on her. Every week we used to study the *Coole Times*, looking for another poem, either a heart-broken 'Lines to D—', saying that Coleman would never see her more, or a 'Song'. 'Song' always meant they were after making it up. The sergeant had them all cut out and pasted in an album; he thought young Coleman was lost in the police.

When I was coming home the row was still on, and I went inside the wall to have a look. There were two Caheraghs: Mike Mountain and his son, Patch. Mike was as lean as a rake, a gaunt old man with mad blue eyes. Patch was an upstanding fellow but drunk to God and the world. The man who was standing up for the honour of the village was Flurry Riordan, another old-age pensioner. Flurry, as you'd expect from a bachelor of that great age, was quarrelsome and scurrilous. Fifteen years before, when he was sick and thought himself dying, the only thing troubling his mind was that a brother he had quarrelled with would profit by his death, and a neighbour had come to his cottage one morning to find Flurry fast asleep with his will written in burnt stick on the whitewashed wall over his bed.

The sergeant, a big, powerful man with a pasty face and deep pouches under his eyes, gave me a nod as I came in.

'Where's Guard Coleman from you?' I asked.

'Over in Coole with the damsel,' he replied.

Apparently the row was about a Caheragh boat that had beaten one of our boats in the previous year's regatta. You'd think a thing like that would have been forgotten, but a bachelor of seventy-six has a long memory for grievances. Sitting on the wall overlooking the jetty, shadowed by the boughs of the ash, Flurry asked with a sneer, with such wonderful sailors in Caheragh wasn't it a marvel that they couldn't sail past the Head – an unmistakable reference to the supposed Portuguese origin of the clan. Patch replied that whatever the Caheragh people sailed it wasn't bum-boats, meaning, I suppose, the pleasure boat in which Flurry took summer visitors about the bay.

'What sailors were there ever in Caheragh?' snarled Flurry. 'If they had men against them instead of who they had they wouldn't get off so easy.'

'Begor, 'tis a pity you weren't rowing yourself, Flurry,' said the sergeant gravely. 'I'd say you could still show them a few things.'

'Ten years ago I might,' said Flurry bitterly, because the sergeant had touched on another very sore subject; his being dropped from the regatta crews, a thing he put down entirely to the brother's intrigues.

'Why then, indeed,' said the sergeant, 'I'd back you still against a man half your age. Why don't you and Patch have a race now and settle it?'

'I'll race him,' shouted Patch with the greatest enthusiasm, rushing for his own boat. 'I'll show him.'

'My boat is being mended,' said Flurry shortly.

'You could borrow Sullivan's,' said the sergeant.

Flurry only looked at the ground and spat. Either he wasn't feeling energetic or the responsibility was too much for him. It would darken his last days to be beaten by a Caheragh. Patch sat in his shirt-sleeves in the boat, resting his reeling head on his oars. For a few minutes it looked as if he was out for the evening. Then he suddenly raised his face to the sky and let out the wild Caheragh war-whoop, which sounded like all the seagulls in Ireland practising unison-shrieking. The effect on Flurry was magical. At that insulting sound he leaped from the wall with an oath, pulled off his coat, and rushed to the slip to another boat. The sergeant, clumsy and heavy-footed, followed, and the pair of them sculled away to where Sullivan's boat was moored. Patch followed them with his eyes.

'What's wrong with you, you old coward?' he yelled. 'Row your own boat, you old sod, you!'

'Never mind,' said Mike Mountain from the top of the slip. 'You'll beat him, boat or no boat. . . . He'll beat him, ladies and gentlemen,' he said confidently to the little crowd that had gathered. 'Ah, Jase, he's a great man in a boat.'

'I'm a good man on a long course,' Patch shouted modestly, his eyes searching each of us in turn. 'I'm slow getting into my stroke.'

'At his age I was the same,' confided his father. 'A great bleddy man in a boat. Of course, I can't do it now – eighty-one; drawing on for it. I haven't the same energy.'

'Are you ready, you old coward?' shrieked Patch to Flurry who was fumbling savagely in the bottom of Sullivan's boat for the rowlocks.

'Shut up, you foreign importation!' snarled Flurry.

He found the rowlocks and pulled the boat round in a couple of neat strokes; then hung on his oars till the sergeant got out. For seventy-six he was still a lively man.

'Ye know the race now?' said the sergeant. 'To the island and back.'

'Round the island, sergeant,' said Mike Mountain plaintively. 'Patch is like me; he's slow to start.'

'Very good, very good,' said the sergeant. 'Round the island it is, Flurry. Are ye ready now, both of ye?'

'Ready,' grunted Flurry.

'Yahee!' shrieked Patch again, brandishing an oar over his head like a drumstick.

'Mind yourself now, Patch!' said the sergeant who seemed to be torn between his duty as an officer of the peace and his duty as umpire. 'Go! – ye whoors,' he added under his breath so that only a few of us heard him.

They did their best. It is hard enough for a man with a drop in to go straight even when he's facing his object, but it is too much altogether to expect him to do it backwards. Flurry made for the *Red Devil*, the doctor's sailing boat, and Patch, who seemed to be fascinated by the very appearance of Flurry, made for him, and the two of them got there almost simultaneously. At one moment it looked as if it would be a case of drowning, at the next of manslaughter. There was a splash, a thud, and a shout, and I saw Flurry raise his oar as if to lay out Patch. But the presence of the sergeant probably made him self-conscious, for instead he used it to push off Patch's boat.

'God Almighty!' cried Mike Mountain with an air of desperation, 'did ye ever see such a pair of misfortunate bosthoons? Round the island, God blast ye!'

But Patch, who seemed to have an absolute fixation on Flurry, interpreted this as a command to go round him, and, seeing that Flurry wasn't at all sure what direction he was going in, this wasn't as easy as it looked. He put up one really grand spurt, and had just established himself successfully across Flurry's bow when it hit him and sent him spinning like a top, knocking one oar clean out of his hand. Sullivan's old boat was no good for racing, but it was grand for anything in the nature of tank warfare, and as Flurry had by this time got into his stroke, it would have taken an Atlantic liner to stop him. Patch screamed with rage, and then managed to retrieve his oar and follow. The shock seemed to have given him new energy.

Only gradually was the sergeant's strategy beginning to reveal itself to me. The problem was to get the Caheraghs out of the village without a fight, and Flurry and Patch were spoiling for one. Anything that would exhaust the pair of them would make his job easier. It is not a method recommended in Police Regulations, but it has the distinct advantage of leaving no unseemly aftermath of summonses and cross-summonses which, if neglected, may in time turn into a regular vendetta. As a spectacle it really wasn't much. Darkness had breathed on the mirror of the water. A bonfire on the island set a pendulum reflection swinging lazily to and fro, darkening the bay at either side of it. There was a milky light over the hill of Croghan; the moon was rising.

The sergeant came up to me with his hand over his mouth and his big head a little on one side, a way he had of indicating to the world that he was speaking aside.

'I see by the paper how they're after making it up again,' he whispered anxiously. 'Isn't she a changeable little divil?'

It took me a moment or two to realize that he was referring to Coleman and the publican's daughter; I always forget that he looks on me as a fellow-artist of Coleman's.

'Poets prefer them like that,' I said.

'Is that so?' he exclaimed in surprise. 'Well, everyone to his own taste.' Then he scanned the bay thoughtfully and started suddenly. 'Who the hell is that?' he asked.

Into the pillar of smoky light from the bonfire a boat had come, and it took us a little while to identify it. It was Patch's, and there was Patch himself pulling leisurely to shore. He had given up the impossible task of going round Flurry. Some of the crowd began to shout derisively at him but he ignored them. Then Mike Mountain took off his bowler hat and addressed us in heart-broken tones.

'Stone him!' he besought us. 'For Christ's sake, ladies and gentlemen, stone him! He's no son of mine, only a walking mockery of man.'

He began to dance on the edge of the slip and shout insults at Patch who had slowed up and showed no inclination to meet him.

'What the hell do you mean by it?' shouted Mike. 'You said you'd race the man and you didn't. You shamed me before everyone. What sort of misfortunate old furniture are you?'

'But he fouled me,' Patch yelled indignantly. 'He fouled me twice.'

'He couldn't foul what was foul before,' said his father. 'I'm eighty-one, but I'm a better man than you. By God, I am.'

A few moments later Flurry's boat hove into view.

'Mike Mountain,' he shouted over his shoulder in a sobbing voice, 'have you any grandsons you'd send out against me now? Where are the great Caheragh sailors now, I'd like to know?'

'Here's one of them,' roared Mike, tearing at the lapels of his coat. 'Here's a sailor if you want one. I'm only a feeble old man, but I'm a better man in a boat than either of ye. Will you race me, Flurry? Will you race me now, I say?'

'I'll race you to hell and back,' panted Flurry contemptuously.

Mike excitedly peeled off his coat and tossed it to me. Then he took off his vest and hurled it at the sergeant. Finally he opened his braces, and, grabbing his bowler hat, he made a flying leap into his own boat and tried to seize the oars from Patch.

''Tisn't fair,' shouted Patch, wrestling with him. 'He fouled me twice.'

'Gimme them oars and less of your talk,' snarled his father.

'I don't care,' screamed Patch. 'I'll leave no man lower my spirit.'

'Get out of that boat or I'll have to deal with you officially,' said the sergeant sternly. 'Flurry,' he added, 'wouldn't you take a rest?'

'Is it to beat a Caheragh?' snarled Flurry viciously as he brought Sullivan's boat round again.

Again the sergeant gave the word and the two boats set off. This time there were no mistakes. The two old men were rowing magnificently, but it was almost impossible to see what happened then. A party of small boys jumped into another boat and set out after them.

'A pity we can't see it,' I said to the sergeant.

'It might be as well,' he grunted gloomily. 'The less witnesses the better. The end of it will be a coroner's inquest, and I'll lose my bleddy job.'

Beneath us on the slip, Patch, leaning against the slimy wall, seemed to have fallen asleep. The sergeant looked down at him greedily.

'And 'tis only dawning on me that the whole bleddy lot of them ought to be in the lock-up,' he muttered.

'Sergeant,' I said, 'you ought to be in the diplomatic service.'

He brought his right hand up to shield his mouth, and with his left elbow he gave me an agonizing dig in the ribs that nearly knocked me.

'Whisht, you divil you! Whisht, whisht, whisht!' he said.

The pendulum of firelight, growing a deeper red, swayed with the gentle motion of an old clock, and from the bay we could hear the excited voices of the boatful of boys, cheering on the two old men.

''Tis Mike,' said someone, staring out into the darkness.

''Tisn't,' said a child's voice. ''Tis Flurry. I sees his blue smock.'

It was Flurry. We were all a little disappointed. I will say for our people that whatever quarrel they may have with the Portuguese, in sport they have a really international outlook. When old Mike pulled in a few moments later he got a rousing cheer. The first to congratulate him was Flurry.

'Mike,' he shouted as he tied up Sullivan's boat, 'you're a better man than your son.'

'You fouled me,' shouted Patch.

In response to the cheer Mike rose in the rocking boat. He stood in the bow and then, recollecting his manners, took off his hat. As he removed his hand from his trousers, they fell about his scraggy knees, but he failed to perceive that.

'Ladies and gentlemen,' he said pantingly, ''twasn't a bad race. An old man didn't wet the blade of an oar these twelve months, 'twasn't a bad race at all.'

'Begod, Mike,' said Flurry, holding out his hand from the slip, 'you were a good man in your day.'

'I was, Flurry,' said Mike, taking his hand and staring up affectionately at him. 'I was a powerful man in my day, my old friend, and you were a powerful man yourself.'

It was obvious that there was going to be no fight. The crowd began to disperse in an outburst of chatter and laughter. Mike turned to us again, but only the sergeant and myself were listening to him. His voice had lost its carrying power.

'Ladies and gentlemen,' he cried, 'for an old man that saw

such hard days, 'tis no small thing. If ye knew what me and my like endured ye'd say the same. Ye never knew them, and with the help of the Almighty God ye never will. Cruel times they were, but they're all forgotten. No one remembers them, no one tells ye, the troubles of the poor man in the days gone by. Many's the wet day I rowed from dawn to dark, ladies and gentlemen; many's the bitter winter night I spent, ditching and draining, dragging down the sharp stones for my little cabin by starlight and moonlight. If ye knew it all, ye'd say I was a great man. But 'tis all forgotten, all, all, forgotten!'

Old Mike's voice had risen into a wail of the utmost poignancy. The excitement and applause had worked him up, and all the past was rising in him as in a dying man. But there was no one to hear him. The crowd drifted away up the road. Patch tossed the old man's clothes into the boat, and, sober enough now, stepped in and pushed off in silence, but his father still stood in the bow, his bowler hat in his hand, his white shirt flapping about his naked legs.

We watched him till he was out of sight, but even then I could hear his voice bursting out in sharp cries of self-pity like a voice from the dead. All the loneliness of the world was in it. A flashlight glow outlined a crest of rock at the left-hand side of the bay, and the moonlight, stealing through a barrier of cloud, let a window of brightness into the burnished water. The peace was safe for another week. I handed the sergeant a cigarette and he fell into step beside me.

'He's in the wrong job altogether,' he whispered, and again I had to pull myself together to realize the way his mind had gone on, working quietly along its own lines. ''Tis in Dublin he ought to be. There's nothing for a fellow like that in our old job. Sure, you can see for yourself.'

A THING OF NOTHING

I

NED LYNCH was a decent poor slob of a man with a fat purple face, a big black moustache like the villain in a melodrama, and a paunch. He had a brassy voice that took an effort of his whole being to reduce it by a puff, sleepy bloodshot eyes, and a big head. Katty, who was a well-mannered, convent-educated girl, thought him very old-fashioned. He said the country was going to the dogs and the land being starved to put young fellows into professions, 'educating them out of their knowledge,' he said. 'What do they want professions for?' he asked. 'Haven't they the hills and the fields – God's great, wonderful book of Nature?' He courted her in the same stiff sentimental way, full of poetic nonsense about 'your holy delicate white hands' and 'the weaker sex'.

The weaker sex indeed! You should see him if he had a head-ache. She havered for years about marrying him at all. Her family thought he was a very good catch, but Katty would have pre-ferred a professional man. At last she suggested that they should separate for a year to see whether they couldn't do better for themselves. He put on a sour puss at that, but Katty went off to business in Dublin just the same. Except for one drunken medical who borrowed money from her, she didn't meet any professional men, and after lending the medico more money than she could afford, she was glad enough to come back and marry Ned. She didn't look twenty-five, but she was thirty-nine. The day of the marriage he handed her three anonymous letters about herself and the medico.

Katty thought a lot about the anonymous letters. She thought she knew the quarter they had come from. Ned had a brother called Jerry who was a different class of man entirely. He was tall and dark and lean as a rake, with a high colour and a pair of bright-blue eyes. Twenty years before, himself and Ned had had some disagreement about politics and he had opened Ned with a poker. They hadn't spoken since, but as Jerry had two sons and only one farm, Katty saw just why it mightn't suit him that Ned and herself would marry.

She was a good wife and a good manager; a great woman to send to an auction. She was pretty and well behaved; she dressed younger than her years in short coloured frocks and wide hats that she had to hold the brim of on a windy morning. She managed to double the business inside two years. But before the first year was well out she began to see rocks ahead. First there was Ned's health. He looked a giant of a man, but his sister had died of blood pressure, and he had a childish craze for meat and pastries. You could see him outside the baker's, looking in with mournful, bloodshot eyes. He would saunter in and stroll out with a little bag of cakes behind his back, hide them under the counter, and eat them when she wasn't looking. Sometimes she came into the shop and found him with his whole face red and one cheek stuffed. She never said anything then; she was much too much a lady, but afterwards she might reproach him gently with it.

And then to crown her troubles one day Father Ring called and Ned and himself went connyshuring in the parlour. A few days later – oh, dear, she thought bitterly, the subtlety of them! – two country boys walked in. One was Con Lynch, Jerry's second son. He was tall and gawkish, with a big, pale, bony face; he walked with a pronounced stoop as if his sole amusement was watching his feet, his hands behind his back, his soft hat down the back of his neck, and the ragged ends of his trousers trailing round the big boots.

He looked at Katty and then looked away; then looked at her again and said: 'Good morra.' Katty put her hands on the counter and said with a smile: 'How d'ye do?' 'Oh, all right,' said Con, as if he thought she was presuming. Ned didn't say anything. He was behind the counter of the bar in his shirt-sleeves.

'Two bottles of stout, i' ye plaze,' said Con with a take-it-or-leave-it air, planking down the two-shilling piece he had squeezed in the palm of one hand. Ned looked at the money and then at Con. Finally he turned to the shelves and poured out three stiff glasses of Irish.

'Porter is a cold drink between relations,' he said in his kind, lazy way.

'Begor, 'tis true for you,' said Con, resting his two elbows on the counter while his whole face lit up with a roguish smile. ''Tis a thin, cold, unneighbourly Protestant sort of drink.'

After that Con and his brother Tom dropped in regularly. Tom was secretary of some political organization and, though very uncouth, able to hold his own by sheer dint of brass, but Con was uncouth without any qualification. He sat with one knee in the air and his hands locked about it as if he had sprained his ankle, or crouched forward with his hands joined between his legs in a manner that Katty would have been too lady-like to describe, and he jumped from one position to another as if a flea had bitten him. When she gave him salad for tea he handed it back to her. 'Take that away and gi' me a bit o' mate, i' ye plaze,' he said with no shyness at all. And the funny thing was that Ned, who in his old-fashioned way knew so much better, only smiled. When he was going, Ned always slipped a packet of cigarettes into his pocket, but Con always pulled them out again. 'What are thim? Faga? Chrisht! Ah, the blessings of God on you!' And then he smiled his rogue's smile, rubbed his hands vigorously, lowered his head as if he were going to butt the first man he met, and plunged out into the street.

It was easy to see how the plot was developing. She was a year married and no child!

II

One day a few weeks later Katty heard a scuffle. She looked out the shop window and saw Jerry with the two boys holding him by the arms while he let on to be trying to break free of them.

'Come on, come on, and don't be making a show of us!' said Tom angrily.

'I don't give a Christ in hell,' cried his father in a shrill tremolo, his wild blue eyes sweeping the sunlit street in every direction except the shop. 'I'll go where I'm asked.'

'You'll go where you're told,' said Con with great glee – clearly he thought his father was a great card. 'Come on, you ould whore you, come on!'

Ned heard the scuffle and leaned over the counter to see what it was. He gave no sign of being moved by it. There was a sort of monumental dignity about Ned, about the slowness of his thoughts, the depth of his sentiment, and the sheer volume of his voice, which enabled him to time a scene with the certainty of an old stage hand. He lifted the flap of the counter and moved slowly out into the centre of the shop and then stopped and held out his hand. That, by the way, did it. Jerry gave a whinny like a young colt and sprang to take the proffered hand. They stood like that for a full minute, moryah they were too overcome to speak! Katty watched them with a bitter little smile.

'You know the fair lady of my choice,' said Ned at last.

'I'm very glad to meet you, ma'am,' said Jerry, turning his knife-blue eyes on her, his dropped chin and his high, small perfect teeth making it sound like the greeting of a well-bred weasel to a rabbit. They all retired to the back parlour, where Katty brought the drinks. The atmosphere was maudlin. After arranging for Katty and himself to spend the next Sunday at the farm, Ned escorted them down the street. When he came back there were tears in his eyes – a foolish man!

'Well,' he said, standing in the middle of the shop with his hands behind his back and his bowler hat well down over his eyes, ''twas nice being all under the one roof again.'

'It must have been grand,' said Katty, affecting to be very busy. 'I suppose 'twas Father Ring did it,' she added over her shoulder with subtle mockery.

'Ah,' said Ned, looking stolidly out at the sunlit street with swimming eyes, 'we're getting older and wiser. What fools people are to embitter their lives about nothing! There won't be much politics where we're going.'

'I wonder if 'tis that,' said Katty, as if she were talking to herself while inwardly she fumed at the stupidity of the man.

'Ah, what else could it be?' asked Ned, wrapped up in whatever sentimental fantasies he was weaving.

'I suppose 'twould never be policy?' she asked archly, looking up from under her brows with a knowing smile.

'How could it be policy, woman?' asked Ned, his voice harsh with indignation. 'What has he to gain by policy?'

'Ah, how would I know?' she said, reaching towards a high shelf. 'He might be thinking of the shop for Con.'

'He'd be thinking a very long way ahead,' said Ned after a pause, but she saw it had gone home.

'Maybe he's hoping 'twouldn't be so long,' she said smoothly.
'How's that?' said Ned.

'Julia, God rest her, went very suddenly,' said Katty.

'He'd be a very foolish man to count on me doing the same,' boomed Ned, but his face grew purple from shame and anger – shame that he had no children of his own, anger that she had pricked the sentimental bubble he had blown about Jerry and the boys.

It was a warning to Katty. Twice in the next year she satisfied herself that she was having a baby, and each time put the whole house into confusion. She lay upstairs on the sofa with a handbell at her side, made baby clothes, ordered the cradle, even got an option on a pram. To secure herself against accidents she slept in the spare room. And then it passed off and with a look like murder she returned to the big bedroom. Ned stared at her over the bedclothes with an incredulous, long-suffering air and then heaved a heavy sigh and turned in.

She knew he blamed her. After being taken in like that it would be weeks before he started again. Weaker sex, indeed! One would think it was he that was trying to start the baby. But Katty blamed herself as well. It was the final year in Dublin and the goings-on with the drunken medico that had finished her. For days on end she sat over the range in the kitchen with a little shawl over her shoulders, shivering and tight-lipped, taking little tots of brandy when Ned's back was turned and complaining of him to the servant girl. To make it worse, the daughter of another shopkeeper came home on holidays from England; a nurse with fast, flighty ways that appealed to Ned. He was always in and out there, full of old-fashioned gallantries. He kissed her hand and even called her 'a rose'. It reached Katty's ears and she clamped her lips. She was far too well bred to make vulgar scenes. Instead, with her feet on the fender, hands joined in her lap, she asked in the most casual friendly way:

'Ned, do you think that was a proper remark to make to the Dunne girl?'

'What remark?' asked Ned, growing crimson – it showed his guilty conscience.

'Well, Ned, you can hardly pretend you don't know, considering that the whole town is talking about it.'

'Are you mad, woman?' he shouted, his voice brassy with rage.

'I only asked a simple question, Ned,' she said with resigna-
tion, fixing him with her clear blue eyes. 'Of course, if you prefer
not to answer there's no more to be said.'

'You have me driven distracted!' cried Ned. 'I can't be polite
to a neighbour's daughter but you sulk for days on me.'

'Polite!' said Katty to the range. 'However,' she added, 'I sup-
pose I have no cause to complain. The man that would do worse
to me wouldn't be put out by a little thing like that.'

'Do worse to you?' shouted Ned, going purple as if he was in
danger of congestion. 'What did I ever do to you?'

'Aren't you planning to leave me in my old age without a roof
over my head?' she asked suddenly, turning on him.

'I'm not planning to leave anything to anyone yet,' roared
Ned. 'With the help of the Almighty God, when I do 'twill be
to a child of my own.'

'Indeed, I hope so,' said Katty, 'but after all, if the worst came
to the worst –'

'If the worst came to the worst,' he interrupted solemnly, 'we
don't know which of us the Lord – glory and praise to His holy
name – might take first.'

'Amen, O Lord,' breathed Katty piously, and then went on in
her original tone. 'I'm not saying you'll be the first to go, and
the way I am, Ned,' she added bitterly, 'I wouldn't wish it. But
'tis only common prudence to be prepared for the worst. You
know yourself how Julia went.'

'My God,' he said mournfully, addressing his remarks out the
empty hall, 'the foolishness of it! We have only a few short years
on the earth; we come and go like the leaves of the trees, and
instead of enjoying ourselves, we wear our hearts out with plan-
ning and contriving.'

'Ah, Ned,' she said, goaded to fury, as she always was by his
philosophizing and poetry talk, ''tis easy it comes to you. I only
wish the money would come as easy. I didn't work myself to the
bone in the shop to be left a beggar in my old age.'

'A beggar?' he cried. 'Do you think I wouldn't provide for
you?'

'Provide for me?' she gibed. 'Con Lynch in the shop and me
in the back room! Fine provisions I'd get!'

'I never said I'd leave it to Con Lynch,' said Ned chokingly.

'Then what is he coming here for?' she shrieked, suddenly

bounding into the middle of the kitchen and spreading out her arms. 'What is he doing in my home? Can't you do what any other man would do and let them know you're leaving the shop to me?'

'I can't,' he shouted back, 'and you know I can't.'

'Why not?' she said, stamping.

'Because 'tis an old custom. The property goes with the name.'

'Not with the people I was brought up with,' she said proudly.

'Well, 'twas with those I was brought up with,' said Ned. 'Women as good as you were satisfied. Ay, and better than you! Better than you,' he added with a backward glance as he went out.

She dropped back beaten into her chair. She was afraid to cross him further. He looked like a man that might drop dead at any moment. She was only a stranger, a foreigner, with no link at all between herself and him. Con Lynch was more to him now than she was. It was only then she realized it was time to stop looking after the shop and look after herself instead.

In the autumn she said she was going to Dublin to see a specialist. Ned didn't say anything to dissuade her, but it was clear he had no faith in it. She didn't see a specialist. Instead she saw a nurse she had known in Dublin, another old flame of the medico's. Nurse O'Mara kept a maternity home on the canal. She was a tall, handsome woman with a fine figure and a long face that was growing just the least shade hard. She listened to Katty with screwed-up eyes and a good-natured smile. She was tickled by the situation. After all, if she hadn't got much out of the medico, Katty hadn't got much more.

'And you don't think that 'tis any use?' asked Katty doubtfully.

'I wouldn't say so,' said the nurse.

'And I suppose there's nothing else I can do?' asked Katty in a low voice and an almost playful tone, never taking her blue eyes from the nurse's face.

'Unless you'd borrow one,' said the nurse mockingly.

'That's what I mean,' said Katty slyly.

'You're not serious?' said the nurse, her smile withering.

'Haven't I reason?' asked Katty, her smile growing broader.

'You'd never get away with it.'

'Why not, girl?' asked Katty almost inaudibly. 'Who's to know? If there was someone that was willing.' '

'Oh, hundreds of them,' said the nurse, with the bitterness of the childless woman.

'You'd know where to find one I could ask,' murmured Katty, still with her eyes steadily fixed.

'I suppose so,' said the nurse doubtfully. 'There's nothing illegal about it. I'm not supposed to know what you're up to.'

'And to have my letters addressed to your place,' continued Katty.

'Why not?' asked Nurse O'Mara with a shrug. 'For that matter, you can come and stay any time you like.'

'That's all I want,' said Katty with blazing eyes. 'I have a hundred or so put on one side. I'll give it to you, and you can make whatever arrangements you like.'

She returned to town triumphant with two new hats, wider and more girlish than those she usually wore. Then she set about a reorganization of the house, running up and down stairs and chattering with the maid.

'Well?' said Ned lazily, interpreting her behaviour with a touch of anxiety. 'He gave you some hope?'

'I don't know if you'd call it hope,' said Katty, furrowing her brow. 'He thought I mightn't come out of it. Of course, I'll have to go back to him if anything happens.'

'But he thought it might?' asked Ned.

'Wisha,' said Katty, 'like the rest of them he wouldn't like to give an opinion.'

That, she saw, impressed Ned more than any more favourable verdict could have done. Almost from that on, he looked at her every morning with a solicitous, questioning air. Katty kept her mouth shut and went on with the housework. One night she said with her nunlike air: 'I think I'll sleep in the spare room for the present.' Even then she could see he only half believed her, but as the weeks passed, he started coming up to her in the evenings, settling the fire, and retailing whatever gobbets of gossip he had picked up in the bar. He started to tell her about his own boyhood, a thing he had never done before.

Jerry called once with Con and was brought upstairs with appropriate solemnity. She knew he had only come to see for himself, and she watched while the electric-blue eyes roved distractedly about the room till they alighted like a bluebottle on her stomach. That settled it so far as Jerry was concerned. He was crafty but not long-sighted. When the game looked like going against him he threw in his hand. He didn't come back, nor did Tom, though Con dropped in once or twice out of pure good nature. To Katty's surprise, Ned noticed and resented it.

'Ah,' she said charitably, 'I wouldn't mind that. They're probably busy on the farm this weather.'

'They weren't so busy they couldn't go to Hartnett's,' said Ned, who made it his business to know all they did.

'Ah, well, Hartnett's is near enough to them,' said Katty, protesting against his unreasonableness.

'This place was near enough to them too when they thought they had a chance of the money,' said Ned resentfully.

She looked at him archly from under her brows. She felt the time was ripe to say what she had to say.

'They didn't send you any more anonymous letters?' she asked lightly.

'They can say what they like now,' said Ned, growing red.

Her smile faded as she watched him go out of the room. She knew now she had made herself secure against any suspicions the Lynches might have of her, but the change in Ned himself was something she hadn't allowed for and it upset her.

It even frightened her the day she was setting out for Dublin. She saw him in the bedroom packing a little case.

'What do you want that for?' she asked, going cold.

'You don't think I'm going to let you go to Dublin alone?' he replied.

'But I may be there for weeks,' she said despairingly.

'Ah, well,' he said as he continued to pack, 'I'm due a little holiday. I have it fixed up with Bridie.'

Katty sat on the bed and bit her lip. Somehow or other the Lynches had succeeded in instilling their suspicions into him and he was coming to see for himself. What could she do? Nothing. She knew O'Mara wouldn't be a party to any deception; it would be too much of a risk. 'Mother of God, direct me!' she prayed, joining her hands in her lap.

'You're not afraid I'll run off with a soldier?' she asked lightly.

'That's the very thing I am afraid of,' said Ned, turning round on her. Suddenly his eyes clouded with emotion. 'It won't be wishing to anyone that tries to get you,' he added, with a feeble attempt to keep up the joke.

'Wisha, Ned,' she cried, rushing across the room to him, her heart suddenly lightened of a load, ''tisn't the way you think anything will happen to me?'

'No, little girl,' he said, putting his arm about her. 'Nor I wouldn't wish it for a thousand pounds.'

'Ah, is it a fine strong woman like me?' she cried skittishly, almost insane with relief. 'What fear there is of me! Maybe I'll let you come up when the next one is arriving.'

III

From Kingsbridge she took a taxi to the maternity home and got rid of some of her padding on the way. O'Mara opened the door for her herself. Katty sat on the edge of a sofa by the window, her hands joined in her lap, and looked expectantly up at the nurse.

'Well,' she asked in a low voice, 'any luck?'

'You'd better not try this game on too often,' said O'Mara with amusement. 'You'd never get past me with that complexion.'

'I'm not likely to try, am I?' asked Katty complacently. 'That girl you wrote about,' she added in the same conspiratorial tone, 'is she still here?'

'She is. You can see her now.'

'I suppose you don't know anything about her?' Katty asked wistfully.

'She's a school-teacher,' replied the nurse cautiously.

'Oh, Law!' said Katty in surprise. She hadn't expected anyone of her own class; it sounded too good to be true; and as plain as if it were written there, her pinched little face registered the doubt whether there wasn't a catch in it somewhere. 'I don't know her by any chance, do I ?' she added innocently.

'I hope not,' replied the nurse smoothly. 'What you don't know won't harm you.'

'Oh, I'm not asking for information,' protested Katty a shade too eagerly. 'But you think she'll agree?' she said, dropping her voice again.

'She'll be a fool if she doesn't.'

'Of course, I'll pay her well,' said Katty. 'I wouldn't ask anyone to do a thing like that for nothing.'

'I wouldn't mention that, if I was you,' said O'Mara dryly. 'She's not trying to make a profit on it.'

'Oh,' said Katty, suddenly beginning to shiver all over, 'I'd give all I ever had in the world to be out of it.'

'But why?' asked O'Mara in surprise. 'You're over the worst of it now.'

'It's Ned,' said Katty with a haggard look. 'He'd murder me.'

'Ah, well,' said O'Mara with gruff kindness, 'it's a bit late in the day to be thinking of that,' and she led Katty up the stairs past a big Venetian window that lit the well and overlooked the canal bank. The lights were already lit outside. Through the trees she saw brown-red houses with flights of steps leading to hall doors, and a hump-backed limestone bridge.

There was a girl in bed in the room they entered; a young woman of twenty-eight or thirty with a plump pale face and a helmet of limp brown hair. Her face at any rate was innocent enough.

'This is the lady I was speaking about, Monica,' said the nurse with a crooked smile. (Obviously she took a certain malicious pleasure in the whole business.) 'I'll leave ye to discuss it for a while.'

She went out, switching on the electric light as she did. Katty shook hands with the girl and then glanced shyly at the cot.

'Oh, isn't he lovely?' she cried with genuine admiration.

'He's sweet,' said the girl called Monica, in a curiously common voice, and then reached out for a cigarette.

'I never smoke, thanks,' said Katty, and then hastily drew a chair over to the bed, resting her hands on her lap and smiling under her big hat in a guilty, schoolgirl way that was curiously attractive.

'I suppose,' she said, throwing back her head, 'you must think I'm simply terrible?'

It wasn't intended to be a good opening but it turned out that way. The girl smiled, and her broad face crinkled.

'And what about me?' she asked, putting them both at once on a common level. 'Will you get away with it though?'

'Oh, I'll have to get away with it, girl,' said Katty flatly. 'My livelihood depends on it. Did nurse tell you?'

'She did, but I still don't understand what you did to your husband to make him do that to you.'

'Oh, that's an old custom,' said Katty eagerly, seeing at once the doubt in the girl's mind. 'Now, I know what you're thinking,' she added with a smile, raising her finger in warning, 'but 'tisn't that at all. Ned isn't a bit like that. I won't wrong him. He is a country boy, and he hasn't the education, but apart from that he's the best poor slob that ever lived.' She was surprised herself at the warmth that crept into her voice when she spoke of him. 'So you see,' she added, dropping her voice and smiling discreetly, 'you needn't be a bit afraid of us. We'd both be mad about him.'

'Strange as it may seem,' said Monica, her voice growing sullen and resentful, 'I'm a bit mad about him myself.'

'Oh, you are, to be sure,' said Katty warmly. 'What other way would you be?' At the same time she was bitterly disappointed. She began to realize that it wasn't going to be so easy after all. Worse than that, she had taken a real fancy to the baby. The mother, whatever her faults, was beautiful; she was an educated woman; you could see she wasn't common. 'Of course,' she added, shaking her head, 'the idea would never have crossed my mind only that nurse thought you might be willing. And then, I felt it was like God's doing. . . . You are one of us, I suppose?' she asked, raising her brows discreetly.

'God alone knows what I am,' said the girl, taking a deep pull of the cigarette. 'A bloody atheist or something.'

'Oh, how could you?' asked Katty in a shocked tone. 'You're convent-educated, aren't you?'

'Mm.'

'I'd know a convent girl anywhere,' said Katty, shaking her head with an admiring smile. 'You can always tell. I went to the Ursulines myself. But you see what I mean? There was I looking for a child to adopt, and you looking for a home for yours, and Nurse O'Mara bringing us together. It seemed like God's doing.'

'I don't know what you want bringing God into it for,' said Monica impatiently. 'The devil would do as well.'

'Ah,' said Katty with a knowing smile, 'that's only because you're feeling weak. . . . But tell me,' she added, still wondering whether there wasn't a catch in it, 'I'm not being curious or anything – but isn't it a wonder the priest wouldn't make him marry you?'

'Who told you he wouldn't marry me?' asked Monica quietly.

'Oh, Law!' cried Katty, feeling that this was probably the catch. 'Was it the way he was beneath you?' she asked with the least shade of disappointment.

'Not that I know of,' said Monica brassily. Then she turned her eyes to the ceiling and blew out another cloud of smoke. 'He asked me was I sure he was the father,' she added lightly, almost as if it amused her.

'Fancy that!' said Katty in bewilderment. 'But what made him say that, I wonder.'

'It seems,' said Monica in the same tone, 'he thought I was going with another fellow at the same time.'

'And you weren't?' said Katty knowingly.

'Not exactly,' said Monica dryly, giving Katty a queer look that she didn't quite understand.

'And you wouldn't marry him?' said Katty, knowing perfectly well that the girl was only trying to take advantage of her simplicity. Katty wasn't as big a fool as that though. 'Hadn't you great courage?' she added.

'Oh, great,' said Monica in the same ironic tone.

'The dear knows,' said Katty regretfully, thinking of her own troubles with the medico, 'they're a handful, the best of them! But are you sure you're not being hasty?' she added with girlish coyness, cocking her little head. 'Don't you think when you meet him again and he sees the baby, ye might make it up?'

'If I thought that,' said the girl deliberately, 'I'd walk out of this into the canal, and the kid along with me.'

'Oh, Law!' said Katty, feeling rather out of her depth and the least bit frightened. At the same time she now wanted the baby with something like passion. It was the same sort of thing she sometimes felt at auctions for little gewgaws from women's dressing-tables or bits of old china; as if she couldn't live without it. No other child would ever satisfy her. She'd bid up to the last farthing for it – if only she knew what to bid.

Then Nurse O'Mara came back and leaned on the end of the bed, her knees bent and her hands clasped.

'Well,' she asked, looking from one to the other with a mocking smile, 'how did ye get on?'

'Oh, grand, nurse,' said Katty with sudden gaiety. 'We were only waiting for yourself to advise us.'

'Why?' asked the nurse. 'What is there between ye?'

'Only that I don't want to part with him,' said Monica steadily.

'Aren't you tired of him yet?' asked the nurse ironically.

'Jesus, woman, be a bit human!' said Monica with exasperation. 'He's all I have and I had trouble enough having him.'

'That's nothing to the trouble you'll have keeping him,' said the nurse.

'I know that well enough,' said Monica in a more reasonable tone, 'but I want to be able to see him. I want to know that he's well and happy.'

'Oh, if that's all that's troubling you,' said Katty eagerly, 'you can see him as much as you like at our place.'

'She could not,' said the nurse angrily. 'The less the pair of you see of one another, the better for both. . . . Listen, Mon,' she said pleadingly, 'I don't care what you do. I'm only speaking for your good.'

'I know that, Peggy,' said Monica.

'I know you think you're going to do marvels for that kid, but you're not. I know the sort of places they're brought up in and the sort that bring them up – the ones that live. I tell you, after the first time, you wouldn't be so keen on seeing him again.'

Monica was staring at the window, which had faded in the pale glare of the electric light. There was silence for a few moments. Katty heard the night wind whistling across the rooftops from the bay. The trees along the canal heard it too and sighed. Something about it impressed her; the wind, and the women's voices, and the sleeping baby, and the heart contracted inside her as she thought of Ned, waiting at home. She pulled herself together with fictitious brightness.

'Now, nurse,' she said firmly, 'it isn't fair to push the young lady too hard. We'll give her till tomorrow night, and I'll say a prayer to Our Lady of Good Counsel to direct her.'

'I'll give her all the good counsel she wants,' said the nurse coarsely. If you're thinking of yourself, Monica, you might as well say no now. We won't have to look far for someone else. If you're thinking of the kid and want to give him a fair chance in life after bringing him into it, you'd better say yes while you have the chance.'

Monica suddenly turned her face away, her eyes filling with tears.

'She can have him,' she said in a dull voice.

'Oh, thank you, thank you,' said Katty eagerly. 'And I give you my word you'll never have cause to regret it.'

'But for Christ's sake don't leave him in the room with me tonight,' cried the girl, leaping up in bed and turning her wild eyes on Nurse O'Mara. 'I'm warning ye now, don't leave him where I can lay my hands on him. I tell ye I won't be responsible.'

Katty bit her lip and her face went white.

'There's supper waiting for you downstairs,' said the nurse, beckoning her to go.

'You're sure I couldn't be of any assistance?' whispered Katty.

'Certain,' said the nurse dryly.

As Katty turned to look back, the girl threw herself down again, holding her head in her hands. The nurse from the end of the bed looked at her with a half-mocking, half-pitying smile, the smile of a childless woman. The baby was still asleep.

NEWS FOR THE CHURCH

WHEN FATHER Cassidy drew back the shutter of the confessional he was a little surprised at the appearance of the girl at the other side of the grille. It was dark in the box but he could see she was young, of medium height and build, with a face that was full of animation and charm. What struck him most was the long pale slightly freckled cheeks, pinned high up behind the grey-blue eyes, giving them a curiously Oriental slant.

She wasn't a girl from the town, for he knew most of these by sight and many of them by something more, being notoriously an easy-going confessor. The other priests said that one of these days he'd give up hearing confessions altogether on the ground that there was no such thing as sin and that even if there was it didn't matter. This was part and parcel of his exceedingly angular character, for though he was kind enough to individual sinners, his mind was full of obscure abstract hatreds. He hated England; he hated the Irish government, and he particularly hated the middle classes, though so far as anyone knew none of them had ever done him the least bit of harm. He was a heavy-built man, slow-moving and slow-thinking with no neck and a Punchinello chin, a sour wine-coloured face, pouting crimson lips, and small blue hot-tempered eyes.

'Well, my child,' he grunted in a slow and mournful voice that sounded for all the world as if he had pebbles in his mouth, 'how long is it since your last confession?'

'A week, father,' she replied in a clear firm voice. It surprised him a little, for though she didn't look like one of the tough shots, neither did she look like the sort of girl who goes to Confession every week. But with women you could never tell. They were all contrary, saints and sinners.

'And what sins did you commit since then?' he asked encouragingly.

'I told lies, father.'

'Anything else?'

'I used bad language, father.'

'I'm surprised at you,' he said with mock seriousness. 'An educated girl with the whole of the English language at your disposal! What sort of bad language?'

'I used the Holy Name, father.'

'Ach,' he said with a frown, 'you ought to know better than that. There's no great harm in damning and blasting but blasphemy is a different thing. To tell you the truth,' he added, being a man of great natural honesty, 'there isn't much harm in using the Holy Name either. Most of the time there's no intentional blasphemy but at the same time it coarsens the character. It's all the little temptations we don't indulge in that give us true refinement. Anything else?'

'I was tight, father.'

'Hm,' he grunted. This was rather more the sort of girl he had imagined her to be; plenty of devilment but no real badness. He liked her bold and candid manner. There was no hedging or false modesty about her as about most of his women penitents. 'When you say you were "tight" do you mean you were just merry or what?'

'Well, I mean I passed out,' she replied candidly with a shrug.

'I don't call that "tight", you know,' he said sternly. 'I call that beastly drunk. Are you often tight?'

'I'm a teacher in a convent school so I don't get much chance,' she replied ruefully.

'In a convent school?' he echoed with new interest. Convent schools and nuns were another of his phobias; he said they were turning the women of the country into imbeciles. 'Are you on holidays now?'

'Yes. I'm on my way home.'

'You don't live here then?'

'No, down the country.'

'And is it the convent that drives you to drink?' he asked with an air of unshakable gravity.

'Well,' she replied archly, 'you know what nuns are.'

'I do,' he agreed in a mournful voice while he smiled at her through the grille. 'Do you drink with your parents' knowledge?' he added anxiously.

'Oh, yes. Mummy is dead but Daddy doesn't mind. He lets us take a drink with him.'

'Does he do that on principle or because he's afraid of you?' the priest asked dryly.

'Ah, I suppose a little of both,' she answered gaily, responding to his queer dry humour. It wasn't often that women did, and he began to like this one a lot.

'Is your mother long dead?' he asked sympathetically.

'Seven years,' she replied, and he realized that she couldn't have been much more than a child at the time and had grown up without a mother's advice and care. Having worshipped his own mother, he was always sorry for people like that.

'Mind you,' he said paternally, his hands joined on his fat belly, 'I don't want you to think there's any harm in a drop of drink. I take it myself. But I wouldn't make a habit of it if I were you. You see, it's all very well for old jossers like me that have the worst of their temptations behind them, but yours are all ahead and drink is a thing that grows on you. You need never be afraid of going wrong if you remember that your mother may be watching you from Heaven.'

'Thanks, father,' she said, and he saw at once that his gruff appeal had touched some deep and genuine spring of feeling in her. 'I'll cut it out altogether.'

'You know, I think I would,' he said gravely, letting his eyes rest on her for a moment. 'You're an intelligent girl. You can get all the excitement you want out of life without that. What else?'

'I had bad thoughts, father.'

'Ach,' he said regretfully, 'we all have them. Did you indulge them?'

'Yes, father.'

'Have you a boy?'

'Not a regular: just a couple of fellows hanging round.'

'Ah, that's worse than none at all,' he said crossly. 'You ought to have a boy of your own. I know there's old cranks that will tell you different, but sure, that's plain foolishness. Those things are only fancies, and the best cure for them is something real. Anything else?'

There was a moment's hesitation before she replied but it was enough to prepare him for what was coming.

'I had carnal intercourse with a man, father,' she said quietly and deliberately.

'You what?' he cried, turning on her incredulously. 'You had carnal intercourse with a man? At your age?'

'I know,' she said with a look of distress. 'It's awful.'

'It is awful,' he replied slowly and solemnly. 'And how often did it take place?'

'Once, father – I mean twice, but on the same occasion.'

'Was it a married man?' he asked, frowning.

'No, father, single. At least I think he was single,' she added with sudden doubt.

'You had carnal intercourse with a man,' he said accusingly, 'and you don't know if he was married or single!'

'I assumed he was single,' she said with real distress. 'He was the last time I met him but, of course, that was five years ago.'

'Five years ago? But you must have been only a child then.'

'That's all, of course,' she admitted. 'He was courting my sister, Kate, but she wouldn't have him. She was running round with her present husband at the time and she only kept him on a string for amusement. I knew that and I hated her because he was always so nice to me. He was the only one that came to the house who treated me like a grown-up. But I was only fourteen and I suppose he thought I was too young for him.'

'And were you?' Father Cassidy asked ironically. For some reason he had the idea that this young lady had no proper idea of the enormity of her sin and he didn't like it.

'I suppose so,' she replied modestly. 'But I used to feel awful, being sent up to bed and leaving him downstairs with Kate when I knew she didn't care for him. And then when I met him again the whole thing came back. I sort of went all soft inside. It's never the same with another fellow as it is with the first fellow you fall for. It's exactly as if he had some sort of hold over you.'

'If you were fourteen at the time,' said Father Cassidy, setting aside the obvious invitation to discuss the power of first love, 'you're only nineteen now.'

'That's all.'

'And do you know,' he went on broodingly, 'that unless you can break yourself of this terrible vice once and for all it'll go on like that till you're fifty?'

'I suppose so,' she said doubtfully, but he saw that she didn't suppose anything of the kind.

'You suppose so!' he snorted angrily. 'I'm telling you so. And what's more,' he went on, speaking with all the earnestness at his command, 'it won't be just one man but dozens of men, and it won't be decent men but whatever low-class pups you can find who'll take advantage of you – the same horrible, mortal sin, week in week out till you're an old woman.'

'Ah, still, I don't know,' she said eagerly, hunching her shoulders ingratiatingly, 'I think people do it as much from curiosity as anything else.'

'Curiosity?' he repeated in bewilderment.

'Ah, you know what I mean,' she said with a touch of impatience. 'People make such a mystery of it!'

'And what do you think they should do?' he asked ironically. 'Publish it in the papers?'

'Well, God knows, 'twould be better than the way some of them go on,' she said in a rush. 'Take my sister, Kate, for instance. I admit she's a couple of years older than me and she brought me up and all the rest of it, but in spite of that we were always good friends. She showed me her love letters and I showed her mine. I mean, we discussed things as equals, but ever since that girl got married you'd hardly recognize her. She talks to no one only other married women, and they get in a huddle in a corner and whisper, whisper, whisper, and the moment you come into the room they begin to talk about the weather, exactly as if you were a blooming kid! I mean you can't help feeling 'tis something extraordinary.'

'Don't you try and tell me anything about immorality,' said Father Cassidy angrily. 'I know all about it already. It may begin as curiosity but it ends as debauchery. There's no vice you could think of that gets a grip on you quicker and degrades you worse, and don't you make any mistake about it, young woman! Did this man say anything about marrying you?'

'I don't think so,' she replied thoughtfully, 'but of course that doesn't mean anything. He's an airy, lighthearted sort of fellow and it mightn't occur to him.'

'I never supposed it would,' said Father Cassidy grimly. 'Is he in a position to marry?'

'I suppose he must be since he wanted to marry Kate,' she replied with fading interest.

'And is your father the sort of man that can be trusted to talk to him?'

'Daddy?' she exclaimed aghast. 'But I don't want Daddy brought into it.'

'What you want, young woman,' said Father Cassidy with sudden exasperation, 'is beside the point. Are you prepared to talk to this man yourself?'

'I suppose so,' she said with a wondering smile. 'But about what?'

'About what?' repeated the priest angrily. 'About the little matter he so conveniently overlooked, of course.'

'You mean ask him to marry me?' she cried incredulously. 'But I don't want to marry him.'

Father Cassidy paused for a moment and looked at her anxiously through the grille. It was growing dark inside the church, and for one horrible moment he had the feeling that somebody was playing an elaborate and most tasteless joke on him.

'Do you mind telling me,' he inquired politely, 'am I mad or are you?'

'But I mean it, father,' she said eagerly. 'It's all over and done with now. It's something I used to dream about, and it was grand, but you can't do a thing like that a second time.'

'You can't what?' he asked sternly.

'I mean, I suppose you can, really,' she said, waving her piously joined hands at him as if she were handcuffed, 'but you can't get back the magic of it. Terry is lighthearted and good-natured, but I couldn't live with him. He's completely irresponsible.'

'And what do you think you are?' cried Father Cassidy, at the end of his patience. 'Have you thought of all the dangers you're running, girl? If you have a child who'll give you work? If you have to leave this country to earn a living what's going to become of you? I tell you it's your bounden duty to marry this man if he can be got to marry you – which, let me tell you,' he added with a toss of his great head, 'I very much doubt.'

'To tell you the truth I doubt it myself,' she replied with a shrug that fully expressed her feelings about Terry and nearly drove Father Cassidy insane. He looked at her for a moment or two and then an incredible idea began to dawn on his bothered old brain. He sighed and covered his face with his hand.

'Tell me,' he asked in a faraway voice, 'when did this take place?'

'Last night, father,' she said gently, almost as if she were glad to see him come to his senses again.

'My God,' he thought despairingly, 'I was right!'

'In town, was it?' he went on.

'Yes, father. We met on the train coming down.'

'And where is he now?'

'He went home this morning, father.'

'Why didn't you do the same?'

'I don't know, father,' she replied doubtfully as though the question had now only struck herself for the first time.

'Why didn't you go home this morning?' he repeated angrily. 'What were you doing round town all day?'

'I suppose I was walking,' she replied uncertainly.

'And of course you didn't tell anyone?'

'I hadn't anyone to tell,' she said plaintively. 'Anyway,' she added with a shrug, 'it's not the sort of thing you can tell people.'

'No, of course,' said Father Cassidy. 'Only a priest,' he added grimly to himself. He saw now how he had been taken in. This little trollop, wandering about town in a daze of bliss, had to tell someone her secret, and he, a good-natured old fool of sixty, had allowed her to use him as a confidant. A philosopher of sixty letting Eve, aged nineteen, tell him all about the apple! He could never live it down.

Then the fighting blood of the Cassidys began to warm in him. Oh, couldn't he, though? He had never tasted the apple himself, but he knew a few things about apples in general and that apple in particular that little Miss Eve wouldn't learn in a whole lifetime of apple-eating. Theory might have its drawbacks but there were times when it was better than practice. 'All right, my lass,' he thought grimly, 'we'll see which of us knows most!'

In a casual tone he began to ask her questions. They were rather intimate questions, such as a doctor or priest may ask, and, feeling broad-minded and worldly wise in her new experience, she answered courageously and straightforwardly, trying to suppress all signs of her embarrassment. It emerged only once or twice, in a brief pause before she replied. He stole a furtive look at her to see how she was taking it, and once more he couldn't withhold his admiration. But she couldn't keep it up. First she grew uncomfortable and then alarmed, frowning and shaking herself in her clothes as if something were biting her. He grew graver and more personal. She didn't see his purpose; she only saw that he was stripping off veil after veil of romance, leaving her with nothing but a cold, sordid, cynical adventure like a bit of greasy meat on a plate.

'And what did he do next?' he asked.

'Ah,' she said in disgust, 'I didn't notice.'

'You didn't notice!' he repeated ironically.

'But does it make any difference?' she burst out despairingly, trying to pull the few shreds of illusion she had left more tightly about her.

'I presume you thought so when you came to confess it,' he replied sternly.

'But you're making it sound so beastly!' she wailed.

'And wasn't it?' he whispered, bending closer, lips pursed and brows raised. He had her now, he knew.

'Ah, it wasn't, father,' she said earnestly. 'Honest to God it wasn't. At least at the time I didn't think it was.'

'No,' he said grimly, 'you thought it was a nice little story to run and tell your sister. You won't be in such a hurry to tell her now. Say an Act of Contrition.'

She said it.

'And for your penance say three Our Fathers and three Hail Marys.'

He knew that was hitting below the belt, but he couldn't resist the parting shot of a penance such as he might have given a child. He knew it would rankle in that fanciful little head of hers when all his other warnings were forgotten. Then he drew the shutter and didn't open the farther one. There was a noisy woman behind, groaning in an excess of contrition. The mere volume of sound told him it was drink. He felt he needed a breath of fresh air.

He went down the aisle creakily on his heavy policeman's feet and in the dusk walked up and down the path before the presbytery, head bowed, hands behind his back. He saw the girl come out and descend the steps under the massive fluted columns of the portico, a tiny, limp, dejected figure. As she reached the pavement she pulled herself together with a jaunty twitch of her shoulders and then collapsed again. The city lights went on and made globes of coloured light in the mist.

As he returned to the church he suddenly began to chuckle, a fat good-natured chuckle, and as he passed the statue of St Anne, patron of marriageable girls, he almost found himself giving her a wink.

THE MAD LOMASNEYS

NED LOWRY and Rita Lomasney had, one might say, been lovers from childhood. The first time they had met was when he was fourteen and she a year or two younger. It was on the North Mall on a Saturday afternoon, and she was sitting on a bench under the trees; a tall, bony string of a girl with a long, obstinate jaw. Ned was a studious young fellow in a blue and white college cap, thin, pale and spectacled. As he passed he looked at her owlishly and she gave him back an impudent stare. This upset him – he had no experience of girls – so he blushed and raised his cap. At that she seemed to relent.

'Hello,' she said experimentally.

'Good afternoon,' he replied with a pale smile.

'Where are you off to?' she asked.

'Oh, just up the dike for a walk.'

'Sit down,' she said in a sharp voice, laying her hand on the bench beside her, and he did as he was told. It was a lovely summer evening, and the white quay walls and tall, crazy, claret-coloured tenements under a blue and white sky were reflected in the lazy water, which wrinkled only at the edges and seemed like a painted carpet.

'It's very pleasant here,' he said complacently.

'Is it?' she asked with a truculence that startled him. 'I don't see anything very pleasant about it.'

'Oh, it's very nice and quiet,' he said in mild surprise as he raised his fair eyebrows and looked up and down the Mall at the old Georgian houses and the nursemaids sitting under the trees. 'My name is Lowry,' he added politely.

'Oh, are ye the ones that have the jeweller's shop on the Parade?' she asked.

'That's right,' replied Ned with modest pride.

'We have a clock we got from ye,' she said. ''Tisn't much good of an old clock either,' she added with quiet malice.

'You should bring it back to the shop,' he said in considerable concern. 'It probably needs overhauling.'

'I'm going down the river in a boat with a couple of chaps,' she said, going off at a tangent. 'Will you come?'

'Couldn't,' he said with a smile.

'Why not?'

'I'm only left go up the dike for a walk,' he said complacently. 'On Saturdays I go to Confession at St Peter and Paul's, then I go up the dike and back the Western Road. Sometimes you see very good cricket matches. Do you like cricket?'

'A lot of old sissies pucking a ball!' she said shortly. 'I do not.'

'I like it,' he said firmly. 'I go up there every Saturday. Of course, I'm not supposed to talk to anyone,' he added with mild amusement at his own audacity.

'Why not?'

'My mother doesn't want me to.'

'Why doesn't she?'

'She comes of an awfully good family,' he answered mildly, and but for his gentle smile she might have thought he was deliberately insulting her. 'You see,' he went on gravely in his thin, pleasant voice, ticking things off on his fingers and then glancing at each finger individually as he ticked it off – a tidy sort of boy – 'there are three main branches of the Hourigan family: the Neddy Neds, the Neddy Jerrys and the Neddy Thomases. The Neddy Neds are the Hayfield Hourigans. They are the oldest branch. My mother is a Hayfield Hourigan, and she'd have been a rich woman only for her father backing a bill for a Neddy Jerry. He defaulted and ran away to Australia,' he concluded with a contemptuous sniff.

'Cripes!' said the girl. 'And had she to pay?'

'She had. But, of course,' he went on with as close as he ever seemed likely to get to a burst of real enthusiasm, 'my grandfather was a well-behaved man. When he was eating his dinner the boys from the National School in Bantry used to be brought up to watch him, he had such beautiful table manners. Once he caught my uncle eating cabbage with a knife and he struck him with a poker. They had to put four stitches in him after,' he added with a joyous chuckle.

'Cripes!' the girl said again. 'What did he do that for?'

'To teach him manners,' Ned said earnestly.

'He must have been dotty.'

'Oh, I wouldn't say, so,' Ned exclaimed in mild surprise.

Everything this girl said came as a shock to him. 'But that's why my mother won't let me mix with other children. On the other hand, we read a good deal. Are you fond of reading, Miss – I didn't catch the name.'

'You weren't told it,' she said, showing her claws. 'But if you want to know, it's Rita Lomasney.'

'Do you read much, Miss Lomasney?'

'I couldn't be bothered.'

'I read all sorts of books,' he said enthusiastically. 'And as well as that, I'm learning the violin from Miss Maude on the Parade. Of course, it's very difficult, because it's all classical music.'

'What's classical music?' she asked with sudden interest.

'*Maritana* is classical music,' he replied eagerly. He was a bit of a puzzle to Rita. She had never before met anyone with such a passion for handing out instruction. 'Were you at *Maritana* in the opera house, Miss Lomasney?'

'I was never there at all,' she said curtly.

'And *Alice Where Art Thou* is classical music,' he added. 'It's harder than plain music. You see,' he went on, composing signs in the air, 'it has signs on it like this, and when you see the signs, you know it's after turning into a different tune, though it has the same name. Irish music is all the same tune and that's why my mother won't let us learn it.'

'Were you ever at the opera in Paris?' she asked suddenly.

'No,' said Ned. 'I was never in Paris. Why?'

'That's where you should go,' she said with airy enthusiasm. 'You couldn't hear any operas here. The staircase alone is bigger than the whole opera house here.'

It seemed as if they were in for a really informative conversation when two fellows came down Wyse's Hill. Rita got up to meet them. Lowry looked up at them and then rose too, lifting his cap politely.

'Well, good afternoon,' he said cheerfully. 'I enjoyed the talk. I hope we meet again.'

'Some other Saturday,' said Rita.

'Oh, good evening, old man,' one of the two fellows said in an affected drawl, pretending to raise a top hat. 'Do come and see us soon again.'

'Shut up, Foster!' Rita said sharply. 'I'll give you a puck in the gob.'

'Oh, by the way,' Ned said, coming back to hand her a number of the *Gem* which he took from his coat pocket, 'you might like to look at this. It's not bad.'

'Thanks, I'd love to,' she said insincerely, and he smiled and touched his cap again. Then with a polite and almost deferential air he went up to Foster. 'Did you say something?' he asked.

Foster looked as astonished as if a kitten had suddenly got on its hind legs and challenged him to fight.

'I did not,' he said, and backed away.

'I'm glad,' Ned said, almost purring. 'I was afraid you might be looking for trouble.'

It came as a surprise to Rita as well. Whatever opinion she might have formed of Ned Lowry, fighting was about the last thing she would have associated him with.

The Lomasneys lived in a house on Sunday's Well, a small house with a long, sloping garden and a fine view of the river and city. Harry Lomasney, the builder, was a small man who wore grey tweed suits and soft collars several sizes too big for him. He had a ravaged brick-red face with keen blue eyes, and a sandy, straggling moustache with one side going up and the other down, and his workmen said you could tell his humour by the side he pulled. He was nicknamed 'Hasty Harry'. 'Great God!' he fumed when his wife was having her first baby. 'Nine months over a little job like that! I'd do it in three weeks if I could only get started.' His wife was tall and matronly and very pious, but her piety never got much in her way. A woman who had survived Hasty would have survived anything. Their eldest daughter, Kitty, was loud-voiced and gay and had been expelled from school for writing indecent letters to a boy. She had copied the letters out of a French novel but she failed to tell the nuns that. Nellie was placider and took more after her mother; besides, she didn't read French novels.

Rita was the exception among the girls. There seemed to be no softness in her. She never had a favourite saint or a favourite nun; she said it was soppy. For the same reason she never had flirtations. Her friendship with Ned Lowry was the closest she ever got to that, and though Ned came regularly to the house, and the pair of them went to the pictures together, her sisters would have found it hard to say whether she cared any more for

him than she did for any of her girl acquaintances. There was
something in her they didn't understand, something tongue-
tied, twisted and unhappy. She had a curious raw, almost timid
smile as though she felt people desired no better sport than hurt-
ing her. At home she was reserved, watchful, almost mocking.
She could listen for hours to her mother and sisters without
once opening her mouth, and then suddenly mystify them by
dropping a well-aimed jaw-breaker – about classical music, for
instance – before relapsing into a sulky silence; as though she had
merely drawn back the veil for a moment on depths in herself
which she would not permit them to explore.

After taking her degree, she got a job in a convent school in
a provincial town in the west of Ireland. She and Ned corre-
sponded and he even went to see her there. He reported at home
that she seemed quite happy.

But this didn't last. A few months later the Lomasney family
were at supper one evening when they heard a car stop, the
gate squeaked, and steps came up the long path to the front
door. Then came the sound of a bell and a cheerful voice from
the hall.

'Hullo, Paschal, I suppose ye weren't expecting me?'

''Tis never Rita!' said her mother, meaning that it was but that
it shouldn't be.

'As true as God, that one is after getting into trouble,' Kitty
said prophetically.

The door opened and Rita slouched in, a long, stringy girl with
a dark, glowing face. She kissed her father and mother lightly.

'Hullo,' she said. 'How's tricks?'

'What happened you?' her mother asked, rising.

'Nothing,' replied Rita, an octave up the scale. 'I just got the
sack.'

'The sack?' said her father, beginning to pull the wrong side
of his moustache. 'What did you get the sack for?'

'Give me a chance to get something to eat first, can't you?'
Rita said laughingly. She took off her hat and smiled at herself
in the mirror over the mantelpiece. It was a curious smile as
though she were amused by the spectacle of what she saw. Then
she smoothed back her thick black hair. 'I told Paschal to bring
in whatever was going. I'm on the train since ten. The heating
was off as usual. I'm frizzled.'

'A wonder you wouldn't send us a wire,' said Mrs Lomasney as Rita sat down and grabbed some bread and butter.

'Hadn't the tin,' replied Rita.

'Can't you tell us what happened?' Kitty asked brightly.

'I told you. You'll hear more in due course. Reverend Mother is bound to write and tell ye how I lost my character.'

'But what did you do, child?' her mother asked placidly. Her mother had been through all this before, with Hasty and Kitty, and she knew God was very good and nothing much ever happened.

'Fellow that wanted to marry me,' said Rita. 'He was in his last year at college, and his mother didn't like me, so she got Reverend Mother to give me the push.'

'And what has it to do with Reverend Mother?' Nellie asked indignantly. 'What business is it of hers?'

'That's what I say,' said Rita.

But Kitty looked suspiciously at her. Rita wasn't natural; there was something wild about her, and this was her first real love affair. Kitty just couldn't believe that Rita had gone about it the same as anyone else.

'Still, I must say you worked pretty fast,' she said.

'You'd have to in that place,' said Rita. 'There was only one possible man in the whole village and he was the bank clerk. We called him "The One". I wasn't there a week when the nuns ticked me off for riding on the pillion of his motorbike.'

'And did you?' asked Kitty.

'I never got the chance, girl. They did it to every teacher on principle to give her the idea that she was well watched. I only met Tony Donoghue a fortnight ago – home after a break-down.'

'Well, well, well!' her mother exclaimed without rancour. 'No wonder his poor mother was upset. A boy that's not left college yet! Couldn't ye wait till he was qualified anyway?'

'Not very well,' said Rita. 'He's going to be a priest.'

Kitty sat back with a superior grin. Of course, Rita could do nothing like anyone else. If it wasn't a priest it would have been a Negro, and Rita would have made theatre of it in precisely the same deliberate way.

'A what?' asked her father, springing to his feet.

'All right, don't blame me!' Rita said hastily. 'It wasn't my fault. He told me he didn't want to be a priest. It was his mother was driving him into it. That's why he had the breakdown.'

'Let me out of this,' said her father, 'before I −'

'Go on!' Rita said with tender mockery (she was very fond of her father). 'Before you what?'

'Before I wish I was a priest myself,' he snarled. 'I wouldn't be saddled with a family like I am.'

He stumped out of the room, and the girls laughed. The idea of their father as a priest appealed to them almost as much as the idea of him as a mother. Hasty had a knack of stating his grievances in such a way that they inevitably produced laughter. But Mrs Lomasney did not laugh.

'Reverend Mother was perfectly right,' she said severely. 'As if it wasn't hard enough on the poor boys without girls like you throwing temptation in their way. I think you behaved very badly, Rita.'

'All right, if you say so,' Rita said shortly with a boyish shrug of her shoulders, and refused to answer any more questions.

After her supper she went to bed, and her mother and sisters sat on in the front room discussing the scandal. Someone rang and Nellie opened the door.

'Hullo, Ned,' she said. 'I suppose you came up to congratulate us on the good news?'

'Hullo,' Ned said, smiling with his mouth primly shut. With a sort of automatic movement he took off his coat and hat and hung them on the rack. Then he emptied the pockets with the same thoroughness. He hadn't changed much. He was thin and pale, spectacled and clever, with the same precise and tranquil manner, 'like an old Persian cat,' as Nellie said. He read too many books. In the last year or two something seemed to have happened him. He didn't go to Mass any longer. Not going to Mass struck all the Lomasneys as too damn clever. 'What good news?' he added, having avoided any unnecessary precipitation.

'You didn't know who was here?'

'No,' he replied, raising his brows mildly.

'Rita!'

'Oh!' The same tone. It was part of his cleverness not to be surprised at anything.

'She's after getting the sack for trying to run off with a priest,' said Nellie.

If Nellie thought that would shake him she was mistaken. He merely tossed his head with a silent chuckle and went in, adjusting his pince-nez. For a fellow who was supposed to be in love with her since they were kids, he behaved in a very peculiar manner. He put his hands in his trouser pockets and stood on the hearth with his legs well apart.

'Isn't it awful, Ned?' Mrs Lomasney asked in her deep voice.

'Is it?' Ned purred, smiling.

'With a priest?' cried Nellie.

'Now, he wasn't a priest, Nellie,' said Mrs Lomasney reprovingly. ''Tis bad enough as it is without making it any worse.'

'Suppose you tell me what happened,' suggested Ned.

'But we don't know, Ned,' cried Mrs Lomasney. 'You know what that one is like in one of her sulky fits. Maybe she'll tell you. She's up in bed.'

'I'll try,' said Ned.

Still with his hands in his pockets, he rolled after Mrs Lomasney up the thickly carpeted stairs to Rita's little bedroom on top of the house. She left him on the landing and he paused for a moment to look out over the river and the lighted city behind it. Rita, wearing a pink dressing-jacket, was lying with one arm under her head. By the bed was a table with a packet of cigarettes she had been using as an ashtray. He smiled and shook his head reprovingly at her.

'Hullo, Ned,' she cried, reaching him a bare arm. 'Give us a kiss. I'm quite kissable now.'

He didn't need to be told that. He was astonished at the change in her. Her whole bony, boyish face seemed to have gone mawkish and soft and to be lit up from inside. He sat on an armchair by the bed, carefully pulling up the bottoms of his trousers, then put his hands in his trouser pockets again and sat back with crossed legs and shoulders slightly hunched.

'I suppose they're all in a floosther downstairs?' Rita asked with amusement.

'They seem a little excited,' said Ned with bowed head cocked a little sideways, looking like a wise old bird.

'Wait till they hear the details and they'll have something to be excited about,' said Rita grimly.

'Why?' he asked mildly. 'Are there details?'

'Masses of them,' said Rita. 'Honest to God, Ned, I used to

laugh at the glamour girls in the convent. I never knew you could get like that about a fellow. It's like something busting inside you. Cripes, I'm as soppy as a kid!'

'And what's the fellow like?' Ned asked curiously.

'Tony Donoghue? His mother had a shop in the Main Street. He's decent enough, I suppose. I don't know. He kissed me one night coming home. I was furious. I cut the blooming socks off him. Next evening he came round to apologize. I never got up or asked him to sit down or anything. I suppose I was still mad with him. He said he never slept a wink. "Didn't you?" said I. "It didn't trouble me much." Bloody lies, of course. "I did it because I was fond of you," says he. "Is that what you told the last one too?" said I. Then he got into a wax too. Said I was calling him a liar. "And aren't you?" said I. Then I waited for him to hit me, but, begor, he didn't, and I ended up sitting on his knee. Talk about the Babes in the Wood! First time he ever had a girl on his knee, he said, and you know how much of it I did.'

They heard a step on the stairs and Mrs Lomasney smiled benevolently at them both round the door.

'I suppose 'tis tea Ned is having?' she asked in her deep voice.

'No. I'm having the tea,' said Rita. 'Ned says he'd sooner a drop of the hard tack.'

'Oh, isn't that a great change, Ned?' cried Mrs Lomasney.

''Tis the shock,' Rita explained lightly, throwing him a cigarette. 'He didn't think I was that sort of girl.'

'He mustn't know much about girls,' said Mrs Lomasney.

'He's learning now,' said Rita.

When Paschal brought up the tray, Rita poured out tea for Ned and whiskey for herself. He made no comment. Things like that were a commonplace in the Lomasney household.

'Anyway,' she went on, 'he told his old one he wanted to chuck the Church and marry me. There was ructions, of course. The people in the shop at the other side of the street had a son a priest. She wanted to be as good as them. So away with her up to Reverend Mother, and Reverend Mother sends for me. Did I want to destroy the young man's life and he on the threshold of a great calling? I told her 'twas they wanted to destroy him. I asked her what sort of priest Tony would make. Oh, 'twas a marvellous sacrifice, and after it he'd be twice the man. Honest to God, Ned, the way that woman went on, you'd think she was talking about doctoring an old tomcat. I told her that was all she knew about Tony, and she said they knew him since he was an altar boy in the convent. "Did he ever tell you how he used to slough the convent orchard and sell the apples in town?" says I. So then she dropped the Holy Willie stuff and told me his ma was after getting into debt to put him in for the priest-hood, and if he chucked it, he'd never be able to get a job at home to pay it back. Three hundred quid! Wouldn't they kill you with style?'

'And what did you do then?' asked Ned with amusement.

'I went to see his mother.'

'You didn't!'

'I did. I thought I might work it with the personal touch.'

'You don't seem to have been very successful.'

'I'd as soon try the personal touch on a traction engine, Ned. That woman was too tough for me altogether. I told her I wanted to marry Tony. "I'm sorry," she said; "you can't." "What's to stop me?" said I. "He's gone too far," says she. "If he was gone farther it wouldn't worry me," says I. I told her then what Reverend Mother said about her being three hundred pounds in debt and offered to pay it back to her if she let him marry me.'

'And had you the three hundred?' Ned asked in surprise.

'Ah, where would I get three hundred?' she replied ruefully. 'And she knew it too, the old jade! She didn't believe a word I said. After that I saw Tony. He was crying; said he didn't want to break his mother's heart. As true as God, Ned, that woman had as much heart as a traction engine.'

'Well, you seem to have done it in style,' Ned said approvingly as he put away his teacup.

'That wasn't the half of it. When I heard the difficulties his mother was making, I offered to live with him instead.'

'Live with him?' asked Ned. Even he was startled.

'Well, go away on holidays with him. Lots of girls do it. I know they do. And, God Almighty, isn't it only natural?'

'And what did he say to that?' asked Ned curiously.

'He was scared stiff.'

'He would be,' said Ned, wrinkling up his nose and giving his superior little sniff as he took out a packet of cigarettes.

'Oh, it's all very well for you,' Rita cried, bridling up. 'You may think you're a great fellow, all because you read Tolstoy and don't go to Mass, but you'd be just as scared if a girl offered to go to bed with you.'

'Try me,' Ned said sedately as he lit her cigarette for her, but somehow the notion of suggesting such a thing to Ned only made her laugh.

He stayed till quite late, and when he went downstairs the girls and Mrs Lomasney fell on him and dragged him into the sitting room.

'Well, doctor,' said Mrs Lomasney, 'how's the patient?'

'Oh, I think the patient is coming round nicely,' said Ned.

'But would you ever believe it, Ned?' she cried. 'A girl that wouldn't look at the side of the road a fellow was at, unless 'twas to go robbing orchards with him. You'll have another drop of whiskey?'

'I won't.'

'And is that all you're going to tell us?' asked Mrs Lomasney.

'Oh, you'll hear it all from herself.'

'We won't.'

'I dare say not,' he said with a hearty chuckle, and went for his coat.

'Wisha, Ned,' said Mrs Lomasney, 'what'll your mother say when she hears it?'

' "All *quite* mad," ' said Ned, sticking his nose in the air and giving an exaggerated version of what Mrs Lomasney called 'his Hayfield sniff'.

'The dear knows, I think she's right,' she said with resignation, helping him with his coat. 'I hope your mother doesn't notice the smell of whiskey from your breath,' she added dryly, just to show him that she couldn't be taken in, and then stood at the door, looking up and down, as she waited for him to wave from the gate.

'Ah,' she sighed as she closed the door behind her, 'with the help of God it might be all for the best.'

'If you think he's going to marry her, I can tell you now he's not,' said Kitty. 'I'd like to see myself trying it on Bill O'Donnell. He'd have my sacred life. That fellow only enjoys it.'

'Ah, God is good,' her mother said cheerfully, kicking a mat into place. 'Some men might like that.'

*

Inside a week Kitty and Nellie were sick to death of the sight of Rita round the house. She was bad enough at the best of times, but now she just brooded and mooned and snapped the head off you. In the afternoons she strolled down the dike and into Ned's little shop, where she sat on the counter, swinging her legs and smoking, while Ned leaned against the side of the window, tinkering at the insides of a watch with some delicate instrument. Nothing seemed to rattle him. When he had finished work, he changed his coat and they went out to tea. He sat at the back of the teashop in a corner, pulled up the legs of his trousers, and took out a packet of cigarettes and a box of matches, which he placed on the table before them with a look that almost commanded them to stay there and not get lost. His face was pale and clear and bright, like an evening sky when the last light has drained from it.

'Anything wrong?' he asked one evening when she was moodier than usual.

'Just fed up,' she said, thrusting out her jaw.

'What is it?' he asked gently. 'Still fretting?'

'Ah, no. I can get over that. It's Kitty and Nellie. They're bitches, Ned; proper bitches. And all because I don't wear my heart on my sleeve. If one of them got a knock from a fellow she'd take two aspirins and go to bed with the other one. They'd have a lovely talk – can't you imagine? "And was it then he said he loved you?" I can't do that sort of stuff. And it's all because they're not sincere, Ned. They couldn't be sincere.'

'Remember, they have a long start on you,' Ned said smiling.

'Is that it?' she asked without interest. 'They think I'm batty. Do you?'

'I've no doubt that Mrs Donoghue, if that's her name, thought something of the sort,' replied Ned with a tight-lipped smile.

'And wasn't she right?' asked Rita with sudden candour. 'Suppose she'd agreed to take the three hundred quid, wouldn't I be in a nice pickle? I wake in a sweat whenever I think of it. I'm just a blooming chancer, Ned. Where would I get three hundred quid?'

'Oh, I dare say someone would have lent it to you,' he said with a shrug.

'They would like fun. Would you?'

'Probably,' he said gravely after a moment's thought.

'Are you serious?' she whispered earnestly.

'Quite.'

'Cripes,' she gasped, 'you must be very fond of me.'

'It looks like it,' said Ned, and this time he laughed with real heartiness, a boy's laugh of sheer delight at the mystification he was causing her. It was characteristic of Rita that she should count their friendship of years as nothing, but his offer of three hundred pounds in cash as significant.

'Would you marry me?' she asked frowningly. 'I'm not proposing to you, only asking,' she added hastily.

'Certainly,' he said, spreading out his hands. 'Whenever you like.'

'Honest to God?'

'Cut my throat.'

'And why didn't you ask me before I went down to that kip? I'd have married you then like a shot. Was it the way you weren't keen on me then?'

'No,' he replied matter-of-factly, drawing himself together like an old clock preparing to strike. 'I think I've been keen on you as long as I've know you.'

'It's easily seen you're a Neddy Ned,' she said with amusement. 'I go after mine with a scalping knife.'

'I stalk mine,' said Ned.

'Cripes, Ned,' she said with real regret, 'I wish you'd told me sooner. I couldn't marry you now.'

'No?'

'No. It wouldn't be fair to you.'

'Isn't that my look-out?'

'It's my look-out now.' She glanced around the restaurant to make sure no one was listening and then went on in a dry voice, leaning one elbow on the table. 'I suppose you'll think this is all cod, but it's not. Honest to God, I think you're the finest bloody man I ever met – even though you do think you're an atheist or something,' she added maliciously with a characteristic Lomasney flourish in the cause of Faith and Fatherland. 'There's no one in the world I have more respect for. I think I'd nearly cut my throat if I did something you really disapproved of – I don't mean telling lies or going on a skite,' she added hastily, to prevent misunderstandings. 'They're only gas. Something that really shocked you is what I mean. I think if I was tempted to do anything like that I'd ask myself: "What would that fellow Lowry think of me now?"'

'Well,' Ned said in an extraordinary quiet voice, squelching the butt of his cigarette on his plate, 'that sounds to me like a very good beginning.'

'It is not, Ned,' she said sadly, shaking her head. 'That's why I say it's my look-out. You couldn't understand it unless it happened to yourself; unless you fell in love with a girl the way I fell in love with Tony. Tony is a scut, and a cowardly scut, but I was cracked about him. If he came in here now and said: "Come on, girl, we're going to Killarney for the weekend," I'd go out and buy a nightdress and toothbrush and be off with him. And I wouldn't give a damn what you or anybody thought. I might chuck myself in the lake afterwards, but I'd go. Christ, Ned,' she exclaimed, flushing and looking as though she might burst into tears, 'he couldn't come into a room but I went all mushy inside. That's what the real thing is like.'

'Well,' Ned said sedately, apparently not in the least put out – in fact, looking rather pleased with himself, Rita thought – 'I'm in no hurry. In case you get tired of scalping them, the offer will still be open.'

'Thanks, Ned,' she said absent-mindedly, as though she weren't listening.

While he paid the bill, she stood in the porch, doing her face in the big mirror that flanked it, and paying no attention to the crowds, coming homeward through streets where the shop windows were already lit. As he emerged from the shop she turned on him suddenly.

'About that matter, Ned,' she said, 'will you ask me again, or do I have to ask you?'

Ned just refrained from laughing outright. 'As you like,' he replied with quiet amusement. 'Suppose I repeat the proposal every six months.'

'That would be the hell of a long time to wait if I changed my mind,' she said with a thoughtful scowl. 'All right,' she said, taking his arm. 'I know you well enough to ask you. If you don't want me by that time, you can always say so. I won't mind.'

Ned's proposal came as a considerable comfort to Rita. It bolstered up her self-esteem, which was always in danger of collapse. She might be ugly and uneducated and a bit of a chancer, but the best man in Cork – the best in Ireland, she sometimes thought – wanted to marry her, even after she had been let down by another man. That was a queer one for her enemies! So while her sisters made fun of her, Rita considered the situation, waiting for the best possible moment to let them know she had been proposed to and could marry before either of them if it suited her. Since her childhood Rita had never given anything away without extracting the last ounce of theatrical effect from it. She would tell her sisters, but not before she could make them sick with the news.

That was a pity, for it left Rita unaware that Ned, whom she respected, was far from being the only one who liked her. For instance, there was Justin Sullivan, the lawyer, who had once been by way of being engaged to Nellie. He hadn't become engaged to her, because she was as slippery as an eel, and her fancy finally lit on a solicitor called Fahy whom Justin despised with his whole heart and soul as a light-headed, butterfly sort of man. But Justin continued to visit the house as a friend of the girls. There happened to be no other house that suited him half as well, and besides he knew that sooner or later Nellie would make a mess of her life with Fahy, and his services would be required.

Justin, in other words, was a sticker. He was a good deal older than Rita, a tall, burly man with a broad face, a brow that was rising from baldness as well as brains, and a slow, watchful ironic air. Like many lawyers, he tended to conduct conversation as though the person he was speaking to were a hostile witness who had either to be coaxed into an admission of perjury or bullied into one of mental deficiency. When Justin began, Fahy simply clutched his head and retired to sit on the stairs. 'Can't anyone shut that fellow up?' he would moan with a martyred air. Nobody could. The girls shot their little darts at him, but he only brushed them aside. Ned Lowry was the only one who could even stand up to him, and when the pair of them argued about religion, the room became a desert. Justin, of course, was a pillar of orthodoxy. 'Imagine for a moment,' he would declaim in a throaty rounded voice that turned easily to pomposity, 'that I am Pope.' 'Easiest thing in the world, Justin,' Kitty assured him. He drank whiskey like water, and the more he drank, the more massive and logical and orthodoxly Catholic he became.

At the same time, under his truculent air he was exceedingly gentle, patient and understanding, and disliked the ragging of Rita by her sisters.

'Tell me, Nellie,' he asked one night in his lazy, amiable way, 'do you talk like that to Rita because you like it, or because you think it's good for her?'

'How soft you have it!' Nellie cried. 'We have to live with her. You haven't.'

'That may be my misfortune, Nellie,' said Justin with a broad smile.

'Is that a proposal, Justin?' asked Kitty shrewdly.

'Scarcely, Kitty,' said Justin. 'You're not what I might call a good jury.'

'Better be careful or you'll have her dropping in on your mother, Justin,' Kitty said maliciously.

'Thanks, Kitty,' Rita said with a flash of cold fury.

'I hope my mother would have sufficient sense to realize it was an honour, Kitty,' Justin said severely.

When he rose to go, Rita accompanied him to the hall.

'Thanks for the moral support, Justin,' she said in a low voice, and then threw her overcoat over her shoulders to go as far as the gate with him. When he opened the door they both stood and gazed about them. It was a moonlit night; the garden, patterned in black and silver, sloped to the quiet roadway, where the gas lamps burned with a dim green light, and in the farther walls gateways shaded by black trees led to flights of steps or to steep-sloping avenues which led to moonlit houses on the river's edge.

'God, isn't it lovely?' Rita said in a hushed voice.

'Oh, by the way, Rita,' he said, slipping his arm through hers, 'that was a proposal.'

'Janey Mack, they're falling,' she said, giving his arm a squeeze.

'What are falling?'

'Proposals.'

'Why? Had you others?'

'I had one anyway.'

'And did you accept it?'

'No,' Rita said doubtfully. 'Not quite. At least, I don't think I did.'

'You might consider this one,' Justin said with unusual humi-lity. 'You know, of course, that I was very fond of Nellie. At one time I was very fond of her indeed. You don't mind that, I hope.

It's all over and done with now, and there are no regrets on either side.'

'No, Justin, of course I don't mind. If I felt like marrying you I wouldn't give it a second thought. But I was very much in love with Tony too, and that's not all over and done with yet.'

'I know that, Rita,' he said gently. 'I know exactly what you feel. We've all been through it.' If he had left it at that everything might have been all right, but Justin was a lawyer, which meant that he liked to keep things absolutely shipshape. 'But that won't last forever. In a month or two you'll be over it, and then you'll wonder what you saw in that fellow.'

'I don't think so, Justin,' she said with a crooked little smile, not altogether displeased to be able to enlighten him on the utter hopelessness of her position. 'I think it will take a great deal longer than that.'

'Well, say six months, even,' Justin went on, prepared to yield a point to the defence. 'All I ask is that in one month or six, whenever you've got over your regrets for this – this amiable young man' (momentarily his voice took on its familiar ironic ring), 'you'll give me a thought. I'm old enough not to make any more mistakes. I know I'm fond of you, and I feel pretty sure I could make a success of my end of it.'

'What you really mean,' said Rita, keeping her temper with the greatest difficulty, 'is that I wasn't in love with Tony at all. Isn't that it?'

'Not quite,' Justin said judiciously. Even if he'd had a serenade as well as the moonlight and the girl, it couldn't have kept him from correcting what he considered to be a false deduction. 'I've no doubt you were very much attracted by this – this clerical Adonis; this Mr Whatever-his-name-is, or that at any rate you thought you were, which in practice comes to the same thing, but I also know that that sort of thing, though it's painful enough while it lasts, doesn't last very long.'

'You mean yours didn't, Justin,' Rita said tartly.

'I mean mine or anybody else's,' Justin said pompously. 'Because love – the only sort of thing you can really call love – is something that comes with experience. You're probably too young yet to know what the real thing is.'

As Rita had only recently told Ned that he didn't yet know what the real thing was, she found this rather hard to stomach.

'How old would you say you'd have to be?' she asked viciously. 'Thirty-five?'

'You'll know soon enough – when it hits you,' said Justin.

'Honest to God, Justin,' she said, withdrawing her arm and looking at him with suppressed fury, 'I think you're the thickest man I ever met.'

'Good night, my dear,' said Justin with perfect good humour, and he raised his cap and took the few steps to the gate at a run.

Rita stood gazing after him with folded arms. At the age of eighteen to be told that there is anything you don't know about love is like a knife in your heart.

Kitty and Nellie grew so tired of her moodiness that they persuaded her mother that the best way of distracting her mind was to find her another job. A new environment was also supposed to be good for her complaint, so Mrs Lomasney wrote to her sister who was a nun in England, and the sister found her work in a convent there. Rita let on to pay no attention, though she let Ned see something of her resentment.

'But why England?' he asked wonderingly.

'Why not?' replied Rita challengingly.

'Wouldn't any place nearer do you?'

'I suppose I wouldn't be far enough away from them.'

'But why not make up your own mind?'

'I'll probably do that too,' she said with a short laugh. 'I'd like to see what's in theirs first though.'

On Friday she was to leave for England, and on Wednesday the girls gave a farewell party. This, too, Rita affected to take no great interest in. Wednesday was the half-holiday, and it rained steadily all day. The girls' friends all turned up. Most were men: Bill O'Donnell of the bank, who was engaged to Kitty; Fahy, the solicitor, who was Justin's successful rival for Nellie; Justin himself, who simply could not be kept out of the house by anything short of an injunction; Ned Lowry, and a few others. Hasty soon retired with his wife to the dining-room to read the evening paper. He said all his daughters' young men looked exactly alike and he never knew which of them he was talking to.

Bill O'Donnell was acting as barman. He was a big man, bigger even than Justin, with a battered boxer's face and a Negro smile, which seemed to well up from depths of good humour with life

rather than from any immediate contact with others. He carried
on loud conversations with everyone he poured out drink for,
and his voice overrode every intervening tête-à-tête, and chal-
lenged even the piano, on which Nellie was vamping music-hall
songs.

'Who's this one for, Rita?' he asked. 'A bottle of Bass for
Paddy. Ah, the stout man! Remember the New Year's Day in
Bandon, Paddy? Remember how you had to carry me up to the
bank in evening dress and jack me up between the two wings of
the desk? Kitty, did I ever tell you about that night in Bandon?'

'Once a week for the past five years, Bill,' said Kitty philo-
sophically.

'Nellie,' said Rita, 'I think it's time for Bill to sing his song.
"Let Me like a Soldier Fall", Bill!'

'My one little song!' Bill said with a roar of laughter. 'My one
and only song, but I sing it grand. Don't I, Nellie? Don't I sing
it fine?'

'Fine!' agreed Nellie, looking up at his big, beaming moonface
shining at her over the piano. 'As the man said to my mother,
"Finest bloody soprano I ever heard."'

'He did not, Nellie,' Bill said sadly. 'You're making that
up. . . . Silence please!' he shouted joyously, clapping his hands.
'Ladies and gentlemen, I must apologize. I ought to sing some-
thing like Tosti's "Good-bye", but the fact is, ladies and gentle-
men, that I don't know Tosti's "Good-bye".'

'Recite it, Bill,' said Justin amiably.

'I don't know the words of it either, Justin,' said Bill. 'In fact,
I'm not sure if there's any such song, but if there is, I ought to
sing it.'

'Why, Bill?' Rita asked innocently. She was wearing a long
black dress that threw up the unusual brightness of her dark,
bony face. She looked happier than she had looked for months.
All the evening it was as though she were laughing to herself.

'Because 'twould be only right, Rita,' said Bill with great
melancholy, putting his arm about her and drawing her closer to
him. 'You know I'm very fond of you, don't you, Rita?'

'And I'm mad about you, Bill,' said Rita candidly.

'I know that, Rita,' he said mournfully, pulling at his collar
as though to give himself air. 'I only wish you weren't going,
Rita. This place isn't the same without you. Kitty won't mind

my saying that,' he added with a nervous glance at Kitty, who
was flirting with Justin on the sofa.

'Are you going to sing your blooming old song or not?' Nellie
asked impatiently, running her fingers over the keys.

'I'm going to sing now in one minute, Nellie,' Bill said
ecstatically, stroking Rita fondly under the chin. 'I only want
Rita to know the way we'll miss her.'

'Damn it, Bill,' Rita said, snuggling up to him with her dark
head on his chest, 'if you go on like that I won't go at all. Tell
me, would you really prefer me not to go?'

'I would prefer you not to go, Rita,' he replied, stroking her
cheeks and eyes. 'You're too good for the fellows over there.'

'Oh, go on doing that,' she said hastily, as he dropped his hand.
'It's gorgeous, and you're making Kitty mad jealous.'

'Kitty isn't jealous,' Bill said fondly. 'Kitty is a lovely girl and
you're a lovely girl. I hate to see you go, Rita.'

'That settles it, Bill,' she said, pulling herself free of him with
a determined air. 'I simply couldn't cause you all that suffering.
As you put it that way, I won't go.'

'Won't you, just?' said Kitty with a grin.

'Now, don't worry your head about it any more, Bill,' said
Rita briskly. 'It's all off.'

Justin, who had been quietly consuming large whiskeys,
looked round lazily.

'Perhaps I ought to have mentioned,' he boomed, 'that the
young lady has just done me the honour of proposing to me and
I've accepted her.'

Ned Lowry, who had been enjoying the scene between Bill
and Rita, looked at him for a moment in surprise.

'Bravo! Bravo!' cried Bill, clapping his hands with childish
delight. 'A marriage has been arranged and all the rest of it –
what? I must give you a kiss, Rita. Justin, you don't mind if I give
Rita a kiss?'

'Not at all, not at all,' replied Justin with a lordly wave of his
hand. 'Anything that's mine is yours, old man.'

'You're not serious, Justin, are you?' Kitty asked incredulously.

'Oh, I'm serious all right,' said Justin. 'I'm not quite certain
whether your sister is. Are you, Rita?'

'What?' Rita asked as though she hadn't heard.

'Serious,' repeated Justin.

'Why?' asked Rita. 'Trying to give me the push already?'

'We're much obliged for the information,' Nellie said ironic-ally as she rose from the piano. 'Now, maybe you'd oblige us further and tell us does Father know.'

'Hardly,' said Rita coolly. 'It was only settled this evening.'

'Well, maybe 'twill do with some more settling by the time Father is done with you,' Nellie said furiously. 'The impudence of you! How dare you! Go in at once and tell him.'

'Keep your hair on, girl,' Rita advised with cool malice and then went jauntily out of the room. Kitty and Nellie began to squabble viciously with Justin. They were convinced that the whole scene had been arranged by Rita to make them look ridiculous, and in this they weren't very far out. Justin sat back and began to enjoy the sport. Then Ned Lowry struck a match and lit another cigarette, and something about the slow, careful way in which he did it drew everyone's attention. Just because he was not the sort to make a fuss, people realized from his strained look that his mind was very far away. The squabble stopped as quickly as it had begun and a feeling of awkwardness ensued. Ned was too old a friend of the family for the girls not to feel that way about him.

Rita returned, laughing.

'Well?' asked Nellie.

'Consent refused,' growled Rita, bowing her head and pulling the wrong side of an imaginary moustache.

'What did I say?' exclaimed Nellie, but without rancour.

'You don't think it makes any difference?' Rita asked dryly.

'I wouldn't be too sure of that,' said Nellie. 'What else did he say?'

'Oh, he hadn't a notion who I was talking about,' Rita said lightly. ' "Justin who?" ' she mimicked. ' "How the hell do you think I can remember all the young scuts ye bring to the house?" '

'Was he mad?' asked Kitty with amusement.

'Hopping.'

'He didn't call us scuts?' asked Bill in a wounded tone.

'Oh, begor, that was the very word he used, Bill,' said Rita.

'Did you tell him he was very fond of me the day I gave him the tip for Golden Boy at the Park Races?' asked Justin.

'I did,' said Rita. 'I said you were the stout block of a fellow with the brown hair that he said had the fine intelligence, and he said he never gave a damn about intelligence. He wanted me to marry the thin fellow with the specs. "Only bloody gentleman that comes to the house." '

'Is it Ned?' cried Nellie.

'Who else?' said Rita. 'I asked him why he didn't tell me that before and he nearly ate the head off me. "Jesus Christ, girl, don't I feed ye and clothe ye? Isn't that enough without having to coort for ye as well? Next thing, ye'll be asking me to have a few babies for ye." Anyway, Ned,' she added with a crooked, almost malicious smile, 'you can always say you were Pa's favourite.'

Once more the attention was directed to Ned. He put his cigarette down with care and sprang up with a broad smile, holding out his hand.

'I wish you all the luck in the world, Justin,' he said.

'I know that well, Ned,' boomed Justin, catching Ned's hand in his own two. 'And I'd feel the same if it was you.'

'And you too, Miss Lomasney,' Ned said gaily.

'Thanks, Mr Lowry,' she replied with the same crooked smile.

Justin and Rita got married, and Ned, like all the Hayfield Hourigans, behaved in a decorous and sensible manner. He didn't take to drink or break the crockery or do any of the things people are expected to do under the circumstances. He gave them a very expensive clock as a wedding present, went once or twice to visit them and permitted Justin to try and convert him, and took Rita to the pictures when Justin was away from home. At the same time he began to walk out with an assistant in Halpin's; a gentle, humorous girl with a great mass of jet-black hair, a snub nose, and a long, pointed melancholy face. You saw them everywhere together.

He also went regularly to Sunday's Well to see the old couple and Nellie, who wasn't yet married. One evening when he called, Mr and Mrs Lomasney were at the chapel, but Rita was there, Justin being again away. It was months since she and Ned had met; she was having a baby and very near her time; and it made her self-conscious and rude. She said it made her feel like a yacht that had been turned into a cargo boat. Three or four times she said things to Ned which would have maddened anyone else, but he took them in his usual way, without resentment.

'And how's little Miss Bitch?' she asked insolently.

'Little Miss who?' he asked mildly.

'Miss – how the hell can I remember the names of all your dolls? The Spanish-looking one who sells the knickers at Halpin's.'

'Oh, she's very well, thanks,' Ned said primly.

'What you might call a prudent marriage,' Rita went on, all on edge.

'How's that, Rita?'

'You'll have the ring and the trousseau at cost price.'

'How interested you are in her!' Nellie said suspiciously.

'I don't give a damn about her,' said Rita with a shrug. 'Would Señorita What's-her-name ever let you stand godfather to my footballer, Ned?'

'Why not?' Ned asked mildly. 'I'd be delighted, of course.'

'You have the devil's own neck to ask him after the way you treated him,' said Nellie. Nellie was interested; she knew Rita and knew that she was in one of her emotional states, and was determined on finding out what it meant. Ordinarily Rita, who also knew her sister, would have delighted in thwarting her, but now it was as though she wanted an audience.

'How did I treat him?' she asked with amusement.

'Codding him along like that for years, and then marrying a man that was twice your age.'

'Well, how did he expect me to know?'

Ned rose and took out a packet of cigarettes. Like Nellie he knew that Rita had deliberately staged the scene and was on the point of telling him something. She was leaning very far back in her chair and laughed up at him while she took a cigarette and waited for him to light it.

'Come on, Rita,' he said encouragingly. 'As you've said so much you might as well tell us the rest.'

'What else is there to tell?'

'What you had against me.'

'Who said I had anything against you? Didn't I distinctly tell you when you asked me to marry you that I didn't love you? Maybe you thought I didn't mean it.'

He paused for a moment and then raised his brows.

'I did,' he said quietly.

She laughed.

'The conceit of that fellow!' she said to Nellie, and then with a change of tone: 'I had nothing against you, Ned. This was the

one I had the needle in. Herself and Kitty were forcing me
into it.'

'Well, the impudence of you!' cried Nellie.

'Isn't it true for me?' Rita said sharply. 'Weren't you both
trying to get me out of the house?'

'We weren't,' Nellie replied hotly, 'and anyway that has noth-
ing to do with it. It was no reason why you couldn't have married
Ned if you wanted to.'

'I didn't want to. I didn't want to marry anyone.'

'And what changed your mind?'

'Nothing changed my mind. I didn't care about anyone, only
Tony, but I didn't want to go to that damn place, and I had no
alternative. I had to marry one of you, so I made up my mind
that I'd marry the first of you that called.'

'You must have been mad,' Nellie said indignantly.

'I felt it. I sat at the window the whole afternoon, looking at
the rain. Remember that day, Ned?'

He nodded.

'The rain had a lot to do with it. I think I half hoped you'd
come first. Justin came instead – an old aunt of his was sick and
he came for supper. I saw him at the gate and he waved to me with
his old brolly. I ran downstairs to open the door for him. "Justin,"
I said, grabbing him by the coat, "if you still want to marry me,
I'm ready." He gave me a dirty look – you know Justin! "Young
woman," he said, "there's a time and place for everything." And
away with him up to the lavatory. Talk about romantic engage-
ments! Damn the old kiss did I get off him, even!'

'I declare to God!' said Nellie in stupefaction.

'I know,' Rita cried, laughing again over her own irrespon-
sibility. 'Cripes, when I knew what I was after doing I nearly
dropped dead.'

'Oh, so you came to your senses?' Nellie asked ironically.

'What do you think? That's the trouble with Justin; he's always
right. That fellow knew I wouldn't be married a week before I
didn't give a snap of my fingers for Tony. And me thinking my
life was over and that was that or the river! God, the idiots we
make of ourselves over men!'

'And I suppose 'twas then you found out you'd married the
wrong man?' Nellie asked.

'Who said I married the wrong man?' Rita asked hotly.

'I thought that was what you were telling us,' Nellie said innocently.

'You get things all wrong, Nellie,' Rita replied shortly. 'You jump to conclusions too much. If I did marry the wrong man I wouldn't be likely to tell you – or Ned Lowry either.'

She looked mockingly at Ned, but her look belied her. It was plain enough now why she wanted Nellie as an audience. It kept her from admitting more than she had to admit, from saying things which, once said, might make her own life impossible. Ned rose and flicked his cigarette ash into the fire. Then he stood with his back to it, his hands behind his back, his feet spread out on the hearth.

'You mean if I'd come earlier you'd have married me?' he asked quietly.

'If you'd come earlier, I'd probably be asking Justin to stand godfather to your brat,' said Rita. 'And how do you know but Justin would be walking out the señorita, Ned?'

'Then maybe you wouldn't be quite so interested whether he was or not,' said Nellie, but she didn't say it maliciously. It was now only too plain what Rita meant, and Nellie was sorry for her.

Ned turned and lashed his cigarette savagely into the fire. Rita looked up at him mockingly.

'Go on!' she taunted him. 'Say it, blast you!'

'I couldn't,' he said bitterly.

A month later he married the señorita.

I

'THERE!' SAID the sergeant's wife. 'You would hurry me.'

'I always like to be in time for a train,' replied the sergeant with the equability of one who has many times before explained the guiding principle of his existence.

'I'd have had heaps of time to buy that hat,' added his wife.

The sergeant sighed and opened his evening paper. His wife looked out on the dark platform, pitted with pale lights under which faces and faces passed, lit up and dimmed again. A uniformed lad strode up and down with a tray of periodicals and chocolates. Farther up the platform a drunken man was being seen off by his friends.

'I'm very fond of Michael O'Leary,' he shouted. 'He is the most sincere man I know.'

'I have no life,' sighed the sergeant's wife. 'No life at all! There isn't a soul to speak to, nothing to look at all day but bogs and mountains and rain – always rain! And the people! Well, we've had a fine sample of them, haven't we?'

The sergeant continued to read.

'Just for the few days it's been like heaven. Such interesting people! Oh, I thought Mr Boyle had a glorious face! And his voice – it went through me.'

The sergeant lowered his paper, took off his peaked cap, laid it on the seat beside him, and lit his pipe. He lit it in the old-fashioned way, ceremoniously, his eyes blinking pleasurably like a sleepy cat's in the match-flame. His wife scrutinized each face that passed, and it was plain that for her life meant faces and people and things and nothing more.

'Oh dear!' she said again. 'I simply have no existence. I was educated in a convent and play the piano; my father was literary man, and yet I am compelled to associate with the lowest types of humanity. If it was even a decent town, but a village!'

'Ah,' said the sergeant, gapping his reply with anxious puffs, 'maybe with God's help we'll get a shift one of these days.' But he said it without conviction, and it was also plain that he was well pleased with himself, with the prospect of returning home, with his pipe and with his paper.

'Here are Magner and the others,' said his wife as four other policemen passed the barrier. 'I hope they'll have sense enough to let us alone ... How do you do? How do you do? Had a nice time, boys?' she called with sudden animation, and her pale, sullen face became warm and vivacious. The policemen smiled and touched their caps but did not halt.

'They might have stopped to say good evening,' she added sharply, and her face sank into its old expression of boredom and dissatisfaction. 'I don't think I'll ask Delancey to tea again. The others make an attempt, but really, Delancey is hopeless. When I smile and say "Guard Delancey, wouldn't you like to use the butter-knife?" he just scowls at me from under his shaggy brows and says without a moment's hesitation "I would not." '

'Ah, Delancey is a poor slob,' said the sergeant affectionately.

'Oh yes, but that's not enough, Jonathon. Slob or no slob, he should make an attempt. He's a young man; he should have a dinner-jacket at least. What sort of wife will he get if he won't even wear a dinner-jacket?'

'He's easy, I'd say. He's after a farm in Waterford!'

'Oh, a farm! A farm! The wife is only an incidental, I suppose?'

'Well, now from all I hear she's a damn nice little incidental.'

'Yes, I suppose many a nice little incidental came from a farm,' answered his wife, raising her pale brows. But the irony was lost on him.

'Indeed, yes; indeed, yes,' he said fervently.

'And here,' she added in biting tones, 'come our charming neighbours.'

Into the pale lamplight stepped a group of peasants. Not such as one sees in the environs of a capital but in the mountains and along the coasts. Gnarled, wild, with turbulent faces, their ill-cut clothes full of character, the women in pale brown shawls, the men wearing black sombreros and carrying big sticks, they swept in, ill at ease, laughing and shouting defiantly. And, so much part of their natural environment were they, that for a moment they seemed to create about themselves rocks and bushes, tarns, turf-ricks and sea.

With a prim smile the sergeant's wife bowed to them through the open window.

'How do you do? How do you do?' she called. 'Had a nice time?'

At the same moment the train gave a jolt and there was a rush in which the excited peasants were carried away. Some minutes passed; the influx of passengers almost ceased, and a porter began to slam the doors. The drunken man's voice rose in a cry of exultation.

'You can't possibly beat O'Leary!' he declared. 'I'd lay down my life for Michael O'Leary.'

Then, just as the train was about to start, a young woman in a brown shawl rushed through the barrier. The shawl, which came low enough to hide her eyes, she held firmly across her mouth, leaving visible only a long thin nose with a hint of pale flesh at either side. Beneath the shawl she was carrying a large parcel.

She looked hastily around, a porter shouted to her and pushed her towards the nearest compartment which happened to be that occupied by the sergeant and his wife. He had actually seized the handle of the door when the sergeant's wife sat up and screamed.

'Quick! Quick!' she cried. 'Look who it is! She's coming in! Jonathon! Jonathon!'

The sergeant rose with a look of alarm on his broad red face. The porter threw open the door, with his free hand grasping the woman's elbow. But when she laid eyes on the sergeant's startled countenance, she stepped back, tore herself free, and ran crazily up the platform. The engine shrieked, the porter slammed the door with a curse, somewhere another door opened and shut, and the row of watchers, frozen into effigies of farewell, now dark now bright, began to glide gently past the window, and the stale, smoky air was charged with the breath of open fields.

II

The four policemen spread themselves out in a separate compartment and lit cigarettes.

'Ah, poor old Delancey!' said Magner with his reckless laugh. 'He's cracked on her all right.'

'Cracked on her,' agreed Fox. 'Did ye see the eye he gave her?'

Delancey smiled sheepishly. He was a tall, handsome, black-haired young man with the thick eyebrows described by the sergeant's wife. He was new to the force and suffered from a mixture of natural gentleness and country awkwardness.

'I am,' he said in his husky voice, 'cracked on her. The devil admire me, I never hated anyone yet, but I think I hate the living sight of her.'

'Oh, now! Oh, now!' protested Magner.

'I do. I think the Almighty God must have put that one in the world with the one main object of persecuting me.'

'Well, indeed,' said Foley, 'I don't know how the sergeant puts up with the same damsel. If any woman up and called me by an outlandish name like Jonathon when all knew my name was plain John, I'd do fourteen days for her – by God, I would, and a calendar month!'

The four men were now launched on a favourite topic that held them for more than an hour. None of them liked the sergeant's wife, and all had stories to tell against her. From these there emerged the fact that she was an incurable scandal-monger and mischief-maker, who couldn't keep quiet about her own business, much less that of her neighbours. And while they talked the train dragged across a dark plain, the heart of Ireland, and in the moonless night tiny cottage windows blew past like sparks from a fire, and a pale simulacrum of the lighted carriages leaped and frolicked over hedges and fields. Magner shut the window, and the compartment began to fill with smoke.

'She'll never rest till she's out of Farranchreesht,' he said.

'That she mightn't!' groaned Delancey.

'How would you like the city yourself, Dan?' asked Magner.

'Man, dear,' exclaimed Delancey with sudden brightness, 'I'd like it fine. There's great life in a city.'

'You can have it and welcome,' said Foley, folding his hands across his paunch.

'Why so?'

'I'm well content where I am.'

'But the life!'

'Ah, life be damned! What sort of life is it when you're always under someone's eye? Look at the poor devils in court!'

'True enough, true enough,' said Fox.

'Ah, yes, yes,' said Delancey, 'but the adventures they have!'

'What adventures!'

'Look now, there was a sergeant in court only yesterday telling me about a miser, an old maid without a soul in the world that died in an ould loft on the quays. Well, this sergeant I'm talking about put a new man on duty outside the door while he went back to report, and all this fellow had to do was to kick the door and frighten off the rats.'

'That's enough, that's enough!' cried Foley.

'Yes, yes, but listen now, listen, can't you? He was there about ten minutes with a bit of candle in his hand and all at once the door at the foot of the stairs began to open. "Who's there?" says he, giving a start. "Who's there, I say?" There was no answer and still the door kept opening quietly. Then he gave a laugh. What was it but a cat? "Puss, puss," says he, "come on up, puss!" Thinking, you know, the ould cat would be company. Up comes the cat, pitter-patter on the stairs, and then whatever look he gave the door the hair stood up on his head. What was coming in but another cat? "Coosh!" says he, stamping his foot and kicking the door to frighten them. "Coosh away to hell out of that!" And then another cat came in and then another, and in his fright he dropped the candle and kicked out right and left. The cats began to hiss and bawl, and that robbed him of the last stitch of sense. He bolted down the stairs, and as he did he trod on one of the brutes, and before he knew where he was he slipped and fell head over heels, and when he put out his hand to grip something 'twas a cat he gripped, and he felt the claws tearing his hands and face. He had strength enough to pull himself up and run, but when he reached the barrack gate down he dropped in a fit. He was a raving lunatic for three weeks after.'

'And that,' said Foley, with bitter restraint, 'is what you call adventure!'

'Dear knows,' added Magner, drawing himself up with a shiver, ''tis a great consolation to be able to put on your cap and go out for a drink any hour of the night you like.'

''Tis, of course,' drawled Foley scornfully. 'And to know the worst case you'll have in ten years is a bit of a scrap about politics.'

'I dunno,' sighed Delancey dreamily. 'I'm telling you there's great charm about the Criminal Courts.'

'Damn the much charm they had for you when you were in the box,' growled Foley.

'I know, sure, I know,' admitted Delancey, crestfallen.

'Shutting his eyes,' said Magner with a laugh, 'like a kid afraid he was going to get a box across the ears.'

'And still,' said Delancey, 'this sergeant fellow I'm talking about, he said, after a while you wouldn't mind it no more than if 'twas a card party, but talk up to the judge himself.'

'I suppose you would,' agreed Magner pensively.

There was silence in the smoky compartment that jolted and rocked on its way across Ireland, and the four occupants, each touched with that morning wit which afflicts no one so much as state witnesses, thought of how they would speak to the judge if only they had him before them now. They looked up to see a fat red face behind the door, and a moment later it was dragged back.

'Is thish my carriage, gentlemen?' asked a meek and boozy voice.

'No, 'tisn't. Go on with you!' snapped Magner.

'I had as nice a carriage as ever was put on a railway thrain,' said the drunk, leaning in, 'a handsome carriage, and 'tis losht.'

'Try farther on,' suggested Delancey.

'Excuse me interrupting yeer conversation, gentlemen.'

'That's all right, that's all right.'

'I'm very melancholic. Me besht friend, I parted him thish very night, and 'tish known to no wan, only the Almighty and Merciful God' (here the drunk reverently raised his bowler hat and let it slide down the back of his neck to the floor), 'if I'll ever lay eyes on him agin in thish world. Good night, gentlemen, and thanks, thanks for all yeer kindness.'

As the drunk slithered away up the corridor Delancey laughed. Fox resumed the conversation where it had left off.

'I'll admit,' he said, 'Delancey wasn't the only one.'

'He was not,' agreed Foley. 'Even the sergeant was shook. When he caught up the mug he was trembling all over, and before he could let it down it danced a jig on the table.'

'Ah, dear God! Dear God!' sighed Delancey, 'what killed me most entirely was the bloody ould model of the house. I didn't mind anything else but the house. There it was, a living likeness, with the bit of grass in front and the shutter hanging loose, and every time I looked down I was in the back lane in Farran-chreesht, hooshing the hens and smelling the turf, and then I'd look up and see the lean fellow in the wig pointing his finger at me.'

'Well, thank God,' said Foley with simple devotion, 'this time tomorrow I'll be sitting in Ned Ivers' back with a pint in my fist.'

Delancey shook his head, a dreamy smile playing upon his dark face.

'I dunno,' he said. ' 'Tis a small place, Farranchreesht, a small, mangy ould *fothrach* of a place with no interest or advancement in it.'

'There's something to be said on both sides,' added Magner judicially. 'I wouldn't say you're wrong, Foley, but I wouldn't say Delancey was wrong either.'

'Here's the sergeant now,' said Delancey, drawing himself up with a smile of welcome. 'Ask him.'

'He wasn't long getting tired of Julietta,' whispered Magner maliciously.

The door was pushed back and the sergeant entered, loosening the collar of his tunic. He fell into a corner seat, crossed his legs and accepted the cigarette which Delancey proffered.

'Well, lads,' he exclaimed. 'What about a jorum!'

'By Gor,' said Foley, 'isn't it remarkable? I was only talking about it!'

'I have noted before now, Peter,' said the sergeant, 'that you and me have what might be called a simultaneous thirst.'

III

The country folk were silent and exhausted. Kendillon drowsed now and again, but he suffered from blood-pressure, and after a while his breathing grew thicker and stronger until at last it exploded in a snort, and then he started up, broad awake and angry. In the silence rain spluttered and tapped along the roof, and the dark window-panes streamed with shining runnels of water that trickled on to the floor. Moll Mor scowled, her lower lip thrust out. She was a great flop of a woman with a big coarse powerful face. The other two women, who kept their eyes closed, had their brown shawls drawn tight about their heads, but Moll's was round her shoulders and the gap above her breasts was filled by a blaze of scarlet.

'Where are we?' asked Kendillon crossly, starting awake after one of his drowsing fits.

Moll Mor glowered at him.

'Aren't we home yet?' he asked again.

'No,' she answered. 'Nor won't be. What scour is on you?'

'Me little house,' moaned Kendillon.

'Me little house,' mimicked Moll. ''Twasn't enough for you to board the windows and put barbed wire on the ould bit of a gate!'

''Tis all dom well for you,' he snarled, 'that have someone to mind yours for you.'

One of the women laughed softly and turned a haggard virginal face within the cowl of her shawl.

''Tis that same have me laughing,' she explained apologetically. 'Tim Dwyer this week past at the stirabout pot!'

'And making the beds!' chimed in the third woman.

'And washing the children's faces! Glory be to God, he'll blast creation!'

'Ay,' snorted Moll, 'and his chickens running off with Thade Kendillon's roof.'

'My roof, is it?'

'Ay, your roof.'

''Tis a good roof. 'Tis a better roof than ever was seen over your head since the day you married.'

'Oh, Mary Mother!' sighed Moll, ''tis a great pity of me this three hours and I looking at the likes of you instead of me own fine bouncing man.'

''Tis a new thing to hear you praising your man, then,' said a woman.

'I wronged him,' said Moll contritely. 'I did so. I wronged him before the world.'

At this moment the drunken man pulled back the door of the compartment and looked from face to face with an expression of deepening melancholy.

'She'sh not here,' he said in disappointment.

'Who's not here, mister?' asked Moll with a wink at the others.

'I'm looking for me own carriage, ma'am,' said the drunk with melancholic dignity, 'and, whatever the bloody hell they done with it, 'tish losht. The railways in thish counthry are gone to hell.'

'Wisha, if 'tis nothing else is worrying you wouldn't you sit here with me?' asked Moll.

'I would with very great pleasure,' replied the drunk, 'but 'tishn't on'y the carriage, 'tish me thravelling companion ... I'm a lonely man, I parted me besht friend this very night, I found wan to console me, and then when I turned me back – God took her!'

And with a dramatic gesture the drunk closed the door and continued on his way. The country folk sat up, blinking. The smoke of the men's pipes filled the compartment, and the heavy air was laden with the smell of homespun and turf smoke, the sweet pungent odour of which had penetrated every fibre of their garments.

'Listen to the rain, leave ye!' said one of the women. 'We'll have a wet walk home.'

''Twill be midnight before we're there,' said another.

'Ah, sure, the whole country will be up.'

''Twill be like daylight with collogueing.'

'There'll be no sleep in Farranchreesht tonight.'

'Oh, Farranchreesht! Farranchreesht!' cried the young woman with the haggard face, the ravished lineaments of which were suddenly transfigured. 'Farranchreesht and the sky over you, I wouldn't change places with the Queen of England this night!'

And suddenly Farranchreesht, the bare bog-lands with the hump-backed mountain behind, the little white houses and the dark fortifications of turf that made it seem the flame-blackened ruin of some mighty city, all was lit up within their minds. An old man sitting in a corner, smoking a broken clay pipe, thumped his stick upon the floor.

'Well, now,' said Kendillon darkly, 'wasn't it great impudence in her to come back?'

'Wasn't it now?' answered a woman.

'She won't be there long,' he added.

'You'll give her the hunt, I suppose?' asked Moll Mor politely, too politely.

'If no one else do, I'll give her the hunt myself.'

'Oh, the hunt, the hunt,' agreed a woman. 'No one could ever darken her door again.'

'And still, Thade Kendillon,' pursued Moll with her teeth on edge to be at him, 'you swore black was white to save her neck.'

'I did of course. What else would I do?'

'What else? What else, indeed?' agreed the others.

'There was never an informer in my family.'

'I'm surprised to hear it,' replied Moll vindictively, but the old man thumped his stick three or four times on the floor requesting silence.

'We told our story, the lot of us,' he said, 'and we told it well.'

'We did, indeed.'

'And no one told it better than Moll Mor. You'd think to hear her she believed it herself.'

'God knows,' answered Moll with a wild laugh, 'I nearly did.'

'And still I seen great changes in my time, and maybe the day will come when Moll Mor or her likes will have a different. story.'

A silence followed his words. There was profound respect in all their eyes. The old man coughed and spat.

'Did any of ye ever think the day would come when a woman in our parish would do the like of that?'

'Never, never, ambasa!'

'But she might do it for land?'

'She might then.'

'Or for money?'

'She might so.'

'She might, indeed. When the hunger is money people kill for money, when the hunger is land people kill for land. There's a great change coming, a great change. In the ease of the world people are asking more. When I was a growing boy in the barony if you killed a beast you made six pieces of it, one for yourself and the rest for the neighbours. The same if you made a catch of fish, and that's how it was with us from the beginning of time. And now look at the change! The people aren't as poor as they were, nor as good as they were, nor as generous as they were, nor as strong as they were.'

'Nor as wild as they were,' added Moll Mor with a vicious glare at Kendillon. 'Oh, glory be to You, God, isn't the world a wonderful place!'

The door opened and Magner, Delancey and the sergeant entered. Magner was drunk.

'Moll,' he said, 'I was lonely without you. You're the biggest and brazenest and cleverest liar of the lot and you lost me my sergeant's stripes, but I'll forgive you everything if you'll give us one bar of the "Colleen Dhas Roo".'

IV

'I'm a lonely man,' said the drunk. 'And now I'm going back to my lonely habitation.

'Me besht friend,' he continued, 'I left behind me – Michael O'Leary. 'Tis a great pity you don't know Michael, and a great pity Michael don't know you. But look now at the misfortunate way a thing will happen. I was looking for someone to console me, and the moment I turned me back you were gone.'

Solemnly he placed his hand under the woman's chin and raised her face to the light. Then with the other hand he stroked her cheeks.

'You have a beauful face,' he said, 'a beauful face. But whass more important, you have a beauful soul. I look into your eyes and I see the beauty of your nature. Allow me wan favour. Only wan favour before we part.'

He bent and kissed her. Then he picked up his bowler which had fallen once more, put it on back to front, took his dispatch case and got out.

The woman sat on alone. Her shawl was thrown open and beneath it she wore a bright blue blouse. The carriage was cold, the night outside black and cheerless, and within her something had begun to contract that threatened to crush the very spark of life. She could no longer fight it off, even when for the hundredth time she went over the scenes of the previous day; the endless hours in the dock; the wearisome speeches and questions she couldn't understand and the long wait in the cells till the jury returned. She felt it again, the shiver of mortal anguish that went through her when the chief warder beckoned angrily from the stairs, and the wardress, glancing hastily into a hand-mirror, pushed her forward. She saw the jury with their expressionless faces. She was standing there alone, in nervous twitches jerking back the shawl from her face to give herself air. She was trying to say a prayer, but the words were being drowned within her mind by the thunder of nerves, crashing and bursting. She could feel one that had escaped dancing madly at the side of her mouth but she was powerless to recapture it.

'The verdict of the jury is that Helena Maguire is not guilty.' Which was it? Death or life? She couldn't say. 'Silence! Silence!'

shouted the usher, though no one had tried to say anything. 'Any other charge?' asked a weary voice. 'Release the prisoner.' 'Silence!' shouted the crier again. The chief warder opened the door of the dock and she began to run. When she reached the steps she stopped and looked back to see if she were being followed. A policeman held open a door and she found herself in an ill-lit, draughty, stone corridor. She stood there, the old shawl about her face. The crowd began to emerge. The first was a tall girl with a rapt expression as though she were walking on air. When she saw the woman she halted suddenly, her hands went up in an instinctive gesture, as though she wished to feel her, to caress her. It was that look of hers, that gait as of a sleep-walker that brought the woman to her senses . . .

But now the memory had no warmth in her mind, and the something within her continued to contract, smothering her with loneliness and shame and fear. She began to mutter crazily to herself. The train, now almost empty, was stopping at every little wayside station. Now and again a blast of wind from the Atlantic pushed at it as though trying to capsize it.

She looked up as the door was slammed open and Moll Mor came in, swinging her shawl behind her.

'They're all up the train. Wouldn't you come?'

'No, no, no, I couldn't.'

'Why couldn't you? Who are you minding? Is it Thade Kendillon?'

'No, no, I'll stop as I am.'

'Here! Take a sup of this and 'twill put new heart in you.' Moll fumbled in her shawl and produced a bottle of liquor as pale as water. 'Wait till I tell you what Magner said! That fellow's a limb of the divil. "Have you e'er a drop, Moll?" says he. "Maybe I have then," says I. "What is it?" says he. "What do you think?" says I. "For God's sake," says he, "baptize it quick and call it whiskey." '

The woman took the bottle and put it to her lips. She shivered as she drank.

''Tis powerful stuff entirely,' said Moll with respect.

Next moment there were loud voices in the corridor. Moll grabbed the bottle and hid it under her shawl. The door opened and in strode Magner, and behind him the sergeant and Delancey, looking rather foolish. After them again came the two country women, giggling. Magner held out his hand.

'Helena,' he said, 'accept my congratulations.'

The woman took his hand, smiling awkwardly.

'We'll get you the next time, though,' he added.

'Musha, what are you saying, mister?' she asked.

'Not a word, not a word. You're a clever woman, a remarkable woman, and I give you full credit for it. You threw dust in all our eyes.'

'Poison,' said the sergeant by way of no harm, 'is hard to come by and easy to trace, but it beat me to trace it.'

'Well, well, there's things they're saying about me!'

The woman laughed nervously, looking first at Moll Mor and then at the sergeant.

'Oh, you're safe now,' said Magner, 'as safe as the judge on the bench. Last night when the jury came out with the verdict you could have stood there in the dock and said "Ye're wrong, ye're wrong, I did it. I got the stuff in such and such a place. I gave it to him because he was old and dirty and cantankerous and a miser. I did it and I'm proud of it!" You could have said every word of that and no one would have dared to lay a finger on you.'

'Indeed! What a thing I'd say!'

'Well, you could.'

'The law is truly a remarkable phenomenon,' said the sergeant, who was also rather squiffy. 'Here you are, sitting at your ease at the expense of the State, and for one word, one simple word of a couple of letters, you could be lying in the body of the gaol, waiting for the rope and the morning jaunt.'

The woman shuddered. The young woman with the ravished face looked up.

''Twas the holy will of God,' she said simply.

''Twas all the bloody lies Moll Mor told,' replied Magner.

''Twas the will of God,' she repeated.

'There was many hanged in the wrong,' said the sergeant.

'Even so, even so! 'Twas God's will.'

'You have a new blouse,' said the other woman in an envious tone.

'I seen it last night in a shop on the quay,' replied the woman with sudden brightness. 'A shop on the way down from the court. Is it nice?'

'How much did it cost you?'

'Honour of God!' exclaimed Magner, looking at them in

stupefaction. 'Is that all you were thinking of? You should have been on your bended knees before the altar.'

'I was too,' she answered indignantly.

'Women!' exclaimed Magner with a gesture of despair. He winked at Moll Mor and the pair of them retired to the next compartment. But the interior was reflected clearly in the corridor window and they could see the pale, quivering image of the policeman lift Moll Mor's bottle to his lips and blow a long silent blast on it as on a trumpet. Delancey laughed.

'There'll be one good day's work done on the head of the trial,' said the young woman, laughing.

'How so?' asked the sergeant.

'Dan Canty will make a great brew of poteen while he have yeer backs turned.'

'I'll get Dan Canty yet,' replied the sergeant stiffly.

'You will, as you got Helena.'

'I'll get him yet.'

He consulted his watch.

'We'll be in in another quarter of an hour,' he said. ''Tis time we were all getting back to our respective compartments.'

Magner entered and the other policemen rose. The sergeant fastened his collar and buckled his belt. Magner swayed, holding the door frame, a mawkish smile on his thin, handsome, dissipated face.

'Well, good night to you now, ma'am,' said the sergeant primly. 'I'm as glad for all our sakes things ended up as they did.'

'Good night, Helena,' said Magner, bowing low and promptly tottering. 'There'll be one happy man in Farranchreesht tonight.'

'Come! Come, Joe!' protested the sergeant.

'One happy man,' repeated Magner obstinately. ''Tis his turn now.'

'Come on back, man,' said Delancey. 'You're drunk.'

'You wanted him,' said Magner heavily. 'Your people wouldn't let you have him, but you have him at last in spite of them all!'

'Do you mean Cady Driscoll?' hissed the woman with sudden anger, leaning towards Magner, the shawl drawn tight about her head.

'Never mind who I mean. You have him.'

'He's no more to me now than the salt sea!'

The policeman went out first, the women followed, Moll Mor

laughing boisterously. The woman was left alone. Through the window she could see little cottages stepping down through wet and naked rocks to the water's edge. The flame of life had narrowed in her to a pin-point, and she could only wonder at the force that had caught her up, mastered her and thrown her aside.

'No more to me,' she repeated dully to her own image in the window, 'no more to me than the salt sea!'

7 ABROAD

A READER uninterested in biography might conclude, from a lengthy survey of O'Connor's fiction, that he never left Ireland in his life. On learning that he loved France, knew England well, and had lived in the United States for many years, the same reader might conclude that it was native caution which restricted his topographical range. The truth is more complicated. 'I prefer to write about Ireland and Irish people,' he explained in the *New York Herald Tribune* in 1952, 'merely because I know to a syllable how everything in Ireland can be said; but that doesn't mean that the stories themselves were inspired by events in Ireland. Many of them should really have English backgrounds; a few should even have American ones.'

Some writers seek universality by ranging the world, by depicting the different cultures they claim or hope to have assimilated. O'Connor went in for a kind of reverse universality: the importation into Ireland of stories picked up elsewhere. Thus in early 1955 he was living in Annapolis with his wife Harriet, who later recalled how Annapolitans had provided him with themes for three of his stories: '"The Man of the World" from my cousin, "Music When Soft Voices Die" from the memories of my first job, and "The Impossible Marriage" from a friend of my mother's.' The universality of a story lies in its truth, not in its language or circumstances. O'Connor liked to quote the story of Lord Edward Fitzgerald meeting an aged Native American woman who told him that, as far as she was concerned, humanity was 'all one Indian'.

But Abroad wasn't merely a source of Irishable stories. The Ireland O'Connor knew and wrote about, though cut off from the rest of the world, was also marked by generations of exile. Poverty, famine and repression had meant parochialism and enclosure, but also emigration. The Irish went to England to work, and to America to start life again. To write about Ireland therefore also meant to write about the longing for departure, the pain or pleasure of absence, and the mixed blessing of return. 'Michael's Wife', O'Connor's great story of return, is here followed by the author's account of its origin: not in order to 'explain' it (though to some extent it does), but as an example of how the writer sees what others – even those centrally involved – may miss in their own story.

Abroad was also where O'Connor earned money – had he been obliged to exist on his Irish earnings he would have been impoverished – and a renown which confirms that fiction travels because of its art and truth rather than its location. In the late 1950s he was flying home from Paris when the Commissioner of Police at Le Bourget recognized him, proudly identified himself as a reader, and personally escorted the writer and his wife through the airport controls. The part which pleased him the most was being addressed as '*maître*'. Even more flatteringly, when John F. Kennedy opened the School of Aerospace Medicine at Brooks Airforce Base on 21 November 1963, he found a metaphor for the space race in *An Only Child*: 'Frank O'Connor, the Irish writer, tells in one of his books how, as a boy, he and his friends would make their way across the countryside, and when they came to an orchard wall that seemed too high and too doubtful to try and too difficult to permit their voyage to continue, they took off their caps and tossed them over the wall – and then they had no choice but to follow them.' Three days later, O'Connor wrote in the *Irish Independent*: 'On Thursday night I was called to the telephone to hear: "President Kennedy is quoting you in San Antonio, Texas"; on Friday night I was called to the telephone to hear: "President Kennedy is dead".'

THE BABES IN THE WOOD

WHENEVER Mrs Early made Terry put on his best trousers and gansey he knew his aunt must be coming. She didn't come half often enough to suit Terry, but when she did it was great gas. Terry's mother was dead and he lived with Mrs Early and her son, Billy. Mrs Early was a rough, deaf, scolding old woman, doubled up with rheumatics, who'd give you a clout as quick as she'd look at you, but Billy was good gas too.

This particular Sunday morning Billy was scraping his chin frantically and cursing the bloody old razor while the bell was ringing up the valley for Mass, when Terry's aunt arrived. She come into the dark little cottage eagerly, her big rosy face toasted with sunshine and her hand out in greeting.

'Hello, Billy,' she cried in a loud, laughing voice, 'late for Mass again?'

'Let me alone, Miss Conners,' stuttered Billy, turning his lathered face to her from the mirror. 'I think my mother shaves on the sly.'

'And how's Mrs Early?' cried Terry's aunt, kissing the old woman and then fumbling at the strap of her knapsack in her excitable way. Everything about his aunt was excitable and high-powered; the words tumbled out of her so fast that sometimes she became incoherent.

'Look, I brought you a couple of things – no, they're fags for Billy' ('God bless you, Miss Conners,' from Billy) '– this is for you, and here are a few things for the dinner.'

'And what did you bring me, Auntie?' Terry asked.

'Oh, Terry,' she cried in consternation, 'I forgot about you.'

'You didn't.'

'I did, Terry,' she said tragically. 'I swear I did. Or did I? The bird told me something. What was it he said?'

'What sort of bird was it?' asked Terry. 'A thrush?'

'A big grey fellow?'

'That's the old thrush all right. He sings in our back yard.'

'And what was that he told me to bring you?'

'A boat!' shouted Terry.

It was a boat.

After dinner the pair of them went up the wood for a walk. His aunt had a long, swinging stride that made her hard to keep up with, but she was great gas and Terry wished she'd come to see him oftener. When she did he tried his hardest to be grown-up. All the morning he had been reminding himself: 'Terry, remember you're not a baby any longer. You're nine now, you know.' He wasn't nine, of course; he was still only five and fat, but nine, the age of his girl friend Florrie, was the one he liked pretending to be. When you were nine you understood everything. There were still things Terry did not understand.

When they reached the top of the hill his aunt threw herself on her back with her knees in the air and her hands under her head. She liked to toast herself like that. She liked walking; her legs were always bare; she usually wore a tweed skirt and a pullover. Today she wore black glasses, and when Terry looked through them he saw everything dark; the wooded hills at the other side of the valley and the buses and cars crawling between the rocks at their feet, and, still farther down, the railway track and the river. She promised him a pair for himself next time she came, a small pair to fit him, and he could scarcely bear the thought of having to wait so long for them.

'When will you come again, Auntie?' he asked. 'Next Sunday?'

'I might,' she said and rolled on her belly, propped her head on her hands, and sucked a straw as she laughed at him. 'Why? Do you like it when I come?'

'I love it.'

'Would you like to come and live with me altogether, Terry?'

'Oh, Jay, I would.'

'Are you sure now?' she said, half-ragging him. 'You're sure you wouldn't be lonely after Mrs Early or Billy or Florrie?'

'I wouldn't, Auntie, honest,' he said tensely. 'When will you bring me?'

'I don't know yet,' she said. 'It might be sooner than you think.'

'Where would you bring me? Up to town?'

'If I tell you where,' she whispered, bending closer, 'will you swear a terrible oath not to tell anybody?'

'I will.'

'Not even Florrie?'

'Not even Florrie.'

'That you might be killed stone dead?' she added in a blood-curdling tone.

'That I might be killed stone dead!'

'Well, there's a nice man over from England who wants to marry me and bring me back with him. Of course, I said I couldn't come without you and he said he'd bring you as well. . . . Wouldn't that be gorgeous?' she ended, clapping her hands.

''Twould,' said Terry, clapping his hands in imitation. 'Where's England?'

'Oh, a long way off,' she said, pointing up the valley. 'Beyond where the railway ends. We'd have to get a big boat to take us there.'

'Chrisht!' said Terry, repeating what Billy said whenever something occurred too great for his imagination to grasp, a fairly common event. He was afraid his aunt, like Mrs Early, would give him a wallop for it, but she only laughed. 'What sort of a place is England, Auntie?' he went on.

''Oh, a grand place,' said his aunt in her loud, enthusiastic way. 'The three of us would live in a big house of our own with lights that went off and on, and hot water in the taps, and every morning I'd take you to school on your bike.'

'Would I have a bike of my own?' Terry asked incredulously.

'You would, Terry, a two-wheeled one. And on a fine day like this we'd sit in the park – you know, a place like the garden of the big house where Billy works, with trees and flowers and a pond in the middle to sail boats in.'

'And would we have a park of our own, too?'

'Not our own; there'd be other people as well; boys and girls you could play with. And you could be sailing your boat and I'd be reading a book, and then we'd go back home to tea and I'd bath you and tell you a story in bed. Wouldn't it be massive, Terry?'

'What sort of story would you tell me?' he asked cautiously. 'Tell us one now.'

So she took off her black spectacles and, hugging her knees, told him the story of the Three Bears and was so carried away that she acted it, growling and wailing and creeping on all fours with her hair over her eyes till Terry screamed with fright and pleasure. She was really great gas.

Next day Florrie came to the cottage for him. Florrie lived in the village so she had to come a mile through the woods to see him, but she delighted in seeing him and Mrs Early encouraged her. 'Your young lady' she called her and Florrie blushed with pleasure. Florrie lived with Miss Clancy in the Post Office and was very nicely behaved; everyone admitted that. She was tall and thin, with jet-black hair, a long ivory face, and a hook nose.

'Terry!' bawled Mrs Early. 'Your young lady is here for you,' and Terry came rushing from the back of the cottage with his new boat.

'Where did you get that, Terry?' Florrie asked, opening her eyes wide at the sight of it.

'My auntie,' said Terry. 'Isn't it grand?'

'I suppose 'tis all right,' said Florrie, showing her teeth in a smile which indicated that she thought him a bit of a baby for making so much of a toy boat.

Now, that was one great weakness in Florrie, and Terry regretted it because he really was fond of her. She was gentle, she was generous, she always took his part; she told creepy stories so well that she even frightened herself and was scared of going back through the woods alone, but she was jealous. Whenever she had anything, even if it was only a raggy doll, she made it out to be one of the seven wonders of the world, but let anyone else have a thing, no matter how valuable, and she pretended it didn't even interest her. It was the same now.

'Will you come up to the big house for a pennorth of goose-gogs?' she asked.

'We'll go down the river with this one first,' insisted Terry, who knew he could always override her wishes when he chose.

'But these are grand goosegogs,' she said eagerly, and again you'd think no one in the world but herself could even have a gooseberry. 'They're that size. Miss Clancy gave me the penny.'

'We'll go down the river first,' Terry said cantankerously. 'Ah, boy, wait till you see this one sail – ssss!'

She gave in as she always did when Terry showed himself headstrong, and grumbled as she always did when she had given in. She said it would be too late; that Jerry, the under-gardener, who was their friend, would be gone and that Mr Scott, the head gardener, would only give them a handful, and not even ripe ones. She was terrible like that, an awful old worrier.

When they reached the river bank they tied up their clothes and went in. The river was deep enough, and under the trees it ran beautifully clear over a complete pavement of small, brown, smoothly rounded stones. The current was swift, and the little sailing-boat was tossed on its side and spun dizzily round and round before it stuck in the bank. Florrie tired of this sport sooner than Terry did. She sat on the bank with her hands under her bottom, trailing her toes in the river, and looked at the boat with growing disillusionment.

'God knows, 'tisn't much of a thing to lose a pennorth of goosegogs over,' she said bitterly.

'What's wrong with it?' Terry asked indignantly. ''Tis a fine boat.'

'A wonder it wouldn't sail properly so,' she said with an accusing, schoolmarmish air.

'How could it when the water is too fast for it?' shouted Terry.

'That's a good one,' she retorted in pretended grown-up amusement. ''Tis the first time we ever heard of water being too fast for a boat.' That was another very aggravating thing about her – her calm assumption that only what she knew was knowledge. ''Tis only a cheap old boat.'

''Tisn't a cheap old boat,' Terry cried indignantly. 'My aunt gave it to me.'

'She never gives anyone anything only cheap old things,' Florrie replied with the coolness that always maddened other children. 'She gets them cost price in the shop where she works. Everyone knows that.'

'Because you're jealous,' he cried, throwing at her the taunt the village children threw whenever she enraged them with her supercilious airs.

'That's a good one too,' she said in a quiet voice, while her long thin face maintained its air of amusement. 'I suppose you'll tell us now what we're jealous of?'

'Because Auntie brings me things and no one ever brings you anything.'

'She's mad about you,' Florrie said ironically.

'She is mad about me.'

'A wonder she wouldn't bring you to live with her so.'

'She's going to,' said Terry, forgetting his promise in his rage and triumph.

'She is, I hear!' Florrie said mockingly. 'Who told you that?'

'She did; Auntie.'

'Dont mind her at all, little boy,' Florrie said severely. 'She lives with her mother, and her mother wouldn't let you live with her.'

'Well, she's not going to live with her any more,' Terry said, knowing he had the better of her at last. 'She's going to get married.'

'Who is she going to get married to?' Florrie asked casually, but Terry could see she was impressed.

'A man in England, and I'm going to live with them. So there!'

'In England?' Florrie repeated, and Terry saw he had really knocked the stuffing out of her this time. Florrie had no one to bring her to England, and the jealousy was driving her mad. 'And I suppose you're going?' she asked bitterly.

'I am going,' Terry said, wild with excitement to see her overthrown; the grand lady who for all her airs had no one to bring her to England with them. 'And I'm getting a bike of my own. So now!'

'Is that what she told you?' Florrie asked with a hatred and contempt that made him more furious still.

'She's going to, she's going to,' he shouted furiously.

'Ah, she's only codding you, little boy,' Florrie said contemptuously, splashing her long legs in the water while she continued to fix him with the same dark, evil, round-eyed look, exactly like a witch in a storybook. 'Why did she send you down here at all so?'

'She didn't send me,' Terry said, stooping to fling a handful of water in her face.

'But sure, I thought everyone knew that,' she said idly, merely averting her face slightly to avoid the splashes. 'She lets on to be your aunt but we all know she's your mother.'

'She isn't,' shrieked Terry. 'My mother is dead.'

'Ah, that's only what they always tell you,' Florrie replied quietly. 'That's what they told me too, but I knew it was lies. Your mother isn't dead at all, little boy. She got into trouble with

a man and her mother made her send you down here to get rid
of you. The whole village knows that.'

'God will kill you stone dead for a dirty liar, Florrie Clancy,'
he said and then threw himself on her and began to pummel
her with his little fat fists. But he hadn't the strength, and she
merely pushed him off lightly and got up on the grassy bank,
flushed and triumphant, pretending to smooth down the front
of her dress.

'Don't be codding yourself that you're going to England at
all, little boy,' she said reprovingly. 'Sure, who'd want you? Jesus
knows I'm sorry for you,' she added with mock pity, 'and I'd like
to do what I could for you, but you have no sense.'

Then she went off in the direction of the wood, turning once
or twice to give him her strange stare. He glared after her and
danced and shrieked with hysterical rage. He had no idea what
she meant, but he felt that she had got the better of him after all.
'A big, bloody brute of nine,' he said, and then began to run
through the woods to the cottage, sobbing. He knew that God
would kill her for the lies she had told, but if God didn't, Mrs
Early would. Mrs Early was pegging up clothes on the line and
peered down at him sourly.

'What ails you now didn't ail you before?' she asked.

'Florrie Clancy was telling lies,' he shrieked, his fat face black
with fury. 'Big bloody brute!'

'Botheration to you and Florrie Clancy!' said Mrs Early. 'Look
at the cut of you! Come here till I wipe your nose.'

'She said my aunt wasn't my aunt at all,' he cried.

'She what?' Mrs Early asked incredulously.

'She said she was my mother – Auntie that gave me the boat,'
he said through his tears.

'Aha,' Mrs Early said grimly, 'let me catch her round here again
and I'll toast her backside for her, and that's what she wants,
the little vagabond! Whatever your mother might do, she was a
decent woman, but the dear knows who that one is or where she
came from.'

All the same it was a bad business for Terry. A very bad business!
It is all very well having fights, but not when you're only five
and live a mile away from the village, and there is nowhere for
you to go but across the footbridge to the little railway station

and the main road where you wouldn't see another kid once in a week. He'd have been very glad to make it up with Florrie, but she knew she had done wrong and that Mrs Early was only lying in wait for her to ask her what she meant.

And to make it worse, his aunt didn't come for months. When she did, she came unexpectedly and Terry had to change his clothes in a hurry because there was a car waiting for them at the station. The car made up to Terry for the disappointment (he had never been in a car before), and to crown it, they were going to the seaside, and his aunt had brought him a brand-new bucket and spade.

They crossed the river by the little wooden bridge and there in the yard of the station was a posh grey car and a tall man beside it whom Terry hadn't seen before. He was a posh-looking fellow too, with a grey hat and a nice manner, but Terry didn't pay him much attention at first. He was too interested in the car.

'This is Mr Walker, Terry,' his aunt said in her loud way. 'Shake hands with him nicely.'

'How're ye, mister?' said Terry.

'But this fellow is a blooming boxer,' Mr Walker cried, letting on to be frightened of him. 'Do you box, young Samson?' he asked.

'I do not,' said Terry, scrambling into the back of the car and climbing up on the seat. 'Hey, mister, will we go through the village?' he added.

'What do you want to go through the village for?' asked Mr Walker.

'He wants to show off,' said his aunt with a chuckle. 'Don't you, Terry?'

'I do,' said Terry.

'Sound judge!' said Mr Walker, and they drove along the main road and up through the village street just as Mass was ending, and Terry, hurling himself from side to side, shouted to all the people he knew. First they gaped, then they laughed, finally they waved back. Terry kept shouting messages but they were lost in the noise and rush of the car. 'Billy! Billy!' he screamed when he saw Billy Early outside the church. 'This is my aunt's car. We're going for a spin. I have a bucket and spade.' Florrie was standing outside the Post Office with her hands behind her back. Full of magnanimity and self-importance, Terry gave her a special shout and his aunt leaned out and waved, but though Florrie looked up she let on not to recognize them. That was Florrie all out, jealous even of the car!

Terry had not seen the sea before, and it looked so queer that he decided it was probably England. It was a nice place enough but a bit on the draughty side. There were whitewashed houses all along the beach. His aunt undressed him and made him put on bright blue bathing-drawers, but when he felt the wind he shivered and sobbed and clasped himself despairingly under the armpits.

'Ah, wisha, don't be such a baby!' his aunt said crossly.

She and Mr Walker undressed too and led him by the hand to the edge of the water. His terror and misery subsided and he sat in a shallow place, letting the bright waves crumple on his shiny little belly. They were so like lemonade that he kept on tasting them, but they tasted salt. He decided that if this was England it was all right, though he would have preferred it with a park and a bicycle. There were other children making sandcastles and he decided to do the same, but after a while, to his great annoyance, Mr Walker came to help him. Terry couldn't see why, with all that sand, he wouldn't go and make castles of his own.

'Now we want a gate, don't we?' Mr Walker asked officiously.

'All right, all right, all right,' said Terry in disgust. 'Now, you go and play over there.'

'Wouldn't you like to have a daddy like me, Terry?' Mr Walker asked suddenly.

'I don't know,' replied Terry. 'I'll ask Auntie. That's the gate now.'

'I think you'd like it where I live,' said Mr Walker. 'We've much nicer places there.'

'Have you?' asked Terry with interest. 'What sort of places?'

'Oh, you know – roundabouts and swings and things like that.'

'And parks?' asked Terry.

'Yes, parks.'

'Will we go there now?' asked Terry eagerly.

'Well, we couldn't go there today; not without a boat. It's in England, you see; right at the other side of all that water.'

'Are you the man that's going to marry Auntie?' Terry asked, so flabbergasted that he lost his balance and fell.

'Now, who told you I was going to marry Auntie?' asked Mr Walker, who seemed astonished too.

'She did,' said Terry.

'Did she, by Jove?' Mr Walker exclaimed with a laugh. 'Well, I think it might be a very good thing for all of us, yourself included. What else did she tell you?'

'That you'd buy me a bike,' said Terry promptly. 'Will you?'

'Sure thing,' Mr Walker said gravely. 'First thing we'll get you when you come to live with me. Is that a bargain?'

'That's a bargain,' said Terry.

'Shake,' said Mr Walker, holding out his hand.

'Shake,' replied Terry, spitting on his own.

He was content with the idea of Mr Walker as a father. He could see he'd make a good one. He had the right principles.

They had their tea on the strand and then got back late to the station. The little lamps were lit on the platform. At the other side of the valley the high hills were masked in dark trees and no light showed the position of the Earlys' cottage. Terry was tired; he didn't want to leave the car, and began to whine.

'Hurry up now, Terry,' his aunt said briskly as she lifted him out. 'Say night-night to Mr Walker.'

Terry stood in front of Mr Walker, who had got out before him, and then bowed his head.

'Aren't you going to say good-night, old man?' Mr Walker asked in surprise.

Terry looked up at the reproach in his voice and then threw himself blindly about his knees and buried his face in his trousers. Mr Walker laughed and patted Terry's shoulder. His voice was quite different when he spoke again.

'Cheer up, Terry,' he said. 'We'll have good times yet.'

'Come along now, Terry,' his aunt said in a brisk official voice that terrified him.

'What's wrong, old man?' Mr Walker asked.

'I want to stay with you,' Terry whispered, beginning to sob. 'I don't want to stay here. I want to go back to England with you.'

'Want to come back to England with me, do you?' Mr Walker repeated. 'Well, I'm not going back tonight, Terry, but if you ask Auntie nicely we might manage it another day.'

'It's no use stuffing up the child with ideas like that,' she said sharply.

'You seem to have done that pretty well already,' Mr Walker said quietly. 'So you see, Terry, we can't manage it tonight. We must leave it for another day. Run along with Auntie now.'

'No, no, no,' Terry shrieked, trying to evade his aunt's arms. 'She only wants to get rid of me.'

'Now, who told you that wicked nonsense, Terry?' Mr Walker said severely.

'It's true, it's true,' said Terry. 'She's not my auntie. She's my mother.'

Even as he said it he knew it was dreadful. It was what Florrie Clancy said, and she hated his auntie. He knew it even more from the silence that fell on the other two. His aunt looked down at him and her look frightened him.

'Terry,' she said with a change of tone, 'you're to come with me at once and no more of this nonsense.'

'Let him to me,' Mr Walker said shortly. 'I'll find the place.'

She did so and at once Terry stopped kicking and whining and nosed his way into Mr Walker's shoulder. He knew the Englishman was for him. Besides he was very tired. He was half asleep already. When he heard Mr Walker's step on the planks of the wooden bridge he looked up and saw the dark hillside, hooded with pines, and the river like lead in the last light. He woke again in the little dark bedroom which he shared with Billy. He was sitting on Mr Walker's knee and Mr Walker was taking off his shoes.

'My bucket,' he sighed.

'Oh, by gum, lad,' Mr Walker said, 'I'd nearly forgotten your bucket.'

Every Sunday after, wet or fine, Terry found his way across the footbridge and the railway station to the main road. There was a pub there, and men came from up from the valley and sat on the wall outside, waiting for the coast to be clear to slip in for a drink. In case there might be any danger of having to leave them behind, Terry brought his bucket and spade as well. You never knew when you'd need things like those. He sat at the foot of the wall near the men, where he could see the buses and cars coming from both directions. Sometimes a grey car like Mr Walker's appeared from round the corner and he waddled up the road towards it, but the driver's face was always a disappointment. In the evenings when the first buses were coming back he returned to the cottage and Mrs Early scolded him for moping and whining. He blamed himself a lot because all the trouble began when he broke his word to his aunt.

One Sunday, Florrie came up the main road from the village. She went past him slowly, waiting for him to speak to her, but he wouldn't. It was all her fault, really. Then she stopped and turned to speak to him. It was clear that she knew he'd be there and had come to see him and make it up.

'Is it anyone you're waiting for, Terry?' she asked.

'Never mind,' Terry replied rudely.

'Because if you're waiting for your aunt, she's not coming,' Florrie went on gently.

Another time Terry wouldn't have entered into conversation, but now he felt so mystified that he would have spoken to anyone who could tell him what was keeping his aunt and Mr Walker. It was terrible to be only five, because nobody ever told you anything.

'How do you know?' he asked.

'Miss Clancy said it,' replied Florrie confidently. 'Miss Clancy knows everything. She hears it all in the Post Office. And the man with the grey car isn't coming either. He went back to England.'

Terry began to snivel softly. He had been afraid that Mr Walker wasn't really in earnest. Florrie drew closer to him and then sat on the grass bank beside him. She plucked a stalk and began to shred it in her lap.

'Why wouldn't you be said by me?' she asked reproachfully. 'You know I was always your girl and I wouldn't tell you a lie.'

'But why did Mr Walker go back to England?' he asked.

'Because your aunt wouldn't go with him.'

'She said she would.'

'Her mother wouldn't let her. He was married already. If she went with him he'd have brought you as well. You're lucky he didn't.'

'Why?'

'Because he was a Protestant,' Florrie said primly. 'Protestants have no proper religion like us.'

Terry did his best to grasp how having a proper religion made up to a fellow for the loss of a house with lights that went off and

on, a park and a bicycle, but he realized he was too young. At
five it was still too deep for him.

'But why doesn't Auntie come down like she always did?'

'Because she married another fellow and he wouldn't like it.'

'Why wouldn't he like it?'

'Because it wouldn't be right,' Florrie replied almost pityingly.
'Don't you see the English fellow have no proper religion, so he
wouldn't mind, but the fellow she married owns the shop she
works in, and Miss Clancy says 'tis surprising he married her at
all, and he wouldn't like her to be coming here to see you. She'll
be having proper children now, you see.'

'Aren't we proper children?'

'Ah, no, we're not,' Florrie said despondently.

'What's wrong with us?'

That was a question that Florrie had often asked herself, but
she was too proud to show a small boy like Terry that she hadn't
discovered the answer.

'Everything,' she sighed.

'Florrie Clancy,' shouted one of the men outside the pub,
'what are you doing to that kid?'

'I'm doing nothing to him,' she replied in a scandalized tone,
starting as though from a dream. 'He shouldn't be here by him-
self at all. He'll get run over. . . . Come on home with me now,
Terry,' she added, taking his hand.

'She said she'd bring me to England and give me a bike of my
own,' Terry wailed as they crossed the tracks.

'She was only codding,' Florrie said confidently. Her tone
changed gradually; it was becoming fuller, more scornful. 'She'll
forget all about you when she has other kids. Miss Clancy says
they're all the same. She says there isn't one of them worth
bothering your head about, that they never think of anyone only
themselves. She says my father has pots of money. If you were in
with me I might marry you when you're a bit more grown-up.'

She led him up the short cut through the woods. The trees
were turning all colours. Then she sat on the grass and sedately
smoothed her frock about her knees.

'What are you crying for?' she asked reproachfully. 'It was all
your fault. I was always your girl. Even Mrs Early said it. I always
took your part when the others were against you. I wanted you
not to be said by that old one and her promises, but you cared

more for her and her old toys than you did for me. I told you what she was, but you wouldn't believe me, and now, look at you! If you'll swear to be always in with me I'll be your girl again. Will you?'

'I will,' said Terry.

She put her arms about him and he fell asleep, but she remained solemnly holding him, looking at him with detached and curious eyes. He was hers at last. There were no more rivals. She fell asleep too and did not notice the evening train go up the valley. It was all lit up. The evenings were drawing in.

THE PARAGON

I

JIMMY GARVIN lived with his mother in a little house in what we called the Square, though there wasn't much of a square about it. He was roughly my own age, but he behaved as if he were five years older. He was a real mother's darling, with pale hair and eyes, a round, soft, innocent face that seemed to become rounder and softer and more innocent from the time he began to wear spectacles, and one of those astonishingly clear complexions that keep their owners looking years younger than their real age. He talked slowly and carefully in a precise, old-fashioned way and hardly mixed at all with the other kids.

His mother was a pretty, excitable woman, with fair hair like Jimmy's, a long, thin face, and a great flow of nervous chatter. She had been separated for years from her husband, who was supposed to be in England somewhere. She had been a waitress in a club on the South Mall, and he was reputed to be of a rather better class, as class is understood in Cork, which is none too well. His family made her a small allowance, but it was not enough to support herself and Jimmy, and she eked it out with housework. It was characteristic of our poverty-stricken locality that the little allowance made her an object of great envy and that people did not like her and called her 'Lady Garvin'.

Each afternoon after school you would see Jimmy making for one of the fashionable districts where his mother worked, raising his cap and greeting any woman he knew in his polite old-fashioned way. His mother brought him into the kitchen and gave him whatever had been left over from lunch, and he read there till it was time for them to go home. He was no trouble; all he ever needed to make him happy was a book – any book – from the shelves or the lumber room, and he read with his head resting on his hands, which formed a screen between him and the domestic world.

'Mum,' he would say, beaming, 'this book is about a very

interesting play they have every year in a place called Oberam-
mergau. Oberammergau is in Germany. In Germany the
language they speak is German. Don't you think I should learn
German?'

'Should you, Jimmy?' she would ask tenderly. 'Don't you
think you're learning enough as it is?'

'But if we go to Germany,' he would exclaim with his trium-
phant smile, 'one of us has to know German. If we don't know
how to ask our way to the right platform, how will we know we're
on the right train? Perhaps they'll take us to Russia.'

'Oh, dear,' she would say, 'that would be dreadful.'

At the same time she was, of course, terribly proud of him,
particularly if the maid was there to hear him. For as Jimmy told
the story, his mother was always the heroine and he Prince
Charming. In a year or two he would begin to earn a lot of money,
and then they would have a big house on the river, exactly like
the one they were in, with a maid to wait on them who would
be paid more than any maid in the neighbourhood, and they
would spend their holidays in France and Italy. If his mother was
friendly with the maid she was working with, he even offered
the position to her. There was nothing like having the whole
thing arranged.

This was how he liked to pass the time while his mother
worked, reading, or – if she had the house to herself – wandering
gravely from room to room and imagining himself already the
owner, looking at himself in the dressing-table mirrors as he
poured bay rum on his hair and brushed it with the silver brushes,
and speaking to himself in a lingo he took to be German, touch-
ing the keys of the piano lightly, or watching from the tall
windows as people hurried by along the river bank in the rainy
dusk. Late in the evening his mother and he would go home
together, holding hands, while he still chattered on in his grave,
ancient, innocent way, the way of a child on whom Life has
already laid too heavy a burden.

But as time went on things grew easier. The monks saw that
Jimmy was out on his own as a student. Finally, Mrs Garvin gave
up the housework and took in boarders. She rented a big house
on the road near the tram-stop and accepted only lodgers of the
best class. There at last Jimmy could have a piano of his own,
though the instrument he did take up was the violin.

II

By the time he was ready for the University he had developed into a tall, gangling, good-looking boy, though his years of study had left their mark on him. He had a pleasant tenor voice and sang in one of the city choirs. He had got the highest mark in Ireland in the Intermediate exams, and his picture had appeared in the *Examiner*, with his right arm resting on a pedestal and his left hand supporting it to keep it from shaking.

And this, of course, was where the trouble really began, for his father's family saw the picture and read the story and realized that they – poor innocent, good-natured, country folk – were being done out of something by the city slickers. The Garvins were a family you couldn't do out of much, and they coveted their share of Jimmy's glory, all the more because they saw that he had got it all from the Garvins, who had always been intellectual – witness Great Uncle Harvey, who had been the greatest scholar in the town of Macroom, consulted even by the parish priest. Some sort of reconciliation was necessary; Mrs Garvin's allowance was increased, and she was almost silly with happiness since it seemed so much like a foretaste of all the things Jimmy had promised to do for her.

At the same time she feared the Garvins, a feeling with which Jimmy could not sympathize because he had no fear whatever of his father's family. He was mildly curious, that was all. To him they were just another audience for whom he could perform on the violin or to whom he could explain the facts of the international situation. At her request he called on his Aunt Mary, who lived in a new red-brick house a stone's throw from the College. Aunt Mary had been involved in a peculiar marriage with a middle-aged engineer, who had left her some money but no children. She was a shrewd, coaxing old West Cork woman with a face that must once have been good-looking. No sooner did she realize that Jimmy was presentable as well as 'smart' than she saw that it was the will of God that she should annex him. She was the family genealogist, and while she fed him excellently on tea, home-made scones, and cake, she filled in for him in a modest and deprecating way the family background he had missed.

It never occurred to her that this might come as an anticlimax to Jimmy. He listened to her with a vacant smile, and even made fun of Great Uncle Harvey to her face, a thing no one had ever presumed to do before, and when he left her she sat, looking out the window after his tall, swinging figure, and wondered if it was really worth her while to pay the call she had promised.

Mrs Garvin had even worse misgivings.

'I don't want that woman in the house, Jimmy,' she said, clasping her hands feverishly. 'She's the one I really blame for the trouble with your father.'

'Well, she's hardly going to make trouble between you and me,' said Jimmy, who had privately decided that his aunt was a fool.

'That's all you know,' his mother said bitterly.

In this she was right, but even she did not realize the full extent of the trouble Aunt Mary was preparing for them when she called. From Jimmy's point of view there was nothing wrong. Aunt Mary cluck-clucked with astonishment when he played the violin for her, when he sang, and when he really explained what was happening in Europe.

'Oh, Jimmy,' she said, 'I'd love your father to hear you sing. You have his voice. I can hear him in you.'

'Oh, no, I don't think so, Mrs Healy,' his mother said hastily. 'Jimmy has far too much to do.'

'Ah, I was only thinking of a week or ten days,' Aunt Mary said. ''Twould be a change for him.'

'I think he's much too young to travel alone,' Mrs Garvin said, quivering. 'In a year or two, perhaps.'

'Oh, really, Mum!' exclaimed Jimmy, cast down from the heights of abstract discussion. 'I think I'm able to travel alone by now.'

Aunt Mary had engaged his interest, and well she knew it. He had always been curious in a human way about the father he did not remember, and, being a born learner, was even more curious about England, a country he was always reading about and hearing of, but had never seen. He had more than his share of boyish vanity, and he knew that English contacts would assure him prestige among his fellow-students.

For twelve months, off and on, he argued with his mother about it, but each time it alarmed her again. When she finally did consent, it was only because she felt that it might be unfair to deprive him of a chance of widening his knowledge of the world.

So, at least, she said. But whatever she might say, and for all her fears, she was flattered, and with every bit of feminine vanity in her she desired the opportunity of showing off to her husband and his family the child they had abandoned and whom she had made into a paragon.

III

Jimmy's first sight of his father in Paddington Station came as a considerable shock to him. Somehow, whenever he had imagined his father it had been as a heavy man with a big red face and a grey moustache, slow-spoken and portentous; but the man who met him in a bowler hat and a pale grey tie was tall and stringy with a neat dark moustache and an irritable, worried air. His speech was pleasant and well-bred; his manner was unaffected without being demonstrative; and he had a sense of quiet fun that put Jimmy at his ease. But he didn't like to see such a distinguished-looking man carrying his cheap suitcase for him.

'Do let me carry that!' he said anxiously.

'Oh, that's all right, son,' his father said lightly. 'By the way,' he added smoothly, 'you'll find I talk an awful lot, but you don't have to pay any attention. If you talk, too, we'll get on fine. That's a hell of a heavy bag. We'd better get a taxi.'

It was another surprise to Jimmy when, instead of taking him to some boarding house in the suburbs, his father took him on an electric train to a station twenty-odd miles from London. To Jimmy it seemed that this must be the heart of the country, but the big houses and the tall red buses he saw did not seem countrified. There was a car waiting outside the station, and his father drove him over high hilly country full of woods and streams down into a little red-brick market town, with a market house on stilts in the middle of the street, and up the hills again. To Jimmy it was all new and exciting, and he kept looking out and asking intelligent questions to which he rarely got satisfactory answers.

'Oh, this damn country!' his father said testily. 'You have to drive five miles out of your way to avoid a hole in the road that's preserved because Alfred the Great fell into it. For God's sake, look at this for a main road!'

While Jimmy was still wondering how you would preserve a

hole in the road, they reached a village on top of the hills, a long, low street open on to a wide common, with a school, a church, a row of low cottages, and a public-house with a brightly painted inn-sign and with green chairs and tables ranged in front of it. They stopped a little up the road outside a cottage with high pilastered chimneys and diamond-paned windows, and a row of tall elms behind.

'You'd want to mind your head in this damn hole,' his father said as he pushed in the door. 'It may have been all right for Queen Elizabeth, but it's not all right for me.'

Jimmy found himself in a combination living- and dining-room with a huge stone fireplace and low oak beams. A door on the right led into a modern kitchen, and another at the end of the room seemed to lead on to a stairway of sorts. A woman and a little girl of four or five came slowly through this door, the woman lowering her head.

'This is Martha, Jim,' his father tossed off lightly as he kissed her. 'Any time you want her, just let me know. She's on the youthful side for me. Gussie, you old humbug,' he added to the little girl, 'this is your big brother. If you're nice to him he might give you five bob.'

Jimmy was stunned, and his face showed it. This was something he had never anticipated and did not know how to deal with. He was too innocent to know even if it was right or wrong. Of course, things might be different in England. But, whatever he believed, his behaviour had been conditioned by years of deference, and he smiled shyly and shook hands with Martha, a heavy, good-looking woman, who smiled back without warmth. As for Gussie, she stood in a corner with her legs splayed and a finger in her mouth.

'Sherry for you, son,' his father called from the farther room. 'I have to take this damn whiskey for my health.'

'Before you take it, I'd better show you your room,' said Martha, picking up his case. 'You'll need to mind your head.'

'Oh, please, Martha!' he said anxiously, but she preceded him with the bag, through the farther room where his father was measuring whiskey in a glass against the light and up a staircase similar to that in the dining-room. In spite of the warning, Jimmy bumped his head badly, and looked in good-humoured disgust at the low doorway. The stairs opened on to an attic room with high beams, a floor that sloped under the grey rug as though the house were on the point of collapse, and a low window that overlooked the garden, the roadway, and the common beyond, a cold blue green compared with the golden green of home. Beyond the common was a row of distant hills.

When he went downstairs again they all sat in the big room under his, and he took the sherry his father offered him. He was too shy to say he didn't drink. It was a nice room, not too heavily furnished, with its diamond-paned windows looking on to the gardens at the front and back, and with a small piano. This gave Jimmy the opening he needed. It seemed that Martha played the piano. In spite of their common interest, he found her very disconcerting. She was polite, and her accent was pleasant, but there seemed to him to be no warmth in her. He had trained himself to present a good impression without wasting time; he knew that he was polite, that he was intelligent, and that he had a fine voice; and it was a new experience for him to find his friendliness coming back to him like a voice in an empty house. It made him raise his voice and enlarge his gestures until he felt that he was even creating a disturbance. His father seemed to enjoy his loud-voiced caricature of Aunt Mary extolling the scholarship of Great Uncle Harvey, a character who struck Jimmy as being pure farce, but a moment later, having passed from amusement to indignation, he was irritably denouncing Great Uncle Harvey as the biggest bloody old humbug that had ever come out of Macroom. He was a man who seemed to move easily from mood to mood, and Jimmy, whose own moods were static and monumental, found himself laughing outright at the sheer unexpectedness of his remarks.

After supper, when Martha had gone to put Gussie to bed, his father stood with his hands behind his back before the big stone fireplace (which, according to him, had already asphyxiated three historical personages and would soon do for him). He was developing a stomach and a double chin, and Jimmy noticed a fundamental restlessness about him, as when he failed to find some letter he was searching for and called petulantly for Martha. She came in with an expressionless air, found the letter, and went out again. He was a man of many enthusiasms. At one moment he was emotional about Cork and its fine schools, so different from English ones, where children never learned anything but insolence, but a few minutes later, almost without a change of tone, he seemed to be advising Jimmy to get out as quick as he could before the damn place smothered him. When Jimmy, accustomed to an adoring feminine audience, gave him the benefit of his views on the Irish educational system, its merits and drawbacks, he sat with crossed legs, looking away and smiling as though to himself while he twirled the glass in his long sensitive fingers. He was something of a puzzle to Jimmy.

'I suppose you must think me a bit of a blackguard,' he said gruffly, rising again to give the fire a kick. 'The truth is, I hadn't the faintest idea what was happening you. Your mother wouldn't write – not that I'm criticizing her, mind you. We didn't get on, and she deserves every credit for you, whatever your aunt or anyone else may say. I'd be proud of her if she was my mother.'

'So I am,' said Jimmy with a beaming smile.

'All I mean is that she put herself to a lot of unnecessary trouble, not letting me help you. I can easily see you through college if that's all you want.'

'Thanks,' Jimmy replied with the same air of triumph. 'But I think I can manage pretty well on scholarships.'

'All the better. Anyway, you can have the money. It's an investment. It always pays to have one member of the family with brains: you never know when you'll need them. I'm doing fairly well,' he added complacently. 'Not that you can be sure of anything. Half the people in a place like this are getting by on credit.'

It was all very strange to Jimmy. He bumped his head again going up to bed, and chuckled to himself. From far away he heard the whistle of a train, probably going north on its way up the valley towards Ireland, and for a long time he lay in bed, his hands joined on his stomach, wondering what it all meant and what he should do about it. It became plainer when he contemplated it like this. He would just ask his father as man to man whether or not he and Martha were married, and if the answer was unsatisfactory, he would pack his bag and go, money or no money. No doubt his father would make a scene, and it would all be very unpleasant, but later on he would realize that Jimmy was right. Jimmy would explain this to him, and make it clear that anything he did was done as much in his father's interests as his own; that nothing was to be gained by defying the laws of morality and the church. Jimmy knew he had this power of dominating people; he had seen old women's eyes filled with tears when he had sung 'I'll Take You Home Again, Kathleen', and, though he rejoiced in the feeling of confidence it gave him, he took care never to abuse it, never to try and convince unless he was first convinced himself. He fell asleep in a haze of self-righteousness.

Next morning, after his father had driven him to Mass in the gymnasium of the local club, it did not seem quite so easy. His father seemed a more formidable character than any he had yet met. But Jimmy had resolution and obstinacy. He summed it all up and asked in a casual sort of way: 'Was it there you were married?'

His father's face grew stern, but he answered urbanely enough. 'No. Why?'

'Nothing,' Jimmy said weakly. 'I just wondered.'

'Whether a marriage in a gymnasium would be binding? I was wondering the same thing myself.'

And, as he got into the car, Jimmy realized that this was as far as ever he would get with his big scene. Whatever the reason was, he was overawed by his father. He put it down partly to the difference in age, and partly to the inflexibility of his own reactions. His father's moods moved too fast for him; beside him he felt like a knight in heavy armour trying to chase a fleet-footed mountainy man. He resolved to wait for a more suitable opportunity. They drove on, and his father stopped the car near the top of the hill, where there was a view of the valley up which the railway passed. Grey trees squiggled across it in elaborate patterns, and grey church towers and red-tiled roofs showed between them in the sunlight that overflowed into it from heavy grey-and-white clouds.

'Lovely, isn't it?' his father said quietly.

Then he smiled, and suddenly his face became extraordinarily young and innocent. There was a sort of sweetness in it that for a moment took Jimmy's breath away.

'You see, son,' he said, 'when I was sixteen my father should have taken me aside and told me something about women. But he was a shy man, and my mother wouldn't have liked it, so, you see, I'm in a bit of a mess. I'd have done the same for you, but I never got the chance, and I dare say when you're a bit older you'll find yourself in a thundering big mess, too. I wouldn't worry too much about it if I were you. Time enough for that when it happens.'

Then he drove on to the pub, apparently under the impression that he had now explained everything. It struck Jimmy that perhaps he would never reach the point of asking his father for an explanation.

His father had changed again and become swaggering and insolent. He made Jimmy play a game of darts with him, flirted with the woman of the house, and made cutting remarks to her husband about the local cricket team which her husband seemed to enjoy. Jimmy had the impression that for some reason they all liked his father.

'Silly bloody game, anyway,' he added with a snort. 'More like a serial story than a game. Give me a good rousing game of hurling where somebody's head gets split.'

'God, this is a beautiful country,' he muttered to Jimmy, standing at the door with one hand in his trousers pocket, the other holding his pint, while he smiled across the sunlit common, and again his face had the strange sweetness that Jimmy had noticed on it before. 'You'd be a long time at home before you could go into a country pub on Sunday and meet a crowd like this.'

There was a sort of consistency about his father's inconsistencies that reminded Jimmy of the sky with its pennants of blue and cascades of silver, but he found he did not like him any the less for these. He did not feel quite so comfortable on the train back to Ireland, wondering what he should tell his mother, feeling that he should tell her nothing, and knowing at the same time that this was something he was almost incapable of doing.

Naturally, he told her everything in the first half-hour, and, when she grew disgusted and bitter, felt he had betrayed a confidence.

'What did I say about your aunt?' she exclaimed. 'All the time she was pressing you to go there, she knew what it was like.'

'I'm not so sure that she did know,' Jimmy said doubtfully. 'I don't think Father tells her much.'

'Oh, Jimmy, you're too innocent to know what liars and cheats they all are, all the Garvins.'

'I didn't think there was much of the cheat about Father,' Jimmy protested. 'He was honest enough about it with me.'

'He was brazen about it,' his mother said contemptuously. 'Like all liars. 'Tisn't alike.'

'I'm not sure that he was brazen,' Jimmy protested weakly, trying in vain to assert himself again in his old authoritative way. 'It's just that he's not a good liar. And, besides,' he added knowingly, folding his hands on his lap and looking at her owlishly over his spectacles, 'we don't know the sort of temptations people have in a place like England.'

'Temptations aren't confined to England,' she said with a flash of temper.

By this time she was regretting bitterly her own folly in allowing him to visit his father. She resented, too, his father's having brought him to a public-house, even though Jimmy explained that he had only drunk cider, and that public-houses there were different. But her full bitterness about this was reserved till later, when Jimmy started going to public-houses on his own. He now had a small allowance from his father, and proceeded to indulge his mother and himself. He had made friends with a group that centred on the College: a couple of instructors, some teachers, some Civil Servants – the usual run of small-town intellectuals. Up to now, Jimmy had been a young fellow with no particular friends, partly because he had had no time for them, partly because, like most kids who have no time for friends, he was scared of them when they made advances to him.

It was about this time, too, that he acknowledged my existence, and the pair of us went for occasional walks together. I admired him almost extravagantly. Whatever he did, from the way he chose his ties to the way he greeted a woman on the road or the way he climbed a fence, was done with an air, while I stumbled over all of them. It was the same with ideas; by the time I had picked myself up after making a point, Jimmy would be crossing the next obstacle, looking back at me and laughing triumphantly. He had a disciplined personality and a trained mind, and, though he was sometimes impressed by my odd bits of knowledge, he was puzzled by my casual, impractical interests and desultory reading. He was a good teacher, so he lent me some elementary books and then started to take me through them step by step, but without much effect. I had not even the groundwork of knowledge, while he was a natural examination-passer with a power of concentration that I lacked completely.

At the same time I was put off by his other friends. They argued as people do who spend too much of their time in public-houses – for effect. They were witty and clever and said wounding things. In spite of my shortcomings, I had a sort of snobbery all my own. I felt they were failures, and I had the feeling that Jimmy only liked them for that very reason. His great weakness was showing off. I sat with them one evening, watching Jimmy lower his beer and listening to him defend orthodoxy against a couple of the others who favoured various forms of agnosticism. He argued well enough in the stubborn manner of a first-year philosophy student. Then he sang for us, a little too well for the occasion. I did not like it, the picture of the fellow I had known as a slim-faced, spectacled school-boy, laying down the law and singing in a pub. He was idling, he was drinking – though not anything like as much as his mother believed – and he had even picked up a girl, a school-teacher called Anne Reidy with whom he went to Crosshaven on week-ends. In fact, for the first time in his life Jimmy was enjoying himself, and, like all those who have not enjoyed themselves in childhood, he was enjoying himself rather too much.

At first his mother was bewildered; then she became censorious and bitter. Naturally she blamed his father for it all. She even told Jimmy that his father had deliberately set out to corrupt him just to destroy whatever she had been able to do for him, which wasn't exactly tactful as Jimmy felt most of the credit was due to himself. And then she, who for all those years had managed to keep her mind to herself, started to complain to Jimmy about her marriage, and the drinking, cheating, and general light-mindedness of his father, exactly as though it had all just newly happened. Jimmy listened politely but with a wooden face, which would have revealed to anyone but her that he thought she was obsessed by the subject.

She was a pathetic figure because, though she was proud and sensitive beyond any woman I knew – the sort who would not call at all unless she brought some little gift, and who took flight if you put on the kettle or looked at the clock – she haunted our house. She was, I think, secretly convinced that I had influence over Jimmy. It made me uncomfortable because not only did I realize how much it cost her to plead for her paragon with a nonentity like myself, but I knew I had no influence over him.

He was far too clever to be influenced by anyone like me. He was also, though I do not mean it in a derogatory way, too conceited. Once when I did try in a clumsy way to advise him, he laughed uproariously.

'Listen to him!' he said. 'Listen to the steady man! Why, you slug, you never in your whole life put in one week's connected work at anything.'

'That may be true enough, Jimmy,' I said without rancour, 'but all the same you should watch out. You could lose that scholarship.'

'Oh, I don't think so,' he said with a smile which expressed his enormous self-confidence. 'But at any rate, even if I did, the old man has plenty.'

But, though his mother continued to appeal to me silently, in conversation she developed a sort of facile pessimism that I found harder to understand. It was a kind of cynicism which failed to come off.

'Oh, I know what will happen,' she said with a shrug. 'I've seen it happen before. His father will get tired of him as he gets tired of everybody, and then he'll find himself with nothing.'

IV

That was not quite how it happened. One month Jimmy's allowance failed to arrive, and when he wrote his father a bantering letter, threatening to refer the matter to his lawyers, it was Martha who replied. There was no banter about her. His father had been arrested for embezzlement, and house, furniture, and business had all been swallowed up. Martha wrote as though she blamed his father for everything.

'I suppose God's vengeance catches up on them all sooner or later,' Mrs Garvin said bitterly.

'Something caught up on him,' Jimmy said with a stunned air. 'The poor devil must have been half out of his mind for years.'

'And now it's the turn of the widows and orphans he robbed,' said his mother.

'Oh, he didn't rob anybody,' Jimmy said.

'You should tell the police that.'

'I'm sure the police know it already,' said Jimmy. 'People like Father don't steal. They find themselves saddled with an expensive wife or family, and they borrow, intending to put it back. Everybody does it one way or another, but some people don't know where to stop. Then they get caught up in their own mistakes. I wish to God I'd known when I was there. I might have been able to help him.'

'You'll have enough to do to help yourself,' she said sharply.

'Oh, I'll manage somehow,' he said doubtfully. 'I dare say I can get a job.'

'As a labourer?' she asked mockingly.

'Not necessarily,' he said steadily, looking at her with some surprise. 'I can probably get an office job.'

'Yes,' she said bitterly, 'as a clerk. And all your years of study to go for nothing.'

That was something she scarcely needed to remind him of, though when he tried to get help he was reminded even more forcefully of the fact which most paragons learn sooner or later: that a cracked paragon is harder to dispose of than plain delft. He had made too much of a fool of himself. The County Council scholarship would not be renewed, and the College would promise nothing.

Even his mother had lost confidence in him, and as time went on his relations with her became more strained. She could not resist throwing the blame for everything on his father, and here she found herself up against a wall of obstinacy in him. He had already silently separated himself from his Aunt Mary, who had thrown herself on him in tears and told him his father had dragged the good name of the Garvins in the gutter. Jimmy didn't know about the good name of the Garvins, but somewhere in the back of his mind was a picture of his father facing a police officer alone with that weak innocent smile on his face, and whenever he thought of it a cloud came over his mind. He even wrote affectionately to his father in prison – something his mother found it hard to forgive. Her taunts had become almost a neurosis because she could not stop them, and when she began, nothing was too extravagant for her. Not only had his father deliberately corrupted Jimmy, but it would almost seem as if he had got himself gaoled with no other object than that of disgracing him.

'Oh, give it a rest, Mum,' Jimmy said, glowering at her from over his book. 'I made a bit of a fool of myself, but Father had nothing to do with that.'

'Don't tell me it wasn't his fault, Jimmy,' she said cuttingly. 'Is it you who never touched drink till you set foot in his house? You who never looked at the side of the road a girl walked at till you stayed with that – *filthy* thing?'

'All right, all right,' he said angrily. 'Maybe I am a blackguard, but if I am, that's my fault, not his. He only did what he thought was the best thing for me. Why do you always assume that everybody but yourself is acting with bad motives?'

'That's what the police seem to think, too,' she said.

Jimmy suddenly lost all control of himself. Like all who have missed the safety-valves of childhood, he had an almost insane temper. He flung his book to a corner of the room and went to the door, white and shaking.

'Damn you!' he said in a low bitter voice. 'I think you're almost glad to see that poor unfortunate devil ruined.'

It scared her, because for the first time she saw that her son, the boy for whom she had slaved her life away, was no better than a stranger. But it scared Jimmy even more. He had become so accustomed to obedience, gentleness, and industry that he could not even imagine how he had come to speak to his mother in such a tone. He, too, was a stranger to himself, a stranger who seemed to have nothing whatever to do with the Jimmy Garvin who had worked so happily every evening at home, and all he could do was to get away from it all with a couple of cronies and drink and argue till he was himself again.

What neither of them saw was that the real cause of the breach was that his mother wanted him back, wanted him all to herself as in the old days, and to forget that he had ever met or liked his foolish, wayward father, and that this was something he could not forget, even for her.

The situation could not last, of course. One evening he came in, looking distressed and pale.

'Mum,' he said with a guilty air, 'I have the offer of a room with a couple of students in Sheares' Street. I can help them with their work, and I'll have a place to myself to do my own. I think it's a good idea, don't you?'

She sat in the dusk, looking into the fire with a strained air, but when she spoke her voice was even enough.

'Oh, is that so, Jimmy?' she said. 'I suppose this house isn't good enough for you any longer?'

'Now, you know it's not that, Mum,' he replied. 'It's just that I have to work, and I can't while you and I are sparring. This is only for the time being, and, anyway, I can always spend the week-ends here.'

'Very well, Jimmy,' she said coldly. 'If the house is here you'll be welcome. Now, I'd better go and pack your things.'

By the time he left, he was in tears, but she was like a woman of ice. Afterwards she came to our house and sat over the fire in the kitchen. She tried to speak with calm, but she was shivering all over.

'Wisha, child, what ails you?' Mother asked in alarm.

'Nothing, only Jimmy's left me,' Mrs Garvin answered in a thin, piping voice while she tried to smile.

'Who?' Mother asked in horror, clasping her hands. 'Jimmy?'

'Packed and left an hour ago. He's taken a room with some students in town. . . . I suppose it was the best thing. He said he couldn't stand living in the same house with me.'

'Ah, for goodness' sake!' wailed Mother.

'That's what he said, Mrs Delaney.'

'And who cares what he said?' Mother cried in a blaze of anger. 'How can you be bothered with what people say? Half their time they don't know what they're saying. Twenty-five years I'm living in the one house with Mick Delaney, and where would I be if I listened to what he says? . . . 'Tis for the best, girl,' she added gently, resting her hand on Mrs Garvin's knee. ''Tisn't for want of love that ye were hurting one another. Jimmy is a fine boy, and he'll be a fine man yet.'

Almost immediately Jimmy got himself a small job in the courthouse with the taxation people. In the evenings he worked, and over the week-ends he came home. There was no trouble about this. He enjoyed his good meals and his soft bed, and in the evenings you could hear him bellowing happily away at the piano. His mother and he were better friends than they had been for a long time, but something seemed to have broken in her. Nothing, I believe, could now have roused her to any fresh effort. At the best of times she would have taken her son's liberation hard, but now the facile pessimism that had only been a crust over her real feelings seemed to have become part of her. It wasn't obtrusive or offensive; when we met she still approached me with the same eagerness, but suddenly she would give a bitter little smile and shrug and say: 'It's well to be you, Larry. You still have your dreams.' She seemed to me to spend more of her time in the church.

The rooms in Sheares' Street were not all they might have been, and Jimmy finally married Anne Reidy, the girl he had been walking out with. Anne had always struck me as a fine, jolly, bouncing girl. They lived in rooms on the Dyke Parade with the gas stove in the hall and the bathroom up the stairs, and even for these small comforts Anne had to hold down a job and dodge an early pregnancy, which, according to her, was 'a career in itself'. Jimmy was studying for a degree from London University, and doing the work by post. They were two hot-blooded people and accustomed to comfort, and the rows between them were shattering. Later they reported them in detail to me, almost as though they enjoyed them, which perhaps they did. Sometimes I met them up the tree-shadowed walk late at night, and went back for an hour to drink tea with them. Jimmy was thin, and there was a translucency about his skin that I didn't like. I guessed they were pretty close to starvation, yet in their queer way they seemed to be enjoying that, too.

By this time Jimmy could have had a permanent job in the County Council – people like him have the knack of making themselves indispensable – but he turned it down, foolishly, I thought. He wanted a degree, though he seemed to me to have no clear notion of what use it was going to be to him when he got it. He talked of Anne and himself getting jobs together in England, but that struck me as no more than old talk. It was only later that I understood it. He wanted a degree because it was the only pattern of achievement he understood, and the only one that could re-establish him in his own esteem. This was where he had failed, and this was where he must succeed. And this was what they were really fighting for, living on scraps, quarrelling like hell, dressing in old clothes, and cracking jokes about their poverty till they had the bailiffs in and Anne's career of childlessness had broken down with a bang.

Then one night I found them at supper in a little restaurant in a lane off Patrick Street. Jimmy was drunk and excited, and when he saw me he came up to me demonstratively and embraced me.

'Ah, the stout man!' he shouted with his eyes burning. 'The steady Delaney! Look at him! Thirty, if he's a day, and not a letter to his name!'

'He's celebrating,' Anne said rather unnecessarily, laughing at me with her mouth full. 'He's got his old degree. Isn't it a blessing? This is our first steak in six months.'

'And what are you going to do now?' I asked.

'Tomorrow,' said Jimmy, 'we're going on our honeymoon.'

'Baby and all!' Anne said, and exploded in laughter. 'Now tell him where!'

'Why wouldn't I tell him where?' shouted Jimmy. 'Why wouldn't I tell everybody? What's wrong with going to see the old man in gaol before they let him out? Nobody else did, even that bitch of a woman. Never went to see him and never sent the kid.'

'That's right,' Anne said almost hysterically. 'Now tell him about baby sister Gussie. That's the bit my mother is dying to hear.'

'You know what your mother can do!' Jimmy said exultantly. 'Where's that waitress?' he called, his long, pale face shining. 'Delaney needs drink.'

'Garvin has too much drink,' said Anne. 'And I'll be up all night putting wet cloths on his head. . . . You should see him when he's sick,' she said indignantly. ' "Oh, I'm finished! Oh, I'm going to die!" That's what his mother did for him!'

That may have been what his mother had done for him – I didn't know – but what interested me was what his father had done for him. All that evening, while they chattered and laughed in a sort of frenzy of relief, I was thinking of the troubles that Jimmy's discovery of his father had brought into his life, but I was thinking, too, of the strength it had given him to handle them. Now whatever he had inherited from his parents he had combined into something that belonged to neither of them, that was his alone, and that would keep him master of his destiny till the day he died.

DARCY IN THE LAND OF YOUTH

ONE OF the few things Mick Darcy remembered of what the monks in the North Monastery had taught him was the story of Oisin, an old chap who fell in love with a fairy queen called Niamh and went to live with her in the Land of Youth. Then, one day when he was a bit homesick, he got leave from her to come back and have a look at Ireland, only she warned him he wasn't to get off his horse. When he got back, he found his pals all dead and the whole country under the rule of St Patrick, and, seeing a poor labourer trying to lift a heavy stone that was too big for him but that would have been nothing at all to fellows of his own generation, Oisin bent down to give him a hand. While he was doing it, the saddle-girth broke and Oisin was thrown to the ground, an old, tired, spiritless man with nothing better to do than get converted and be thinking of how much better things used to be in his day. Mick had never thought much of it as a story. It had always struck him that Oisin was a bit of a mug, not to know when he was well off.

But the old legends all have powerful morals though you never realize it till one of them gives you a wallop over the head. During the war, when he was out of a job, Mick went to England as a clerk in a war factory, and the first few weeks he spent there were the most miserable of his life. He found the English as queer as they were always supposed to be; people with a great welcome for themselves and very little for anyone else.

Then there were the air-raids, which the English pretended not to notice. In the middle of the night Mick would be awakened by the wail of a siren, and the thump of faraway guns like all the window-panes of Heaven rattling: the thud of artillery, getting louder, accompanied a faint buzz like a cat's purring that seemed to rise out of a corner of the room and mount the walls to the ceiling, where it hung, breathing in steady spurts, exactly like a cat. Pretending not to notice things like that struck Mick as too much of a good thing. He would rise and dress himself and sit lonesome by the gas fire, wondering what on earth had induced him to leave his little home in Cork, his girl, Ina, and his pal, Chris – his world.

The daytime was no better. The works were a couple of miles outside the town, and he shared an office with a woman called Penrose and a Jew called Isaacs. Penrose called him 'Mr Darcy', and when he asked her to call him 'Mick' she wouldn't. The men all called him 'Darcy', which sounded like an insult. Isaacs was the only one who called him 'Mick', but it soon became plain that he only wanted to convert Mick from being what he called 'a fellow traveller', whatever the hell that was.

'I'm after travelling too much,' Mick said bitterly.

He wasn't a discontented man, but he could not like England or the English. On his afternoons off, he took long, lonesome country walks, but there was no proper country either, only red-brick farms and cottages with crumpled oak frames and high red-tiled roofs; big, smooth, sick-looking fields divided by low, neat hedges which made them look as though they all called one another by their surnames; handsome-looking pubs that were never open when you wanted them, with painted signs and non-sensical names like 'The Star and Garter' or 'The Shoulder of Mutton'. Then he would go back to his lodgings and write long, cynical, mournful letters home to Chris and Ina, and all at once he and Chris would be strolling down the hill to Cork city in the evening light, and every old house and bush stood out in his imagination as if spotlit, and everyone who passed hailed them and called him Mick. It was so vivid that when his old landlady came in to draw the black-out, his heart would suddenly turn over.

But one day in the office he got chatting with a girl called Janet who had something to do with personnel. She was a tall, thin, fair-haired girl with a quick-witted laughing air. She listened to him with her head forward and her eyebrows raised. There was nothing in the least alarming about Janet, and she didn't seem to want to convert him to anything, unless it was books, which she seemed to be very well up in, so he asked her politely to have supper with him, and she agreed eagerly and even called him Mick without being asked. She seemed to know as if by instinct that this was what he wanted.

It was a great ease to him; he now had someone to argue with, and he was no longer scared of the country or the people.

Besides, he had begun to master his job, and that always gave him a feeling of self-confidence. He had a quiet conviction of his own importance and hated servility of any sort. One day a group of them, including Janet, had broken off work for a chat when the boss's brisk step was heard, and they all scattered – even Janet hastily said: 'Good-bye.' But Mick just gazed out the window, his hands still in his pockets, and when the boss came in, brisk and lantern-jawed, Mick looked at him over his shoulder and gave him a greeting. The boss only grinned. 'Settling in, Darcy?' he asked. 'Just getting the hang of things,' Darcy replied modestly. Next day the boss sent for him, but it was only to ask his advice about a scheme of office organization. Mick gave his opinions in a forthright way. That was another of his little weaknesses; he liked to hear himself talk. Judging by the way the boss questioned him, he had no great objection.

But country and people still continued to give him shocks. One evening, for instance, he had supper in the flat which Janet shared with a girl called Fanny, who was an analyst in one of the factories. Fanny was a good-looking, dark-haired girl with a tendency to moodiness. She asked how Mick was getting on with Mrs Penrose.

'Oh,' Mick said with a laugh, sitting back with his hands in his trouser pockets, 'she still calls me Mister Darcy.'

'I suppose that's only because she expects to be calling you something else before long,' said Fanny.

'Oh, no, Fanny,' said Janet. 'You wouldn't know Penrose now. She's a changed woman. With her husband in Egypt, Peter posted to Yorkshire, and no one to play with but George, she's started to complain of people who can't appreciate the simple things of life. Any day now she'll start talking about primroses.'

'Penrose?' Mick exclaimed with gentle incredulity, throwing himself back farther in his chair. 'I never thought she was that sort. Are you sure, Janet? I'd have thought she was an iceberg.'

'An iceberg?' Janet said gleefully, rubbing her hands. 'Oh, boy! A blooming fireship!'

'You're not serious?' murmured Mick, looking doubtfully at the two girls and wondering what fresh abyss might remain beneath the smooth surface of English convention.

Going home that night through the pitch-dark streets, he no longer felt a complete stranger. He had made friends with two of the nicest girls a man could wish for – fine broad-minded girls you could talk to as you'd talk to a man. He had to step in the roadway to make room for a couple of other girls, flicking their torches on and off before them; schoolgirls, to judge by their voices. 'Of course, he's married,' one of them said as they passed, and then went off into a rippling scale of laughter that sounded almost unearthly in the sinister silence and darkness.

A bit too broad-minded, thought Mick, coming to himself. Freedom was all very well, but you could easily have too much of that too.

But the shock about Penrose was nothing to the shocks that came on top of it. In the spring evenings Janet and he cycled off into the near-by villages and towns for their drinks. Sometimes Fanny came too, but she didn't seem very keen on it. It was as though she felt herself in the way, but at the same time she saw them go off with such a reproachful air that she made Janet feel bad.

One Sunday evening they went to church together. It seemed to surprise Janet that Mick insisted on going to Mass every Sunday morning, and she wanted him to see what a Protestant service was like. Her own religion was a bit mixed. Her father had been a Baptist lay preacher; her mother a Methodist; but Janet herself had fallen in love with a parson at the age of eleven and become Church for a while till she joined the Socialist Party and decided that Church was too conservative. Most of the time she did not seem to Mick to have any religion at all, for she said that you were just buried and rotted and that was all anyone knew. That seemed the general view. There were any amount of religions, but nobody seemed to believe anything.

It was against Mick's principles, but Janet was so eager that he went. It was in a little town ten miles from where they lived, with a brown Italian fountain in the market-place and the old houses edging out the grey church with its balustraded parapet and its blue clock-face shining in the sun. Inside there was a young sailor playing the organ while another turned over for him. The parson rang the bell himself. Only three women, one of whom was the organist, turned up.

The service, to Mick's mind, was an awful sell. The parson turned his back on them and read prayers at the east window; the organist played a hymn, which the three people in church took up, and then the parson read more prayers. There was no religion in it that Mick could see, but Janet joined in the hymns and seemed to get all worked up.

'Pity about Fanny,' she said when they were drinking their beer in the inn yard later. 'We could be very comfortable in the flat only for her. Haven't you a friend who'd take her off our hands?'

'Only in Ireland,' said Mick.

'Perhaps he'd come,' said Janet. 'Tell him you've a nice girl for him. She really is nice, Mick.'

'Oh, I know,' said Mick in surprise. 'But hasn't she a fellow already?'

'Getting a fellow for Fanny is the great problem of my life,' Janet said ruefully. 'I'll never be afraid of a jealous husband after her. The sight of her johns with the seat up is enough to depress her for a week.'

'I wonder if she'd have him,' Mick said thoughtfully, thinking how very nice it would be to have a friend as well as a girl. Janet was excellent company, and a good woman to learn from, but there were times when Mick would have been glad of someone from home with whom he could sit in judgment on the country of his exile.

'If he's anything like you, she'd jump at him,' said Janet.

'Oh, there's no resemblance,' chuckled Mick, who had never before been buttered up like this and loved it. 'Chris is a holy terror.'

'A terror is about what Fanny needs,' Janet said grimly.

It was only as the weeks went on that he realized that she wasn't exaggerating. Fanny always received him politely, but he had the feeling that one of these days she wouldn't receive him at all. She didn't intend to be rude, but she watched his plate as Janet filled it, and he saw she begrudged him even the food he ate. Janet did her best to shake her out of it by bringing her with them.

'Oh, come on, Fanny!' she said one evening with a weary air. 'I only want to show Mick the Plough in Alton.'

'Well, who'd know it better?' Fanny asked sepulchrally.

'There's no need to be difficult,' Janet replied with a flash of temper.

'Well, it's not my fault if I'm inhibited, is it?' Fanny asked with a cowed air.

'I didn't say you were inhibited,' Janet replied in a ringing tone. 'I said you were difficult.'

'Same thing from your point of view, isn't it?' Fanny asked. 'Oh, I suppose I was born that way. You'd better let me alone.'

All the way out, Janet was silent and Mick saw she was in a flaming temper, though he failed to understand what it was all about. It was distressing about Fanny, no doubt, but things were pleasanter without her. The evening was fine and the sun in wreath and veil, with the fields a bright blue-green. The narrow road wound between bulging walls of flint, laced with brick, and rows of old cottages with flower-beds in front that leaned this way and that as if they were taking life easy. It wasn't like Ireland, but still it wasn't bad. He was getting used to it as he was to being called Darcy. At the same time the people sometimes left him as mystified as ever. He didn't know what Fanny meant about being inhibited, or why she seemed to think it wrong. She spoke of it as if it was some sort of infectious disease.

'We'll have to get Chris for Fanny all right,' he said. 'It's extraordinary, though. An exceptional girl like that, you'd think she'd have fellows falling over her.'

'I don't think Fanny will ever get a man,' Janet replied in the shrill, scolding voice she used when upset. 'I've thrown dozens of them in her way, but she won't even make an effort. I believe she's one of those quite attractive women who go through life without ever knowing what it's about. She's just a raging mass of inhibitions.'

There it was again – prohibitions, exhibitions, inhibitions! He wished to God Janet would use simple words. He knew what exhibitions were from one old man in the factory who went to jail because of them. You would assume that inhibitions meant the opposite, but if so, what were the girls grousing about?

'Couldn't we do something about them?' he asked helpfully, not wishing to display his ignorance.

'Yes, darling,' she replied with a mocking air. 'You can take her away to Hell and give her a good roll in the hay.'

Mick was so staggered that he didn't reply. Even then it took a long time for Janet's words to sink in. By this time he was used to English dirty jokes, but he knew that this was something different. No doubt Janet was joking about the roll in the hay – though he wasn't altogether sure that she was joking about that either and didn't half hope that he might take her at her word – but she was not joking about Fanny. She really meant that all that was wrong with Fanny was that she was still a virgin, and that this was a complaint she did not suffer from herself.

The smugness horrified him as much as the savagery with which it was uttered. Put in certain way, it might be understandable, and even forgivable. Girls of Janet's kind were known at home as 'damaged goods', but he had never permitted the expression to pass. He had a strong sense of justice and always tended to take the side of the underdog. Some girls had not the same strength of character as others; some were subjected to greater temptation than others; he had never met any, but he was quite sure that if he had he would have risen to the occasion. But to have a girl like that stand up and treat her own weakness as strength and another girl's strength as weakness was altogether too much for him to take. It was like asking him to stand on his head.

Having got rid of her spite, Janet began to brighten. 'This is wonderful,' she sighed with tranquil pleasure as they floated downhill towards Alton and the Plough, a pleasant little inn, standing at the bridge, half-timbered above and stone below, with a big yard to one side where a dozen cars were parked, and at the other a long garden with rustic seats overlooking the river. Mick didn't feel it was so very wonderful. He felt as lonely as he had done in his first weeks there. While Janet sat outside, he went to the bar for beer and stood there for a few minutes unnoticed. There was a little crowd at the bar; a bald fat man in an overcoat, with a pipe, a good-looking young man with a fancy waistcoat, and a local with a face like a turnip. The landlord, a man of about fifty, had a long, haggard face with horn-rimmed glasses, and his wife, apparently twenty years younger, was a good-looking young woman with bangs and a Lancashire accent. They were discussing a death in the village.

'I'm not against religion,' the local spluttered excitedly. 'I'm chapel myself, but I never tried to force me views on people. All them months poor Harry was paralysed, his wife and daughter never so much as wet his lips. That idn't right, is it? That idn't religion?'

'No, Bill,' the landlord said, shaking his head. 'Going too far, I call that.'

'Everyone is entitled to his views, but them weren't old Harry's views, were they?'

'No, Bill,' sighed the landlord's wife, 'they weren't.'

'I'm for freedom,' Bill said, tapping his chest. 'The night before he died, I come in here and got a quart of old and mild, didn't I, Joe?'

'Mild, wadn't it, Bill?' the publican asked anxiously, resettling his glasses.

'No, Joe, old and mild was always Harry's drink.'

'That's right, Joe,' the landlady expostulated. 'Don't you remember?'

'Funny,' said her husband. 'I could have swore it was mild.'

'And I said to Millie and Sue, "All right," I said. "You got other things to do. I'll sit up with old Harry." Then I took out the bottle. His poor eyes lit up. Couldn't move, couldn't speak, but I shall never forget the way he looked at that bottle. I had to hold his mouth open' – Bill threw back his head and pulled one side of his mouth awry in illustration – 'and let it trickle down. No. If that's religion give me beer!'

'Wonder where old Harry is now?' the fat man said, removing his pipe reverently. 'It's a mystery, Joe, i'nt it?'

'Shocking,' the landlord said, shaking his head.

'We don't know, do we, Charles?' the landlady said sadly.

'Nobody knows,' Bill bawled scornfully as he took up his pint again. 'How could they? Parson pretends to know, but he don't know any more than you and me. Shove you in the ground and let the worms get you – that's all anybody knows.'

It depressed Mick even more, for he felt that in some way Janet's views and those of the people in the pub were of the same kind and only the same sort of conduct could be expected from them. Neither had any proper religion and so they could not know right from wrong.

'Isn't it lovely here?' Janet sang out when he brought the drinks.

'Oh, grand,' said Mick without much enthusiasm.

'We must come and spend a few days here some time. It's wonderful in the early morning. . . . You don't think I was too bitchy about Fanny, do you, Mick?'

'Oh, it's not that,' he said, seeing that she had noticed his depression. 'I wasn't thinking of Fanny particularly. It's the whole set-up here that seems so queer to me.'

'Does it?' she asked with interest.

'Well, naturally – fellows and girls from the works going off on weekends together, as if they were going to a dance.'

He looked at her with mild concern as though he hoped she might enlighten him about a matter of general interest. But she didn't respond.

'Having seen the works, can you wonder?' she asked, and took a long drink of her beer.

'But when they get tired of one another, they go off with someone else,' he protested. 'Or back to the fellow they started with. Like Hilda in the packing shed. She's knocking round with Dorman, and when her husband comes back she'll drop him. At least, she says she will.'

'Isn't that how it usually ends?' she asked politely, raising her brows and speaking in a superior tone that left him with nothing to say. This time she really succeeded in scandalizing him.

'Oh, come, come, Janet!' he said scornfully. 'You can't take that line with me. You're not going to pretend there's nothing more than that in it?'

'Well, I suppose, like everything else, it's just what you make of it,' she replied with a sophisticated shrug.

'But that's not making anything at all of it,' he said, beginning to grow heated, 'If it's no more than a roll in the hay, as you call it, there's nothing in it for anybody.'

'And what do you think it should be?' she asked with a politeness that seemed to be the equivalent of his heat. He realized that he was not keeping to the level of a general discussion. He could distinctly hear how common his accent had become, but excitement and a deep-seated feeling of injury carried him away.

'But look here, Janet,' he protested, sitting back stubbornly with his hands in his trouser pockets, 'learning to live with somebody isn't a thing you can pick up in a weekend. It's a blooming job for life. You wouldn't take up a job somewhere in the middle, expecting to like it, and intending to drop it in a few months' time if you didn't, would you?'

'Oh, Mick,' she groaned in mock distress, 'don't tell me you have inhibitions too!'

'Oh, you can call them what you like,' retorted Mick, growing commoner as he was dragged down from the heights of abstract discussion to the expression of his own wounded feelings. 'I saw the fellows who have no inhibitions, as you call them, and they didn't seem to me to have very much else either. If that's all you want from a man, you won't have far to go.'

By this time Janet had realized that she was dealing with feelings rather than with general ideas and was puzzled. After a moment's thought she began to seek for a point of reconciliation.

'But after all, Mick, you've had affairs yourself, haven't you?' she asked reasonably.

Now, of all questions, this was the one Mick dreaded most, because, owing to a lack of suitable opportunities, for which he was in no way to blame, he had not. For the matter of that, so far as he knew, nobody of his acquaintance had either. He knew that in the matter of experience, at least, Janet was his superior, and, coming from a country where men's superiority – affairs or no affairs – was unchallenged, he hesitated to admit that, so far as experience went, Fanny and he were in the one boat. He was not untruthful, and he had plenty of moral courage. There was no difficulty in imagining himself settling deeper down on to his bench and saying firmly and quietly: 'No, Janet, I have not,' but he did not say it.

'Well, naturally, I'm not an angel,' he said in as modest a tone as he could command and with a shrug intended to suggest that it meant nothing in particular to him.

'Of course not, Mick,' Janet replied with all the enthusiasm of a liberal mind discovering common ground with an opponent. 'But then there's no argument.'

'No argument, maybe,' he said coldly, 'but there are distinctions to be made.'

'What distinctions?'

'Between playing the fool and making love,' he replied with a weary air as though he could barely be bothered explaining such matters to a girl as inexperienced as she. From imaginary distinctions he went on to out-and-out prevarication. 'If I went out with Penrose, for instance, that would be one thing. Going out with you is something entirely different.'

'But why?' she asked as though this struck her as a doubtful compliment.

'Well, I don't like Penrose,' he said mildly, hoping that he sounded more convincing than he felt. 'I'm not even vaguely interested in Penrose. I am interested in you. See the difference?'

'Not altogether,' Janet replied in her clear, unsentimental way. 'You don't mean that if two people are in love with one another, they should have affairs with somebody else, do you?'

'Of course I don't,' snorted Mick, disgusted by this horrid example of English literal-mindedness. 'I don't see what they want having affairs at all for.'

'Oh, so that's what it is!' she said with a nod.

'That's what it is,' Mick said feebly, realizing the cat was out of the bag at last. 'Love is a serious business. It's a matter of responsibilities. If I make a friend, I don't begin by thinking what use I can make of him. If I meet a girl I like, I'm not going to begin calculating how cheap I can get her. I don't want anything cheap,' he added with passion. 'I'm not going to rush into anything till I know the girl well enough to try and make a decent job of it. Is that plain?'

'Remarkably plain,' Janet replied icily. 'You mean you're not that sort of man. Let me buy you a drink.'

'No, thanks.'

'Then I think we'd better be getting back,' she said, rising and looking like the wrath of God.

Mick, crushed and humiliated, followed her at a slouch, his hands still in his trouser pockets. It wasn't good enough. At home a girl would have gone on with the argument till one of them fell unconscious, and in argument Mick had real staying power, so he felt she was taking an unfair advantage. Of course, he saw that she had some reason. However you looked at it, she had more or less told him that she expected him to be her lover, and he had more or less told her to go to hell, and he had a suspicion that this was an entirely new experience for Janet. She might well feel mortified.

But the worst of it was that, thinking it over, he realized that even then he had not been quite honest. He had not told her he already had a girl at home. He believed all he had said, but he did not believe it quite so strongly as all that; not so as not to make exceptions. Given time, he might quite easily have made an exception of Janet. She was the sort of girl people made an exception of. It was the shock that had made him express himself so violently; the shock of realizing that a girl he cared for had lived with other men. He had reacted that way almost in protest against them.

But the real shock had been the discovery that he minded so much what she was.

They never resumed the discussion openly, on the same terms, and it seemed as though Janet had forgiven him, but only just. The argument was always there beneath the surface, ready to break out again. It flared up whenever she mentioned Fanny – 'I suppose one day she'll meet an Irishman, and they can discuss one another's inhibitions.' Or when she mentioned other men she had known, like Bill, with whom she had spent a holiday in Dorset, or an American called Tom with whom she had gone to the Plough in Alton, she seemed to be contrasting the joyous past with the dreary present, and she became cold and insolent.

Mick gave as good as he got. He had a dirty tongue, and he had considerable more ammunition than she. The canteen was always full of gossip about who was living with whom, or who had stopped living with whom, or whose wife or husband had returned and found him or her living with someone else, and he passed it on with a quizzical air. The first time she said 'Good!' in a ringing voice. After that, she contented herself with a shrug, and Mick suggested ingenuously that perhaps it took all those religions to deal with so much fornication. 'One religion would be more than enough for Ireland,' she retorted, and Mick grinned and admitted himself beaten.

But, all the same, he could not help feeling that it wasn't nice. He remembered what Fanny had said about nobody's knowing the Plough better, and Janet about how nice it was in the early morning. Really, really, it wasn't nice! It seemed to show a complete lack of sensibility in her to think of bringing him to a place where she had stayed with somebody else, and made him suspicious of every other place she brought him. He had never been able to share her enthusiasm for old villages of red-brick cottages, all coloured like geraniums, grouped about a grey church tower, but he lost even the desire to share it when he found himself wondering what connection it had with Bill or Tom.

At the same time, he could not do without her. They met every evening after work, went off together on Saturday afternoons, and she even came to Mass with him on Sunday mornings. Nor was there any feeling that she was critical of it. She followed the service with great devotion. As a result, before he returned home on his first leave, everything seemed to have changed between them. She no longer criticized Fanny's virginity and ceased altogether to refer to Bill and Tom. Indeed, from her conversation it would have been hard to detect that she had ever known such men, much less been intimate with them. Mick wondered whether it wasn't possible for a woman to be immoral and yet remain innocent at heart and decided regretfully that it wasn't likely. But no wife or sweetheart could have shown more devotion than she in the last week before his return, and when they went to the station and walked arm-in-arm to the end of the long, drafty platform to say good-bye, she was stiff with unspoken misery. She seemed to feel it was her duty to show no sign of emotion.

'You will come back, Mick, won't you?' she asked in a clear voice.

'Why?' Mick asked banteringly. 'Do you think you can keep off Americans for a fortnight?'

That she spat out a word that showed only too clearly her intimacy with Americans and others. It startled Mick. The English had strong ideas about when you could joke and when you couldn't, and she seemed to think this was no time for joking. To his surprise, he found she was trembling all over.

At any other time he would have argued with her, but already in spirit he was half-way home. There, beyond the end of the line, was Cork, and with it home and meat and butter and nights of tranquil sleep. When he leaned out of the window to wave good-bye, she was standing like a statue, looking curiously desolate. Her image faded quickly, for the train was crowded with Irish servicemen and women, clerks and labourers, who gradually sorted themselves out into north and south, country and town, and within five minutes, Mick, in a fug of steam heat and tobacco smoke, was playing cards with a group of men from the South Side who were calling him by his Christian name. Janet was already farther away than any train could leave her.

It was the following evening when he reached home. He had told no one of his coming and arrived in an atmosphere of sensation. He went upstairs to his own little whitewashed room with the picture of the Sacred Heart over his bed and lost himself in the study of his shelf of books. Then he shaved and, without waiting for more than a cup of tea, set off down the road to Ina's.

Ina was the youngest of a large family, and his arrival there created a sensation too. Elsie, the eldest, a fat, jolly girl, just home from work, shouted with laughter at him.

'He smelt the sausages.'

'You can keep your old sausages,' Mick said scornfully. 'I'm taking Ina out to supper.'

'You're what?' shouted Elsie. 'You have high notions like the goats in Kerry.'

'But I have to make my little brothers' supper, honey,' Ina said laughingly as she smoothed his hair. She was a slight, dark, radiant girl with a fund of energy.

'Tell them make it themselves,' Mick said scornfully.

'Tell them, you!' cried Elsie. 'Someone ought to have told them years ago, the caubogues! They're thirty, and they have no more intention of marrying than flying. Have you e'er an old job for us over there? I'm damned for the want of a man.'

Ina rushed upstairs to change. Her two brothers came in, expressed astonishment at Mick's appearance, satisfaction at his promotion, incredulity at his view that the English weren't beaten, and began hammering together on the table with their knives and forks.

'Supper up! Supper up!' shouted the elder, casting his eyes on the ceiling. 'We can't wait all night. Where the hell is Ina?'

'Coming out to dinner with me,' replied Mick with a sniff, feeling that for the first time in his life he was uttering a curtain line.

They called for Chris, an undersized lad with a pale face like a fist and a voice like melted butter. He expressed pleasure at seeing them, but gave no other signs of it. It was part of Chris's line never to be impressed by anything. In a drawling voice he commented on priests, women, and politicians, and there was little left of any of them when he had done. He had always regarded Mick as a bit of a softy because of his fondness for Ina. For himself, he would never keep a girl for more than a month because it gave them ideas.

'What do you want going to town for supper for?' he drawled incredulously, as though this were only another indication that Mick was a bit soft in the head. 'Can't ye have it at home?'

'You didn't change much anyway,' said Mick with a snort of delight. 'Hurry up!'

He insisted on their walking so as not to miss the view of the city he had been dreaming of for months; the shadowy perspective of winding road between flowering trees, and the spires, river, and bridges far below in evening light. His heart was overflowing. Several times they were stopped by neighbours who wanted to know how things were in the outside world. Because of the censorship, their ideas were very vague.

'Oh, all right,' Mick replied modestly.

'Ye're having it bad.'

'A bit noisy at times, but you get used to it,' he said lightly.

'I dare say, I dare say.'

There was pity rather than belief in their voices, but Mick didn't mind. It was good to be back where people cared whether you were having it bad or not. But in his heart Mick felt you didn't get used to it, that you never could, and that all of it, even Janet, was slightly unreal. He had a suspicion that he would not return. He had had enough of it.

Next morning, while he was lying in bed in his little attic, he received a letter from Janet. It must have been written while he was still on the train. She said that trying to face things without him was like trying to get used to an amputated limb; she kept on making movements before realizing that it wasn't there. He dropped the letter at that point without trying to finish it. He couldn't help feeling that it sounded unreal too.

Mick revisited all his old haunts. 'You should see Fair Hill,' his father said with enthusiasm. ''Tis unknown the size that place is growing.' He went to Fair Hill, to the Lough, to Glanmire, seeing them with new eyes and wishing he had someone like Janet to show them off to. But he began to realize that without a job, without money, it would not be very easy to stay on. His parents encouraged him to stay, but he felt he must spend another six months abroad and earn a little more money. Instead, he started to coax Chris into coming back with him. He knew now that his position in the factory would ensure a welcome for anyone he brought in. Besides, he grew tired of Ina's brothers telling him how the Germans would win the war, and one evening was surprised to hear himself reply in Chris's cynical drawl: 'They will and what else?' Ina's brothers were surprised as well. They hadn't expected Mick to turn his coat in that way.

'You get the feeling that people here never talk of anything only religion and politics,' he said one evening to Chris as they went for their walk up the Western Road.

'Ah, how bad it is!' Chris said mockingly. 'Damn glad you were to get back to it. You can get a night's sleep here anyway.'

'You can,' Mick said in the same tone. 'There's no one to stop you.'

Chris looked at him in surprise, uncertain whether or not Mick meant what he seemed to mean. Mick was developing out of his knowledge entirely.

'Go on!' he said with a cautious grin. 'Are they as good-natured as that?'

'Better come and see,' Mick said sedately. 'I have the very girl for you.'

'You don't say so!' Chris exclaimed with the smile of a child who has ceased to believe in Santa Claus but likes to hear about it just the same.

'Fine-looking girl with a good job and a flat of her own,' Mick went on with a smile. 'What more do you want?'

Chris suddenly beamed.

'I wouldn't let Ina hear me talking like that if I was you,' he said. 'Some of them quiet-looking girls are a terrible hand with a hatchet.'

At that moment it struck Mick with cruel force how little Ina had to reproach him with. They were passing the college, and pairs of clerks and servant girls were strolling by, whistling and calling to one another. There was hardly another man in Ireland who would have behaved as he had done. He remembered Janet at the station with her desolate air, and her letter, which he had not answered. Perhaps, after all, she meant it. Suddenly everything seemed to turn upside down in him. He was back in the bar in Alton, listening to the little crowd discussing the dead customer, and carrying out the drinks to Janet on the rustic seat. It was no longer this that seemed unreal, but the Western Road and the clerks and the servant girls. They were like a dream from which he had wakened so suddenly that he had not even realized that he was awake. And he had waked up beside a girl like Janet and had not even realized that she was real.

He was so filled with consternation that he almost told Chris about her. But he knew that Chris would no more under-stand him than he had understood himself. Chris would talk sagaciously about 'damaged goods' as if there were only one way in which a woman could be damaged. He knew that no one would understand, for already he was thinking in a different language. Suddenly he remembered the story of Oisin that the monks had told him, and it began to have meaning for him. He wondered wildly if he would ever get back or if, like Oisin in the story, he would suddenly collapse and spend the rest of his days walking up and down the Western Road with people as old and feeble as himself, and never see Niamh or the Land of Youth. You never knew what powerful morals the old legends had till they came home to you. On the other hand, their heroes hadn't the advantages of the telephone.

'I have to go back to town, Chris,' he said, turning in his tracks. 'I've just remembered I have a telephone call to put through.'

'Good enough,' Chris said knowingly. 'I suppose you might as well tell her I'm coming too.'

When Chris and himself got in, the alert was still on and the station was in pitch-darkness. Outside, against the clear summer sky, shadowy figures moved with pools of light at their feet, and searchlights flickered like lightning over the battlements of the castle. For Chris, it had all the novelty it had once had for Mick, and he groaned. Mick gripped his arm and steered him confidently.

'This is nothing,' he said cheerfully. 'Probably only a scouting plane. Wait till they start dropping a few wagons of high explosive and you'll be able to talk.'

It was sheer delight to Mick to hear himself speak in that light-hearted way of high explosives. He seemed to have become forceful and cool all at once. It had something to do with Chris's being there, as though it gave occupation to all his protective instincts. But there was something else as well. It was almost as though he were arriving home.

There was no raid, so he brought Chris round to meet the girls, and Chris groaned again at the channel of star-shaped traffic signals that twinkled between the black cliffs of houses whose bases opened mysteriously to reveal pale stencilled signs or caverns of smoky light.

Janet opened the door, gave one hasty, incredulous glance at Chris, and then hurled herself at Mick's neck. Chris opened his eyes with a start – he later admitted to Mick that he had never before seen a doll so quick off the mark. But Mick was beyond caring for appearances. While Chris and Fanny were in the throes of starting a conversation, he followed Janet into the kitchen, where she was recklessly tossing a week's rations into the pan. She was hot and excited and used two dirty words in quick succession, but he didn't mind these either. He leaned against the kitchen wall with his hands in his trouser pockets and smiled at her.

'I'm afraid you'll find I've left my principles behind me this time,' he said with amusement.

'Oh, good!' she said – not as enthusiastically as he might have expected, but he put that down to the confusion caused by his unexpected arrival.

'What do you think of Chris?'

'A bit quiet, isn't he?' she asked doubtfully.

'Scared,' replied Mick with a sniff of amusement. 'He'll soon get over that. Should we go off somewhere for the weekend?'

'Next weekend?' she asked aghast.

'Or the one after. I don't mind.'

'You're in a hurry, aren't you?'

'So would you be if you'd spent a fortnight in Cork.'

'All of us?'

'The more the merrier. Let's go somewhere really good,' he went on enthusiastically. 'Take the bikes and make a proper tour of it. I'd like Chris to see a bit of the country.'

It certainly made a difference, having Chris there. And a fortnight later the four of them set off on bicycles out of town. It was a perfect day of early summer. Landscape and houses gradually changed; old brick and flint giving place to houses of small yellow tile, tinted with golden moss, and walls of narrow tile-like stone with deep bands of mortar that made them seem as though woven. Out of the woven pullovers rose gables with coifs of tile, like nuns' heads. It all came over Mick in a rush; the presence of his friend and of his girl and a country that he had learned to understand. While they sat on a bench outside a country public-house, he brought out the beer and smiled with quiet pride.

'Good?' he asked Chris with a slight lift of his brows.

'The beer isn't up to much, if that's what you mean,' replied Chris, who still specialized in not being impressed.

In the late evening they reached their destination, having

cycled through miles of suburb with gardens in flower, and dismounted in the cobbled yard of an inn where Queen Elizabeth was supposed to have stayed and Shakespeare's company performed; the walls of the narrow, twisting stairs were dark with old prints, and the windows deep embrasures that overlooked the yard. The dining-room had great oak beams and supports. At either end there was an oak dresser full of window-ware, with silver sauceboats hanging from the shelves and brass pitchers on top.

'You'd want to mind your head in this hole,' Chris said with an aggrieved air.

'But this place is four hundred years old, man,' protested Mick.

'Begor, in that time you'd think they'd make enough to rebuild it,' said Chris.

He was still acting in character, but Mick was just the least bit disappointed in him. He hit it off with Fanny, who had been thrown into such a panic that she was prepared to hit it off with anyone, but he seemed to have lost a lot of his dash. Mick wasn't quite sure yet but that he would take fright before Fanny. He would certainly do so if he knew what a blessed innocent she was. Whenever Mick looked at her, her dark, sullen face broke into a wistful smile that made him think of a Christian martyr's first glimpse of the lion. No doubt he would lead her to paradise, but the way was messy and uncomfortable.

After supper Janet showed them the town and finally led them to a very nice old pub which was on no street at all but was approached by a system of alleyways. The little bar-room was full, and Janet and he were crowded into the yard, where they sat on a bench in the starlight. Beyond the clutter of old tiled roofs a square battlemented tower rose against the sky. Mick was perfectly happy.

'You're certain Fanny will be all right with Chris?' Janet asked anxiously.

'Oh, certain,' replied Mick with a slight feeling of alarm lest his troops had opened negotiations behind his back. 'Why? Did she say anything?'

'No,' said Janet in a bustle of motherly solicitude, 'but she's in a flat spin. I've told her everything, but she's afraid she'll get it mixed up, and if anyone could that girl will. He does understand, doesn't he?'

'Oh, perfectly,' said Mick with a confidence he did not feel, but his troops were already sufficiently out of hand. If Janet started to give orders they would undoubtedly cut and run.

When they returned to the hotel and the boys retired to their room, the troops were even more depressed.

'A fellow doesn't know how well off he is,' said Chris mournfully.

He said it by way of a joke, but Mick knew it was something more. Chris was even more out of his element than he had been. All his life he had practised not being impressed by anything, but in this new country there was far too much not to be impressed about.

'Why?' Mick asked from his own bed. 'Would you sooner be up the Western Road?'

'Don't talk to me about the Western Road!' groaned Chris. 'I think I'll never see it.'

He didn't sound in the least dashing, and Mick only hoped he wouldn't break down and beg Fanny to let him off. It would be a sad end to the picture he had built up of Chris as the romantic Irishman.

Then the handle of their door turned softly and Janet tiptoed in in her bathing-wrap, her usual competent self, as though arriving in men's bedrooms at that hour of night was second nature to her. 'Ready Chris?' she whispered. Chris was a lad of great principle and Mick couldn't help admiring his manliness. With a face like death on him he went out, and Janet closed the door cautiously behind him. Mick listened to make sure he didn't hide in the toilet. Then Janet switched off the light, drew back the black-out, and, shivering slightly, opened the window on the darkened inn yard. They could hear the Klaxons from the street, while the stuffy room filled with the smells and rustlings of a summer night.

In the middle of the night Mick woke up and wondered where he was. When he recollected, it was with a feeling of profound satisfaction. It was as if he had laid down a heavy burden he had been carrying all his life, and in the laying down had realized that the burden was quite unnecessary. For the pleasantest part of it was that there was nothing particular about the whole business and that it left him the same man he had always been.

With a clearness of sight which seemed to be part of it, he realized that all the charm of the old town had only been a put-up job of Janet's because she had been here already with someone else. He should have known it when she took them to the pub. That, too, was her reason for suggesting this pleasant old inn. She had stayed there with someone else. It was probably the American and possibly the same bed. Women had no interest in scenery or architecture unless they had been made love to in them. And, Mick thought with amusement, that showed very good sense on their part. If he ever returned with another woman, he would also bring her here, because he had been happy here. Happiness, that was the secret the English had and the Irish lacked.

It was only then that he realized that what had wakened him was Janet's weeping. She was crying quietly beside him. At first it filled him with alarm. In his innocence he might quite easily have made a mess of it without even knowing. It was monstrous, keeping men in ignorance up to his age. He listened till he could bear it no longer.

'What is it, Jan?' he asked in concern.

'Oh, nothing,' she replied, dabbing her nose viciously with her handkerchief. 'Go to sleep.'

'But how can I and you like that?' he asked plaintively. 'Was it anything I did?'

'No, of course not, Mick.'

'Because I'm sorry, if it was.'

'Oh, it's not that, it's not that,' she replied, shaking her head miserably. 'I'm just a fool, that's all.'

The wretchedness of her tone made him forget his own doubts and think of her worries. Being a man of the world was all right, but Mick would always be more at home with other people's troubles. He put his arm about her and she sighed and threw a bare leg over him. It embarrassed him for a moment, but then he remembered that now he was a man of the world.

'Tell me,' he whispered gently.

'Oh, it's what you said that night at the Plough,' she sobbed.

'The Plough?' he echoed in surprise.

'The Plough at Alton.'

Mick found it impossible to remember what he had said at the Plough, but he was used to the peculiar way women remembered things which some man had said and forgotten, and which he would have been glad if they had forgotten too.

'Remind me of it,' he said.

'Oh, when you said love was a matter of responsibilities.'

'Oh, yes, yes,' he said. 'I remember now.' But he didn't. What he remembered mostly was that she had told him about the other men, and he had argued with her. 'But you shouldn't take that too seriously, Jan.'

'Oh, what else could I do but take it seriously?' she asked fiercely. 'I was mad with you, but I knew you were right. I knew that was the way I'd always felt myself, only I blinded myself. Just as you said; taking up love like a casual job you could drop whenever you pleased. I'm well paid for my own bloody folly.'

She began to sob again. Mick found it very difficult to readjust his mind to the new situation. One arm about her and the other supporting his head, he looked out the window and thought about it.

'Oh, of course, that's perfectly true, Janet,' he agreed, 'but, on the other hand, you can take it to the fair. You have to consider the other side of the question. Take people who're brought up to look at the physical facts of love as inhuman and disgusting. Think of the damage they do to themselves by living like that in superstitions. It would be better for them to believe in fairies or ghosts if they must believe in some sort of nonsense.'

'Yes, but if I had a daughter, I'd prefer to bring her up like that than in the way I was brought up, Mick. At least she wouldn't fool with serious things, and that's what I've done. I made fun of Fanny because she didn't sleep around like the rest of us, but if Fanny falls for Chris, the joke will be on me.'

Mick was silent again for a while. The conversation was headed in a direction he had not foreseen, and he could not yet see the end of it.

'You don't mean you didn't want to come?' he asked in astonishment.

'Oh, it's not that,' she cried, beating her forehead with her fist. 'Don't you see that I wanted to prove to myself that I could be a decent girl for you, and that I wasn't just one of the factory janes who'll sleep with anything? I wanted to give you something worth while, and I have nothing to give you.'

'Oh, I wouldn't say that,' Mick said in embarrassment. He

was feeling terribly uncomfortable. Life was like that. At one moment you were on top of the world, and the next you were on the point of tears. At the same time it was hard to sacrifice his new-found freedom from inhibitions, all in a moment, as you might say. Here he had lain, rejoicing at being at last a man of the world, and now he was being asked to sacrifice it all and be an ordinary decent fellow again. That was the worst of dealing with the English, for the Irish, who had to be serious whether they liked it or not, only wanted to be frivolous, while the one thing in the world that the English seemed to demand was the chance of showing themselves serious. But the man of the world was too new a development in Mick to stand up to a crisis.

'Because you don't have to do it unless you like,' he added gently. 'We could always be married.'

That threw her into positive convulsions, because if she agreed to this, she would never have the opportunity of showing him what she was really like, and it took him a long time to persuade her that he had never really thought her anything but a serious-minded girl – at least, for most of the time. Then she gave a deep sigh and fell asleep in the most awkward manner on his chest. Outside, the dawn was painting the old roofs and walls in the stiff artless colours of a child's paint-box. He felt a little lonely. He would have liked to remain a man of the world for just a little longer, to have had just one more such awakening to assure him that he had got rid of his inhibitions, but clearly it was not to be. He fell asleep soon after, and was only wakened by Chris, who seemed to have got over his ordeal well.

Chris was furious when Mick told him, and Mick himself realized that as a man of the world he had been a complete wash-out. Besides, Chris felt that now Fanny would expect him to marry her as well. She had already given indications of it.

Later, he became more reconciled to the idea, and when last heard of was looking for a house. Which seems to show that marriage comes more natural to us.

THE AMERICAN WIFE

ELSIE COLLEARY, who was on a visit to her cousins in Cork, was a mystery even to them. Her father, Jack Colleary's brother, had emigrated when he was a kid and done well for himself; he had made his money in the liquor business, and left it to go into wholesale produce when Elsie was growing up, because he didn't think it was the right background for a girl. He had given her the best of educations, and all he had got out of it was to have Elsie telling him that Irishmen were more manly, and that even Irish-Americans let their wives boss them too much. What she meant was that *he* let her mother boss him, and she had learned from other Irish people that this was not the custom at home. Maybe Mike Colleary, like a lot of other Americans, did give the impression of yielding too much to his wife, but that was because she thought she knew more about things than he did, and he was too soft-hearted to disillusion her. No doubt the Americans, experienced in nostalgia, took Elsie's glorification of Irishmen good-humouredly, but it did not go down too well in Cork, where the men stood in perpetual contemplation of the dangers of marriage, like cranes standing on one leg at the edge of the windy water.

She stood out at the Collearys' quiet little parties, with her high waist and wide skirts, taking the men out to sit on the stairs while she argued with them about religion and politics. Women having occasion to go upstairs thought this very forward, but some of the men found it a pleasant relief. Besides, like all Americans, she was probably a millionaire, and the most unworldly of men can get a kick out of flirting with a real millionaire.

The man she finally fell in love with did not sit on the stairs with her at all, though, like her, he was interested in religion and politics. This was a chap called Tom Barry. Tom was thirty-five, tall and thin and good-looking, and he lived with his mother and two good-looking sisters in a tiny house near the Barrack, and he couldn't even go for a walk in the evening without the three of them lining up in the hallway to present him with his hat, his gloves, and his clean handkerchief. He had a small job in the courthouse, and was not without ambition; he had engaged in several small business enterprises with his friend Jerry Coakley, but all they had ever got out of these was some good stories. Jerry was forty, and *he* had an old mother who insisted on putting his socks on for him.

Elsie's cousins warned her against setting her cap at Tom, but this only seemed to make her worse. 'I guess I'll have to seduce him,' she replied airily, and her cousins, who had never known a well-bred Catholic girl to talk like that, were shocked. She shocked them even more before she was done. She called at his house when she knew he wasn't there and deluded his innocent mother and sisters into believing that she didn't have designs on him; she badgered Tom to death at the office, gave him presents, and even hired a car to take him for drives.

They weren't the only ones who were shocked. Tom was shocked himself when she asked him point-blank how much he earned. However, he put that down to unworldliness and told her.

'But that's not even a street cleaner's wages at home,' she said indignantly.

'I'm sure, Elsie,' he said sadly. 'But then, of course, money isn't everything.'

'No, and Ireland isn't everything,' she replied. It was peculiar, but from their first evening together she had never ceased talking about America to him – the summer heat, and the crickets chattering, and the leaves alive with fireflies. During her discussions on the stairs, she had apparently discovered a great many things wrong with Ireland, and Tom, with a sort of mournful pleasure, kept adding to them.

'Oh, I know, I know,' he said regretfully.

'Then if you know, why don't you do something about it?'

'Ah, well, I suppose it's habit, Elsie,' he said, as though he weren't quite sure. 'I suppose I'm too old to learn new tricks.'

But Elsie doubted if it was really habit, and it perplexed her that a man so clever and conscientious could at the same time be so lacking in initiative. She explained it finally to herself in terms of an attachment to his mother that was neither natural nor healthy. Elsie was a girl who loved explanations.

On their third outing she had proposed to him, and he was so astonished that he burst out laughing, and continued to laugh whenever he thought of it again. Elsie herself couldn't see anything to laugh at in it. Having been proposed to by men who were younger and better-looking and better off than he was, she felt she had been conferring an honour on him. But he was a curious man, for when she repeated the proposal, he said, with a cold fury that hurt her, 'Sometimes I wish you'd think before you talk, Elsie. You know what I earn, and you know it isn't enough to keep a family on. Besides, in case you haven't noticed it, I have a mother and two sisters to support.'

'You could earn enough to support them in America,' she protested.

'And I told you already that I had no intention of going to America.'

'I have some money of my own,' she said. 'It's not much, but it would mean I'd be no burden to you.'

'Listen, Elsie,' he said, 'a man who can't support a wife and children has no business marrying at all. I have no business marrying anyway. I'm not a very cheerful man, and I have a rotten temper.'

Elsie went home in tears, and told her astonished uncle that all Irishmen were pansies, and, as he had no notion what pansies were, he shook his head and admitted that it was a terrible country. Then she wrote to Tom and told him that what he needed was not a wife but a psychiatrist. The writing of this gave her great satisfaction, but next morning she realized that her mother would only say she had been silly. Her mother believed that men needed careful handling. The day after, she waited for Tom outside the courthouse, and when he came out she summoned him with two angry blasts on the horn. A rainy sunset was flooding the Western Road with yellow light that made her look old and grim.

'Well,' she said bitterly, 'I'd hoped I'd never see your miserable face again.'

But that extraordinary man only smiled gently and rested his elbows on the window of the car.

'I'm delighted you came,' he said. 'I was all last night trying to write to you, but I'm not very good at it.'

'Oh, so you got my letter?'

'I did, and I'm ashamed to have upset you so much. All I wanted to say was that if you're serious – I mean really serious – about this, I'd be honoured.'

At first she thought he was mocking her. Then she realized that he wasn't, and she was in such an evil humour that she was tempted to tell him she had changed her mind. Then common sense told her the man would be fool enough to believe her, and after that his pride wouldn't let him propose to her again. It was the price you had to pay for dealing with men who had such a high notion of their own dignity.

'I suppose it depends on whether you love me or not,' she replied. 'It's a little matter you forgot to mention.'

He raised himself from the car window, and in the evening light she saw a look of positive pain on his lean, sad, gentle face. 'Ah, I do, but –' he was beginning when she cut him off and told him to get in the car. Whatever he was about to say, she didn't want to hear it.

They settled down in a modern bungalow outside the town, on the edge of the harbour. Elsie's mother, who flew over for the wedding, said dryly that she hoped Elsie would be able to make up to Tom for the loss of his mother's services. In fact, it wasn't long before the Barrys were saying she wasn't, and making remarks about her cooking and her lack of tidiness. But if Tom noticed there was anything wrong, which is improbable, he didn't mention it. Whatever his faults as a sweetheart, he made a good husband. It may have been the affection of a sensitive man for someone he saw as frightened, fluttering, and insecure. It could have been the longing of a frustrated one for someone that seemed to him remote, romantic, and mysterious. But whatever it was, Tom, who had always been God Almighty to his mother and sisters, was extraordinarily patient and understanding with Elsie, and she needed it, because she was often homesick and scared.

Jerry Coakley was a great comfort to her in these fits, for Jerry had a warmth of manner that Tom lacked. He was an insignificant-looking man with a ravaged dyspeptic face and a tubercular complexion, a thin, bitter mouth with bad teeth, and long lank hair; but he was so sympathetic and insinuating that at times he even gave you the impression that he was changing his shape to suit your mood. Elsie had the feeling that the sense of failure had eaten deeper into him than into Tom.

At once she started to arrange a match between him and Tom's elder sister, Annie, in spite of Tom's warnings that Jerry would never marry till his mother died. When she realized that Tom was right, she said it was probably as well, because Annie wouldn't put his socks on him. Later she admitted that this was unfair, and that it would probably be a great relief to poor Jerry to be allowed to put on his socks himself. Between Tom and him there was one of those passionate relationships that spring up in small towns where society narrows itself down to a handful of erratic and explosive friendships. There were always people who weren't talking to other people, and friends had all to be dragged into the disagreement, no matter how trifling it might be, and often it happened that the principals had already become fast friends again when *their* friends were still ignoring one another in the street. But Jerry and Tom refused to disagree. Jerry would drop in for a bottle of stout, and Tom and he would denounce the country, while Elsie wondered why they could never find anything more interesting to talk about than stupid priests and crooked politicians.

Elsie's causes were of a different kind. The charwoman, Mrs Dorgan, had six children and a husband who didn't earn enough to keep them. Elsie concealed from Tom how much she really paid Mrs Dorgan, but she couldn't conceal that Mrs Dorgan wore her clothes, or that she took the Dorgan family to the seaside in the summer. When Jerry suggested to Tom that the Dorgans might be doing too well out of Elsie, Tom replied, 'Even if they were, Jerry, I wouldn't interfere. If 'tis people's nature to be generous, you must let them be generous.'

For Tom's causes she had less patience. 'Oh, why don't you people do something about it, instead of talking?' she cried.

'What could you do, Elsie?' asked Jerry.

'At least you could show them up,' said Elsie.

'Why, Elsie?' he asked with his mournful smile. 'Were you thinking of starting a paper?'

'Then, if you can't do anything about it, shut up!' she said. 'You and Tom seem to get some queer masochistic pleasure out of these people.'

'Begor, Elsie, you might have something there,' Jerry said, nodding ruefully.

'Oh, we adore them,' Tom said mockingly.

'You do,' she said. 'I've seen you. You sit here night after night denouncing them, and then when one of them gets sick you're round to the house to see if there's anything you can do for him, and when he dies you start a collection for his wife and family. You make me sick.' Then she stamped out to the kitchen.

Jerry hunched his shoulders and exploded in splutters and giggles. He reached out a big paw for a bottle of stout, with the air of someone snaring a rabbit.

'I declare to God, Tom, she has us taped,' he said.

'She has you taped anyway,' said Tom.

'How's that?'

'She thinks you need an American wife as well.'

'Well, now, she mightn't be too far out in that, either,' said Jerry with a crooked grin. 'I often thought it would take something like that.'

'She thinks you have *problems*,' said Tom with a snort. Elsie's favourite word gave him the creeps.

'She wouldn't be referring to the mother, by any chance?'

For a whole year Elsie had fits of depression because she thought she wasn't going to have a baby, and she saw several doctors, whose advice she repeated in mixed company, to the great embarrassment of everybody except Jerry. After that, for the best part of another year, she had fits of depression because she was going to have a baby, and she informed everybody about that as well, including the occasion of its conception and the probable date of its arrival, and again they were all embarrassed only Jerry. Having reached the age of eighteen before learning that there was any real difference between the sexes, Jerry found all her talk fascinating, and also he realized that Elsie saw nothing immodest in it. It was just that she had an experimental interest in her body and mind. When she gave him bourbon he studied its taste, but when he gave her Irish she studied its effect – it was as simple as that. Jerry, too, liked explanations, but he liked them for their own sake, and not with the intention of doing anything with them. At the same time, Elsie was scared by what she thought was a lack of curiosity on the part of the Cork doctors, and when her mother learned this she began to press Elsie to have the baby in America, where she would feel secure.

'You don't think I should go back, Tom?' she asked guiltily. 'Daddy says he'll pay my fare.'

It came as a shock to Tom, though the idea had crossed his mind that something of the kind might happen. 'If that's the way you feel about it, I suppose you'd better, Elsie,' he replied.

'But you wouldn't come with me.'

'How can I come with you? You know I can't just walk out of the office for a couple of months.'

'But you could get a job at home.'

'And I told you a dozen times I don't want a job in America,' he said angrily. Then, seeing the way it upset her, he changed his tone. 'Look, if you stay here, feeling the way you do, you'll work yourself into a real illness. Anyway, sometime you'll have to go back on a visit, and this is as good an occasion as any.'

'But how can I, without you?' she asked. 'You'd only neglect yourself.'

'I would not neglect myself.'

'Would you stay at your mother's?'

'I would not stay at my mother's. This is my house, and I'm going to stop here.'

Tom worried less about the effect Elsie's leaving would have on him than about what his family would say, particularly Annie, who never lost the chance of a crack at Elsie. 'You let that girl walk on you, Tom Barry,' she said. 'One of these days she'll walk too hard.' Then, of course, Tom walked on *her,* in the way that only a devoted brother can, but that was no relief to the feeling that something had come between Elsie and him and that he could do nothing about it. When he was driving Elsie to the liner, he knew that she felt the same, for she didn't break down until they came to a long grey bridge over an inlet of water, guarded by a lonely grey stone tower. She had once pointed it out to him as the first thing she had seen that represented Ireland to her, and now he had the feeling that this was how she saw him – a battered old tower by a river mouth that was no longer of any importance to anyone but the sea gulls.

She was away longer than she or anyone else had expected. First there was the wedding of an old school friend; then her mother's birthday; then the baby got ill. It was clear that she was enjoying herself immensely, but she wrote long and frequent letters, sent snapshots of herself and the baby, and – most important of all – had named the baby for Jerry Coakley. Clearly Elsie hadn't forgotten them. The Dorgan kids appeared on the road in clothes that had obviously been made in America, and whenever Tom met them he stopped to speak to them and give them the pennies he thought Elsie would have given them.

Occasionally Tom went to his mother's for supper, but otherwise he looked after himself. Nothing could persuade him that he was not a natural housekeeper, or that whatever his sisters could do he could not do just as well himself. Sometimes Jerry came and the two men took off their coats and tried to prepare a meal out of one of Elsie's cookbooks. 'Steady, squad!' Tom would murmur as he wiped his hands before taking another peep at the book. 'You never know when this might come in handy.' But whether it was the result of Tom's supervision or Jerry's helplessness, the meal usually ended in a big burnup, or a tasteless mess from which some essential ingredient seemed to be missing, and they laughed over it as they consoled themselves with bread and cheese and stout. 'Elsie is right,' Jerry would say, shaking his head regretfully. 'We have problems, boy! We have problems!'

Elsie returned at last with trunks full of new clothes, a box of up-to-date kitchen stuff, and a new gaiety and energy. Every ten minutes Tom would make an excuse to tiptoe upstairs and take another look at his son. Then the Barrys arrived, and Elsie gave immediate offence by quoting Gesell and Spock. But Mrs Barry didn't seem to mind as much as her daughters. By some extra-ordinary process of association, she had discovered a great similarity between Elsie and herself in the fact that she had married from the south side of the city into the north and had never got used to it. This delighted Elsie, who went about proclaiming that her mother-in-law and herself were both displaced persons.

The next year was a very happy one, and less trying on Elsie, because she had another woman to talk to, even if most of the time she didn't understand what her mother-in-law was telling her, and had the suspicion that her mother-in-law didn't under-stand her either. But then she got pregnant for the second time, and became restless and dissatisfied once more, though now it wasn't only with hospitals and doctors but with schools and schoolteachers as well. Tom and Jerry had impressed on her that the children were being turned into idiots, learning through the medium of a language they didn't understand – indeed, according to Tom, it was a language that nobody understood. What chance would the children have?

'Ah, I suppose the same chance as the rest of us, Elsie,' said Jerry in his sly, mournful way.

'But you and Tom don't want chances, Jerry,' she replied earnestly. 'Neither of you has any ambition.'

'Ah, you should look on the bright side of things. Maybe with God's help they won't have any ambition either.'

But this time it had gone beyond a joke. For days on end, Tom was in a rage with her, and when he was angry he seemed to withdraw into himself like a snail into a shell.

Unable to get to him, Elsie grew hysterical. 'It's all your damned obstinacy,' she sobbed. 'You don't do anything in this rotten hole, but you're too conceited to get out of it. Your family treat you as if you were God, and then you behave to me as if you were God! God! God!' she screamed, and each time she punched him viciously with her fist, till suddenly the humour of their situation struck him and he went off into laughter.

After that, he could only make his peace with her and make excuses for her leaving him again, but he knew that the excuses wouldn't impress his sisters. One evening when he went to see them, Annie caught him, as she usually did, when he was going out the front door, and he stood looking sidewise down the avenue.

'Are you letting Elsie go off to America again, Tom?' she asked.

'I don't know,' Tom said, pulling his long nose with an air of affected indifference. 'I can't very well stop her, can I?'

'Damn soon she'd he stopped if she hadn't the money,' said Annie. 'And you're going to let her take young Jerry?'

'Ah, how could I look after Jerry? Talk sense, can't you!'

'And I suppose we couldn't look after him either? We're not sufficiently well read.'

'Ah, the child should be with his own mother, Annie,' Tom said impatiently.

'And where should his mother be? Ah, Tom Barry,' she added bitterly, 'I told you what that one was, and she's not done with you yet. Are you sure she's going to bring him back?'

Then Tom exploded on her in his cold, savage way. 'If you want to know, I am not,' he said, and strode down the avenue with his head slightly bowed.

Something about the cut of him as he passed under a street lamp almost broke Annie's heart. 'The curse of God on that bitch!' she said when she returned to her mother in the kitchen.

'Is it Elsie?' her mother cried angrily. 'How dare you talk of her like that!'

'He's letting her go to America again,' said Annie.

'He's a good boy, and he's right to consider her feelings,' said her mother anxiously. 'I often thought myself I'd go back to the south side and not be ending my days in this misfortunate hole.'

The months after Elsie's second departure were bitter ones for Tom. A house from which a woman is gone is bad enough, but one from which a child is gone is a deadhouse. Tom would wake in the middle of the night thinking he heard Jerry crying, and be half out of bed before he realized that Jerry was thousands of miles away. He did not continue his experiments with cooking and housekeeping. He ate at his mother's, spent most of his time at the Coakleys', and drank far too much. Like all inward-looking men he had a heavy hand on the bottle. Meanwhile Elsie wavered and procrastinated worse than before, setting dates, cancelling her passage, sometimes changing her mind within twenty-four hours. In his despondency Tom resigned himself to the idea that she wouldn't return at all, or at least persuaded himself that he had.

'Oh, she'll come back all right,' Jerry said with a worried air. 'The question is, will she stay back. . . . You don't mind me talking about it?' he asked.

'Indeed no. Why would I?'

'You know, Tom, I'd say ye had family enough to last ye another few years.'

Tom didn't look up for a few moments, and when he did he smiled faintly. 'You think it's that?'

'I'm not saying she knows it,' Jerry added hastily. 'There's nothing calculating about her, and she's crazy about you.'

'I thought it was something that went with having the baby,' Tom said thoughtfully. 'Some sort of homing instinct.'

'I wouldn't say so,' said Jerry. 'Not altogether. I think she feels that eventually she'll get you through the kids.'

'She won't,' Tom said bitterly.

'I know, sure, I know. But Elsie can't get used to the – the irremediable.' The last word was so unlike Jerry that Tom felt he must have looked it up in a dictionary, and the absurdity of this made him feel very close to his old crony. 'Tell me, Tom,' Jerry added gently, 'wouldn't you do it? I know it wouldn't be easy, but wouldn't you try it, even for a while, for Elsie's sake? 'Twould mean a hell of a lot to her.'

'I'm too old, Jerry,' Tom said so deliberately that Jerry knew it had been in his mind as well.

'Oh, I know, I know,' Jerry repeated. 'Even ten years ago I might have done it myself. It's like jail. The time comes when you're happier in than out. And that's not the worst of it,' he added bitterly. 'The worst is when you pretend you like it.'

It was a strange evening that neither of them ever forgot, sitting in that little house to which Elsie's absence seemed a rebuke, and listening to the wind from the harbour that touched the foot of the garden. They knew they belonged to a country whose youth was always escaping from it, out beyond that harbour, and that was middle-aged in all its attitudes and institutions. Of those that remained, a little handful lived with defeat and learned fortitude and humour and sweetness, and these were the things that Elsie, with her generous idealism, loved in them. But she couldn't pay the price. She wanted them where she belonged herself, among the victors.

A few weeks later, Elsie was back; the house was full of life again, and that evening seemed only a bad dream. It was almost impossible to keep Jerry Og, as they called the elder child, away from Tom. He was still only a baby, and a spoiled one at that, but when Tom took him to the village Jerry Og thrust out his chest and took strides that were too big for him like any small boy with a father he admired. Each day, he lay in wait for the postman and then took the post away to sort it for himself. He sorted it by the pictures on the stamps, and Elsie noted gleefully that he reserved all the pretty pictures for his father.

Nobody had remembered Jerry's good advice, even Jerry himself, and eighteen months later Elsie was pregnant again. Again their lives took the same pattern of unrest. But this time Elsie was even more distressed than Tom.

'I'm a curse to you,' she said. 'There's something wrong with me. I can't be natural.'

'Oh, you're natural enough,' Tom replied bitterly. 'You married the wrong man, that's all.'

'I didn't, I didn't!' she protested despairingly. 'You can say anything else but that. If I believed that, I'd have nothing left, because I never cared for anyone but you. And in spite of what you think, I'm coming back,' she went on, in tears. 'I'm coming back if it kills me. God, I hate this country; I hate every God damn thing about it; I hate what it's done to you and Jerry. But I'm not going to let you go.'

'You have no choice,' Tom said patiently. 'Jerry Og will have to go to school, and you can't be bringing him hither and over, even if you could afford it.'

'Then, if that's what you feel, why don't you keep him?' she cried. 'You know perfectly well you could stop me taking him with me if you wanted to. You wouldn't even have to bring me into court. I'll give him to you now. Isn't that proof enough that I'm coming back?'

'No, Elsie, it is not,' Tom replied, measuring every word. 'And I'm not going to bring you into court either. I'm not going to take hostages to make sure my wife comes back to me.'

And though Elsie continued to delude herself with the belief that she would return, she knew Tom was right. It would all appear different when she got home. The first return to Ireland had been hard, the second had seemed impossible. Yet, even in the black hours when she really considered the situation, she felt she could never resign herself to something that had been determined before she was born, and she deceived herself with the hope that Tom would change his mind and follow her. He must follow her. Even if he was prepared to abandon her, he would never abandon Jerry Og.

And this, as Big Jerry could have told her, was where she made her biggest mistake, because if Tom had done it at all it would have been for her. But Big Jerry had decided that the whole thing had gone beyond his power to help. He recognized the irremediable, all right, sometimes perhaps even before it became irremediable. But that, as he would have said himself, is where the ferryboat had left him.

Thanks to Elsie, the eldest of the Dorgans now has a job in Boston and in the course of years the rest of them will probably go there as well. Tom continues to live in his little bungalow beside the harbour. Annie is keeping house for him, which suits her fine, because Big Jerry's old mother continued to put his socks on for him a few years too long, and now Annie has only her brother to worship. To all appearances they are happy enough, as happiness goes in Cork. Jerry still calls, and the two men discuss the terrible state of the country. But in Tom's bedroom there are pictures of Elsie and the children, the third of whom he knows only through photographs, and apart from that, nothing has changed since Elsie left five years ago. It is a strange room, for one glance is enough to show that the man who sleeps there is still in love, and that everything that matters to him in the world is reflected there. And one day, if he comes by the dollars, he will probably go out and visit them all, but it is here he will return and here, no doubt, he will die.

A STORY BY MAUPASSANT

PEOPLE WHO have not grown up in a provincial town won't know what I mean when I say what Terry Coughlan meant to me. People who have won't need to know.

As kids we lived a few doors from each other on the same terrace, and his sister, Tess, was a friend of my sister, Nan. There was a time when I was rather keen on Tess myself. She was a small plump gay little thing, with rosy cheeks like apples, and she played the piano very well. In those days I sang a bit, though I hadn't much of a voice. When I sang Mozart, Beethoven, or even Wagner Terry would listen with brooding approval. When I sang commonplace stuff Terry would make a face and walk out. He was a good-looking lad with a big brow and curly black hair, a long, pale face, and a pair of intense dark eyes. He was always well-spoken and smart in his appearance. There was nothing sloppy about him.

When he could not learn something by night he got up at five in the morning to do it, and whatever he took up, he mastered. Even as a boy he was always looking forward to the day when he'd have money enough to travel, and he taught himself French and German in the time it took me to find out I could not learn Irish. He was cross with me for wanting to learn it; according to him it had 'no cultural significance', but he was crosser still with me because I couldn't learn it. 'The first thing you should learn to do is to work,' he would say gloomily. 'What's going to become of you if you don't?' He had read somewhere that when Keats was depressed, he had a wash and brushup. Keats was his God. Poetry was never much in my line, except Shelley, and Terry didn't think much of him.

We argued about it on our evening walks. Maybe you don't remember the sort of arguments you had when you were young. Lots of people prefer not to remember, but I like thinking of them. A man is never more himself than when he talks nonsense about God, eternity, prostitution, and the necessity for having mistresses. I argued with Terry that the day of poetry was over, and that the big boys of modern literature were the fiction writers – the ones we'd heard of in Cork at that time, I mean – the Russians and Maupassant.

'The Russians are all right,' he said to me once. 'Maupassant you can forget.'

'But why, Terry?' I asked.

'Because whatever you say about the Russians, they're noble,' he said. 'Noble' was a great word of his at the time: Shakespeare was 'noble', Turgenev was 'noble', Beethoven was 'noble'. 'They are a religious people, like the Greeks, or the English of Shakespeare's time. But Maupassant is slick and coarse and commonplace. Are his stories literature?'

'Ah, to hell with literature!' I said. 'It's life.'

'Life in this country?'

'Life in his own country, then.'

'But how do you know?' Terry asked, stopping and staring at me. 'Humanity is the same here as anywhere else. If he's not true of the life we know, he's not true of any sort of life.'

Then he got the job in the monks' school and I got the job in Carmody's and we began to drift apart. There was no quarrel. It was just that I liked company and Terry didn't. I got in with a wild group – Marshall and Redmond and Donnelan, the solicitor – and we sat up until morning, drinking and settling the future of humanity. Terry came with us once but he didn't talk, and when Donnelan began to hold forth on Shaw and the Life Force I could see his face getting dark. You know Donnelan's line – 'But what I mean – what I want to say – Jasus, will somebody let me talk? I have something important to say.' We all knew that Donnelan was a bit of a joke, and when I said good-night to Terry in the hall he turned on me with an angry look.

'Do those friends of yours do anything but talk?' he asked.

'Never mind, Terry,' I said. 'The Revolution is coming.'

'Not if they have anything to say to it,' Terry said and walked away from me. I stood there for a while feeling sorry for myself, as you do when you know that the end of a friendship is in sight. It didn't make me happier when I went back to the room and Donnelan looked at me as if he didn't believe his eyes.

'Magner,' he asked, 'am I dreaming or was there someone with you?'

Suddenly, for no particular reason, I lost my temper.

'Yes, Donnelan,' I said. 'But somebody I wouldn't expect you to recognize.'

That, I suppose, was the last flash of the old love, and after that it was bogged down in argument. Donnelan said that Terry lacked flexibility – flexibility!

Occasionally I met Tess with her little shopping basket and her round rosy cheeks, and she would say reproachfully, 'Ah, Ted, aren't you becoming a great stranger? What did we do to you at all?' And a couple of times I dropped around to sing a song and borrow a book, and Terry told me about his work as a teacher. He was a bit disillusioned with his job, and you wouldn't wonder. Some of the monks kept a mackintosh and muffler handy so that they could drop out to the pictures after dark with some doll. And then there was a thundering row when Terry discovered that a couple of his brightest boys were being sent up for public examinations under the names of notorious ignoramuses, so as to bolster up the record. When Brother Dunphy, the headmaster, argued with Terry that it was only a simple act of charity, Terry replied sourly that it seemed to him more like a criminal offence. After that he got the reputation of being impossible and was not consulted when Patrick Dempsey, the boy he really liked, was put up for examination as Mike Mac-Namara, the county councillor's son – Mike the Moke, as Terry called him.

Now, Donnelan is a gasbag, and speaking charitably, a bit of a fool, but there were certain things he learned in his Barrack Street slum. One night he said to me, 'Ted, does that fellow Coughlan drink?'

'Drink?' I said, laughing outright at him. 'Himself and a sparrow would have about the same consumption of liquor.' Nothing ever embarrassed Donnelan, who had the hide of a rhinoceros.

'Well, you might be right,' he said reasonably, 'but, begor, I never saw a sparrow that couldn't hold it.'

I thought myself that Donnelan was dreaming, but next time I met Tess I sounded her. 'How's that brother of yours keeping?' I asked.

'Ah, fine, Ted, why?' she asked, as though she was really surprised.

'Oh, nothing,' I said. 'Somebody was telling me that he wasn't looking well.'

'Ah, he's that way this long time, Ted,' she replied, 'and 'tis nothing only the want of sleep. He studies too hard at night, and then he goes wandering all over the country, trying to work off the excitement. Sure, I'm always at him!'

That satisfied me. I knew Tess couldn't tell a lie. But then, one moonlight night about six months later, three or four of us were standing outside the hotel – the night porter had kicked us out in the middle of an argument, and we were finishing it there. Two was striking from Shandon when I saw Terry coming up the pavement towards us. I never knew whether he recognized me or not, but all at once he crossed the street, and even I could see that the man was drunk.

'Tell me,' said Donnelan, peering across at him, 'is that a sparrow I see at this hour of night?' All at once he spun round on his heels, splitting his sides with laughing. 'Magner's sparrow!' he said. 'Magner's sparrow!' I hope in comparing Donnelan with a rhinoceros I haven't done injustice to either party.

I saw then what was happening. Terry was drinking all right, but he was drinking unknown to his mother and sister. You might almost say he was drinking unknown to himself. Other people could be drunkards but not he. So he sat at home reading, or pretending to read, until late at night, and then slunk off to some low pub on the quays where he hoped people wouldn't recognize him, and came home only when he knew his family was in bed.

For a long time I debated with myself about whether I shouldn't talk to him. If I made up my mind to do it once, I did it twenty times. But when I ran into him in town, striding slowly along, and saw the dark, handsome face with the slightly ironic smile, I lost courage. His mind was as keen as ever – it may even have been a shade too keen. He was becoming slightly irritable and arrogant. The manners were as careful and the voice was as pleasant as ever – a little too much so. The way he raised his hat high in the air to some woman who passed and whipped the big handkerchief from his breast pocket reminded me of an old actor going down in the world. The farther down he went the worse the acting got. He wouldn't join me for a drink; no, he had this job that simply must be finished tonight. How could I say to him,

'Terry, for God's sake, give up trying to pretend you have work to do. I know you're an impostor and you're drinking yourself to death.' You couldn't talk like that to a man of his kind. People like him are all of a piece; they have to stand or fall by something inside themselves.

He was forty when his mother died, and by that time it looked as though he'd have Tess on his hands for life as well. I went back to the house with him after the funeral. He was cruelly broken up. I discovered that he had spent his first few weeks abroad that summer and he was full of it. He had stayed in Paris and visited the cathedrals round, and they had made a deep impression on him. He had never seen real architecture before. I had a vague hope that it might have jolted him out of the rut he had been getting into, but I was wrong. It was worse he was getting.

Then, a couple of years later, I was at home one evening, finishing up some work, when a knock came to the door. I opened it myself and saw old Pa Hourigan, the policeman, outside. Pa had a schoolgirl complexion and a white moustache, china-blue eyes, and a sour elderly mouth, like a baby who has learned the facts of life too soon. It surprised me because we never did more than pass the time of day.

'May I speak to you for a moment, Mr Magner?' he asked modestly. ''Tis on a rather private matter.'

'You can be sure, sergeant,' I said, joking him. 'I'm not a bit afraid. 'Tis years since I played ball on the public street. Have a drink.'

'I never touch it, going on night duty,' he said, coming into the front room. 'I hope you will pardon my calling, but you know I am not a man to interfere in anyone else's private affairs.'

By this time he had me puzzled and a bit anxious. I knew him for an exceptionally retiring man, and he was clearly upset.

'Ah, of course you're not,' I said. 'No one would accuse you of it. Sit down and tell me what the trouble is.'

'Aren't you a friend of Mr Coughlan, the teacher?' he asked.

'I am,' I said.

'Mr Magner,' he said, exploding on me, 'can you do nothing with the man?'

I looked at him for a moment and had a premonition of disaster.

'Is it as bad as that?' I asked.

'It cannot go on, Mr Magner,' he said, shaking his head. 'It cannot go on. I saved him before. Not because he was anything to me, because I hardly knew the man. Not even because of his poor decent sister, though I pity her with my whole heart and soul. It was for the respect I have for education. And you know that, Mr Magner,' he added earnestly, meaning (which was true enough) that I owed it to him that I had never paid a fine for drinking during prohibited hours.

'We all know it, sergeant,' I said. 'And I assure you, we appreciate it.'

'No one knows, Mr Magner,' he went on, 'what sacrifices Mrs Hourigan and myself made to put that boy of ours through college, and I would not give it to say to him that an educated man could sink so low. But there are others at the barracks who don't think the way I do. I name no names, Mr Magner, but there are those who would be glad to see an educated man humiliated.'

'What is it, sergeant?' I asked. 'Drink?'

'Mr Magner,' he said indignantly, 'when did I ever interfere with an educated man for drinking? I know when a man has a lot on his mind he cannot always do without stimulants.'

'You don't mean drugs?' I asked. The idea had crossed my mind once or twice.

'No, Mr Magner, I do not,' he said, quivering with indignation. 'I mean those low, loose, abandoned women that I would have whipped and transported.'

If he had told me that Terry had turned into a common thief I couldn't have been more astonished and horrified. Horrified is the word.

'You don't mind my saying that I find that very hard to believe, sergeant?' I asked.

'Mr Magner,' he said with great dignity, 'in my calling a man does not use words lightly.'

'I know Terry Coughlan since we were boys together, and I never as much as heard an unseemly word from him,' I said.

'Then all I can say, Mr Magner, is that I'm glad, very glad, that you've never seen him as I have, in a condition I would not compare to the beasts.' There were real tears in the old man's eyes. 'I spoke to him myself about it. At four o'clock this morning I separated him from two of those vile creatures that I knew well were robbing him. I pleaded with him as if he was my own brother. "Mr Coughlan," I said, "what will your soul do at the judgment?" And Mr Magner, in decent society I would not repeat the disgusting reply he made me.'

'Corruptio optimi pessima,' I said to myself.

'That is Latin, Mr Magner,' the old policeman said with real pleasure.

'And it means "Lilies that fester smell far worse than weeds," sergeant,' I said. 'I don't know if I can do anything. I suppose I'll have to try. If he goes on like this he'll destroy himself, body and soul.'

'Do what you can for his soul, Mr Magner,' whispered the old man, making for the door. 'As for his body, I wouldn't like to answer.' At the door he turned with a mad stare in in his blue eyes. 'I would not like to answer,' he repeated, shaking his grey pate again.

It gave me a nasty turn. Pa Hourigan was happy. He had done his duty, but mine still remained to be done. I sat for an hour, thinking about it, and the more I thought, the more hopeless it seemed. Then I put on my hat and went out.

Terry lived at that time in a nice little house on College Road; a little red-brick villa with a bow window. He answered the door himself, a slow, brooding, black-haired man with a long pale face. He didn't let on to be either surprised or pleased.

'Come in,' he said with a crooked smile. 'You're a great stranger, aren't you?'

'You're a bit of a stranger yourself, Terry,' I said jokingly. Then Tess came out, drying her hands in her apron. Her little cheeks were as rosy as ever but the gloss was gone. I had the feeling that now there was nothing much she didn't know about her brother. Even the nervous smile suggested that she knew what I had come for – of course, old Hourigan must have brought him home.

'Ah, Ted, 'tis a cure for sore eyes to see you,' she said. 'You'll have a cup? You will, to be sure.'

'You'll have a drink,' Terry said.

'Do you know, I think I will, Terry,' I said, seeing a nice natural opening for the sort of talk I had in mind.

'Ah, you may as well have both,' said Tess, and a few minutes later she brought in the tea and cake. It was like old times until she left us, and then it wasn't. Terry poured out the whiskey for me and the tea for himself, though his hand was shaking so badly that he could scarcely lift his cup. It was not all pretence; he didn't want to give me an opening, that was all. There was a fine print over his head – I think it was a Constable of Salisbury Cathedral. He talked about the monastery school, the usual clever, bitter contemptuous stuff about monks, inspectors and pupils. The whole thing was too carefully staged, the lifting of the cup and the wiping of the moustache, but it hypnotized me. There was something there you couldn't do violence to. I finished my drink and got up to go.

'What hurry is on you?' he asked irritably.

I mumbled something about its getting late.

'Nonsense!' he said. 'You're not a boy any longer.'

Was he just showing off his strength of will or hoping to put off the evil hour when he would go slinking down the quays again?

'Ah, they'll be expecting me,' I said, and then, as I used to do when we were younger, I turned to the bookcase. 'I see you have a lot of Maupassant at last,' I said.

'I bought them last time I was in Paris,' he said, standing beside me and looking at the books as though he were seeing them for the first time.

'A deathbed repentance?' I asked lightly, but he ignored me.

'I met another great admirer of his there,' he said sourly. 'A lady you should meet some time.'

'I'd love to if I ever get there,' I said.

'Her address is the Rue de Grenelle,' he said, and then with a wild burst of mockery, 'the left-hand pavement.'

At last his guard was down, and it was Maupassant's name that had done it. And still I couldn't say anything. An angry flush mounted his pale dark face and made it sinister in its violence.

'I suppose you didn't know I indulged in that hideous vice?' he snarled.

'I heard something,' I said. 'I'm sorry, Terry.'

The angry flush died out of his face and the old brooding look came back.

'A funny thing about those books,' he said. 'This woman I was speaking about, I thought she was bringing me to a hotel. I suppose I was a bit muddled with drink, but after dark, one of these places is much like another. "This isn't a hotel," I said when we got upstairs. "No," she said, "it's my room."'

As he told it, I could see that he was living it all over again, something he could tell nobody but myself.

'There was a screen in the corner. I suppose it's the result of reading too much romantic fiction, but I thought there might be somebody hidden behind it. There was. You'd never guess what?'

'No.'

'A baby,' he said, his eyes boring through me. 'A child of maybe eighteen months. I wouldn't know. While I was looking, she changed him. He didn't wake.'

'What was it?' I asked, searching for the message that he obviously thought the incident contained. 'A dodge?'

'No,' he said almost grudgingly. 'A country girl in trouble, trying to support her child, that's all. We went to bed and she fell asleep. I couldn't. It's many years now since I've been able to sleep like that. So I put on the light and began to read one of these books that I carried round in my pocket. The light woke her and she wanted to see what I had. "Oh, Maupassant," she said. "He's a great writer." "Is he?" I said. I thought she might be repeating something she'd picked up from one of her customers. She wasn't. She began to talk about *Boule de Suif*. It reminded me of the arguments we used to have in our young days.' Suddenly he gave me a curious boyish smile. 'You remember, when we used to walk up the river together.'

'Oh, I remember,' I said with a sigh.

'We were terrible young idiots, the pair of us,' he said sadly. 'Then she began to talk about *The Tellier Household*. I said it had poetry. "Oh, if it's poetry you want, you don't go to Maupassant. You go to Vigny, you go to Musset, and Maupassant is life, and life isn't poetry. It's only when you see what life can do to you that you realize what a great writer Maupassant is."' ... Wasn't that an extraordinary thing to happen?' he asked fiercely, and again the angry colour mounted his cheeks.

'Extraordinary,' I said, wondering if Terry himself knew how extraordinary it was. But it was exactly as if he were reading the thoughts as they crossed my mind.

'A prostitute from some French village; a drunken old waster from an Irish provincial town, lying awake in the dawn in Paris, discussing Maupassant. And the baby, of course. Maupassant would have made a lot of the baby.'

'I declare to God, I think if I'd been in your shoes, I'd have brought them back with me,' I said. I knew when I said it that I was talking nonsense, but it was a sort of release for all the bitterness inside me.

'What?' he asked, mocking me. 'A prostitute and her baby? My dear Mr Magner, you're becoming positively romantic in your old age.'

'A man like you should have a wife and children,' I said.

'Ah, but that's a different story,' he said malevolently. 'Maupassant would never have ended a story like that.'

And he looked at me almost triumphantly with those mad, dark eyes. I knew how Maupassant would have ended that story all right. Maupassant, as the girl said, was life, and life was pretty nearly through with Terry Coughlan.

THE CONVERSION

'The Conversion' draws on a 1950 cycling trip through France with O'Connor's friend Stan Stewart.

GÉRONTE AND I landed in Dieppe on the afternoon of Holy Thursday. Géronte is the companion of all my cycling trips; we have covered together most of Ireland and a lot of England, but this was our first trip to France, and we were rather scared.

On the whole, we make a good mixture; I, in my late forties, tall, gaunt and seedy; Géronte, in the neighbourhood of sixty, a pipe smoker, small and stout, and with the digestion and temper necessary to handle a chronic dyspeptic. He was brought up in an Irish Protestant house where it was a sin to play on Sunday, I, in an Irish Catholic one where I was encouraged to give the Infant Jesus in the Christmas crib a clockwork engine as a present. In our cynical middle age, the difference of upbringing still comes out. I, restive and fiery, can be led a great part of the way by anyone who will talk soothingly to me and pat me on the nose; Géronte, the most good-natured of men, remains the complete individualist, and will submit to dictation from nobody.

There was, for instance, the awful half-hour in Warwick Castle. While the guard showed us the armour, Géronte discovered what he took to be a Breughel; when the guide reached the Breughel, I found Géronte in the castle chapel looking at the ceiling and muttering 'Contra-Buhl' between his teeth. In the great hall, when the guide showed the furniture, Géronte affected interest in a gittern presented by Queen Elizabeth to Leicester, and when the guide, noticing his apparent interest, began to tell us about it, Géronte grabbed me by the arm and hissed, 'Tell the damn fellow we're not going to look at any more of his damn rubbish!' Eventually I had to tell the guide that my friend was ill.

Travelling with a man like Géronte has its advantages as well as its embarrassments, for of all men he is the most completely unaffected by propaganda. He can look at the most famous work of art in the world, first through his spectacles and then over them, and finally sum it up without self-consciousness, as though nobody in the world had ever seen it before. It is the story of 'The Emperor's New Clothes' eternally renewed.

Only two others on the ship had bicycles; we parted from them with regret on the quay, and, full of suspicions of French traffic, pushed our bicycles up the main street. We were so scared we even left the parish church on our left unvisited. Géronte did buy himself a pair of insoles for his shoes, and that struck me as great boldness, for even in England I had found it hard to make myself understood when I wanted insoles, and it wasn't until afterwards that I realized the natives call them 'socks'. Instead, I bought a kilo of apples under the mistaken impression that a kilo was a pound, and then wondered what I was to do with them.

Even after we had walked into the open country, Géronte insisted on cycling in single file, a most unsociable practice, and he didn't really relax till after our first meal in a wayside pub, when he, with a French shakier even than mine, had boldly gone out and bought what he called 'a yard of bread'. That gave him confidence. In the evening light the downland country we cycled through became magical, Sussex with a slight accent. In the village churches there was a mass of baroque and rococo statuary, second-rate work, but wonderful after the bareness of Irish and English parish churches where Géronte's ancestors had smashed everything with a face. But none of the statues were draped in purple. It was Holy Thursday, and I thought it strange to find the statues undraped and the churches empty. It gave me the feeling that something was wrong.

Next day, no longer feeling like foreigners, we cycled on in the direction of Beauvais. It was Good Friday, but the story was the same. We came to a beautiful church and found it locked. Through the plain glass windows we saw that the woodwork and statues inside were excellent. By this time I was becoming really inquisitive, and while Géronte went off with two children from a near-by cottage to locate the key of the church, I remained behind and questioned the children's mother.

'Tell me,' I asked, 'is there no service here today?'

'No, sir.'

'But surely you have Mass here?'

'No. We only hear Mass occasionally. Once in six months, perhaps.'

'But why?'

'We have no priest.'

So that was it! That was why the statues remained undraped. Here the enemy of the churches was not puritanism, but something more deadly because more logical, something which left them their beauty but removed their significance.

At the next village we found the parish church open because the organist was practising. He was a young man, good-looking, with a slight moustache, and after a few minutes he got up and joined us. He might have been the expression in the flesh of the logic we had seen at work on the other churches. He proceeded politely to tell us the life stories of the more unfamiliar saints, and by the time he was finished there was little left of the saints. Yet we liked him, as we shouldn't have liked a puritan.

'You're English, I suppose?' he asked as we were leaving.

'No, Irish.'

'Ah,' he said with a shrug, 'of Ireland I know nothing but James Joyce.'

'You know quite a lot if you know that,' I replied, and again we fell into talk, and he told us how he had read *Ulysses* in the Ste Geneviève Library in the evenings and given up *Finnegans Wake* as a bad job. He was the sort of young man who makes France worth while, the sort who takes naturally to culture and not because he doesn't feel himself capable of business or games. We parted from him with real regret.

But the parting was not complete. We had cycled some miles farther and found yet another locked church, when he caught up on us. He, too, was riding a bicycle, and he excused himself in terms that were familiar enough to me from having heard them so often in rural Ireland from young country priests and teachers. The poor devil was dying of loneliness; there wasn't a soul in the village he could talk to about books or music except his uncle, the parish priest, a severe, old-fashioned man who still looked on Flaubert and De Maupassant as 'immoral writers' and kept their books locked up. How well I knew that old uncle! How often I had argued with him in the days when I was a librarian, trying to get the hospitable, saintly, pig-headed old devil to let me start a library in his godforsaken parish where the unfortunate people were drinking themselves to death for want of something to do! And failed! It isn't the bad priests who break your heart, but the good ones.

'Anyway,' said the organist, 'as if he couldn't find all the vices of Flaubert and De Maupassant among his own parishioners!'

'Do you think so?' I asked. 'I've always wondered if there really were people like De Maupassant's Normans.'

'You needn't,' said the organist. 'Look at me!'

I asked him about the locked churches and our chances of hearing Tenebrae anywhere along the road.

'You won't hear Tenebrae anywhere outside Beauvais,' he replied. 'You couldn't get a choir together in this whole country. My uncle is having the Stations of the Cross tonight. That was why I was practising. I'm the one who has to carry the cross.'

He tried out his irreverent jokes on us just to see how we responded. He was full of curiosity about us cycling round, look-ing at statues, wanting to hear Tenebrae – obviously a pious pair and yet laughing at his jokes about religion. It wasn't right.

'You Irish are all Catholics, aren't you?' he asked with mock innocence.

'Not all,' I replied. 'My friend is a Protestant.'

'He has all my sympathy,' the organist replied gravely. 'That, I suppose, explains his interest in statues?'

'Except modern ones,' said Géronte.

'Bah!' said the organist. 'Iconoclast!'

Whatever else he may not have shared with De Maupassant's Normans, he certainly had all their inquisitiveness. He wasn't satisfied with my attempts at an explanation. He went on with his probing. As for him, he was an atheist – with an uncle a parish priest, what else could he be? He was a delightful young fellow and excellent company in a strange country.

We cycled on for some miles till we came to a really attractive village green where we halted for tea. It had a wall of trees round it, and behind a hedge at the back rose a great parish church. This was really only the choir of a large church begun by the English during their occupation of Normandy and never com-pleted. There were a few labourers at work on the road. We rested our bicycles against the hedge before the church and got out the coffee and rolls and Irish whiskey. Géronte explained to the organist how he must drink the whiskey to get the full effect of it, 'without hitting his tonsils', and the organist compared it (I thought, without much conviction) to *fine*. We sat on the grass enjoying the meal and the evening sunlight, when suddenly the organist, who seemed to have been following up his own train of thought all the time, began to chuckle.

'I understand it all now,' he explained. '*You* are a very bad Catholic; *he* is a very bad Protestant, and so, you can be very good friends.'

At last the French intellect had found its formula, and there was sufficient truth in it to make Géronte and myself laugh, too. We were still laughing when one of the labourers hailed us.

'Aren't you fellows going to the flicks?' he shouted.

'Flicks?' the organist shouted back, looking puzzled. 'What flicks?'

'In there,' said the labourer, jerking his thumb in the direction of the church.

'Flicks,' the organist repeated to us.

'The Stations of the Cross,' shouted the labourer.

'Ah,' said the organist, beginning to laugh apologetically, 'the Stations of the Cross.'

We listened, but we could hear no organ or anything else from the church.

'Why don't we go in?' I asked, and we packed up our food and went into the church.

It was a huge church, bigger even than it had appeared from outside, and only a bay or two of the nave had been completed before the west wall had been roughly put in to finish it off. It was as bare as it was high, with no ornament but one excellent modern statue of the Blessed Virgin on a crossing pier at the south side of the choir.

I went into the pew farthest from the altar and was followed by Géronte and the organist. It was only then I realized why we had heard no sound from outside. There was no organ. A young priest was celebrating the Stations of the Cross accompanied by two acolytes, and the whole congregation in that great church consisted of three women and two little girls – mothers, aunts and sisters of the acolytes – who had obviously come not to join in the service but to see Jean and Louis perform. I hope they enjoyed them more than I did. There is a frustrated acolyte somewhere in me, and it rose within me like a wave of fury at the incompetence and silliness of those two horrible children. The young priest had to steer them. They didn't know where to go, didn't know what to do, didn't know when to genuflect and when not. Louis was just a plain born idiot; Jean was a show box who knew the music of two whole bars of the canticles, and whenever they turned up joined in in a lusty 'la-la-la' and then looked round to his family for approval.

What made the flightiness of the acolytes more striking was the recollection of the young priest. I watched him and found myself falling under a spell. He looked small and lost in that great bare barrack of a church. His voice was weak and toneless. His face wasn't the face of a priest, and it took me some minutes to remember where and when I had seen faces like his before. Then I remembered. It was among young airmen during the war.

But the really extraordinary thing was that he was creating a congregation for himself out of his head. He was not celebrating a service for three reluctant women and two small girls who had merely been dragged in to see members of their family perform in a countryside where God was dead. He was celebrating it in a crowded church in some cathedral town of the Middle Ages. The hypnotic influence he exerted came from the fact that he had hypnotized himself. You saw it in his extraordinary recollection, in the way he managed to push those acolytes about without once letting go the spell. I wondered if I wasn't imagining it all. I looked at Géronte to see how he was taking it. He, whose usual response to a church service is like his response to a conducted tour, was half-kneeling, his eyes fixed on the priest as though he were some work of art which had to be sized up.

'This is one of the most wonderful things I've ever seen,' he whispered without looking round.

The organist heard the whisper without understanding it. He was sitting back gloomily, his hand over his face. He bent across Géronte's arched back to whisper to me.

'I must apologize.'

'Apologize for what?' I asked.

'This,' he said with a wave of the hand. 'I'm ashamed. Really, I'm ashamed.'

'But of what?' I asked. 'The Church of the Catacombs?'

'I beg your pardon?'

'The Church of the Catacombs.'

He said nothing to that, and the service went on, disorderly, disconnected, ridiculous, but for the young priest who held it all together by some sort of inner power. What I felt then I have felt on other occasions, but it is hard to describe. I have felt it about a picture of a nun which has been standing before me for some days. I felt it about another picture, which I took in a Fever Hospital when a family whose child had died asked me to photograph the little body for them one summer morning in the mortuary chapel. The photographs I took were beautiful, but I could not live with them. In a peculiar way the positions had been reversed; the object had become the subject; the dead child had photographed the camera. It is the sudden reversal of situation which is familiar in dreams and which sooner or later happens to all of us and to the civilizations to which we belong. Bethlehem itself was merely an interesting object which the Roman Empire had studied with amusement, till suddenly it opened its eyes and the Roman Empire was no more.

The priest finished, went up to the altar, came down again with the cross in his arms and stood there patiently. It was only then that I realized that none of the congregation had attended the Stations of the Cross before, and that the only two people in the church who had were an Irish agnostic and a French atheist. 'I can't stand this,' I said to Géronte and pushed hastily out past him and the organist. As I went up the nave the priest signalled to the three women. While I stood aside and waited for them to kiss the cross, I suddenly heard the steps behind me. 'Iconoclast!' I thought. 'Whatever would they say of us in Ireland.' But when I turned, I saw that the man behind me was not Géronte but the organist. 'So all De Maupassant's people are not like that!' I thought.

After the service we chatted for a while with the young priest. There was nothing remarkable about him; we hadn't expected it. The young organist was the bigger man. To him we said good-bye outside the church: it was getting late and we wanted to reach Beauvais before dark.

'You know,' he said with sudden emotion as we shook hands, 'I thought that service hideous till I suddenly saw it through the eyes of you and your friend. Then I realized how beautiful it was. Perhaps that is conversion.'

'Let's be honest,' I said. 'It's not conversion for me.' My French would not rise to an explanation of what it really was.

'I'm younger than you,' he replied gravely. 'For me, perhaps, it is complete conversion.'

'I hope so,' I said, and Géronte and I plugged on our way to Beauvais.

THE LATE HENRY CONRAN

'I'VE ANOTHER little story for you,' said the old man.

'I hope it's a good one,' said I.

'The divil a better. And if you don't believe me you can go down to Courtenay's Road and see the truth of it with your own eyes. Now it isn't every wan will say that to you?'

'It is not then.'

'And the reason I say it is, I know the people I'm talking about. I knew Henry in the old days – Henry Conran that is, otherwise known as "Prosperity" Conran – and I'll say for him he had the biggest appetite for liquor of any man I ever met or heard of. You could honestly say Prosperity Conran would drink porter out of a sore heel. Six foot three he was, and he filled it all. He was quiet enough when he was sober, but when he was drunk – Almighty and Eternal, you never knew what divilment he'd be up to!

'I remember calling for him wan night to go to a comity meeting – he was a great supporter of John Redmond – and finding him mad drunk, in his shirt and drawers; he was trying to change out of his old working clothes. Well, with respects to you, he got sick on it, and what did he do before me own two eyes but strip off every stitch he had on him and start wiping up the floor with his Sunday clothes. Oh, every article he could find he shoved into it. And there he was idiity drunk in his pelt singing,

"Up the Mollies! Hurray!
We don't care about Quarry Lane,
All we want is our own Fair Lane."

'Well, of course, poor Henry couldn't keep any job, and his own sweet Nellie wasn't much help to him. She was a nagging sort of woman, if you understand me, an unnatural sort of woman. She had six children to rear, and, instead of going quietly to work and softening Henry, she was always calling in the priest or the minister to him. And Henry, to get his own back, would smash every bit of china she had. Not that he was a cross man by any manner of means, but he was a bit independent, and she could never see how it slighted him to call in strangers like that.

'Henry hung round idle for six months. Then he was offered a job to go round the town as a walking advertisement for somebody's ale. That cut him to the heart. As he said himself, "Is it me, a comity man of the Ancient Order of Hibernians, a man dat shook hands with John Dillon, to disgrace meself like dat before the town? And you wouldn't mind but I couldn't as much as stomach the same hogwash meself!"

'So he had to go to America, and sorry I was to lose him, the decent man! Nellie told me after 'twould go through you to see him on the deck of the tender, blue all over and smothered with sobs. "Nellie," says he to her, "Nellie, give the word and I'll trow me ticket in the water." "I will not," says Nellie, "for you were always a bad head to me."

'Now that was a hard saying, and maybe it wasn't long before she regretted it. There she was with her six children, and wan room between the seven of them, and she trying to do a bit of laundry to keep the life in their bodies.

'Well, it would be a troublesome thing for me to relate all that happened them in the twenty-five long years between that day and this. But maybe you'd remember how her son, Aloysius, mixed himself up in the troubles? Maybe you would? Not that he ever did anything dangerous except act as clerk of the court, and be on all sorts of relief comities, and go here and go there on delegations and deputations. No shooting or jailing for Aloysius. "Lave that," says he, "to the rank and file!" All he ever had his eye on was the main chance. And grander and grander he was getting in himself, my dear! First he had to buy out the house, then he had an electric bell put in, then he bought or hobbled a motor car, then he found tidy jobs for two of his sisters and one for his young brother. Pity to God the two big girls were married already or he'd have made a rare haul! But God help them, they were tied to two poor boozy sops that weren't half nor quarter the cut of their father! So Aloysius gave them the cold shoulder.

'Now Nellie wasn't liking this at all in her own mind. She often said to me, "For all me grandeur, I'd be better off with poor Henry," and so she would, for about that time Aloysius began to think of choosing a wife. Of course, the wife-to-be was a flashy piece from the country, and Nellie, who didn't like her at all, was forever crossing her and finding fault with her. Sure, you ought to remember the row she kicked up when the damsel appeared wan night in wan of them new fangled sleeping things with trousers. Nellie was so shocked she went to the priest and complained her, and then complained her to all the neighbours, and she shamed and disgraced Aloysius so much that for months he wouldn't speak to her. But begod, if she didn't make that girl wear a plain shift every other time she came to stay with them!

'After the scandal about the trousers nothing would content Aloysius but that they must live away from the locality, so they got another house, a bigger wan this time, and it was from the new house that Aloysius got married. Nellie, poor woman, couldn't read nor write, so she had nothing at all to do with the preparations, and what was her surprise when the neighbours read out the marriage announcement to her! "Aloysius Gonzaga Conran, son of Ellen Conran, Courtenay's Road" – and divil the word about poor Henry! The whole town was laughing at it, but what annoyed Nellie most was not the slight on herself, but the slight on her man. So up with her to Aloysius, and "this and that," she says, "I didn't pick you up from under a bush, so give your father the bit of credit that's due to him or I'll put in the note meself!" My dear, she was foaming! Aloysius was in a cleft stick, and they fought and fought, Aloysius calling his father down and Nellie praising him, and then the young wife drops the suggestion that they should put in "the late Henry Conran". So Nellie not having a word to say against that, next day there is another announcement – nothing about Nellie this time only plain "son of the late Henry Conran".

'Well, the town is roaring yet! Wan day the man have no father to speak of and the next day he have a dead father and no mother at all. And everybody knowing at the same time that Henry was in America, safe and sound, and wilder than ever he was at home.

'But that's not the end of it. I was in me bed the other night when a knock came to the door. My daughter-in-law opened it and I heard a strange voice asking for me. Blast me if I could place it! And all at once the stranger forces his way in apast her and stands in the bedroom door, with his head bent down and wan hand on the jamb. "Up the Mollies!" says he in the top of his voice. "Me ould flower, strike up the antem of Fair Lane! Do you remember the night we carried deat and destruction into Blackpool? Shout it, me hearty man – Up the Mollies!"

'But 'twas the height I recognized.

' "'Tis Prosperity Conran," says I.

' "Prosperity Conran it is," says he.

' "The same ould six foot three?" says I.

' "Every inch of it!" says he, idioty drunk.

' "And what in the name of God have you here?" says I.

' "Me wife dat put a notice in the papers saying I was dead. Am I dead, Larry Costello? Me lovely man, you knew me since I was tree – tell me if I'm dead. Feel me! Feel dat muscle of mine and tell me the trute, am I alive or dead?"

' "You're not dead," says I after I felt his arm.

' "I'll murder her, dat's what I'll do! I'll smash every bone in her body. Get up now, Larry, and I'll show you the greatest bust-up dat was ever seen or heard of in dis city. Where's the All-for-Ireland Headquarters till I fling a brick at it?"

' "The All-for-Irelands is no more," says I.

'He looked at me unsteadily for a minute.

' "Joking me you are," says he.

' "Divil a joke," says I.

' "The All-for-Irelands gone?"

' "All gone," says I.

' "And the Mollies?"

' "All gone."

' "All gone?"

' "All gone."

' "Dat you might be killed?"

' "That I might be killed stone dead."

' "Merciful God! I must be an ould man then, huh?"

' "'Tisn't younger we're getting," says I.

' "An ould man," says he, puzzled-like. "Maybe I'm dead after all? Do you think I'm dead, Larry?"

' "In a manner of speaking you are," says I.

' "Would a court say I was dead?"

' "A clever lawyer might argue them into it," says I.

' "But not *dead*, Larry? Christ, he couldn't say I was *dead*?"

' "Well, as good as dead, Henry."

' "I'll carry the case to the High Courts," says he, getting excited. "I'll prove I'm not dead. I'm an American citizen and I can't be dead."

' "Aisy! Aisy!" says I, seeing him take it so much to heart.

' "I won't be aisy," says he, flaring up. "I've a summons out agin me wife for defaming me character, and I'll never go back to Chicago till I clear me name in the eyes of the world."

' "Henry," says I, "no wan ever said wan word against you. There isn't as much as a shadow of an aspersion on your character."

' "Do you mane," says he, "'tis no aspersion on me character to say I'm dead? God damn you, man, would you like a rumour like dat to be going round about yourself?"

' "I would not, Henry, I would not, but 'tis no crime to be dead. And anyway, as I said before, 'tis only a manner of speaking. A man might be stone dead, or he might be half dead, or dead to you and me, or, for the matter of that, he might be dead to God and the world as we've often been ourselves."

' "Dere's no manner of speaking in it at all," says Henry, getting madder and madder. "No bloody manner of speaking. I might be dead drunk as you say, but dat would be no excuse for calling me the late Henry Conran. . . . Dere's me charge sheet," says he, sitting on the bed and pulling out a big blue paper. "Ellen Conran, for defamation of character. Wan man on the boat wanted me to charge her with attempted bigamy, but the clerk wouldn't have it."

' "And did you come all the way from America to do this?" says I.

' "Of course I did. How could I stay on in America wit a ting like dat hanging over me? Blast you, man, you don't seem to know the agony I went trough for weeks and weeks before I got on the boat!"

' "And do Nellie know you're here?" says I.

' "She do not, and I mane her not to know till the policeman serves his warrant on her."

' "Listen to me, Henry," says I, getting out of bed, "the sooner you have this out with Nellie the better for all."

' "Do you tink so?" says he a bit stupid-like.

' "How long is it since you put your foot aboard the liner in Queenstown, Henry?"

' "'Tis twenty-five years and more," says he.

' "'Tis a long time not to see your own lawful wife," says I.

' "'Tis," says he, "'tis, a long time," and all at wance he began to cry, with his head in his two hands.

' "I knew she was a hard woman, Larry, but blast me if I ever tought she'd do the like of dat on me! Me poor ould heart is broke! And the Mollies – did I hear you say the Mollies was gone?"

' "The Mollies is gone," says I.

' "Anyting else but dat, Larry, anyting else but dat!"

' "Come on away," says I.

'So I brought him down the road by the hand just like a child. He never said wan word till I knocked at the door, and all at wance he got fractious again. I whispered into Nellie to open the door. When she seen the man with me she nearly went through the ground.

' "Who is it?" says she.

' "An old friend of yours," says I.

' "Is it Henry?" says she, whispering-like.

' "It is Henry," says I.

' "It is not Henry!" bawls out me hero. "Well you know your poor ould Henry is dead and buried without a soul in the world to shed a tear over his corpse."

' "Henry!" says she.

' "No, blast you!" says he with a shriek, "but Henry's ghost come to ha'ant you."

' "Come in, come in the pair of ye," says I. "Why the blazes don't ye kiss wan another like any Christian couple?"

'After a bit of trouble I dragged him inside.

' "Ah, you hard-hearted woman!" says he moaning, with his two paws out before him like a departed spirit. "Ah, you cruel, wicked woman! What did you do to your poor ould husband?"

' "Help me to undress him, Nellie," says I. "Sit down there on the bed, Henry, and let me unlace your boots."

'So I pushed him back on the bed, but, when I tried to get at his boots, he began to kick his feet up in the air, laughing like a kid.

' "I'm dead, dead, dead, dead," says he.

' "Let me get at him, Larry," says Nellie in her own determined way, so, begod, she lifted his leg that high he couldn't kick without falling over, and in two minits she had his boots and stockings off. Then I got off his coat, loosened his braces and held him back in the bed while she pulled his trousers down. At that he began to come to himself a bit.

' "Show it to her! Show it to her!" says he, getting hot and making a dive for his clothes.

' "Show what to her?" says I.

' "Me charge sheet. Give it to me, Larry. There you are, you jade of hell! Seven and six-pence I paid for it to clear me character."

' "Get into bed, sobersides," says I.

' "I wo' not go into bed!"

' "And there's an old nightshirt all ready," says Nellie.

' "I don't want no nightshirt. I'll take no charity from any wan of ye. I wants me character back, me character that ye took on me."

' "Take off his shirt, Larry," says she.

'So I pulled the old stinking shirt up over his grey pate, and in a tick of the clock she had his nightshirt on.

' "Now, Nellie," says I, "I'll be going. There's nothing more I can do for you."

' "Thanks, Larry, thanks," says she. "You're the best friend we ever had. There's nothing else you can do. He'll be asleep in a minit, don't I know him well?"

' "Good-night, Henry," says I.

' "Good-night, Larry. Tomorrow we'll revive the Mollies."

'Nellie went to see me to the door, and outside was the two ladies and the young gentleman in their nighties, listening.

' "Who is it, Mother?" says they.

' "Go back to bed the three of ye!" says Nellie. "'Tis only your father."

' "Jesus, Mary and Joseph!" says the three of them together.

'At that minit we heard Henry inside bawling his heart out.

' "Nellie, Nellie, where are you, Nellie?"

' "Go back and see what he wants," says I, "before I go."

'So Nellie opened the door and looked in.

' "What's wrong with you now?" says she.

' "You're not going to leave me sleep alone, Nellie," says he.

' "You ought to be ashamed of yourself," says she, "talking like that and the children listening. . . . Look at him," says she to me, "look at him for the love of God!" The eyes were shining in her head with pure relief. So I peeped in, and there was Henry with every bit of clothes in the bed around him and his back to us all. "Look at his ould grey pate!" says she.

' "Still in all," says Henry over his shoulder, "you had no right to say I was dead!" '

MICHAEL'S WIFE

I

THE STATION – it is really only a siding with a shed – was empty but for the station-master and himself. When he saw the station-master change his cap he rose. From far way along the water's edge came the shrill whistle of the train before it puffed into view with its leisurely air that suggested a trot.

Half a dozen people alighted and quickly dispersed. In a young woman wearing a dark-blue coat who lingered and looked up and down the platform he recognized Michael's wife. At the same moment she saw him but her face bore no smile of greeting. It was the face of a sick woman.

'Welcome, child,' he said, and held out his hand. Instead of taking it, she threw her arms about him and kissed him. His first impulse was to discover if anyone had noticed, but almost immediately he felt ashamed of the thought. He was a warm-hearted man and the kiss silenced an initial doubt. He lurched out before her with the trunk while she carried the two smaller bags.

''Tis a long walk,' he said with embarrassment.

'Why?' she asked wearily. 'Can't I drive with you?'

'You'd rather have McCarthy's car, but 'tisn't back from Cork yet.'

'I would not. I'd rather drive with you.'

''Tis no conveyance,' he said angrily, referring to the old cart. Nevertheless he was pleased. She mounted from behind and sat on her black trunk. He lifted himself in after her, and they jolted down the village with the bay on their left. Beyond the village the road climbed a steep hill. Through a hedge of trees the bay grew upon the sight with a wonderful brightness because of the dark canopy of leaves. On and up, now to right, now to left, till the trees ceased, the bay disappeared over the brow of a hill, and they drove along a sunlight upland road with sunken fences. Hills like mattresses rose to their right, a brilliant green except where they were broken by cultivated patches or clumps of golden furze; a bog, all brown with bright pools and tall grey reeds, flanked the road.

'Ye were in about eight, I'd say,' he commented, breaking the silence.

'Oh yes. About that.'

'I seen ye.'

'You did?'

'I was on the look out. When she rounded the head I ran in and told the wife "Your daughter-in-law's coming." She nearly had me life when she seen 'twas only the ould liner.'

The girl smiled.

'Ah, now,' he added proudly, a moment later, 'there's a sight for you!'

She half raised herself on the edge of the cart and looked in the direction his head indicated. The land dropped suddenly away from beneath their feet, and the open sea, speckled white with waves and seagulls' wings, stretched out before them. The hills, their smooth flanks patterned with the varying colours of the fields, flowed down to it in great unbroken curves, and the rocks looked very dark between their wind-flawed brightness and the brightness of the water. In little hollows nestled houses and cottages, diminutive and quaint and mostly of a cold, startling whiteness that was keyed up here and there by the spring-like colour of fresh thatch. In the clear air the sea was spread out like a great hall with all its folding doors thrown wide; a dancing floor, room beyond room, each narrower and paler than the last, till on the farthest reaches steamers that were scarcely more than dots jerked to and fro as on a wire.

Something in the fixity of the girl's pose made Tom Shea shout the mare to a standstill.

''Tis the house beyond,' he said, brandishing his stick. 'The one with the slate roof on the hill.'

With sudden tenderness he looked quizzically down at her from under his black hat. This strange girl with her American clothes and faintly American accent was his son's wife and would some day be the mother of his grandchildren. Her hands were gripping the front of the cart. She was weeping. She made no effort to restrain herself or conceal her tears, nor did she turn her eyes from the sea. He remembered a far-away evening when he had returned like this, having seen off his son.

'Yes,' he said after a moment's silence, '' tis so, 'tis so.'

A woman with a stern and handsome face stood in the doorway. As everything in Tom seemed to revolve about a fixed point of softness; his huge frame, his comfortable paunch, his stride, his round face with the shrewd, brown twinkling eyes and the big grey moustache, so everything in her seemed to obey a central reserve. Hers was a nature refined to the point of hardness, and while her husband took colour from everything about him, circumstances or acquaintance would, you felt, leave no trace on her.

One glance was enough to show her that he had already surrendered. She, her look said, would not give in so easily. But sooner than he she recognized the signals of fatigue.

'You're tired out, girl!' she exclaimed.

'I am,' replied the younger woman, resting her forehead in her hands as though to counteract a sudden giddiness. In the kitchen she removed her hat and coat and sat at the head of the table where the westering light caught her. She wore a pale-blue frock with a darker collar. She was very dark, but the pallor of illness had bleached the dusk from her skin. Her cheek-bones were high so that they formed transparencies beneath her eyes. It was a very Irish face, long and spiritual, with an inherent melancholy that might dissolve into sudden anger or equally sudden gaiety.

'You were a long time sick,' said Maire Shea, tossing a handful of brosna on the fire.

'I was.'

'Maybe 'twas too soon for you to travel?'

'If I didn't, I'd have missed the summer at home.'

'So Michael said, so Michael said.'

'Ah,' declared Tom with burning optimism, 'you won't be long pulling round now, with God's help. There's great air here, powerful air.'

'You'll be finding us rough, simple poor people,' added his wife with dignity, taking from him a parcel that contained a cheap glass sugar-bowl to replace the flowered mug without a handle that had served them till now. 'We're not used to your ways nor you to ours but we have a great will to please you.'

'We have,' agreed Tom heartily. 'We have indeed.'

The young woman ate nothing, only sipped her tea that

smelled of burned wood, and it was clear, as when she tried to pour milk from the large jug, that she was completely astray in her new surroundings. And that acute sense of her discomfort put a strain on the two old people, on Tom especially, whose desire to make a good impression was general and strong.

After tea she went upstairs to rest. Maire came with her.

''Tis Michael's room,' she said. 'And that's Michael's bed.'

It was a bare, green-washed room with a low window looking on to the front of the house, an iron bed and an oleograph of the Holy Family. For a moment an old familiar feeling of wild jealousy stole over Maire Shea, but when the girl, in undressing, exposed the scar across her stomach, she felt guilty.

'You'll sleep now,' she said softly.

'I ought to.'

Maire stole down the straight stair. Tom was standing in the doorway, his black hat over his eyes, his hands clasped behind his back.

'Well?' he asked in a whisper.

'Whist!' she replied irritably. 'She shouldn't be travelling at all. I don't know what come over Michael, and to leave her and he knowing well we have no facility. The cut in her stomach – 'tis the length of your arm.'

'Would I run up and tell Kate not to come? Herself and Joan will be in soon.'

''Twould be no use. All the neighbours will be in.'

'So they will, so they will,' he admitted in a depressed tone.

He was very restless. After a while he stole upstairs and down again on tiptoe.

'She's asleep. But whisper, Moll, she must have been crying.'

''Tis weakness.'

'Maybe she'd be lonely.'

''Tis weakness, 'tis weakness. She should never be travelling.'

Later Kate and Joan arrived and after them three or four other women. Twilight fell within the long whitewashed kitchen; and still they talked in subdued voices. Suddenly the door on the stair opened and Michael's wife appeared. She seemed to have grown calmer, though she still retained something of the air of a sleep-walker, and in the half-light with her jet-black eyes and hair, her long pale face had a curious ethereal beauty.

The sense of strain was very noticeable. Tom fussed about her in a helpless fidgety way till the women, made nervous by it, began to mock and scold him. Even then a question put at random caused him to fret.

'Can't ye leave her alone, now can't ye? Can't ye see she's tired? Go on with yeer ould talk, leave ye, and don't be bothering her any more.'

'No, no,' she said. 'I'm not so tired now.' Her voice retained a memory of her native Donegal in a certain dry sweetness.

'Have a sup of this,' urged Tom. 'A weeshy sup – 'twill do you no harm.'

She refused the drink, but two of the other women took it, and Tom, having first toasted 'her lovely black eyes,' drank a glass without pausing for breath. He gave a deep sigh of content.

'The curate was drunk and the midwife was tipsy
And I was baptized in a basin of whiskey,'

he hummed. He refilled his glass before sitting down beside the open door. The sky turned deep and deeper blue above the crown of a tree that looked in the low doorway and a star winked at the window-pane. Maire rose and lit the wall-lamp with its tin reflector. From far away in a lag between two headlands a voice was calling and calling on a falling cadence 'Taaaamie! Taaaamie!' and in the distance the call had a remote and penetrating sweetness. When it ceased there came to their ears the noise of the sea, and suddenly it was night. The young woman drew herself up. All were silent. One of the women sighed. The girl looked up, throwing back her head.

'I'm sorry, neighbours,' she said. 'I was only a child when I left Ireland and it's all strange to me now.'

''Tis surely,' replied Kate heartily. ''Tis lonely for you. You're every bit as strange as we'd be in the heart of New York.'

'Just so, just so,' exclaimed Tom with approval.

'Never mind,' continued Kate. 'You have me to take your part.'

'You be damned!' retorted Tom in mock indignation. 'No one is going to look after that girl but meself.'

'A deal she have to expect from either of ye!' added Maire coldly. 'It wouldn't occur to ye she should be in bed.'

She dipped a candle in the fire and held it above her head. The girl followed her. The others sat on and talked; then all took their leave together. Maire, busy about the house and yard for a long time, heard voices and footsteps coming back to her on the light land wind.

She was thinking in her dispassionate way of Michael's wife. She had thought of her often before but now she found herself at sea. It wasn't only that the girl was a stranger and a sick one at that, but – and this Maire had never allowed for – she was the child of a strange world, the atmosphere of which had come with her, disturbing judgement. Less clearly than Kate or Tom, yet clearly enough, she realized that the girl was as strange amongst them as they would be in New York. In the bright starlight a cluster of whitewashed cottages stood out against the hillside like a frame of snow about its orange window-squares. For the first time Maire looked at it, and with a strange feeling of alienation wondered what it was like to one unused to it.

A heavy step startled her. She turned in to see that Tom had disappeared. Heated with drink and emotion he had tiptoed up the stairs and opened the girl's door. He was surprised to find her sitting on the low window-ledge in her dressing-gown. From the darkness she was looking out with strange eyes on the same scene Maire had been watching with eyes grown too familiar, hills, whitewashed cottages and sea.

'Are 'oo awake?' he asked – a stupid question.

'Wisha, for goodness' sake will you come down and leave the girl sleep?' came Maire's voice in irritation from the foot of the stairs.

'No, no, no,' he whispered nervously.

'What is it?' asked the girl.

'Are 'oo all right?'

'Quite, thanks.'

'We didn't disturb 'oo?'

'Not at all.'

'Come down out of that, you ould fool!' cried Maire in an exasperated tone.

'I'm coming, I'm coming – Jasus, can't you give us a chance?' he added angrily. 'Tell me,' this in a whisper, 'the ould operation, 'twont come again you?'

He bent over her, hot and excited, his breath smelling of whiskey.

'I don't understand you.'

'Ah,' he said in the same low tone, 'wouldn't it be a terrible misfortune? A terrible misfortune entirely! 'Tis great life in a house, a child is.'

'Oh, no,' she answered hastily, nervously, as though she were growing afraid.

'Are 'oo sure? What did the doctors say?'

'It won't, it won't.'

'Ah, glory be to the hand of God!' he said, turning away, ''tis a great ease to my mind to know that. A great ease! A great ease! I'm destroyed thinking of it.'

He stumbled downstairs to face his wife's anger that continued long after he had shut up the house for the night. She had a bitter tongue when she chose to use it, and she chose now. For weeks they had been screwing themselves up, to make a good impression on Michael's wife, and now it was spoiled by a drunken fool of a man.

He turned and tossed, unable to sleep at the injustice of it. As though a man wouldn't want to know a thing like that, as though he mightn't ask his own daughter-in-law a civil question, without being told he was worse than a black, a heathen savage from Africa, without niceness or consideration except for his own dirty gut!

He, Tom Shea, who tried to leave a good impression on every hog, dog and devil that came the road!

II

In the morning Michael's wife was somewhat better. The sun appeared only at intervals, but for the greater part of the day she was able to sit by the gable where she had a view of the sea in shelter from the wind. A stream ran just beneath her, and a hedge of fuchsia beside it bordered a narrow stony laneway leading to the strand. The chickens raced about her with a noise like distant piping and from the back of the house came the complaining voice of a hen saying without pause, 'Oh, God! God! God! God!'

Occasionally Maire came and sat beside her on a low stool. Maire asked no questions – her pride again – and the conversation was strained, almost hostile, until the girl became aware of what ailed her: curiosity for the minute trifles of their life in

America, hers and Michael's; the details that had become so much part of her that she found it difficult to remember them. How much the maid was paid, how the milk was delivered, the apartment house with its central heating, the negro lift-hop, the street-cars and the rest of it. At last her mind seemed to embrace the old woman's vivid and unlettered mind trying to construct a picture of the world in which her son lived, and she continued to talk for the sake of talking, as though the impersonality of it was a relief.

It was different when at dinner-time Tom came in from the strand in a dirty old shirt and pants, his black hat well forward on his eyes.

'Listen, girleen,' he said in a gruff voice, very different from that of the previous night, as with legs crossed and hands joined behind his back he leaned against the wall. 'Tell that husband of yours he should write oftener to his mother. Women are like that. If 'twas your own son now, you'd understand.'

'I know, I know,' she said hastily.

'Of course you do. You're a fine big-hearted girl, and don't think we're not thankful to you. The wife now, she's a fine decent woman but she have queer ways. She wouldn't thank God Almighty if she thought He was listening, and she'll never say it to you but she said it to others, how good you are to us.'

'Don't blame Michael,' she replied in a low voice. 'It isn't his fault.'

'I know, sure, I know.'

'He never has time.'

'Mention it to him though, you! Mention it to him. The letter to say you were coming, 'twas the first we had from himself for months. Tell him 'tis his mother, not me at all.'

'If only you knew how he wanted to come!' she exclaimed with a troubled glance.

'Yes, yes, yes; but 'twill be two years more before he can. Two years to one at his hour of life 'tis only like tomorrow, but for old people that never know the time or the place . . . ! And that same, it may be the last he'll see of one or the other of us. And we've no one but him, girleen, more's the pity.'

It was certainly different with Tom, who had but one approach to any situation.

*

In a few days she had regained something of her strength. Tom cut her a stout ashplant and she went for short walks, to the strand, to the little harbour or to the post office which was kept by Tom's sisters. Mostly she went alone. To his delight the weather turned showery, but it never completely broke.

All day long the horizon was peopled by a million copper-coloured cloudlets, rounded and tiny and packed back to the very limits of the sky like cherubs in a picture of the Madonna. Then they began to swell, bubble on bubble, expanding, changing colour; one broke away from the mass and then another; it grew into a race; they gathered, sending out dark streamers that blackened the day and broke the patina of the water with dark-green stormy paths; lastly, a shrill whistle of wind and wild driving rain enveloped everything in mist. She took shelter under a rock or at the lee-side of a fence, and watched the shower dissolve in golden points of light that grew into a sunlit landscape beyond, as the clouds like children in frolic terror scampered back pell-mell to the horizon, the blue strip of sky they left broadening, the rain thinning, the fields and sea stripping off their scum of shadow till everything was sparkling and steaming again.

What it meant to her they could only guess when she returned. Whenever she remained too long in the house the shadow came on her again. Kate bade them take no notice.

She seemed to be very drawn towards Kate. Her walks often took her to the post office, and there she sat for hours with the two sisters, frequently sharing their meals, and listening to Kate's tales of old times in the parish, about her parents and her brother Tom, but most frequently about Michael's youth.

Kate was tall and bony with a long nose, long protruding chin and wire spectacles. Her teeth, like her sister's, were all rotten. She was the sort country people describe as having a great heart, a masterful woman, always busy, noisy and good-humoured. Tom, who was very proud of her, told how she had gone off for a major operation carrying a basket of eggs to sell so that she wouldn't have her journey for nothing. Her sister Joan was a nun-like creature who had spent some time in an asylum. She had a wonderfully soft, round, gentle face with traces of a girlish complexion, a voice that seldom rose above a whisper and the most lovely eyes; but when the cloud came on her she was perverse and obstinate. On the wall of the living-room, cluttered thick with pictures, was a framed sampler in ungainly letter-ing, 'Eleanor Joan Shea, March 1881'. She was nominally post-mistress, but it was Kate who did the work.

As much as Michael's wife took to them, they took to her. Joan would have wept her eyes out for a homeless dog, but Kate's sympathy was marked by a certain shrewdness.

'You had small luck in your marriage,' she said once.

'How?' The young woman looked at her blankly.

'For all you're only married a year you had your share of trouble. No honeymoon, then the sickness and now the separation.'

'You're right. It's nothing but separations.'

'Ye had only seven months together?'

'Only seven.'

'Ah, God help you, I never saw a lonelier creature than you were the night you came. But that's how we grow.'

'Is it, I wonder?'

''Tis, 'tis. Don't I know it?'

'That's what Father Coveney says,' wailed Joan, 'but I could never understand it myself. All the good people having all the misfortunes − that don't deserve them, and the bad ones get-ting off.'

'You'll be happier for it in the latter end, and you've a good boy in Michael . . . Musha, listen to me talking about Michael again. One'd think I was his mother.'

'You might be.'

'How so?'

'He has a lot of your ways.'

'Ah, now, I always said it! Didn't I, Joan? And why wouldn't he? When his mother leathered him 'twas up to me he came for comfort.'

'He often said it − you made a man of him.'

'I did,' said Kate proudly. 'I did so. Musha, he was a wild boy and there was no one to understand him when he was wild. His mother − not judging her − was born heavy with the weight of sense.'

Kate rarely lost the chance of a jeer at Maire.

'You're getting to like us, I think?' she said at last.

'I am,' admitted the girl. 'When I came first I was afraid.'

'You won't be so glad to get back to the States.'

'I wish I never saw the States again.'

'Och, aye!'

'It's true.'

'Ah, well. Two years more and ye'll be back together. And what's a couple of years to one of your age?'

'More than you think.'

'True, true, years are only as you feel them.'

'And I'll never come back here again.'

'Ach, bad cess to you, you're giving into it again! And now, listen to me. 'Tis a thing I often said to Tom Shea, why wouldn't ye come back? What's stopping ye? Never mind that ould fool telling you Michael wouldn't get a job! Why wouldn't he? And only Tom was such a gligin he'd never have left the boy go away.'

To Tom's disgust the weather cleared without heavy rain, though there was little sun, and that wandering, bursting out here and there on the hills or in mirror-like patches on the water and then fading into the same grey sultry light. Now, early and late, Michael's wife was out, sitting on the rocks or striding off to the village. She became a familiar figure on the roads in her blue dress with her ashplant. At first she stood far off, watching the men at the nets or sitting at the crossroads; as time went on she drew nearer, and one day a fisherman hailed her and spoke to her.

After that she went everywhere, into their houses, on to the quay and out in the boats when they went fishing. Maire Shea didn't like it, but all the men had known Michael as a boy and had tales of him and his knowledge of boats and fishing, and after a few days it was as though she too had grown up with them. It may be also that she gathered something from those hours on the water, in silent coves on grey days when the wind shook out a shoal of lights, or in the bay when the thunderous light moved swiftly, starting sudden hares of brightness from every hollow, blue from the hills, violet from the rocks, primrose from the fields, and here and there a mysterious milky glow that might be rock or field or tree. It may be these things deepened her knowledge so that she no longer felt a stranger when she walked in the morning along the strand, listening to the tide expand the great nets of weed with a crisp, gentle, pervasive sound like rain, or from her window saw the moon plunge its silver drill into the water.

But there was a decided change in her appearance and in her

manner. She had filled out, her face had tanned and the gloomy, distraught air had left it.

'There,' said Tom, 'didn't I tell ye we'd make a new woman of her? Would anyone know her for the girl she was the night she came? Would they? I declare to me God, the time she opened the door and walked down the stairs I thought her own were calling.'

Kate and Joan, too, were pleased. They liked her for her own sake and Michael's sake, but they had come to love her for the sake of her youth and freshness. Only Maire held her peace. Nothing had ever quite bridged the gap between the two women; in every word and glance of hers there was an implicit question. It was some time before she succeeded in infecting Tom. But one day he came for comfort to Kate. He was downcast, and his shrewd brown eyes had a troubled look.

'Kate,' he said, going to the heart of things as his way was, ''tis about Michael's wife.'

'Och, aye! What about her?' asked Kate, pulling a wry face. ''Tisn't complaining you are?'

'No, but tell me what you think of her.'

'What I think?'

''Tis Maire.'

'Well?'

'She's uneasy.'

'Uneasy about what, aru?'

'She thinks the girl have something on her mind.'

'Tom Shea, I tell you now as I told you many a time before, your wife is a suspicious woman.'

'Wisha, wisha, can't you forget all that? I never seen such a tribe for spite. We know ye never got on. But now, Kate, you can't deny she's a clever woman.'

'And what do the clever woman think?'

'She thinks the pair of them had a row; that's what she thinks now plain and straight, and I won't put a tooth in it.'

'I doubt it.'

'Well now, it might be some little thing a few words would put right.'

'And I'm to say the few words?'

'Now Kate, 'twas my suggestion, my suggestion entirely. The way 'tis with Moll, she'd say too much or say too little.'

'She would,' agreed Kate with grim amusement. Maire Shea had the reputation for doing both.

Next day she reported that the idea was absurd. He had to be content, for Kate too was no fool. But the question in Maire's manner never ceased to be a drag on him, and for this he did not know whether to blame her or the girl. Three weeks had passed and he began to find it intolerable. As usual he came to Kate.

'The worst of it is,' he said gloomily, 'she's making me as bad as herself. You know the sort I am. If I like a man, I don't want to be picking at what he says like an ould hen, asking "What did he mean by this?" or "What's he trying to get out of me now?" And 'tisn't that Moll says anything, but she have me so bothered I can hardly talk to the girl. Bad luck to it, I can't even sleep ... And last night –'

'What happened last night?'

He looked at her gloomily from under his brows.

'Are you making fun of me again?'

'I am not. What happened last night?'

'I heard her talking in her shleep.'

'Michael's wife?'

'Yes.'

'And what harm if she do in itself?'

'No harm at all!' howled Tom in a sudden rage, stamping up and down the kitchen and shaking his arms. 'No harm in the bloody world, but, Chrisht, woman, I tell you it upsot me.'

Kate looked at him over her wire spectacles with scorn and pity.

'Me mother's hood cloak that wasn't worn since the day she died, I must get it out for you. You'll never be a proper ould woman without it!'

'Moll,' said Tom that night as they were going to bed, 'you're dreaming.'

'How so?'

'About Michael's wife.'

'Maybe I am,' she admitted grudgingly, yet surprising him by any admission at all.

'You are,' he said, to clinch it.

'I had my reasons. But this while past she's different. Likely Kate said something to her.'

'She did.'

'That explains it so,' said Maire complacently.

Two nights later he was wakened suddenly. It happened now that he did waken like that at any strange noise. He heard Michael's wife again speaking in her sleep. She spoke in a low tone that dwindled drowsily away into long silences. With these intervals the voice went on and on, very low, sometimes express- ing – or so it seemed to him – a great joy, sometimes as it were, pleading. But the impression it left most upon him was one of intimacy and tenderness. Next day she came down late, her eyes red. That same day a letter came from Donegal. When she had read it she announced in a halting way that her aunt was expecting her.

'You won't be sorry to go,' said Maire, searching her with her eyes.

'I will,' replied the girl simply.

'If a letter comes for you!'

''Tisn't likely. Any letters there are will be at home. I never expected to stay so long.'

Maire gave her another long look. For the first time the girl gave it back, and for a moment they looked into one another's eyes, mother and wife.

'At first,' said Maire, turning her gaze to the fire, 'I didn't trust you. I'm a straight woman and I'll tell you that. I didn't trust you.'

'And now?'

'Right or wrong, whatever anyone may say, I think my son chose well for himself.'

'I hope you'll always think it,' replied the girl in the same serious tone. She looked at Maire, but the older woman's air repelled sentiment. Then she rose and went to the door. She stood there for a long time. The day was black and heavy, and at intervals a squall swept its shining net over the surface of the water.

And now the positions of Tom and his wife were reversed, as frequently happens with two such extremes of temperament. Before dusk rain began to fall in torrents. He went out late to the post office and sat between his two sisters, arguing.

'There's a woman all out,' he said bitterly. 'She upsets me and then sits down on me troubles. What's on the girl's mind?

There's something queer about her, something I can't make out. I've a good mind to send word to Michael.'

'And what would you say?' asked Kate. 'Disturbing him without cause! Can't you be sensible!'

'I can't be sensible,' he replied angrily. 'She's here in my charge and if anything happened her—'

'Nothing will happen her.'

'But if it did?'

'She's all right. She got back her health that none of us thought she would. Besides, she's going away.'

'That's what's worrying me,' he confessed. 'She'll leave me with the trouble on me, and I haven't the words to walk back and have it out with her.'

He returned late through the driving rain. The women had gone to bed. He turned in but could not sleep. The wind rose gradually from the squalls that shook the house and set the window-panes rattling.

All at once he caught it again, the damned talking. He lay perfectly still in order not to wake Maire. Long intervals of silence and then the voice again. In a sudden agony of fear he determined to get up and ask what was on her mind. Anything was better than the fear that was beginning to take hold of him. He lifted himself in the bed, hoping to crawl out over Maire's feet without waking her. She stirred, and he crouched there listening to the wind and the voice above his head, waiting till his wife should settle out again. And then, suddenly in a moment when wind and sea seemed to have died down to a murmur, the voice above him rose in three anguished mounting breaths that ended in a suppressed scream. 'Michael! Michael! Michael!'

With a groan he sank back and covered his eyes with his hands. He felt another hand coldly touching his forehead and his heart. For one wild, bewildering moment it was as though Michael had really entered the room above his head, had passed in his living body across all those hundreds of miles of waves and storm and blackness; as though all the inexpressible longing of his young wife had incarnated him beside her. He made the sign of the cross as if against some evil power. And after that there was silence but for the thunder of the rising storm.

*

Next morning he would have avoided her eyes, but there was something about her that made him look and look in spite of himself. A nervous exaltation had crystallized in her, making her seem ethereal, remote and lovely. Because of the rain that still continued to pour Maire would have had her remain, but she insisted.

She went out in heavy boots and raincoat to say good-bye to Kate and Joan. Joan wept. 'Two years,' said Kate in her hearty way, ''twill be no time passing, no time at all.' When she left it was as if a light had gone out in the childless house.

Maire's good-bye was sober but generous too.

'I know Michael is in good hands,' she said.

'Yes,' replied the girl with a radiant smile, 'he is.'

And they drove off through the rain. The sea on which she looked back was blinded by it, all but a leaden strip beside the rocks. She crouched over her black trunk with averted head. Tom, an old potato bag over his shoulders, drove into it, head down. The fear had not left him. He looked down at her once or twice, but her face was hidden in the collar of her raincoat.

They left the seemingly endless, wind-swept upland road and plunged down among the trees that creaked and roared above their heads, spilling great handfuls of water into the cart. His fear became a terror.

When he stood before the carriage door he looked at her appealingly. He could not frame the question he looked; it was a folly he felt must pass from him unspoken; so he asked it only with his eyes, and with her eyes she answered him – a look of ecstatic fulfilment.

The whistle went. She leaned out of the carriage window as the train lurched forward, but he was no longer looking. He raised his hands to his eyes and swayed to and fro, moaning softly to himself. For a long time he remained like that, a ridiculous figure with the old potato bag and the little pool of water that gradually gathered in the platform about his feet.

I ENJOYED having him [Father] with us because he was an even better walker than myself, though a more perfunctory one. On a visit to the country his trained military eye sized up the number of roads, and he liked to inspect each once, and when the inspection was complete to go home. The fact that a road was attractive did not mean it needed a second inspection.

One of these walks in Courtmacsherry is very vivid in my memory, and I wrote a story about it long after. We had climbed a hill overlooking the sea, and on the horizon, apparently moving across it in a series of jerks, like the swan in *Lohengrin*, was an American liner on its way into Cobh. A farmer working in a field by the road joined us; he too had been watching the liner and it had reminded him of his son who had emigrated to America when he was quite young. After a few years the boy had married an Irish-American girl whose family had come from Donegal, and soon after ceased to write home, though his wife continued to write. Then she fell ill and her doctor suggested a holiday in Ireland. She had arrived one day on a liner like the one we were watching, and her father-in-law had met her at the station with his horse and cart. She had stayed with them for weeks, regained her health, and gradually won the affection of the family. After that she had set off to visit her parents' family in Donegal, and it was only then that the old Cork couple had learned from a letter to a neighbour that their son was dead before ever she left America.

Up there on the hill in the evening with the little whitewashed farmhouse beside us and the liner disappearing in the distance, it was an extraordinarily moving story, all the more so because the farmer was obviously still bewildered and upset by it.

'Why would she do a thing like that to us?' he asked. 'It wasn't that we weren't fond of her. We liked her, and we thought she liked us.'

Clearly he suspected that some motive of self-interest was involved, and I was afraid to tell him my own romantic notion that the girl might have liked them all too well and kept her husband alive in their minds as long as she could and – who knows? – perhaps kept him alive in her own.

I knew that some time I should have to write that story, but Father only listened with the polite and perfunctory smile that he gave to the scenery. Both, no doubt, were suitable for people living in backward places, but did not call for closer inspection, and next morning he was up at six to make sure of catching the noon bus for Cork.

He was the most complete townie I ever knew.

8 LAST THINGS

PREFACE

ON THE last page of *An Only Child* O'Connor wrote:

All our arguments about the immortality of the soul seem
to me to be based on one vast fallacy – that it is our vanity
that desires eternity. Vanity! As though any reasonable man
could be vain enough to believe himself worth immortality!
From the time I was a boy and could think at all, I was
certain that for my own soul there was only nothingness.
I knew it too well in its commonness and weakness. But I
knew that there were souls that were immortal, that even
God, if He wishes, could not diminish or destroy, and per-
haps it was the thought of these that turned me finally from
poetry to story-telling, to the celebration of who for me
represented all I should ever know of God.

O'Connor seems rarely, if ever, to have defined himself in
religious terms. Was he a reluctant, sceptical believer? Possibly.
A questioning agnostic? Probably. He had a great deal to say
about the Catholic Church, much of it critical; but in his writing
life he was brother in God to the believer and the disbeliever
alike. Nor did he bring any dogmatism, let alone propagandizing,
to his depiction of the individual priests who people his stories.
They are not, to be sure, the twinkly, gentle, overarchingly wise
fellows who inhabit sentimental Catholic fiction; they tend to
be bristly, fierce, manipulative. Some are lonely voices, despair-
ingly consumed by the life they have chosen; some are social
voices, worldly, drink-loving, temptable. They are also, at times,
analogues of the writer:

The attraction of the religious life for the story-teller is
overpowering. It is the attraction of a sort of life lived, or
seeking to be lived, by standards other than those of this
world, one which, in fact, resembles that of the artist. The
good priest, like the good artist, needs human rewards, but
no human reward can ever satisfy him.

From LEINSTER, MUNSTER AND CONNAUGHT
– MONASTERY

THE ROAD runs through it [Cappoquin] up the mountain to the modern Cistercian monastery of Melleray, architecturally to be clearly distinguished from its mediaeval prototype, for it sprawls there on the mountainside, as unsightly as any other modern Irish ecclesiastical building. In my youth Melleray used to be the place where drunks were sent for a yearly cure, but now I believe the distinction has passed to the other Cistercian monastery of Mount St Joseph, near Roscrea. There is a wayside pub half-way up, where these unfortunates halted to undo a little of the monks' cure. The stories they tell about them are endless. One (which was the basis of a story of my own, called 'Song without Words') was of an English clerical student who was sent there by his bishop to study a little Latin. The life didn't suit him at all, and he complained to the abbot that he was feeling unwell for lack of exercise. Instead of allowing him to take a daily walk to the pub, the abbot suggested that he might give himself some exercise by taking a hand in the stables. At first the English student didn't at all appreciate the abbot's sense of humour, until he discovered that an outside carrier called at the stables and could be persuaded to leave a quart bottle of beer in hiding there for a small consideration. He was then perfectly happy until he found his bottle emptied for several mornings running. One of the monks had nosed out his hiding-hole and was taking advantage of the blessing God had sent him. At this point the English student decided that he knew enough Latin and returned home.

Another English priest went there after a nervous upset and remained for months, enchanted by its solitude and peace. But he still continued to have sleepless nights and practised shadow-boxing to weary himself. One night a poor chronic from Dublin arrived in the last stages of intoxication and was put to bed. The thirst woke him. He went to the washstand and emptied the carafe. As this failed to satisfy him, he started on the water-jug and finished that. In the early hours of the morning he found himself still mad with thirst and with nothing to drink, so he took the water-jug and set off in search of a bathroom. In the corridor outside his cell he saw the English priest shadow-boxing. At first he thought it must be he who had the d.t.'s, but after watching the apparition for several minutes decided it must be the other man.

'How – how long are you here for, sir?' he asked.

'Oh, I've been here six months,' said the apparition.

'Jasus!' said the chronic.

I am sorry it is losing that old distinction. It was part of its quality. Now the place of the drunks is taken by pilgrims from all over Ireland. There were charabancs of them outside the guest-house when I visited it last. The apartments weren't very clean and the food which was served out by the guest-master and another monk wasn't very good, but it probably is not fair to judge it by so busy a day. The gaiety of the monks themselves made up for a lot. After dinner we men were taken on a con-ducted tour of the monastery, the women being left behind. They are allowed to eat in the guest-house; there is even an apart-ment labelled 'Ladies' Wash-hand and Toilet Room', but if they wish to stay they must go and sleep at a safe distance. They are not allowed within the monastery precincts. There seemed to be no vocations among the party which I accompanied through the bare dormitories, the refectory with the name-plates on the tables, the hall with its labelled hangers, where silent monks passed us with bowed heads.

'What do you think of it?' asked the pleasant young monk who acted as guide.

'Cripes, brother,' said one young man in a horrified tone, 'I think 'tis *awful*!'

I noticed that there were no dissenting voices. Afterwards I stayed for Compline in the ugly little chapel with its screen decorated with pictures of the Blessed Virgin, and was bitterly disappointed with the chant. No doubt it was all in a very good tradition, but I don't like traditions which scamper through the Gregorian Credo. I want to hear it thundered out as though someone believed in it. Above all, in the gallery of that horrid little church, with the dusk falling on the desolate mountainside behind me, and behind the screen, invisible, those men who had abandoned the world, I felt the *Et Expecto Resurrectionem*

Mortuorum should at least suggest that they had something to look forward to.

But that is only a superficial view, and even as a superficial view it is not without impressiveness. Looking deeper, you see what Melleray means to Ireland. In its extremest form it is an expression of the conflict between the soul and the world, and every ugly stone of it is a story, tragic or comic. As on any other battlefield, comedy exists in its own right, and nobody enjoys it more than the monks themselves. I once knew two men in Cork who decided to leave the world for ever and become Cistercian monks. They left their comfortable jobs and disposed of their worldly goods. Their male relatives drove them down. The occasion was grave, and the gravity of it necessitated a little alcoholic encouragement. After all, it is not every day that a chap leaves the world for ever. The more they discussed it, the more encouragement they found they needed, and they were finally presented to the novice-master in the monastery in no state to care where they were. Later they returned to the jobs they had left and took up their worldly lives again. That incident just misses tragedy, but it is a real tragedy when a monk who has been for years in the order leaves it. Clerics in general who have all their lives been accustomed to obedience are badly fitted to face the world, and a worse training for the world than a Cistercian monastery affords is inconceivable. For the most part the comedy confines itself to those romantic spirits who imagine themselves equipped for so gruelling a life. One, who got the horrors on the first evening, slipped out of a window during the night, stole a suit of overalls belonging to a painter employed in the monastery, and then raced for dear life over the mountains. That, I fancy, would be my own reaction.

But those who get over their horror learn to love the life, and their piety is of an altogether different type from that of more worldly orders. Like soldiers who themselves have been tested so far that they become almost incapable of criticizing one another, they have a large charity which approaches worldliness in everything but its source.

SONG WITHOUT WORDS

EVEN IF there were only two men left in the world and both of them saints they wouldn't be happy. One of them would be bound to try and improve the other. That is the nature of things.

I am not, of course, suggesting that either Brother Arnold or Brother Michael was a saint. In private life Brother Arnold was a postman, but as he had a great name as a cattle doctor they had put him in charge of the monastery cows. He had the sort of face you would expect to see advertising somebody's tobacco; a big, innocent, contented face with a pair of blue eyes that were always twinkling. According to the rule he was supposed to look sedate and go about in a composed and measured way, but he could not keep his eyes downcast for any length of time and wherever his eyes glanced they twinkled, and his hands slipped out of his long white sleeves and dropped some remark in sign language. Most of the monks were good at the deaf and dumb language; it was their way of getting round the rule of silence, and it was remarkable how much information they managed to pick up and pass on.

Now, one day it happened that Brother Arnold was looking for a bottle of castor oil and he remembered that he had lent it to Brother Michael, who was in charge of the stables. Brother Michael was a man he did not get on too well with; a dour, dull sort of man who kept to himself. He was a man of no great appearance, with a mournful wizened little face and a pair of weak red-rimmed eyes – for all the world the sort of man who, if you shaved off his beard, clapped a bowler hat on his head and a cigarette in his mouth, would need no other reference to get a job in a stable.

There was no sign of him about the stable yard, but this was only natural because he would not be wanted till the other monks returned from the fields, so Brother Arnold pushed in the stable door to look for the bottle himself. He did not see the bottle, but he saw something which made him wish he had not come.

Brother Michael was hiding in one of the horse-boxes; standing against the partition with something hidden behind his back and wearing the look of a little boy who has been caught at the jam. Something told Brother Arnold that at that moment he was the most unwelcome man in the world. He grew red, waved his hand to indicate that he did not wish to be involved, and returned to his own quarters.

It came as a shock to him. It was plain enough that Brother Michael was up to some shady business, and Brother Arnold could not help wondering what it was. It was funny, he had noticed the same thing when he was in the world; it was always the quiet, sneaky fellows who were up to mischief. In chapel he looked at Brother Michael and got the impression that Brother Michael was looking at him, a furtive look to make sure he would not be noticed. Next day when they met in the yard he caught Brother Michael glancing at him and gave back a cold look and a nod.

The following day Brother Michael beckoned him to come over to the stables as though one of the horses was sick. Brother Arnold knew it wasn't that; he knew he was about to be given some sort of explanation and was curious to know what it would be. He was an inquisitive man; he knew it, and blamed himself a lot for it.

Brother Michael closed the door carefully after him and then leaned back against the jamb of the door with his legs crossed and his hands behind his back, a foxy pose. Then he nodded in the direction of the horse-box where Brother Arnold had almost caught him in the act, and raised his brows inquiringly. Brother Arnold nodded gravely. It was not an occasion he was likely to forget. Then Brother Michael put his hand up his sleeve and held out a folded newspaper. Brother Arnold shrugged his shoulders as though to say the matter had nothing to do with him, but the other man nodded and continued to press the newspaper on him.

He opened it without any great curiosity, thinking it might be some local paper Brother Michael smuggled in for the sake of the news from home and was now offering as the explanation of his own furtive behaviour. He glanced at the name and then a great light broke on him. His whole face lit up as though an electric torch had been switched on behind, and finally he burst out laughing. He couldn't help himself. Brother Michael did not laugh but gave a dry little cackle which was as near as he ever got to laughing. The name of the paper was *The Irish Racing News*.

Now that the worst was over Brother Michael grew more relaxed. He pointed to a heading about the Curragh and then at himself. Brother Arnold shook his head, glancing at him expectantly as though he were hoping for another laugh. Brother Michael scratched his head for some indication of what he meant. He was a slow-witted man and had never been good at the sign talk. Then he picked up the sweeping brush and straddled it. He pulled up his skirts, stretched out his left hand holding the handle of the brush, and with his right began flogging the air behind him, a grim look on his leathery little face. Inquiringly he looked again and Brother Arnold nodded excitedly and put his thumbs up to show he understood. He saw now that the real reason Brother Michael had behaved so queerly was that he read racing papers on the sly and he did so because in private life he had been a jockey on the Curragh.

He was still laughing like mad, his blue eyes dancing, wishing only for an audience to tell it to, and then he suddenly remembered all the things he had thought about Brother Michael and bowed his head and beat his breast by way of asking pardon. Then he glanced at the paper again. A mischievous twinkle came into his eyes and he pointed the paper at himself. Brother Michael pointed back, a bit puzzled. Brother Arnold chuckled and stowed the paper up his sleeve. Then Brother Michael winked and gave the thumbs-up sign. In that slow cautious way of his he went down the stable and reached to the top of the wall where the roof sloped down on it. This, it seemed, was his hiding-hole. He took down several more papers and gave them to Brother Arnold.

For the rest of the day Brother Arnold was in the highest spirits. He winked and smiled at everyone till they all wondered what the joke was. He still pined for an audience. All that evening and long after he had retired to his cubicle he rubbed his hands and giggled with delight whenever he thought of it; it was like a window let into his loneliness; it gave him a warm, mellow feeling, as though his heart had expanded to embrace all humanity.

It was not until the following day that he had a chance of looking at the papers himself. He spread them on a rough desk under a feeble electric light bulb high in the roof. It was four years since he had seen a paper of any sort, and then it was only a scrap of local newspaper which one of the carters had brought wrapped about a bit of bread and butter. But Brother Arnold had palmed it, hidden it in his desk, and studied it as if it were a bit of a lost Greek play. He had never known until then the modern appetite for words – printed words, regardless of their meaning. This was merely a County Council wrangle about the appointment of seven warble-fly inspectors, but by the time he was done with it he knew it by heart.

So he did not just glance at the racing papers as a man would in the train to pass the time. He nearly ate them. Blessed words like fragments of tunes coming to him out of a past life; paddocks and point-to-points and two-year-olds, and again he was in the middle of a racecourse crowd on a spring day with silver streamers of light floating down the sky like heavenly bunting. He had only to close his eyes and he could see the refreshment tent again with the golden light leaking like spilt honey through the rents in the canvas, and the girl he had been in love with sitting on an upturned lemonade box. 'Ah, Paddy,' she had said, 'sure there's bound to be racing in heaven!' She was fast, too fast for Brother Arnold, who was a steady-going fellow and had never got over the shock of discovering that all the time she had been running another man. But now all he could remember of her was her smile and the tone of her voice as she spoke the words which kept running through his head, and afterwards whenever his eyes met Brother Michael's he longed to give him a hearty slap on the back and say: 'Michael, boy, there's bound to be racing in heaven.' Then he grinned and Brother Michael, though he didn't hear the words or the tone of voice, without once losing his casual melancholy air, replied with a wall-faced flicker of the horny eyelid, a tick-tack man's signal, a real, expressionless, horsy look of complete understanding.

One day Brother Michael brought in a few papers. On one he pointed to the horses he had marked, on the other to the horses who had won. He showed no signs of his jubilation. He just winked, a leathery sort of wink, and Brother Arnold gaped as he saw the list of winners. It filled him with wonder and pride to think that when so many rich and clever people had lost, a simple little monk living hundreds of miles away could work it all out. The more he thought of it the more excited he grew. For one wild moment he felt it might be his duty to tell the Abbot, so that the monastery could have the full advantage of Brother Michael's intellect, but he realized that it wouldn't do. Even if Brother Michael could restore the whole abbey from top to bottom with his winnings, the ecclesiastical authorities would disapprove of it. But more than ever he felt the need of an audience.

He went to the door, reached up his long arm, and took down a loose stone from the wall above it. Brother Michael shook his head several times to indicate how impressed he was by Brother Arnold's ingenuity. Brother Arnold grinned. Then he took down a bottle and handed it to Brother Michael. The ex-jockey gave him a questioning look as though he were wondering if this wasn't cattle-medicine; his face did not change but he took out the cork and sniffed. Still his face did not change. All at once he went to the door, gave a quick glance up and a quick glance down and then raised the bottle to his lips. He reddened and coughed; it was good beer and he wasn't used to it. A shudder as of delight went through him and his little eyes grew moist as he watched Brother Arnold's throttle working on well-oiled hinges. The big man put the bottle back in its hiding-place and indicated by signs that Brother Michael could go there himself whenever he wanted and have a drink. Brother Michael shook his head doubtfully, but Brother Arnold nodded earnestly. His fingers moved like lightning while he explained how a farmer whose cow he had cured had it left in for him every week.

The two men were now fast friends. They no longer had any secrets from one another. Each knew the full extent of the other's little weakness and liked him the more for it. Though they couldn't speak to one another they sought out one another's company and whenever other things failed they merely smiled. Brother Arnold felt happier than he had felt for years. Brother Michael's successes made him want to try his hand, and whenever Brother Michael gave him a racing paper with his own selections marked, Brother Arnold gave it back with his, and they waited impatiently till the results turned up three or four days late. It was also a new lease of life to Brother Michael, for what comfort is it to a man if he has all the winners when not a soul in the world can ever know whether he has or not. He felt now that if only he could have a bob each way on a horse he would ask no more of life.

It was Brother Arnold, the more resourceful of the pair, who solved that difficulty. He made out dockets, each valued for so many Hail Marys, and the loser had to pay up in prayers for the other man's intention. It was an ingenious scheme and it worked admirably. At first Brother Arnold had a run of luck. But it wasn't for nothing that Brother Michael had had the experience; he was too tough to make a fool of himself even over a few Hail Marys, and everything he did was carefully planned. Brother Arnold began by imitating him, but the moment he struck it lucky he began to gamble wildly. Brother Michael had often seen it happen on the Curragh and remembered the fate of those it had happened to. Men he had known with big houses and cars were now cadging drinks in the streets of Dublin. It struck him that God had been very good to Brother Arnold in calling him to a monastic life where he could do no harm to himself or to his family.

And this, by the way, was quite uncalled for, because in the world Brother Arnold's only weakness had been for a bottle of stout and the only trouble he had ever caused his family was the discomfort of having to live with a man so good and gentle, but Brother Michael was rather given to a distrust of human nature, the sort of man who goes looking for a moral in everything even when there is no moral in it. He tried to make Brother Arnold take an interest in the scientific side of betting but the man seemed to treat it all as a great joke. A flighty sort of fellow! He bet more and more wildly with that foolish good-natured grin on his face, and after a while Brother Michael found himself being owed a deuce of a lot of prayers, which his literal mind insisted on translating into big houses and cars. He didn't like that either. It gave him scruples of conscience and finally turned him against betting altogether. He tried to get Brother Arnold to drop it, but as became an inventor, Brother Arnold only looked hurt and indignant, like a child who has been told to stop his play. Brother Michael had that weakness on his conscience too. It suggested that he was getting far too attached to Brother Arnold, as in fact he was. It would have been very difficult not to. There was something warm and friendly about the man which you couldn't help liking.

Then one day he went in to Brother Arnold and found him with a pack of cards in his hand. They were a very old pack which had more than served their time in some farmhouse, but Brother

Arnold was looking at them in rapture. The very sight of them gave Brother Michael a turn. Brother Arnold made the gesture of dealing, half playfully, and the other shook his head sternly. Brother Arnold blushed and bit his lip but he persisted, seriously enough now. All the doubts Brother Michael had been having for weeks turned to conviction. This was the primrose path with a vengeance, one thing leading to another. Brother Arnold grinned and shuffled the deck; Brother Michael, biding his time, cut for deal and Brother Arnold won. He dealt two hands of five and showed the five of hearts as trump. He wanted to play twenty-five. Still waiting for a sign, Brother Michael looked at his own hand. His face grew grimmer. It was not the sort of sign he had expected but it was a sign all the same; four hearts in a bunch; the ace, jack, two other trumps, and the three of spades. An unbeatable hand. Was that luck? Was that coincidence or was it the Adversary himself, taking a hand and trying to draw him deeper in the mire?

He liked to find a moral in things, and the moral in this was plain, though it went to his heart to admit it. He was a lonesome, melancholy man and the horses had meant a lot to him in his bad spells. At times it had seemed as if they were the only thing that kept him sane. How could he face twenty, perhaps thirty, years more of life, never knowing what horses were running or what jockeys were up – Derby Day, Punchestown, Leopardstown, and the Curragh all going by while he knew no more of them than if he were already dead?

'O Lord,' he thought bitterly, 'a man gives up the whole world for You, his chance of a wife and kids, his home and his family, his friends and his job, and goes off to a bare mountain where he can't even tell his troubles to the man alongside him; and still he keeps something back, some little thing to remind him of what he gave up. With me 'twas the horses and with this man 'twas the sup of beer, and I dare say there are fellows inside who have a bit of a girl's hair hidden somewhere they can go and look at it now and again. I suppose we all have our little hiding-hole if the truth was known, but as small as it is, the whole world is in it, and bit by bit it grows on us again till the day You find us out.'

Brother Arnold was waiting for him to play. He sighed and put his hand on the desk. Brother Arnold looked at it and at him. Brother Michael idly took away the spade and added the heart and still Brother Arnold couldn't see. Then Brother Michael shook his head and pointed to the floor. Brother Arnold bit his lip again as though he were on the point of crying, then threw down his own hand and walked to the other end of the cow-house. Brother Michael left him so for a few moments. He could see the struggle going on in the man, could almost hear the Devil whisper in his ear that he (Brother Michael) was only an old woman – Brother Michael had heard that before; that life was long and a man might as well be dead and buried as not have some little innocent amusement – the sort of plausible whisper that put many a man on the gridiron. He knew, however hard it was now, that Brother Arnold would be grateful to him in the other world. 'Brother Michael,' he would say, 'I don't know what I'd ever have done without your example.'

Then Brother Michael went up and touched him gently on the shoulder. He pointed to the bottle, the racing paper, and the cards. Brother Arnold fluttered his hands despairingly but he nodded. They gathered them up between them, the cards, the bottle, and the papers, hid them under their habits to avoid all occasion of scandal, and went off to confess their guilt to the Prior.

FATHER WHELAN the parish priest called on his curate, Father Devine, one evening in autumn. He was a tall stout man, broad-chested, with a head that did not detach itself too clearly from the rest of his body, bushes of wild hair in his ears and the rosy, innocent, good-natured face of a pious old country woman who made a living selling eggs. Devine was pale and worn-looking with a gentle, dreamy face that had the soft gleam of an old piano keyboard and wore pince-nez perched on his unhappy, insignificant little nose. He and his PP got on very well considering – considering, that is to say, that Devine, who didn't know when he was well off, had fathered a dramatic society and an annual festival on old Whelan, who had to attend them both, and that whenever the curate's name was mentioned the parish priest, a charitable old man, tapped his forehead and said poor Devine's poor father was just the same. 'A national teacher – sure, I knew him well, poor man!' What Devine said about Whelan in that crucified drawl of his would take longer to tell, because for the most part it consisted of a repetition of the old man's own words with just the faintest inflection that isolated and underlined their fatuity, so much so that even Devine himself, who didn't often laugh, broke out into a little thin cackle. Devine was clever; he was lonely; he had a few good original water-colours and a book-case full of works that were a constant source of wonder to Whelan. The old man stood in front of them now with his hat in his hands, lifting his warty old nose while his eyes held a wondering, hopeless, charitable look.

'Nothing there in your line, I'm afraid,' said Devine with his maddeningly respectful, deprecating air as if he really thought the schoolboy adventure stories which were the only thing his parish priest read were worth his consideration.

'I see you have a lot of foreign books,' said Whelan in a hollow far-away voice. 'I suppose you know the languages well?'

'Well enough to read,' said Devine wearily, his handsome head on one side. 'Why?'

'That foreign boat at the jetties,' said Whelan without looking round. 'What is it? French or German? There's terrible scandal about it.'

'Is that so?' drawled Devine, his dark eyebrows going up his narrow slanting forehead. 'I didn't hear.'

'Oh, terrible,' said Whelan mournfully, turning on him the full battery of his round, rosy old face and shining spectacles. 'There's girls on it every night. Of course there's nothing for us to do only rout them out, and it occurred to me that you'd be handy, speaking the language.'

'I'm afraid my French would hardly rise to that,' Devine said drily, but he didn't like to go further with his refusal, for except for his old-womanly fits of virtue, Whelan was all right as parish priests go. Devine had had sad experience of how they could go. So he put on his faded old coat and clamped his battered hat down over his pince-nez, and the two of them went down the Main Street to the Post Office corner. It was deserted at that hour, except for two out-of-works like ornaments supporting either side of the door, and a few others hanging hypnotized over the bridge while they looked down at the foaming waters of the weir. The tall, fortress-like gable of an old Georgian house beyond the bridge caught all the light.

'The dear knows,' said Devine with a sigh, 'you'd hardly wonder where they'd go.'

'Ah,' said the old parish priest, holding his head as though it were a flower-pot that might fall and break, 'what do they want to go anywhere for? They're gone mad on pleasure. That girl, Nora Fitzpatrick, is one of them, and her mother at home dying.'

'That might possibly be her reason for going,' said Devine, who knew what the Fitzpatricks' house was like with six children and a mother dying of cancer.

'Ah, sure the girl's place is beside her mother,' said old Whelan without rancour.

They went down past the Technical School to the quays; these too deserted but for a local coal boat and the big foreign grain boat, rising high and dark over the edge of the quay on a full tide. The town was historically reputed to have been a great place – well, about a hundred years ago – and it had masses of grey stone warehouses all staring with lightless eyes across the river. There were two men standing against the wall of the mill, looking up at the grain boat, and as the priests appeared they came to join them on the water's edge. One was a tall gaunt man with a long, sour, melancholy face which looked particularly hideous because it sported a youthful pink-and-white complexion and looked exactly like the face of an old hag heavily made up. He wore a wig and carried a rolled-up umbrella behind his back as though supporting his posterior. His name was Sullivan, the manager of a shop in town, and a man Devine hated. The other was a small, fat, Jewish-looking man with dark skin and hair and an excitable manner. His name was Sheridan. As they met by the boat, Devine looked up and saw two young foreign faces propped on their hands peering at him over the edge of the boat.

'Well, boys?' asked old Whelan.

'There's two of them on it at present, father,' said Sullivan in a shrill, scolding voice. 'Nora Fitzpatrick and Phillie O'Malley.'

'Well, better go aboard and tell them come off,' said Whelan tranquilly.

'I wonder what our legal position is, father?' said Sheridan, scowling at Whelan and Devine. 'Have we any sort of *locus standi*?'

'Oh, in the event of your being stabbed I think the fellow could be tried,' said Devine with bland malice. 'I don't know of course whether your wife and children could claim compensation.'

The malice was lost on the parish priest, who laid one hairy paw on Devine's shoulder and the other on Sheridan's to calm their fears. He exuded a feeling of pious confidence.

'Don't worry your heads about the legal position,' he said paternally. 'I'll be answerable for that.'

'Good enough, father,' said Sheridan with a grim air, and pulling his hat over his eyes and putting his hands behind his back he strode up the gangway while Sullivan, clutching his umbrella against the small of his back, followed him. They went up to the two young sailors.

'Two girls,' said Sullivan in his high-pitched scolding voice. 'We're looking for two girls that came aboard about a half an hour ago.'

Neither of the sailors stirred. One of them turned his eyes lazily and looked Sullivan up and down.

'Not this boat,' he said impudently. 'That boat down there. Always girls on that.'

Then Sheridan, who had glanced downstairs through an open doorway, saw something below.

'Phillie O'Malley,' he shouted in a raucous voice with one arm pointing towards the quay, 'Father Whelan and Father Devine are here. They want a word with you.'

'Tell her if she doesn't come at once I'll go and bring her off,' shouted Father Whelan anxiously.

'He says if you don't come he'll damn soon make you,' shouted Sheridan.

Nothing happened for a moment or two. Then a tall girl with a consumptive face came to the top of the gangway with a hand-kerchief pressed to her eyes. Devine couldn't help a sudden pang of misery at the sight of her wretched finery, her cheap hat and bead necklace. He was angry and ashamed, and a cold fury of sarcasm rose up in him.

'Come on, lads,' said the parish priest encouragingly. 'Where's the second one?

Sheridan, flushed with triumph, was just about to disappear downstairs when one of the sailors turned and flung him aside. Then he stood nonchalantly in the doorway, blocking the way. The parish priest's face grew flushed and he only waited for the girl to leave the gangway before he went up himself. Devine paused to catch her hand and whisper a few words of comfort into her ear before he followed. It was a ridiculous scene: the sailor blocking the door; Sheridan blowing himself up till his dark Jewish face turned purple; the fat old parish priest with his head in the air, trembling with senile anger and astonishment.

'Get out of the way at once,' he said.

'Don't be a fool, man,' Devine said with quiet ferocity. 'If you got a knife in your ribs, it would be your own doing. You don't want to quarrel with these lads. You'll have to talk to the captain.' And then, bending forward with his eyebrows raised and his humble, deprecating manner he asked, 'I wonder if you'd mind showing us the way to the captain's cabin?'

The sailor who was blocking the way looked at him for a

moment and then nodded in the direction of the upper deck. Taking his parish priest's arm and telling Sullivan and Sheridan not to follow them, Devine went up the ship. When they had gone a little way the second young sailor passed them out, knocked at a door and said something which Devine couldn't catch. Then, with a scowl, he held the door open for them to go in. The captain was a middle-aged man with a heavily lined sallow face, close-cropped black hair and a black moustache. There was something Mediterranean about his air.

'*Bonsoir, messieurs*,' he said in a loud business-like tone.

'*Bonsoir, monsieur le capitaine*,' said Devine with the same plaintive, ingratiating manner as he bowed his head and raised his battered old hat. '*Est-ce que nous vous dérangeons?*'

'*Mais pas du tout; entrez, je vous prie*,' the captain said heartily, obviously relieved by the innocuousness of Devine's manner. '*Vous parlez français alors?*'

'*Un peu, monsieur le capitaine*,' Devine said deprecatingly. '*Vous savez, ici en Irlande on n'a pas souvent l'occasion.*'

'Ah, well,' said the captain, 'I speak a little English too, so we will understand one another. Won't you sit down?'

'I wish my French were anything like as good as your English,' said Devine as he took a chair.

'You'll have a drink with me,' said the captain, expanding to the flattery of words and tone. 'Some brandy, eh?'

'I'd be delighted, of course,' said Devine regretfully, 'but I'm afraid I've a favour to ask of you first.'

'Certainly, certainly,' agreed the captain enthusiastically. 'Anything you like. Have a cigar?'

'Never smoke them,' said old Whelan in a dull stubborn voice, looking at the cigar-case and then looking away; and to mask his rudeness Devine, who never smoked them either, took one and lit it.

'Perhaps I'd better explain who we are,' he said, sitting back, his head on one side, his long delicate hands hanging over the arm of the chair. 'This is Father Whelan, who is the parish priest of the town. My name is Devine and I'm the curate.'

'And my name,' said the captain proudly, 'is Platon Demarrais. I bet you never heard before of a fellow called Platon?'

'I can't say I did,' said Devine mildly. 'Any relation to the philosopher?'

'The very man!' exclaimed the captain, holding up his cigar. 'And I have two brothers, Zenon and Plotin.'

'Really?' exclaimed Devine. 'What an intellectual family you are!'

'My father was a school-teacher,' said the captain. 'He called us that to annoy the priest. He was anti-clerical.'

'That's scarcely peculiar to teachers in France,' said Devine drily. 'My own father was a school-teacher, but I'm afraid he never got to the point of calling me Plato. . . . But about this business of ours. There's a girl called Nora Fitzpatrick on the ship, fooling with the sailors, I suppose. She's one of Father Whelan's parishioners and we'd be very grateful if you could see your way to have her put off.'

'Speak for yourself, father,' said Whelan, raising his stubborn old peasant's head and quelling fraternization with a glance. 'I don't see why I should be grateful to any man for doing what 'tis his moral duty to do.'

'Then perhaps you'd better explain your errand yourself, Father Whelan,' said Devine with an abnegation not far removed from waspishness.

'I think so, Father Devine,' said Whelan stubbornly. 'That girl, Captain Whatever-your-name-is,' he went on in a slow voice, 'has no business to be on your ship at all. It is no place for a young unmarried girl to be at this hour of night.'

'I don't understand,' said the captain uneasily, looking at Devine. 'Is this girl a relative of yours?'

'No, sir,' said Whelan. 'She is nothing whatever to me.'

'Then I don't see what you want her for,' said the captain.

'That's as I'd expect, sir,' said Whelan stolidly, studying his nails.

'Oh, for heaven's sake!' exclaimed Devine, exasperated by the old man's boorishness. 'You see, captain,' he said patiently, bending forward with his worried air, his head tilted back as though he feared the pince-nez might fall off, 'this girl, as I said, is one of Father Whelan's parishioners. She's not a very good girl! – not that I mean there's any harm in her,' he added hastily, 'but she is a bit wild, and it's Father Whelan's duty to keep her as far as he can removed from temptation. He is the shepherd and she is one of his stray sheep,' he added with a faint smile at his own eloquence.

The captain bent forward and touched Devine lightly on the knee.

'You are a funny race,' he said. 'I have travelled the whole world. I have met Englishmen everywhere, but I will never understand you. Never!'

'But we're not English, man,' said old Whelan with the first sign of interest he had so far displayed. 'Don't you know what country you're in? This is Ireland.'

'Ah,' said the captain with a shrug, 'it is the same thing.'

'Oh, but surely, captain,' protested Devine gently with his head cocked, sizing up his man, 'surely we admit some distinction?'

'No, no,' said the captain vigorously, shaking his head.

'At the Battle of the Boyne you fought for us,' said Devine persuasively. 'We fought for you at Fontenoy and Ramillies.

When on Ramillies bloody field
The baffled French were forced to yield,
The victor Saxon backward reeled
    Before the charge of Clare's Dragoons.'

He recited the lines with the same apologetic smile he had adopted in speaking of sheep and shepherds, as if to excuse his momentary lapse into literature, but the captain waved him aside impatiently.

'No, no, no, no, no,' he said with a shrug and a groan. 'I know all that. You call yourselves Irish and the others call themselves Scotch, but there is no difference. You all speak English; you all behave like English; you all pretend to be very good boys. You don't do nothing, eh? You do not come to me as man to man and say, "The curé's daughter is on the ship. Send her home." Why?'

'Perhaps,' suggested Devine sarcastically, 'because she doesn't happen to be the curé's daughter.'

'Whose daughter?' asked Whelan with his mouth hanging.

'Yours,' said Devine drily.

'Well, well, well,' the old man said in real distress. 'What sort of upbringing had he at all? Does he even know we can't get married?'

'I should say he takes it for granted,' replied Devine over his shoulder even more drily than before. '*Elle n'est pas sa fille*,' he added to the captain.

'*C'est sûr?*' asked the captain suspiciously.

'*C'est certain,*' said Devine with a nod.

'*Sa maîtresse alors?*' said the captain.

'*Ni cela non plus,*' replied Devine evenly, with only the faintest of smiles on the worn shell of his face.

'*Ah, bon, bon, bon,*' said the captain excitedly, springing from his seat and striding about the cabin, scowling and waving his arms. '*Bon. C'est bon. Vous vous moquez de moi, monsieur le curé. Comprenez-vous, c'est seulement par politesse que j'ai voulu faire croire que c'était sa fille. On voit bien que le vieux est jaloux. Est-ce que je n'ai pas vu les flics qui surveillent mon bateau toute la semaine? Mais croyez-moi, monsieur, je me fiche de lui et de ses agents.*'

'He seems to be very excited,' said Whelan with distaste. 'What's he saying?'

'I'm trying to persuade him that she isn't your mistress,' Devine couldn't refrain from saying with quiet malice. 'He says you're jealous and that you've had spies watching his ship for a week.'

'Well, well, well,' Father Whelan cried, colouring up like a girl and trembling with the indignity that had been put on him. 'We'd better go home, Devine. 'Tis no use talking to a man like that. It's clear that he's mad.'

'He probably thinks the same of us,' said Devine, rising. '*Venez manger demain soir et je vous expliquerai tout,*' he added to the captain.

'*Je vous remercie, monsieur,*' said the captain with a shrug which Devine knew he could never equal; '*c'est très aimable de votre part, mais je n'ai pas besoin d'explications. Il n'y a rien d'inattendu, mais,*' with a smile, '*vous en faites toute une histoire.*' He clapped his hand jovially on Devine's shoulder and almost embraced him. '*Naturellement, je vous rends la fille, parce que vous la demandez, mais comprenez bien que je le fais à cause de vous, et non pas*' – he drew himself up to his full height and glared at old Whelan, who stood there in a dumb stupor – '*à cause de monsieur et de ses agents.*'

'Oh, *quant à moi,*' said Devine with weary humour, '*vous feriez mieux en l'emmenant où vous allez. Et moi-même aussi.*'

'*Quoi?*' shouted the captain in desperation, clutching his forehead. '*Vous l'aimez aussi?*'

'*Non, non, non,*' said Devine good-humouredly, patting him consolingly on the arm. 'It's all very complicated. I really wouldn't try to understand it if I were you.'

'What's he saying now?' asked Whelan with sour suspicion.

'Oh, he thinks she's my mistress as well,' said Devine pleasantly. 'He thinks we're sharing her so far as I can gather.'

'Come on, come on,' said Whelan in dull despair, making for the gangway. 'My goodness, even I never thought they were as bad as that. And we sending missions to the blacks!'

Meanwhile the captain had rushed aft and shouted down the stairway. The girl appeared, small, plump and weeping too, and the captain, quite moved, slapped her encouragingly on the shoulder and said something to her in a gruff voice which Devine suspected was in the nature of advice about choosing younger lovers for the future. Then the captain went up bristling to Sullivan, who was standing by the gangway, leaning on his folded umbrella, and with fluttering hands and imperious nods ordered him off the vessel.

'*Allez-vous-en,*' he said curtly, '*allez, allez, allez!*'

Sullivan went and Sheridan followed. Dusk had crept suddenly along the quays and lay heaped there the colour of blown sand. Over the bright river mouth, shining under a bank of dark cloud, a star twinkled. Devine felt hopeless and lost, as though he were returning to the prison-house of his youth. The parish priest preceded him down the gangway with his old woman's dull face sunk in his broad chest. At the foot he stopped and stood with his hands still clutching the gangway rail and gazed back up at the captain, who was scowling fiercely at him over the edge of the ship.

'Anyway,' he said heavily, 'thanks be to the Almighty God that your accursed race is withering off the face of the earth.'

Devine with a bitter little smile raised his battered old hat and pulled the skirts of his old coat about him as he stepped up on to the gangway.

'*Vous viendrez demain, monsieur le capitaine?*' he said in his gentlest, most ingratiating tone.

'*Avec plaisir. A demain, monsieur le berger,*' replied the captain with a knowing look.

THE FRYING-PAN

FATHER FOGARTY'S only real friends in Kilmulpeter were the Whittons. Whitton was the teacher there. He had been to the seminary and college with Fogarty, and, like him, intended to be a priest, but when the time came for him to take the vow of celibacy, he had contracted scruples of conscience and married the principal one. Fogarty, who had known her too, had to admit that she wasn't without justification, and now, in this lonely place where chance had thrown them together again, she formed the real centre of what little social life he had. With Tom Whitton he had a quiet friendship compounded of exchanges of opinion about books or wireless talks. He had the impression that Whitton didn't really like him and considered him a man who would have been better out of the Church. When they went to the races together, Fogarty felt that Whitton disapproved of having to put on bets for him and thought that priests should not bet at all. Like other outsiders, he knew perfectly what priests should be, without the necessity for having to be that way himself. He was sometimes savage in the things he said about the parish priest, old Father Whelan. On the other hand, he had a pleasant sense of humour and Fogarty enjoyed retailing his cracks against the cloth. Men as intelligent as Whitton were rare in country schools, and soon, too, he would grow stupid and wild for lack of educated society.

One evening Father Fogarty invited them to dinner to see some films he had taken at the races. Films were his latest hobby. Before this it had been fishing and shooting. Like all bachelors, he had a mania for adding to his possessions, and his lumber-room was piled high with every possible sort of junk from chest-developers to field-glasses, and his library cluttered with works on everything from Irish history to Freudian psychology. He passed from craze to craze, each the key to the universe.

He sprang up at the knock, and found Una at the door, all in furs, her shoulders about her ears, her big, bony, masculine face blue with cold but screwed up in an amiable monkey-grin. Tom, a handsome man, was tall and self-conscious. He had greying hair, brown eyes, a prominent jaw, and was quiet-spoken in a way that concealed passion. He and Una disagreed a lot about the way the children should be brought up. He thought she spoiled them.

'Come in, let ye, come in!' cried Fogarty hospitably, showing the way into his warm study with its roaring turf fire, deep leather chairs, and the Raphael print above the mantelpiece, a real bachelor's room. 'God above!' he exclaimed, holding Una's hand a moment longer than was necessary. 'You're perished! What'll you have to drink, Una?'

'Whi-hi-hi –' stammered Una excitedly, her eyes beginning to pop. 'I can't say the bloody word.'

'Call it malt, girl,' said the priest.

'That's enough! That's enough!' she cried laughingly, snatching the glass from him. 'You'll send me home on my ear, and then I'll hear about it from this fellow.'

'Whiskey, Tom?'

'Whiskey, Jerry,' Whitton said quietly with a quick conciliatory glance. He kept his head very stiff and used his eyes a lot instead.

Meanwhile Una, unabashably inquisitive, was making the tour of the room with the glass in her hand, to see if there was anything new in it. There usually was.

'Is this new, father?' she asked, halting before a pleasant eighteenth-century print.

'Ten bob,' the priest said promptly. 'Wasn't it a bargain?'

'I couldn't say. What is it?'

'The old courthouse in town.'

'Go on!' said Una.

Whitton came and studied the print closely. 'That place is gone these fifty years and I never saw a picture of it,' he said. 'This is a bargain all right.'

'I'd say so,' Fogarty said with quiet pride.

'And what's the sheet for?' Una asked, poking at a tablecloth pinned between the windows.

'That's not a sheet, woman!' Fogarty exclaimed. 'For God's sake, don't be displaying your ignorance!'

'Oh, I know,' she cried girlishly. 'For the pictures! I'd forgotten about them. That's grand!'

Then Bella, a coarse, good-looking country girl, announced dinner, and the curate, with a self-conscious, boyish swagger, led them into the dining-room and opened the door of the side-board. The dining-room was even more ponderous than the sitting-room. Everything in it was large, heavy and dark.

'And now, what'll ye drink?' he asked over his shoulder, study-ing his array of bottles. 'There's some damn good Burgundy – 'pon my soul, 'tis great!'

'How much did it cost?' Whitton asked with poker-faced humour. 'The only way I have of identifying wines is by the price.'

'Eight bob a bottle,' Fogarty replied at once.

'That's a very good price,' said Whitton with a nod. 'We'll have some of that.'

'You can take a couple of bottles home with you,' said the curate, who, in the warmth of his heart, was always wanting to give his treasures away. 'The last two dozen he had – wasn't I lucky?'

'You have the appetite of a canon on the income of a curate,' Whitton said in the same tone of grave humour, but Fogarty caught the scarcely perceptible note of criticism in it. He did not allow this to upset him.

'Please God, we won't always be curates,' he said sunnily.

'Bella looks after you well,' said Una when the meal was nearly over. The compliment was deserved so far as it went, though it was a man's meal rather than a woman's.

'Doesn't she, though?' Fogarty exclaimed with pleasure. 'Isn't she damn good for a country girl?'

'How does she get on with Stasia?' asked Una – Stasia was Father Whelan's old housekeeper, and an affliction to the community.

'They don't talk. Stasia says she's an immoral woman.'

'And is she?' Una asked hopefully.

'If she isn't, she's wasting her own time and my whiskey,' said Fogarty. 'She entertains Paddy Coakley in the kitchen every Saturday night. I told her I wouldn't keep her unless she got a boy. And wasn't I right? One Stasia is enough for any parish. Father Whelan tells me I'm going too far.'

'And did you tell him to mind his own business?' Whitton asked with a penetrating look.

'I did, to be sure,' said Fogarty, who had done nothing of the sort.

'Ignorant, interfering old fool!' Whitton said quietly, the ferocity of his sentiments belied by the mildness of his manner.

'That's only because you'd like to do the interfering yourself,' said Una good-humouredly. She frequently had to act as peacemaker between the parish priest and her husband.

'And a robber,' Tom Whitton added to the curate, ignoring her. 'He's been collecting for new seats for the church for the last ten years. I'd like to know where that's going.'

'He had a collection for repairing my roof,' said the curate, 'and 'tis leaking still. He must be worth twenty thousand.'

'Now, that's not fair, father,' Una said flatly. 'You know yourself there's no harm in Father Whelan. It's just that he's certain he's going to die in the workhouse. It's like Bella and her boy. He has nothing more serious to worry about, and he worries about that.'

Fogarty knew there was a certain amount of truth in what Una said, and that the old man's miserliness was more symbolic than real, and at the same time he felt in her words criticism of a different kind from her husband's. Though Una wasn't aware of it she was implying that the priest's office made him an object of pity rather than blame. She was sorry for old Whelan, and, by implication, for him.

'Still, Tom is right, Una,' he said with sudden earnestness. 'It's not a question of what harm Father Whelan intends, but what harm he does. Scandal is scandal, whether you give it deliberately or through absent-mindedness.'

Tom grunted, to show his approval, but he said no more on the subject, as though he refused to enter into an argument with his wife about subjects she knew nothing of. They returned to the study for coffee, and Fogarty produced the film projector. At once the censoriousness of Tom Whitton's manner dropped away, and he behaved like a pleasant and intelligent boy of seventeen. Una, sitting by the fire with her legs crossed, watched them with amusement. Whenever they came to the priest's house, the same sort of thing happened. Once it had been a microscope, and the pair of them had amused themselves with it for hours. Now they were kidding themselves that their real interest in the cinema was educational. She knew that within a month the cinema, like the microscope, would be lying in the lumber-room with the rest of the junk.

Fogarty switched off the light and showed some films he had taken at the last race meeting. They were very patchy, mostly out of focus, and had to be interpreted by a running commentary, which was always a shot or two behind.

'I suppose ye wouldn't know who that is?' he said as the film showed Una, eating a sandwich and talking excitedly and demonstratively to a couple of wild-looking country boys.

'It looks like someone from the Country Club,' her husband said dryly.

'But wasn't it good?' Fogarty asked innocently as he switched on the lights again. 'Now, wasn't it very interesting?' He was exactly like a small boy who had performed a conjuring trick.

'Marvellous, father,' Una said with a sly and affectionate grin.

He blushed and turned to pour them out more whiskey. He saw that she had noticed the pictures of herself. At the same time, he saw she was pleased. When he had driven them home, she held his hand and said they had had the best evening for years – a piece of flattery so gross and uncalled-for that it made her husband more tongue-tied than ever.

'Thursday, Jerry?' he said with a quick glance.

'Thursday, Tom,' said the priest.

The room looked terribly desolate after her; the crumpled cushions, the glasses, the screen and the film projector, everything had become frighteningly inert, while outside his window the desolate countryside had taken on even more of its supernatural animation: bogs, hills, and field, full of ghosts and shadows. He sat by the fire, wondering what his own life might have been like with a girl like that, all furs and scent and laughter, and two bawling, irrepressible brats upstairs. When he tiptoed up to his bedroom he remembered that there would never be children there to wake, and it seemed to him that with all the things he bought to fill his home, he was merely trying desperately to stuff the yawning holes in his own big, empty heart.

On Thursday, when he went to their house, Ita and Brendan, though already in bed, were refusing to sleep till he said good-night to them. While he was taking off his coat the two of them rushed to the banisters and screamed: 'We want Father Fogey.'

When he went upstairs they were sitting bolt upright in their cots, a little fat, fair-haired rowdy boy and a solemn baby girl.

'Father,' Brendan began at once, 'will I be your altar boy when I grow up?'

'You will to be sure, son,' replied Fogarty.

'Ladies first! Ladies first!' the baby shrieked in a frenzy of rage. 'Father, will I be your altar boy?'

'Go on!' Brendan said scornfully. 'Little girls can't be altar boys, sure they can't, father?'

'I can,' shrieked Ita, who in her excitement exactly resembled her mother. 'Can't I, father?'

'We might be able to get a dispensation for you,' said the curate. 'In a pair of trousers, you'd do fine.'

He was in a wistful frame of mind when he came downstairs again. Children would always be a worse temptation to him than women. Children were the devil! The house was gay and spotless. They had no fine mahogany suite like his, but Una managed to make the few coloured odds and ends they had seem deliberate. There wasn't a cigarette end in the ashtrays; the cushions had not been sat on. Tom, standing before the fireplace (not to disturb the cushions, thought Fogarty), looked as if someone had held his head under the tap, and was very self-consciously wearing a new brown tie. With his greying hair plastered flat, he looked schoolboyish, sulky, and resentful, as though he were meditating ways of restoring his authority over a mutinous household. The thought crossed Fogarty's mind that he and Una had probably quarrelled about the tie. It went altogether too well with his suit.

'We want Father Fogey!' the children began to chant monotonously from the bedroom.

'Shut up!' shouted Tom.

'We want Father Fogey,' the chant went on, but with a groan in it somewhere.

'Well, you're not going to get him. Go to sleep!'

The chant stopped. This was clearly serious.

'You don't mind if I drop down to a meeting tonight, Jerry?' Tom asked in his quiet, anxious way. 'I won't be more than half an hour.'

'Not at all, Tom,' said Fogarty heartily. 'Sure, I'll drive you.'

'No, thanks,' Whitton said with a smile of gratitude. 'It won't take me ten minutes to get there.'

It was clear that a lot of trouble had gone to the making of supper, but out of sheer perversity Tom let on not to recognize any of the dishes. When they had drunk their coffee, he rose and glanced at his watch.

'I won't be long,' he said.

'Tom, you're not going to that meeting?' Una asked appealingly.

'I tell you I have to,' he replied with unnecessary emphasis.

'I met Mick Mahoney this afternoon, and he said they didn't need you.'

'Mick Mahoney knows nothing about it.'

'I told him to tell the others you wouldn't be coming, that Father Fogarty would be here,' she went on desperately, fighting for the success of her evening.

'Then you had no business to do it,' her husband retorted angrily, and even Fogarty saw that she had gone the worst way about it, by speaking to members of his committee behind his back. He began to feel uncomfortable. 'If they come to some damn fool decision while I'm away, it'll be my responsibility.'

'If you're late, you'd better knock,' she sang out gaily to cover up his bad manners. 'Will we go into the sitting-room, father?' she asked over-eagerly. 'I'll be with you in two minutes. There are fags on the mantelpiece, and you know where to find the whi-hi-hi – blast that word!'

Fogarty lit a cigarette and sat down. He felt exceedingly uncomfortable. Whitton was an uncouth and irritable bastard, and always had been so. He heard Una upstairs, and then someone turned on the tap in the bathroom. 'Bloody brute!' he thought indignantly. There had been no need for him to insult her before a guest. Why the hell couldn't he have finished his quarrelling while they were alone? The tap stopped and he waited, listening, but Una didn't come. He was a warm-hearted man and could not bear the thought of her alone and miserable upstairs. He went softly up the stairs and stood on the landing. 'Una!' he called softly, afraid of waking the children. There was a light in the bedroom; the door was ajar and he pushed it in. She was sitting at the end of the bed and grinned at him dolefully.

'Sorry for the whine, father,' she said, making a brave attempt to smile. And then, with the street-urchin's humour which he found so attractive: 'Can I have a loan of your shoulder, please?'

'What the blazes ails Tom?' he asked, sitting beside her.

'He – he's jealous,' she stammered, and began to weep again with her head on his chest. He put his arm about her and patted her awkwardly.

'Jealous?' he asked incredulously, turning over in his mind the half-dozen men whom Una could meet at the best of times. 'Who the blazes is he jealous of?'

'You!'

'Me?' Fogarty exclaimed indignantly, and grew red, thinking of how he had given himself away with his pictures. 'He must be mad! I never gave him any cause for jealousy.'

'Oh, I know he's completely unreasonable,' she stammered. 'He always was.'

'But you didn't say anything to him, did you?' Fogarty asked anxiously.

'About what?' she asked in surprise, looking up at him and blinking back her tears.

'About me?' Fogarty mumbled in embarrassment.

'Oh, he doesn't know about that,' Una replied frantically. 'I never mentioned that to him at all. Besides, he doesn't care that much about me.'

And Fogarty realized that in the simplest way in the world he had been brought to admit to a married woman that he loved her and she to imply that she felt the same about him, without a word being said on either side. Obviously, these things happened more innocently than he had ever thought possible. He became more embarrassed than ever.

'But what is he jealous of so?' he added truculently.

'He's jealous of you because you're a priest. Surely, you saw that?'

'I certainly didn't. It never crossed my mind.'

Yet at the same time he wondered if this might not be the reason for the censoriousness he sometimes felt in Whitton against his harmless bets and his bottles of wine.

'But he's hardly ever out of your house, and he's always borrowing your books, and talking theology and church history to you. He has shelves of them here – look!' And she pointed at a plain wooden bookcase, filled with solid-looking works. 'In my b-b-bedroom! That's why he really hates Father Whelan. Don't you see, Jerry,' she said, calling him for the first time by his Christian name, 'you have all the things he wants.'

'I have?' repeated Fogarty in astonishment. 'What things?'

'Oh, how do I know?' she replied with a shrug, relegating these to the same position as Whelan's bank-balance and his own gadgets, as things that meant nothing to her. 'Respect and responsibility and freedom from the worries of a family, I suppose.'

'He's welcome to them,' Fogarty said with wry humour. 'What's that the advertisements say? – owner having no further use for same.'

'Oh, I know,' she said with another shrug, and he saw that from the beginning she had realized how he felt about her and been sorry for him. He was sure that there was some contradiction here which he should be able to express to himself, between her almost inordinate piety and her light-hearted acceptance of his adoration for her – something that was exclusively feminine, but which he could not isolate with her there beside him, willing him to make love to her, offering herself to his kiss.

'It's a change to be kissed by someone who cares for you,' she said after a moment.

'Ah, now, Una, that's not true,' he protested gravely, the priest in him getting the upper hand of the lover who had still a considerable amount to learn. 'You only fancy that.'

'I don't, Jerry,' she replied with conviction. 'It's always been the same, from the first month of our marriage – always! I was a fool to marry him at all.'

'Even so,' Fogarty said manfully, doing his duty by his friend with a sort of schoolboy gravity, 'you know he's still fond of you. That's only his way.'

'It isn't, Jerry,' she went on obstinately. 'He wanted to be a priest and I stopped him.'

'But you didn't.'

'That's how he looks at it. I tempted him.'

'And damn glad he was to fall!'

'But he did fall, Jerry, and that's what he can never forgive. In his heart he despises me and despises himself for not being able to do without me.'

'But why should he despise himself? That's what I don't understand.'

'Because I'm only a woman, and he wants to be independent of me and every other woman as well. He has to teach to keep a home for me, and he doesn't want to teach. He wants to say Mass and hear confessions, and be God Almighty for seven days of the week.'

Fogarty couldn't grasp it, but he realized that there was something in what she said, and that Whitton was really a lonely, frustrated man who felt he was forever excluded from the only things which interested him.

'I don't understand it,' he said angrily. 'It doesn't sound natural to me.'

'It doesn't sound natural to you because you have it, Jerry,' she said. 'I used to think Tom wasn't normal, either, but now I'm beginning to think there are more spoiled priests in the world than ever went into seminaries. You see, Jerry,' she went on in a rush, growing very red, 'I'm a constant reproach to him. He thinks he's a terrible blackguard because he wants to make love to me once a month. . . . I can talk like this to you because you're a priest.'

'You can, to be sure,' said Fogarty with more conviction than he felt.

'And even when he does make love to me,' she went on, too full of her grievance even to notice the anguish she caused him, 'he manages to make me feel that I'm doing all the love-making.'

'And why shouldn't you?' asked Fogarty gallantly, concealing the way his heart turned over in him.

'Because it's a sin!' she cried tempestuously.

'Who said it's a sin?'

'He makes it a sin. He's like a bear with a sore head for days after. Don't you see, Jerry,' she cried, springing excitedly to her feet and shaking her head at him, 'it's never anything but adultery with him, and he goes away and curses himself because he hasn't the strength to resist it.'

'Adultery?' repeated Fogarty, the familiar word knocking at his conscience as if it were Tom Whitton himself at the door.

'Whatever you call it,' Una rushed on. 'It's always adultery, adultery, adultery, and I'm always a bad woman, and he always wants to show God that it wasn't him but me, and I'm sick and tired of it. I want a man to make me feel like a respectable married woman for once in my life. You see, I feel quite respectable with you, although I know I shouldn't.' She looked in the mirror of the dressing-table and her face fell. 'Oh, Lord!' she sighed. 'I don't look it. . . . I'll be down in two minutes now, Jerry,' she said eagerly, thrusting out her lips to him, her old, brilliant, excitable self.

'You're grand,' he muttered.

As she went into the bathroom, she turned in another excess of emotion and threw her arms about him. As he kissed her, she pressed herself close to him till his head swam. There was a mawkish, girlish grin on her face. 'Darling!' she said in an agony of passion, and it was as if their loneliness enveloped them like a cloud.

As he went downstairs, he was very thoughtful. He heard Tom's key in the lock and looked at himself in the mirror over the fireplace. He heard Tom's step in the hall, and it sounded in his ears as it had never sounded before, like that of a man carrying a burden too great for him. He realized that he had never before seen Whitton as he really was, a man at war with his animal nature, longing for some high, solitary existence of the intellect and imagination. And he knew that the three of them, Tom, Una and himself, would die as they had lived, their desires unsatisfied.

THIS MORTAL COIL

EVERY SUNDAY morning, at a time when the rest of the city was at church, a few of us met down the quays. We ranged from a clerical student with scruples to a roaring atheist. The atheist, Dan Turner, was the one I liked best. He was a well-built, fresh-coloured man who looked like a sailor or farmer, but was really a County Council official. Part of my sympathy for him was due to the way he was penalized for his opinions. Long before, at the age of eighteen, he had had to give evidence in a taxation case and refused to take the oath. That finished him. Though he was easily the cleverest man in the Courthouse, he would never be secretary or anything approaching it. And knowing that, and knowing the constant intriguing to keep him from promotion, only made him more positive and truculent. Not that he thought of himself as either; in his own opinion he was a perfect example of the English genius for compromise, but the nearest thing he ever got to ignoring some remark he disagreed with was to raise his eyebrows into his hair, turn his blue eyes the other way, and whistle.

'You take things to the fair, Dan,' I said to him once.

'All I ask,' he replied reasonably enough, 'is that bloody idiots will keep their opinions to themselves and not be working them off on me.'

'If you want bloody idiots to do anything of the kind,' I said, 'you should go somewhere you won't be a target for them.'

'And if we all do that, this country will never be anything, only a home for idiots,' he said.

'Oh, of course, if you want to make a martyr of yourself in the interests of the country, that's a different thing,' I said. 'But it seems to me very queer conduct for a man that calls himself a rationalist. I call that sentimentality.'

He nearly struck me over calling it sentimentality, but, of course, that's what it was. For all the man's brains, he was as emotional as a child. He was cut to the heart by all the intrigues against him. He lived in an old house on the quays with a pious maiden sister called Madge who adored him, cluck-clucked and tut-tutted his most extravagant statements, and went to Mass every morning to pray for his conversion. Though it hurt him that she called in outside aid (even if it was purely imaginary), he was too big a man to hold it against her, and according to his lights he did his best to bring her to some sense of proportion.

'That's not religion at all,' he would shout, slapping the arm of his chair in vexation. 'That's damn superstition,' but Madge only pitied and loved him the more for it, and went on in her own way believing in God, ghosts, fairies and nutmegs for lumbago.

It wasn't until well on in his thirties that Dan fell in love, and then he did it in a way that no rationalist could approve of. Tessa Bridie wasn't very young either, but, as with many another fine girl in the provinces, she found the fellows that wanted to marry her were not always those she wanted to marry. As a last resort she was holding on to a clerk in an insurance office, called Mac-Guinness, with jet-black curly hair, nationalist sentiments, and great aspirations after the religious life, which, I suppose, is the only sort of life a clerk in an insurance office can aspire to.

In spite of the way he had been spoiled by Madge, Tessa was convinced for a long time that Dan was the answer to her prayers. But Dan in his simple, straightforward way wouldn't let her be. He explained that he couldn't be the answer to anyone's prayer, because there was no one to answer prayers, and it was foolishness, foolishness and madness, to imagine they were answered. Now, Tessa wasn't by any means a bigoted girl; she had several brothers and she knew that in the matter of religion and politics every man without exception had some deficiency, but this cut at the very roots of her existence. Because if Dan wasn't the answer to her prayers, what was he? She quietly started a novena for enlightenment, hoping to bring in a verdict in his favour, but so acute was her awareness of his view that there was no enlightenment either, only whatever you wanted to believe yourself, that it ended by convincing her that it was her duty to give him up. He begged and prayed, he cursed and blinded; he assured her he was the most tolerant man in the world and she could believe in any damn nonsense she liked if only she'd marry him, but he had no chance against a direct revelation from heaven. She got engaged to MacGuinness.

I thought it a pity, because she was a really nice girl, and MacGuinness was only a poor dishcloth of a man.

Then I heard through my sister that Dan was behaving very queerly. It seemed he had deserted all his old haunts (he no longer came down the quays on Sundays), refused to eat or talk, and didn't stir out at night until after dark, when he went for long, lonesome walks in the country. People who had met him talked about the way he passed them without looking or the brief nod he gave them. I knew the symptoms. I felt it was up to me to do something. So one fine spring evening I called. Madge opened the door, and I could see that she had been crying.

'I didn't see Dan this long time, Madge,' said I. 'How is he?'

'Come in, Michael John,' she said, taking out her handkerchief. 'He's upstairs. He didn't stir out this last couple of days. Sure, you know the County Council will never stand it.'

I followed her up the stairs. Dan was lying on the bed, dressed but without collar and tie, his two hands under his head, apparently studying the ceiling. When I came in he raised his brows with his usual look of blank astonishment as much as to say: 'What the hell do you want?'

'Would you like a cup of tea, Dan?' Madge asked anxiously.

'If 'tis for me you needn't mind,' said Dan with a patient, long-suffering air that made it only too plain what he thought of the suggestion that he could be snatched back from the gates of the grave by a cup of tea.

'Wisha, I'm sure Michael John would like one,' said Madge.

'You're not feeling well, I hear?' I said.

'I don't know how you heard anything of the kind,' said Dan, rolling his blue eyes to the other side of the room, 'because I'm sure I didn't say anything about it.'

'Wisha, Michael John,' Madge burst out, 'did you ever in all your life hear of a grown man carrying on like that on account of a woman?'

'Now,' Dan said, raising his voice and turning the flat of his hand in her direction like a partition wall, 'I told you I wasn't going to discuss my business with you.'

'Why then, indeed, she discussed it enough,' said Madge, not realizing how every word hurt. 'There wasn't much about you that she didn't repeat. How well I could hear it all from a woman in the market.'

'Well, go back and discuss it with the woman in the market,' he retorted brutally. She gave me a tearful smile and went out.

'You have a grand view,' I said, looking down on the quays and the three-master below the bridge in the dusk.

'Yes,' he said grudgingly, 'but there isn't the traffic there used to be.'

'You never wanted to be a sailor?' I asked.

'I was never asked,' he replied as if this was a grievance that hadn't occurred to him before. 'No one ever consulted me about what I wanted to be.'

'What you need is a holiday,' I said.

'How can I take a holiday?' he asked, turning his blue eyes wonderingly on me as if he had discovered that I, too, had come with a view to persecuting him further.

'If you go on like this you'll take a holiday whether you like it or not,' I said, 'and it won't be by the seaside. We'll go to Ballybunion for a week.'

The eyebrows went up again.

'Parish priests!'

'All right,' I said to humour him. 'We'll go where there are no parish priests.'

'I'd like to see London again,' he admitted. 'I wasn't there for ten years.'

The idea of that almost got him into good humour, and when I was leaving he put on a collar and tie and walked home with me. I could see that Madge was well pleased with the result of my intervention, and I wasn't altogether dissatisfied myself.

But the pleasure didn't last long. Next morning I was in the yard when she called. She could scarcely speak for terror.

'Michael John, something awful is after happening,' she said.

'What?' I asked.

''Tis Dan. I don't know what to do with him. He tried to commit suicide.'

'He what?' I said, aghast.

'He did, Michael John. After he came home last night. He turned on the gas-tap before he went to bed. I know because I could still smell it this morning. He's in bed now with a terrible headache.' Then she began to cry. 'Sure, anyone could have told him you couldn't commit suicide with the gas we have in our house.'

'I'll be down this evening,' I said. 'We'll have to get him away by Saturday without fail.'

I spoke with a good deal more confidence than I felt. Suicide was a thing I had no experience of, because in our class a man's family or friends would never let him go so far. It was only with a freak of nature like Dan that the thing became possible at all, and, knowing the man's obstinacy, I wasn't sure but that he might try the same thing again. I didn't know what was the best thing to do. I bought a bottle of whiskey and a few lively gramophone records to bring him, because whenever I feel like committing suicide myself, I usually go out and buy whatever takes my fancy. After such a tribute of respect to myself, I never feel so inclined to deprive the community of my services.

He was sitting in the front room when I went in, still without his collar and tie, and he barely lifted his head to salute me. With the dusk coming down on the river outside, the man seemed so lonesome, so shut away in his own doubt and gloom, that my heart bled for him.

'Well,' I said, trying to make my voice sound as cheerful and out of doors as possible, 'I got leave from Saturday if you're ready to start.'

'I don't know that I'll be able,' he replied in a dead voice as though the words were merely a momentary interruption of the train of thought that went on in his head.

'You'll have to,' I said. 'You can't go on like this much longer.'

'I wasn't thinking of going on much longer,' he said in the same tone. It was exactly as if there was a wall of cotton-wool between us.

'Why?' I said, raising my voice and trying to make a joke of it. 'You weren't thinking of chucking yourself in the river or anything?'

'I suppose a man might as well do that as anything else,' he said.

'Ah, look here, Dan,' I said, opening the bottle of whiskey, 'we all feel like that at times, and it's only a mug's game. In a week's time you'll be laughing at it.'

'Of course, if you're not there in a week's time, you won't have an opportunity of laughing at it,' he said, positive even in despair.

'That's why it's a mug's game,' I said, filling him out a stiff one. 'Doing something permanent about something temporary is always a mug's game, like burning the house to get rid of a leak in the roof.'

'Temporary?' he said, raising his brows at me and becoming more like himself. 'Is old age a temporary state?'

'Old age?' I said. 'Merciful God, how old are you? Thirty-five?'

'Thirty-eight,' he said in the tone of some old paralytic telling you he's eighty-three and that he wished the Lord would take him soon. 'And what has a man of thirty-eight to look forward to in this country, Mr Dunphy?'

'Being thirty-nine,' said I.

'It's hardly likely to be much pleasanter than being thirty-eight,' he said. 'And that, let me tell you, is no sinecure.'

I took my whiskey and sat opposite him, while he still continued to look at me moodily, a big powerful red-faced man, his hands over the arms of his chair, his head lowered, his eyebrows raised, his blue, smouldering eyes in ambush beneath them.

'The trouble with you, Dan,' I said, 'is that you're under two illusions. One is that everyone except yourself is having a lovely time; the other is that when you're dead your troubles are at an end.'

That roused him.

'That's not an illusion,' he said, raising his voice. 'That's a scientific fact.'

'Fact, my nanny!' I said. 'How could it be a fact?'

''Tis a fact that anyone can see with his own two eyes,' he said, getting angrier and more positive.

'Well, I can't see it for one,' I said.

'You can see it, but you don't want to see it,' he said, tossing his big head at me. 'It doesn't suit you to see it. You're like all the other gentlemen who pretend they can't see it. My God,' he said, beginning to explode on me, 'the vanity and conceit of people, imagining that their own miserable little existence is too valuable to be wiped out!'

Then I began to get angry too. Forgetting the fellow was a sick man, I wanted to take it out of him for his unmannerly arrogance and complacency.

'And who the hell are you?' I said. 'Who told you you were alive in the first place?'

'Who told me?' he asked, a bit shaken. 'No one told me. I am alive. If I didn't know that I wouldn't know anything.'

'And who the blazes said you do know anything?' I shouted. 'As long as you can't tell me who you really are, or what you're doing in this room at this moment, you have no right to tell me in that impudent tone that when you die there's no more about you.'

He thought about that for a moment. I fancy it had never occurred to him in his life before that a man with his strong character mightn't be as real as he thought himself and that he didn't quite know how to answer it.

'I admit there are some things you can't explain yet,' he admitted grudgingly.

'Nor never will be able to explain,' said I.

'Everything can be explained,' he said, getting indignant again.

'Not things that are deliberately intended not to be explained,' said I. 'There are things we don't know, because if we knew them, whatever the answer was, we couldn't go on living.'

'Plenty of people think they know them.'

'They have faith,' said I. 'But faith, without doubt, can't exist.'

'They have more than faith, Mr Dunphy,' he said saucily. 'They have actual knowledge, according to themselves.'

'They pretend to,' I said. 'But they know as little about it as I do. Doubt is the first principle of existence, and you and they go round as if ye had special information trying to destroy it. Yeer own lives prove the opposite. If you really knew what you pretend to know, you wouldn't be planning to go to England on Saturday.'

'I'm not so sure that I'm going to England on Saturday,' he said with sudden despondency, all his load of troubles coming back to his mind.

But the argument did him good. It did me good as well. It was the first time I had stood up to him and if I hadn't exactly floored him, I had at least held my own. The only mistake I made was in thinking it was the argument that impressed him. I should have known that communists and atheists are never impressed by arguments. I continued the treatment with the records; Madge came in to listen, and it was quite like old times. He came to the door to see me off. It was a lovely starlit night, and he leaned against the jamb of the door, talking and listening to the voices of girls and sailors from away down the river.

But next morning I was only in to work when a couple of the men came up to tell me about the body that had been fished out of the river a quarter of an hour before. I didn't need anyone to tell me whose it was. I knew my confounded complacency had put me astray again.

'Below the bridge was this, Jack?' I asked.

'Yes, Mr Dunphy. Why?'

'I'm the man that's responsible, Jack,' I said. 'Tell the boss I probably won't be back this morning.'

I rushed off down the quays. They were very quiet, and the church and the trees were reflected in the water, it was so still. I was blaming myself terribly for the whole thing, for not realizing that a man as headstrong as that would never be diverted from anything he made up his mind to by arguments. When I reached the bridge I saw plainly that it was all as Jack Delea had described it; the knot of women outside the door, and the still undried trail from the quayside to the hall door.

Madge opened the door, and at once she put her finger to her lips. Surprised not to see her looking more concerned, I tiptoed in the hall and up the stairs after her. They were wet too, and there was a shocking smell of gas. She opened the door of Dan's bedroom, but he wasn't there. The window was wide open; the bed had not been slept in; there was a tea-chest in the middle of the floor.

'What did they do with him, Madge?' I whispered, wondering if he had been removed to the morgue.

'Dan?' she said in surprise. 'Oh, he's downstairs, at his breakfast.'

'You mean he's all right?' I gasped.

'It was the mercy of God that the sailor saw him,' she said, her eyes shining. 'I didn't want you to say anything till you knew what happened.'

'But what did happen?' I asked, with an enormous feeling of relief that there wouldn't be any inquest.

'Don't you see?' she said, pointing to the tea-chest. 'He had a length of tubing running through this and a tap at the end.'

She lifted the tea-chest, which had a hole drilled in the side of it for the tubing to go through. Beneath it was a pillow and a rug.

'What in hell is that for?' I asked.

'He bought the tubing and the tap so that he could turn on the gas when he was inside the tea-chest,' said Madge with a smile at the man's innocence. 'The notion of him being kept down by a tea-chest, that two men couldn't control when he had the pneumonia! He must have been lifting it off him the whole time. You can see where he got sick through the window.'

'And was it after that he threw himself in the river?' I said, marvelling at the pertinacity of the man.

'Ah, that was afterwards, Michael John,' said Madge. 'Then he saw a great light.'

'A great what?' said I.

'A great light,' said Madge. 'He saw life was good.'

'He saw a lot,' said I.

'He said he saw everything quite plain at last,' said Madge. 'So to put temptation away from him he took the tube and the tap to throw them in the river. It was while he was doing that that he tripped over the rope.'

'I see,' said I. 'He saw the light, but he didn't see the rope. I hope you don't take that nonsense seriously.'

'Oh, I do, Michael John,' she said, beginning to cry. 'I'm sure 'tis the answer to my prayers. Whatever you do, you mustn't upset him now. He's the best brother in the world only for the misfortunate books he reads. 'Tis them I'd like to throw in the river.'

And she gave a heart-scalded look at the shelf of books by Dan's bed.

I went downstairs in a sort of stupor, and there, in the kitchen, in his best suit with a collar and tie on, was Dan, eating his breakfast and reading the paper at the same time.

'Hullo,' he said, quite friendly.

'Oughtn't you to be damn well ashamed of yourself?' I said, losing all control of myself.

'Ashamed of myself?' he asked, raising his brows and getting on his usual high horse. 'What would I be ashamed of? I suppose an accident can happen to anyone?'

'Accident?' I said. 'Wasn't I sitting in the front room with you last night, trying to keep you away from any more accidents? What sort of way is this to treat your unfortunate sister that has her heart broken trying to look after you in your kimeens?'

Suddenly a strange look came into his face. He bowed his head and nodded.

'I admit that,' he said meekly. 'I admit I was headstrong.'

'Headstrong,' I said, refusing to be curbed, 'and conceited and thinking you were the only one in the world that knew anything.'

'I know, I know,' he said, 'I was very egotistical.' And it was only then it struck me that for the first time in his life he had agreed with me. It was an accident all right.

Of course, Madge wouldn't agree with that. He's a reformed character now. And the funny thing is, he'll run through a key-hole to avoid me. He says I'm a man without any proper faith.

THE WREATH

WHEN FATHER FOGARTY read of the death of his friend Father Devine in a Dublin nursing home, he was stunned. He was a man who did not understand the irremediable.

He took out an old seminary group, put it on the mantelpiece, and spent the evening looking at it. Devine's clever, pale, shrunken face stood out from all the others, not very different from what it had been in his later years except for the absence of pince-nez. He and Fogarty had been boys together in a provincial town where Devine's father was a schoolmaster and Fogarty's mother kept a shop. Even then everybody had known that Devine was marked by nature for the priesthood. He was clever, docile, and beautifully mannered. Fogarty's vocation had come later and was a surprise.

They had been friends over the years, affectionate when together, critical and sarcastic when apart, and had seen nothing of one another for close on a year. Devine had been unlucky. As long as the old Bishop lived he had been fairly well sheltered, but Lanigan, the new one, disliked him. It was partly his own fault; because he could not keep his mouth shut; because he was witty and waspish and said whatever came into his head about his colleagues who had nothing like his gifts. Fogarty remembered the things Devine had said about himself. He affected to believe that Fogarty was a man of many personalities, and asked with mock humility which of them he was now dealing with – Nero, Napoleon or St Francis of Assisi.

It all came back, the occasional jaunts together, the plans for holidays abroad which never came to anything; and now the warm and genuine love for Devine which was natural to him welled up, and realizing that never again in this world would he be able to express it, he began to weep. He was as simple as a child in his emotions. He forgot lightly, remembered suddenly and with exaggerated intensity, and blamed himself cruelly and unjustly for his own shortcomings. He would have been astonished to learn that, for all the intrusions of Nero and Napoleon, his understanding had continued to develop through the years, when that of clever men had dried up, and that he was a better and wiser priest at forty than he had been twenty years before.

Because there was no one else to whom he could communicate his sense of loss, he rang up Jackson, a curate who had been Devine's other friend. He did not really like Jackson, who was worldly, cynical, and a bit of a careerist, and had always wondered what it was that Devine saw in him.

'Isn't that terrible news about Devine?' he said, barely keeping the tears out of his voice.

'Yes,' drawled Jackson in his usual cautious, fishy tone, as though even on such a subject he were afraid of committing himself. 'I suppose it's a happy release for the poor devil.'

This was the sort of talk which maddened Fogarty. It sounded as if Jackson were talking of an old family pet who had been sent to the vet's.

'I dare say,' he said gruffly. 'I was thinking of going to town and coming back with the funeral. You wouldn't come?'

'I don't see how I could, Jerry,' Jackson replied in a tone of concern. 'It's only a week since I was up last.'

'Ah, well, I'll go myself,' said Fogarty. 'I suppose you don't know what happened him?'

'Oh, you know he was always anaemic. He ought to have looked after himself, but he didn't get much chance with that old brute of a parish priest of his. He was fainting all over the shop. The last time, he fainted at Mass.'

'You were in touch with him, then?' Fogarty asked in surprise.

'I just saw him for a while last week. He couldn't talk much, of course.'

And again the feeling of his own inadequacy descended on Fogarty. He realized that Jackson, who seemed to have as much feeling as a mowing machine, had kept in touch with Devine and gone out of his way to see him at the end, while he, the warmhearted, devoted, generous friend, had let him slip from sight into eternity and was now wallowing in the sense of his own loss.

'God, I feel thoroughly ashamed of myself, Jim,' he said with a new humility. 'I never even knew he was sick.'

'I'll see about getting off for the funeral,' Jackson said. 'I think I might manage it.'

*

That evening, the two priests set off in Fogarty's car for the city. Jackson brought Fogarty to a very pleasant restaurant for dinner. He was a tall, thin man with a prim, watchful, clerical air, who knew his way round. He spent at least ten minutes over the menu and the wine list, and the headwaiter danced attendance on him as headwaiters do only when there is a big tip in view or they have to deal with an expert.

'I'm having steak,' Fogarty said to cut it short.

'Father Fogarty is having steak, Paddy,' said Jackson, looking at the headwaiter over his spectacles. 'Make it rare. And stout, I suppose?'

'I'll spare you the stout,' said Fogarty. 'Red wine.'

'Mind, Paddy,' said Jackson warningly. 'Father Fogarty said *red* wine. You're in Ireland now, remember.'

Next morning, they went to the mortuary chapel, where the coffin was resting on trestles before the altar. Beside it, to Fogarty's surprise, was a large wreath of red roses. When they rose from their knees, Devine's uncle Ned had come in with his son. Ned was a broad-faced, dark-haired, nervous man, with the anaemic complexion of the family.

'I'm sorry for your trouble, Ned,' Father Fogarty said.

'I know that, father,' said Ned.

'I don't know if you know Father Jackson. He was a great friend of Father Willie's.'

'I heard him speak of him,' said Ned. 'He talked a lot about both of you. Ye were his great friends. Poor Father Willie!' he added with a sigh. 'He had few enough of them.'

Just then the parish priest entered and spoke to Ned Devine. He was a tall man with a stern, unlined, wooden face. He stood for a few moments by the coffin, then studied the breastplate and the wreath, looking closely at the tag of the wreath. It was only then that he beckoned the two younger priests aside.

'Tell me,' he asked in a professional tone, 'what are we going to do about this?'

'About what?' Fogarty asked in surprise.

'This wreath,' said Father Martin, giving him a candid glare.

'What's wrong with it?'

''Tis against the rubrics.'

'For Heaven's sake!' Fogarty said impatiently. 'What have the rubrics to do with it?'

'The rubrics have a lot to do with it,' Martin said sternly. 'And, apart from that, 'tis a bad custom.'

'You mean Masses bring in more money?' Fogarty asked with amused insolence.

'I do not mean Masses bring in more money,' said Martin, who seemed to reply to every remark verbatim, like a solicitor's letter. 'I mean that flowers are a pagan survival.' He looked at the two young priests with the same innocent, anxious, wooden air. 'And here am I, week in, week out, preaching against flowers, and a blooming big wreath of them in my own church. And on a priest's coffin too, mind you! What am I going to say about that?'

'Who asked you to say anything?' asked Fogarty. 'The man wasn't from your diocese.'

'Oh, now, that's all very well,' said Martin. 'And that's not the whole story, and you know it.'

'You mean, the wreath is from a woman?' broke in Jackson.

'I do mean the wreath is from a woman.'

'A woman?' Fogarty exclaimed in astonishment. 'Does it say so?'

'It does not say so. But 'tis red roses.'

'And does that mean it's from a woman?'

'What else could it mean?'

'It could mean it's from somebody who didn't study the language of flowers the way you seem to have done,' said Fogarty.

'Oh, well,' Jackson intervened again with a shrug, 'we know nothing about it. You'll have to decide about it yourself. It's nothing to do with us.'

'I don't like doing anything when I wasn't acquainted with the man,' said Martin, but he made no further attempt to interfere, and one of the undertaker's men took the wreath and placed it on the hearse. Fogarty controlled himself with difficulty. As he banged open the door of the car and started the engine, his face was very flushed. He drove with his head bowed and his brows jutting down like rocks above his eyes. As they cleared the Main Street he burst out.

'That's the sort of thing that makes me ashamed of myself! "Flowers are a pagan survival." And they take it from him, Jim! They listen to that sort of stuff instead of telling him to shut his ignorant gob.'

'Oh, well,' Jackson said in his nonchalant, tolerant way, 'he was right, of course.'

'Right?'

'I mean, on the appearance of the thing. After all, he didn't know Devine.'

'All the more reason why he shouldn't have interfered. Do you realize that he'd have thrown out that wreath only for us being there? And for what? His own dirty, mean, suspicious mind!'

'Ah, I wouldn't say that. I wouldn't have let that wreath go on the coffin.'

'You wouldn't? Why not?'

'It was from a woman all right.'

Jackson lit his pipe and looked over his spectacles at Fogarty.

'Yes, one of Devine's old maids.'

'Ever heard of an old maid sending a wreath of red roses?'

'To tell you the God's truth,' Fogarty confessed with boyish candour, 'it would never have struck me that there was anything wrong with it.'

'It would have struck the old maid, though.'

Fogarty missed a turning and reversed with a muttered curse.

'You're not serious, Jim?' he said after a few moments.

'Oh, I'm not saying there was anything wrong in it,' Jackson replied with a shrug. 'Women get ideas like that. You must have noticed that sort of thing yourself.'

'These things can happen in very innocent ways,' Fogarty said with ingenuous solemnity. Then he began to scowl again, and a blush spread over his handsome craggy face that was neither anger nor shame. Like all those who live greatly in their imaginations, he was always astonished and shocked at the suggestion that reached him from the outside world: he could live with his fantasies only by assuming that they were nothing more. The country began to grow wilder under the broken spring light; the valley of the river dropped away with a ruined abbey on its bank, and a pine-clad hill rose on their right, the first breath of the mountains. 'I can't believe it,' he said angrily, shaking his head.

'You don't have to believe it,' Jackson said, nursing his pipe. 'I'd nearly be glad if Martin's suspicions were right. If ever a man needed somebody to care for him, Devine did.'

'But not Devine, Jim,' Fogarty said obstinately. 'You could believe a thing like that if it was me. I could nearly believe it if it was you. But I knew Devine since we were kids, and he wouldn't be capable of it.'

'I never knew him like that,' Jackson admitted mildly. 'In fact, I scarcely knew him at all, really. But I'd have said he was as capable of it as we are. He was a good deal lonelier than we'll ever be.'

'God, don't I know it!' Fogarty ground out in self-reproach. 'If it was drinking, I could understand it.'

'Devine was too fastidious.'

'But that's what I say.'

'There's a big difference,' said Jackson. 'A very intelligent woman, for instance, might have appealed to him. You can imagine how he'd appeal to her. After all, you know, what he meant to us; the most civilized chap we could meet. Just fancy what a man like that would mean to some woman in a country town: maybe a woman married to some lout of a shopkeeper or a gentleman farmer.'

'He didn't tell you about her?' Fogarty asked incredulously, because Jackson spoke with such plausibility that it impressed him as true.

'Oh, no, no, I'm only guessing,' Jackson said hastily, and then he blushed too.

Fogarty remained silent, aware that Jackson had confessed something about himself, but he could not get the incredible idea of Devine out of his mind. As the country grew wilder and furze bushes and ruined keeps took the place of pastures and old abbeys, he found his eyes attracted more and more to the wreath that swayed lightly with the swaying of the hearse and seemed to concentrate all the light. It seemed an image of the essential mystery of a priest's life.

What, after all, did he know of Devine? Only what his own temperament suggested, and mostly – when he wasn't being St Francis of Assisi, in Devine's phrase – he had seen himself as the worldly one of the pair, the practical, coarse-grained man who cut corners, and Devine as the saint, racked by his own fastidiousness and asceticism that exploded in his bitter little jests. Now his mind boggled at the agony which could have driven a man like Devine to seek companionship in such a way; yet the measure of his incredulity was that of the conviction which he would soon feel, the new level on which his thought must move.

'God!' he burst out. 'Don't we lead lonely lives. We probably knew Devine better than anyone else in the world, and there's that damn thing in front of us, and neither of us has a notion what it means.'

'Which might be just as well for our own comfort,' Jackson said.

'If you're right, I'll take my oath it did very little for Devine's,' Fogarty said grimly.

'Oh, I don't know,' Jackson said. 'Isn't that the one thing we all really want from life?'

'Would you say so?' Fogarty asked in astonishment. He had always thought of Jackson as a cold fish, a go-getter, and suddenly found himself wondering about that too; wondering what it was in him that had appealed so much to Devine. He had the feeling that Jackson, who was, as he modestly recognized, by far the subtler man, was probing him, and for the same reason. Each of them was looking in the other for the quality which had attracted Devine, and which having made him their friend might make them friends also. 'I couldn't do it though, Jim,' he said sombrely. 'I went as close to it as I'm ever likely to do. It was the wife of one of the chaps that was with me in the seminary. She seemed to be all the things I ever wanted a woman to be. Then, when I saw what her marriage to the other fellow was like, I realized that she hated him like poison. It might have been me she hated that way. It's only when you see what marriages are like, as we do, that you know how lucky we are in escaping them.'

'Lucky?' Jackson repeated with light irony. 'Do you really think we're lucky? Have you ever known a seminary that wasn't full of men who thought themselves lucky? They might be drinking themselves to death, but they never once doubted their luck. Clerical sour grapes. . . . Anyway, you're rather underrating yourself if you think she'd have hated you.'

'You think I might have made her a good husband?' Fogarty asked, flushing with pleasure, for this was what he had always thought himself when he permitted his imagination to rest on Una Whitton.

'Probably. You'd have made a good father at any rate.'

'God knows you might be right,' said Fogarty. 'It's easier to do without a woman than it is to do without kids. My mother was the same. She was wrapped up in us; she always wanted us to be better than anyone else, and when we did badly at school or got into trouble it nearly broke her heart. She said it was the Fogarty blood breaking out in us – the Fogartys were all horse dealers.' His handsome, happy face clouded again with the old feelings of remorse and guilt, unjustified, like most of his self-reproach. 'I'm afraid she died under the impression that I was a Fogarty after all.'

'If the Fogartys are any relation to the Martins, I'd say it was most unlikely,' said Jackson.

'I never really knew till she was dead how much she meant to me,' Fogarty said broodingly. 'I insisted on performing the burial service myself, though Hennessey warned me not to. My God, the way we gallop through it till it comes home to ourselves! I broke down and bawled like a kid and Hennessey got up and finished it.'

Jackson shook his head uncomprehendingly. 'You feel these things more than I do. I'm a cold fish.'

It struck Fogarty that, though this was precisely what he had always believed, he would now believe it no longer. 'That settled me,' he said. 'Up to that, I used to be a bit flighty, but afterwards, I knew I could never care for another woman as I cared for her.'

'Nonsense!' Jackson said lightly. 'That's the best proof you could offer a woman that you'd care for her as much. Love is just one thing, not a half dozen. If I had my eye on a woman, I'd take good care to choose one who cared that way for her father. You're the sort who'd go to hell for a woman if ever you let yourself go. I couldn't go to hell for anybody. The nearest I ever got to it was with one woman in a town I was in. I didn't realize the state she was getting herself into till I found her outside my door at two o'clock one morning. She wanted me to take her away! You can imagine what happened to her afterwards.'

'She went off with someone else?'

'No. Drink. And it was nothing but loneliness. After that, I decided that people of my sort have no business with love.'

At the word 'love' Fogarty felt his heart contract. It was partly the wreath, brilliant in the sunlight, that had drawn him out of his habitual reserve and linked him with a man of even greater reserve, partly the excitement of returning to the little town where he had grown up. He hated it; he avoided it; it seemed to be the complete expression of all the narrowness and mean-ness that he tried to banish from his own thoughts; but at the same time, it contained all the violence and longing that had driven him out of it, and when once he drew near it a tumult of emotions rose in him that half strangled him.

'There it is!' he said triumphantly, pointing to a valley where a tapering Franciscan tower rose from a clutter of low Georgian houses and thatched cabins. 'They'll be waiting for us at the bridge. That's the way they'll be waiting for me when my turn comes.'

'They' were the priests and townspeople who had come out to escort the hearse to the cemetery. Ned Devine steered people to their places. Four men shouldered the coffin over the high-arched bridge past the ruined castle and up the hilly Main Street. Shutters were up on the shop fronts, blinds were drawn, every-thing was at a standstill except here and there where a curtain was lifted and an old woman, too feeble to make the journey, peered out.

A laneway led off the hilly road, and they came to the abbey; a tower and a few walls with tombstones thickly sown in choir and nave. The hearse was already drawn up and people gathered in a semi-circle about it. Ned Devine came hastily up to the car where the two priests were donning their surplices.

'Whisht, Father Jerry,' he muttered in a strained, excited voice. 'People are talking about that wreath. I wonder would you know who sent it?'

'I know nothing at all about it, Ned,' Fogarty replied roughly, and suddenly felt his heart begin to pant violently.

'Come here a minute, Sheela,' Ned called, and a tall, pale girl in black, with the stain of tears on her long, bony face, left the little group of mourners and joined them. 'You know Father Jerry. This is Father Jackson, Father Willie's other friend. They don't know anything about it.'

'Then I'd let them take it back,' she said doggedly.

'What would you say, father?' Ned asked, appealing to Fogarty.

Fogarty suddenly felt his courage desert him. In arguing with Martin, he had felt himself dealing with an equal, but now the intense passions and prejudices of the little town seemed to rise up and oppose him, and he felt himself again an adolescent, rebellious but frightened.

'I can only tell you what I told Father Martin,' he blustered.

'Did Father Martin talk about it too?' Ned asked sharply.

'He did.'

'There!' Sheela said vindictively. 'What did I tell you?'

'Well, the pair of you may be cleverer than I am,' Fogarty said. 'I can only say what I said before: I'd never have noticed anything wrong with it.'

'It was no proper thing to send to a priest's funeral,' she hissed with prim fury. 'Whoever sent it was no friend of my brother.'

'You wouldn't agree with that, father?' Ned asked anxiously.

'But I tell you, Uncle Ned, if that wreath goes into the grave-yard we'll be the laughing-stock of the town,' she said furiously.

'Whisht, girl, whisht, and let Father Jerry talk!' he snapped angrily.

'Well, Ned, it seems to me to be entirely a matter for your-selves,' Fogarty replied. 'I can only tell you what I think.' He was really scared now; he realized that he was in danger of behaving imprudently in public, and that sooner or later the story would get back to the Bishop and it would be suggested that he knew more than he pretended.

'If you'll excuse my interrupting, father,' Jackson said suavely, giving him a warning glance over his spectacles, 'I know it isn't my place to speak –'

'But that's the very thing we want, father,' Ned said passion-ately. 'If you say 'tis all right, that's enough for me.'

'Oh, well, Mr Devine, that would be too great a responsibility for me to take,' Jackson said with a cautious smile, though his pale face had grown flushed. 'You know this town. I don't. I only know what it would mean in my own place. I've told Father Fogarty already that I agree with Miss Devine. I think it was wrong to send it. But,' and his mild voice suddenly grew menacing, and he shrugged his shoulders and spread out his hands with a contemptuous look, 'if you were to send that wreath back from the graveyard, you'd make yourself something far worse than a laughing-stock. You'd throw mud on a dead man's name that would never be forgotten for you, the longest day you lived. . . . Things may be different here, of course,' he added superciliously.

Ned Devine suddenly came to his senses. He clicked his fingers impatiently.

'Of course, of course, of course,' he snarled. 'That's something we should have thought of ourselves. 'Twould be giving tongues to the stones.'

And he took the wreath and carried it behind the coffin to the graveside. That was sufficient to dissipate the growing hysteria which Fogarty felt about him. He touched Jackson's hand lightly.

'Good man, Jim!' he said in a voice that was full of love and tears.

Side by side they stood at the head of the open grave where the other surpliced priests had gathered. Their voices rose in the psalms for the dead. But Fogarty's brooding, curious eyes swept the crowd of faces he had known since childhood, now caricatured by age and pain, and each time they came to rest on the wreath which stood to one side of the grave. Each time it came over him in a flood of emotion that what he and Jackson had saved was something more than a sentimental token. It was the thing which formerly had linked them to Devine and which now linked them with one another; the feeling of their own integrity as men beside their integrity as priests; the thing which gave significance and beauty to their sacrifice.

THEN MY grandmother died. In the early hours of the morning my uncle went for the priest and came in with him looking very pale. As they passed a forge, Father Tierney had said: 'Get off the footpath and let the ghosts go by,' which admittedly was enough to make any man go pale. In the manner of the old country people, my grandmother was well prepared for death. For as long as I remembered her, she had been giving instructions for her funeral, and Father, the tease of the family, had told her he couldn't afford to take her back to her own people, at which Grandmother had told him she would haunt him. In a drawer she had the two bits of blessed candle that were to be lit over her when she died, and her shroud, which she took out regularly to air on the line. She was ill for a week or two and lay upstairs, saying her beads and reciting poetry in Irish. The day before she died she shouted for a mirror, and Mother told her she should be thinking of God, but the old woman only shouted louder. When Mother brought the mirror upstairs, Grandmother studied herself for a few moments in stupefaction and muttered: 'Jesus Christ, there's a face!' before turning to the wall. She had not wanted to rejoin her dead husband, looking like that.

THE LONG ROAD TO UMMERA

Stay for me there. I will not fail
To meet thee in that hollow vale.

ALWAYS IN the evenings you saw her shuffle up the road to Miss
O.'s for her little jug of porter, a shapeless lump of an old woman
in a plaid shawl, faded to the colour of snuff, that dragged her
head down on to her bosom where she clutched its folds in one
hand; a canvas apron and a pair of men's boots without laces.
Her eyes were puffy and screwed up in tight little buds of flesh
and her rosy old face that might have been carved out of a turnip
was all crumpled with blindness. The old heart was failing her,
and several times she would have to rest, put down the jug, lean
against the wall, and lift the weight of the shawl off her head.
People passed; she stared at them humbly; they saluted her; she
turned her head and peered after them for minutes on end. The
rhythm of life had slowed down in her till you could scarcely
detect its faint and sluggish beat. Sometimes from some queer
instinct of shyness she turned to the wall, took a snuffbox from
her bosom, and shook out a pinch on the back of her swollen
hand. When she sniffed it it smeared her nose and upper lip and
spilled all over her old black blouse. She raised the hand to
her eyes and looked at it closely and reproachfully, as though
astonished that it no longer served her properly. Then she
dusted herself, picked up the old jug again, scratched herself
against her clothes, and shuffled along close by the wall, groan-
ing aloud.

When she reached her own house, which was a little cottage
in a terrace, she took off her boots, and herself and the old cob-
bler who lodged with her turned out a pot of potatoes on the
table, stripping them with their fingers and dipping them in
the little mound of salt while they took turn and turn about with
the porter jug. He was a lively and philosophic old man called
Johnny Thornton.

After their supper they sat in the firelight, talking about old times in the country and long-dead neighbours, ghosts, fairies, spells, and charms. It always depressed her son, finding them together like that when he called with her monthly allowance. He was a well-to-do businessman with a little grocery shop in the South Main Street and a little house in Sunday's Well, and nothing would have pleased him better than that his mother should share all the grandeur with him, the carpets and the china and the chiming clocks. He sat moodily between them, stroking his long jaw, and wondering why they talked so much about death in the old-fashioned way, as if it was something that made no difference at all.

'Wisha, what pleasure do ye get out of old talk like that?' he asked one night.

'Like what, Pat?' his mother asked with her timid smile.

'My goodness,' he said, 'ye're always at it. Corpses and graves and people that are dead and gone.'

'Arrah, why wouldn't we?' she replied, looking down stiffly as she tried to button the open-necked blouse that revealed her old breast. 'Isn't there more of us there than here?'

'Much difference 'twill make to you when you won't know them or see them!' he exclaimed.

'Oye, why wouldn't I know them?' she cried angrily. 'Is it the Twomeys of Lackroe and the Driscolls of Ummera?'

'How sure you are we'll take you to Ummera!' he said mockingly.

'Och aye, Pat,' she asked, shaking herself against her clothes with her humble stupid wondering smile, 'and where else would you take me?'

'Isn't our own plot good enough for you?' he asked. 'Your own son and your grandchildren?'

'Musha, indeed, is it in the town you want to bury me?' She shrugged herself and blinked into the fire, her face growing sour and obstinate. 'I'll go back to Ummera, the place I came from.'

'Back to the hunger and misery we came from,' Pat said scornfully.

'Back to your father, boy.'

'Ay, to be sure, where else? But my father or grandfather never did for you what I did. Often and often I scoured the streets of Cork for a few ha'pence for you.'

'You did, amossa, you did, you did,' she admitted, looking into the fire and shaking herself. 'You were a good son to me.'

'And often I did it and the belly falling out of me with hunger,' Pat went on, full of self-pity.

''Tis true for you,' she mumbled, ''tis, 'tis, 'tis true. 'Twas often and often you had to go without it. What else could you do and the way we were left?'

'And now our grave isn't good enough for you,' he complained. There was real bitterness in his tone. He was an insignificant little man and jealous of the power the dead had over her.

She looked at him with the same abject, half-imbecile smile, the wrinkled old eyes almost shut above the Mongolian cheek-bones, while with a swollen old hand, like a pot-stick, it had so little life in it, she smoothed a few locks of yellow-white hair across her temples – a trick she had when troubled.

'Musha, take me back to Ummera, Pat,' she whined. 'Take me back to my own. I'd never rest among strangers. I'd be rising and drifting.'

'Ah, foolishness, woman!' he said with an indignant look. 'That sort of thing is gone out of fashion.'

'I won't stop here for you,' she shouted hoarsely in sudden, impotent fury, and she rose and grasped the mantelpiece for support.

'You won't be asked,' he said shortly.

'I'll haunt you,' she whispered tensely, holding on to the mantelpiece and bending down over him with a horrible grin.

'And that's only more of the foolishness,' he said with a nod of contempt. 'Haunts and fairies and spells.'

She took one step towards him and stood, plastering down the two little locks of yellowing hair, the half-dead eyes twitching and blinking in the candlelight, and the swollen crumpled face with the cheeks like cracked enamel.

'Pat,' she said, 'the day we left Ummera you promised to bring me back. You were only a little gorsoon that time. The neighbours gathered round me and the last word I said to them and I going down the road was: "Neighbours, my son Pat is after giving me his word and he'll bring me back to ye when my time comes." . . . That's as true as the Almighty God is over me this night. I have everything ready.' She went to the shelf under the stairs and took out two parcels. She seemed to be speaking to herself as she opened them gloatingly, bending down her head in the feeble light of the candle. 'There's the two brass candlesticks and the blessed candles alongside them. And there's my shroud aired regular on the line.'

'Ah, you're mad, woman,' he said angrily. 'Forty miles! Forty miles into the heart of the mountains!'

She suddenly shuffled towards him on her bare feet, her hand raised clawing the air, her body like her face blind with age. Her harsh croaking old voice rose to a shout.

'I brought you from it, boy, and you must bring me back. If 'twas the last shilling you had and you and your children to go to the poorhouse after, you must bring me back to Ummera. And not by the short road either! Mind what I say now! The long road! The long road to Ummera round the lake, the way I brought you from it. I lay a heavy curse on you this night if you bring me the short road over the hill. And ye must stop by the ash tree at the foot of the boreen where ye can see my little house and say a prayer for all that were ever old in it and all that played on the floor. And then – Pat! Pat Driscoll! Are you listening? Are you listening to me, I say?'

She shook him by the shoulder, peering down into his long miserable face to see how was he taking it.

'I'm listening,' he said with a shrug.

'Then' – her voice dropped to a whisper – 'you must stand up overright the neighbours and say – remember now what I'm telling you! – "Neighbours, this is Abby, Batty Heige's daughter, that kept her promise to ye at the end of all." '

She said it lovingly, smiling to herself, as if it were a bit of an old song, something she went over and over in the long night. All West Cork was in it: the bleak road over the moors to Ummera, the smooth grey pelts of the hills with the long spider's web of the fences ridging them, drawing the scarecrow fields awry, and the whitewashed cottages, poker-faced between their little scraps of holly bushes looking this way and that out of the wind.

'Well, I'll make a fair bargain with you,' said Pat as he rose. Without seeming to listen she screwed up her eyes and studied his weak melancholy face. 'This house is a great expense to me. Do what I'm always asking you. Live with me and I'll promise I'll take you back to Ummera.'

'Oye, I will not,' she replied sullenly, shrugging her shoulders helplessly, an old sack of a woman with all the life gone out of her.

'All right,' said Pat. ''Tis your own choice. That's my last word; take it or leave it. Live with me and Ummera for your grave, or stop here and a plot in the Botanics.'

She watched him out the door with shoulders hunched about her ears. Then she shrugged herself, took out her snuffbox and took a pinch.

'Arrah, I wouldn't mind what he'd say,' said Johnny. 'A fellow like that would change his mind tomorrow.'

'He might and he mightn't,' she said heavily, and opened the back door to go out to the yard. It was a starry night and they could hear the noise of the city below them in the valley. She raised her eyes to the bright sky over the back wall and suddenly broke into a cry of loneliness and helplessness.

'Oh, oh, oh, 'tis far away from me Ummera is tonight above any other night, and I'll die and be buried here, far from all I ever knew and the long roads between us.'

Of course old Johnny should have known damn well what she was up to the night she made her way down to the cross, creeping along beside the railings. By the blank wall opposite the lighted pub Dan Regan, the jarvey, was standing by his old box of a covered car with his pipe in his gob. He was the jarvey all the old neighbours went to. Abby beckoned to him and he followed her into the shadow of a gateway overhung with ivy. He listened gravely to what she had to say, sniffing and nodding, wiping his nose in his sleeve, or crossing the pavement to hawk his nose and spit in the channel, while his face with its drooping moustaches never relaxed its discreet and doleful expression.

Johnny should have known what that meant and why old Abby, who had always been so open-handed, sat before an empty grate sooner than light a fire, and came after him on Fridays for the rent, whether he had it or not, and even begrudged him the little drop of porter which had always been give and take between them. He knew himself it was a change before death and that it all went into the wallet in her bosom. At night in her attic she counted it by the light of her candle and when the coins dropped from her lifeless fingers he heard her roaring like an old cow as she crawled along the naked boards, sweeping them blindly with her palms. Then he heard the bed creak as she tossed about in it, and the rosary being taken from the bedhead, and the old voice rising and falling in prayer; and sometimes when a high wind blowing up the river roused him before dawn he could hear her muttering: a mutter and then a yawn; the scrape of a match as she peered at the alarm clock – the endless nights of the old – and then the mutter of prayer again.

But Johnny in some ways was very dense, and he guessed nothing till the night she called him and, going to the foot of the stairs with a candle in his hand, he saw her on the landing in her flour-bag shift, one hand clutching the jamb of the door while the other clawed wildly at her few straggly hairs.

'Johnny!' she screeched down at him, beside herself with excitement. 'He was here.'

'Who was there?' he snarled back, still cross with sleep.

'Michael Driscoll, Pat's father.'

'Ah, you were dreaming, woman,' he said in disgust. 'Go back to your bed in God's holy name.'

'I was not dreaming,' she cried. 'I was lying broad awake, saying my beads, when he come in the door, beckoning me. Go down to Dan Regan's for me, Johnny.'

'I will not, indeed, go down to Dan Regan's for you. Do you know what hour of night it is?'

'"Tis morning.'

'"Tis. Four o'clock! What a thing I'd do! . . . Is it the way you're feeling bad?' he added with more consideration as he mounted the stairs. 'Do you want him to take you to hospital?'

'Oye, I'm going to no hospital,' she replied sullenly, turning her back on him and thumping into the room again. She opened an old chest of drawers and began fumbling in it for her best clothes, her bonnet and cloak.

'Then what the blazes do you want Dan Regan for?' he snarled in exasperation.

'What matter to you what I want him for?' she retorted with senile suspicion. 'I have a journey to go, never you mind where.'

'Ach, you old oinseach, your mind is wandering,' he cried. 'There's a divil of a wind blowing up the river. The whole house is shaking. That's what you heard. Make your mind easy now and go back to bed.'

'My mind is not wandering,' she shouted. 'Thanks be to the

Almighty God I have my senses as good as you. My plans are made. I'm going back now where I came from. Back to Ummera.'

'Back to where?' Johnny asked in stupefaction.

'Back to Ummera.'

'You're madder than I thought. And do you think or imagine Dan Regan will drive you?'

'He will drive me then,' she said, shrugging herself as she held an old petticoat to the light. 'He's booked for it any hour of the day or night.'

'Then Dan Regan is madder still.'

'Leave me alone now,' she muttered stubbornly, blinking and shrugging. 'I'm going back to Ummera and that was why my old comrade came for me. All night and every night I have my beads wore out, praying the Almighty God and His Blessed Mother not to leave me die among strangers. And now I'll leave my old bones on a high hilltop in Ummera.'

Johnny was easily persuaded. It promised to be a fine day's outing and a story that would delight a pub, so he made tea for her and after that went down to Dan Regan's little cottage, and before smoke showed from any chimney on the road they were away. Johnny was hopping about the car in his excitement, leaning out, shouting through the window of the car to Dan and identifying big estates that he hadn't seen for years. When they were well outside the town, himself and Dan went in for a drink, and while they were inside the old woman dozed. Dan Regan roused her to ask if she wouldn't take a drop of something and at first she didn't know who he was and then she asked where they were and peered out at the public-house and the old dog sprawled asleep in the sunlight before the door. But when next they halted she had fallen asleep again, her mouth hanging open and her breath coming in noisy gusts. Dan's face grew gloomier. He looked hard at her and spat. Then he took a few turns about the road, lit his pipe and put on the lid.

'I don't like her looks at all, Johnny,' he said gravely. 'I done wrong. I see that now. I done wrong.'

After that, he halted every couple of miles to see how she was and Johnny, threatened with the loss of his treat, shook her and shouted at her. Each time Dan's face grew graver. He walked gloomily about the road, clearing his nose and spitting in the ditch. 'God direct me!' he said solemnly. ''Twon't be wishing to me. Her son is a powerful man. He'll break me yet. A man should never interfere between families. Blood is thicker than water. The Regans were always unlucky.'

When they reached the first town he drove straight to the police barrack and told them the story in his own peculiar way.

'Ye can tell the judge I gave ye every assistance,' he said in a reasonable broken-hearted tone. 'I was always a friend of the law. I'll keep nothing back – a pound was the price agreed. I suppose if she dies 'twill be manslaughter. I never had hand, act or part in politics. Sergeant Daly at the Cross knows me well.'

When Abby came to herself she was in a bed in the hospital. She began to fumble for her belongings and her shrieks brought a crowd of unfortunate old women about her.

'Whisht, whisht, whisht!' they said. 'They're all in safe-keeping. You'll get them back.'

'I want them now,' she shouted, struggling to get out of bed while they held her down. 'Leave me go, ye robbers of hell! Ye night-walking rogues, leave me go. Oh, murder, murder! Ye're killing me.'

At last an old Irish-speaking priest came and comforted her. He left her quietly saying her beads, secure in the promise to see that she was buried in Ummera no matter what anyone said. As darkness fell, the beads dropped from her swollen hands and she began to mutter to herself in Irish. Sitting about the fire, the ragged old women whispered and groaned in sympathy. The Angelus rang out from a nearby church. Suddenly Abby's voice rose to a shout and she tried to lift herself on her elbow.

'Ah, Michael Driscoll, my friend, my kind comrade, you didn't forget me after all the long years. I'm a long time away from you but I'm coming at last. They tried to keep me away, to make me stop among foreigners in the town, but where would I be at all without you and all the old friends? Stay for me, my treasure! Stop and show me the way. . . . Neighbours,' she shouted, pointing into the shadows, 'that man there is my own husband, Michael Driscoll. Let ye see he won't leave me to find my way alone. Gather round me with yeer lanterns, neighbours, till I see who I have. I know ye all. 'Tis only the sight that's weak on me. Be easy now, my brightness, my own kind loving comrade. I'm coming. After all the long years I'm on the road to you at last. . . .'

It was a spring day full of wandering sunlight when they

brought her the long road to Ummera, the way she had come
from it forty years before. The lake was like a dazzle of midges;
the shafts of the sun revolving like a great millwheel poured their
cascades of milky sunlight over the hills and the little white-
washed cottages and the little black mountain cattle among the
scarecrow fields. The hearse stopped at the foot of the lane that
led to the roofless cabin just as she had pictured it to herself in
the long nights, and Pat, looking more melancholy than ever,
turned to the waiting neighbours and said:

'Neighbours, this is Abby, Batty Heige's daughter, that kept
her promise to ye at the end of all.'

THE OTHER friend of those years in Dublin was the curate in the Star of the Sea church in Sandymount, Tim Traynor. I had met him first through Sean O'Faolain when he was curate in Adam and Eve's church. He brought us down to the vaults to see the coffin of Leonard MacN ally, the informer who betrayed Robert Emmett, and as we left he gave the coffin a thundering kick. He did the same with all visitors, and it was something you liked or did not like as the case might be. It was so typical of Traynor that I liked it.

He had the sort of face that I now see oftener in New York and Boston than in Ireland – the pugilistic Irish face, beefy and red and scowling, with features that seemed to have withdrawn into it to guard it from blows; a broad, blunted nose and a square jaw. He was as conspiratorial as Higgins and much more malicious. If you were injured by one of Higgins's intrigues there was nothing much to blame for it but the will of God, but Traynor, in pursuing some imaginary grievance, would invent and carry through cruel practical jokes. When he swaggered into my room of an evening I would sometimes ask, 'Well, which is it to be tonight, Nero, Napoleon, or St Francis of Assisi?' Most often it was Nero.

'It's that fellow Jenkins. Wait till I tell you!'

Yet I never really felt that he was not a good priest, and he gave me an understanding of and sympathy with the Irish priesthood which even the antics of its silliest members have not been able to affect. It was merely that his temperament and imagination constantly overflowed the necessary limits of his vocation as they would have overflowed the limits of almost any calling, short of that of a pirate. Yet they also enriched his character, so that you felt if he lived for another twenty years he would be a very fine priest indeed. It was significant to me that our old friend, the Tailor of Gougane Barra, who had a trick of nicknaming all his acquaintances in ways that stuck instantly, christened Hayes 'The

Old Child' and Traynor 'The Saint'. There *was* an element of childishness in Hayes, and you always underestimated Traynor if you paid attention only to the devil and forgot the saint.

It was characteristic of him that he became really friendly with me only when he discovered that as boys we had both had a romantic crush on the same girl. He had had better fortune than I, for one night he had seen Natalie home from college up Summer Hill, and all the way they had held hands without exchanging a word. When the man she was proposing to marry had held back, she had complained of him to Traynor; he had advised her and they had remained friends until her death.

It was also characteristic of him that when I left his rooms that night he insisted on my taking the only picture he had of her. That was not only the new friend and the outburst of generosity; it was also the priest who knew he should not brood on a dead girl's picture.

But, of course, he brooded just the same. The emotional expansiveness that overflowed the limitations of his profession made him brood on all the might-have-beens of his life, and they were endless. I used to make fun of his rooms, which were a museum of all the might-have-beens: books on science, history, art; paintings, sculptures, a shotgun that needed cleaning and a cinematograph that wouldn't work – all passions pursued with fury for a few weeks till each in turn joined the exhibits on view. It was not only Nero and St Francis who alternated in his strange, complex character, but Einstein, Michelangelo and Gibbon as well. [. . .]

All the imaginative improvisation was only the outward expression of a terrible inward loneliness, loneliness that was accentuated by his calling. In that sense only could I ever admit that he was not a good priest – he should have had a tougher hide. Priests in Ireland are cut off from ordinary intercourse in a way that seems unknown in other countries. Once when we were arguing he made me impatient and I said, 'Ah, don't be a bloody fool, Tim!' His face suddenly went mad, and for a moment I thought he meant to strike me. Then he recollected himself and said darkly, 'Do you know that nobody has called me a bloody fool since I was sixteen?' Then the humour of it struck him, and he described how, once, when he was home on holidays from the seminary he was pontificating at the supper table and suddenly caught his uncle winking at his mother. Then he grew angry again.

'People like you give the impression that it's our fault if the country is priest-ridden. We know it's priest-ridden, but what can we do about it? I can't even get on a tram without some old man or woman getting up to offer me his seat. I can't go into a living-room without knowing that all ordinary conversation stops, and when it starts again it's going to be intended for my ears. That's not a natural life. A man can't be sane and not be called a bloody fool now and again.'

Before I knew him he spent his holidays as a stretcher-bearer in Lourdes: somehow the contact with people who were ill and dying satisfied the gentleness and protectiveness in his nature. There was an enormous amount of this, but it never went on for long because when he felt rebuffed, brooding and anger took its place. In those years he took every chance of spending a few days in Gougane Barra in the mountains of West Cork. He stayed at the inn, abandoned his Roman collar, and served at the bar, went fishing and argued with the visitors and (if I knew him) got involved personally and vindictively in every minor disagreement for miles round. His loneliness was of a sort that made it difficult for him to become involved with anything except as a protagonist. [. . .]

Traynor died while I was in America, and somehow or other his priest friends managed to bury him where he had always wished to be buried, in Gougane Barra: how, I don't know for, being Traynor, he died penniless and intestate; the rules dictated that he should be buried in the town, and the island cemetery he wished to be buried in had been closed by order of the bishop.

But even in death he was a romantic, bending circumstances to his will, and his old friends brought him there on Little Christmas Night, when the snow was on the mountains, and the country people came across the dangerous rocks and streams with their lanterns, and an array of cars turned their headlights on the causeway to the island church where he was to spend his last night above ground.

At the other side of the causeway lies the Tailor, under the noble headstone carved for him by his friend Seamus Murphy, with the epitaph I chose for him – 'A star danced and under it I was born.' I was glad that Traynor permitted that, though he refused to allow Murphy to do what he wanted and replace the cross with an open shears. He himself has no gravestone, but the country people have not forgotten him and on his grave his initials are picked out in little coloured stones. Even in death the things that Traynor would have most liked to know have been hidden from him.

THE MASS ISLAND

WHEN FATHER JACKSON drove up to the curates' house, it was already drawing on to dusk, the early dusk of late December. The curates' house was a red-brick building on a terrace at one side of the ugly church in Asragh. Father Hamilton seemed to have been waiting for him and opened the front door himself, looking white and strained. He was a tall young man with a long, melancholy face that you would have taken for weak till you noticed the cut of the jaw.

'Oh, come in, Jim,' he said with his mournful smile. ''Tisn't much of a welcome we have for you, God knows. I suppose you'd like to see poor Jerry before the undertaker comes.'

'I might as well,' Father Jackson replied briskly. There was nothing melancholy about Jackson, but he affected an air of surprise and shock. ''Twas very sudden, wasn't it?'

'Well, it was and it wasn't, Jim,' Father Hamilton said, closing the front door behind him. 'He was going downhill since he got the first heart attack, and he wouldn't look after himself. Sure, you know yourself what he was like.'

Jackson knew. Father Fogarty and himself had been friends of a sort, for years. An impractical man, excitable and vehement, Fogarty could have lived for twenty years with his ailment, but instead of that, he allowed himself to become depressed and indifferent. If he couldn't live as he had always lived, he would prefer not to live at all.

They went upstairs and into the bedroom where he was. The character was still plain on the stern, dead face, though, drained of vitality, it had the look of a studio portrait. That bone structure was something you'd have picked out of a thousand faces as Irish, with its odd impression of bluntness and asymmetry, its jutting brows and craggy chin, and the snub nose that looked as though it had probably been broken twenty years before in a public-house row.

When they came downstairs again, Father Hamilton produced half a bottle of whiskey.

'Not for me, thanks,' Jackson said hastily. 'Unless you have a drop of sherry there?'

'Well, there is some Burgundy,' Father Hamilton said. 'I don't know is it any good, though.'

''Twill do me fine,' Jackson replied cheerfully, reflecting that Ireland was the country where nobody knew whether Burgundy was good or not. 'You're coming with us tomorrow, I suppose?'

'Well, the way it is, Jim,' Father Hamilton replied, 'I'm afraid neither of us is going. You see, they're burying poor Jerry here.'

'They're what?' Jackson asked incredulously.

'Now, I didn't know for sure when I rang you, Jim, but that's what the brother decided, and that's what Father Hanafey decided as well.'

'But he told you he wanted to be buried on the Mass Island, didn't he?'

'He told everybody, Jim,' Father Hamilton replied with grow-ing excitement and emotion. 'That was the sort he was. If he told one, he told five hundred. Only a half an hour ago I had a girl on the telephone from the Island, asking when they could expect us. You see, the old parish priest of the place let Jerry mark out the grave for himself, and they want to know should they open it. But now the old parish priest is dead as well, and, of course, Jerry left nothing in writing.'

'Didn't he leave a will, even?' Jackson asked in surprise.

'Well, he did and he didn't, Jim,' Father Hamilton said, look-ing as if he were on the point of tears. 'Actually, he did make a will about five or six years ago, and he gave it to Clancy, the other curate, but Clancy went off on the Foreign Mission and God alone knows where he is now. After that, Jerry never bothered his head about it. I mean, you have to admit the man had nothing to leave. Every damn thing he had he gave away – even the old car, after he got the first attack. If there was any loose cash around, I suppose the brother has that.'

Jackson sipped his Burgundy, which was even more Aus-tralian than he had feared, and wondered at his own irritation. He had been irritated enough before that, with the prospect of two days' motoring in the middle of winter, and a night in a godforsaken pub in the mountains, a hundred and fifty miles away at the other side of Ireland. There, in one of the lakes, was an island where in Cromwell's time, before the causeway and the little oratory were built, Mass was said in secret, and it was here that Father Fogarty had wanted to be buried. It struck Jackson as sheer sentimentality; it wasn't even as if it was Fogarty's native place. Jackson had once allowed Fogarty to lure him there, and had hated every moment of it. It wasn't only the discomfort of the public-house, where meals erupted at any hour of the day or night as the spirit took the proprietor, or the rain that kept them confined to the cold dining-and-sitting room that looked out on the gloomy mountainside, with its couple of whitewashed cabins on the shore of the lake. It was the over-intimacy of it all, and this was the thing that Father Fogarty apparently loved. He liked to stand in his shirtsleeves behind the bar, taking turns with the proprietor, who was one of his many friends, serving big pints of porter to rough moun-tainy men, or to sit in their cottages, shaking in all his fat whenever they told broad stories or sang risky folk songs. 'God, Jim, isn't it grand?' he would say in his deep voice, and Jackson would look at him over his spectacles with what Fogarty called his 'jesuitical look', and say, 'Well, I suppose it all depends on what you really like, Jerry.' He wasn't even certain that the locals cared for Father Fogarty's intimacy on the contrary, he had a strong impression that they much preferred their own reserved old parish priest, whom they never saw except twice a year, when he came up the valley to collect his dues. That had made Jackson twice as stiff. And yet now when he found out that the plans that had meant so much inconvenience to him had fallen through, he was as disappointed as though they had been his own.

'Oh, well,' he said with a shrug that was intended to conceal his perturbation, 'I suppose it doesn't make much difference where they chuck us when our time comes.'

'The point is, it mattered to Jerry, Jim,' Father Hamilton said with his curious shy obstinacy. 'God knows, it's not anything that will ever worry me, but it haunted him, and somehow, you know, I don't feel it's right to flout a dead man's wishes.'

'Oh, I know, I know,' Jackson said lightly. 'I suppose I'd better talk to old Hanafey about it. Knowing I'm a friend of the Bishop's, he might pay more attention to me.'

'He might, Jim,' Father Hamilton replied sadly, looking away over Jackson's head. 'As you say, knowing you're a friend of the

Bishop's, he might. But I wouldn't depend too much on it. I talked to him till I was black in the face, and all I got out of him was the law and the rubrics. It's the brother Hanafey is afraid of. You'll see him this evening, and, between ourselves, he's a tough customer. Of course, himself and Jerry never had much to say to one another, and he'd be the last man in the world that Jerry would talk to about his funeral, so now he doesn't want the expense and inconvenience. You wouldn't blame him, of course. I'd probably be the same myself. By the way,' Father Hamilton added, lowering his voice, 'before he does come, I'd like you to take a look round Jerry's room and see is there any little memento you'd care to have – a photo or a book or anything.'

They went into Father Fogarty's sitting-room, and Jackson looked at it with a new interest. He knew of old the rather handsome library – Fogarty had been a man of many enthusiasms, though none of long duration – the picture of the Virgin and Child in Irish country costume over the mantelpiece, which some of his colleagues had thought irreverent, and the couple of fine old prints. There was a newer picture that Jackson had not seen – a charcoal drawing of the Crucifixion from a fifteenth-century Irish tomb, which was brutal but impressive.

'Good Lord!' Jackson exclaimed with a sudden feeling of loss. 'He really had taste, hadn't he?'

'He had, Jim,' Father Hamilton said, sticking his long nose into the picture. 'This goes to a young couple called Keneally, outside the town, that he was fond of. I think they were very kind to him. Since he had the attack, he was pretty lonely, I'd say.'

'Oh, aren't we all, attack or no attack,' Jackson said almost irritably.

Father Hanafey, the parish priest of Asragh, was a round, red, cherubic-looking old man with a bald head and big round glasses. His house was on the same terrace as the curates'. He, too, insisted on producing the whiskey Jackson so heartily detested, when the two priests came in to consult him, but Jackson had decided that this time diplomacy required he should show proper appreciation of the dreadful stuff. He felt sure he was going to be very sick next day. He affected great astonishment at the quality of Father Hanafey's whiskey, and first the old parish priest grew shy, like a schoolgirl whose good looks are being praised, then he looked self-satisfied, and finally he became almost emotional. It was a great pleasure, he said, to meet a young priest with a proper understanding of whiskey. Priests no longer seemed to have the same taste, and as far as most of them were concerned, they might as well be drinking poteen. It was only when it was seven years old that Irish began to be interesting, and that was when you had to catch it and store it in sherry casks to draw off what remained of crude alcohol in it, and give it that beautiful roundness that Father Jackson had spotted. But it shouldn't be kept too long, for somewhere along the line the spirit of a whiskey was broken. At ten, or maybe twelve, years old it was just right. But people were losing their palates. He solemnly assured the two priests that of every dozen clerics who came to his house not more than one would realize what he was drinking. Poor Hamilton grew red and began to stutter, but the parish priest's reproofs were not directed at him.

'It isn't you I'm talking about, Father Hamilton, but elderly priests, parish priests, and even canons, that you would think would know better, and I give you my word, I put the two whiskeys side by side in front of them, the shop stuff and my own, and they could not tell the difference.'

But though the priest was mollified by Father Jackson's maturity of judgement, he was not prepared to interfere in the arrangements for the funeral of his curate. 'It is the wish of the next of kin, father,' he said stubbornly, 'and that is something I have no control over. Now that you tell me the same thing as Father Hamilton, I accept it that this was Father Fogarty's wish, and a man's wishes regarding his own interment are always to be respected. I assure you, if I had even one line in Father Fogarty's writing to go on, I would wait for no man's advice. I would take the responsibility on myself. Something on paper, father, is all I want.'

'On the other hand, father,' Jackson said mildly, drawing on his pipe, 'if Father Fogarty was the sort to leave written instructions, he'd hardly be the sort to leave such unusual ones. I mean, after all, it isn't even the family burying ground, is it?'

'Well, now, that is true, father,' replied the parish priest, and it was clear that he had been deeply impressed by this rather doubtful logic. 'You have a very good point there, and it is one

I did not think of myself, and I have given the matter a great deal of thought. You might mention it to his brother. Father Fogarty, God rest him, was *not* a usual type of man. I think you might even go so far as to say that he was a rather *unusual* type of man, and not orderly, as you say – not by any means orderly. I would certainly mention that to the brother and see what he says.'

But the brother was not at all impressed by Father Jackson's argument when he turned up at the church in Asragh that evening. He was a good-looking man with a weak and pleasant face and a cold shrewdness in his eyes that had been lacking in his brother's.

'But why, father?' he asked, turning to Father Hanafey. 'I'm a busy man, and I'm being asked to leave my business for a couple of days in the middle of winter, and for what? That is all I ask. What use is it?'

'It is only out of respect for the wishes of the deceased, Mr Fogarty,' said Father Hanafey, who clearly was a little bit afraid of him.

'And where did he express those wishes?' the brother asked. 'I'm his only living relative, and it is queer he would not mention a thing like that to me.'

'He mentioned it to Father Jackson and Father Hamilton.'

'But when, father?' Mr Fogarty asked. 'You knew Father Jerry, and he was always expressing wishes about something. He was an excitable sort of man, God rest him, and the thing he'd say today might not be the thing he'd say tomorrow. After all, after close on forty years, I think I have the right to say I knew him,' he added with a triumphant air that left the two young priests without a leg to stand on.

Over bacon and eggs in the curates' house, Father Hamilton was very despondent. 'Well, I suppose we did what we could, Jim,' he said.

'I'm not too sure of that,' Jackson said with his 'jesuitical air', looking at Father Hamilton sidewise over his spectacles. 'I'm wondering if we couldn't do something with that family you say he intended the drawing for.'

'The Keneallys,' said Father Hamilton in a worried voice. 'Actually, I saw the wife in the church this evening. You might have noticed her crying.'

'Don't you think we should see if they have anything in writing?'

'Well, if they have, it would be about the picture,' said Father Hamilton. 'How I know about it is she came to me at the time to ask if I couldn't do something for him. Poor man, he was crying himself that day, according to what she told me.'

'Oh dear!' Jackson said politely, but his mind was elsewhere. 'I'm not really interested in knowing what would be in a letter like that. It's none of my business. But I would like to make sure that they haven't something in writing. What did Hanafey call it – "something on paper"?'

'I daresay we should inquire, anyway,' said Father Hamilton, and after supper they drove out to the Keneallys', a typical small red-brick villa with a decent garden in front. The family also was eating bacon and eggs, and Jackson shuddered when they asked him to join them. Keneally himself, a tall, gaunt, cadaverous man, poured out more whiskey for them, and again Jackson felt he must make a formal attempt to drink it. At the same time, he thought he saw what attraction the house had for Father Fogarty. Keneally was tough and with no suggestion of lay servility towards the priesthood, and his wife was beautiful and scatter-brained, and talked to herself, the cat, and the children simultaneously. 'Rosaleen!' she cried determinedly. 'Out! Out I say! I told you if you didn't stop meowing you'd have to go out. . . . Angela Keneally, the stick! . . . You do not want to go to the bathroom, Angela. It's only five minutes since you were there before. I will not let Father Hamilton come up to you at all unless you go to bed at once.'

In the children's bedroom, Jackson gave a finger to a stolid-looking infant, who instantly stuffed it into his mouth and began to chew it, apparently under the impression that he would be bound to reach sugar at last.

Later, they sat over their drinks in the sitting-room, only inter-rupted by Angela Keneally, in a fever of curiosity, dropping in every five minutes to ask for a biscuit or a glass of water.

'You see, Father Fogarty left no will,' Jackson explained to Keneally. 'Consequently, he'll be buried here tomorrow unless something turns up. I suppose he told you where he wanted to be buried?'

'On the Island? Twenty times, if he told us once. I thought he took it too far. Didn't you, father?'

'And me not to be able to go!' Mrs Keneally said, beginning to cry. 'Isn't it awful, father?'

'He didn't leave anything in writing with you?' He saw in Keneally's eyes that the letter was really only about the picture, and raised a warning hand. 'Mind, if he did, I don't want to know what's in it! In fact, it would be highly improper for anyone to be told before the parish priest and the next of kin were consulted. All I do want to know is whether' – he waited a moment to see that Keneally was following him – 'he did leave any written instructions, of any kind, with you.'

Mrs Keneally, drying her tears, suddenly broke into rapid speech. 'Sure, that was the day poor Father Jerry was so down in himself because we were his friends and he had nothing to leave us, and –'

'Shut up, woman!' her husband shouted with a glare at her, and then Jackson saw him purse his lips in quiet amusement. He was a man after Jackson's heart. 'As you say, father, we have a letter from him.'

'Addressed to anybody in particular?'

'Yes, to the parish priest, to be delivered after his death.'

'Did he use those words?' Jackson asked, touched in spite of himself.

'Those very words.'

'God help us!' said Father Hamilton.

'But you had not time to deliver it?'

'I only heard of Father Fogarty's death when I got in. Esther was at the church, of course.'

'And you're a bit tired, so you wouldn't want to walk all the way over to the presbytery with it. I take it that, in the normal way, you'd post it.'

'But the post would be gone,' Keneally said with a secret smile. 'So that Father Hanafey wouldn't get it until maybe the day after tomorrow. That's what you were afraid of, father, isn't it?'

'I see we understand one another, Mr Keneally,' Jackson said politely.

'You wouldn't, of course, wish to say anything that wasn't strictly true,' said Keneally, who was clearly enjoying himself enormously, though his wife had not the faintest idea of what was afoot. 'So perhaps it would be better if the letter was posted now, and not after you leave the house.'

'Fine!' said Jackson, and Keneally nodded and went out. When he returned, a few minutes later, the priests rose to go.

'I'll see you at the Mass tomorrow,' Keneally said. 'Good luck, now.'

Jackson felt they'd probably need it. But when Father Hanafey met them in the hall, with the wet snow falling outside, and they explained about the letter, his mood had clearly changed. Jackson's logic might have worked some sort of spell on him, or perhaps it was just that he felt they were three clergymen opposed to a layman.

'It was very unforeseen of Mr Keneally not to have brought that letter to me at once,' he grumbled, 'but I must say I was expecting something of the sort. It would have been very peculiar if Father Fogarty had left no instructions at all for me, and I see that we can't just sit round and wait to find out what they were, since the burial is tomorrow. Under the circumstances, father, I think we'd be justified in arranging for the funeral according to Father Fogarty's known wishes.'

'Thanks be to God,' Father Hamilton murmured as he and Father Jackson returned to the curates' house. 'I never thought we'd get away with that.'

'We haven't got away with it yet,' said Jackson. 'And even if we do get away with it, the real trouble will be later.'

All the arrangements had still to be made. When Mr Fogarty was informed, he slammed down the receiver without comment. Then a phone call had to be made to a police station twelve miles from the Island, and the police sergeant promised to send a man out on a bicycle to have the grave opened. Then the local parish priest and several old friends had to be informed, and a notice inserted in the nearest daily. As Jackson said wearily, romantic men always left their more worldly friends to carry out their romantic intentions.

The scene at the curates' house next morning after Mass scared even Jackson. While the hearse and the funeral car waited in front of the door, Mr Fogarty sat, white with anger, and let the priests talk. To Jackson's surprise, Father Hanafey put up a stern fight for Father Fogarty's wishes.

'You have to realize, Mr Fogarty, that to a priest like your brother the Mass is a very solemn thing indeed, and a place where the poor people had to fly in the Penal Days to hear Mass would be one of particular sanctity.'

'Father Hanafey,' said Mr Fogarty in a cold, even tone, 'I am a simple businessman, and I have no time for sentiment.'

'I would not go so far as to call the veneration for sanctified ground mere sentiment, Mr Fogarty,' the old priest said severely. 'At any rate, it is now clear that Father Fogarty left instructions to be delivered to me after his death, and if those instructions are what we think them, I would have a serious responsibility for not having paid attention to them.'

'I do not think that letter is anything of the kind, Father Hanafey,' said Mr Fogarty. 'That's a matter I'm going to inquire into when I get back, and if it turns out to be a hoax, I am going to take it further.'

'Oh, Mr Fogarty, I'm sure it's not a hoax,' said the parish priest, with a shocked air, but Mr Fogarty was not convinced.

'For everybody's sake, we'll hope not,' he said grimly.

The funeral procession set off. Mr Fogarty sat in the front of the car by the driver, sulking. Jackson and Hamilton sat behind and opened their breviaries. When they stopped at a hotel for lunch, Mr Fogarty said he was not hungry, and stayed outside in the cold. And when he did get hungry and came into the dining-room, the priests drifted into the lounge to wait for him. They both realized that he might prove a dangerous enemy.

Then, as they drove on in the dusk, they saw the mountain country ahead of them in a cold, watery light, a light that seemed to fall dead from the ragged edge of a cloud. The towns and villages they passed through were dirtier and more derelict. They drew up at a crossroads, behind the hearse, and heard someone talking to the driver of the hearse. Then a car fell into line behind them. 'Someone joining us,' Father Hamilton said, but Mr Fogarty, lost in his own dream of martyrdom, did not reply. Half a dozen times within the next twenty minutes, the same thing happened, though sometimes the cars were waiting in lanes and byroads with their lights on, and each time Jackson saw a heavily coated figure standing in the roadway shouting to the hearse driver: 'Is it Father Fogarty ye have there?' At last they came to a village where the local parish priest's car was waiting outside the church, with a little group about it. Their headlights caught a public-house, isolated at the other side of the street, glaring with whitewash, while about it was the vague space of a distant mountainside.

Suddenly Mr Fogarty spoke. 'He seems to have been fairly well known,' he said with something approaching politeness.

The road went on, with a noisy stream at the right-hand side of it falling from group to group of rocks. They left it for a by-road, which bent to the right, heading towards the stream, and then began to mount, broken by ledges of naked rock, over which hearse and cars seemed to heave themselves like animals. On the left-hand side of the road was a little whitewashed cottage, all lit up, with a big turf fire burning in the open hearth and an oil lamp with an orange glow on the wall above it. There was a man standing by the door, and as they approached he began to pick his way over the rocks towards them, carrying a lantern. Only then did Jackson notice the other lanterns and flashlights, coming down the mountain or crossing the stream, and realize that they represented people, young men and girls and an occasional sturdy old man, all moving in the direction of the Mass Island. Suddenly it hit him, almost like a blow. He told himself not to be a fool, that this was no more than the desire for novelty one should expect to find in out-of-the-way places, mixed perhaps with vanity. It was all that, of course, and he knew it, but he knew, too, it was something more. He had thought when he was here with Fogarty that those people had not respected Fogarty as they respected him and the local parish priest, but he knew that for him, or even for their own parish priest, they would never turn out in midwinter, across the treacherous mountain bogs and wicked rocks. He and the parish priest would never earn more from the people of the mountains than respect; what they gave to the fat, unclerical young man who had served them with pints in the bar and egged them on to tell their old stories and bullied and ragged and even fought them was something infinitely greater.

The funeral procession stopped in a lane that ran along the edge of a lake. The surface of the lake was rough, and they could hear the splash of the water upon the stones. The two priests got

out of the car and began to vest themselves, and then Mr Fogarty
got out, too. He was very nervous and hesitant.

'It's very inconvenient, and all the rest of it,' he said, 'but
I don't want you gentlemen to think that I didn't know you were
acting from the best motives.'

'That's very kind of you, Mr Fogarty,' Jackson said. 'Maybe
we made mistakes as well.'

'Thank you, Father Jackson,' Mr Fogarty said, and held out his
hand. The two priests shook hands with him and he went off,
raising his hat.

'Well, that's one trouble over,' Father Hamilton said wryly as
an old man plunged through the mud towards the car.

'Lights is what we're looking for!' he shouted. 'Let ye turn her
sidewise and throw the headlights on the causeway the way we'll
see what we're doing.'

Their driver swore, but he reversed and turned the front of the
car till it almost faced the lake. Then he turned on his headlights.
Somewhere farther up the road the parish priest's car did the
same. One by one, the ranked headlights blazed up, and at every
moment the scene before them grew more vivid – the gateway
and the stile, and beyond it the causeway that ran towards the
little brown stone oratory with its mock Romanesque doorway.
As the lights strengthened and steadied, the whole island became
like a vast piece of theatre scenery cut out against the gloomy
wall of the mountain with the tiny whitewashed cottages at
its base. Far above, caught in a stray flash of moonlight, Jackson
saw the snow on its summit. 'I'll be after you,' he said to Father
Hamilton, and watched him, a little perturbed and looking
behind him, join the parish priest by the gate. Jackson resented
being seen by them because he was weeping, and he was a man
who despised tears – his own and others'. It was like a miracle,
and Father Jackson didn't really believe in miracles. Standing
back by the fence to let the last of the mourners pass, he saw the
coffin, like gold in the brilliant light, and heard the steadying
voices of the four huge mountainy men who carried it. He saw
it sway above the heads, shawled and bare, glittering between the
little stunted holly bushes and hazels.

This book is set in BEMBO which was cut
by the punch-cutter Francesco Griffo
for the Venetian printer-publisher
Aldus Manutius in early 1495
and first used in a pamphlet
by a young scholar
named Pietro
Bembo.